TRANSCENDING DARKNESS
By Airicka Phoenix

Transcending Darkness ©2015 by Airicka Phoenix
All rights reserved.

AIRICKA PHOENIX
CEO of Romance Enterprises

www.AirickaPhoenix.com

This book or parts thereof may not be reproduced in any form, stored in or introduced into a retrieval system, or transmitted, in any form, or by any means (electronic, mechanical, photocopying, recording, or otherwise) without prior written permission of the copyright owner and/or the publisher of this book, except as provided by United States of America copyright law.

This book is a work of fiction. Names, characters, places, and incidents are a product of the author's imagination or are used fictitiously. Any resemblance to actual events, locales, or persons, living or dead, is coincidental.

Cover Designer: Airicka's Mystical Creations
Interior Design: Airicka Phoenix
Editor & Formatter: Kathy Eccleston
ISBN-13: 1517595215
ISBN-10: 9781517595210
Published by Airicka Phoenix
Also available in eBook and paperback publication.

Also by Airicka Phoenix

Games of Fire
Betraying Innocence

TOUCH SAGA
Touching Smoke
Touching Fire
Touching Eternity

THE LOST GIRL SERIES
Finding Kia
Revealing Kia

REGENERATION SERIES
When Night Falls

THE BABY SAGA
Forever His Baby
Bye-Bye Baby
Be My Baby
Always Yours, Baby

IN THE DARK SERIES
My Soul For You
Kissing Trouble

SONS OF JUDGMENT SAGA
Octavian's Undoing
Gideon's Promise

ANTHOLOGY
Whispered Beginnings: A Clever Fiction Anthology
Midnight Surrender Anthology

Dedication
To Jessica,
For having my back and not getting me locked up.

TRANSCENDING DARKNESS

Chapter 1

"How badly do you want to be free, Juliette?"

As questions went, it was a redundant one. What sort of person didn't want to be free of the tether binding them to a lifetime of oppression and abuse? What kind of person thrived on the fear of not knowing if they would live to see another day? But Juliette knew it wasn't the answer Arlo was after. For him, it was to remind her just how far beneath his boots she stood and how her life was his to do with as he so wished.

"I'm sorry the payment was late this month," she began, talking to his filthy boots rather than facing the man sitting on the hood of his shiny, black Bentley, or the five other men standing in a perfect circular formation around her, caging her in. "I couldn't pull enough hours—"

"That wasn't my question." Arlo slid off the car, disturbing the dirt beneath their feet as he kicked absently at a soda can. The bit of metal clattered noisily in the late afternoon as it tumbled across the parking lot. "Do you want to be free?"

Arlo wasn't much taller than her. Maybe a foot at the very most, but he had intimidation on his side, which was something Juliette severely lacked. Plus he had the gun tucked into the waistband of his black jeans. The butt stood out against the white material of his t-shirt. It was all Juliette could see despite her best efforts not to stare.

Swallowing the thick chunks of bile pooling at the back of her throat, Juliette nodded. "Yes."

His footsteps drew closer, deliberately slow as the space between them shrank rapidly. He stopped when she could smell the sharp stink of tobacco on his dark clothes and clearly make out the broken road map scarring his boots. The sweet stench of cinnamon rolls curled into the space separating them to claw across her cheeks. It tangled with the stench of stale beer wafting off his breath and taunted the sickness she was fighting so hard to suppress.

"We had a deal you and I, didn't we?" He reached up and it took all her courage not to cringe when he plucked a coil of her hair off her shoulder. He wound it around a dirty finger, tight enough to tug strands from her scalp. "You promised to pay the debt your father owed me and I wouldn't take your pretty little sister as compensation. So far, I have kept my end of the bargain, but you haven't kept yours."

"I'm sorry—"

With the speeds of an angry cobra, his free hand shot out and closed around her jaw. Jagged nails bit into tender skin as she was wrenched closer. His foul breath cut across her cheeks, burning her senses. Tears sprang to her eyes and were quickly blinked back; he already held all the power over her. She refused to let him see her cry. Oh, but he tried every chance he got to break her.

"Sorry doesn't get me my money, Juliette," he murmured in a taunting whisper that was followed by pressure on her face. His cold, brown eyes sliced into her from amongst a messy cap of equally brown hair. Most would have considered him handsome, and maybe he was with his built frame and rugged features, but all Juliette could see was a monster. "I want my money, or something of equal value."

Crippling terror vaulted up the cavity of her body in a numbing lance when his hand dropped the lock of her hair to snake up the side of her thigh, dragging the worn hem of her waitress uniform up her leg in the process. Chills rushed over her in a torrent of hot and cold. She reflexively grabbed his wrist, but it slid effortlessly inward despite her using both hands against only one of his.

"No, please..."

The hand on her face tightened to the point of blinding pain. Her cry went ignored.

"I own you."

The hand tucked between her legs to grind in painful nudges over the slip of cotton covering her mound. Her resistance had no effect on him. She was barely able to push him away and that amused him. It lit the dark glimmer of triumph shimmering across his eyes and radiated in the possessive grip of his fingers bruising her jaw. He pulled her in closer so their mouths were mere inches apart and she was forced to swallow every one of his foul exhales.

"Everything you have, everything you will have … mine, and there is nothing you can do about it, Juliette."

The sickening truth rippled up the length of her to curdle in her chest. It warped around her heart and lungs until she was sure she would suffocate right there at his feet. But even death had abandoned her to his mercy.

"I'm sorry," she choked out, struggling not to fight, while simultaneously restraining his prodding fingers from pushing past the material of her panties. "I'll get your money!" she promised over the loud boom of terror thundering between her ears. "I promise."

"See that you do." His gaze lingered on her mouth, dark and hungry. "And make sure this is the only time we have this conversation."

He released her and Juliette staggered back in a fit of coughs. A sob worked up into her throat and curled into a tight ball that made her want to do the same across the dirt. Cold, clammy hands went to her face to rub the welts he'd left behind on her skin. The muggy, summer breeze slipped beneath her dress to lick tauntingly at the sweat dampening the material. A violent shudder claimed her.

"And to ensure that this never happens again," he pivoted on his heels and meandered back to his car. "I want two months' worth by tomorrow."

"Two months?" Juliette's disbelief came out in a choked gasp. "I can't get six thousand dollars in a day."

Pausing at the driver's side door of his Bentley, Arlo turned. "That's your problem, *puta*." He yanked open his door. "Six thousand or your sister by five o'clock tomorrow."

There was nothing to do but stand back and watch as the group disassembled and peeled off in a plume of dust and exhaust. Around her, the world seemed to roar back into focus with a vengeance. Sights and sounds slammed into her. Their normality paralyzed the breath she was desperately trying to suck in. Despite the heat, her skin prickled in pimples that itched beneath her uniform. Her stomach writhed, a pit of angry snakes struggling for dominance. Nausea pushed against her, threatening to take her under. But she couldn't. She had work and she couldn't go in smelling like vomit and sweat.

Knees wobbled as she staggered her way unsteadily to the *Around the Bend* diner. The squat little burger joint catered mainly to truckers, hookers and the occasional family passing through and was, literally, around the bend before an abrupt drop into the churning Anyox river. It sat off the main highway into the city and was the main stop for most people coming or going. But as tips went, it was questionable. The only ones who actually gave good ones were the truckers and only after spending an hour squeezing her ass. But it was a job and it paid some of her bills.

The afternoon rush had already begun when she stumbled through the door into a wall of palpable heat. Low chatter sweltered through the rancid stench of burnt fries, grease, and stale perfume. Someone had put a quarter into the jukebox and *Dolly Parton* crooned from the crackling speakers bolted into the two corners of the room. Overhead, the twin fans wobbled and creaked as they churned the sour air like dough beneath a blender head. Juliette always wondered when the two would just dislocate from the ceiling and kill somebody. It was only a matter of time.

"Juliette!" More hairspray than person, Charis Paxton slapped the rag in her hands down onto the counter and speared her tiny fists on voluminous hips. The plastic bangles circling twiggy arms clattered noisily. "You're late!"

Automatically, Juliette's gaze darted to the clock behind the auburn beehive adding about two feet to Charis's four foot nothing stature.

"I'm sorry—"

One child-sized hand cut through the air, five slender fingers splayed in a clear warning to stop talking. She stood like an irate traffic guard at an intersection, but meaner. She burned Juliette with her squinty, blue eyes.

"This isn't some charity place," she bit out. "You're not going to get paid for being lazy."

It was on the tip of her tongue to tell the woman that she had never been late a single day in two years and that it was only five minutes, but she knew that would only get her fired.

"Do you have any idea how many applications we get a day for your position?" Charis went on in her chirpy squeak. "We could have you replaced within the hour."

It didn't matter whether or not that was true. Juliette was in no position to test the theory. So she apologized again before ducking her head and hurrying behind the counter. Her worn sneakers squeaked against the grimy linoleum in her haste to get away from the shrewd woman watching her every movement. Charis didn't stop her as Juliette disappeared into the back.

Larry, Charis's husband and their fry cook, looked up from the grill he was scraping with a metal spatula. His pudgy face was flushed and shone with sweat that he wiped off on the hem of his filthy apron. His beady eyes watched Juliette as she darted into the miniature-sized staffroom tucked between the walk-in and the bathroom.

The kitchen was a small, cramped place that barely fit two people. Most of the space was claimed by the grill and deep fryer combo crammed into one corner. It was attached to a sheet of dented metal that ended under the takeout window. The walk-in took up the rest.

Around the Bend was the kind of place she felt like people needed to get a tetanus shot before stepping into, or the sort of place that killed its customers and served them in the burger mix. It was dingy and badly maintained. It made no sense to her why anyone would want to eat there. But people did and so long as they did, she continued to get a paycheck once a week. By no means was it enough to support her, her sister, and the tower of bills that just kept getting bigger each day, but it was something. The rest was made up from her two other jobs that she did throughout the week. Yet no matter how many jobs she worked or how many paychecks she pulled in, it was never enough. Between the mortgage, bills, Viola's tuition, and Arlo, she barely saw a penny of it.

Things hadn't always been bad. There had been a time when she had been a normal carefree teenager with a room full of all the crap girls wanted when their life was perfect. She'd had a mother and a father and an irritating baby sister. They had even had a tiny dog that slept on a velvet cushion on her window seat. Back then, she never had to worry about making ends meet. She never even knew where the money came from, only that they had it and she was popular and rich and the envy of everyone at her elite prep school.

Then her mother had died. No amount of money in the world could save her. The cancer had been too advanced. It had taken over her body seemingly overnight. She barely lasted a year. Juliette's world had fractured the second her mother's heart monitor had flat lined. Her perfectly manicured existence tumbled into dark chaos and no one stayed to hold her hand through it. Her perfect boyfriend had called her an emotionally unresponsive bitch and left her for her best friend. All the kids who had once begged for a second of her time were nowhere to be seen. Her father drowned himself in whiskey, quit his job, and squandered their money on horses. The checks to the school bounced. The bank began to call three times a day. The cupboards had more cobwebs than food and she had a nine year old sister who needed her. Abandoning her dreams of partying it up in college, Juliette had gotten a job, then two, then three. She worked her fingers to the bone and went home exhausted only to wake up an hour later and do it all over again. But that was her life and someone had to do it.

"Larry?" Securing the apron strings around her waist, Juliette faced the giant beast of a man dumping greasy onion rings out of the fryer. "I was wondering if I could get an advance on my paycheck this week?"

Twisting enormous hands in his apron, Larry turned to her. "You're still paying off the last advance I gave you."

"Then an advance on my next week pay? You know I'm good for it," she pressed. "I've been working here for two years. I'm always on time and I come in every time you guys ask me to."

"Always on time?" he mumbled with a raised eyebrow.

Juliette grimaced. "Today was an exception. I ran into some complications."

Larry grunted and went back to scooping onion rings into a paper covered basket. "How much do you need?"

It was a struggle not to look away, to not shift uneasily. "Six thousand."

Larry's tiny eyes nearly bulged from their sockets. "Six *thousand* dollars?"

"You know I'll pay every penny back!" she cut in hurriedly.

"What the hell do you need six thousand dollars for?"

"Bills," she semi-lied.

"I don't have that kind of money," Larry shot back. "Are you crazy? Do I look like a bank to you?"

Already mortified for having even asked, Juliette bristled. "Well, what about three thousand?"

"No!" he barked. "Get to work."

Cheeks hot, she spun on her heels and stormed from the kitchen.

The Twin Peaks Hotel was the crème de la crème of luxury and sat nestled in the heart of the city. Its gleaming walls of glass glinted in the fading afternoon light. Sparks sliced down the sharp lines in blinding winks. The building itself rose from a bed of lavish green like a sword jutting from its magnificent hilt. For miles all around, lush hills rose and dipped. Manicured bushes swayed daintily in a breeze that wouldn't dare be anything but soothing. Even in the winter, the surrounding park and golf course remained the picture of absolute perfection. Back when life had been simple, Juliette had dreamed of renting one of the condos at the very top and entertaining the most exclusive people. She used to drive out with her friends and walk the grounds, chattering on like the world was already hers.

Stupid, she thought now as she shifted the strap on her purse higher and ducked through the staff doors at exactly five.

Unlike the cool scent of lavender, sea breeze, and money wafting through the lobby and corridors, the staff area stank of sweat, harsh cleaners, and desperation. The paint was a little duller there, the carpets a little more rundown. It was the type of place dreams went to die. But it was substantially better than Around the Bend. It was certainly cleaner.

Unhooking her purse from around her shoulders, Juliette marched into the change area and made a beeline through the rows of metal lockers and wooden benches. Her locker was tucked away in the far, left corner, away from the showers, the door, and the bathrooms. The alcove held three other lockers owned by three other women Juliette had never talked to, not once in four years. But she was fine with that. Friends required a level of dedication she didn't have time for.

Grease and sweat left over from her six hour shift at the diner slicked the dial on her lock as she fumbled to get her locker open. It didn't seem to matter how hard she tried, the oily sensation never left her skin.

The lock gave with an audible click and she wrenched the metal door open. Her purse was carelessly hung on one of the spare hooks while she kicked off her shoes and reached with her free hand for the maid uniform. The simple gray and white ensemble was a drastic change from her scratchy waitress one. The material was softer and comfortable with a neat little collar that matched the cuffs on the short sleeves. The flat, pearly buttons slipped easily into each hole from hem to throat. She dusted a hand along the front before tying her apron overtop and starting round two of her day.

Being a room attendant took no real brain power, but the manual exertion of it was exhausting.

Most of the customers weren't too bad, like the older couples who were neat and orderly and only required minimal attending. It was the frat boys, the rich and sleazy assholes who partied hard on their daddy's dollar and thought they owned the damn world that she couldn't stand. Walking into one of *those* rooms always made her want to dress up in a hazmat suit first.

Used condoms, discarded panties with questionable stains, filthy clothes, drug paraphernalia, the stench of sweat, pot, and sex were just some of the things that greeted her when she opened her first room. It was policy to shut the door behind them while they worked, for their own safety as well as the privacy of their clients, but the smell was just unbearable. She wasn't sure she'd survive being locked up in there.

Going against the rules, she propped the door open with her cart and got to work stuffing everything into trash bags. Personal items were put aside or tossed into the laundry pile. The bed was made, all surfaces wiped down and the floors vacuumed. But it was all done with a quickness she normally didn't show in her work. Each room would take an hour, two if it was really bad, but she usually took her time and made sure she did everything perfectly.

She didn't have time for perfect.

Checking the rooms off her clipboard, she grabbed her cart and hurried her way back down through the service elevator. Her foot tapped anxiously on the sheet of metal as she watched the numbers descend.

On five, the doors opened and one of the servers pushed his empty food cart in next to hers. He took ages aligning it perfectly.

"Busy night, huh?" he said unexpectedly as the car started its descent once more.

"Yeah," she mumbled absently, eyes never steering away from the blinking numbers overhead.

"Are you almost off?" he asked.

She looked at him then, taking in his boyish face, mop of golden brown curls, and sparkling green eyes. *Practically still a baby,* she thought, judging his age to be roughly nineteen.

"Almost," she answered.

They approached their level and he let her out first. Juliette propelled her cart straight into the stock room and hurriedly refilled everything she'd used. She emptied the trash, dumped the laundry into the chute and returned her cart to the store room manager, who barely glanced up from his magazine. With five minutes to spare, she bolted towards payroll like her pants were on fire.

"What's the hurry, *chica*?"

She ignored the question thrown her way by one of the servers in passing and pumped faster.

Martin, the floor manager and all around douchebag, took his break at midnight and usually didn't return until six in the morning. If she didn't catch him before that, she would have to wait to see the accounting clerk and those bastards didn't come in until nine.

"Martin!" Panting and wheezing, Juliette skidded to a clumsy halt just outside his door and doubled over. "I need to talk to you."

"You have two minutes," Martin stated, never once glancing up from his paperwork.

"I need an advance," she said, staggering in a few steps deeper into the eight by eight room consumed mainly by the metal desk and wall of filing cabinets.

"I'm not payroll," he muttered.

"No, but they need your verification."

Round, ruddy face lifted and she was pinned by a pair of sharp, clear blue eyes. "Didn't you get an advance last week?"

And the week before that, she thought miserably, but didn't say as much. "It's an emergency."

One eye squinted at her warily. "How much?"

"Six," she said, deciding to go with the high amount and work her way down if he said no.

"Hundred?"

Inwardly, she grimaced. "Thousand."

"Jesus Christ!" The joints of his chair shrieked when he threw himself back. "What the hell do you need that kind of money for?"

"I told you, it's an emergency or I wouldn't be asking."

"Christ!" Martin said again, rubbing his palm over his pudgy face. "No. Absolutely not. I am not going to be responsible for you paying that kind of money back."

"I'll pay it back!" Juliette promised. "You know I will. Come on, Martin. I've been a model employee. I'm always on time. I finish my work. I've never had a complaint. My work is exemplary. You know I'm good for it."

Martin kept rocking his head from side to side. "Can't do it. Not only because I won't, but because payroll will never agree to that amount. Are you crazy?"

"Well, what about three thousand?"

Martin sighed. "The most I can do is maybe five hundred bucks."

"Five hundred?" Disbelief and outrage rang through her voice even as dread coiled in her chest. She felt the urge to burst into frustrated tears and swallowed it back quickly. "Fine."

Five hundred bucks wasn't enough to pay what she owed, nor was it enough to appease Arlo when he came knocking. But maybe it would be enough to give her a few days to come up with the rest.

By the time she shuffled home to the only place she'd ever lived, the clock was sitting at well after three. Shadows spilled along the walls like black paint, obscuring the worn, second hand furniture she'd picked up from street curbs and dumpsters. The original items had been sold off to pay for the overdue mortgage. She hadn't gotten nearly as much as her parents had paid for them, but it had kept the bank off their backs for a little while. The only things she hadn't gotten rid of were her and Vi's bedroom sets. Both had been birthday presents and the last gift their mother had given them. But everything else was gone, leaving empty rooms throughout the house, giving it the appearance of abandonment. Maybe in a way, it was. Juliette certainly no longer lived there. It was a place to keep her things mostly. But it was the one piece of her old life she fought desperately to cling on to.

Careful not to make a sound, she started up the stairs. She knew from the discarded backpack next to the stairway, that Vi was home and already in bed. Her entire body ached. There was a numbness behind her eyeballs that she was certain wasn't normal and all she wanted to do was curl up and sleep. Instead, she staggered her way into the bathroom, careful not to make too much noise as she locked herself inside.

The bags beneath her brown eyes had bags and each one was a darker shade of purple. They stood out against the dull, lifeless white of her complexion. Dirty blonde wisps stood in erratic, frizzy waves where they had escaped the elastic restraining the unruly curls. She'd taken a shower that morning, but the strands were dull and lanky from sweat, humidity, and grease. She ripped the band out and tossed it down on the counter before shoving away from the mirror to undress. Her waitress uniform hit the floor and was left there as she turned away to climb into the tub for a quick shower.

It was after four in the morning by the time she fell face first across the bed.

True to his promise, Martin had left a note with the accounting clerk regarding her five hundred dollars. The check was waiting for her when Juliette returned to the hotel the next morning. She signed for it before making her way to the staff lounge and the coin operated phone mounted to the wall.

Juliette didn't own a cellphone. It was an extra expense that she couldn't afford. Vi had one and only because it gave Juliette some piece of mind knowing her sister could use it in case of an emergency, even though, at the end of the month, Vi racked up a bill fit for six cellphones. But Juliette had no problem using a payphone if she really needed to. She very seldom ever had anyone to call anyway.

There were still three hours before her shift started at the arcade and fun pit. Thankfully, unlike her commute from the diner on the outskirts and the hotel smack dab in the very heart of the city, the arcade was a reasonable twenty minutes from her house by bus. The bank was ten minutes. But she still had to call Arlo and hopefully talk him into taking the five hundred for the time being. The very thought made her insides writhe.

The staff lounge was occupied by one other person, a woman in a maid's uniform. Realistically, for the amount of time Juliette spent at the hotel, she should have at least known some of the others. Some she did recognize on sight, but others were new or she never paid attention. Maybe that made her an antisocial weirdo, but she rarely found time to sit down and have a proper meal, never mind an actual conversation with another human being.

The woman never glanced up when Juliette hurried across the worn carpet to the tiny alcove cut into the other side of the room. The phone booth hung over a small, wooden table containing a tattered phonebook. It was flipped open to a cab company ad. The number was circled with a bright, red pen.

Juliette ignored it as she snatched up the phone, inserted fifty cents and punched in Arlo's number. After seven years, it was as clear to her as her own name. She didn't even need to look at the dial pad.

A man answered on the fourth ring.

"Yeah?"

Juliette had to swallow hard before she could answer. "This is Juliette Romero. I need to speak to Arlo ... please."

The gruff man said something away from the phone. There was some scuffling and then Arlo's voice was in her ear.

"Juliette. Do you have my money?"

Nausea soured the contents of her empty stomach. The plastic handle squished beneath her clammy palm as she gripped the phone harder.

"Not exactly," she murmured unsteadily. "I have some of it, but—"

"Juliette." Feigned disappointment crackled between them in the single exhale of her name. *"I don't like hearing that."*

"I know, and I tried, but it's a lot of money to get in a single night."

Arlo sighed. *"How much do you have?"*

More and more, it was becoming increasingly harder to breath around the sickness climbing up her throat. Dull, gray fingers had begun to creep up around the edges of her vision and she had to struggle not to pass out.

"Juliette."

Oh how she hated when he said her name like that, in that sing-song manner.

"Five hundred," she said. "I have ... it was all I could get."

There was a hiss of air being sucked through clenched teeth.

"Oh that isn't what we agreed to at all, is it, Juliette? That isn't even half."

"I'll get the rest—"

"You know, it's not about the money, Juliette. It's about keeping your word. I was really good to you, wasn't I? I gave you time—"

"One day isn't—"

Arlo kept on talking. *"I thought for sure we had some kind of understanding when we spoke yesterday. But maybe you just don't care about your sister as much as you claim. Maybe you're hoping I'll take the hindrance off your hands."*

"No! Please, Arlo, just give me a little—"

"The time for bargaining is over, Juliette. I want your sister delivered to me by six PM sharp tonight or I will get her myself."

Chapter 2

The shivering wouldn't stop. It ravaged the length of her body in rivulets of hot and cold so severe, it was worse than the time she'd had the flu and had to be admitted to the hospital. Every inch of her hurt with a viciousness that felt stifling and unbearable. She couldn't breathe and the world kept going in and out of focus.

Somehow, by some miracle, she found herself at home. Its emptiness seemed to howl around her in a cruel sort of silence. Puddles of light and shadow spilled across every room in a filmy dark gold. The previous night's supper, something cheesy and creamy, lingered through the space, yet despite the fact that she was starving, the scent made her queasy. Her insides roiled and gave her just enough warning to get her sprinting for the bathroom.

Dear God, this can't be happening.

Partially wheezing and partially sobbing, she huddled down next to the toilet with her legs drawn and her clammy face mashed into her raised knees. Her body heaved with every struggled breath until she was certain she'd pass out from lack of oxygen.

Somewhere deep in the house, hinges squeaked. A floorboard creaked. Any other time, the sounds wouldn't have filled her with unimaginable dread, but in that moment, it only made her want to cry harder.

"Juliette?" The raspy voice soaked up the silence. "Juliette, are you home?"

Pulling herself together and scrubbing away all lingering signs of her weakness, Juliette twisted her face into a smile and stepped out of the washroom.

"Hello Mrs. Tompkins! Did I wake you?"

As small and frail as a child, Abagail Tompkins stood barely at five feet with fine, white hair that hung in straggles around her withered face. Her blue eyes had faded to gray, but still sparkled in a way that always made Juliette envious. She stood in the doorway between the kitchen and dining room, clad in her floral housecoat and pink slippers.

Mrs. Tompkins rented the one bedroom in-law suite in the basement. It worked out for both of them, because Mrs. Tompkins was on a fixed budget that barely covered the cost of a matchbox and Juliette needed someone to be home with Vi when she couldn't be.

"I was up," the woman croaked. "Joint pains," she explained with a miserable shrug. "But how are you?" She looked Juliette over. "You're not at work today?"

The arcade.

Juliette wanted to swear and kick something, but that would only concern Mrs. Tompkins all the more.

"I'm going in a few minutes. I came home to change." She paused before adding. "I'll be working a triple shift tonight. Do you think—?"

Mrs. Tompkins put gnarled hands up. "Don't you worry about a thing. I'll make my chicken casserole and make sure Little Miss does her homework."

Grateful not to have to worry about at least one thing, Juliette smiled. "Thank you." She started for the stairway. "Let Vi know that I put you in charge and she has to listen."

Thin lips pursed and Mrs. Tompkins huffed. "I raised five children and six grandchildren. I know how to put down the law."

Laughing, Juliette climbed the rest of the way to the top. The moment she was out of ear and eye shot, her smile dissolved. Her shoulders drooped. She stumbled into her bedroom and shut the door.

She knew she needed to call Wanda at the arcade and let her know she would be late, but there was a lack of energy to do anything. Normally, each day was done with a sort of numbness that didn't end until she was face flat across the sheets. But that protective veil had been ripped away and

Juliette was exhausted and yet, oddly, highly alert. Her mind was a tangled knot of everything and anything she could possibly do to get Arlo his money. There was still seven hours before she had to see him and she knew she wouldn't be able to rest until she'd tried everything.

She could get an extra two hundred from her overdraft protection at the bank. It was a risk, because the bank had already warned her they would shut her accounts down if she did that again. But what choice did she have? It was either her bank account or her sister. There really was no other option. Still, that left her five thousand, three hundred unaccounted for and nothing short of selling the house was getting her that. Even if that was an option, seven hours wasn't enough time to do it.

Pacing, she slid sweaty fingers back through her hair and fisted, ripping out strands from their roots, but not caring. Below, she could hear Mrs. Tompkins puttering around the kitchen. Cupboards opened and closed. Dishes rattled. She heard the beep of the oven being preheated. Then the quiet hum of some lullaby song Mrs. Tompkins always hummed while cooking.

Juliette dropped down on the edge of her bed and stared absently at her dresser. Most of the drawers were empty whereas once, they barely closed. She had sold most of her high end, brand named stuff and lived off thrifty jeans and t-shirts, much to Vi eternal disgrace. But they were cheap and practical. She withdrew a fresh pair of pants and a top and stripped quickly out of her sweat drenched clothes. She combed out her hair and refastened it in a ponytail before grabbing her purse and hurrying downstairs.

"Mrs. Tompkins, I have to run to the bank, but I'll be right back."

She heard *all right, dear* just before she shut the front door behind her and bounded down the front steps.

The bank was around the corner from the house, a white building lined with sheets of glass that were tinted a green-blue against the sun. Juliette went to the teller first to cash the check before making a straight line for the machines. Her fingers shook as she inserted her card.

The two hundred dollars went into the envelope along with the five hundred from the hotel. It was stuffed back into her purse before she left the building and made her way home.

"I don't want your stupid casserole!" was the first thing Juliette heard when she stepped back into the house. "I'm going out with my friends."

Dropping her purse down on the table next to the door, Juliette followed the shrill sound of her sister's screeching and found the blonde looming over the island while Mrs. Tompkins diced chicken into neat cubes on the cutting board.

"Your sister put me in charge," Mrs. Tompkins said evenly. "That means I want you at that table doing your homework."

"You haggard old c—"

"Hey!" Outrage crackled down the length of Juliette's spine as she barged into the room. "What's the matter with you?"

At sixteen, Vi was the exact build and height as Juliette. They shared everything right down to the dirty blonde hair and brown eyes. The only thing that differed was their attitude. But even that, Juliette had once shared. Vi was exactly how Juliette used to be, shallow, self-centered, and engrossed in the knowledge that nothing bad could possibly ever happen to her. In a lot of ways, Vi was the way she was because Juliette refused to open her eyes to their situation. She knew Vi knew enough, but if she knew the full extent, she never let on. Juliette was fine with that. She had already grown up too fast for the both of them.

"Why do I have to listen to her?" Vi demanded, waving a thin arm in Mrs. Tompkins'ss direction. "She's nobody."

"She's family," Juliette countered sharply. "And you better watch your tone."

Vi's pert little nose wrinkled in a clear show of disgust. "She's not my family and I don't have to do shit." She swatted a strand of hair off her shoulder with a dismissive flick of her wrist. "I'm going out with my friends. I need money."

Juliette shook her head. "I don't have money and you're not going anywhere."

"Are you serious right now?" The deafening volume of Vi's shriek nearly made Juliette wince. "Oh my God, you are trying to ruin my life!"

"I'm trying to get you to finish your schooling," Juliette countered calmly. "You need to graduate, Vi."

"Ugh! I have a life and I have friends and I don't need you—"

"And homework that needs to be done," Juliette finished for her. "I have to go to work so you are going to listen to Mrs. Tompkins, eat your supper, do your homework and watch TV, or something. I don't care. But you're not leaving this house."

"You are not my mother!" Vi roared, flags of crimson flooding her cheeks. "You can't tell me what to do!"

"I can," Juliette said with a note of sadness she couldn't suppress. "I am your legal guardian and that means I'm responsible for you and your wellbeing until you're eighteen. Until then, you listen to what I tell you or—"

"Or what?" Her hiss was mocking and cruel.

Juliette never flinched. "Or I send you to Uncle Jim's farm and let him ruin your life for the next two years."

All color drained from the other girl's face in a single sweep of horror.

"You are such a bitch!"

Eyes glittering, Vi stormed from the kitchen. Juliette listened as the crack of her pink pumps resonated off the hardwood all the way down the hall. Then all the way up the stairs. It ended with the booming bang of the upstairs bedroom.

She sighed heavily into the silence her sister's tantrum had left behind. Mrs. Tompkins studied her with sad, shrewd eyes, but thankfully didn't comment; they had gone through this song and dance before with Vi. Juliette had apologized profusely over and over again for the girl's behavior. There was nothing left to do.

"I'm going to work," she mumbled at last. "You might not be able to reach me, but I'll try to be back some time tomorrow morning."

Mrs. Tompkins nodded. "All right, dear."

Taking her weary frame, Juliette ambled her way upstairs. In Vi's room, the stereo blared something angry and loud that rattled the door. Juliette let it be. She had learned long ago not to fight every battle if she wanted to win the war, and Vi was one giant war.

In her room, she stripped quickly and showered. Then she dressed carefully in a short, black skirt and a white blouse over a white camisole. She combed out her hair and left it in a rippling wave down her back while she applied a fine stroke of makeup, all the while, avoiding her own eyes in the mirror.

There was no longer room to ignore the inevitable. She had done her best, but in the end, there was only one final option. One last thing she could give Arlo to protect Vi. While she lacked the courage to put a name to the unthinkable, she knew what needed to be done.

It had never dawned on her just how much she weighed until her entire weight was being supported by the grace of her unsteady legs. The three inch pumps she'd forced her feet into wrenched and wobbled across gravel as she hobbled her way to the warehouse doors. Lights spilled through the cracked windows on either side of the sheet of metal, a sure sign that someone was home. A burly man stood in front, sucking lightly on a cigarette. Juliette could just make out the crimson little rosebud flare up with every inhale. His dark attire enfolded him in the setting dusk. But the light from inside the factory glinted off the smooth globe of his shaved head and the thick silver hoop stretching his earlobe. Eyes squinting, he watched her approach through the plume of gray smoke he expelled between them.

"I'm here to see Arlo," Juliette said with all the gumption she could muster. "He's expecting me."

He brought the tabacco stick to his mouth again and she caught the sharp glint of a bar piercing through his bottom lip. His free hand slipped behind his back and he withdrew a walkie-talkie.

"Boss? There's a girl here to see you."

There was a long pause of silence where Juliette was forced to see who would blink first. He did when static erupted from the device in his hand.

"What she look like?"

The guard looked Juliette over, assessing her quickly. "Blonde. Kind of hot."

Any other time, any other person, the compliment would have been flattering. But knowing the reason she was there, Juliette wanted to be sick.

"Send her in."

Clipping the walkie-talkie back on his belt, the guard took hold of the iron handle and yanked the heavy doors apart, revealing a patch of dim yellow light against the night.

Juliette stepped carefully over the threshold and onto smooth concrete.

The entrance opened into a wide foyer caged in by slabs of metal. An opening had been cut into one side that led into an eerie darkness.

Her insides quivered with apprehension. Her hands shook as she smoothed them down her skirt. She looked back to see if the guard would at least show her the way, but he gave her one last, almost pitying glance and let the door slam shut between them.

Alone, she started forward through the dingy hue of a single dangling lamp swaying miserably overhead. The opening bent into a narrow corridor that stopped abruptly at several sharp turns. It reminded her of a maze and she was the mouse that had to find the cheese. The click of her heels seemed to echo through the place in a hollow pulse, resounding off the metal and bouncing along each thick beam overhead.

It hadn't been very hard to find where Arlo would be that night. It was a Friday and that meant collection day. Anyone who owed the Dragons made sure that they had their money in before the end of that day. Juliette had been there every last Friday of the month for seven years, but she'd never gone inside. Usually, she gave her money to the guy outside and left. She knew it was safe because no one was stupid enough to double cross Arlo.

The clan had been in the family for generations, getting passed down from father to son. Juan Cruz was still the kingpin of the eastside, but Arlo ran the streets. He was the one who got his hands dirty and had built himself a name that most wouldn't even dare whisper. They were mostly runners, smuggling everything from drugs, to guns, to children and women. Juliette hadn't known that world existed outside of cop shows until the day Arlo had shown up on her doorstep. Now she was in so deep she didn't think she'd ever be able to get out.

The end of the corridor opened to every frat boy's dream playhouse. It was built with the sole purpose of entertainment and comfort. The area was large, large enough to hold two pool tables, a full arcade tucked into one corner, and a lounge in the other. There was also a built in bar with an enormous oak counter that gleamed under the dull fingers of light spilling down from the dangling lamps overhead. A long, wooden table took over the center of the room like an ugly gash. The thing was painted a faded gray and there were no chairs around it. Only men.

There were four standing at the table with Arlo. Six more sat around the lounge area watching some basketball game on the plasma TV mounted into the wall. They all looked up when Juliette stepped into their domain. The TV was muted.

"Juliette." Arlo stepped away from the papers he and the four men had been poring over. "I see your sister isn't with you so I'm assuming you have my money."

Willing her nerves to hold steady, Juliette closed the wide distance between her and the monster watching her. She stopped when there were three steps between them.

"I don't have all of it, but I brought whatever I could raise."

She pulled out the envelope from her purse and held it out. Arlo smoothed a hand over his grinning mouth. He chuckled.

"That wasn't our deal, Juliette."

She nodded, wishing he would take the money because her hand was beginning to tremble.

"I know, but I … I'm willing to work off an extension."

There was no mistaking how scared she was. Everything right down to the tips of her hair shivered with barely suppressed terror.

Arlo arched an eyebrow. He shoved away from the table and started towards her in a slow, almost taunting strides.

"And how do you propose to do that?"

Her arm dropped to her side. A hot wave of mortification rushed up her throat to fill her cheeks. She could feel the eyes burning into her, the ears all listening, waiting for her response.

"In whatever way you want."

Her voice caught on each word like hooks snagging on flesh. She felt each one rip away a piece of her until she was in bloody tatters.

Arlo stopped dead in his tracks. A darkness that made her skin crawl crept into his eyes. They raked over her, a slow progression along the length of her. His teeth caught the corner of his mouth.

"I'm sure we can think of something." He rubbed an absent hand along the curve of his jaw. "Why don't you take all that off and get on the table so I can get a better look at what you're offering?"

Juliette's muscles stiffened.

"Problem?" he challenged.

Her gaze darted to the six men sitting almost motionless across the room.

"Don't worry about them," Arlo said casually. "They don't mind watching." He paused to slide a tongue over his teeth. "And if you're good, I might not even share you."

Crippling panic slammed into her. It rolled down the length of her spine in a serrated wheel of ice. The packet of money slipped from her numb fingers and struck the side of her foot. Bills spilled free from the top. They lay forgotten as she struggled not to join them in a crumpled heap on the ground.

Arlo watched her, dark eyes hooded with a sick sort of pleasure. She knew fear was the thing that gave him his power, but she couldn't stave hers back. It rushed over her, hot and formidable, threatening to drown her. Around the room, silence continued to crackle. But it was the type of silence no one ever wanted to hear.

"Juliette," Arlo purred in that mocking drawl of his. His boots scoffed across concrete as he swaggered forward. "You're making this very hard on yourself."

Heart beating louder than his words, Juliette willed herself not to turn and bolt. She knew that would only make things worse. She knew running would only fuel the whole pack into chasing her. So she stood perfectly still. He stopped before her, smelling of beer and cheap cigarettes. There was a stain—tomato sauce—just on his stubbled chin. Juliette focused on that rather than the predatory glint in his eyes.

"Undress or I will undress you."

He emphasized his promise with a sharp click of a switchblade being snapped open. She hadn't even seen him remove it from his pocket, yet it sat in his hand, glinting menacingly for all it was worth.

Her fingers trembled as she lowered her purse. The bag hit the ground with an almost resounding thump that was nowhere near as loud as it sounded in her head. The sound made her jump despite having expected it. Ignoring it, she reached numbly for the buttons holding her blouse together. The fastens slipped with too much ease through the holes. The V parted inch by painful inch to expose the camisole and the full curves of her breasts. They rose and fell rapidly with her every ragged breath. The sight of them seemed to drag Arlo to her. It took all her strength and courage not to be sick when his heat crawled over her, thick and speckled with his foul stench. Her skin prickled in reaction. Her stomach recoiled. She would have flinched back, but her shoes had fused themselves into the grimy floor. All she could manage to do was avert her face when his pushed all the closer.

"Faster, Juliette," he urged, his voice breathless with anticipation. "I'm not a patient man and I have been waiting a long time for this."

A choked sound escaped. Her mortification was swallowed by the crippling reality of what was about to happen. She was under no illusion that Arlo would be gentle. He wouldn't care that she had never been with a man. No doubt he would relish the fact. She just prayed to God he didn't do it right there in front of his men or worse, let them have her, too.

A sob worked up into her throat, suffocating what little oxygen she'd managed to hang on to. It formed a tight ball in her windpipe, choking her until she was certain she'd blackout. Part of her hoped she did. Then she wouldn't be present for whatever he did to her.

His fingers, rough and almost scaly, brushed against the contour of her cheek, smearing the tear that had slipped past her defenses. The salty tang was smudged across the quivering curve of her bottom lip, bringing with it the taste of pizza and sweat leftover on his skin. The sensation kicked at her stomach, harassing the frothing bile.

"Pretty little Juliette." His fingers curled into her jaw, cutting and biting as her face was wrenched towards his. "Always looking down your nose at me, thinking you were too good to lower yourself to my level and yet…" His grip tightened. His grin broadened. "Here you are, giving me the thing you swore you never would. How mortifying for you this must be."

Juliette said nothing. She could think of nothing to say. Part of her was afraid she might spit on him, or vomit if she even considered opening her mouth.

The hand fell away to close around her upper arm instead. The unevenly cut nails tore at flesh as she was hauled forward. The envelope of money went skidding under her feet, littering bills in all direction. No one seemed to notice. Everyone was too busy watching as Arlo shoved her against the table. The thing must have been bolted into the concrete, because it didn't so much as budge with the impact. But Juliette knew her hip would hold evidence of the assault come morning.

That was all the time she was given to think about it though. The next moment, Arlo had her wrenched down onto her back. His hands grabbed her wrists when her survival instincts kicked in almost automatically and she began flailing. Her arms were slammed down against the wood just above her head with enough force to steal her breath away with the pain. Her thighs were forced apart by lean hips.

"Don't fight me, Juliette," he panted, washing her face with his sour breath. "You came to me, remember? You asked for this."

By *this* he meant the hand he forced between their bodies. The fingers tore at fabric until it found skin. Above her, his grunt was met by her weak sob. He didn't seem to mind when she squeezed her eyes shut tight and twisted her face away. He had found what he'd been searching for. Blunt fingers brutally prodded against her dry opening, jabbing and pinching despite the resistance of her body. Against her thigh, his erection seemed to swell the harder she tried to buck him off. It burned through the rough grain of his jeans to singe her with every grind of his hips.

"Please..." she choked out, desperately trying to wrench away. "Please stop..."

"Are you sure that's what you want?" He ran the flat length of his tongue across her jawline. "I don't mind having your sister instead. Didn't think so," he mocked when she clamped her teeth down on her lip. "So be a good girl and let me in."

Despite every voice in her head screaming for her not to do it, she let her body go limp. She shut her eyes and prayed to God it ended quickly.

"Boss? We got company."

The phantom voice shattered through the sound of labored breathing, of buttons and zippers being undone. It cracked through Juliette's sanity, nearly destroying her as relief speared through her.

Arlo drew away and she wasted no time rolling off the table. Her knees deserted her and she hit the ground hard enough to peel the skin on her knees and palms. The room swam behind a thick film of tears that threatened to fall no matter how hard she tried to battle them back. Her entire body shuddered with a violence that made her feel half crazy, like the only thing keeping her sane was the shock.

Above her, Arlo cursed and reached for the walkie-talkie set somewhere on the table.

"Who is it?" he snapped into the device. "Tell them I'm busy."

"Is that right?"

The voice was deep with a rolling accent that vibrated through the silence as easily as a whip. It was followed by the steady clip of approaching footsteps. A moment later, the entranceway was filled by no less than eight men in sleek, expensive suits in varying shades of gray and black. One man stood at the helm, tall, dark, and breathtaking in a way Juliette couldn't help noticing despite the circumstances. He was the type of man who belonged on the cover of GQ. The kind that romance novels were written about and women longed for. He radiated power, the kind that dominated the space and crackled like the approach of a terrible thunderstorm. Juliette could feel the snap of his presence even from a distance. She could feel the rise of the hairs along her arms. The sharp scrape of it along her skin. It rippled through her veins to pool somewhere deep inside her like a harsh combination of alcohol and fear. Whoever this man was, he was dangerous and he was pissed.

"Are you busy, Cruz?" he spat, slicing through the thickened air with an Irish lilt that she would have found dead sexy any other time. Eyes the voluminous black of absolute night pivoted against a face defined from the very definition of rugged and focused on Juliette still on all fours half under the table. They narrowed. "Is this your idea of busy?"

Nerves frayed beyond repair, Juliette fumbled for the edge of the table and forced her body up. Her knees buckled uncontrollably, sending her staggering into the wood. But she remained upright, which was a miracle in itself.

"Wolf." Arlo set the walkie-talkie down and clapped his hands together once and kept them firmly clasped in front of him as he regarded the group. "I wasn't expecting a visit."

"Weren't you?" The man took a single step deeper into the warehouse. "Bit surprising that considering this is the third time this week your men have been caught doing business on my turf."

"A mistake," Arlo said hurriedly. "I'm dealing with my crew and it won't happen again."

"No, it won't." He moved closer, his strides unnaturally even and calm. "But that doesn't change the facts. You owe us for using my streets to peddle your garbage. I'm here to collect."

A muscle jumped in Arlo's jaw. Juliette recognized it as well concealed rage. She expected him to lash out, to throw the first punch or, at the very least, tell the guy to get out. Instead, she was surprised by the restraint tightening the length of his jaw. It made her wonder just who the newcomer was, because anyone who scared Arlo enough to curb his temper was clearly someone not to screw with.

"Unless you'd rather I took this to your father," the man went on. "I'm sure he'd like to know why I was forced to make this trip."

At the mention of his father, Arlo seemed to straighten and shrink back at the same time. Juliette noticed only because they stood a mere five feet apart. Everyone else seemed to be focused on the scattered envelope of money the man idly nudged with the toe of one shiny dress shoe. He seemed unperturbed by the fact that there was hundreds of dollars just lying across the floor. Juliette showed that type of disinterest to litter on the streets.

"There's no need to involve my father," Arlo said, propping his ass against the ledge of the table and folding his arms. "I'm sure we can come up with a solution that suits us both."

Stepping over the envelope, the man shrugged. "All right then."

He drew to a stop in the strip of space separating Juliette from Arlo. That close, he was a too-close two feet from her. Close enough so that she could stretch out a hand and touch his broad back. So close that she could easily make out the fine, white lines running vertically down his suit and catch the shimmer of light playing amongst the thick strands curling over the collar of his suit. But what she noticed most was that she could no longer see Arlo and she had a feeling he couldn't see her either. It was crazy to think it was deliberate, but she couldn't help feeling relief at the temporary security.

"Seventy."

Arlo's short, hard laugh spoke of his outrage before he even spoke.

"Seventy percent? That's more—"

"More than half," the man cut in. "I've done the math."

"That barely covers the cost of shipment, never mind—"

"Not my problem. That's the cost of doing business in my neighborhood without my say so. Something you should have thought of, clearly. I don't take well to guns being traded in my parks. You're lucky I don't ask for the full hundred."

Juliette couldn't help herself. Curiosity and a whole lot of stupidity had her leaning an inch to the left to peer around the man's looming frame to where Arlo stood looking like someone had just force fed him a cluster of cockroaches. His sour expression only seemed to deepen when her movement caught his attention. The anger in his eyes sharpened even as they narrowed and she knew she'd screwed up.

"Why don't we talk about this in private?" He bit out as he heaved away from the table and reached for her. His hand closed around her wrist and she was dragged to his side forcibly. "Pierre, take Juliette into the other room. This is no place for a woman. We'll continue where we left off when I'm finished."

The notion of picking up where they'd left off churned in the pit of her stomach. Her gaze flicked to the man watching her. His expression was void of everything, but a bored sort of disinterest that assured her she would get no help from him. Not that she had expected it. Nevertheless, she couldn't stop herself from silently begging him not to leave her there. But he made no move to do anything when she was hauled away from the group towards a set of doors across the room. The grimy sheet of metal lay hidden behind a thick curtain of shadow and shrieked like a lost soul when it was wrenched open. She was shoved inside and sealed in.

Chapter 3

If there was anything Killian truly hated in the world it was having his time wasted. Already he'd had to reschedule six different appointments and reorder his calendar just to make the drive east, which was more than a rat like Arlo Cruz deserved. But it was something that needed to be done. Oh, he could have easily sent his men to make the point for him, but something like selling guns in broad daylight, in a park full of children spurred the psychopath in Killian into taking action. Plus a part of him was actually hoping Arlo would refuse, giving Killian an excuse to rid the world of the arrogant little fuck once and for all. It was purely out of respect for Arlo's father that Killian was even willing to negotiate the problem. Juan Cruz was a vicious, violent, and bloodthirsty member of the underworld, but he understood the laws. He, like everyone else in the business, respected those laws. It was how peace was kept. The younger generation like Arlo, they sometimes forgot the order of things.

"Why don't we have a drink and—"

"Why don't you cut the shit and hand over my money," Killian cut in, feeling his nerves reaching their maximum bullshit quota.

Agitation bore into the place just between his shoulder blades like an unreachable itch. It was taking all his resolve not to just kill the fucker and leave. It would certainly solve a lot of problems, but ultimately, it would also create a shit storm Killian was in no mood to deal with.

"I think we can all agree that forty is a more reasonable solution," Arlo was saying when Killian forced himself to pay attention once more. "It's a win for everyone."

"Forty?" Disgust and outrage laced the single snarled word, serrating the edges until they were razor sharp. "This is not a negotiation. You broke the rules. You came into my territory to peddle your crap. Now, I don't do business on your streets, but if I did, I would have the decency to pay the toll. So, give me my money or we will have a serious problem."

There was a subtle sound of movement from the men stationed around the room. Killian was acutely aware of the gun metal and powder smell that stung the air. He knew everyone there, including his own men, were armed. He knew it would be a bloodbath if things went sideways. But he also knew Arlo was too much of a coward to go down in a glorious blaze of gunfire, because he was the type to shoot a man in the back in a dark alley rather than face him. Killian didn't need a gun to destroy a man.

"Maybe we could make it forty and I'll sweeten the pot with a little something extra."

Bargaining. Killian had been expecting it and yet it sent a spike through his head, making his temple pang in pain.

"What could you possibly have that would make me eat thirty percent of a ten million dollar profit?" he demanded.

The leer that twisted Arlo's rat face made his knuckles itch with the desire to clock the other man in the kisser.

"Juliette."

That name meant nothing to him, nor did it elicit even an ounce of interest. If anything, it only irked him all the further.

"The girl?" he said, not bothering to even glance at the door across the room. "Why would I want her?"

"Consider her a peace offering," Arlo cajoled smoothly. "And hopefully, the beginnings of a business partnership."

Now he really did want to hit the little punk.

"I don't dabble in stolen women."

Something sharp and angry flashed behind Arlo's brown eyes that Killian recognized as outrage, but it was quickly smothered down.

"I have a shipment coming in in a week that will make us both very happy men."

"If I let you use my docks," Killian finished, having already had this song and dance with Arlo's father only the night before. "I already told your father, I'm no longer in that business."

Something about that statement seemed to amuse the other man. He shoved away from the table with a low chuckle and pivoted ever so slightly on the heel of his boots to face Killian head on.

"You say you're not in the business and yet ... here you are."

The implication sent a white hot surge of fury rippling through Killian.

"I may not be in the business, but that doesn't mean I'm about to let filth dirty up my streets. The north is still mine to protect."

Arlo gave an almost imperceptible nod. "I can respect that." His gaze roamed over to Killian's men before dropping down to the purse laying forgotten on the ground. "Then take the girl as a token of my apologies for this misunderstanding."

Killian tried not to pinch the bridge of his nose in impatience. He tried. Instead, his hand went up to grind four fingers into his throbbing temple.

"Why on earth would I take a girl that looks barely old enough to tie her own shoelaces over seven million dollars?" He sighed and fixed Arlo with cool, dark eyes. "I am losing my patience, Cruz."

A palm was lifted in some absurd display of peace. "Like I said, a peace offering. Nothing more. I will get you the money, but I can only give you forty now and thirty in a week when my other shipment comes in. The girl is ... a gift."

"Is this a game to you?" Killian growled through his teeth. "Do you think I'm here as a joke?" He drew back. "Perhaps you need an incentive."

Pivoting on his heels, he started towards the exit. His heels cracked noisily against the concrete. His men watched as he approached, but none were looking at him; he didn't pay them to ogle him, but to watch his surroundings.

"Wait!" Arlo called at his back. "I will have the money sent directly to your account in the morning."

Killian stopped. He slowly rounded on his heels. "I said now. Not in a day. Not in an hour or in five minutes. Now."

A muscle wrenched in Arlo's jaw that had his nostrils flaring, but he was smart enough to keep it out of his tone when he spoke.

"David."

One of the men from his crew hurriedly dug out his phone. Killian glanced back at his own man and gave a subtle nod. Max pulled away from the group and went to where David stood. The two exchanged account information while Killian waited. He checked his watch. He was already ten minutes behind.

"Pierre, the girl," Arlo ordered.

It was on the tip of Killian's tongue to tell Pierre not to bother. He didn't want the girl. But the Goliath had already thrown open the door with a shriek of rusted hinges. The steel sheet swung inward to what appeared to be a bedroom of sorts. Killian could just see the girl standing in the middle of the room, small and terrified. Her thin arms were wrapped around her chest, creasing the white material of her blouse. She backed away when Pierre charged into the room with her. Even from a distance, he heard her cry out when a meaty fist closed around her upper arm and wrenched her forward. Her heels scraped on stone as she was dragged before the assembly. She was fighting him, but it was doing no good; he was three times her size.

"Juliette." Arlo took over when Goliath relinquished his grip. He hauled her to him and forcibly twisted her around so she was facing Killian. Enormous brown eyes shot up to his, a stark contrast to the pallor of her face. "This is the Scarlet Wolf. He's going to take you home tonight."

The Scarlet Wolf. Christ sakes. Who the hell introduced another person as *The Scarlet Wolf?* It was pathetic and he would have face palmed if he could do so without looking as moronic as Arlo. Besides, that was the title he had earned. It was the name everyone in the city knew him as, at least, those on the flipside of the law. People like Arlo and Juan. People who needed to be reminded of who he was and what he was capable of. It would forever be a reminder of a past he could never forget.

Across from him, what little color had resided in the girl face bleached to nothing so all that stood out was her eyes, wide and glossy with terror. They stared at Killian as though he were the devil reincarnated. She stood rigid against Arlo, her slight frame trembling hard enough to make Killian wince.

"This is Juliette," Arlo went on. "Juliette here owes me a favor and I would consider it paid in full if she were to help you relax."

Juliette seemed to still before his eyes. Killian could see something churning behind her eyes, a desperate sort of realization that parted her lips in a gasp.

Behind her, Arlo smirked. "Do we have a deal?"

She was thrust forward before she could even respond. Killian watched it happen as though in slow motion. He saw her stagger as her feet caught over each other. Her hands flung out to brace her fall. His own flew out without a shred of hesitation. He caught her—all of her—and hauled her into his chest. Her small frame tucked snuggly against his chest. His arms wound seamlessly around the curve of her narrow waist. Palms flattened against a slim slope of her back as the subtle scent of wildflowers rushed over him on impact. Eyes the rich gold of caramel shot up to his face, half hidden behind a riot of dirty blonde curls. Soft, pink lips parted, revealing just the hint of a slight overbite that seemed to be the only imperfection on an otherwise beautiful face. It was the sort of face that made smart men stupid and rich men poor. Killian wasn't immune, but he wasn't a fool either.

He released her quickly and stepped back.

"Keep her," he muttered, forcing himself to look away. "Please."

The whisper was so low, he momentarily wondered if he'd imagined it. His gaze flicked to the girl with her big, pleading eyes and pitiful plea. Blood welled where her teeth cut a gash in her bottom lip. But it was the tear clinging to her thick lashes that did him in. Something about the sight of it punched him low in the gut. It reminded him of another woman, one that had meant the world to him, one he had lost because he'd been powerless to save her.

"Get your things," Killian told her before his common sense could kick in.

Her throat muscles worked in a deep swallow. Relief shimmered in her eyes before she lowered them and hurried to the purse a few feet away. Her hand trembled as it was twisted around the worn strap. The spilled envelope of cash was left where it lay scattered in the dirt.

"Pleasure doing business with you," Arlo called after him when Killian started to turn away.

The smug arrogance in the single comment hackled along Killian's spine with slimy fingers. He glanced back at the *boy* standing in all his own self-righteous glory and almost scoffed. Arlo Cruz would be nowhere without his father's empire behind him. No doubt he would be just another statistic on the streets, a shit ass kid gunned down for robbing a liquor store. He had no class. He had no respect. The world had been handed to him on a gold platter and he relished in his own self-worth. Men like that seldom lasted very long in their line of work.

It was true that Killian got his own empire through several generations of McClarys before him. His father had trained him from the age of five to one day rule. But he'd been alone since he was ten. He raised himself. The city he owned and ran, he had held together by himself. His father hadn't held his hand or fixed his mistakes. Killian had done it on his own.

"Stay off my turf, Cruz," Killian said evenly. "I very much dislike repeating myself."

Arlo inclined his head, but Killian caught the barely suppressed rage hidden deep in the other man's eyes. He let it go. Arlo had every right to be pissed. Juan Cruz was not going to be pleased that his son managed to lose more than half their payment for a shipment that probably cost them double that to smuggle over. But that wasn't Killian's problem. Arlo was lucky Killian hadn't asked for the full profit, which was in his right to do. There would have been nothing Arlo or Juan could have done about it. They might have been the Dragons of the east, but Killian dominated the north with some deep connections in the south and west. It would have been a bloodbath and the Dragons knew it.

No one moved or spoke as Killian headed to where the girl stood, purse clutched to her stomach. She didn't budge when he stepped around her and started for the door. Max and Jeff led the way with the others left to follow in tight formation around Killian. Killian didn't wait to see if she would follow. If she didn't, well, that wouldn't be his problem either.

At the front entrance, the guard stationed there quickly jumped back when Killian's group emerged. He said nothing as they filed out, but his eyes lingered on the seven foot giant that took the end, guiding the girl through the doorway.

Frank had that effect on most people. He was twice the size of a regular man with hands bigger than Killian's entire head and a body straight out of a bodybuilder magazine. His very presence installed a fear in Killian's enemies no gun ever could. Not that his men didn't carry. They all did. Killian didn't and hadn't in years. It was a personal choice. He had enough blood on his hands and, while he still lived in a world that required a daily dose of violence, he tried to keep the bloodshed to a minimal.

A scuffle from behind him had him glancing back just as the girl's ankle twisted and she stumbled sideways. Frank caught her around the middle and nimbly set her back on her feet. He held on a moment as she limped on her injured foot a second.

"I'm okay," she said at last, pulling away. "Thank you."

Frank did what Frank did best, he inclined his head, but said nothing.

She glanced up to find the caravan had stopped and everyone was watching her. She blushed in the pale light spilling from the grimy light above the warehouse doors. Her hands nervously smoothed down her skirt and she adjusted the purse strap on her shoulder.

Killian took that as a cue to keep moving. All the while, he couldn't help wondering what the hell he'd gotten himself into and how the hell he was going to get out. Unlike Arlo who had no qualms about using and abusing the weak, Killian had no such fetish. The girl was clearly someone in way over her head, or worse, she was some girl kidnapped from her country and shipped over. The Dragons were certainly not averse to human trafficking. It was, after all, their biggest trade, next to drugs and guns. Killian had never, nor would he ever, sell a human. His father hadn't. His grandfather hadn't. It was not the type of business the McClary's had ever dealt in, because, despite how good the money was, they had morals. Oh, there was a time they dabbled in guns and there was an uncle, or cousin who had gotten himself into the drugs business. But he started dipping into his own product and wound up choking on his own vomit and dying and that had been the end of that. But the McClary's had always been shippers. Transporters. They specialized in the safe passage of cargo and took forty percent of every cut, but that was before. All that changed after Killian's dad died. It had taken years, but the entire company had been scrubbed to a near legal cleanse. The McClary Corporation no longer did transportation of the illegal kind. The money was less, but he still made a pretty coin through his many other business ventures. In no way was he a good, upstanding citizen, but he no longer had to play two sides of the law and that was something his family had never done. His grandfather would have been appalled.

Hands buried deep in the bowels of his pockets, Killian stalked to the limo waiting for him just were the gravel smoothed out to solid concrete. Most of the warehouse district was designed the same way, with gravel used as an almost alarm to forewarn the guilty of an oncoming presence. It was a pain in the ass and it left streaks of white on his best pair of trousers.

He glowered down at the white powder marring his hems and ruining his shoes.

That was his punishment for dealing with the matter himself, he thought miserably.

From his right, Marco hurried forward and yanked open the back door and held it.

Like Frank, Marco was one of the trusted employees Killian had kept on even after the purge. Everyone else had been fired the moment Callum McClary had been lowered into the ground. Their inability to protect his father had not been tolerated. But Marco was simply a driver. His father hadn't trusted him with his life and Frank hadn't been there that afternoon. His father had taken to dragging Killian everywhere since his mother's death. Killian wasn't sure if it was just to keep him close or because looking at Killian reminded his father of the woman he'd lost. But he'd sent Frank off to handle a different matter. It was an unusual move. His father rarely ever went anywhere without the giant. Sometimes Killian couldn't help wondering if his father would still be alive had Frank been there.

A cool evening breeze swept through the group. A shiver passed through him that he brushed off with a roll of his shoulders. Behind him, the group stopped when he did. Without their feet disturbing the gravel, silence quickly followed.

He turned to face them and the girl. His gaze moved over their heads to squint at the looming structure and the anxious guard watching them with apprehension. But it was the snake he was guarding that prickled the sixth sense Killian had inherited when stepping into the family business. The one that warned him to be cautious.

"Call Jacob," he told Dominic. "Tell him to be prepared."

The dark haired man on Killian's left inclined his head, but his brows were furrowed. "Think he's stupid enough to double cross you?"

Killian gave an almost imperceptible shrug. "I think he'll do what he can to avoid having to explain this to his father. Not that it will save him." He smoothed a hand down the front of his suit. "I have every intention of letting Juan know exactly why I'm taking his money."

"Arlo won't like that." While it was said with a straight face, there was amusement in the statement.

"That's just too bad for him isn't it now?" He rounded his attention to the other men waiting for instructions. "Take the car. I need a word with our guest."

The girl flinched as though he'd reached out and smacked her. Her grip on her purse intensified until he was sure the cracked and peeling fabric might pop. But she didn't run, or back down when their gazes met. He held hers for a full second before focusing on the figures fanned out behind her.

"Not you, Frank," he said when the giant began to turn his massive frames in the direction of the SUV parked just ahead of the limo. "Ride up front with Marco."

The giant gave a curt bob of his bald head before ambling to the passenger's side door of the limo. But he didn't get in, nor did the others make a move towards the SUV. He knew they were waiting for him to get into the limo first.

He faced the girl. "Ladies first."

Her gaze darted past him to the open door then back, filled with a trepidation that almost made him arch a brow.

"Are you going to sell me?" she blurted.

No accent, he noted. Her English was clear, but that didn't mean anything. Not all kidnapped girls were foreign.

"I don't sell people," he said evenly.

She licked her lips and he was momentarily distracted by the wet sheen across the plump curve. It took him a second to realize she was speaking once more.

"Are you going to hurt me?"

He regarded her calmly, taking in her hollow cheeks, the darkness beneath her eyes and the exhausted slump in her too thin shoulders. She had the look of someone who had once been healthy, but unavoidable circumstances had sucked the life from her body. He wasn't overly picky about the physical appearance of his women. Big or small, they served the same purpose. But this girl ... there was something in her eyes that made him want to stuff her full of food.

He derailed that thought before it could grow roots. For all her big, doe eyes, she wasn't his problem. He refused to make her his problem. He would drive her to the bus station, buy a one way ticket to wherever the hell she wanted to go and never think of her again. That was the plan.

"Are you going to give me a reason to?" he said at last with an almost challenging quirk of his dark eyebrow.

He wouldn't. He'd never hurt a woman in his life. But she didn't need to know that. Maintaining order sometimes required fear, a subtle reminder that he was in control.

She shook her head a little too quickly, sending loose tendrils of hair swinging wildly around her ashen face. "I won't. I promise."

He motioned her forward with a sweeping brush of his hand. "Then we shouldn't have any problems."

With a reluctant jerk of her head in a nod, she started for the gaping hole waiting for her to climb into. Around her legs, her skirt twisted with the breeze. It lifted her hair around her face in a tangle. Her knees shuddered visibly with every step. But she made it to the door when Marco stepped forward. Killian had been expecting it. The girl had not.

She jumped and scrambled back away from him.

"I just want your purse," he told her in an almost gentle murmur.

Rather than abide, her gaze shot to Killian's. "Why do you need my purse?" she asked. "I don't have any money."

"I don't want your money," he told her. "It's merely a precaution."

She hesitated a full second longer before gingerly unhooking the strap off her shoulder and passing it over. Marco wasted no time tearing it open and rifling around inside. Killian had a suspicion there wouldn't be much in there, especially not a gun. Somehow he doubted Arlo armed his whores. But he had learned from experience to never trust a pretty face.

As he expected, the purse was returned to her.

"Against the car, please," Marco said, motioning with his chin towards the side of the limo.

"Seriously?" Juliette blurted, horrified. Her wide eyes jumped back to Killian. "I'm not carrying."

"Precaution," he said again.

Visibly biting back the retort he could see shining in her eyes, she moved to where Marco pointed and set her purse down on the ground. Then she planted both palms on the hood, smudging the spotless black paint with sweat. But even while she braced herself for his hands, she jumped when they lightly brushed her shoulders and started down her sides. Her eyes squeezed shut tight when they moved along her hips and down her legs. Then back up the inside to her thighs. Marco was quick. It ended reasonably fast and she jerked away the moment Marco stepped back. She snatched up her purse, her face bright with the first sign of color Killian had seen on her.

She glared at Killian. "I don't like guns," she told him sharply. "I'm not a threat."

Unconsciously, the word *threat* drew his eyes to her mouth and he almost snorted at her outright lie. Everything about her was a threat and made even more dangerous by the fact that she clearly didn't realize it.

"Precaution," he said yet again, oddly fascinated by the fire reflecting in her eyes. He found he preferred it to the fear and emptiness he'd seen there so far. "You can never be too careful."

Her gaze slanted to where his men still stood, silent and watchful. She caught her bottom lip between her teeth and nibbled anxiously before returning her attention to Killian. Lips he couldn't seem to keep his eyes off of opened only to be snapped shut by the resounding bang of metal that split the evening silence. The explosion sent a flurry of chaos into motion. Killian leapt into action without even pausing to consider.

He grabbed the girl. His bruising hands cut strips into her skin as he jerked her forward into his chest. One arm closed firmly about her middle as the other lifted to thread rough fingers through her hair and cup the base of her skull. Her face was shoved into the soft fabric of his dress shirt even as he whipped them around in a fluid and powerful twist of his body. Her back slammed up against the side of the limo and held there by the solid length of him as he tried to shield her from whatever was happening in the background.

"Whoa! Easy. It's just me!" someone shouted into the chaos they'd created.

Killian pulled back from the girl just enough for a quick once over to make sure she was all right. He was met with those big eyes of hers and parted lips. Even with heels, she barely came to his shoulders and the slightness of her affected him far more than he was comfortable admitting. But it was the feel of the rest of her that had him jerking away. It was the graze of her taut little nipples through both their clothes that temporarily made him forget why he didn't pick girls like her. He tried not to let himself look, knowing full well that it would end with her flat on her back across the limo floor and him tearing at her clothes like some starved animal.

Christ, what was wrong with him? Sure it had been a while since he'd been with a woman, but it hadn't been *that* long.

He turned away, quickly and struggled to assess the situation. His men stood in a half circle around him and the girl, guns drawn and aimed at a kid barely eighteen, waving a white envelope in the air.

"Arlo wanted me to give this to her."

He gestured at the girl. Her eyes flicked towards Killian, uncertain and dark. He stepped aside and let her accept the envelope the boy handed to Dominic, who passed it to her. She took it with a quiet murmur of thanks and frowned. Her gaze shot up to the boy, questioningly.

"Boss said to hang on to this," the boy answered with an airy shrug.

It was clear from the bemused line crinkling the place between her brows that she had not expected the gesture. She turned it over in her hand and froze. Killian couldn't see what she'd spotted, but whatever it was had her head jerking up and her eyes going as round as the O shape of her mouth in surprise. She forgot the boy and turned her attention towards Killian. Part of him wanted to ask, while the other determined they'd been in that driveway long enough and his skin was beginning to itch.

"Get in the car," he told her, his hand already on her elbow, propelling her.

She didn't fight him. She let him nudge her into the leather seat. Killian followed her as she abandoned the bench and moved to the one adjacent. The harsh halo of light spilling over them from the single bulb overhead shimmered through her unbound hair and illuminated the bleakness of her face. It intensified the rings beneath her eyes and the smudge of dried blood still staining her lip from her earlier nibbling. She wedged herself into the seat, perching rigidly on the edge with her purse stuffed into her lap and her back unnaturally stiff.

She watched him the way most people watched a chainsaw wielding maniac.

Not far off, the voice in his head said dryly, and was ignored.

The door was shut behind them and they were alone in the semi silence. Somewhere ahead, he could just hear Marco and Frank climbing into their seats in front.

"What's your name?" he asked as the car started its smooth departure.

"Juliette," she whispered.

"Juliette what?"

"Romero."

A dark eyebrow lifted. "Juliette Romero?"

She met his gaze with a warning he found immensely amusing. "My mom really liked Shakespeare."

She seemed to think of something and quickly dropped her gaze. Her hands trembled as she stuffed the envelope into her purse.

"Where are you from?" he pressed.

She zipped the top of her bag before lifting her eyes to him. "Yorksten."

Surprise flickered through him. "That's only twenty minutes from here."

Juliette nodded.

Clearly not kidnapped then, he thought, sitting back. "How much are you in with Arlo?"

She blinked as though he'd caught her mid thought. "I'm sorry?"

"How much do you owe him," he clarified.

Genuine offence pursed her brow. "Why does that matter?"

"Because I said so."

She looked like she was ready to argue, but thought better of it. She grudgingly averted her eyes when she spoke.

"Hundred thousand."

He knew to most people that would have been shocking; a hundred grand was a lot of money. But in his world, that barely sparked an ounce of surprise. The crackheads and dope fends ran that bill up easy.

"Drugs?"

Juliette shook her head. "It's not my debt."

Curiosity had his head tilting a notch to the side. "Whose is it?"

His question seemed to bother her. Her lashes lowered to her lap where her hands were twisting restlessly into the strap of her purse. Her teeth assaulted her already brutalized lip, uncaring that she was agitating the wound. She stayed that way for several long minutes. Killian waited, refusing to budge on the question.

"My father's," she murmured at last. "He got in deep after my mother passed away from cancer. He started playing the tables and the machines and..." she trailed off with a twist of her lips. "Anything that promised a big payout really."

"He gambled," he finished for her.

Juliette nodded. "And he drank heavily. I didn't know about Arlo until he showed up at our house after my dad was shot during a drive by and demanded money or my sister."

He said nothing for a damn long time. Instead he studied the woman across from him, traced the beaten lines of her body. She had a very nice body. He was certainly not immune to it. She had long legs and curvy hips. Truthfully, there was nothing about her he found remotely unattractive, nor could he deny his own body's awareness of her.

He wanted her.

It was jarring because he didn't normally find girls like her remotely appealing. The women he was used to were professionals, clean and carefully selected by him. They knew what he wanted. They knew the role. Girls like Juliette, girls who came off the streets and gave themselves to men for whatever little money they considered themselves worth, were a risk. They were dangerous.

"Are you lying?" He squinted at her through the shadows, scrutinizing her every movement carefully. "Because if I find out you're lying…"

He didn't finish. He didn't need to. She struck him as a clever girl who would get his meaning without him needing to paint a picture.

Instead, she frowned at him like he just asked her to reenact Swan Lake.

"Why would I lie about having a sister?" she wondered with a hint of annoyance.

"You'd be surprised the things people lie about," he stated evenly. "But I meant about why you owe Cruz. Is it drugs?"

Juliette shook her head. "I don't do drugs and I'm not lying."

It was impossible to tell if she was telling the truth or not. She didn't falter or even bat an eyelash, yet something about her continued to nag at him. Something about her just didn't fit everything he was seeing and it was pissing the fuck out of him.

Outside, city lights flared past the windows, coloring the glass the electric pink and blue of the neon signs. The weekend had the younger crowd haunting the busy streets, club hopping and living their carefree lives. Juliette's attention was snapped away by a group of scantily clad women darting down the sidewalk, arm in arm, laughing and staggering drunkenly into each other. A taxi honked noisily when they bolted blindly across the intersection. They laughed riotously and disappeared down the block.

She continued to watch them long after they had vanished from sight and the longing in her eyes only intensified his curiosity. The shadows of sadness haunted the corners of her downward tilted mouth. Her teeth were back to nipping at her bottom lip and it took all his restraint not to reach over and pry it free, not to smooth his thumb over her self-inflicted injury. The leather beneath him rustled when the temptation had him shifting in his seat. The sound turned her focus back on him and their eyes met across the distance. Hers were so impossibly open. The vulnerability in them filled him with a frustration he had no idea what to do with, yet wanting to do something.

"Is your name really the Scarlet Wolf?" she asked quietly.

Despite the knot in his chest, Killian felt his mouth twitch.

"Killian," he said.

She nodded slowly. "Why do they call you the Scarlet Wolf?"

It was his turn to shift his gaze to the window, away from the question and those damn eyes. The surreal sensation of being asked was a new one; no one had ever asked him before and he was ill prepared with a response.

She didn't push.

"Thank you for not leaving me with Arlo," she murmured. She dropped her chin to study the clasp on her purse. "I don't know how to repay—"

"I don't want repayment," he cut in sharply, annoyed by the very idea. "And I didn't do it for you." And he hadn't.

His reasons for not leaving her alone in that warehouse had nothing to do with him being a good guy. Honestly, he would have left her there without a thought if it weren't for the fact that she reminded him of someone he had once loved. Maybe that made him an asshole, but there were hundreds of different groups of organized crime in the city. No way in hell was it possible to save every single victim. Juliette was no exception. It made no difference to him that his body was willing to overlook all his own rules for one night with her. He wouldn't be who he was if he let his cock do all the thinking.

"How long have you been in the Dragon's debt?" he cut into the awkward silence that had descended upon the car.

Juliette moistened her lips. "Seven years."

Seven years to pay off a hundred grand made sense. She wasn't paying the loan. She was paying the eighty percent interest and probably would be for the rest of her life. It was how loan sharks made a big chunk of their profits, by bullying and milking their victims for all they were worth. Odds were she would never be free of Arlo.

"So you've done this before then."

"This?" she asked, genuinely puzzled.

"Been with a man," he clarified.

She hesitated a full heartbeat before answering, "Yes."

Killian studied her. "How many?"

She shifted in her seat. "How many…?"

"Men."

She licked her lips again. "I … I don't know."

Normally, he didn't ask the woman he was planning on fucking for a number of past lovers. Most being escorts, he assumed had had plenty and that was how he preferred his women—experienced. Asking was just redundant. Virgins were messy and delicate and he wasn't gentle. He didn't possess the patience a virgin would require. But he sincerely wanted to know with Juliette. It was insane, but the thought of her having so many men she couldn't possibly keep count annoyed him. While he was perfectly aware that it was the twenty first century and women were allowed to have as many lovers as they wanted—it was her body after all—the idea of any man touching her pricked him with an irrational sense of irritation.

"You don't know?"

"I never thought to keep track," she snapped, her cheeks a deep scarlet. "A few."

He willed his voice to remain calm. "Are you clean?"

"Of course!" she snapped.

"When was your last john?"

The look of absolute horror and outrage would have been highly entertaining if he wasn't serious about his question.

"My ... *john*?" Disgust curled her lips. "I'm not a prostitute!"

"Your last *lover* then," he corrected, refusing to let her back out of the question.

"I don't know," she retorted with a sharpness that would have gotten her smacked if he were anyone else. "A while."

A moment passed while he contemplated his next question. One arm lifted and he propped the elbow on the handle of the door. His chin rested lightly on his loosely fisted fingers. He observed her through the three feet separating them with a solemn curiosity that made Juliette fidget. But she kept his gaze, unwavering and unflinching. The hypnotic dance of fire in her eyes pulled at him. The allure was too tempting to ignore as was the hot pool of desire forming in the pit of his stomach.

Mind made up, he lowered his hand and pushed the buttons built into the door. Juliette gave a startled jolt when the privacy window behind her rolled down, revealing Frank and Marco.

"Pull over, Marco."

The limo cut seamlessly off the road and came to a gentle stop. Juliette was watching him, her eyes filled with that fear he hated so much.

"You're free to go," he told, motioning with a jerk of his chin towards the door. "You can leave now and not have to go through with this. I won't stop you. But if you choose to stay, you will not be given a second chance to say no."

Confusion folded the skin between her eyebrows. Her eyes darted from him to the door and back. He didn't need to read minds to know she didn't understand why he was giving her the option of leaving. He let her wonder. He let her decide. He had never, not once ever forced a woman to do something she didn't want to do. He didn't hurt women. If Juliette wanted to leave, he would let her and never think of her again.

"I want to stay," she whispered, after what felt like hours of deliberation. "Please."

The quiver in her voice made him doubt her, but the determination in her eyes … oh, it was powerful and fierce. Whether she wanted him or not, she would give herself to him and he wanted her enough not to stop her a second time.

"Remove your blouse."

Chapter 4

As though that were the cue, the privacy window geared to life and rolled back up. The limo eased onto the road and they were moving once more. It made her wonder just how many other girls he'd had in his fancy limo. How many other girls had been given the option to leave and opted to stay? She wondered how many of them were still alive.

Pushing them and everything else from her thoughts, her fingers lifted to the buttons on her blouse. They trembled and refused to bend as she struggled to undo the fastens.

Across from her, he painted a hot path with his eyes along every inch that was exposed over the U-shaped collar of her camisole. Against the material, her nipples hardened as the air conditioned temperature nipped at sticky flesh. Her heart beat hard against her chest, cracking with a vengeance that could no doubt be heard for miles. There were no other sounds in her ears. Not the grind of rubber over asphalt. Not the purr of the engine. Not the rustle of clothing as her blouse came free and slid off her shoulders. She shut her eyes and willed herself not to yank it back on.

It was Arlo's promise that kept her mouth clamped shut tight. It was the promise of freedom. In return, all she had to do was sell her soul and belittle everything about herself. But it was worth it. It had to be. It would be, because it meant no longer being under Arlo's crushing thumb. It meant not working herself into the ground with nothing to show for it. It meant no longer walking down the street in fear. There was nothing she wouldn't do for that. One night with a stranger meant nothing in comparison.

But maybe she should tell him she'd never been with a man. While she wasn't sure that would make any sort of difference, it still terrified her. She had lied to him and he had warned her about that. It was just that he seemed like the sort who wanted someone experienced. Confessing to be a virgin would have no doubt either turned him on or turned him off and Juliette couldn't risk her sliver of hope on a hunch. So the lie had slipped a little too easily from her lips. A little too casual. It had curdled in the pit of her stomach like sour milk. It burned her cheeks with shame. While she wasn't a saint and had told plenty of lies in her life, they had been petty lies. Things she could easily walk away from. Things that didn't include lying to a man who held her life in his hands. But she couldn't risk the alternative. She needed to do this and she needed to do it well. Plus, who was to say he would even notice? It couldn't be too hard to fake being experienced.

Yet the idea made her stomach churn. It wasn't so much the idea of sleeping with Killian as it was the fact that it wasn't by choice. There was nothing remotely wrong with him, except him being a stranger ... and a criminal. The latter kept prodding at her. She silenced it by reminding herself that he didn't traffic in people. He had said as much. While she had no reason to believe him, she found that she actually did. That made her decision slightly easier. That and the knowledge that he was her only hope of survival.

"Come here," he instructed once she had bunched the fabric in her clammy hands. "Stay on your knees."

Setting aside her purse and blouse, Juliette slipped unsteadily off the bench. The soft carpet whispered against her knees as she slid the first step forward. The slight burn of her skin was nothing compared to the mortification of kneeling before another person. A stranger no less. There was nothing remotely romantic or sexual about it as most people would assume. It was degrading.

"Closer," he prompted when her body refused to follow the urging of her brain.

Sucking in a breath that smelled of new leather, liqueur, expensive cologne and wood polish, Juliette shuffled across the distance keeping her separate from the wolf. She stopped when his body heat washed over her and his knees were mere inches from brushing against her. She held her breath and waited for her next set of instructions.

"Closer."

Bemused, Juliette lifted her eyes to his face. The question sat poised on her lips when it was answered with a simple parting of his knees.

Alarms jingled between her ears with the ferocity of fire alarms. Her spit turned to ashes pouring down her throat with her audible gulp. She stared at his thighs, clad beneath material that probably cost more than her entire house and felt the urge to vomit in his lap.

You can do this, she willed herself when it became painfully apparently just what he wanted. *Don't think about it. Just do it!*

But it was easier said than done when she caught sight of the long, hard bulge outlined by the front of his dark trousers. Her stomach muscles seized in an odd mixture of surprise, terror, and curiosity. The latter was a knee jerk reaction that was quickly smacked down before it could take hold.

Juliette wasn't a stranger to a man's cock. While one had never been inside her, she had seen plenty of them. Possibly too many. It was the hazards of being a maid. She'd lost count of the number of times she'd walked into a room with the intent to clean only to find some asshole standing naked waiting for her. But aside from that, she'd been in what she had foolishly considered a steady and passionate relationship for three years. Stan had loved his penis. So much so that it had rarely seen the inside of his pants. Plus there was that weekend his parents had gone away and they had spent the better part of two days doing everything but have sex. Oh, but he had begged her to change her mind. It was the one decision she had prided herself on when things went to hell and Stan found solace between Karen's pasty white thighs ... until she found herself kneeling between the knees of a man she didn't even know, prepared to do more than suck his cock to keep from being killed or worse.

Maybe she really was a prostitute.

The thought was in no way comforting. It only made her all the more anxious to leave.

Stop thinking! The voice in her head hissed and she had to agree with it. Thinking wasn't helping.

Sucking in a deep breath, she reached for his buckle. The cool metal kissed trembling fingers only to be captured a second later. Long, tapered fingers curled effortlessly around the expanse of her hands. The hold was firm, but gentle in his restraint.

Confusion and surprise flicked her gaze to his face, to those intense, black eyes and full mouth. It was probably a bad time to notice when she was trying to keep her mind blank, but he really was ridiculously beautiful. The knowledge didn't ease the anxiety eating at her insides, but the fact that he wasn't some fat, hairy slob was a kind of small comfort.

"I thought…"

She was drawn off her knees and pulled up onto his lap. His toned thighs cradled her backside as she was made to straddle his hips. Cool leather shifted beneath her knees, a contrast to the scalding hot palms that released her hands to curl around her waist. She was pulled closer. So close, they shared the same air with every exhale. So close she could count each individual lash circling his darkened eyes. One hand pulled forward and captured her chin between long fingers. Her face was tipped even closer.

Juliette gasped, a weak, pitiful sound that seemed to ignite the fire in his eyes. The light flickered with a glimmer of triumph that stole a shiver through her.

"You should have left, *a ghrá*." His low, seductive drawl snagged on the few wisps of air she'd managed to coax into her lungs and tore them from her. She floundered while he watched her with those predatory eyes. "You should have escaped whilst you had the chance. Now you're mine, little lamb."

Mesmerized by his eyes, lured by his scent, captivated by the feel of his hands gliding to her hips, Juliette could only hold her breath while he dared her to do something she had no experience in. Every prickling sensation was brutally aware of his calloused fingers inching up the soft skin of her thighs and dipping beneath the fabric of her skirt to graze her hips. Juliette's whimper crashed into the back of the teeth she clamped over her lip, but the sound still filtered from her throat in an embarrassing moan.

Damn it. She wasn't supposed to be enjoying herself. That hadn't been part of the plan. But there was no stopping it now. Her body was freefalling into a whirlwind of everything it had been deprived of for the last seven year. It was thrumming for everything he was offering her without a shred of care. It made no difference that her mind was against the whole thing when he had so expertly tamed her body to his will.

Hard hands curled into the globes of her backside and she was dragged over the hard lump nestled beneath his pants. The heat of their bodies coming together burned through fabric. The rigid length of him slid perfectly up the heart of her being, hitting every critical point right to the taut muscle at the top. The slow grind elicited a rush of unexpected heat to plow into her. It welled up through her in a single swoop of arousal that had her grabbing for his shoulders. One of them groaned, low and guttural that sounded infinitely too loud in the fraught silence. It was only when he pushed down on her hips while lifting his and she gasped that she realized—with some degree of horror—that the sounds were coming from her.

"That a girl," he drawled in that delicious accent of his. "Tell me what you like."

She couldn't think of a single response to that. She couldn't think period. Her mind had become a wasteland of desire and guilt. The two coiled around each other in a vicious war that made her want to cry.

It had been years since she'd come anywhere near an orgasm. Years where she hadn't even touched herself and the need was killing her. Worse than that was the knowledge that she had all but abandoned her morals in the time it took to climb into a stranger's lap, but she wanted this. She wanted him. As wrong as it was.

Yet the moment she peered into those impossibly dark eyes, there was no denying the sweet flutter of arousal that swept through her belly. She couldn't ignore the ache. Her body was lost in a sea of desire and nothing else mattered. The fact that his eyes were promising things that made her pussy clench and her nipple tighten didn't help calm the waves washing over her.

His hands felt their way over her eager body, fanning the fires bursting through her in a rainbow of colors. Against her mound, his cock worked her approaching climax with a skill that had her delirious for something only he could provide. All the while, he continued to fuck her with his eyes. He plunged deep inside her and rode her emotions hard. She could have orgasmed from the look alone.

"I want a taste of your pussy, little lamb," Killian hissed into her ear as he twisted his fingers around the straps of her camisole. "I want to open you wide right here and feast on you until you can't walk straight."

Christ, how was she supposed to keep her head when he was saying things like that?

"Please," she breathed. She begged. Her fingers tightened around fabric of his blazer. Her body arched deeper into his. "I need—"

"Up," he commanded.

Juliette wasted no time scrambling off him. The roof of the limo grazed the top of her head, forcing her to stay stooped as she dropped unceremoniously into the seat next to him. She waited with her breath held as he shrugged out of his blazer and carelessly pitched it aside. His tie followed in a streak of solid emerald slashing into the air before fluttering to the ground. Juliette hurriedly kicked off her shoes. The black heels struck the carpet with a muffled thud and lay forgotten.

Killian lowered himself down on his knees in front of her. It didn't seem to bother him in the least to be kneeling at her feet. He didn't seem to care about anything but getting his hands on her hips and jerking her roughly down the leather seat. Her skirt bunched in a wrinkled mess about her waist, exposing the painfully plain material of her panties stretched over the lips of her pussy.

"You've soaked through." The pad of one thumb traced the wet patch in lazy circles from hole to clit. Each pass over the nub they could both clearly see poking up against her panties increased the flow. "Can you feel just how wet you are?"

He gave her no chance to respond when his hands closed around the supple flesh of her thighs. Her knees were lewdly splayed and the place in between was filled by his lean hips. Her choked gasp was met by the vicious glint in his eyes as he pressed over her, pinning her to the leather with his torso. For a moment, she thought he was going to kiss her. Her lips parted. They tingled in eager anticipation as he drew closer. Her fingers tightened in the sleeve of his dress shirt. The fabric wrinkled and she knew she was damaging it beyond repair, but the only thing she could bring herself to focus on was the mouth a heartbeat away from hers.

He shifted his weight higher. The leather beneath her squeaked with the adjustment. On either side of her hips, the seat dipped beneath his hands as he settled, aligning the full weight of his erection against her mound once more. A sound escaped her that she couldn't even identify. It was something between a whine and a whimper, but it came from somewhere deep in the pit of her body. Her companion rocked his hips forward and her entire body jerked. Her cry was louder, desperate, and it rang through the car.

"Like that?" he murmured, doing it again, but slower.

Cotton mouthed and irrationally dizzy, Juliette gave a single, rapid nod. "Yes."

Hungry eyes devoured her through the thick fringes of his lashes. His hands lifted. They wrapped in the straps of her top and dragged them leisurely over the slopes of her shoulders. The painfully slow descent tugged the hem down her chest, over the swell of her breasts to catch on the puckered tips, tugging and teasing before popping free. Juliette's hiss was met with triumph before he was focused on the flesh he'd uncovered.

His face darkened.

"Christ, the things I'm going to do to you," he breathed, untangling his hands from her top to slide around her back. They flattened against her shoulder blades. The heat of his palms soaked through the bunched material of her top and bit into skin. "The things I'm going to make you do."

He attacked with bruising hands and greedy lips. He assaulted and tore into one nipple while plucking and rolling the other with an anger that should have been painful if she wasn't silently begging him for more.

"God, that feels good!"

Her breathless whimper was rewarded by the sharp nip of his teeth that sent hot embers scattering up her body. Her involuntary jerk tightened his grip on her, a clear warning that she wasn't going anywhere. Black eyes bore up into hers, unwavering, unflinching, and unabashed by the fact that he was lazily circling the sensitive peak with the tip of his tongue. One hand slid forward and worked the other nipple into a hard, tingling nub under a taunting thumb.

It was wrong.

Letting him … wanting it … wanting him … it was all so wrong. But him stopping was even worse. The very idea had her fingers threading through all that thick, rich hair and clasping him to her. Her hips fought to lift, to rub, to ease the unbearable pang humming between her thighs. But his weight kept her immobilized and in unbearable pain.

"Please..." she whispered.

Gaze still cutting into hers, he relinquished his assault, leaving her breasts tingling and wet as he ascended. Hot lips followed the flush staining her chest to her collarbone. Soft, satiny strands tickled the underside of her chin and throat and forced her neck back. Her spine arched, pushing out her breasts into the hand still lazily toying with her sensitive peak.

"Move your panties," he commanded against her skin. "Show me where you want me."

Panting, her fingers trembled as they moved between their bodies to do as she was told. Beneath the coaxing strum of his fingers, her heart thundered against his palm. Her insides twisted as she hooked a finger into the damp stitch of fabric concealing her sex. Cool air kissed her exposed flesh and she shivered. The tremor coursed through her with a vengeance that had her teeth closing down on her lip and her every breath come out impossibly too fast. Killian never took his eyes off hers. He didn't seem to care that every private part of her was bare before him. His only focus was on her eyes, watching every shift of light play across their surface with a shrewd sort of fascination that made her fidget uncomfortably.

"Touch yourself," he instructed.

It was easier said than done when his weight was restraining her, but she managed to skim a single finger over the hard muscle of her clit. The back of her hand brushed over the rock hard bulge denting the front of his trousers and his irises expended. His nostrils gave a sharp flare, but his gaze remained dauntingly firm. He forced her thighs further apart and slowly drew back. Those incredible eyes drifted over her languidly until they stopped at her fingers.

Heat drifted over her in a surge of embarrassment and her initial instinct was to shut her legs, but she couldn't with him wedged firmly between them. Instead, all she could do was cup herself in some pathetic attempt at modesty that had his attention drifting back to her face with an almost questioning quirk of his eyebrow.

He didn't ask. He didn't say anything. But his fingers curled around her wrist and gently drew her hand away. Powerless to stop him—part of her not wanting to—she watched as he shifted lower, as his dark head bent until his hot breath whispered over her sensitive flesh. Her body jerked simultaneously in two different reactions. The first was longing. The second was surprise. But it was nothing compared to the shock and the sharp zing that shot up her at the lazy sweep of his tongue.

Juliette gasped. Her hands flew to his head. Her fingers closed in his hair. Maybe she'd meant to stop him, but it was lost the moment his lips suctioned over the crest of her sex and sucked.

"Killian!" his name burst out of her in a tortured whine that was followed by the violent shudder that ripped through her.

Her fingers tightened as her hips rose to meet the demanding coaxing of his mouth. He devoured her like a man who had been given a second chance at life. It was passionate and insistent and full of so much everything she couldn't breathe.

When he coaxed a finger past the tight ring of her opening, Juliette froze at the pressure. The subtle pain was nowhere near enough to make her want to stop, but it was enough to make her grunt a little and shift uncomfortably.

Killian lifted his head. The light overhead shone off the moisture smeared across his mouth and chin. It glinted across the surface of his eyes, reminding her of the ocean at night.

"Am I hurting you?" he asked.

Juliette shook her head. "No." She wet her lips hurriedly. "It's been a while," she whispered, not really lying. It *had* been a while since anyone had been down there. "I'm okay."

He gave an understanding nod before bending his head back to his task. His finger worked gingerly, but with purpose, relaxing the muscles of her opening. Between his tongue and his hand, it took no time at all for Juliette to start thrashing again. Her hips shifted restlessly for more, but he kept at his teasing pace until she was sure she was going to burst into frustrated tears.

"Killian, please…" she begged, tugging at his hair. Her thigh muscles were beginning to quiver uncontrollably and her heart was beating against her ribcage with a vengeance she was sure wasn't safe. Still, Killian kept on tormenting her. "God, please! I'm so close!"

His answer was to ease a second finger inside her and flick lazily at her blood filled clit. It wasn't nearly enough to ease the pain.

Juliette swore viciously and bucked. It did nothing, but get him to stop.

He drew back and swiped his forearm casually over his mouth. She watched him with confusion and more than a mild sense of panic. Inside her, his fingers continued to move, stretching her and working the unused muscles of her pussy.

"Do you make a mess when you come?"

Panting, Juliette had to swallow hard before she could respond. "Mess?"

He nodded. "Do you squirt?"

Scalding hot blood rushed to her face that seemed to amuse him. She averted her eyes.

"I haven't before," she mumbled, wishing he wouldn't watch her with such intensity.

"Never?"

She shook her head. She started to open her mouth when his fingers bent inside her. It wasn't subtle. Whatever he did, whatever he pushed up against nearly had her leaping out of the seat. Her entire body involuntarily bowed off the leather. Her wail burst up her chest to lodge in her throat, becoming a silent scream she couldn't control. Her fingers clawed into the bench as she lifted and slammed her hips into his hand.

"Oh my God!" she sobbed.

"No one's done that before either?" he taunted with a sly cock of his head.

Dying for more, Juliette convulsed between shaking her head and trying to gain control of her body again. Her channels sucked greedily at his fingers still moving inside her, but going anywhere near that place again. And she wanted him to. God, she needed it so badly.

"What sort of men have you been with?" he pondered darkly, giving the spot a gentle nudge that sent her head flinging back and her vision blurring.

"What are you doing?" she gasped, writhing shamelessly into his palm.

Something hot and liquid trickled free and pooled beneath her. It soaked into her panties and dribbled over his fingers.

"I'm going to make you squirt."

"Oh!" she choked out, breathless. "Okay."

He drew the pads of his fingers expertly along her walls, bypassing the button she never knew she had. He did this a few times until she was certain she'd lose her fucking mind. Then he pulled out, without warning or reason. His fingers slipped free of her body and he sat back, still kneeling between her sprawled and quivering thighs. Her channel felt unusually empty without him. More than that, her clit was on fire.

"What … why…?"

Her bafflement tugged on one corner of his mouth. It wasn't exactly a smile, but it was close.

"We're at my place."

Sure enough, the limo had stopped moving. She couldn't make anything out through the windows, except an overcast of clouds. It took her a moment to realize she was slumped as low as she could possibly go on the seat, practically on the limo floor with him.

Flushing, she wiggled up, dragging her clothes and shoes back into place as she did so. The higher she got, the more of her surroundings came into view.

A building of blinding white stucco glowed beneath the evening sky. The Mediterranean style mansion sat at the end of a glittering carpet of polished stone and was surrounded by lush lawns, towering trees and gleaming lamps. A stone fountain bubbled melodiously at the foot of marble steps leading to a set of wide, wooden doors. It was that that propelled Juliette from the car, the woman standing on a stone dais in the center of the fountain, pouring water out of a clay pot. She wore a flowing gown with thick straps and while the whole sculpture was flawless white, Juliette pictured the dress to be purple to match the band keeping back the riot of curls spilling recklessly down a slender back. The hair would be dark … black and the eyes…

Juliette crossed the cobblestone to stand at the base.

Brown, she decided. The woman's eyes would be a soft, hazel brown.

It was ridiculous to imagine colors on a colorless statue, but there was something about the whole piece that didn't seem random.

"She's so beautiful," Juliette said, as Killian came up beside her. "Did she come with the fountain or was she specially made?"

"It's my mother." His hands dipped into the pockets of his trousers and he tipped his head back to peer into the statue's smiling face. "My father had it made after she passed."

"I'm sorry," she murmured, knowing all too well the pains of losing a mother.

She started to open her mouth and tell him she knew how he felt, but he was already walking away. She didn't stop him. Instead, she turned towards the limo, intending to go back and get her things, but the car was gone. The giant they'd driven back with stood a few feet away, solemnly watching something over her head.

Again, her mouth opened to ask him where her stuff was.

"Marco will bring everything inside," Killian said before she could get the words out.

Left with no other choice, she followed him towards the house and the steps. He offered her his hand, taking her completely by surprise.

"The stones can be slippery," he told her when she peered up at him.

Gingerly, she settled her fingers into his palm and watched as her entire hand was seamlessly swallowed with just a mere curl of his long fingers. He guided her up and through the doors, which pulled open before he could touch them.

Two men dressed in navy suits stood stationed just inside. Neither glanced at Juliette when she and Killian walked through. The doors were shut behind them.

"Would you like a drink?" Killian glanced back over his shoulder as he made his way deeper through the spacious foyer.

Like the outside, the inside was a sprawling catacomb of gleaming stone and iron. The front entrance opened in three separate sections that led into rooms that could easily fit her entire house. At first glance the two open doorways on either side of her opened to a pair of sitting areas and she couldn't fathom why anyone needed two when she noticed one had a TV and the other didn't. It still made no sense, but then decorating his house wasn't why she was there.

Her gaze went to the man waiting for her a few feet away.

"Water, please."

He eyed her a moment. "I have champagne."

Juliette shook her head. "No, thank you."

Her response seemed to confuse him, but he didn't ask. He motioned her to follow him past an elegant set of stairs sweeping upwards to the second floor. They walked in silence through a wide corridor lined with windows looking out onto what appeared to be a garden barely illuminated in the darkness. It ended at a wide opening and a doorway.

Juliette stayed just outside, balancing on the threshold as he walked to the fridge and yanked it open.

The kitchen, like all the other rooms, was enormous. Much too big for the single corner it took up. An island was bolted in the center, cutting the kitchen away from the rest of the space. Across the room, lights spilled through the sheer drapes hanging over a series of French doors and cut patches into the marble floors.

"Don't like it?" Killian was walking towards her, a frosty glass bottle of water in hand.

Juliette shook her head. "It's nice."

A snort left him. "It's a waste of space, but I rarely entertain ... or cook."

Not knowing what to say to that, Juliette accepted the bottle and broke the seal on the cap. She took a long sip. The ice cold liquid cut a path down the center of her chest to fill her stomach. It didn't put the fire out that he'd lit there, but it calmed some of it.

She replaced the cap. "Thank you."

He peered at her while she offered him the bottle back. He seemed, as always, to be waiting for something, like somehow, she hadn't conducted herself the way he'd expected and that made her nervous. She needed for that night to go well. Really well. She needed for him to have the time of his life. Otherwise, she would never be free of Arlo.

He took the water and peered down at the clear, white glass. He weighed it a moment in his hand before walking to the island and setting the bottle down. The muffled crack echoed in the silence.

Juliette fidgeted nervously. "So..." she murmured. "This is a nice house. Have you lived here long?"

Killian's head lifted slowly and turned in her direction. One eyebrow lifted, but there was amusement in his eyes.

"Are you making small talk?"

A flush worked up her throat to fill her face. "What? No … maybe," she mumbled at last. She offered him a sheepish half grin. "Sorry."

His mouth twitched and for a moment, she honestly thought he was going to smile. But it was gone as he started towards her, though the light remained shimmering in his eyes.

"Come."

She followed him back the way they'd come. In the foyer, he turned left and started up the staircase. Juliette faltered at the bottom. Her fingers were sweaty when she closed them around the polished banister. Her knees wobbled and her grip tightened.

God, this was it. He was taking her to his room where he would … panic lodged in her throat, making her heart drum wildly between her ears. Ahead of her, Killian paused and glanced back. His gaze was questioning.

I can do this! she told herself. *It'll be okay. It's only one night.*

But a lot could happen in a night. He was a perfect stranger. He could be a serial killer, or worse. He could tie her down and do whatever he wanted and no one knew where she was.

Oh God … no one knew where she was. Hell, she didn't know where she was. He had distracted her the entire drive. They could be in another city for all she knew.

"Juliette?" Killian took one step down.

Get a grip! The voice in her head hissed, jolting her out of her crippling terror.

It was a wonder when her legs didn't fold beneath her with her first unsteady attempt. She managed to make it all the way to the step beneath his without tumbling down to her death.

Killian stayed put for a full heartbeat, looking like he wanted to say something, but seemed to think better of it as he turned and lead the way down a long corridor.

At the end, the hallway split off in two separate directions before looping around and coming to a full circle on the other side of a large opening that looked down into a whole other section of the place. Juliette peered over the iron railing and saw only the rose marble flooring below. On the other side of the circle was a set of wrought iron stairs leading downward.

"It leads to the sunroom and conservatory," Killian said, catching her. "The gym and media room are on the other side."

On the other side of what? Juliette was about to ask, but did it really matter? She wasn't there for a tour.

He led her down a hallway that widened down yet another corridor lined with doors. The cold feeling of dread took over again, making her strides sloppy; every step rattled, making her heels scrape noisily in the silence. She tried to pull herself together, but the further they went, the less she wanted to be there.

This was not how she had envisioned her first time, with a guy whose last name she didn't even know. It definitely wasn't out of obligation or fear. But she didn't know how to stop it now, how to walk away without putting Vi or herself in danger. She had to go through with it. She had to finally end the nightmare. It was clear from the drive up that Killian knew what he was doing where women were concerned so maybe it wouldn't be so bad. Maybe she might even like it. Then she would forget all about it and everything would be okay.

"You don't have to do this." Killian's voice snapped her out of her own pep talk. It jerked her head up to find him standing in the open doorway of a room, watching her. "You can leave if you like. Frank will call you a cab."

Yes! She wanted to cry. Better yet, she wanted to spin on her heels and make a mad dash back down to the foyer. But she stayed.

"You said I couldn't back out once I said yes in the limo," she reminded him.

Killian nodded slowly. "I meant it, but I don't force women either."

Something about that statement and the ferocity darkening his face calmed the unease snapping through her. His offer to let her get out coaxed her closer.

She shook her head. "I don't want to leave."

To prove it, she slipped past him into the room.

It didn't surprise her to see the enormous bed taking up most of the space. But it did surprise her that there was very little else in the room. A set of French doors took up one wall. There were two doors on the other and a dresser against the wall next to the door. Two end tables with lamps flagged the bed. The room itself was bathed in a mute darkness held at bay solely by the white light pouring through the French doors. The rectangular patch of light spilled across the white fabric of the neatly made bed and her stomach twisted.

"Take your clothes off and get on the bed," he instructed, coming up behind her.

But rather than touch her, he moved past her towards the glass doors. He unhooked the latch keeping them closed and let the panels swing open to the humid night. The movement rippled across the wide expense of his back. Even through the dress shirt, the toned muscles were painfully visible. He had an amazing build, she thought, catching her bottom lip between her teeth. He had an amazing face and hands and eyes and … Christ, he was just all kinds of lust worthy. It was almost a shame that they had to meet that way. That he couldn't be just some normal guy who walked into the diner one afternoon and struck up a conversation with her. But that would have been too easy and nothing about her life had been easy in years.

Juliette was still studying him when he turned back to her. His black eyes roamed over her and she blinked.

"Oh!"

Blushing, she reached for the straps on her camisole. It was an act she'd done a million times before in the privacy of her own bedroom. Plus there had been that weekend with Stan, but it hadn't been weird. She'd been with Stan a whole year before he saw her naked. Stripping for a stranger was a whole different experience. It didn't help that he refused to look away. That his eyes were burning holes through her.

Her hands trembled as the material was pulled down her arms and her breasts sprung free. He'd already seen them … hell, he'd seen all of her, yet she had to suppress the urge to cover herself when her nipples pulled tight, tugging at some invisible wire connected to her lower region. She left the material bunched around her waist as she picked at the zipper holding her skirt in place. The tongue tugged down without any effort and the circle of fabric fluttered to the floor in a halo around her ankles. Her top followed. She stepped out of both to stand before him in her heels and panties. Tentatively, she hooked her thumbs into the elastic of her panties.

He was across the room and looming over her before the material could even pass the sharp edges of her hipbones. His large hands settled over hers, stilling the descent. Juliette tipped back her head in surprise. He met her gaze unwavering and sharp while sliding lean fingers under the elastic with hers. Together, they eased the material all the way to her knees. He released and it slipped down the rest of the way to catch at her ankles.

She was naked.

He wasn't.

The sensation was odd.

He took her hand and helped her step out of her discarded panties. He kept holding her up while she kicked out of her shoes. Feet planted flat on the floor, she was forced to tip her head back drastically to peer up into his face.

"On the bed," he told her quietly.

Swallowing audibly, Juliette made her way around him and started to the four poster bed with its handcrafted posts and satin sheets. It was the sort of bed she would have loved any other time.

Behind her, Killian followed. The floorboards creaked beneath his slow strides. Each step closer sent her heart pattering just a little faster until it was a wild drum banging between her ears. She stopped when her knees bumped into the mattress. She didn't dare turn, not even when she felt the prickle of his presence skim the full length of her spine.

"How do you like it?" The question whispered hot along the slope of her shoulder.

"Like it?" Her voice sounded weak and small even to her own ears.

His lips skipped her shoulder and Juliette jumped.

"To be fucked," he clarified against the spot connecting her neck to her shoulder.

Juliette wondered if he could feel just how hard her pulse was beating against the soft skin of her throat. It was practically trying to tear free.

"Um…" She licked her dry lips. "I'm not picky. They're all nice."

His mouth stopped. It lifted off her neck, leaving the spot feeling chilled. She felt him draw back. Then she was being turned to face him.

There was silent laughter dancing in his eyes when she dared herself to peek up and his mouth did that twitching thing, like he was fighting not to let them curve, which she didn't understand.

"They're nice?" he mimicked.

Feigning experience was a lot harder than she had anticipated. She probably should have put more enthusiasm in her statement.

"I … I just want you inside me," she blurted, hoping to God he didn't hear the quiver in her voice.

He was still biting back his grin when he spoke. "Get on your back."

Gingerly, Juliette lowered herself down on the cool sheets and watched as he stayed looming over her. Shadows concealed his eyes, but she could feel the path of their attention working lazily up and down the hills and valleys of her body. The silent scrutiny worked along her skin like phantom fingers. Heat rippled through her, teasing her nipples and reigniting the fire he'd lit back in the limo. It was intensified when he began to undress, when his fingers began the progression down the front of his dress shirt, undoing each button in their path. The fabric was shrugged off wide shoulders and pitched carelessly aside. He wore nothing under and the play of shadows across smooth ivory made her shift restlessly. It pooled in the hallows and indents of his hard chest and the neat cut of his stomach. Toned muscle roped and shifted along strong arms and she was momentarily distracted by the thought of having them close around her. It was the jingle of his belt buckle and the hiss of his zipper that brought her back.

No underwear.

Dark trousers opened to lean hips and the fat head of his cock. The thick shaft jutted out from a neat circle of coarse, black hair that wove a fine path up the flat surface of his pelvis to his navel. The pants were tossed aside and he stood before her as naked as she was.

"Like what you see?" One hand closed around his erection. He stroked it deliberately, all the while studying her.

It was a task not to blush or look away. It took a lot of reminding herself she was supposed to know about this stuff. But she kept his gaze and steeled herself to respond.

"Yes."

The mattress dipped beneath his weight as he joined her. Automatically, her knees parted, already expecting him to climb over her. Instead, he stayed kneeling between them, peering over her splayed body. Firm hands rested on her hips, holding her down as he shifted closer.

"I promised you something, didn't I?" he said evenly. "Back in the limo. What was it?"

Body thrumming in that way only he seemed to be able to make it, Juliette fought not to buck and wiggle and demand he just end the suffering already.

"You promised to make me squirt," she whispered, breathless.

"Aye." His hands slid inward, dipping into her pelvis and stopping when his thumbs could peel apart her lips. "But are you still wet?"

She was. She knew she was. She could feel the thick puddle of arousal collecting against her opening, begging for him to make use of it.

"Yes!"

Rather than check like she wanted him to, his hands fell away and he leaned over her for the light next to the bed. It flared on with a deft flick of his fingers, flooding part of the room, the bed and them. Juliette winced at the sudden invasion of illumination. She blinked a few times before turning her eyes on the man leaning over her.

She'd been wrong. He wasn't gorgeous. He was something so beyond such a simple term. He was breathtaking.

Propped above her on his hands, dark tendrils slipped over his brow and fell recklessly over his eyes. God, his eyes. They were just so unimaginably powerful, like the sky during a dangerous storm. Peering into them from a distance, she hadn't realized just how vulnerable he could make her feel with only a look. Up close, she felt small and helpless ... and so fucking turned on.

He pulled back until he was kneeling once more. His gaze went down the length of her to her mound.

"Open her for me," he ordered. "And stay open until I tell you otherwise."

Her hands moved without a shred of hesitation. They shot between her thighs and parted her lips. Her clit poked out, swollen and slick.

Killian cocked his head to the side and studied the tiny muscle throbbing for his attention through heavily hooded eyes. One hand lifted off the sheets. Four fingertips glided down the inside of her thigh, leaving a trail of goose bumps in their wake. She shivered.

He didn't notice. His whole focus trained on the feather light caress of his finger over her clit. It was barely a whisper. Barely made contact. Yet Juliette cried out. Her hips bucked off the mattress in desperation that went ignored as Killian repeated the motion. Each time was slower, lighter. She could scarcely feel the contact, but each one rocked her closer to the orgasm she could feel snapping inside her.

"Please…" she whined, too far gone in the haze to care about how pathetic she sounded.

Killian raised his head and his eyes met hers. His finger slipped away from the sliver of air just above her button and traveled down to her opening. It pushed in just to the tip and Juliette sobbed as the tight ring suckled greedily at the invader, willing it in deeper. But he didn't.

"What do you want?" he asked.

God, how could he not know?

"That … that thing you did in the limo," she panted. "With your fingers. Please."

His lashes lowered, cutting her off from the black flames leaping across his eyes. His finger withdrew and went back to terrorizing her clit, pushing her right to the edge before pulling back. It was a sort of psychological torture to see just how much she could take before she lost her fucking mind. It was more effective than water boarding or electrocution. She was ready to tell him anything, do anything to make it stop. She would have given him her first born if it meant easing the unbearable pang. Beneath her, the sheets were soaked and growing wetter with every passing second he toyed with her.

"Do you want me inside you yet?"

"Yes!" she sobbed, close to tears. "God, please! I can't take anymore."

His response was to take his cock in hand and stroke it while she writhed beneath him. The fat, purple head was leaking and the sight had her legs widening even further.

"Put your hands up," he said. "Palms flat against the headboard."

Nerves trembling uncontrollably, she raised her arms and flattened her palms against the headboard. The motion thrust out her breasts.

"Don't take them down," he warned, bending at the waist and taking a nipple in his mouth.

He sucked lightly while palming his erection. She couldn't understand why he wasn't already inside her when he was rock hard, but he seemed to be waiting for something.

That something became evident when he drew back and reached for the end table. She watched as the light caught the silver foil he pulled out from inside the drawer. The magnificent appendage jutting from the center of his body was wrapped tight in rubber.

Now, she thought, anticipation making her dizzy. Now he would finally quench the fire.

She didn't get his cock.

Two blunt fingers worked a lazy path down the quivering planes of her stomach, circled her navel before descending further. Juliette barely caught the whine working its way up her throat. It slammed into the teeth she clamped down hard on her bottom lip. Beneath his touch, her hips writhed against the sheets. The muscles of her thighs ached from holding them open for so long, but she didn't care.

The tip of his middle finger dipped between her lips and traced a teasing O around her clit. The caress was so close to where she wanted him and yet he deliberately kept away. Anger and frustration tore a growl from her. The sound drew his eyes upwards to her face. The right corner of his mouth actually lifted in a half grin.

"Patience," he said, his voice dripping with silent laughter.

"I have been patient!" she snapped. "Christ, just fuck me already!"

The left corner lifted and his mouth stretched into the first smile she'd seen him give and it was overshadowed by the fact that she wanted to hit him.

Eyes still on her face, his finger slipped downward to skim her opening. The gesture immediately made her forget her anger. All remnants of it washed away with her gasp as he broke through and pushed all the way inside. A second finger joined the first and Juliette swore colorfully. Her heels dug into the mattress, lifting her hips into his palm as he pumped his fingers slowly. But that wasn't what she wanted!

"Do it!" she hissed.

"What?"

Breathing hard, she glowered at him down the length of her sweat drenched and flushed body. "That thing with your fingers!"

One, thick eyebrow lifted in innocent questioning. "This?"

He grazed against the spot, just a light skim that sent sparks flashing behind the eyes she squeezed shut tight.

"Yes! Yes! That. Fuck!"

She no longer had any control over her body. It was a mindless mess of desire rutting and thrashing for every little thing he saw fit to bestow her.

To her surprise, he worked the spot without driving her out of her mind first. His thrusts grew faster, harder. His palm slapped into her clit with stinging pain, but it was perfect.

Juliette came with a vicious scream of someone under some violent torture. It muffled the screech of her nails raking into the wood above her head and the rustle of sheets as her entire body convulsed with a ferocity that couldn't possibly be natural. The world around her shattered and shimmered and exploded and still, he continued to destroy her with only two fingers.

It felt like hours before the shrieking between her ears dimmed to a simmering roar. Hours before she could let her toes uncurl against the roped sheets. She had no sense in her head to think or move. All she could do was lie there in a limp, sated haze while her body continued to shudder every so often with some inner electric current that refused to quit.

"Killian..." His name was the first thing she could get her tongue to work around.

The fingers eased out from inside her and she whimpered. She shivered and shut her eyes as exhaustion threatened to take her under.

"That's what good girls get when they are patient," she vaguely heard him murmur.

She could only muster a moan in response.

Something sharp and blunt closed around her nipple and tugged. Juliette jolted awake with a cry of pain. Her chin jerked down to find Killian's dark head moving over her breast. It lifted just enough so their eyes met.

"Not done yet," he told her.

"So tired," she whispered.

He lowered his mouth and nuzzled the nipple he'd assaulted, making it tingle and her moan. Her hands instinctively went to the back of his skull, cradling him to her as he worked her body back awake. Against her side, his hand drifted along the curve of her waist to rest against her hip. It eased under and she was lifted to him. His pelvis aligned with hers and she was gifted with the full weight of his cock settling against her mound. His head lifted and hovered over hers. Most of his weight was supported by the forearm he planted on the pillow next to her head, but the majority of it was on her, molding her into the mattress. She found that she didn't mind it. There was something incredibly comfortable about it.

Juliette smiled up at him. She wasn't sure why. Maybe because she'd just had the most incredible, earth shattering climax of her life, but whatever it was, she felt an overwhelming sense of contentment for the first time in forever and it refused to stay contained.

"Did I squirt?" she asked, not really sure when everything down there felt wet and tingly.

Killian made a sound that could have been a snort or a chuckle. "No, but we still have time."

She burst out laughing and, without thinking, lifted her head and kissed him.

Immediately, she knew she'd done something wrong when he jerked back. Hot, intense eyes bore down into hers with a look of stunned anger. His entire body had gone rigid.

Juliette shrank back against the pillow. "I'm sorry. Is that not allowed—?"

His response was a snarl of rage before his mouth slammed down over hers, violent and starving. Fingers closed into her hair, dragging her head back as he consumed her. His body shifted against hers, opening her even wider to his hard hips. The arm beneath her tightened and dragged her down to him as he pushed up against her. His cock beat into her clit with every downward descent, getting harder and crueler with every second.

He broke the kiss when her pained whimper hummed between them. He began to draw back, but Juliette grabbed him, yanked him back down.

"Don't stop!" she panted, bringing his mouth back to hers.

His growl vibrated against her swollen lips, making them tingle and part for the invasion of his tongue. The arm beneath her pulled out and the hand settled her writhing hips, forcing her against the mattress. He bit her lip sharply when she whined in protest.

"I need to be inside you!"

He gave her no time to brace when his cock drove home deep inside her with a single, powerful thrust.

Juliette gave a cry that had nothing to do with pleasure as he tore through the thin membrane protecting her innocence. The bulging length of him filled her with a pressure that brought tears to her eyes and drew blood from the skin of his back where her nails raked.

Above her, Killian had gone rigid. His eyes were wide with stunned realization as he stared down at her. His heart slammed into hers. The two mirrored each other perfectly in the fraught silence.

"You're a virgin," he panted, his tone accusatory.

"I'm sorry…"

He snapped out a curse that made her flinch. His nostrils flared as he glowered down at her. He swore again and gripped her tighter when she tried to pull away.

"Too late for that, love," he said tightly. "The damage is done. I'm inside you."

As though to prove it, he shifted his hips. The uncomfortable pang made Juliette groan and tighten her hold on his shoulders. She gritted her teeth and struggled to block it out, but every thrust, no matter how slow or careful felt like he was tearing her in two. Each one grated against her tender flesh and she fought not to let herself cry.

Face as tight as the corded muscles of his arms trembling on either side of her, Killian exhaled through his nose. He drew back just enough to reach for the end table. Juliette watched him as he yanked open the drawer and rummaged inside. He returned with a white bottle in hand. He flicked the cap open with his thumb and rose higher to bring the bottle between their bodies.

Juliette watched as it was tipped and clear liquid drizzled over her mound. The unexpected coolness made her jump as it ran over her clit to drench his cock.

"What—?"

"Hold still," he told her when she started to shift.

The top was snapped back into place and the bottle was pitched aside. His hand returned to her hip. He drew back and she winced at the slight burn. But as the lube began to work its way inside her with every gradual thrust, the friction became fluid and intense.

"Better?" he asked when she gasped.

It was. It was better than she had ever imagined. The hard feel of him filling her slick walls, the teasing little bursts of pleasurable pain that exploded every time he hit the end, it was incredible.

"Yes."

"Good."

His grip tightened. His movement quickened. Juliette panted as a new burn began to build deep inside her. Her fingers threaded through his hair, gripping him close as the familiar surge of euphoria began to build.

"Killian…"

Without a word, one hand slipped between their bodies and rested flat against her pelvis. His thumb found the hardened little muscle slick with arousal and lubrication and stroked. Each flick was followed by a thrust of his hips. The combination had her back arching and her toes curling. She squeezed her eyes shut tight as an overwhelming burst of ecstasy rushed over her. His name hitched out of her, again and again, growing louder and more desperate with every second that passed and she teetered on that colorful brink.

"Come on, love," he coaxed, his own voice ragged. "Let go. I've got you."

With a sound between a sob and a wail, Juliette fell. It was the sort of collision that pulled every nerve ending in her body into a knot. She might have cried out, but the sound was lost in a buzz of aftershock that dulled everything but the implosion of her very soul. Killian kept the steady pace, never in a hurry as she gripped at him with her walls and sucked him in deeper. She was vaguely aware of his grunt, of the bruising clamp of his fingers. Then he collapsed over her while the world continued to spin.

Neither moved for several minutes. They lay in a tangled knot of damp limbs and pulsing sexes. She could feel the clench of her pussy every time his embedded cock twitched inside her. She could feel the crack of his heart clapping in time with hers. His weight was a hot, solid blanket draped over her, molding her possessively in the confines of his fierce embrace. He cradled her to him even when he pulled free and she whimpered her protest into the corded muscle of his shoulder.

"You lied to me," he said into the unsteady pulse at her throat.

Juliette closed her eyes. "I'm sorry."

Carefully, he pulled out of her arms and left the bed. She watched him move with confidence to the door across the room on the left. A light was switched on before he disappeared inside and shut the door. A moment later, water hitting basin filled the silence. A toilet flushed. The water was shut off, then the lights and he was walking towards her once more, still naked, with a white cloth in hand.

Killian returned to her side of the bed and took a seat next to her hip. His free hand parted her sore thighs and filled the space in between with the damp square of fabric. The icy coldness of it made her squeak and jolt, but he remained firmly pressed against her tender sex.

"You should've told me," he muttered. "I would've taken better care."

Juliette studied the man gingerly cleaning her with a gentleness she would never have expected.

"Would you have?"

He shot her a glance. "No. I would've taken you home. I don't bed children."

Juliette blinked. "I'm not a child! I'm twenty three."

His eyes narrowed. "And you're still a virgin?" He shook his head. "What the hell were you waiting for?"

"I wasn't waiting for anything. I just never had anyone I wanted to give myself to before."

Not entirely the truth, but not entirely a lie either. She had wanted to give it to Stan. After that, she never had time for sex and it had never been an issue.

"Christ," was all he said.

"It wasn't really that bad, was it?"

His gaze stayed on her face for much longer this time. "No, but that isn't the point," he said at last. "I could have hurt you."

"You were wonderful," she assured him softly.

He looked away. "Again, not the point."

"Thank you," she murmured for lack of anything better.

"For hurting you? You're welcome."

She grabbed his wrist when he rose to his feet. "You didn't hurt me. It really was amazing."

He searched her face and settled on her lips before letting his gaze roam down the length of her splayed across his bed. The appendage hanging between his legs hardened and Juliette didn't miss it. Her skin prickled with heat and awareness. Her breasts swelled as her nipples tightened.

Christ, she wanted him again.

"Get dressed."

It was stupid, but she hadn't expected that. Judging from the dark heat in his eyes to the fully hardened cock at his midsection, she had honestly believed he would join her again. Instead, he was turning away from her.

Disappointment and an irrational twang of hurt built up inside her chest as she bit her lip and sat up. The chill that swept through the room made her painfully aware of her nakedness and she reached for the rumpled sheets. The fabric rustled too loudly in the silence as she drew it around herself in some weird attempt at protecting the rest of her tattered dignity.

"Can I use your washroom first?" she asked.

Without looking at her, he nodded before moving towards the open terrace.

Gripping the sheets tight, Juliette made her way to the bathroom and slipped inside.

It was as lavish as she would have expected of such a grand place. Ivory and gold gleamed under sharp lights, drenching the inlaid Jacuzzi built into one wall, a glass shower in the other and a counter with two sinks taking up the third. It was five times the size of hers. It even had a bench wedged between the Jacuzzi and the sinks. There was a trash bin next to the toilet, a row of folded towels on a rack next to the shower and an assortment of man products cluttered neatly on the counter. But it was the plush bathroom mat that really sold her. She could practically burrow into the thing and sleep.

Still wondering why anyone needed a bathroom that big, she moved to the sink. She washed up the best she could before leaving the room to find Killian at the veranda once more. He stood stark naked with both hands curled around the wrought iron railing. Tension pulled at the bulging muscles along his back, making them ripple with his frustration. She wondered what he was thinking about. She wondered if she should say something. Not sure what the protocol was for moments like that, she went to her clothes instead. She scooped them up off the floor and straightened. She jumped to find Killian standing right behind her, beautiful, naked, and hard. The latter had her heart leaping. Her core muscles clenched and she had to bite down hard on her lip to keep from making a sound. She clutched her clothes to her chest in some pathetic attempt to muffle the erratic cracks of her heart.

"Hi," she whispered for lack of anything better.

Killian didn't move. He stayed directly in her path, forcing her to tilt her chin and meet the exasperation and lust crackling across his face. Her body gave a shiver of longing that it had no right to considering she could feel the tenderness pulsing between her legs. But the twang wasn't all pain, she realized with a start. There was a familiar pulse of want there that surprised her.

He was suddenly on her. His mouth cut viciously against hers as she was lifted and dumped unceremoniously on the bed once more. The sheets were torn away, leaving her naked and vulnerable before the wolf. She barely managed a gasp when he forced apart her thighs and filled them with his hips.

"Tell me to stop!" he snarled at her.

Hurting with the force of her need for him, Juliette wound her legs around his ribs and locked her ankles in place at his back.

"No." She licked her lips. "Please don't."

Chapter 5

The silence seemed somehow impossibly too loud as seconds passed. In the space next to him, Juliette lay with her face mashed into the pillow. Her back rose and fell but not with the same intensity as it had only moments before. The smooth curve of her spine glistened with sweat and held the remnants of their love making.

Sex, Killian reminded himself. He didn't make love. He didn't do gentle. Making love implied emotions and he did not possess that ability. He didn't have the luxury. Love and family were a liability he couldn't afford. It was why he never chose virgins. Why the women he took to his bed always had experience and knew what to expect.

Honestly, he wasn't sure he would have stopped even if he had known about Juliette. Being inside her, buried in all that wet heat had been irresistible and addictive ... and dangerous, like leaping off a bridge with only a piece of thread keeping him from hitting the jagged rocks below. It had been an unimaginable thrill, one he knew he needed to step away from before he forgot why he had rules. He had already broken too many of them for her. But no more. She needed to get away from him.

Yet he made no move to make it happen. He lay there, propped on his elbow, transfixed by the shape of Juliette's silhouette half concealed beneath the sheets. Her hair was a tangled riot tumbling across the pillow, the color of pale yellow under the light of the lamp. He knew from memory that the rich strands smelled of wildflowers and felt like silk. But it was nothing compared to her skin. The miles of pale, supple flesh had felt like satin gliding beneath his fingers. He had especially loved the feel of her wrapped around him as he drove into her with the urgency of a wild animal. And she had let him. God, she had begged for more. Again and again, until she had passed out from exhaustion.

Against his will, his fingertips ghosted the smooth slant, following the ridges of her spine from nape to tailbone. The woman made a sound between a moan and a sigh and shifted. One long, toned leg slipped out from beneath the sheets. Killian studied the limb and the triangle of fabric barely concealing her ass and second leg. He already knew what lay beneath; he had been thorough in his consumption of her. Nevertheless, he tore away the hindrance and took his fill of her naked flesh before he never saw it again.

Beautiful. Absolute perfection. Every inch of her stirred his blood and reawakened his cock for another round. Having her so near, so completely vulnerable to the animal already hard for her was a new sort of torture he'd never felt before. Sure there had been women who he had lusted for, but a roll or two between the sheets and that hunger was always sated. There had yet to be a woman he had wanted a third or fourth time.

But he wanted Juliette. He wanted her to stay. He wanted to keep her tied to the bed until his body no longer burned for her. He wanted to feel her bow and writhe and shatter beneath him until every ounce of his need for her was sated. God, he wanted to tear into her and consume her until there was nothing left. He wanted to own and mark every inch of that flawless body so that there was never a doubt of who she belonged to. He wanted to do things to her, dark and dirty things that would horrify her if she ever knew. What the hell was it about her that made the beast in him so crazy?

"Killian?" As though awakened by the mere power of his thoughts, Juliette shifted. The sheets rustled beneath her as she lifted her head and searched for him. Pools of murky brown fixed on his face. Hers softened into a sweet, shy smile that made it all the harder to let go. "Hi."

The knot in his stomach tightened. His jaw creaked. The frustration built into an unbearable thrum. It must have shown on his face because the smile on hers slipped. She drew away, pulling the sheets up with her.

"What?" she whispered. "What's wrong?"

Most of the women he took to bed knew the rules. They knew when it was time to get their things and depart without being asked. Juliette wasn't one of them and yet that wasn't the actual problem. The problem was that he didn't want her to leave. Not yet. But he knew it wouldn't be one more time or another six more times. Something about her was making it impossible to get enough and that alone sent the red flags waving.

"It's time to go," he blurted with a bit more heat then was necessary. "Your things will be by the door. Frank will call you a cab."

It was impossible to pinpoint an exact emotion; so many flickered across her face in rapid succession. But the one that kicked him in the throat was the hurt and confusion that crinkled the skin between dainty eyebrows. A small hand lifted and pushed coils of tangled hair out of her eyes as she tried to process what he was saying. It didn't take very long.

"Oh," she whispered finally. "Right. Sorry."

He made no move to stop her when she scrambled off the bed with the sheets and searched for her clothes. She dressed quickly before turning to the bed. She wet her swollen lips and adjusted the hem of her skirt to cover those beautiful legs. Her eyes never touched on him, he noted. They clung to the space just above his head when she spoke.

"Thank you for everything," she murmured quietly. "I'll see myself out."

One more time, the beast pleaded. *Just one more.*

But she was already gone. The doorway stood empty and dark. In the silence that followed her departure, he could just hear the soft clip of footsteps as she hurried away. He knew she had reached the corridor leading to the stairs when the sound stopped and then there was nothing but his own breathing.

Unfurling himself from the bed, Killian got to his feet. He yanked on his trousers and dress shirt, not bothering to tuck in or button either. Aside from his security, no one else lived in the three story estate. He could walk around naked for all the difference it would have made.

The place held the chill of predawn. Killian wandered the hallways as he too often did when his insomnia was at its worst. That night was no exception and it had nothing to do with Juliette and everything to do with the nightmares. There were too many and they hounded him like dogs. There were pills, he knew. Medication to dull the senses for a few hours and knock him out cold. He had tried a few, but it was a loss of control he couldn't allow himself. Not in his line of work when his senses were all he had keeping him alive. So he wandered an estate that had become his prison too early in life. He followed the ghosts of his past through the empty corridors and listened to his lost childhood echo through every room.

Despite all the money and power, it was a solitary existence. It was a self-proclaimed isolation and it was how he liked it. People had a tendency of dying around him and he already had too many deaths on his hands. He knew he would wind up killing Juliette if he didn't keep her away.

At the top of the backstairs, Killian paused. His hand tightened around the cold iron banister until the knuckles blazed a harsh white in the semi darkness. He stared at the pool of black at the bottom with a numb sort of trepidation, a fear that reared its head every time the idea of being forever alone gripped him. It wasn't ideal. Who in their right mind wanted to die alone? But how could he allow an innocent into his world knowing he would ultimately destroy them? How could he let himself love when he knew it would eventually get torn away? He knew he could easily fall for someone like Juliette. They might not have shared more than a few steamy hours together, but he could see a tomorrow with her. He could also see her broken and bloody in his arms and that nearly made him double over as pain wrenched through him.

Why are you even thinking about this? The voice in his head demanded viciously. *One night with the girl and you're hearing church bells?*

Not exactly church bells, he thought absently as he started downward, his fingers moving unsteadily over the buttons of his clothes, fastening them and tucking his top into the waistband of his trousers. But it did make him want things he had no business wanting.

At the bottom, he turned right and headed in the direction of the conservatory. The chamber of glass and steel had been his mother's favorite place, aside from the gardens. Every happy memory circled around that room, memories of kneeling next to her while she filled the place with every bloom imaginable, memories of her stories. She was forever telling him stories of the impossible. His father would tease her about filling Killian's head with nonsense, but she would swat him away and continue with her tales.

"The world is already an ugly place," Killian had overheard her telling his father once. *"Our son deserves to know happiness."*

His father had shook his head, but he'd been smiling. He would have given her anything. Even as a child, Killian had known his parents were the center of each other's universes. It was in every glance, in every smile and caress. They looked at each other the way his mother used to tell him about in her stories, like there was no oxygen in the world until the other was in the same room. And he had wanted that for himself. He had wanted to love like that.

"One day, you will find your fairytale, a mhuirnín," his mother would tell him when his father would go away on business and he would find her curled up in the window seat of the front room, watching the driveway with a look of absolute heartbreak on her face. She would pull him into her lap and cuddle him close. *"When you do, don't let anything in this world touch her."*

At the time, he had thought she meant not to let another man take away what belonged to him. It wasn't until much later that he realized she meant his world was poisoned and everything brought into it would die. He had just been too young to understand it sooner.

He made it as far as the sunroom when his progress was interrupted by the hulking silhouette moving towards him from the opposite direction. It was impossible not to recognize it immediately.

"Frank?" Killian waited for the giant to draw closer. "Everything all right?"

Frank gave the faintest inclination of his head. "Yes sir. Just walking the girl to the gates."

Killian frowned. "Did a cab pick her up already?"

It was well after midnight and most cab companies rarely ventured that far north and if they did, it usually took at least thirty minutes. It hadn't been that long since Juliette had left his bed.

Frank shook his head. "I offered to call her one. She insisted on taking the bus."

"The bus?" Killian checked his watch, not that he needed to. "It's three in the morning. If the bus even runs this far out of the city, I don't think it actually runs this late."

The other man simply gave a shrug like the matter was completely out of his hands.

"Did she say why?" he asked.

Frank shook his head. "No sir."

It really wasn't his problem. She wasn't his problem. If she refused a cab then what was he supposed to do about it?

Yet the gnawing in his stomach wouldn't allow him to brush the matter off so easily. It kept building and knotting up inside him until it was all he could do to keep from snarling his frustrations.

"Sir, I can—"

Killian waved Frank's offer aside, his body already turning away. "Tell Marco to get the car."

A frown deepened the creases already etched around the bigger man's round face. "Maybe I should come—"

"Rest, Frank," Killian said. "We have a long day tomorrow. I won't be gone long."

Leaving his head of security scowling in disapproval, Killian stalked back towards the stairs. There was an opening at the other end of the corridor that opened to the gym area and another that led to the indoor pool, but then he'd have to circle around and Juliette had already been out there alone for too long. His hurried strides took the stairs two at a time to the top. Without missing a beat, he jogged down the corridor to the second set of stairs leading downward to the foyer.

Marco was already parked at the bottom of the stairs when Killian stepped out the front doors. Despite the late hour, the other man was dressed without a crease in sight and looked far more alert than anyone at that hour should. Behind him, the black BMW shone beneath the bright illumination circling the property. The engine was running, which meant the keys were in the ignition and saved Killian from asking for them.

Marco started to open the back door, but Killian waved him away.

"I got it. Thank you, Marco."

Without waiting to be stopped and reminded of the dangers of going anywhere alone, he circled around the back and ducked into the driver's seat.

"Sir—"

"It's fine," he promised his driver as he slammed the door shut behind him and propelled the car into drive.

The estate sat at the very peak of Chacopi Point, overlooking the entire city. It was the only house for nearly twenty minutes and was surrounded by miles of wilderness and a steep plummet to certain death. Overhead, above the smog and pollution, the sky was a flawless carpet of navy blue littered with stars. Below, the city was a glittering gem of lights despite the hour. But it was the silence his mother had loved when she had picked the spot. There was no sound for miles, except the secrets the wind would whisper to the leaves.

Killian kept both hands on the wheel as he shot down the winding spiral, careful to take each new bend at a slow embrace just in case she was on the other side. His apprehension grew with every second he didn't spot her, knowing she couldn't have gone very far and there was nowhere to go but down.

His patience paid off when he caught sight of her white blouse. It seemed to glow with its own light in the darkness. She was on the side of the road, arms folded against the early morning chill as she stumbled her way over broken gravel. She jumped when Killian sped up and swerved onto the shoulder several feet ahead of her.

He threw open the car door and leapt out.

"Juliette."

She stood before him, small and confused with red rimmed eyes and tangled hair. The fact that she'd been crying hit him much harder than he ever thought possible and for a moment, he wasn't sure what he was supposed to do.

She broke the silence.

"What are you doing here?" she asked, her voice hoarse.

"What did you expect I would do?" he shot back, his anger overruling his common sense. "Let you wander the streets in the dead of night?" He stalked closer, stopping when there was enough space between them to keep his hands in check. "Why didn't you let Frank call you a cab?"

"Because I didn't want a stupid cab," she retorted. "The bus is fine."

"It most certainly is not fine," he said sharply. "What, you think the world is safer when everyone is sleeping? Do you know what could have happened to you?"

She simply stared at him a long moment, her eyes narrowed beneath furrowed eyebrows.

"And why would you care? You certainly didn't seem to consider my wellbeing when you kicked me out of bed like some whore you were done using. Heaven forbid if you waited until morning."

His muscles tightened at her accusation. "I have my reasons, all right? You knew what you were getting into when you got into my car."

She scoffed and gave her head a little shake. "You're right. I did know. I also know that I don't want anything else from you."

With that, she pushed past him. The crunch of gravel beneath her feet drowned out the rustle of leaves. Killian briefly wondered if he should just let her go. He certainly wasn't responsible for her and if she didn't want his help, what was he supposed to do? Force her?

But leaving her didn't seem to be an option either.

"Ah for fuck sakes!" He muttered under his breath before twisting around on his heel. "Wanting it or not, I'm not letting you go off on your own."

She never slowed her angry strides. "You can't stop me."

It was a challenge that made the darkness in him crackle awake. It made his insides tremble with excitement. Every line of his body went taut with anticipation.

"Get in the car, Juliette."

"No!" she shot over her shoulder.

"Don't test me, little lamb," he warned, his voice barely audible and yet unmistakable. "I'm not like the soft men you're used to. I will put you over my knee."

For a moment, she seemed unfazed by his words. Her feet took her three more steps before she stopped. Her back was rigid and her movement stiff when she turned too slowly to face him. The sharp beams of the headlights shone off her eyes, illuminating their wetness and the anger and defeat shining off their surface. She stared at him for so long he couldn't help wondering if she was ever going to speak. Then she opened her mouth.

"I'm so tired," she whispered at last, sounding it. "I am tired of people like you and Arlo who think you can go through life bullying and threatening people into doing what you want."

All thoughts of taking her on the hood of his car vanished with the pain radiating off her.

"That was not—"

But she wasn't finished.

"I know I'm not a good person. I know I probably even deserve all of this, but I just ... I can't..." She broke off with a choked gasp. Her hand flattened against her stomach as though the pain was too much to take. "I can't do this anymore." Her chin wobbled once before she mashed her lips together tightly. Her hands went to the buttons on her blouse and began undoing them roughly. "So whatever you want, just take it and leave me alone."

Killian had no knowledge of moving, but he suddenly found himself right in front of her. His fingers closed around the frail bones of her wrists and he wrenched them away on the forth button.

He was breathing hard. Fury crashed into him with every second he stood there peering into her wet eyes and breathing in her scent; the despair coming off her nearly killed him.

"Don't you ever do that again!" he heard himself snarl. His hands released her wrists and moved into her hair. He cupped the back of her head and yanked her the rest of the way to him. Her gasp ripped through him. "Don't you ever give up, do you hear me? Do you?" He gave her a light shake. "Juliette!"

Eyes wide with fear and confusion, she nodded quickly. "Yes."

He continued to hold her until he was certain she meant it. Then he let go and stepped back, shaken by how much seeing her broken had affected him.

Christ, what was the matter with him?

But he knew. He knew exactly what had gone wrong and he couldn't look at her.

"Get in the car," he mumbled, needing to move, needing to do something other than stand there and feel her eyes burning into him with confusion and, God help him, pity.

"I don't—"

"Don't!" he warned, already turning away. "Just don't. Get in."

He didn't wait for her to follow him. He stalked to the passenger's side door and yanked it open.

There was a moment of pause. Then he heard the quiet shuffle of her feet crossing to him. She slid into the seat and he shut the door behind her. He rounded the hood and climbed in behind the wheel. Neither spoke as he maneuvered the car back onto the road.

She sat huddled against the door, her face painted in lines and shadows. Exhaustion seemed to pour off her in waves to suffocate the air around them. Killian had never found himself in that position before and had no idea what to say or do to make her stop twisting up his insides.

"Are you hungry?" he asked at last.

"No, thank you," she whispered.

The leather beneath his grasp squeaked as his grip tightened around the wheel. They reached the base of the hill and started down the road in the direction of the city.

"The bus stop is at the end of that block," she murmured, never lifting her head off the glass.

"Not leaving you at the bus stop," he said evenly.

She sighed and straightened. "You don't have to take me all the way home. I live an hour out of the city."

Without taking his eyes off the road, he activated the GPS built into the car.

"Put your address in," he told her.

She hesitated and he wondered if she was worried he might rob her in the dead of night. After all, in her eyes, he was no better than a good for nothing lowlife like Arlo. She'd said so herself. The thought annoyed him far more than was rational. He was nothing like Arlo and for her to think he was, was insulting. He may not have been the sort of man she deserved, but he sure as hell wasn't Arlo.

She put her address into the machine and sat back. The map on the screen swirled until it synced their location and shot a purple arrow through the streets they needed to take.

"*In six kilometers, turn—*"

He set it on mute.

Juliette lay her head back against the headrest and stared out the window as they shot through a near empty city lit by lamps and the pale fingers of dawn. Pink and pale blue bled into navy blue and black as they hit Main Street. Every so often, she'd grind her knuckles into her eyes and yawn, but remained awake the whole way to her house, a squat two story that had clearly seen better days. It sat in a neat little neighborhood, surrounded by manicured lawns and well kept houses.

It wasn't exactly a rich area, but reasonably well off. Juliette's house seemed to be an exception. The paint was flaking. The grass was dead in patches. There were several shingles missing off the roof and the whole place radiated with a sort of hollow despair normally found in abandoned places. For a moment, he thought maybe the GPS had taken him to the wrong place. But Juliette was taking off her belt as he pulled into the empty driveway. She grabbed her purse up off the car floor and reached for the door handle.

"Thank you," she said as she threw the door open. "And I'm sorry about my breakdown earlier. I shouldn't have yelled at you."

The thought that *that* was her way of yelling almost made him laugh. But he could only shake his head as she climbed out. He stayed until she had stepped inside and the door had shut firmly behind her. Only then did he pull away.

Chapter 6

There was a level of soreness most people didn't know existed. It was the sort that started in the thighs and splintered across the length of the body in bunched knots of agony. Juliette had never felt so used. Everything hurt and not in the good way romance novels always portrayed after a serious fuckfest.

Her thighs throbbed as though she had spent the night riding a stone horse. Her breasts felt tender and held the lingering remains of Killian's demanding fingers, as did her waists, thighs, arms, and ass. Her lips were swollen from his and felt oddly numb. But it was her pussy that hurt the most. Granted, it wasn't all bad, but there was enough soreness to make Juliette wince every time she attempted to sit down. Having seven inches of hard, angry man meat rammed into untouched territories no doubt had that effect. But he had been gentle as well, she mused. He hadn't been pleased about the state of her experience, that was for sure, but she knew Arlo would not have cared one way or another whether she was in pain or not. Killian had practically been a saint in comparison. He had also been thorough and attentive. He had put her pleasure above his own each time. Pain aside, it had been the best first time a girl could ask for. She had come … often and hard. She had felt the sharp sting of passion as her body had been ripped apart and rebuilt. It may not have been a night she willingly wanted, but it was a night she would never forget either.

Until it was over. Exhaustion and pain had broken her and she had fallen to pieces for the first time in ages. She had said things she regretted, but what was worse, she had let him see her cry. That was something she regretted most. People like him, people who lived on power and the throats of their victims, thrived on the show of weakness. While she didn't believe Killian was like that, not entirely, she couldn't help wondering if he would use what happened the night before to his advantage somehow.

She prayed she was wrong. She prayed that would be the last time she ever saw Arlo or ... no. Not Killian. It was horrible and contradictory to everything her brain was telling her, but the thought of seeing him again didn't fill her with dread. If anything, the thought made her body prickle with awareness and her breast tingle.

Stop it! She scolded herself, trying not to dwell on things she couldn't change.

Instead, she focused on pulling on a light summer dress and a pair of flats. She brushed out her hair, swept on some makeup and hurried downstairs to start on the mile long list of errands she'd written out a week ago before having to face work later that evening.

In the kitchen, Mrs. Tompkins looked up from the previous night's chicken casserole she was scrapping into the trash and smiled.

"Hello dear. How was your evening?"

"Exhausting," Juliette confessed. "How was yours? Did Vi behave herself?"

"Didn't hear a peep from her the whole night. Didn't eat her supper of course, but went up to her room and didn't come out."

Juliette nodded. "I'm glad she didn't give you a hard time." She sighed and checked her watch. "I have to run to the bank and then the grocery store before heading out to work. I'll be back some time after midnight."

Mrs. Tompkins smiled and nodded. "All right, dear. Be safe."

With a wave, Juliette left the house. She hurried along the sidewalk in the direction of the bank. The day was warm with just the right amount of breeze to make it beautiful. It was the sort of day she would have spent in the park, on the towel in nothing but a bikini and sunscreen while her friends chattered on around her and Stan played football with his buddies a few yards away. It had been years since she had been so frivolous, but the pain was still so raw, so fresh. It always felt like she'd lost everything only yesterday.

But she did what she always did when the lingering fingers of depression began creeping across her chest, she reminded herself she had a sister who needed her. She and Vi may not have ever gotten along, but the girl was the only family Juliette had. It was her job to protect her. Something she couldn't do if she let the darkness consume her.

Forcing aside her sadness, she squared her shoulders and ducked into the frigid interior of the bank. The place was nearly empty with only an elderly woman at the teller depositing a check. Juliette followed the neatly painted arrow across the floor to the *please wait here* sign. She was there a full second before she was waved over.

Nena smiled as Juliette approached her window, the kind of smile that was reflexive and a little dead.

"Hello Juliette."

Juliette offered her own smile, but it felt strained. "Hello. I would like to make a deposit, please."

Nena fixed her with cool gray eyes. "Do you have your bank card?"

Juliette shifted. She dug out her card and passed it along.

"I know I'm overdrawn, but I'm going to cover that."

To prove it, she pulled out the envelope of cash Arlo had sent back and set it on the counter between them, deliberately keeping Arlo's message pressed into the glass. It wouldn't have meant anything to Nena, but Juliette didn't want to see it. She didn't want to remember anything from the night before that involved Arlo. She didn't even care that she'd been sold to pay off Arlo's debt to Killian. In her mind, to be away from Arlo, to never have to see or hear him again ... it was worth it. She was officially free. She could finally cut back on working. She could refurnish the house. She could maybe get a car and new clothes. The possibilities were endless and she wanted to cry she was so happy.

"I see the overdrawn." Nena cut into her thoughts. "But it was covered by the deposit made this morning."

Juliette blinked. "What deposit?"

French manicured nails clicked on keys as Nena pulled up the information. She had on her blank bank teller face, making it impossible to tell what she was thinking. Plus she took so long, Juliette was ready to grab the screen and look for herself.

"It looks like it came from a company…" She rapped some more on the keyboard. Thinly penciled eyebrows tangled together. "It looks like it was deposited by the McClary Corporation."

"Who?" Juliette demanded, leaning forward in attempt to see into the screen. "How much?"

Rather than answer, Nena printed off a copy of the balance and slid it gingerly across the divide.

Juliette snatched it up and peered at the long parade of numbers that she initially mistook for a computer malfunction, but realized it wasn't an accident.

"Jesus Christ! What is this?" she exclaimed loud enough to draw attention from the other customers and employees.

Nena's mouth opened, but nothing came out. She shrugged and shook her head.

"Is there a note?" Juliette snapped, anger slicing with white hot speed through her shock.

Nena shook her head a second time.

Grabbing her card, the envelope of cash and the scrap of paper containing more dollars than Juliette had ever seen in her life, she stormed from the bank. All the way downtown, she boiled in a rage that refused to be hampered. If she had hoped the hour long bus ride into the city followed by the twenty minute cab ride to the front gates of Killian's enormous estate would at least bank some of the fire snapping through her with a vengeance, she had been sorely mistaken. It only seemed to bunch around her throat in vice that strangled the air from her lungs.

"Don't leave," she told the cabbie when he rolled up the cobblestone driveway and braked. "I won't be long."

Kicking open her door, Juliette rolled out and charged for the grand doors. Two men stood outside, cigarettes in hand. Both stepped forward when she approached.

"I need to see Killian. Now!" she snarled at them.

"Not without an appointment you ain't," one retorted evenly.

"I am not leaving until I see him," Juliette said, planting her feet and crossing her arms.

Each taking a long drag of their smokes, they eyed her through the tendrils that coiled from their nostrils and the corners of their mouths. Both seemed to be the same height but one clearly spent much more time in the gym. Each of his biceps were the size of watermelons and he had the chest of some rogue pirate off a romance novel. The other was more slender and lean. But neither was one of the men from the previous night, at least that she recognized.

"Look, I was here last night. Killian knows me."

Leers that she did not appreciate twisted their mouths. They slanted each other knowing glances that prickled Juliette's temper several degrees hotter.

"Let it go, sweetheart," Steroid said, chuckling. "This makes you look desperate."

Juliette bristled. "What is that supposed to mean?" she snapped.

"It means you've had your night so move along. The boss doesn't fuck the same whore twice."

Humiliation burned behind her eyes, drawing tears that made her hands tremble with the effort not to let them spill. Blood roared in her ears, muting everything else.

"I'm not leaving until I talk to him," she ground out.

The two snorted and shook their heads. One flicked his cigarette at her feet, missing the top her big toe by mere inches. The top blazed a molten red that billowed smoke.

Steriods nudged him hard in the side. "You crazy? Boss'll kill you if he sees that. Pick it up."

Flushing, the smaller one stalked over and picked up the smoking butt. That close, Juliette had to stave off the urge to knee him in the face. Instead, she watched as he straightened and ambled around the side of the house, leaving Juliette alone with Steroids, who got a call through the mic clipped to his belt.

"Yeah?"

"Problem?" The voice asked.

Steroids stole a peek at Juliette. "Nope."

He turned away to mumble into the device. While she couldn't hear him, Juliette knew exactly what he was telling them and the red hot anger returned. She considered smashing his head in with one of the potted plants lining the pathway, but opted it wasn't worth going to jail over. Instead, she made a split second decision to run. She ran like her life depended on it. She didn't stop until she had slammed into the front doors. The knob was ice cold in her grasp as she wrenched it sharply to the right. Behind her, Steroids shouted for her to stop. But Juliette threw herself into the foyer and slammed the door shut behind her. For good measure, she snapped the lock into place. Then she whirled on her heels and ran forward, past the curved stairway towards the back of the house only to skid to a halt at the sound if raised voices coming at her from the kitchen.

Cursing, she whipped around and bolted up the stairs, taking two at a time to the top. Below, the voices rose, as did the sound of running footsteps. Panting, she tore down the corridor, trying to remember if that was the way from the night before. She didn't expect Killian to still be in the bedroom but it was a place to start.

"Hey!"

With a startled scream, Juliette tore past the second set of stairs and sprinted down the hall in the opposite direction of the small army chasing after her. The thunder of footsteps echoed like bombs going off. It mirrored the pounding of her heart. The bottoms of her feet stung with every slap of her sandal. She ignored it as she ran blindly down the endless hallway. In the end, out of sheer desperation, she ducked into the first open door and slammed the doors shut behind her. The lock cracked into place, sounding oddly muffled to her ringing ears.

Panting, she staggered away from the barricade just as the whole thing shuddered with the weight that slammed into it from the other side. A sound escaped her that was something between a moan and a whimper; the door wouldn't hold. Odds were they had a key. She was trapped.

"Shit!" she panted, lifting a shaky and swiping away the stands of plastered hair off her sweaty brow.

"Juliette?" The break in the silence ripped a frantic scream from her before she even spun around. Killian sat behind an enormous desk, surrounded by papers and wearing an expression that insisted he had not been expecting her.

"Killian..."

The door gave another violent shudder that made her flinch and back away from it.

Killian looked from her to the door before reaching for the phone on his desk. He hit a button and put the receiver to his ear.

"Stand down," he told the person on the other end, never once taking his eyes off Juliette. "No. I'll handle it." He set the phone down and rose. "What are you doing breaking into my house?"

"I didn't break in!" she shot back. "I ran in," she finished lamely. She sighed when he merely arched a brow. "I needed to see you." She moved across the room. It was almost twenty steps from the door to the desk. She dug onto her purse. "It's not a gun!" She snapped, losing her cool the moment his eyes narrowed warily. She ripped out the bank slip and slapped it down on the desk between them. "Is this yours? Did you do this?"

He gave it a fleeting glance. "Aye," he said. "I had it transferred this morning."

"Why?" Her fingers tightened around her purse strap. "Why would you put this or anything into my account? Why..?" She licked her lips when they caught on her dry teeth. "How did you even get my account information?"

"It's not very hard if you know the right people to ask," he answered simply.

"Why?" she said again, louder. "Why the hell would you think I would want your money?"

"Who doesn't want money?" he said.

"I don't!" She raked ten fingers back through her hair. "I don't want anything from you. I sure as hell don't want your … your prostitution…" she broke off, realizing with some horror that she was about to burst into tears. "I'm not a whore! I didn't sleep with you for money!"

But she had, she thought miserably. Just not Killian's money. She had slept with him to get away from Arlo. She had sold herself for freedom.

"That's not why—"

"Take it back!" She tried to ignore the tears clinging dangerously to her lashes as she glowered at him from across the desk. "Take it back. All of it." She shoved the slip at him. It caught the air and drifted over the lip of the desk and disappeared from sight. "Now. Please!"

He didn't reach for the paper, nor did he look away from her.

"I can't," he said with that same level of calm that was beginning to grate on her nerves. "It's already been transferred."

"Fine." She straightened. "I'll have the bank send it back to you. Give me your account number."

He hesitated and, for a moment, she thought he was going to refuse.

"If you don't, I will have it all withdrawn and I will leave it on your doorstep," she threatened.

It must have shown on her face that she meant it, because he reluctantly took up a pen and a piece of stationary. But he continued to watch her even when the pen was poised over paper.

"Are you sure about this?" he asked, which made her want to hurl something at his face.

"The fact that you can ask me that is an insult on its own," she said with as much calm as she could muster. "I don't sleep with men for money. I didn't sleep with you so you could pay me afterwards. Do you honestly think my body has a price, Mr. McClary? That is your name, isn't it?"

He gave a mute nod.

Juliette pressed on. "I may not have a lot in this world, but I have my pride and this isn't okay." She sucked in a breath. "Account information, please."

He scribbled it down without even looking and passed it over. Juliette took it.

"Can I use your phone?"

He gave another silent nod.

Not meeting his gaze, she dialed her bank and made the transfer back to his account. She double checked with the clerk that it was all sent, every penny before hanging up. She set the paper with his account number down on his desk and took a careful step back. Her hands twisted in the strap of her purse as she contemplated what to say next. There didn't seem to be anything. While most people would have found the gesture of him dumping an insane amount of money into their account as charming or sweet, she found it wrong and violating. Why couldn't he just tell her he wanted to give her money? Sure she would have said no, but the alternative was somehow so much worse.

Without braving a single word, she turned on her heels and stalked to the door. Her fingers were sticky with sweat when she disengaged the lock and yanked the doors open. No less than five men moved forward simultaneously to block her path when she stepped out of the room. One even reached for her and she braced to slap it aside.

"Let her go." Killian's voice cut through the space and the hand dropped away.

Juliette shot the owner of the hand a glower before storming off in the direction she had come.

She returned to her part of town with only a hundred wasted on cab fare. Apparently the rich part of town didn't believe in buses or saving the environment. The cabbie had kept the meter going while Juliette had been running for her life through Killian's house. It did make her wonder what he would have done if she'd been killed. Would he still be waiting?

Deciding not to think about it, Juliette went back to the bank. Killian's money was gone and Juliette couldn't help the twang of regret that prickled through her. That money could have solved so many of her problems. She could have paid the mortgage for a whole year and Vi's tuition for the next three years. Plus have money left over. But if she had learned anything from her father's mistake, it was that no one just gave away money and Juliette wasn't stupid enough to let herself fall into that trap with yet another loan shark. Not now when she had finally freed herself. Besides, her virginity didn't have a price tag and she wouldn't let Killian give it one.

"There is only four hundred here," Nena told her, counting the money from the envelope out onto the counter.

"No," Juliette said, leaning over to see. "That's not right. I had seven in there last night. I paid the cabbie a hundred. There should be six."

Nena looked down at the four hundred dollar bills pointedly.

"Sorry, love. Maybe you spent it somewhere without thinking."

Juliette shook her head. "No, I..." But she had no answer. The evidence was right in front of her. Four measly bills.

It made no sense why Arlo would keep two hundred and give back the rest. Had she accidently dropped it somewhere?

She ransacked her purse and came up empty handed.

Had she given the cabbie three hundred? The thought made her stomach hurt. But there was nothing she could do. The money was gone.

Depositing what was left, she hurried home to grab her things for work, her mind still wrapped in the missing two hundred. The house was dark and quiet. Mrs. Tompkins was probably resting. Vi was either in her room or out with her friend. Juliette opted for out because the house wasn't shaking with the sound of some angry girl band. Part of her was actually relieved. As much as she loved her sister, she could never bring herself to like her very much. Not out of jealousy that Vi was free to do what she wanted and possessed an ignorance Juliette wished she still had, but because Vi was a brat, a spoiled, useless brat. Juliette knew her sister knew the extent of their situation. She knew Juliette worked three jobs to pay for their home and food and clothes. Not to mention Vi's tuition and yet that didn't stop the girl from whining about everything and demanding more. And after working eighteen hours days and dealing with everything, Juliette had no patience for her sister's crap.

In her room, she quickly grabbed the bag with her freshly laundered uniform. The stress of losing money tangled with the worry of buying food for the next month and paying bills. She didn't know how they were going to do both with only four hundred. At least with seven she'd had some wiggle room. Maybe she could pick up another shift at the arcade, or get another job. The *Walmart* down the street was hiring stock crew for the evening shift. It was an option.

Tying up her hair, she left her room and headed for the stairs just as the front door opened with a bang and Vi charged in on her chunky heels. She tossed her purse down next to the door and pitched her keys into the glass dish with a deafening clang.

"Jesus!" Juliette hissed, hurrying down the steps. "Mrs. Tompkins is sleeping. Keep it down."

Brown eyes rolled. "Please. She's like a hundred years old. She can sleep all she wants when she's dead."

It took all her willpower not to smack her sister.

"You're unbelievable," she said instead. "Where have you been?"

"With friends," was her answer with a flip of blonde curls.

Juliette opened her mouth to speak when she noticed the smooth leather jacket pulled on over a pretty red top and crisp new jeans.

"Where did you get those?" she demanded.

"What? These?" Vi tugged on the hem of the midriff baring jacket. "I've had them ages."

"No, I do laundry," she reminded the girl sharply. "I've never seen those. Where did you get them?"

"I borrowed them."

"From whom?"

"Oh my god! Are you like my mother or something? I don't need to tell you."

Juliette moved to stand in the girl's path when Vi started for the stairs.

"Did you take money from my purse last night? Two hundred dollars?"

The smooth slant of her gaze, the absent shift of her hand moving up to scratch at her ear, said it without a word.

"Do you have any idea what you've done? Do you have any idea—?"

"What?" A pale hand speared a slim hip. "You're the one who lied and said you didn't have money. And so what? I only took like two bills."

"That money wasn't mine!" Juliette screamed. "You taking that money could have gotten me killed! What is the matter with you? Why are you such a horrible—?"

"Horrible?" Vi shrieked. "Me? I'm not the one who lies and goes off all hours of the day and night—"

"To work!" Juliette said back. "I work so you can stay in that stupid school with your stupid friends, so you can have a house and food. I have sacrificed everything—"

"What the hell have you sacrificed? You've done nothing for me!"

Juliette walked away before she could punch the girl in the mouth. The unstoppable anger was unlike anything she'd ever felt in her life. Not once had she ever physically wanted to hurt her sister before and yet, in that moment, it was all she wanted. Vi had no idea what would have happened if Arlo had opened that envelope and found two hundred missing. Juliette couldn't even imagine what he would have done. She had barely made it out of there alive as it was.

The very idea had her doubling over, body wet with cold sweat. Her stomach heaved, but there was nothing in it to throw up. She closed her eyes against the tears and waited for world to stop spinning.

People moved around her, but not one stopped to ask if she was all right. No one seemed to care that she was clinging to a *no parking* post, doubled over with tears streaming down her face. And why would they? She thought miserably. No one cared about anyone else. The most she could ask for was someone reporting her decaying body if she were to wind up dead on the street one day. Even then, it probably wouldn't happen without someone first stopping to take a selfie.

The thought disgusted her more than the fact that her own sister had stolen from her after Juliette had taken that money out to protect her. It only solidified her feelings towards the girl. But there was nothing to do now but get to work and hopefully get through the night in one piece.

Marie Lopez, a maid Juliette had spoken to on the odd occasion they were cleaning the same level was waiting for her when she arrived. The woman must have just gotten off the morning shift. She was pulling her coat on over her maid uniform. She spotted Juliette and made her way over.

"A man was looking for you," she said, following Juliette to her locker.

Juliette stopped and faced her. "What man?"

Marie shrugged. "White. Dark hair."

Reflexively, her heart gave a leap in her chest. The sensation was foreign, but she recognized it as excitement.

"Black eyes? Beautiful to look at?"

Marie arched an eyebrow. "I don't know about beautiful to look at, but he had nice hair."

Not Killian, she thought, excitement deflating. Marie would definitely remember a face like his.

Juliette frowned. "What did he want?"

Marie shrugged again. "Miss Candy Ass took a message."

Miss Candy Ass was Celina Swanson, the bitter hostess rumored to be sleeping with Harold Whitefield, the manager. She acted like she was hotel royalty when in fact she was the bane of everyone's existence.

Juliette groaned. "Great. Thanks, Marie."

Turning away from the direction she'd been heading, she made her way out of the change room.

Celina was in her usual place at the front counter, her million dollar smile wide and dazzling as she passed room keys over to the couple on the other side. Everything from her sleek, blonde mane to her sapphire blue eyes was flawless and probably cost her daddy—and several rich lovers—a pretty penny to maintain. She always reminded Juliette of a soap opera star, all teeth and big boobs. Plus, she did this thing where she batted her eyelashes like a little girl every time she thanked a guest for coming to the Twin Peaks Hotel. For whatever reason, it drove Juliette nuts.

She was also the reason Juliette could never get a hostess position no matter how hard she tried. For four years, her application had been denied and she knew it was because Harold had given Celina infinite God powers over who got the position. There were only two slots, one for day host and one for the evening shift. Celina owned the day slot so no one ever had any hopes of getting that one unless Celina mysteriously keeled over one day. The position paid double what Juliette was making as a maid and there was more to do than sit around waiting for guests to arrive. But Juliette wouldn't mind the night position. It meant she could keep her job at the diner, quit her job at the arcade and actually get a decent day's sleep for once. But Celina only ever hired her friends, who always wound up getting fired within a week. It was enough to make Juliette want to write a formal complaint, but since the complaint would go to Harold ... it was just a waste of time.

She waited until the couple had ambled away, luggage in tow before making her way forward to address the *Queen*.

"Hey Celina."

The smile immediately twisted into a sneer. "You shouldn't be here! It hotel policy—"

"Did someone come looking for me today?"

Glossy, pink lips pulled together tight in clear annoyance at being interrupted. But she snatched up a piece of hotel stationary and slapped it down on the counter.

"I'm not your receptionist. Tell your friends to get their messages to you themselves."

Ignoring that, Juliette grabbed the paper and hurried into the back.

Call me.
Arlo.

Juliette's insides writhed. Her hands trembled. The nausea she'd been fighting back the whole way to work slammed up into her throat. She barely managed to coax it back down as she reread the note. It couldn't be possible. She'd done everything he'd asked. When she'd left, Killian had been happy. Unless he'd called Arlo that morning and … no. No. God, was that it? Had he complained to Arlo about her behavior? Damn it. She should have just kept the fucking money. Her dignity meant nothing if she was dead.

Heart thumping, she raced for the staffroom and the payphone. Her fingers shook as she inserted the required fifty cents and punched in Arlo's cell number.

He answered on the second ring.

"Yeah?"

Juliette swallowed audibly once to moisten her throat. "It … it's me. Juliette."

"Juliette!" he sounded delighted, like they were old friends who hadn't spoken in a long time. *"Got my message, eh? How was your night?"*

Woozy, she slumped against the wall and shut her eyes. "Fine."

"Yeah? Did you show our friend a good time?"

Having no idea what a *good time* was supposed to be like, Juliette answered, "I think so."

"You think so? Think so isn't good enough, Juliette."

"Yes," she corrected. "I did."

"Good, because I need you to do something else for me."

A frown tightened Juliette's brow. "What?"

"Yeah, it's easy."

"No," she gasped. "You said we were done. That if I … that if I did what you said, you'd forget the debt."

"And I meant it," he promised smoothly. *"The month you owed me is forgiven. Done. You don't need to worry about it ever again."*

No. No!

She sunk to the ground under the phone booth. "No, that's not what you said…"

"Yes, it was." He laughed, long and hard. *"Did you really think I meant the whole debt? Jesus, Juliette, that's crazy. But I have a way where you can get rid of the whole thing in a matter of a couple of weeks."*

It was curdling inside her to say no and hang up, but that was just suicide.

"What?" Even to her own ears, the single word sounded jagged and hollow.

"I knew you'd like that." She heard something crack in the background. Pool balls maybe. *"I need you to see Killian again."*

"Killian? Why?"

"Because he has something I need and only you can get it for me."

"What?"

"Don't worry about that right now. Just get yourself back in his good graces and I will tell you what when the time is right."

"Wait. How do I—?"

"Oh come, come, Juliette. You're a woman. Aren't you guys hardwired with the ability to lure men into your web?" He laughed when she said nothing. *"Okay, look, you're at work, right? What time do you get off?"*

"My first shift ends at midnight," she choked out.

"Great. Call me when you're done."

With that, he hung up.

Chapter 7

Killian studied the bank slip Juliette had left behind and thought of the woman who had evaded his men and risked her life to tell him to take back something most people would have never questioned. Money was the thing that turned his world. It was something everyone worked very hard to obtain and keep, including murder. Yet she had thrown it back in his face even though it was obvious from her bank slip that she had none. With his amount gone there would be nothing in there. So why had she given it back? Why all of it?

He set the slip down on his desk and stared at it some more, determined to make sense of the mystery that was Juliette Romero, because it made no sense. She made no sense and the more he thought about her the less sense she made.

"Sir?" Frank darkened the open doorway of Killian's office, hands clasped neatly in front of him. He regarded Killian with cool, black eyes. "The car is ready."

"Already?" Automatically, his gaze dropped to his watch.

"Yes sir."

Jesus, it was already after eleven. Where the hell had the time gone?

He glanced at the mound of papers spread out across the expanse of his great grandfather's favorite desk. None of it was finished. He had started, but at some point his mind had wandered back to that morning and Juliette and hadn't returned.

Juliette.

He eyed the slip just sitting there, mocking him and shook his head. Damn if that didn't just prove his theory about her.

Dangerous. Definitely. Absolutely. No doubt about it.

Dragging the slip into the top drawer of his desk, Killian rose. He fastened the button on his blazer and made his way to where the other man stood. Neither said another word as Killian made his way downstairs and out the front doors. The limo and BMW had been switched for a simple town car in gunmetal gray. Marco stood at the door, holding it open. He tipped his head forward slightly in indication when Killian approached.

"Would you like to make any stops before we hit the club, sir?"

Killian shook his head. "No, thank you, Marco. Straight there, please."

Marco bowed his head again as Killian took the backseat and the door was shut behind him. Frank crammed his large frame into the passenger's side, rattling the frame and making the little pine air freshener swing beneath the rear view mirror.

Killian drew out his phone and scrolled absently through the emails he would spend the night combing through. There never seemed to be a shortage in crap people sent him. He made a mental note to get someone to go through the mess for him. It was time consuming and he already had too little of it to waste.

"Sir, would you like me to double security at the house?" Frank broke through the silence, attention fixed on the tiny phone in his massive palm. "I think after the incident this morning—"

"No," Killian said, pocketing his phone and turning his gaze to the window. "If Juliette returns, I am to be informed immediately."

Frank lifted his head and turned it ever so slightly over the seat. "Sir, that is not advisable. To be lax about security—"

"She is not a threat," he cut in and almost laughed; she was nothing if not the biggest threat Killian had ever faced. "I want to be informed."

Frank inclined his head once before keying the instruction into the phone. Killian knew it would be sent to every member of his security team as an update.

"Max has just informed me that the money transfer you requested be sent this morning was returned." Frank paused to scroll more carefully through the message. "Perhaps there was an error with the bank or the account numbers Domino retrieved. Would you like him to resend or look into the matter?"

Killian shook his head. "No."

Frank sent the message to Max.

There were no more questions as they drove into the heart of the city and Killian's brand new nightclub. Ice was only one of fifteen, but so far, it was his favorite. The glass and steel motif reminded him of living in an ice castle. The place was spacious with three full floors for dancing, a fully stocked bar and menu and a bartender that could make just about every drink under the sun. Plus it was the first establishment he'd bought with money that didn't belong to his family. It had come from his own hard work and that alone made it special.

The car was pulled up behind the building and Killian climbed out before Marco could get the door for him. The night was humid with the promise of rain. Already the streets glittered like black diamonds and crunched beneath his soles as he made his way inside.

The backdoor opened just behind the dance floor and was guarded by a beefy bouncer who kept people from sneaking inside without paying admission. He gave Killian a fleeting glance before turning narrowed eyes back on the crowd.

Marco took lead, paving a path along the edges of the packed floor towards the stairs tucked in a corner towards the back. Beneath their feet, lights blasted neon tones that reflected off the glass tables, walls and ceilings. Strobe lights pulsed in time to the heavy thunder of bass and swung wildly over sweaty skin and glittering dresses. The place was full and he knew outside would already have a lineup. He paid no attention to anyone as he followed the stairs to the third floor. Frank was at his back, moving with a quiet sort of grace a man his size should never possess.

At the top, Killian opened the metal door leading into his office and stepped into the box overlooking the entire club. Most of it was one sided glass that glinted a deep purplish blue that matched the plush carpet tucked beneath the leather sofa and glass coffee table. There was an onyx bar pushed up against the right side with glass shelving built into the wall behind it. At the head of the room sat a desk with a computer.

It wasn't the most original or fancy club he owned, but it was his.

He moved to the wall of glass and peered down at the moving figures below. Beautiful women with glistening bodies barely covered by scraps of fabric swayed and sashayed to music he couldn't hear in the soundproof confines of his haven. He could have any one of them, he thought. He wasn't ignorant to his looks or the fact that he was one of the wealthiest men in the country. Women liked both and he had used both in the past to get what he wanted. But money hadn't worked with Juliette. Nothing he did seemed to impress her and he wasn't sure what that said about him or her.

Below, a red head in a slinky green dress grinded against a brunette. The two were drawing a lot of male admirers and Killian couldn't blame any of them. The pair were beautiful, young and drunk. He was half tempted himself to join them. Tempted, but not exactly motivated to follow through. Not even when the redhead slipped her hand up the brunette's skirt and had the brunette catching her bottom lip between her teeth.

"Who's manning the floors?"

Frank checked his phone. "A new guy, Brock. Why?"

"Tell him to get the two porn stars off the dance floor before we have an orgy on our hands."

He heard Frank heave himself off the sofa and walk up behind Killian's shoulder. He found the two and shook his head. Without a word, he turned and left the room. Killian watched as his head of security hit the main level and cut a wide path through to where the girls stood, passionately lip locked and oblivious of everything until they were torn apart. They pouted. The men around them booed. But the two were still escorted off the floor towards the exit.

Killian shook his head.

As fun as it all was to watch, he didn't run that type of business. Sure he knew it happened. He knew there would be discarded condom wrappers in the bathroom by the time the night was over, but it didn't mean he turned a blind eye to it.

Show over, he turned his attention to the rest of the place. He watched the waitresses, the bartender, the DJ. He took note of the lighting and the way the customers moved around the glass tables. There was still plenty of work that needed to be done, but so far nothing that caught his immediate attention.

Distractedly, he pulled out his phone and checked the time. It was still fairly early, yet he had no desire to be there. After a sleepless night, part of him wanted to head home and attempt a few hours of shut eye, not that it would do him any good. He knew he would merely toss and turn until frustration propelled him up and pacing the estate. Occasionally, he got lucky and managed an hour or two. Those nights were rare and usually disturbed by visions of blood, screaming, and death. There were times he forced himself to stay awake just to not have to see that.

That night, he was exhausted. His head felt full of cotton and lead and he had no sense to concentrate like he knew he ought to.

Maybe he should go home, he decided vaguely while glancing at the eight new messages flashing across his screen. A few he knew he needed to respond to immediately while the rest could wait until morning. But it was the text message from an unknown number that gave him pause.

It was a series of seemingly random letters and numbers that were mashed together to form two paragraphs. Anyone not familiar with the secret language he and Maraveet had spent an entire summer inventing as children would automatically assume the sender's phone had accidentally pocket texted him. But Killian knew exactly who the sender was and what the message said and it made him snort in response.

"*I hate ducks,*" it began in true Maraveet fashion. "*Vicious, unlikable creatures. Why couldn't they go extinct instead of the white tigers? Oh, that's right, because they are useless. I bought new shoes from a little store in Paris and stopped at a café for some coffee and one of the little fuckers stole my box. Snatched it right up from under the table and took off. It was lucky I wasn't carrying or I would be having duck for supper.*

What is this I hear about your insane idea to open a nightclub in New York? Nothing ever lasts there, except questionable road conditions and those hotdog venders. I'm telling you, I'm not convinced they're all beef. Still can't believe you bought one that summer we went there to see The Statue of Liberty. *I thought Mother was going to die right there on the street. Don't be too much of a brat, hm?*"

Maraveet was the closest thing he had to a sibling. They shared no blood, but their parents had been close friends and Maraveet was the only child of his parent's business partners that he was allowed to play with. He had never minded. She'd been a pain most days, but she had also kept him company, which was a big deal when there was no one else.

But all that changed when her parents were killed and Maraveet was brought to live with them. They'd only been seven, but she had been devastated. For months, she'd wandered the estate, crying at the drop of a hat. He hadn't understood it at the time, he'd had his own parents so her loss was something he couldn't relate to. But when he lost his mom, then his dad in the span of a few short years, he understood it too well. That was the year Maraveet considered them cursed and told him to stay away from her. That as long as they kept apart, they wouldn't be used as pawns against the other.

"If it looks like we have no one, we won't have to go to another funeral." That had been her logic.

Killian had let her go. He couldn't keep her even though he'd tried. She'd already made up her mind and on the night of her seventeenth birthday, she'd packed her bags and left for Paris to take over her family's obtaining business. She was good at it and it made her happy. Occasionally, she would send him an encrypted text message with clues to her newest adventure, but he hadn't laid eyes on her in years.

"Maybe the duck smelled that revolting perfume you're so fond of and thought you were its mate," he wrote back, grinning to himself. "And there is nothing wrong with New York. That hot dog tasted delicious, even if it might not have been beef. Also, I can be a brat all I want. It's not like you're here to stop me."

Hitting send, Killian pocketed the phone and glanced at the glass again. He knew Maraveet wouldn't answer again. Not for several months, maybe even years. But at least she wrote. It eased his mind that one of the criminals she was always hanging around with hadn't killed her. It really was a matter of time, especially when she spent her time smuggling hot goods from country to country and encountering drug cartels and murderers. And telling her to quit was out of the question; she had a criminal nose like her father and refused to acknowledge the possibility of being double crossed. She was too good at what she did, and there was the fact that she knew dirt on just about everyone. Her connections were limitless and kept her well protected, which gave him some peace of mind.

The phone buzzed in his pocket, momentarily surprising him. He knew it wouldn't be Maraveet even before he fished it out, but a part of him hoped it was. It was ridiculous and pitiful, but he hadn't had anyone to talk to in years. Sure, he talked plenty of business with many people, but he hadn't had a normal conversation with a normal person in so long, he couldn't even remember it. Maybe it was with Maraveet before she left. Maybe it was with his dad before he died. Both had faded into the double digits. No one really understood just how lonely an island of one really was.

As quickly as the thought penetrated, he shoved it aside. The serrated fingers of weakness and doubt cut into flesh before it was forced back into the deep recesses of his mind. He focused instead on the new message and the many more waiting for his attention.

It was on the forefront of his mind to spend the remainder of the night going over correspondences when a flutter of white caught the corner of his eye. Flashes of color in a club full of people and lights wasn't so uncommon, yet it was compelling enough to catch his attention and coax his gaze down to the dance floor.

Amongst the sea of oversexed women, she practically glowed with a radiance that seemed to outshine every single person there. It was as though she had her own spotlight gleaming down over her, following her as she cut through the throng of people in the direction of the bar. In the semi darkness, her pale dress radiated an almost purple. Her tied back hair shone a soft gold. Strands had escaped to frame her flushed face and the anxious look in her eyes.

For several confounded moments, Killian could only stand there and stare with open mouth wonder. His brain couldn't seem to comprehend whether or not she was an illusion conjured by the state of his unstoppable need for her or if she had somehow found him. Both filled him with a certain level of dread and excitement. He watched as she slid into a corner and looked out over the floor. He waited to make sure she wouldn't move from the spot before making his way out of the office and down the stairs. Marco glanced up from the bottom. He straightened when Killian drew closer.

"It's fine," he told the other man as Killian moved past him towards the front of the bar.

He spotted Frank making his way back, saw the confusion on the man's face as he caught sight of Killian. But he didn't try to stop him, nor did he—as Killian expected—let him go alone.

She was exactly where she'd been when he'd first seen her from the office, tucked alongside the bar with her purse hugged to her midsection and her eyes moving rapidly over the crowd. Killian paused to study her, taking note of the fine lines knotting the place between her eyebrows and the restless gnawing of her teeth along her lip. It was clear she was waiting for someone and he couldn't help wondering if it was him. Had she somehow found him? More importantly, what did she want? She had already made it perfectly clear that she wanted nothing from him, not him, not his money. He wasn't sure what else he could possibly offer. Unless she was there for another night of intense, mind blowing sex. He normally didn't bed the same woman twice, but he knew he wouldn't say no to her if that was what she wanted. Truth be told, he couldn't stop wanting her either.

A man broke away from the dancers and meandered his way over to where Juliette stood. His approach wasn't expected. Juliette tensed and narrowed her eyes as he approached. Her grip on her purse tightened as the man stopped mere feet from her. He said something that had her shaking her head and backing up a step. He followed her retreat and Killian stiffened. Sharp blades of anger crawled along his spine. It curled his fingers into fists at his sides and tensed the lines of his shoulders in a sensation Killian hadn't allowed himself to feel in years.

The man continued to grin as Juliette unsuccessfully tried to sidestep around him. She said something and he shrugged, slow and deliberate. He moved into her space again and Juliette lifted one hand against his chest, holding him back even as he ignored it. He captured her wrist and used it to jerk her into his arms. His hands went around her, gliding and stroking her back, sides and arms while he swayed his body against hers in grinding rotations. Juliette twisted and finally shoved him back. She said something and, even from the distance, Killian recognized the heat. The anger. Not many women could pull off sexy when they were pissed. The way her eyes lit up when she was furious was the same fire that shone in her eyes when she was aroused. It was hot and intense and it fueled him with a powerful surge of adrenaline he knew could either be really good or really bad.

He reached for her again. This time with an insistence that had even Frank stiffening at Killian's back. He reached for Juliette and was met with a resounding crack of her palm across his cheek. The snap echoed over the music, drawing the attention of a few dancers, but no one made any move to intervene. No doubt in their minds, the two were having a lover's quarrel.

Killian knew better.

He charged forward before the guy had a chance to react. He got there just as one arm was being drawn back in retaliation. His hand closed around the wrist and, in the same momentum, dragged the arm back and around. He twisted it against the man's back and shoved him forward, slamming him into the corner of the bar. Taken by surprise, he had no chance to react before Killian's free hand had grabbed hold of the back of his head and slammed his face into the table.

"I really hope you weren't about to do what I think you were," he hissed low into the man's ear. "Otherwise, I might need to teach you a lesson about raising your hand to a lady."

Arm restrained, face mashed against the table, the man had no room to struggle, but he gasped.

"You're going to leave," Killian went on. "And if I see you again, no one will ever find your body." And he meant it.

Not bothering to wait for a response, he shoved the man. A few dancers nearby scuttled back as he hit the floor at their feet. No one seemed particularly interested by the scene as they shifted further away and resumed their evening. Frank grabbed hold of the guy struggling to his feet and dragged him out of sight.

Killian turned to Juliette. She stood staring at him with a look of wide eyed confusion.

"Killian?" She glanced around them as though something in their surroundings might explain what was happening. Finding nothing, her gaze returned to him. "What are you doing here?"

It was clear that she hadn't come looking for him, but it did make him all the more curious.

"Friend of yours?" he asked instead, gesturing with his head towards the direction the asshole.

Juliette shook her head. "I don't know him." She licked her lips and the plump curves glistened tauntingly under the light. "What are you doing here?"

He almost laughed at the question. "I own it."

"You own...?" She trailed off as her gaze lowered to the piece of paper in her hand. She studied it a long moment before something seemed to click and her shoulders slumped as though she were afraid of that. "You own the place," she mumbled with a sad sort of acceptance.

"Aye." He studied her, trying to pinpoint what exactly she was thinking, but the lights and shadows kept shifting on and off the lines of her face, distracting him. "Come upstairs."

He didn't wait to see if she would follow. He turned and started back the way he'd come. It was only at the stairs that he paused and waited for her to catch up. Marco stepped aside as Killian offered Juliette his hand. At the top, he held the door open and waited for her to pass through first before following and shutting them in.

She groaned the moment the door sealed shut and silence descended. "That's so much better."

"Don't like music?"

He moved to the bar, needing a drink. Or six.

"I love music," she answered, stepping up to the glass wall and peering down. "I just don't want to be deafened by it."

"Then a nightclub is clearly not the right place to be," he deduced, reaching for a bottle of whiskey.

Her chuckle made him glance up.

"Maybe," she mused.

Drink forgotten, he found his gaze tracing the soft curves of her back, the womanly shape of her hips, the long, slender lines of her legs. Even scooped up, her hair reached the small of her back. It seemed darker in the dimness of the club. Then, as though sensing his eyes on her, she turned her head over her shoulder. Her brown eyes met his from across the room and held. The innocent gesture pierced through him with an intensity that shook him straight to the core.

"It's beautiful up here," she said quietly. "The lights look great off all the glass."

He fixed his focus on pouring the drink. "Who are you here to meet?" he asked, struggling to keep his voice even. "A lover?"

The dry look she sent him was unnecessary. He knew what a stupid question that had been before he'd even spoken; of course there was no lover.

"There is no lover," she answered anyway.

"Boyfriend then," he corrected.

She shook her head. "No boyfriend." She faced forward. "Last night would not have happened if there was one."

"Of course," he mused quietly. "He would never have allowed it."

Her eyes found him once more over the smooth curve of her shoulder. "I would never have allowed it." The corner of her mouth quirked. "And no, he wouldn't. Would you?"

His drink paused midway to his mouth. "If you were mine?"

Color darkened the contours of her cheeks, but she held his gaze firmly. "If the person you were with was in my position."

He didn't even attempt to consider his answer. "Never. I would have skinned Cruz alive. But also, my woman would never have been a virgin."

She did avert her eyes that time. Killian threw down a much too large gulp of whiskey and refilled his glass.

"Would you like a drink?"

She shook her head. "No, thank you. I don't drink."

Nerves calmed, he circled the bar and made his way to where she stood.

"You don't drink." He twirled his own drink absently. "You don't carry a gun. You don't have a lover. You don't like loud music. Do you smoke?"

She shook her head.

He stopped when there was a full foot between them and peered down into her upturned face.

"Just what do you do, Juliette?"

"Work," she murmured quietly.

His gaze drifted over the top of her head and settled on his desk without seeing it. He took a sip of his drink and contemplated his next question. He had so many.

"What kind of work?"

She drew in a breath that made her breasts swell against the material of her dress. She held it a moment before releasing it in a rush to answer.

"I'm a waitress at Around the Bend," she said evenly. "And a maid at the Twin Peaks hotel. On weekends, I work at Fun Time Arcade and Fun Pit."

"Jesus." He lowered his glass. "When do you sleep?"

She gave a wry smile. "Coffee and I are very close."

"Surely you don't only always work," he cajoled.

"Pretty much," she stated with a small shrug. "What about you?"

He met her gaze. "Do I work or do I do all those things?"

"The latter."

He glanced at the glass. "Yes, I drink. In moderation. I do carry a gun. Yes, it's registered and, yes, I do know how to use it. I used to smoke." He threw back the rest of his drink and set the empty glass down on the coffee table. "It was a nasty habit I picked up after my mother died. It was either smoke or drink and…" And he had needed all his senses to do what needed to be done. "Smoking was an easier habit to kick," he finished.

She watched him with those eyes that seemed to see too much and he looked away.

"Why did you quit?"

"My father's death, ironically." He felt his mouth twist into humorless grin. "He hated that I smoked and begged me to quit for years. When he died … I quit."

"How old were you?" she asked.

"Ten when my mom died and sixteen when I lost my dad."

"I'm sorry," she whispered. "I lost both my parents around that age as well."

He started to tell her it wasn't the same thing. That her mother's cancer wasn't the same as how his mother was brutally beaten, raped, and tortured, nor was her father's gambling problems anything like watching his father die in his arms after taking a bullet meant for Killian. Yes, they had both lost their parents at a young age, but her loss was nothing like his. Yet there was something on her face, a shadow of pain he recognized that made him stop.

"You have your sister," he reminded her instead.

Her bottom lip was caught between her teeth and she turned away. Neither spoke for several long moments.

"I love my sister," she said, but it was the way she said it, like she was reminding herself that made him glance her way. "Sometimes it's just hard to remember why." She seemed to remember he was still standing there, because her head jerked up and she faced him with a sheepish little grin. "Sisters can be a pain, that's all."

He said nothing.

"Do you have siblings?" she asked when the silence deepened for too long.

"Sort of," he said, thinking of Maraveet. "We're not related though and I haven't seen her in years. She'll drop by occasionally, unannounced, but it's a hard thing getting a hold of her otherwise."

Something in his tone, maybe a note of wistfulness had her peering back at him, a glimmer of sympathy in her eyes he did not appreciate.

"Does she live very far?"

Killian shook his head. "She travels a lot."

Thankfully, she didn't push. Instead, she glanced at her watch.

"I should go. My second shift starts in an hour."

He turned as she started away from him. "Second?"

Juliette paused to glance back. "I have two hours between shifts and I'm down to the last hour."

"When do you get off?"

She adjusted the staple on her purse. "Six."

"Where?"

"The Twin Peaks hotel on—"

"I know where it is." He had no recollection of moving until he found the space between them gone and he was standing a mere foot away. "But you never told me why you're here."

Juliette hesitated. Her lashes lowered to the gap between their feet. Her fingers knotted in her strap. The knuckles blistered white before she released them and lifted her eyes to his face.

"Arlo sent me. You have something he wants and he's trying to use me to get it."

The declaration collided square with his gut, expelling all his oxygen and making his insides ache. At the same time, it filled him with a familiar sort of rage he hadn't felt in a long damn time. The latter had him turning away from her. It had his clenched fists sliding into his pockets as he moved to put an entire room between them. It wasn't because he doubted his restraint. He just chose not to test himself.

"I see," he murmured quietly. "And what does he want?"

Juliette shook her head. "He never told me."

He glanced at her. He took in her doe brown eyes and weary expression. She stood so small and determined. But it was the way she was watching him back that had his curiosity bristling.

"What do you want?" he wondered out loud. "Were you hoping that by telling me, I would hand over whatever it is that little fuck wants?"

"No." She held his gaze squarely. "I don't want anything."

Irritation spiked up the cavity of his body. He twisted around to face her fully, all the while, resisting the urge to march over and shake her.

"So, you're telling me out of the goodness of your own heart."

"No," she said again. "I'm telling you so you know to be careful."

That only seemed to intensify the burning coil winding up inside him. But it was the jagged thorns of something else, something foreign and deadly that had him tensing.

"And why would you do that, eh?" He edged around her carefully. "Why would I be a concern of yours? Were you hoping I would owe you? Were you hoping you could play me?"

For the first time since her confession, Juliette's face twisted into one of absolute disgust.

"Play you? What on earth do you have that I would want?" she threw back at him. "I'm trying to get away from the lot of you, not get in deeper."

That intrigued him enough to let go of some of his anger. But he kept a firm grip on his suspicion.

"What then? What would you like for this wee bit of information?"

He thought he had her when her gaze broke away from his and lowered to her feet. He thought for sure that she would ask him for money or protection. Part of him secretly hoped she would ask him to kill Arlo and end her problems. That was something he would do without hesitation. He still might depending on how the night ended.

"I don't want anything," she murmured at last with a weariness that made her voice come out strained. Her chin lifted and she peered at him once more. "But I don't want Arlo to get what he wants either. Maybe it's suicidal and stupid of me, but I realized something today after I talked to him, that I would never be free of him. That he would never let me go. He already lied once and I don't believe he won't do it again if it means getting what he wants. I know telling you was dangerous, but if I have to pick the lesser of two evils, I pick you."

With that, she turned on her heels and slipped out the door.

Chapter 8

The arcade was in chaos. The Sunday crowd was especially chaotic as they stuffed their tokens into the machines and filled the space with the shrill of bells, whistles and lights. It was Juliette's least favorite of places to work, but it filled the Sunday gap that neither the diner nor the hotel covered. It wasn't much in paychecks—barely anything at all—but it was still something, which was still better than nothing.

Some orange haired kid with an infestation of freckles was having his eleventh birthday party in one of the corners. He and his friends had taken over the place in a cacophony of noise and smells. One boy, Juliette was certain, had shit himself in all his excitement. Juliette wasn't sure which of the twenty-five boys it was, but Wanda, the day manager, had taken one sniff and left Juliette to fend for herself, which honestly she could handle. It was the dads she wanted to stab with a rusted knife.

"Can we get another pitcher over here, sweetheart?"

No! Juliette wanted to scream at them. *Get your own fucking pitcher.* But smiles and friendly service was how she made her tips, which unfortunately sometimes also included having bored, horny men think she was one of the games.

"Sure."

With a smile that hurt her jaw, she reached for the pitcher placed a bit too far on the opposite side of the table where the four men sat watching, waiting to get a peek down her top as she bent forward. She could feel their eyes burning into her, stripping away the tight black t-shirt and equally tight mini that rode uncomfortably high up her bare thighs.

The uniform, while not stated as such, was designed to entertain the male cliental over the age of sixteen. It was cut low in the bodice to reveal more cleavage than Juliette was comfortable showing and the skirt hem had a two inch slit up one side that made the bit of fabric even shorter.

The women that occasionally made the trip with their children eyed the outfits with raised eyebrows and pursed lips while shooting their husbands warning glares not to look. Juliette always felt bad for being the cause of all the friction that followed those visits, especially when they were there to have fun.

The men loved it—when their wives weren't around.

"Coke, right?" she clarified as she dragged the pitcher to her.

"Unless you got something stronger," one man said and laughed like he'd made the best joke ever.

Juliette chuckled because it was her job to do so.

"No, sorry," she said and made her way to the kitchen, fully aware of their eyes on her backside.

Barely five feet with wiry black hair and intense brown eyes, Wanda looked up when Juliette pushed her through the swinging doors. A basket of fries sat clasped between her hands. Her dark, mocha skin was beaded with sweat from the deep fryer and the unnatural heat that never seemed to leave the cooking area. Purple lips pursed as she set the basket down on a tray already heaped with four other baskets and arched an eyebrow.

"I'm fine," Juliette answered the unasked question. "Really. It's not so bad."

Wanda snorted and went back to her tray. "Don't know what they're feeding that child, but, Lord, he stank."

Juliette laughed. "Well, hopefully they'll leave soon."

"Girl, ain't that the truth. I got no more patience for them little bastards."

It always hit Juliette as ironic that Wanda partially owned an establishment designed to cater to children and hate children. Wanda had none of her own and swore she'd hang herself if that unfortunate day ever came. It was unclear whether the woman had always felt that way or if it was something that deepened the longer she worked at the arcade. Whatever it was, it always made Juliette chuckle.

"I need another refill," she said, waving the pitcher and rattling the few pieces of ice at the bottom.

"Another one? Jesus."

Juliette shrugged. "Twenty-five kids. Four parents. It adds up."

Leaving the woman to finish her task, Juliette headed for the freezer in the back. She dumped the melted ice out into the sink and refilled with fresh cubes before pouring in the pop.

While the machine gurgled and sputtered brown liquid, she busied her sweaty hands refastening her hair. Strands had begun to escape the elastic since her heroic crawl through one of the tubes after a girl of six who had gotten herself mixed up and frightened. Oddly enough, the mother had been more frantic than the child once Juliette had lured her out.

The soda machine clunked to a stop. The drink fizzed inside the pitcher and she waited a full heartbeat before forcing herself to pick it up.

One more hour, she reminded herself.

It wasn't the greatest motivator, but it got her moving. At the kitchen doors, she sucked in a breath and plastered a smile on her face before pushing through.

"One pitcher of Coke." She set it down in the middle of the table, wiped the moisture off her hands on her skirt and peered around at the group. "Can I get you guys anything else?"

The father of the birthday boy leaned forward after casting furtive smirks at his buddies. "Yeah, the time you get off tonight."

It was a struggle to maintain her smile, but it was worse trying to restrain the urge to dump the pitcher down on his head.

"Sorry. I'm already seeing someone," she lied, which usually was enough to deter further propositions but he seemed to be adamant.

"And we're married." He sat back and shrugged. "No harm in a little bit of fun, right? We could pick you up and check out that little motel down the block."

Juliette couldn't help it. Her brow lifted.

"We?"

Maybe he mistook her outrage for interest, because his grin blossomed wide. "Yeah, a little something extra."

She looked over at them carefully, not because she was considering it, but because the very notion was hilarious and laughing outright would no doubt get her fired.

"Sorry. I'm very happily taken."

Not waiting for a comeback, she started edging away, hoping to get the rest of her section cleaned up before her shift was over. Plus there was that kid with the mess in his pants she had to find before he got shit all over the play area and she had to clean it up.

"Well, how about you help us take care of our bill?" Birthday Boy's dad suggested, drawing Juliette to a stop.

She had half a mind to get Wanda to take care of that, but there was a good chance Wanda might decide that qualified as an opening to share the tips fifty-fifty and Juliette had worked fucking hard for every cent. At least, if they wanted their bill tallied, that meant they were leaving and Juliette was more than happy to comply.

Smile tight, she turned back. "Would you like me to bring the debit machine to your table or will you be paying in cash?"

The man in charge stooped to the side and tugged his wallet free of his back pocket. His murky gray eyes stayed fixed on her face as he withdrew a wad of bills. One by one, they were counted out across the table in a row that crackled hot along her skin.

"That should about cover it, plus a little something extra for your troubles," he said with an evenness that made her want to punch him. Carefully, he took each bill and folded them in half once and waved them at her as though she were some stripper on a pole. "Where would you like me to put it?"

Up your fucking ass! Juliette was about to tell him when another voice answered for her.

"That all really depends," said the low, chilling voice laced with a familiar accent she had no trouble placing. "How badly would you like to keep your hands?"

Juliette whirled around, her heart already somersaulting in her chest before she even set eyes on him.

Painfully beautiful with his dark hair swept back and his face flawlessly shaven, Killian joined the circle that was her, the table and the four men, with Frank at his back like a hulking shadow. He scrutinized the four blinking back at him with a steely glower that made Juliette shiver.

"I suggest you reconsider your method of payment very carefully, gentleman," he drawled in that same icy tone.

The birthday boy's father came out of his shock first.

"Who the hell are you?"

Killian fixed him with those dark, penetrating eyes. "I am the man who could make this a very bad day for your son."

"Killian…" Her breathy whisper was silenced by a single sidelong glance shot her way from over his shoulder before he went back to addressing the men at the table.

Gleaming, black sunglasses were set neatly on the table and bracketed by long, square palms planted flat on either side as Killian leaned forward.

"Pick up your money," he told the other man. "You've decided you'll be paying by debit. Juliette, get the machine."

Left with no other option, Juliette left the group quickly and returned barely a minute later to find all four men ashen faced and trembling as plastic cards were practically thrown at her. The birthday boy's father looked nearly in tears and there was a faint, red welt circling his throat that she was almost certain hadn't been there before she'd left.

Her gaze shot to Killian, who stood a few feet away from the table, hands clasped together around his glasses as he waited for her to finish. He met her gaze from a face carved in absolute calm, but it was the barely suppressed fury crashing behind his eyes that captured her.

The party paid for their bill and, as Juliette noted, left a very generous tip before scrambling out of their booth to find their children. Part of her wondered if they would ever come back and realized she hoped not.

With nothing left to occupy her attention, she had no choice but to face the man she hadn't seen in over a week, a man she hadn't thought she would ever see again, honestly. And while the sight of him filled her with a sort of lightness she wasn't sure what to do with, she was also apprehensive and a little scared; she highly doubted Killian McClary made courtesy calls to people who were sent to betray him.

"Hi," she whispered for lack of anything better.

"Hello," he replied with that same scary calm voice she wished he would stop using.

He studied her face before dipping down past her shoulders and taking in the rest of her. She could feel the careful glide of his eyes along every contour like hungry hands. The intensity made her painfully aware of all the skin not covered by the uniform, all the skin branded by his touch. There were nights she could still feel the phantom caress of his fingers skating, tracing … teasing, and she'd wake up gasping and throbbing for more. So many times she pondered the idea of going to his house or the club and begging him to take her again, just once more, but common sense had always prevailed and she had been forced to take matters into her own clumsy and far less adequate hands.

"What are you doing here?" she asked when he said nothing else.

"I need to know something," he said, dragging his attention back up her flushed and embarrassingly aroused body to settle on her eyes. "Why did you come home with me that night? Why didn't you get out when I gave you the chance?"

Heat crept up her neck to spill into her cheeks and burn behind her eyes. "This isn't the time or place—"

"Why?" he cut in not unkindly. "I could have been worse than Arlo. I could have done horrible things to you, but you still didn't run. Tell me why, Juliette."

Nerves and something sharp and coppery like fear roiled in the pit of her stomach. It flexed up fill her chest with a weight that made it impossible to breath. Yet it never crossed her mind to lie.

"Arlo promised that if I slept with you, he would consider my father's debt paid." She bit her lip hard enough to ward back the prickle of tears. "I wouldn't have otherwise. I'm not like that. I don't sleep with men for money or…" She turned away with the pretenses of clearing away the discarded plastic cups and napkins left behind by the party. "I'm not a whore."

His hand closed around her wrist just as she snatched at a wad of used napkin. She released it as she was drawn around to face him.

"Who would know that better than me?" he asked quietly.

It was true. He had firsthand knowledge of her innocence. Yet it didn't ward away the flood of shame she could feel stinging her cheeks.

"It was you or him," she whispered.

"And I was the lesser of two evils," he finished with a sort of humor that she couldn't bring herself to share.

She shook her head. "He was going to give me to his men after he finished." She lowered her eyes to the sharp point of his Adam's apple. "I don't regret it being you."

It was only when she felt the hot glide of his palm following the curve of her side to splay between her shoulder blades that she realized he had taken over the space between them. His heat and scent curled around her like comforting arms and it took all her restraint not to close whatever distance was left and surrender. As it were, all she could manage was to fall recklessly into his eyes and pray to God she wouldn't regret it later.

"Good," he murmured, drawing back.

The hand around her wrist released and extended to the man standing mutely a few feet away, seemingly having gone deaf and blind throughout the entire interaction. A white envelope was passed over and Killian held it out to Juliette.

She took the legal sized packet and flipped open the top. She peered inside at the small stack of papers.

"Contract of Agreement?" she read out loud before lifting her head to him questioningly. "What's this?"

"That is the solution to our problem," he stated, dropping his arm from around her as well and taking a step back. "It will get rid of Arlo from both our lives for good."

Juliette gasped. She shoved the envelope back against his chest, horrified.

"I am not going to … to contract you to kill him!" she hissed. "Are you crazy? This is so wrong, not to mention illegal!"

Killian's mouth twitched as silent laughter glittered in his eyes. "It's not a hit contract," he said gently. "I wouldn't need your consent to kill him if that was what I wanted. This," he placed the envelope back in her hands, "is me giving you what you want."

Wary, but intrigued, Juliette reached into the packet and removed the papers. The document had all the beginnings and markings of a normal, legal contract, but she still didn't understand.

"I don't get it." She raised her head. "What is this?"

"I'm going to pay off your father's debt."

Juliette's muscles tensed. Her fingers wrinkled the papers clutched tightly between them.

"In exchange for…?"

His eyes were dark pits of hunger and fire boring into hers in a way that left no doubt in her mind that he was remembering every dirty, heart stopping thing he'd done to her.

The phantom sensation sent a hot shiver through her that fanned the inferno he'd lit in the pit of her stomach all those nights ago, the one that had never fully extinguished.

"You." His shoulders rose with his deep inhale. "I want you and in return, I will clear all your debt. I will give you a monthly allowance that will surpass everything you make working three jobs and I will take care of all your wants and needs without question."

"If I ... what? Sleep with you again?"

"Yes!" His nostrils flared like a wolf at the scent of delicious blood. "But not once more. I want you to be mine for a full year."

Juliette blinked. "A year? Why—?"

"Because that night wasn't enough. Because I can't stop wanting you and that is a problem. A year will ensure that I have successfully fucked you out of my system."

Her heart escalated in rhythm. "And if it doesn't?"

"It has to." His dark gaze jumped from her eyes to her mouth, which parted obediently. Yet their traitorous actions were nothing compared to the familiar tingle that vaulted recklessly up her body, tightening and pinching places aching for him. "Read it. Sign it. Bring it to me. If you don't bring it yourself in one week, then I will consider that your rejection."

It was moments like that where Juliette wished she had a friend. Another person she could trust enough to confess her worries and pains. As it were, all decisions were left on her exhausted shoulders.

The contract lay in her lap as she watched the flow of people strolling the hotel grounds. The afternoon sun was a brilliant, yellow ball of joy glistening against a flawless blue sky. Rays shimmered off the surface of the lake where children pitched in rocks and scrambled back and forth over the stone bridge. Couples wandered the trails, exploring the lush landscape the brochure promised while Juliette sat out of sight on a shady bench, deliberating what was sure to be yet another epic twist in her life.

The rational thing was to accept Killian's offer. One year with him was practically a carnival ride compared to a lifetime with Arlo. But the idea of belonging to another person, of signing her entire life over to someone she didn't know for a whole year scared the shit out of her. Even if it meant getting out of the hell she was in, who was to say Killian wouldn't turn out to be even worse?

While no part of her believed that for even a moment, she debated her decision. Part of her wished she had Killian's number so she could talk some of the contract over with him. Not that there was a single unclarified line in the whole thing.

Since offering her an escape almost three days before, all Juliette had done was read and reread every paragraph. She skimmed and circled and dissected every word and still she was no closer to solidifying her resolve. Even as she sat there and watched children play, she was not ready.

Gingerly, she pried open the top of the envelope and drew out the wad of papers from inside. There were a lot, practically a small book and each page had an extensive amount of writing that seemed to surpass a mere sleeping arrangement for a year. But she tucked her legs under her and read over his conditions.

This agreement is between Killian McClary (hereafter called The Primary) and

_____,

(hereafter called The Secondary.) For a one year agreement: Hereafter referred to as The Agreement.

Anal, was the first thing that came to her mind. Every condition was explained to an inch of its life, leaving no mistake in the reader's mind that there was no exception to those rules, nor should there be an excuse to not follow them to the letter. There were only fifteen, but well over thirty pages.

i.

The Secondary:

1. The Agreement will begin from the time the two parties (The Primary and The Secondary) have signed the contract and both have agreed on the conditions.

2. By signing The Agreement, The Secondary has agreed that she will make herself readily available to The Primary at any and all hours of the day or night within the one year cycle with the exception of her respite.

3. The Secondary will not have relations with outside parties at any time during the year stated in The Agreement. Failure to abide will results in severe consequences as well as termination of The Agreement.

4. The Secondary acknowledges the fact that this arrangement is in no way a relationship and thus has no rights, holdings or say in business ventures overseen by The Primary. She has no legal or financial jurisdiction over any companies, holdings, bonds or institutions other than that to which is agreed upon.

5. By agreeing to The Agreement, The Secondary has accepted that she will, to the best of her abilities, maintain a certain level of appearance, hygiene, and decorum. Regular physicals and maintenance must be made and provided to The Primary upon request.

6. The Secondary acknowledges that she will be given one week a month in respite where she is free to spend her time as she so chooses. The week is chosen by The Secondary at the start of each month and disclosed to The Primary in writing.

7. The Secondary has accepted and acknowledged that at no point in the year stated in the Agreement will she knowingly manipulate The Agreement into a relationship, which also includes spending the night, monopolizing The Primary's time outside the agreed upon slots stated and, or extending The Agreement after the initial year period. The Secondary has acknowledged that at the end of the year stated in The Agreement, she will remove all articles of herself, her

possessions and belongings of all places resided by The Primary. No furrther contact shall be made henceforth that isn't initiated by The Primary.

8. The Secondary has agreed that at no time during the year stated in The Agreement will she allow herself to produce children. Precautions must be taken at all times through the year stated in The Agreement. Failure to do so will result in termination of The Agreement and penalties will be applied. Evidence must be given of contraception once a month without exceptions.

ii.

The Primary:

9. The Primary has agreed that by signing The Agreement, he has taken upon himself the responsibility of The Secondary's wellbeing financially, mentally, emotionally, and physically. At no given time can this be altered or negotiated.

10. The Primary is responsible for regular health examinations which will be given to The Secondary upon request.

11. The Primary will cease all relations outside The Agreement for the year stated.

12. Should The Primary and/or The Secondary wish to terminate The Agreement at any point or time, a thirty day written notice must be submitted to the other party and notarized by a witness present.

13. The Primary will abide by all boundaries in or out of all agreed slots stated in The Agreement. The Primary will cease all acts immediately upon The Secondary's request without question. The Primary will not force, coerce, or harm The Secondary at any time or point in the year stated in The Agreement.

14. The Primary will respect and acknowledge The Secondary's respite once a month and never question her time away from The Primary.

iii.

15. Both parties acknowledge that The Agreement is temporary and will terminate promptly one year to the day. Both parties acknowledge that they are in the right state of mind while signing The Agreement. They acknowledge that they were not coerced or under the influence of alcohol or narcotics while signing The Agreement.

_____
Primary

_____
Secondary

Juliette reread the thing from the start, trying to find even a hint of something strange, but it was all so fair and precise. There was no reason at all why she couldn't easily follow the rules, why she couldn't make it work. If it meant being away from Arlo and not having to work as much ... why not?

Nevertheless, she slipped the papers into the envelope and rose to her feet, her break over.

He's crazy, Juliette told herself a few hours later as she tore the sheets off a queen sized mattress and tossed them in pile next to the door. Of course she wasn't going to accept. Who the hell would? A year with a guy she barely knew and only as his fuck toy. Where the hell was the dignity in that? Did he really think she would just jump at the chance to be his mistress?

"Crazy!" she grumbled under her breath as she pitched the pillowcases in after the sheets.

It didn't matter how handsome he was or how incredible in bed, he was a criminal. She didn't even know what kind. He could sell children for all she knew. He could be a killer. A rapist. An expert in black market organ trade. How the hell was she supposed to overlook that? It wasn't as though she could ask. Even if she did, odds were he would probably lie.

But it was tempting. God, was it ever tempting. The thought of no more Arlo made her insides shiver with excitement and longing. It was all she wanted. She didn't care about the rest. She would be Killian's slave for the rest of her life if it meant never having to see Arlo again. It wasn't something she would ever tell him, of course, but it was all she could think about and it was making her decision to stay immune increasingly harder.

Maybe ... no!

She kicked the wad of fabric with her foot in vicious anger at her own weakness. It didn't help, but it did send them a foot closer to her laundry hamper, which, in a way, helped.

Scooping them up, she marched to the basket and tossed the bundle in. She shoved the cart out into the hallway before ducking back into the room to finish the bathroom.

It was well after four in the morning by the time her shift finally ended. The hotel was a dark, silent place full of strangers. Juliette hated the nightshift. The dark corridors and eerie hum of phantom noises always gave her the chills. But she did her job quickly and thoroughly with the end goal being going home and getting two hours of sleep before heading to the diner for a six hour shift. Then it was back to the hotel. The endless rat race made her want to cry. But it was necessary.

Last bed made, Juliette did the one thing they were forbidden to ever do: she lay across the cool sheets and stared up at the ceiling. The knots along her spine wrenched as her back straightened for what felt like the first time in days. She didn't dare shut her eyes. She knew they would never open again if she did.

Seconds ticked into minutes. She gave herself five before rolling to her feet and grabbing her things.

Downstairs, she took the laundry hamper to the laundry room, her cleaning cart to the storage closet and made her way to the change room. Marie was nowhere in sight, but there were a few other staff members changing back into their normal clothes. No one spoke as they went about their business. Juliette went straight to her locker and stripped out of her uniform. She hung it neatly on the hook before redressing in jeans and a t-shirt. She let her hair down from its elastic and ran a quick brush through it before grabbing her bag and making her way out of the hotel.

"Juliette."

That voice, that loud, obnoxious drawl of her name sent an explosion of terror scattering across the length of her spine. The fear grew as the metal door locked shut behind her and a single shadow split off into five different figures all making their way towards her in a cluster. They fanned out, leaving no room for her to maneuver around them in the tight alley behind the hotel. Trapped, she stood waiting for them to reach her.

"Juliette," Arlo said again as he came to a sickening halt two feet from her. "Where have you been, Juliette?"

"Working," she murmured for lack of anything better.

It had been a blissful week and a half since her talk with Arlo over the phone, a week since he'd sent her to Killian's club in hopes of her seducing him. She had begun to hope that maybe he'd forgotten about her, or better yet, that he'd been shot and was now dead.

Arlo exhaled and dropped his head to the side. In the thick shadows of the buildings surrounding them, it was impossible to see his face, but she didn't need to. The single light over the staffroom door seemed to catch on his brown eyes and reflect like cold metal.

"You haven't been answering my calls."

"I don't have a phone," she reminded him.

Arlo chuckled. "True. True. But you should have made an effort to stay in touch. I needed you."

She pulled her purse closer into her stomach. "Why?"

"It's been almost two weeks," he reminded her. "How are things coming with Killian?"

Juliette didn't know what to say, didn't know how to tell him she hadn't seen Killian in three days or that she hadn't even attempted to get on his good side. But she thought of his proposition burning a hole inside her purse.

"Okay."

A dark brow lifted. "Just ... *okay*? Didn't I tell you to soften him up?"

"I did," she blurted.

That seemed to satisfy Arlo.

"Good, because I have your first assignment."

Juliette's head rocked before she could stop it. "I won't use Killian."

"Use?" Arlo pivoted around on his heel to face his crew with his arms open. "Who said anything about using him?" He turned back to her. "I just need you to get his signature on something. That's all. See? I even have all information written down for you."

He pulled out a folded piece of paper from his back pocket and held it out to her.

"What is this?" she asked, taking the slip and opening it. "Ownership papers?" Her head jerked up. "You want him to sell you his port?"

"Not *sell*," Arlo corrected. "I want to own it."

"But ... how?" she asked. "He's not just going to—"

"Make it happen, Juliette." The happy go lucky tone was gone from his voice. "Seduce him, drug him, beat him, I don't care. I want that shipping yard."

"I ... I can't—"

"That's not what I want to hear, Juliette," he warned slowly. "Imagine how much easier obeying can make your life. Get me what I want and you can have your life back. But if you so much as breathe a word of this to McClary or anyone, I will rip you open like a Thanksgiving turkey, you get me?"

Juliette nodded quickly. "I won't tell anyone." Else, she added silently to herself.

She wasn't stupid enough to tell him she'd already told Killian everything.

"Good." He leaned back, did a little bounce on the heels of his feet and clasped his hands behind his back. "Now, how did things go with you and him at the club the other night? Did he find you?"

"Yes." The single word caught in her throat.

"My cousin said he did. He said you played your part very well."

"I didn't know I had a part," she whispered. "Your ... cousin, didn't tell me who he was. He just grabbed me and—"

"Luan likes to improvise," Arlo cut in. "It needed to look authentic." He waved a hand. "That's not important. Tell me what McClary said."

Juliette swallowed. "He didn't really say anything about ... anything."

Arlo stopped. His head tilted back a notch. "My cousin said you were up in his office for an hour."

Had it really been an hour? It hadn't felt that long.

"We didn't do very much talking," she lied.

"Oh, I see." He snickered when she flushed. "Had you on your knees, did he?" He shook his head. "Well, whatever helps you get him to sign that paper..."

"I'm not going to help you steal from Killian," she blurted weakly, but with a confidence she had to dig deep for. "I'll keep paying you what I owe, but—"

She never saw the backhand coming until the crack of it resonated through the alley like a gunshot. Unimaginable pain erupted up the entire left side of her face with a fire that seemed to possess its very own heartbeat. It seared through her, filling her mouth with the tang of copper and shattering the world in a brilliant shower of stars. Juliette had barely caught her breath when violent hands closed around her throat. The wet concrete she had no recollection of meeting scrapped up her back as she was hoisted into the air and slammed into something equally hard.

"What did you say to me, you little bitch?" The foul stench of unwashed mouth cut into her whirling senses and it took her several desperate attempts before she realized she was shoved into the side of the hotel by her throat and he was leaning right into her face. "Did you seriously say no to me?" he snarled. "I own you, do you hear me? You will do whatever the fuck I tell you. You will fuck whoever I tell you. You will obey my every command without question." The pressure on her windpipe increased until she was gasping for air. Her legs kicked fruitlessly. The heels smacked rapidly against the wall pressed into her back. She clawed at the hands holding her, but he seemed immune to the blood she was drawing. "The next time you open that mouth of yours, it had better be because you're going to suck my cock or you're going to say, *yes, Arlo, whatever you want*. This is the only warning I'm going to give you, Juliette. Next time, I will make sure they never find your body."

With a final squeeze, he released her. She collapsed to the ground in a gagging, gasping, sobbing mess. Her entire body convulsed in pain and fear. She flinched when he crouched down next to her.

"So what are you going to do for me, Juliette?" He cocked his head to the side to peer through her hair into her tearstained and bloodied face. "You're going to cozy up to Killian McClary and get me my shipping yard, right?"

Not sure what else to do, she nodded vigorously.

"Good girl. Now, go home and rest. You have a big day ahead of you tomorrow."

With that, he got to his feet and strolled over to where his men stood. The group turned together and followed him back into the shadows.

Juliette stayed huddled against the building, her face radiating with its own heat and heartbeat. She couldn't even tell if anything was broken, but she could feel the steady trickle of blood pouring from one or possibly both of her nostrils. The flow was dripping down her chin to stain her shirt and jeans.

She wiped numbly at the flow with her bare forearm, smearing wet crimson across her skin. The sight of it brought a sob to her numb lips that she quickly bit back, knowing if she started, she'd never stop.

Shakily, she used the wall to heave herself up onto unsteady legs. She grabbed her purse and the folded piece of paper off the ground and picked her way carefully out of the alley. The staffroom doors were usually locked from the inside after six o'clock or she would have gone back in to clean up. Instead, she was forced to make her way home in an almost drunken haze. People glanced her way, but no one made any move to see if she was all right, to which she was eternally grateful for. She wasn't sure she could trust herself not to fall apart if anyone stopped her before she got home.

At home, she went straight to her room and stripped. Her clothes were left scattered across the floor in a long row to the bathroom. She climbed into the tub without glancing in the mirror. She knew she would never be able to stand it if she saw herself in that state. The jets hit her like hot pins piercing flesh. Juliette sank to the bottom and stayed there until the feeling returned to her otherwise numb body.

It could have been five minutes or five hours, but the water had gone cold when she finally dragged her throbbing self back into her room and pulled on a t-shirt and panties. She threw back three aspirins, downed it with water and steeled every nerve in her body for the inevitable. Only when she was steady did she allow herself a peek at her own reflection.

The left side of her face was an explosion of colors that expanded across her cheekbone, starting from the gash. It bled across her temple and stopped just inches from the corner of her mouth. Her nose was swollen and tender and there was a split in her bottom lip. Otherwise, aside from the glossy sheen in her eyes, she seemed fine.

Moving away from the mirror, she headed for the bed and the sweet promise of a brief nap. Her entire body felt raw and she knew that was only the tip of the iceberg.

Arlo had never hit her before. He'd manhandled and assaulted her, but had never physically struck out. Certainly, she never believed it beneath him. He was a monumental asshole riding on a power trip that he didn't seem to realize would ultimately end with his death, a fate she couldn't wait for. Not that it would end the reign of terror that was the Dragons. Arlo had three younger brothers and a slew of cousins and other relations, all just dying to get in on the pie. So Juliette was under no fantasy that the nightmare would ever end.

Unless she made it end.

Reaching for the foot of the bed and the purse flopped over in one corner, she dragged the ancient piece of garbage over to her and tore out the envelope Killian had given her. The corners were bent from being shoved into her bag, but it was otherwise smooth and a shade of white that actually hurt her eyes.

There were two great evils in the world and both wanted a piece of her. The question as always was: which one was the lesser of the two?

She could stay with Arlo and be his punching bag or worse, his whore for the rest of her life or she could throw her hat in with Killian. While he was a criminal, he hadn't hurt her and she had meant it when she said she would pick his side. If anything, he had gone out of his way to make sure he was gentle, something she knew he didn't have to do. Arlo certainly wouldn't have. Had Killian not taken her away that night … she couldn't even think about it. The very idea made her want to curl up in a ball and sob.

Instead, she drew out the contract and followed the familiar lines through each page. She had already memorized most of it, but still she kept rereading until her pounding head reached its splitting point and she had to stop. She stuffed the agreement back into the envelope and tossed it down onto the nightstand to reread again in the morning.

Without looking at it, she rolled onto her side and drifted off into an immediate and dreamless sleep.

Chapter 9

Killian could never be mistaken for a patient man when it came to incompetence. People who went through life living on excuses of injustice and righteous indignation infuriated him beyond a reasonable measure of doubt. The man across from him was no exception.

Peter Jacoby was a minor nobody Killian had no time for. He ran some insignificant little group of marauders that peddled drugs from province to province. In the food chain of things, he was somewhere just above dirt. Most minor groups and gangs circled around a bigger organization. Each district had its monarchy and every monarchy had its ruler. Killian just so happened to be the monarchy for the north and that meant that, just because he would like nothing better than to shut it all down and take it all apart brick by brick, that wouldn't happen overnight. It was a slow and agonizing process that required patience and the gentle snip of ties being cut. While toes were bound to be tread upon, when Killian finally threw off the final chain holding him to that life, it would be such a clean cut that he could live the rest of his life without ever looking over his shoulder. But before that could happen, first he needed to focus on the minor things, like Jacoby.

"As you can see, it's a fairly large shipment," Jacoby stated with a breathless sort of urgency.

Killian drew in a breath for what felt like the first time in ages and sat even further back into the soft leather of his chair. The hinges squeaked slightly and he made a mental note to get the joints greased.

"Mr. Jacoby, I honestly have no idea what you're asking of me," he stated simply, lifting his gaze to pin them on the man who looked like he was in desperate need of a shower, not to mention a shave.

Small and shriveled with skin sagging off bony limbs, Peter Jacoby reminded Killian of a grandfather biker. He wore dark shades, even though they were inside and a bandana over a receding hairline that had just enough straggly strands to be shoved into a greasy ponytail down the back of his leather vest. Underneath that was a white t-shirt and pale jeans that Killian had a feeling were his best attire. Unlike the goons he'd brought with him, Jacoby had six tattoos along his arms, though Killian could just make out the hint of more beneath the collar of his shirt. Most of them he recognized as prison ink.

Maybe he'd been more intimidating in his younger years, Killian mused.

"What exactly is it you want?"

Jacoby pursed dry, cracked lips, clearly annoyed by the lack of focus Killian was giving him. "I have a shipment coming in," Jacoby repeated slowly, and Killian prayed to God he didn't start his story over again. "All the main highways have upped their security after that incident a while back. I need a safe transpo and I was told you were the man to talk to."

Normally he would be. Since the incident where a truck full of cocaine over turned right in the middle of Highway 1 between Alberta and Saskatchewan, the authorities had upped their security by about a hundred percent. People in Jacoby's line of business were forced to find new and more creative ways to transport their cargo. Most turned to Killian. What with his family owning one of the largest port in the west plus several private cargo planes, there really was no one better.

"And what type of shipment are you looking to transport?" he countered.

There was a time in his ancestry that it didn't really matter what was in the container so long as the money was green. Killian didn't run his business like that. He needed to know exactly what was in each container, right down to the last straw, and something told him Peter Jacoby wasn't transporting melons.

True enough, Jacoby shifted. "Just a few odds and ends."

"What kind of odds and ends?" Killian pressed. "If you want to use my ships, I need to know just how hot the merchandise being moved actually is."

"Just a few kilos of angel powder," Jacoby said with a casual shrug.

"Cocaine." Killian clarified and waited for the man to give a nod before rubbing the tips of his four fingers over his mouth. "Mr. Jacoby, I don't—"

A movement from the open doorway caught his attention. His head jerked up just as a small, pale figure stepped onto the threshold. Brown eyes met his from a face that had been haunting his every waking hour and all his thoughts scattered. Everything faded, but how the sun from the wide windows seemed to halo her, turning her white dress nearly translucent and her hair a riot of spun gold. The silky strands were unbound, spilling in curls around bare shoulders to stop teasingly over firm breasts. She'd parted it differently, with half being tucked behind her ear while the rest hung deliberately over one side of her face. But it was her mere presence he noticed above all else and the purpose behind it.

She reached into her monstrous purse and pulled free the envelope he'd given her. Color worked into her cheeks as she held it in front of her for him to see. But the euphoric bliss that rushed over him was short lived by the off coloring on her face. How the one side hidden by hair was darker and how she seemed to be … smaller, like she had somehow shrunk into herself overnight. He didn't for a second believe it was her decision to accept his terms that had her looking so shaken and defeated.

Jacoby started to rise from his seat. "Mr. McClary?"

"Leave." he said without a shred of care as he shot out of his chair and marched to where Juliette stood. His hands found her face before it even registered that he was reaching. He tipped it up to the light behind him and swept back the hair.

There was no telling just how bad the injuries were when she had about ten pounds of makeup slapped down over it. But he could see enough of it to make his nostrils flare.

"Who did this?" Even to his own ears, the words hummed with barely suppressed fury. It vibrated with rage and a type of danger that he could feel crackling up his spine. "Who put their fucking hands on you?"

He saw the fear in her eyes, the tremor in her chin before she pushed it behind a shaky smile.

"I brought the agreement," she whispered, putting the envelope between them. "I do have some questions—"

He ignored her pathetic attempts to misdirect his focus and dragged her into his private bathroom despite her protest. He shut the door behind them and reached for a clean washcloth.

"Killian—"

"Quiet!"

He dampened the cloth and reached for her once more. One hand cupped the base of her skull while the other swiped gingerly at her face, rubbing until every last bit of makeup was removed all the way down her throat where the smooth skin was a maze of red, purple, green and yellow welts the exact shape of a man's violent hands. Every new mark filled him with a new color of red that was making it impossible to breathe. Every time she winced, every time he saw pain in her eyes, it was all he could do to keep the need for blood at bay.

"Take it off," he bit out, giving her the option before he tore the clothes off her back with his bare hands.

"Killian, please—"

"Take it off, Juliette, or so help me I will."

She was trembling and God help him, but he didn't care if it was from fear of him. In that moment, all he cared about was seeing just how far her injuries went. From there, he was going to hunt the bastard down and kill him like a rabid dog.

Carefully, her clothes were removed and she stood before him in her plain bra and panties. Any other time, the sight of her body naked would have driven him mad with lust. But all he felt instead was a choking rage every time she removed an article and her breath caught with pain.

He turned her around, taking careful consideration not to hurt her further. His gaze roamed up the backs of her legs to the blossoming smear of hues splashed across her shoulder blades. Skin had been peeled away, leaving the spot jagged and scabbed. There was torn flesh along her right elbow and right knee, but nothing else.

"Who did this?" It took all his strength to keep his touch gentle when he made her face him once more. "Tell me."

She shook her head. "I fell."

"Bullshit!" His snarl made her jump. "I know a man's hands, Juliette. Tell me his name."

"Killian, please, don't—"

He kissed her. There was nothing remotely gentle or warm about the vicious grind of his mouth over hers. It was brutal and merciless. But it was either that or shake her and he couldn't trust himself with the latter.

"I will find him," he vowed against her lips. "And I will end him!"

He kissed her one last time before throwing open the bathroom door. He shot her one last glance before closing it behind him and marching across the office.

Frank met him at the door as though summoned by the mere power of Killian's mind. Jacoby, Killian noted absently and without much care, was gone.

"Sir?"

"Get the car," he bit out, charging past the other man and storming down the corridor. "We're going to pay the east a little visit."

Frank didn't ask. He fell into step alongside Killian while he dug out his phone and made the call. Killian knew Marco would already be outside, waiting.

"We need to make a stop first." He told Marco before climbing into the back. He paused closing the door to peer up at Frank. "Make sure she doesn't leave."

Inclining his head, Frank pressed his phone to his ear again and muttered instructions quickly as he rounded the trunk of the car and climbed in next to Killian.

Killian preferred doing his business from home, but Juan Cruz did his from the front parlor of the Dragon's Palace. The eight story hotel of ivory and gold had been gutted into a lavish palace equipped with gilded stairways, priceless art, and the entire Cruz family, blood related or not. Three of them patted Killian down upon entering the sprawling foyer. They weren't exactly gentle about it, but Killian let it go as he was ushered through the entrance towards a room swept into one corner of the main floor.

Juan sat on a velvet settee with one leg reclined across the scarlet expense while a girl of sixteen knelt on the floor and rubbed the other. He looked up when Killian was brought in. The copper tone of his complexion seemed even darker beneath the black cap of wavy hair. It was swept back to expose deep lines on a face that could have once been considered handsome before time and prison took over. Six teardrops inked his right cheek just beneath the contours of his dark eyes. More tattoos colored his throat and disappeared beneath the buttoned collar of his *shalwar kameez*. It wasn't traditionally something worn on the streets of Mexico, but Juan had a love for the loose trousers and baggy top and wore it everywhere.

"Killian." He motioned for the girl to go away with a dismissive flick of his wrist. The girl ducked her head and scurried out of the room. "What brings you to the east?"

Killian moved to the matching seat on the other side of the gilded coffee table and sat.

"It seems we have some business to discuss," he said evenly.

Dark eyebrows winging up, Juan lowered both feet to the worn carpet and leaned forward to rest his elbows on his knees.

"Do we?"

Killian glanced over at Frank and motioned the man over with a curt nod. Frank stepped over and gingerly set the silver briefcase down on the coffee table. Juan gave it a fleeting glance before fixing his curious gaze on Killian once more.

"If this is the amount you obtained from Arlo for his idiotic indiscretions, I won't lie, I am surprised."

Killian shook his head. "It's not, though I hope that has not soured our friendship."

Juan waved a hand dismissively and sat back. "The boy must learn the business. We have all done foolish things in our youth and we paid the consequences. But I can assure you that it will not happen again."

It was on the tip of his tongue to ask what kind of consequences Arlo was forced to endure, but that wasn't his business.

"Thank you."

Nodding, Juan flicked a glance down at the case between them. "So, what can I do for you?"

"I am here to pay the debt of Antonio Romero," Killian said.

Frank unsnapped the locks and turned the briefcase over for Juan to look inside.

"It's all there," Killian assured him. "Plus a little something extra for your troubles."

Juan never bothered even glancing at the briefcase. "And why does this matter to you?"

Killian folded one leg over the other and leaned into the firm back of the sofa. "The girl and her family are under my protection."

The other man's face immediately broke into a grin that created even more folds to appear around his eyes. "Ah, the girl. I have seen the girl. Very pretty. I can see why you would want her, but this…?" He waved a gold studded hand at the briefcase. "Surely she is not worth this much."

Killian didn't so much as bat an eyelash. "She's mine."

Both hands went up in a show of surrender. "Alexandro!"

One of the men stationed around the room hurried forward and bowed low.

"Antonio Romero," Juan said evenly. "He's done."

Without batting an eye, Alexandro dug out his phone and found Antonio's name. He crossed it out and typed in paid next to it. Then he presented the screen to Killian, who gave it a brief glance.

He turned back to Juan. "Appreciate it."

Juan waved Alexandro away. "Now that we finish with business, you must stay for supper. Maria is always making too much."

"There is something else," Killian cut in. "A problem."

All amusement faded from Juan's face. "What sort of problem?"

"Arlo," Killian said shortly. "He's been giving Juliette a hard time."

"It is the way of things," Juan said instantly. "You don't scare the people, they take your money and never pay."

"No." Killian let the full force of his anger shimmer to the surface. "Not like this. He put his hands on her. He hurt her."

"I will talk to him," the other man promised.

"See that you do." He rose gracefully to his feet. "I don't like my things touched, Juan. And I would hate for your wife to bury a son so early."

There was warranted indignation in the older man's eyes, but they both knew the laws of the streets. They knew how bloody a turf war could get and how dangerous. Juan was old enough and wise enough to recognize a friendly warning opposed to a threat.

"It will be done."

Inclining his head in farewell, Killian started for the door.

"Killian." Juan's voice stopped him, had him turning around. "I do not take lightly the friendship we have between our homes, but I will not look favorably should something befall my family."

"Nor will I," Killian answered evenly. "Juliette and her family no longer owe the Dragons. I don't ever want to hear that she was bothered. Please give Maria my best and tell her I will come another night to see her."

With that, Killian walked out with Frank right on his heels.

The drive back was done in a silence that was broken by the occasional chirp of Frank's phone. Killian watched the scenery zip past the window in a blur of buildings and people. His temples throbbed in a familiar drum of agony that made him close his eyes and shut off his thoughts. But images of Juliette's bruised face, the marks on her body, rose up behind his eyelids and the scorching grip of rage returned with a vengeance. It made him want to throw friendship and years of careful planning into the wind, hunt Arlo down, and break every bone in his fucking body. It made him want to do all the things that had given him the nickname The Scarlet Wolf.

"Boss?" Frank's booming voice pulled him from the brink.

"Home," he mumbled without opening his eyes.

Marco veered the car north. In the distance, sirens blared and Killian reflexively winced. The sound grated on all his nerves with serrated claws. It gouged up memories he fought so hard to bury. But all it took was that sound, a sound meant to assure and calm. For him, it was a sound that had failed his father. The sound that carried his mother away to save only to fail in route. It was a bad sound. He loathed that sound.

At the manor, Killian opened his own door before Marco could even draw to a full stop at the base of the stone stairs. Frank followed. Together, they started up.

"Can you find out why Jacoby was here?" he told the other man. "I think he wants to bring a shipment into the city. Help him off the books then make sure the proper authorities stop him before he gets close. I don't want his garbage running my streets," Killian muttered, trudging over the threshold and into the foyer. "But be sure it doesn't come back on the company."

Head bent over his phone, Frank nodded. "Yes sir."

Killian turned to the stairs.

"Kitchen," Frank said without looking up or being asked.

Redirecting his steps, Killian made his way down the corridor towards the back of the house. Patches of sunlight trickled down the white walls and lay in a slump half across the marble floors like a drunk. It shone and flickered when he passed through. On the left, rows of high glass overlooked the garden his mother had practically lived in. After her death, he'd hired the best gardeners and landscapers to maintain the grounds, to keep everything exactly as she had. Truth be told, he had changed nothing in the entire house.

His mother had handpicked and designed every inch of the manor from the faucets to the little doorstoppers behind every door. It had been her project for over thirteen years and probably would have still been had she not been taken from him. Killian would have sold the place after his father's death, and had contemplated it several times, but it had so much of his parents woven into every grain and piece of wood that parting with it would be like losing them all over again.

The hall ended at the brightly lit kitchen. The rich scent of meat and gravy greeted him before rolling laughter. It had been so long since that sound had filled the estate that he wasn't sure what to expect when he walked through the doorway.

Juliette sat at the stone island, head thrown back as she filled the room with the sweet chime of her delight. His part time cook, full time substitute aunt, Molly Coghlan stood on the opposite end of the counter, hands waving as she gave elaborate gestures in description. Lights sparked off the bangles cluttering her arms. The sound rattled through the room, making a world of noise.

Molly was a stout woman with a head full of Irish red curls and broad shoulders. Years of spending too many hours in the sun gardening without proper cover had forever imprinted folds around gleaming green eyes. Yet despite her love of the outdoors, her skin was a doughy white that emphasized the gray creeping through the russet curls cut and permed stubbornly short. She stood three full feet shorter than Killian even with three inch heels, but her aura dominated, fierce and resilient. She was a woman who feared nothing, not even death and it circled her like a shroud.

"Of course me mum took that second to walk into the kitchen," Molly went on, eyes the color of sea foam wide and shining with amusement. "And there I was, scissors in one hand, me sister's hair in the other, and me wee brother dangling from the cupboard. Ma just about had a fit."

Juliette broke out in another fit of uncontrollable giggles that had her rocking back on her stool. The sound was a thing of magic. It echoed with such an abundance of joy that Killian, who had heard the story a million times before, couldn't help feeling his own laughter tickling his chest.

"That is horrible and hilarious!" Juliette gasped, pressing a palm to her chest.

Her shoulders were still trembling when she spotted him in the doorway. Her smile immediately vanished and was replaced by something he could have mistaken for concern if he could look past the bloom of colors splashed across her face.

"Killian." She turned in her seat to face him properly. "You're back."

"Aye," he murmured. "I am."

"And about time." Molly rounded on him, one hand planted on the full curve of her hip. "Know how hard it was to keep this one calm? Practically had to sedate her."

Juliette blushed. "I was calm," she argued. "I was ... worried." The last word was said so quietly he nearly didn't hear it. "I wasn't sure you were okay."

As though realizing the extent of her confession, she averted her eyes and fell quiet.

Every warning bell in Killian's head simultaneously went off at the exact same moment. They all screamed for him to turn and run, or better yet, tell her to leave before she further contaminated his perfectly set world. All the signs were there, flashing before his eyes and yet the words refused to come. Maybe it was cowardice. Maybe it was stupidity. But he couldn't turn her away. Not yet.

"Just handling some business," he said, struggling to maintain a level tone.

Juliette remained fixated by the fingers knotted in her lap and Killian wasn't sure he was ready to have her attention return to him just yet.

"So found this one locked up in that dungeon o' yers," Molly cut in when the tension stretched into a full, agonizing minute. "Is that how your da taught you to keep a woman?"

"Nah, he taught me to keep'em tied to the bed," he said honestly.

Molly laughed. "Aye, that sounds more like him." She dusted her hands and sighed. "Well, I'll be off then."

"You're leaving?" Juliette said, sounding genuinely disappointed.

"Aye, I'm done me job for the week."

"Bless you that." Killian replied, moving deeper into the room. "Molly's been in the family since I was a boy," he told Juliette. "Used to sneak me sweets when me mum wasn't looking. Now she stays to make sure I don't accidently starve myself to death. Makes the best lamb stew on this side of the pond."

Juliette glanced from one to the other. "So basically, you get your food precooked and delivered in weekly batches?" She looked to Killian. "You can't cook?"

It was Molly's booming voice roared in laughter. "Aw, love, I wouldn't trust him in the kitchen if you paid me. Boy can't even boil water."

While embarrassingly true, Killian tried not to take offense to amusement being had on his behalf. Instead, he eased his hands into his pockets and shot silent glowers at the woman who had practically raised him. Molly was unmoved.

"I can't cook," Juliette confessed. "I mean, I can boil water, but I think the last meal I made was a sandwich."

Molly made a sound of pain. Her hand flew to her chest.

"Lord, save me." She eyed the pair of them. "It's any wonder you two haven't wasted away. Do I need to start making double?"

"No!" Juliette burst out before Killian could open his mouth. "No, thank you, but I won't be here very much and I don't want you to go through the trouble."

Molly tipped her head towards Killian. "Don't matter. He eats like a dainty bird."

Killian straightened. "You know, that's the second time you've insulted me in a matter of an hour."

Molly laughed, unfazed. "Only second? I must be losing me touch." She tossed on her coat and purse. "I best be on me way. Got a house to clean and a man at home to feed." She narrowed her eyes at Killian. "Don't eat all that in a day, you hear me? I won't be making more."

She would. Killian knew she would. But not without a lot of complaining.

"Weren't you the one who used to tell me I was a growing boy who needed to eat more?" Killian challenged with an arch of his eyebrows.

Molly pursed her lips. "I also told you you'd never be too old to put over me knee."

From the counter, Juliette made a sound that was quickly stifled behind a cough.

"It was nice to meet you," she told Molly, tactfully avoiding Killian's gaze. "Thank you for the stew."

Molly released Killian from her death glare and focused on Juliette. "You take care now." she said, already starting for the door. "Walk me," she said to Killian.

Killian glanced at Juliette. "Stay here," he told her before following Molly out.

"Mind telling me what happened to her face?"

"It wasn't me."

Molly shot him a glance. "I'da beaten your hide bloody if I thought you had it in you to put your hands on a woman." She stopped walking and peered closely into Killian's face. "My question is, what are you intending to do about it?"

It was a question Killian had expected the moment he'd seen Molly in the kitchen with Juliette. He had almost been waiting for it.

Molly had been raised by a father who used his fists more than his mouth. Killian had never met the man, but he suspected it had been bad; Molly always got that look in her eyes whenever mentions of abuse came up. It was the look Killian had seen in the mirror every day for three years before he'd put a stop to it. It was something that surpassed fury, conquered rage, and passed that line beyond the haze of red. But unlike him, she had no one to punish. She had no way to make it stop. Her father had drank himself to death in a gutter when she'd been thirteen.

"I'm taking care of it."

Molly straightened her shoulders. Her chin went up in a defiance he knew all too well.

"Be sure you do. There's a special place in hell for men who hurt women and children."

"Aye." He eased his hands into his pockets to keep from touching her. "And I intend to make sure he gets there sooner rather than later."

Her shoulders rose with her deep inhale. "Good lad." She twisted away towards the doors. Her hands were unsteady when she adjusted her purse strap. "Until next week then."

With a kiss to his cheek, she shuffled away. Killian watched her until she had descended the front steps and made her way to the car Marco brought around for her. He shook his head at the piece of crap Toyota. The thing was older than he was and yet she refused to let him get her anything better. It rumbled and shrieked like a banshee all the way through the front gates.

"Sir? You have a conference call booked in an hour." Frank appeared seemingly out of nowhere, phone in hand. He stopped at Killian's shoulder. "Should I reschedule?"

Killian glanced down the sunbathed corridor leading towards the kitchen.

"No." He unbuttoned his cuffs and rolled the sleeves on his dress shirt. "Give me thirty minutes."

Leaving the man to punch that into his phone, Killian made his way through the strobes of sunlight. His feet clipped on marble with an almost skip to each step.

The excitement he felt coursing through him was an unfamiliar one. He'd never been the cause of another person's happiness. He'd never been able to give someone something that meant a damn. Telling Juliette she was free of Arlo was practically burning a hole through his chest.

She stood at the sink. The water ran as she scrubbed her bowl and spoon. Killian followed the lines of her back in the soft material of her dress. The light from the French doors shimmered through the silky strands falling around thin shoulders. One foot was arched up on the toes while the other remained flat. He knew the moment she was finished when the foot was settled down next to the other one and she snapped off the faucet. The bowl and spoon were settled inside the dishwasher. She dried her hands and turned.

"Jesus!" One hand jumped to her chest. "I didn't hear you come back."

"There's no need for that," he said instead, gesturing with a jerk of his chin towards the dishwasher. "I have someone that takes care of those duties every day."

Still breathing hard enough to make her chest rise and fall rapidly, she moved to the stove and hooked the rag back through the oven handle bar.

"I would feel bad if I left it for someone else." A smile curled the corners of her mouth as she turned to him. "You sound like her," she said. "Molly," she clarified when he raised a brow. "I mean, you already have a deep accent, but when you were talking with her, it was very thick."

It was a fact his father used to tease him over mercilessly. Unlike his mother and Molly, his father hadn't been raised in Dublin. His accent had been more refined, audible and understandable by most. Killian had been raised by the three and together, they had given him something in between. While he couldn't hear it, he'd been told several times that his accent was more pronounced in his anger or when Molly was around.

For Juliette, he snorted. "I haven't got an accent."

She chuckled. "Of course not." She started towards him. Her smile faded and she was eyeing him with those furrowed brows of concern. "Are you okay?"

His hands moved into his pockets. "Why wouldn't I be?"

One shoulder lifted in an indecisive shrug. "You seemed angry when you left and I—"

"You can't," he cut her off with more sharpness then was probably necessary. "You can't worry. You can't ask. You can't know. Those are the rules. You're not my girlfriend or my wife. There is nothing between us but sex."

It was cold. Molly would have hit him for less, but it needed to be said. She needed to understand her place. The delusion of women who believed there was more to be had when there wasn't was a problem. He wanted no problems. Not where Juliette was concerned. She needed to know right from the beginning what he expected. She needed to be aware of just how limited and emotionless their arrangement would be.

But Juliette, if she was hurt or angry, revealed nothing outwardly beyond the tilt of her chin.

"I only worried because if something happens to you before my debt is paid, I'll be stuck with Arlo forever."

It was a legit response, whether it was the truth or not made little difference; he would let her keep her secrets as he would keep his. After all, he wasn't there to trade diaries.

He drifted deeper into the room, moving as close to her as he dared without touching.

"You can stop worrying then," he said. "Arlo won't be bothering you anymore. He sure as hell won't be putting his hands on you again."

His news didn't have the affect he'd expected. Instead, her eyes went enormous. All the blood spilled from her face, making the bruises grotesquely bright.

"Oh God…" She stumbled back, away from him, her hands flying to her mouth. "You killed him?"

It was insulting and amusing that that was the first place her mind always seemed to go where Arlo and Killen were concerned.

"And if I did?" He circled around her slowly, taking a sort of pleasure in her panic.

She rounded on him. "Then you gave up a bit of your soul for someone who didn't deserve it. Yes, Arlo deserves to die. Yes, I imagined doing it myself a million times. But he has no right to taint any part of you with his … his evil."

That made him pause. His head tilted as he observed the woman standing before him.

"My soul."

The two words sounded foreign and strange leaving his lips. It reminded him of the time his mother had hired lumpy Mr. Delavan to teach him German. Every syllable had come out gruff and clumsy and ultimately ended with Mr. Delavan throwing his coffee mug at the wall and storming out.

Intrigued by the novelty of him with a soul, Killian moved to the French doors and peered out at the sheen of light glinting off the polished marble. The late afternoon sun hung low and tired in the cloudless sky. The hint of a breeze made the leaves shiver on their branches, but never made it past the glass to touch his skin.

"I'm not entirely certain I possess one of those," he murmured more to himself than the woman watching him.

"Everyone has a soul," Juliette said quietly. "Even Arlo, although, I'm sure his is black and shriveled to nothing."

He glanced back over his shoulder at her. "How do you know mine isn't?"

"I don't know you well enough to answer that."

What had he expected? Had he honestly expected her to tell him he was redeemable? That he could somehow be forgiven for his past crimes? Did he want to be? It had never occurred to him before. What he'd done, he knew he would do again given the chance. He made no apologies for taking those lives. Did that make him evil? Did that make his soul black and shriveled?

His mother used to tell him stories of brave knights who would seek justice for their kingdom, for their king and princess. They were deemed as heroes, as a thing of honesty and integrity.

Killian wasn't a hero. He wasn't a white knight in shiny armor riding a white horse. He didn't save king and country. He also knew the difference between fantasy and reality; only in a fantasy did the hero stalk, torture and murder nine men and expect a parade. Killian expected nothing. He had no illusions. None. His world was black and white and splattered by crimson.

"Killian?" The quiet click of her shoes moving, closing the distance pulled him from his thoughts. "Did you kill him?"

Turning away from the glass, Killian watched her draw ever closer and wondered what she would say if he told her yes. Would she call him a monster? Would she throw the contract back into his face and scream for him to leave her alone?

"No," he heard himself say before his brain could finish wondering. "He continues to live, unfortunately."

He saw her shoulders sag with her exhale. A fine crinkle formed between her brows that emphasized the relief and worry in her eyes.

"Okay." She licked her lips. "Good." She ran a hand through her hair, exhaled again and started to turn away. But she paused and turned back to him. "What ... what did you mean he won't be bothering me again?"

"I mean that I've handled the matter," he said evenly. "It's been dealt with. You and your family will be left alone."

Her breathing grew steadily louder. "It's done? It's over?"

He inclined his head. "Aye. You're free, Juliette."

There was a distinct tremor in her hands when they lifted and flattened to her chest. Wet eyes darted away from him to focus on something just over his shoulder. He knew she wasn't seeing anything, but she stood that way, unmoving as the impact of his words finally sunk in.

She finally turned those glossy eyes back to him, glimmering with panic and fear.

"I haven't signed the contract. I..." She broke off with a strangled gasp. "I have questions and..."

He put his hand up. "That isn't important right now."

The smooth column of her throat bobbed rapidly. "I ... I don't ... I can't." One hand lifted, trembling violently before settling on her brow. "Seven years..." She looked to him, desperation haunting every line of her face. "It's over?"

"It's over."

Killian caught her when she swayed. He almost didn't. Almost wasn't fast enough. She gave him no warning. But he had her. His arms were around her, lifting her limp weight into his chest. Hot, ragged breath burned against his throat with her first sob. Her back heaved. Slender fingers curled viciously into the crisp material of his shirt, wrinkling and tearing at the fabric as she clung to him.

She smelled of wildflowers. The scent clung to her hair. It surrounded him, filled his senses. He knew he should be focusing on her, on comforting her, but he was drowning in her instead.

"I never thought I would hear those words," she choked out. "I thought I would die being his slave. I thought…"

"It's over now," he promised. "He won't ever touch you again."

With a deep inhale that lifted her back against his stroking palms, she tipped her face up to his. Her eyes were rimmed red. The lashes were sharp, wet spikes. Tendrils of hair clung to her damp cheeks and were hastily wiped away as she peered up at him.

"Thank you," she whispered. "I can never repay you."

He started to shake his head, started to tell her he wanted no repayment when she moved into his space once more. Her hands went to his shoulders, balancing her weight as she rose up on her toes. Then her mouth was on his in a delicate kiss.

It was soft and filled with a tenderness that scared the shit out of him. Her sweet hesitance rocked him all the way to his toes in a wave. It distracted him from the hand she lifted to the side of his stubbled cheek until she deepened her kiss. The honeyed taste of her mouth, the heady scent of her body swelled up around him in a flood of everything he didn't want, but could find no sense to stop.

But she did. She stopped. She broke the meeting of their lips and blinked open her eyes. The irises expanded across the gold. But it was the wet and swollen state of her mouth that preoccupied his thoughts.

"I have to go," she whispered.

The statement automatically tightened his hold on her. "Why?"

"I have to work in an hour," she said. "I only came to tell you that I will accept your contract if—"

"You're still going to work?" he cut in.

"Of course. Why wouldn't I?"

"Because you no longer need to if you're accepting the agreement," he said. "I will make sure you are paid well above what you are making now with all your jobs."

She pulled out of his embrace and took a step back. Her arms folded over her midsection.

"That's very kind, but I haven't signed the papers yet so I still need to work."

He started to protest, but decided against it. Instead, he said, "Marco will drive you."

She shook her head. "I don't need—"

He silenced her with a look. "Marco will drive you," he repeated very slowly. "Then we will talk about getting you your own driver."

Her eyes practically bulged out of her skull. "My own … why on earth would I need my own driver?"

"Because if you insist on working unholy hours, then I'm not letting you walk around in the dark alone."

"I don't need my own—"

"Please," he interjected sharply. "For me."

Her lips pursed together and he could see the refusal raging behind her eyes, but she nodded. "Okay. Thank you."

She started towards the doorway.

"Juliette." She stopped a few feet away and turned. "I will have someone pick you up tomorrow for lunch. We'll go over your questions."

She frowned at him. "You don't have to send…" She broke off when he arched an eyebrow. The corners of her mouth twisted downward. "Fine," she mumbled grudgingly. "I'll see you tomorrow."

Chapter 10

True to Killian's promise, Marco stood waiting at the bottom of the stairs, next to a sleek, white car. He inclined his head when Juliette made her way to him. His expression stayed blank, even as he took in the side of her face.

It had taken her an hour to apply enough concealer to … well, conceal. In the span of five minutes, Killian had wiped it all away, leaving her exposed for all to see. It annoyed her; she didn't have time to go home and reapply. Thankfully, she seldom came into contact with people at the hotel that late at night.

"Thank you," she said to Marco when he yanked open the backdoor.

He bobbed his head once and waited for her to slide in before shutting the door behind her.

Juliette didn't watch him round the car. Her gaze stayed fixed on the open doorway at the top of the staircase. The one void of Killian. But she could sense him. She could feel his presence filling the space and spilling out into the settling evening.

He'd freed her. He'd done it even before she'd signed his contract. He had done it for her. A voice in her head had argued that he'd most likely done it to strong arm her into submission, but she didn't believe it. Truthfully, she didn't care.

Her goal, her dream, her entire mission in life for seven years had been to get away from Arlo, to never again have to see his smug, cruel face. Killian had given her that, all of that, and he'd done so without a moment's hesitation.

It still nagged at her that she was now indebted to him, that she was quite possibly in no better situation than she had been. But she was. No one and nothing was worse than Arlo. It didn't seem to matter if Killian used his good deed to shackle her all over again. At least not in that moment. In that moment, all that mattered was that Arlo could never touch her or her sister again.

"Ma'am?"

Juliette blinked and turned her head to Marco, who was politely watching her through the rearview mirror.

"Yes?"

"Where would you like to go?"

Flustered, Juliette shifted. "Oh, right. I'm sorry. Twin Peaks Hotel, please."

Marco put the car into drive and rolled them away from the estate.

It took less time than she'd anticipated to reach the hotel. Maybe it was because she was used to public transportation taking hours sometimes to reach a certain destination, but arriving without the hassle had a unique sort of thrill to it she partially didn't appreciate; the last thing she needed was to get comfortable with someone else driving her around.

But she undid her belt and reached for the door handle when Marco pulled to a stop next to the hotel. In the front seat, Marco did the same, but Juliette was already throwing herself out of the car. She stuck her head back inside and peered at the man.

"Thank you for driving me."

Marco nodded. "You're welcome, ma'am."

With a smile, she shut the door and hurried inside.

It was a trick keeping her head down and her hair falling over the side of her face. She wasn't sure they could actually fire her for having bruises on her face, but the last thing she needed was to get reported. She'd be fine once she was up in the rooms, away from the prying eyes of the staff.

It worked. She grabbed her cart and started her shift on the fourth floor without anyone asking what happened to her face. After that, the night went by smoothly. She finished her rooms, took her cart back down and signed out like she'd done a million times before. She changed back into her regular clothes and left the building.

The air outside was wet, like it had rained at some point. The concrete was wet, black and stained by distorted rainbows. It shimmered beneath the dull light hanging over the backdoor.

It was the only light. The only source of safety and it illuminated the exit, leaving the entire alleyway drenched in shadows. To the right, a light flow of traffic passed by the opening leading onto the street. The left led into the staff parking area around back and sat in absolute darkness. The hotel didn't much care what happened to its night staff. There were cameras, but none of them worked. The lights were few and far between. Most of the women left at night in packs. But Juliette had no car and thus no reason to go anywhere near the parking area.

She turned right. If she hurried, she could reach the bus stop at the end of the block and be home before four AM.

"Beautiful night for a walk, eh, Juliette?"

The familiar voice snapped through the silence like a whip. It ripped through Juliette. She staggered to a stop and whipped around. Her hand almost instinctively went to her purse, even though it was useless. Her heart scuttled up into her throat while her mind tried to put reasoning to Arlo's presence at her work.

"What are you doing here?" she demanded, struggling to keep her voice calm.

Like a demon from a horror movie, Arlo pulled away from the shadows and descended upon her with slow, even strides. The thump of his boots echoed off the slimy walls, the sound almost deafening.

"I came to see you, Juliette," he said simply.

"No." She staggered back a step. "We're done. You got your money."

He chuckled and it was cold and brittle. "I got McClary's money," he corrected. "But that's not why I'm here." He paused when there were three steps between them. His closeness drove against her sanity. "We had so many years together. It wouldn't have been right if we just parted ways without a proper goodbye, would it, Juliette?"

"What do you want?" she said.

His hands vanished into the pockets of his jeans. The posture was relaxed, unhurried.

"I want to know why you betrayed me. I thought we were friends."

Anger rode over the rational voice telling her to stay calm. It knotted her in its fiery grip until all she could taste was the need to sink her nails into his face and tear off his skin. She wanted to stab him until he stopped moving. Seven years she fought to get away from him, to never again see that vile face of his and finally … *finally* she was free and he was still terrorizing her. He was still finding ways to make her feel two inches tall.

"We were never friends!" she hissed. "And you need loyalty and respect in order to betray someone. I have neither for you." She swallowed past the desert drying up her throat. "We are done. I owe you nothing. My family owes you nothing! So stay the—"

His hand whipped out with the strength, speed and viciousness of a coiled cobra and closed around her throat. It wasn't hard, but there was enough force behind it to warn her not to struggle. There was enough bite to render her silent. Beneath his fingertips, her pulse quickened.

"Do you think that just because you're McClary's whore you no longer belong to me? That I won't continue to use you in whatever manner I see fit?" His fingers tightened until she cried out. "You're mine for the rest of your life, Juliette. It doesn't matter how much he paid for you."

"You can't touch me!" she bit out with what little remaining courage she had left. "Killian will—"

"Will what?" His fingertips gouged into her esophagus, cutting new bruises over the old ones. "Kill me?" He snickered.

"He can't, not without starting a war. Most he can do is rat on me to my dad, but what is he going to do? Spank me and send me to my room? You're nobody, Juliette. I could kill you right now and no one would care. You're a filthy whore that no one will miss."

"What do you want?" she asked yet again for the third time. "You got your money."

Arlo's blunt fingers loosened and she sucked in a quick breath to sooth the burn in her lungs.

"It wasn't just the money between us, Juliette," he said, sounding genuinely hurt. "I thought we had a connection. I know I always thought very highly of you." He sighed when she said nothing. His hand fell away from her esophagus and he took a step back. "I came to warn you. You made a big mistake taking McClary's side."

Rubbing at the fresh bruise staining her throat, Juliette stared at him. "Are you threatening me?"

Arlo rolled his eyes. "I'm warning you. Didn't I just say that?" He shook his head slowly as though she were stupid. "You have no idea what kind of guy he is."

"And you're suddenly all about protecting me?" she shot back. "You gave me to him."

"That was business!" he retorted. "I never thought you'd be dumb enough to become his full time whore."

"Why do you care?"

"Because I consider us friends and friends don't let other friends get in bed with the enemy."

There was so many things fucked up about the whole scenario that Juliette couldn't think of a single thing to say for a moment. Instead, she stood there and stared at the man who had basically sold her for his own profit, who had beaten and abused her and had threatened her and her family. Just to name a few things. In no shape or form did she believe for a second that he had her best interest at heart. For one, Arlo didn't have a heart.

"Fine. You've warned me. Thank you."

She started to turn away.

"He's dangerous," Arlo called after her. "He's worse than I am."

No one is worse than you are, she wanted to say.

"He's been nothing but kind to me," she said instead.

"He's a killer," Arlo cut in. "He's not called the Scarlet Wolf because of his sparkling personality."

The image made her blood run cold. It made her stomach roil and her mouth go dry. But outwardly, she fought hard to remain impassive.

"I don't believe you."

Truth was, she wasn't sure what to believe. She didn't know Killian. Not really. Arlo could be telling her the truth for all she knew. But for whatever Killian was, for whatever he'd done in the past, he had saved her life. He had done so when he had no reason to. He had given her a future, one free of pain and suffering. He may not have yet earned her respect, but he had her trust and her loyalty, and both went a long way with her.

"Ask him," Arlo said with a shrug. "Or don't. I really don't care. I have cleared my consciences. Have a good life, Juliette."

With a salute, he spun on his heel and disappeared back the way he'd come. Several minutes later, she heard the slam of a car door, followed by the roar of an engine. She didn't wait to see him come out. She didn't wait to see if he would run her over. She turned quickly and ran towards the opening just as piercing headlights exploded behind her as the Bentley turned down the alleyway after her. He didn't stop or slow down. He hit the street and swerved left. Juliette watched as the car hit a bump and disappeared from sight down the next street.

"He's a stone cold killer."

Those five words looped through her mind the whole way home. It wouldn't stop even when she showered and got ready for bed. The whole time, she kept asking herself what she'd gotten herself into and what was she going to do to get out.

But did she want to get out? Had she not already owed Killian her life, had he not already paid a small fortune for her freedom, would she want to get away from him? It was insane, but the answer was always no. It didn't seem to matter how much logic and reasoning she threw at herself, how many times she tried to discourage the unwavering force that had become her resolve where Killian was concerned, her answer was always the same.

She didn't want to go back on her promise to be his for a year. She didn't want to stop seeing him, maybe even after the year was up. And it wasn't even because of what he'd done or how good looking he was. Those things were remarkably insignificant compared to the fact that she just wanted to see him.

Maybe she was crazy. Maybe it was some hybrid Stockholm syndrome type thing or she just felt supremely indebted to him, but the truth remained the same—she liked him, which was no doubt ludicrous and dangerous and her death waiting to happen.

Nevertheless, she had every intention of signing his contract, of becoming his for an entire year. But not until she had clarified a few things first.

A man in a green polo t-shirt stood on Juliette's porch the next morning. He beamed a million watt smile and offered her an inclination of his head when she opened the door. A massive SUV sat on the street behind him, looking oddly in place amongst all the other SUVs and BMWs belonging to her neighbors.

"Hello Ms. Romero. I'm Ted," he said, continuing to blind her with all those sparkly teeth. "Mr. McClary sent me to retrieve you for your lunch meeting."

Juliette nodded. "Thank you. I'll just grab my purse."

Vi appeared at Juliette's shoulder, forcing her way into the conversation. Despite being younger, she towered over Juliette by a full two inches thanks to the soft, leather boots strapped on over her tight, black leggings. The dark contrasted with the buttercup yellow dress she wore overtop, adorned by rows of silver chains and a fat, yellow bracelet. Overtop, she wore a midriff baring jacket in faded black. She looked more like she was on her way to some upscale photoshoot and not high school.

"Who's Mr. McClary?" she demanded, squinting at Ted. "Who are you?"

"Don't be rude." Juliette pushed her sister back into the house. "Get your things or you'll be late getting back to school. Lunch will be over in twenty minutes."

"Who's McClary?" Vi pressed, refusing to let the matter drop.

"No one that is any of your business."

She stalked around the girl towards the kitchen. She paused in the bathroom to double check her face and the heavy weight of makeup concealing Arlo's handiwork. It was all mostly covered, unless a person got very close and saw the faint shadowing no amount of makeup could conceal. But thankfully, Vi never bothered to pay close attention to anything that didn't regard her, Mrs. Tompkins was nearsighted, and Killian had already seen them. It was just the rest of the world she hoped to fool.

"Is he rich?" Vi followed her, her heels cracking against hardwood. "Are you sleeping with him?"

"That is none of your business!" Juliette spun away from the mirror to confront her shadow. "And I don't appreciate you asking me these questions."

Pushing past her sister, she left the bathroom.

Rolling her eyes, Vi stalked into the kitchen after her and grabbed her backpack off the kitchen table.

"Whatever. He's probably fat and hairy anyway."

Saying nothing, Juliette got her own purse off the counter, double checked to make sure she had everything she would need, and then followed Vi to the front door.

The man was still standing there. He ushered Juliette to the SUV as Vi hurried down the block to meet up with her friends, who she refused to let anywhere near their *dumpster house,* which suited Juliette just fine. Normally, she wouldn't even come home for lunch, except she had no money and thus couldn't go out to eat like she wanted to. It was mortifying, Vi always said, because she was the only one of her friends who had to make up excuses as to why she couldn't go out to eat like everyone else. Juliette wasn't sure what excuse she gave, and frankly, didn't care.

"Where are we going?" she asked Ted as he hurried ahead of her and yanked open the backdoor of the SUV for her.

"Ocean and Park," he told her.

Ocean and Park was a high end country club that catered to celebrities, drug lords, and royalty. The pristine acreage stretched an almost unreal green far out of the city and overlooked the marina. Juliette had once had friends whose fathers had owned fancy boats and yachts and would spent entire summers sunbathing out on the lake. Ocean and Park had been too exclusive though, even for her circle of friends.

The SUV rolled to a gentle stop before a set of gleaming gold gates guarded by ivory stone walls. Ted rolled down his window and a melodious voice spoke through the intercom spearing up from the white gravel.

"Welcome to Ocean and Park, where our only priority is to help you unwind. Please state your name and client ID number for our records."

Juliette was impressed and oddly intimidated.

"Ted Webster. I have Mr. McClary's guest, who he is expecting."

There was several seconds of silence where Juliette assumed Ted's story was being validated. It must have checked out, because the voice returned.

"Thank you. Please continue and have a wonderful day."

The gold gates swept open without a sound, revealing miles of lush, green that spanned on forever. In the distance, she could just make out the glimmer of water. Sitting regal and impressive, sat the estate with its stucco walls and enormous bay windows. The winding path cut a white gash all the way to the circular driveway and the marble fountain that bubbled and frothed in the beautiful afternoon sun. Ted pulled the SUV to a stop just beneath a wide set of stairs. A boy of nineteen hurried down them in his crisp black and gold uniform and yanked open her door. He bowed his head once without a word before hopping back to allow her to exit.

She thanked him and got another bow before he motioned her mutely upward.

Killian was waiting for her in the grand foyer when she passed over the threshold. He looked incredible in his black trousers and white dress shirt. A black blazer was pulled on over top and hung unbuttoned over a black belt. No tie, she noted and wondered if that went against the club's dress code. If it did, she was sure he paid them enough to overlook it.

Around him, the soft whisper of jazz lingered in the delicate scent of lilacs and honeysuckle. It flowed harmoniously through the vast chamber, filling it with a calming tone that complimented the cream and gold décor. Everything looked so expensive, it made her feel very out of place. The fact that she was drawing curious attention from the few people loitering about didn't help matters.

Her strides faltered. Her fingers tightened in the straps of her worn purse. She was suddenly so very aware of her thrift store dress with its faded colors and the lack of pedicure on the toes that were peeking out of her dollar store sandals. She wondered if it was too late to back out and wait for Killian outside, when he closed the rest of the distance and claimed all her attention.

"I don't think I should be here," she whispered.

"Why?"

Her gaze darted past him to a group of older women standing a few feet away in their thousand dollar dress suits and hundred dollar haircuts. They were watching her with frowns that said very clearly that they didn't understand her audacity. Their scrutiny had her skin prickling with heat. It worked up the column of her throat to burn beneath the skin of her face, to sear behind her eyes.

She started to lower her chin, shame a bright, red flag against her cheeks. Only to be stopped by firm fingers. Her face was tilted and held tipped up to his.

"Are you ashamed of me?"

The absurdity of the question had her eyes going round. "What? No! Of course not."

The rough pad of his thumb glided lightly along her jawline, sending a shiver through her.

"Then why does it matter what they think?"

She started to shake her head. "It doesn't. At least not because of you."

The tip of his thumb stopped just beneath her bottom lip. His fingers tightened their hold on her chin.

"These people," he said slowly, "mean nothing to me. Their thoughts are as small and insignificant as they are. But if you would like to leave, we will."

She was dying to say yes. It welled up inside her like a flood, threatening to drag her under if she didn't. Her gaze went to the women again who, judging from their outraged expressions, had heard everything Killian had said about them and were none too pleased about being called small and insignificant. The sight of their shock and anger inexplicably tapered back her urge to flee. If anything, it only solidified her need to stay and continue to piss them off.

"No," she whispered. She lifted her eyes to the man lightly caressing her mouth with his thumb. "I'd like to stay."

Something intense and consuming sparked behind his eyes. It reflected in the tightening of his fingers and in the slight flare of his nostrils. Whatever it meant was left a mystery as he released her and stepped back. But not far.

"I have lunch waiting on the terrace," he said, then offered her his arm, which had never happened to her before. The sight of it brought a grin to her face.

"How *Jane Austin* of you," she teased, slipping her hand into the crook of his elbow.

Killian made a quiet, humming sound of agreement as he led her deeper into the place.

"I could amaze you by how gallant I can be." He peered down at her, his eyes dancing with silent laughter. "I might even toss my coat over a puddle for you."

Against her will, Juliette burst out laughing. The sound followed them all the way through an extravagant dining area full of men and women enjoying fancy bowls of lettuce and soups. A few heads lifted and turned in their direction. The unwanted attention had her lifting a hand to her mouth to stifle the sound.

"Don't," Killian said, and her hand obeyed; it dropped down to her side.

He hadn't been joking about lunch on the terrace. He led her through the dining area and out through a set of magnificent French doors. The navy carpet halted and cobblestone took over, leading the way across a wide platform ringed by marble columns and overlooking a sprawling garden. They made their way along the side to a single table dwelling, tucked beneath a beautiful canopy of gauze. The circular table was draped in soft, white linen and topped by a plate of glass. A bowl of floating tea candles sat in the center, unlit. Two wrought iron chairs sat tucked into place on either side. Killian took her to one and drew it out for her.

"Thank you," she said, easing into it.

He tucked her in before claiming his own seat.

"I took the liberty of ordering," he told her. "I didn't want to waste time since you have to leave soon."

Juliette nodded and stuffed her purse beneath her chair. "That's fine."

As though on cue, their meal and drinks were brought out by two girls in tight, white t-shirts and white tennis skirts. Everything was set down perfectly before the pair left without saying a word.

The plates consisted of steak burgers and fries with a side order of salad. Everything smelled incredible and it was the remaining shred of her dignity that kept her from lunging ravenously on the table.

Instead, she chuckled and gave her head a slight shake of amusement.

"Don't like my choice?" Killian asked.

She shook her head again. "I actually really like steak burgers. I'm just surprised you ordered it."

He met her gaze. "It's my favorite," he said. "I always get it when I'm here."

"Are you here often?" she wondered.

"No." He grabbed the bottle of ketchup and doused his fries. "I normally don't have time."

He set the ketchup bottle down and reached for his fork. Juliette didn't bother with a fork as she reached for a fry.

"I honestly don't think I could come here every day like some people," she admitted. "I had a friend whose mom practically lived at their country club and she brought me along once. It was awful."

He speared a blade of lettuce from his salad bowl, but didn't bring it to his mouth. "Why?"

"Just being under that kind of attention all the time." She shrugged. "She always had to be so careful about what she said and what she wore and who she talked to. It just seemed like so much unnecessary work."

Neither said anything for a moment while they ate. Juliette fought hard not to stuff it all into her mouth like some starved maniac. She couldn't even remember the last time she'd had a full meal that didn't consist of Mrs. Tompkins'ss casserole. It had been ages since she'd had real meat. It was a little disturbing just how much she wanted to cuddle her plate and weep.

"Did you bring the agreement?" Killian asked, cutting into her thoughts.

She nodded. "Yes."

Reluctantly setting her fork down, she reached beneath her seat and fished out the envelope. She set it on the table.

Killian barely spared it a glance. "We'll go over it after we eat."

Lowering her gaze, Juliette poked at the blade of lettuce peeking out from beneath her bun. "It was very well thought out," she mused, tearing a piece of the green and popping it into her mouth. "Do you write contracts like that often?"

He shook his head. "Not like that exactly, no. But the concept is usually the same." He lifted his eyes to her face. "Did it all make sense?"

"Oh, yes, it was very … thorough. Thank you." She lifted a fry and studied the long, golden strip. "There were a lot of rules."

He wiped his fingers on his napkin. "I didn't want to leave anything to chance. This way, we both know what to expect." He met her gaze. "If you have any stipulations you want to add or—"

She shook her head. "No, what you have is fine. Actually." A thought occurred to her and she leaned forward. "There is something."

He stopped eating and waited.

"It might have already been implied, but I would rather get it out in the open just in case."

"All right?"

She took a deep breath. "If this is only about sex, then you can have no say in what I do when I'm not with you."

His eyes narrowed. "Clarify."

"I want to keep working," she stated simply. "Yes, I know you said you would provide an allowance, but at the end of the year, when we are over, I will be without a job and an income. While I'm fairly apt at budgeting, I don't want to fall into a situation where my sister will suffer."

Something on his face shifted. "I wouldn't allow you to suffer, Juliette."

"Well, you were very clear that we would not have any contact after the year was up."

Killian sighed. "I wouldn't simply leave you to fend for yourself."

Annoyance prickled the length of her spine. "I feel wrong taking your money as it is. If anything, I should be paying you for saving my life."

"Stop." He rubbed a hand over his face. "Juliette…"

"It's okay." She offered him a small smile. "I read the agreement. I know what's expected of me and I'm okay with the terms. I just want you to know that I am going to keep working. I will work time in for you whenever you want, but the jobs stay. Also, I don't want you telling me what to wear or where I can go and what I can't do. I have responsibilities outside of our agreement and I have to find a balance between the two."

He said nothing for a long damn time. His dark eyes bore into her. She wondered if he would refuse her request. But he surprised her by giving a reluctant nod.

"Fair enough, but before you accept the terms…" He reached into the inside pocket of his blazer and drew out a thin envelope, the sort people used to send bills and letters. He set it down next to the hand she'd settled on the table. "I have a second agreement I think you should look over."

Juliette blinked. "A second?"

He nodded, but said nothing as she lifted the envelope and tugged free the letter. He continued to watch her while she unfolded the paper and read.

It started off exactly like the first one.

This agreement is between Killian McClary (hereafter called The Primary) and

_____

_____ *,*

(hereafter called The Secondary.)   For a one year agreement: Hereafter referred to as The Agreement.

But it went on to detail a completely different agreement, one that still included a year of her life to him, but in a manner that completely shocked her.

Her head jerked up to him. "I don't understand."

Wiping his mouth and hands with the napkin, even though he hadn't eaten anything, Killian settled his gaze on her.

"It's exactly as the contract states." He set the napkin down and leaned back, folding his arms. "In order to pay what you owe, you will work for me for the next twelve months."

"Work for you?"

She looked down at the paper in her hand again and reread it carefully a third time.

The conditions were clear. She had no problem understanding them. But it was the exact opposite of the original contract.

"My club needs waitresses," he said as she ran over the lines again. "The position is available to you for as long as you want it. You will be paid accordingly with the exception of a hundred and fifty dollars every month that will be automatically withheld from your check. That money will go towards the amount you owe. This will continue for twelve months, after which you will be freed of your obligations. You are free to continue your position at the club, or you can find something else. The decision is yours."

Clear, yet…

"But…" She lowered her arm and lifted her head. "A hundred fifty a month, every month for a single year doesn't come anywhere close to paying you off. Not even by half."

It was his turn to drop his gaze. He studied the fine thread of gold circling the plate containing his half eaten lunch.

"Do you know what happens when I die?" He lifted his chin and cocked his head so he could peer at her through narrowed, contemplating eyes. "All my money, every bit of property I own, goes to various charities and organizations. I don't have any family or anyone to leave any of it to and I don't want to. So money and possession means nothing to me. What I gave Juan for you will never be missed. I honestly couldn't give a damn if I never see a penny of it again, but I know you will disagree with me."

"Of course I disagree!" she shot back, horrified and disturbed by his disregard of something most people would kill to have more of. "That was a lot of money. A lot!" she stressed. "I can't just let you toss away that much without paying it back. I won't."

A ghost of a smile shadowed the corners of his mouth, it lingered behind his eyes before he looked away with a sound that could have passed for a chuckle.

"I didn't think so, which is why we now have two agreements." He motioned to the one in her hand. "Both are essentially the same, but gives you the option to pick what you want to do."

She did have options, which momentarily intimidated her. It had been too long since she was given the choice to do what she wanted. No one had ever given her that, not since her parents. For a moment, it was all too much and she had to drop the letter before he could see the tremor in her hand.

"This one is the most logical," she began, barely in control of her tone as she nudged the letter to one side. "The other one makes no mention of you being paid, except by … by giving you me." Heat swelled in her cheeks and she stubbornly kept her eyes lowered. "I also, while not rational, kind of like the idea of only having to work one job for once."

"Is that the one you've decided on?"

The rational part of her said yes. It reminded her that it would mean not having to use her body and degrading herself even more. But the bigger envelope, the one binding her to him and not a job kept pulling her eyes, kept coaxing her to reach for it.

The truth was that she had really liked her single night with him. She had liked his hands on her, had liked the feel of his mouth. Accepting the job may have been logical, but it didn't come with the added bonus of being with him, and she already had a job. She had three. And without having to give Arlo seventy percent of her income every month, that left her with more than enough money to support herself and Vi. But she still needed to give Killian something. He deserved something for everything he'd done for her.

"What do you want?" she asked him. She shoved her dishes away and placed the two agreements side by side. "Which one would you pick?"

If her question surprised him, he never showed it, nor did he even glance at the two contracts.

"I would pick the job," he said after several long minutes of silence.

That surprised her. She had been so certain he would ask for her.

"Why?"

Dull fingers of grief flittered across his features before they were shuttered out and he averted his eyes.

"I'm cursed and those who get too close always wind up dead."

Juliette thought of what Arlo had told her about Killian being a stone cold killer and shivered despite the warm summer breeze wafting around them.

"Can I ask you something?"

He looked at her, waiting.

"Have you ever killed anyone?"

It was a dangerous question to ask. He had every right to get up and walk away. No one in their right mind would confess to murder.

"Yes."

Except maybe Killian McClary. He never so much as batted an eyelash.

She licked her lips. "Did they deserve it?"

Most people didn't think anyone had the right to take a life. Most people would think her question ridiculous and maybe even appalling. How did one justify murder? But there were people in the world who deserved to die. Sometimes even horribly. Juliette truly believed that. People like Arlo. People who beat and raped women. People who hurt children. Their lives were cancer on society and there was no rehabilitation. Once a child molester, always a child molester. It was a sickness that had no cure, contrary to what the law might say.

"Yes," Killian murmured. "They raped, tortured, and murdered my mother and shot my father."

Juliette sucked in a sharp breath. Her fingers tightened in her lap. She thought of what Killian had said to her the night they'd met, when she'd thanked him for saving her and he'd said he hadn't done it for her. She thought of the beautiful stone fountain, a monument his father had created for the woman they'd both lost and the pain on Killian's face when he'd stood before it.

"Did you make them suffer?" she heard herself ask.

He never broke eye contact and she could see the raw anger and pain he was fighting back. "Yes."

Swallowing hard, Juliette nodded. She lowered her gaze to the agreements before her without seeing them.

"Good." She whispered. She moistened her lips again and pushed the bigger envelope forward. "This one."

Killian studied her selection a long while before focusing on her once more.

"Why?"

Steeled in her decision, Juliette sat back. She straightened her shoulders and met his gaze unflinching.

"I don't need a job," she told him matter of factly. "And what I do want, it's not listed in the second contract."

One hand lifted. The elbow was propped against the armrest as the fingers curled lightly near his mouth. He studied her from over the curves of his knuckles, his eyes dark with challenge.

"And what is it you want, Juliette?"

Self-consciousness had her gaze flicking away for a split second before she bolted down her courage and faced him squarely.

"You." She ignored the crack of her heart pounding against her chest and the way his face seemed to grow all the more intense with her declaration. "I understand this isn't a relationship and that it's only for a year, but I'm okay with that. I just want what we shared the other night."

Juliette wasn't certain if it was her imagination, but the very air around them seemed to vibrate. Time itself had pulled to a stop as she waited with her breath held for him to respond. Each second that passed coiled in the pit of her stomach, winding tighter around her nerves until she was terrified the whole thing would snap and she'd bolt out of her chair and run.

Finally, after what felt like eons, he lowered his arm. The long fingers settled on the edge of the glass, reminding her of a pianist preparing to perform.

"Is that what you choose?" he asked at last.

Juliette nodded. "But with the corrections I mentioned. I get to keep my jobs and you don't get to tell me where to go or what to wear when we're not together."

"Fine." Reaching over, he plucked up the second envelope and tucked it away inside his blazer once more. "But I have my own conditions."

Surprised, Juliette blinked. "Okay?"

The clatter of dishes being shoved aside filled the stretch of silence as he took up the remaining envelope and emptied the papers onto the table. He withdrew a pen from the inside pocket of his blazer and turned the papers over to the blank underside.

He began to write.

Juliette watched the fluid and flawless flow of his penmanship. Every loop and curve flashed with power and authority. He didn't stop until one whole page was filled.

He passed her the sheet.

The first half was her conditions in exact terms in which she had placed them. The second half was his.

I, The Primary, acknowledge and accept all the above terms issued by The Secondary with the condition that The Secondary allows The Primary to take the necessary precautions as listed in page twelve under term nine.

Frowning, Juliette found page twelve and skimmed over the conditions to number nine.

"The Primary has agreed that by signing The Agreement, he has taken upon himself the responsibilities of The Secondary's wellbeing financially, mentally, emotionally, and physically. At no given time can this be altered or negotiated." She read out loud. "I don't understand."

"I'm getting you a car," he stated. "As is my right under The Agreement."

Her frown deepened. "It says nothing about a car in The Agreement."

Killian leaned over and pointed. "The Secondary's wellbeing financially, mentally, emotionally, and physically." He sat back. "I consider you getting to and from work safely a physical wellbeing."

"That is cheating!" she snapped. "You're manipulating the contract."

"I am enforcing the contract," he corrected. "Do you not agree that walking around downtown, waiting for a bus full of questionable characters in the dead of night is risky? Not to mention dangerous?"

She could think of no answer to that.

"So, case and point, it's a safety issue and since I am responsible for your physical wellbeing, it's my right to provide you with an alternative. It's either a car or a driver. Which would you prefer?"

She shoved the contract back at him. "I've been doing this for seven years and I have never—"

"You didn't have me then," he reminded her. "Now that you do, I won't take chances with that which is mine."

She loved and hated the tingles that crackled along her skin at the quiet, guttural murmur. It elicited a shiver she just barely concealed.

"Car," she mumbled with more than a touch of grudging reluctance. "But only because I don't want some person catering around after me."

"Excellent." He took the contract back and scribbled her decision down next to the paragraph. "Okay, the next matter."

The contract was pushed back to her. Juliette took it.

"The Primary reserves the right to occasionally attire The Secondary." She raised her head. "What?"

"There will be times over the course of the year when I will require you to join me at certain events which will require a specific type of attire."

"Fine," she mumbled.

His eyebrows shot up. "No argument?"

She glowered at him. "Would it do any good? You'll just fancy talk your way around it anyway."

"Fancy talk?" The corner of his mouth quirked. "That's interesting." He pulled the contract over to him and continued writing. When he was finished, he glanced up at her with one eyebrow lifted. "Would you like to read it or will you just agree to it in case I use my fancy talk again?"

She jerked the papers away from him. "You're a real brat, you know that?" Ignoring his snicker, she read the final line. "The Primary will not dictate the comings and goings of The Secondary unless in the event that The Secondary is placing herself in danger." Juliette chuckled dryly and shook her head. "You are the master of words, I swear to God."

"Do you disagree?"

She shook her head and passed the pages back. "It sounds fine, but one final thing."

"Just one?"

She ignored that. "I want it to be made clear that I don't want any money from you, like at all and I'm not going to sleep with you to pay off what you paid Juan." She paused to better collect her explanation. "If I accept, it needs to be made perfectly clear that our arrangement to sleep together has nothing to do with paying you back. I'm not a prostitute. And you won't pay me for spending time with you or whatever else you think you're paying me for. I will however take one stipulation from the second contract where I will pay you, but more than a hundred fifty a month."

Killian analyzed this a long moment. She could see the deep deliberation in the furrow of his brow and in the narrowness of his eyes.

"Let me get this straight, you want to pay me for sleeping with you?" he finally asked with an amused quirk of his eyebrow.

"No!" she said a bit too loudly. "No one is paying anyone to sleep with them. I'm paying off what you paid Juan for me. I'm sleeping with you because I want to."

"You're an odd sort of woman, do you know that?" he said at last, but reached for the contract and wrote the rest of her request along the bottom.

It was passed over to her to read over.

"Good," she said, nudging it back.

With a satisfied nod, he lowered his hand and signed at the bottom. Then the pages and the pen were passed to her to do the same.

"I will get a copy made up for you," he told her as he took the freshly signed contract and slipped it back into the envelope. "We can always adjust should you think of something else later."

Juliette nodded. "Thank you."

"Oh, before I forget." He reached into the lapel of his blazer and removed a sleek, black card and slid it across the tablecloth towards her. "That's for you."

"What is it?"

She picked it up and examined what should have been painfully obvious.

"There is a limit," he told her. "If you need more than what is on the card, just let me know—"

"Oh for the love of God!" She shoved the card back at him.

Killian sighed. "Juliette…"

She shook her head. "Did I just not finish telling you I wanted no money from you? Zero. Nada. Zip!"

"You also said I could cloth you," he pointed out.

Anger sizzling just beneath her skin, she snatched the card from him and held it up. "How much is on here?"

It would have been amusing to see how quickly he averted his eyes and focused on tugging down the lapel of his blazer.

"Just a small amount," he mumbled, smoothing a hand over his chest.

"How much?" she pressed.

He inhaled deeply. "Ten."

Juliette's eyes widened. "Dollars?"

"Grand," he retorted with a bit of a bite.

"Jesus Christ!" She slapped the card down on the table. "Where the hell am I going to wear ten thousand dollars' worth of clothes? No." She shoved the card back to him. "I have already degraded myself in letting you help me with Arlo in an amount that I can't possibly payback and I have agreed to let you get me a car. I won't take this. I can buy my own clothes."

He set his hand over his and gently pushed it and the card back towards her.

"Just hang on to it. If you don't use it, fine. But I'll feel better knowing you have it."

Juliette stared at him. Really stared at him through narrowed, wary eyes.

"Are you crazy?" she blurted. "Or some weird pervert? What's wrong with you?"

Killian's eyes darkened as he jerked back. "Excuse me?"

She yanked her hand out from under his. "Why do you keep giving me things? Do you have some weird fetish I should know about and this is your way of easing me into it?"

"I have quite a few fetishes, but none that are overly ... weird," he muttered. "I like eating pussy. A lot. I especially like eating yours. It's all I've thought about since we sat down. Right here." He touched the table top directly in front of him. "With your legs over my shoulders. Then I'd take you to that wall there," he pointed to a nearby slab of granite making up a sort of bench joined to the railings along the terrace, "have you straddle it and lean forward so I can fuck you from behind." He said it all so casually, like he was discussing nothing more than how lovely the scenery was. "In that position, every thrust would rub your pussy and nipples against the rough stone. I think you'd like it."

"Shit..." She had no recollection of speaking out loud until the words blurted out of her. In her seat, her ass wiggled slightly, the pressure between her legs too intense to hold still. "That..." she broke off to run an anxious tongue over her lips.

Amused by the rise of color in her face, Killian leaned closer and lowered his voice. "I like sex," he whispered. "I plan on having a lot of it with you. Starting tonight."

"Tonight?" Her voice was barely above a croak.

He rose out of his seat in a single, fluid motion. His black eyes never left hers as he extended one hand to her. Juliette accepted before she could even think to stop herself and he tugged her to her feet.

For a moment, for one heart stopping second, she almost thought he would follow through with his promise to take her on the stone bench. Her entire body tightened with anticipation. Her breasts swelled. The nipples tingled. She almost begged. She could feel it bubbling up her chest.

He pulled her into his chest with one gentle tug of his arm around her middle. The collision of their bodies ripped a moan from her that tightened his grip.

"Tonight," he murmured quietly into her upturned face, "you will come to the estate, take off your clothes, climb into bed and play with yourself until I arrive. You will make yourself wet for me and bring yourself to the very brink, but you will not come, do you understand?"

Cotton mouthed, Juliette could only nod furiously.

"Good." The hand holding hers uncurled and lifted to pinch her chin. He forced her head back even further. "Welcome to the next twelve months, little lamb."

Chapter 11

Killian hadn't been sleeping when Frank announced Juliette's arrival at four in the morning. He hadn't realized how late it was until he'd lifted his gritty eyes off the merger contract he'd been working on and found the bigger man darkening the doorway of Killian's office.

He set his pen down and winced at the pain that lanced through his hand. His fingers creaked as he forced them open.

"Take her to my room, please, Frank," he instructed, massaging the stiffness from his joints.

Inclining his head, Frank stalked away.

Killian rose and ventured to the window. The world outside was illuminated by a pregnant moon and a skyline glowing with golden light. The predawn hour had his lips pursing; had he known how late it would be when she arrived, he would have … what? Told her to come tomorrow night? No doubt she was working then, too. And in the morning and afternoon. When did the girl plan on sleeping? He wondered, undoing his cuffs and rolling the sleeves up.

It baffled him beyond reasoning why she was so desperate to cling on to how she'd been living all those years. Maybe it was habit. Maybe it was the fear of letting go and having everything falling apart. He knew there were nights he felt that way. Control was a demon that always found a way to demand more. He could understand that. He could understand her need to keep surviving. He would respect that. If she thought she could do it, then who was he to say otherwise? But the moment it started to drag her under, all bets were off.

Abandoning his place, he left the office and made his way across the estate to his room. It was a bit of a walk, but it was the only room in the entire place with a bed he actually enjoyed sleeping on. There were guestrooms he could take his company to, and he had in the past. They were closer to the front door and convenience was everything. But he usually tried to make it to his own room whenever possible. The women never stayed the night, not in his bed, not in his home, so it was usually just him in bed anyway; overnight visits hinted at a deeper sort of intimacy he refused to have.

The door to the room was shut firmly closed. There was no sound on the other side and he suspected she was probably just getting comfortable.

She wasn't in bed when he let himself in. The room was empty and he was beginning to wonder if Frank had taken her to a different room when the bathroom door opened and she emerged, looking drawn and ashen. The hairs at her temples were damp, indicating she'd probably been splashing water on her face, possibly to elevate some of the puffiness. There were dark, purple halos around her eyes and fine pinch lines around her mouth. Yet, despite that, she smiled when she saw him.

"Hi!" she said, her voice gravelly with exhaustion. "I thought I would have more time to get ready."

He went to her before she could reach for the first button on her maid uniform. His hands lifted and he took her chin in his palms. He peered into her eyes, into the warm pools of brown amongst a sea of faint red.

"You're tired," he observed.

She started to shake her head. "No, I'm fine—"

"That wasn't a question," he cut in sharply. "Are you working tomorrow?"

"Yes, but—"

He released her and took a step back. "Go home."

She blinked. "What? But you said—"

"I won't have you like this," he told her evenly. "You're barely able to keep on your feet."

"I'm fine!" she protested. "I've gone days without sleeping before."

That only managed to piss him off all the further.

"Those days are over," he said, willing his temper down. "I know we agreed you could keep your jobs, but I won't have this. I won't have you coming to me like this when you have to work again in a few hours. I won't have you spending the precious few minutes you have to sleep fighting to stay awake in my bed."

She stared at him with apprehension. "What are you saying?"

"That you need to pick one job, Juliette. Only one. I prefer the one that leaves your nights open for me, but I'll leave the decision to you. And before you begin arguing, this isn't a request. Your health and wellbeing is the only things that matter and you're running yourself into the ground. I won't let you."

Her mouth opened and closed, but nothing came out. Whether it was because she didn't know what to say or because she was too tired to think of anything, he wasn't sure.

"Have you even eaten?" he broke in before she could find her voice.

"Eaten?" she mimicked like the thought had never occurred to her. "What—?"

"Food," he explained. "You barely touched your plate at lunch. Have you eaten since?"

The confusion crinkling her brow said it for her.

Killian exhaled with a growl. He scrubbed viciously at his face and turned away from her before he did something unforgivable, like shake her.

"I don't understand what the problem is," Juliette said, her voice high.

"The problem," he said, forcing himself to face her once more, "is that when I have you on that bed, I want you awake and ready to take everything I do to you. I want you alive in my arms. I want you writhing and screaming and begging me for more. What I don't want is to worry about how much sleep you're going to get before you have to work another sixteen hour shift or if you're going to remember to eat properly. That is the problem."

A muscle flexed at her jaw. He could see the tension vibrating along the length of her. He wasn't sure what she wanted to do more, yell, cry, or leave the room. But she stayed. She didn't yell or cry.

"You seemed fine when I told you just this afternoon that I was keeping my jobs," she reminded him in a deadly calm voice.

"Aye," he agreed with a subtle nod. "But I didn't see you looking like this then or I would have told you hell no."

That sparked the anger in her eyes. "That's not your decision to make and don't you dare bring up that crap about being personally in charge of my wellbeing. I'm twenty-three years old. I've been taking care of myself and my sister since I was sixteen. I know my limits."

Killian didn't know what to say or do that didn't involve tying her to the bed and forcing her to take better care of herself. While the thought was tempting, he knew she would never forgive him for it.

"Clearly we will reach no mutual decision tonight," he decided, willing himself to keep his composure. "We'll discuss this again tomorrow."

"There is nothing to discuss!" she shot back. "I'm not quitting my job."

It was on the tip of his tongue to snap out, *we'll see about that*. But he opted against it. He was a business man and he dealt with challenges every day. He would fix this. He just needed to find a common ground for both of them.

"Fine."

Surprise flickered across her face before suspicion set in. "Really?"

He nodded. "But I reserve the right to bring this up at a later date when we have both had time to cool down." He put his hand up when she opened her mouth, no doubt to argue. "No more arguing. I'll have Marco drive you home."

"I thought…" She stopped. Her shoulders lifted with her deep inhale. "Fine."

He let her walk out, because the alternative was to lock her up and apparently that was kidnapping. He told himself it wasn't his business how she juggled her life or how much it was killing her, but it was. The moment she had signed that contract, she had become his business. She had become his and that meant something. It meant he took care of things, made sure she was safe and protected, even if it meant from herself. But damn, the woman was stubborn. He had honestly never met a woman who made him want to strangle her and kiss her at the same time.

However, her abilities to infuriate him wasn't the thing up for question. He needed to fix the problem while respecting her decision. That was going to take some doing. But solving impossible situations was what Killian did best.

"What did you do?"

Scrawling down the last line of the agreement before he forgot, Killian glanced up just as Juliette charged into his office, her face set in the type of anger women got just before they started throwing things. Killian did a quick sweep of his desk to make sure there was nothing sharp before gathering up the contract he'd been working on for most of the night. He stowed them and his pen inside a drawer—just in case she decided to stab him with it—and faced her.

"Sorry?"

She stopped just on the other side of his desk. Her chest heaved rapidly beneath the thin material of her maid's uniform. The top button had popped open and he was momentarily distracted by the hollow of her throat.

"I got called into the manager's office today," she was saying when he broke out of his thoughts to rip open the rest of the buttons and take her across his desk. "I have never been called into the manager's office."

He sat back in his chair, more to observe her fully than anything else. "All right?"

Slender palms pressed flat against the top of his desk as she leaned forward, her eyes narrowed.

"Do you know what he told me?" She didn't wait for him to respond. "That I've been promoted to front desk duty with a raise and a clothing bonus. Oh, and coincidently, the amount I'm now making is double what I was originally making as a maid *and* it's more than I'm making at the diner, plus some."

Killian portrayed the proper expression. He widened his eyes with interest and nodded.

"That's great. Congratulations."

His attempts to soothe her didn't seem to work when her eyes only narrowed further, in suspicion now.

"What did you do?"

He kept his features neutral. Completely blank of everything but a mild confusion.

"What do you mean?"

"Don't give me that!" She slapped his desk with one hand. "I know you did something. The timing is just too weird. Just the night before, you were telling me I had to pick one and now, suddenly, I'm getting a raise and a promotion?"

He lifted one shoulder in a brief shrug. "Maybe management finally realized what an asset you were."

"That's bullshit." She straightened and folded her arms. "I've been there almost four years and they never once accepted my front desk application."

"Well, there it is then." He rose. "Yours finally hit the top of the pile." Casually, he circled around to her side of the desk. "When do you start?"

She watched him with a wariness that was amusing as hell. He would have laughed if he didn't value his life.

"Tomorrow," she mumbled at long last. "I got the day shift slot, which I'm sure is going to piss Celina off big time."

But there was a sort of quirk in her mouth, a devious tilt that made the glint in her eyes appear almost mischievous.

"Not a fan?" he pressed, oddly endeared by the grin unfolding across her face.

Her smile was full blown when she met his gaze. "I think I just found the silver lining in this situation."

"That's your silver lining?"

He had thought for sure it would be the money or the new position or the not having to work late at night cleaning up other people's filth.

"Yes!" she hissed with a laugh that was more of an evil cackle. "Celina Swanson is getting demoted to night duty and it's beautifully horrible."

Killian couldn't help it, he laughed. "You're an odd woman."

She snorted and rolled her eyes. "You don't know Celina. She's a bi … witch," she corrected quickly, amusing him all the further. "No one likes her, except Harold. But everyone knows they're sleeping together so she's going to be furious when she finds out he gave me the position." Her smile faded into a wide eyed panic. "Right before she slits my throat." She met his gaze with a frown. "Not sure Harold did me any favors, now that I think about it."

Bottling back a second laugh, he swept back a coil of hair off her temple and tucked it behind her ear.

"It'll be fine."

"Maybe." She squinted up at him. "You laughed. I don't think I've ever heard you laugh."

He stepped around her and headed for the window, the back of his neck prickling with discomfort.

"I don't normally have a secret sadist in my office."

"I'm not a sadist!" she gasped in feigned outrage.

He tossed a dry glance over his shoulder. "Have you heard yourself cackle? It's Disney villain material."

Her glower melted into a wide smile that dissolved into a brilliant shower of giggles. She gave a little squeal that came with an odd little dance like a four year old who finally got the doll she wanted.

"Do you know how long I've waited for this position?" she gasped, beaming so wide he was certain she'd rip her face open. "Years!" She slapped both hands over her chest and gasped. "I think I'm having a heart attack."

Chuckling, Killian turned fully to face her, charmed and endeared and absolutely enchanted by the euphoria wafting off her and filling every sparse corner of his office. It was unabashed joy in a form he was unaccustomed to seeing.

"Well, try not to," he teased. "My CPR is rusty."

Laughing, she walked over to join him in the patch of sunlight crashing through the window. The rays tangled through her hair, turning the downy strands into a halo around her flushed face. It illuminated the gold flecks in her eyes and the happiness shimmering across their surface.

"Do you know what this means?" she said quietly.

Captivated by how much she reminded him of a pixie, Killian could only muster a weak, "What?" in response.

"I don't have to keep my job at the diner, or the arcade." She paused to roll her eyes. "Thank God. I hated that place." She bit her lip and his cock tightened. "I need to go shopping. Do you know how long it's been since I've stepped inside a mall? I don't even know what size I am anymore."

He could have told her. He'd always been fairly decent when it came to estimating the size of things. It was a family talent when one was in the transporting business. But he also valued his ability to reproduce and while he knew he could never have children, it was the thought that mattered most.

"How old is your sister?" he asked instead.

"Vi? Sixteen. Why?"

He rolled a shoulder casually. "Maybe you could take her with you. Make a day of it."

He saw the spark of interest in her eyes, the contemplation before she nodded.

"I should. She's a brat, but she's a brat with really good taste in clothes." Her grin became sheepish and a bit pained. "I'm taking up all your time, aren't I? You seemed busy when I arrived."

"You mean when you stormed in hell bent on putting the wrath of God in me ... again?"

Her cheeks turned a dark shade of scarlet. "I'll work on remembering to knock next time."

"Next time?" He forced his hands into his pockets and rocked back on his heels. "Is this going to become a regular thing then?"

"That depends." She gave him a smile that was pure mischief. "Are you going to keep going behind my back and doing things for me?"

One of them drew closer, closing the foot of space separating them. He only became aware because he was suddenly drowning in the scent of her, in the temptation of her mouth being offered to him. The single motion brought her right beneath his height. It forced her neck back so her face was tipped up to him.

"Possibly." He forced his attention up to her eyes. "Unless you've decided to let me take care of you?"

She shook her head. "No."

He had expected nothing less.

"Too bad." His hand snaked free of its confines and lifted to ghost the soft contour of her cheek. It traced the apple and dipped into the hollow. The palm settled along her jaw, aligning the pad of his thumb over the parted curves of her mouth. "I take very good care of my things."

Slim fingers curled around his wrist, but made no move to brush him aside as she peered unwaveringly up at him.

"I'm not a thing," she whispered, bathing his skin with the heat of her breath.

"No," he agreed in an equally low murmur. "But I would spoil you if you let me. I would give you everything you could ever possibly want. Just let me, Juliette."

It was beyond him why it was so important she submit. He honestly couldn't understand why he needed her to let him shower her in all the things she deserved. But it thrummed through him like a physical wound. It coursed through him like poison. The more she denied him, the more demanding the need became.

"I only want you." The hand not holding his wrist cradled the side of his face, mirroring the one he held to hers. Her thumb grazed his bottom lip and he felt it like a punch in the chest. "Only you, Killian."

He kissed her.

No. He pummeled her mouth with an unhampered sense of urgency that shocked even him. It rolled up and over him, taking him under in a current of electrified waves that snapped at his sanity. Beneath his assault, Juliette whimpered. A small, weak part of him prickled with the fear of hurting her, but the madness was too strong. It had him in its clutches and he was powerless to think or do anything but claim the woman clinging to him.

"Killian."

Her soft voice washed through the red haze in a wave of calming blue. It soothed the burn eating him up inside in a way he had never experienced before. It was as though she possessed the power to ease the storm he'd been fighting his entire life with just the whisper of his name. The mere thought had him tearing out of her arms in a panic.

"What are you doing?" The question was an unintentional snarl that cracked through the room as loud as the uneven pants coming from the both of them.

"I..." Mouth wet and swollen, Juliette stared at him, bemused and afraid. "I wasn't ... I didn't..."

He grabbed her and hauled her back into his arms. His mouth slanted across hers, demanding and hungry. She didn't push him away, not even when he lifted her up and carted her to his desk. He set her down on the cool surface and reached for the tiny V at the hollow of her throat, the one that had been mocking him from the moment she'd stalked into his office.

Buttons flew in all directions. Their pathetic clatter went unnoticed as the fabric was torn over her shoulders and down her arms. Full, firm breasts barely covered by black lace sprung free. The last of the buttons were ripped from their holes and he had her across the desk clad in nothing but her bra and panties. Her uniform was pitched somewhere across the room. He briefly heard it hit the floor and skid. But it was the woman splayed out before him that had his main focus.

There were no words to describe the sight she made. Every inch of her was cut from the very depths of his fantasies. It was as though someone had reached deep inside him and crafted a woman far more dangerous than any weapon on earth and the only one she could potentially destroy was him.

How are you doing this to me? Every fiber of his being begged the question. But the words remained firmly lodged in his chest. Instead, all he could do was bow his head and worship the smooth valley of her belly with his lips. Then his tongue. He followed the delicate curves of her ribs one by one to the rough fabric of her bra. Her breasts rose with the arching of her back, a silent offering that included the feather light trailing of her fingertips along his shoulders, up the back of his neck to thread through his hair. He ignored her urging and worked his way back down, pausing to circle her navel with his tongue before stopping at her mound.

Heat rose off the stretch of cotton covering her. He could feel it burning his lips even before he was near enough to plant an open mouth kiss to apex of her thighs. Juliette moaned. Her hips shifted with an anticipation he had to still with a hand on her hip.

"Patience," he reminded her and earned a groan of frustration in return.

He concealed his grin in the toned muscle of her inner right thigh. He sank his teeth into warm flesh just hard enough to make her cry out. He kissed the spot before tracing a path along the elastic of her panties to repeat it on the other side. Her fingers tightened in his hair.

"Killian..."

Compelled by the pain in her whimper, his head lifted. His body shifted over hers, weight balanced on his palms as he leaned in close. Eyes an opaque black with arousal met his. Swollen lips parted, possibly to speak. But he nipped sharply on the bottom curve, hard enough to make her buck beneath him and gasp.

"Are you going to make me spank you?" he demanded.

She didn't say yes, but she didn't say no, either. Instead, she stared up at him with a wide eyed sort of interest that was an almost physical caress along the rigid length of his erection. It wrapped around every nerve ending like a challenge and tugged. He would have groaned if she hadn't taken that moment to reach for his pants.

Her eyes never left his as his belt was tugged open. Then the button. He continued to watch her with his heart hammering as she dragged down the zipper and freed him. She broke the connection first. She looked away, looked down at the skin she'd bared, at the part of him that was throbbing with a searing pain that was almost unbearable. The delicate column of her throat bobbed with her swallow. Her cheeks darkened. Her lashes lifted and their eyes locked once more.

"Can I have him now?"

His cock swelled, a fate that should have been impossible considering the raw shade it was already in and the amount of clear liquid that was coating the top and trickling down the shaft.

Fucking woman! Killian thought as he dragged her to him by the hips. She was going to be the death of him. He knew it even as he forcibly twisted her over onto her stomach. Her feet hit the floor and he kicked them apart as wide as they would go. The worn elastic of her panties snapped easily beneath his violent yank. He knew there would be marks on her hips from the assault, but that was the last thing on his mind when he cupped her, turning her cry of surprise into a mewl of pleasure with just a flick of his fingers.

"Killian!"

Liquid heat rushed over his fingers, burning skin and drawing him to the pool at her opening. The tight ring gave easily, greedily sucking him into the slick channel of her body. Her ass thrust back into his palm, her back arching like a cat begging to be stroked. Her incoherent sobbing fanned in a white fog across the desk and he knew he wouldn't last. What hot blooded male would when his woman was dripping all over his floor and mewling like a vixen in heat?

Christ!

Abandoning her welcoming heat, Killian stalked to the other side of his desk. The drawer rattled with the anticipation vibrating through him. His entire body was fraught with a dark, endless need that gripped him like ropes of fire driving him to claim what was his. The craving came from somewhere deep in the pit of his stomach, a dormant evil prowling to claw free. For years he had fought back the beast, had kept it in check and away from innocent life and for years it had obeyed without complaint. It had sat subdued and hungry in the dark corner of his soul.

Until now. Until Juliette. Damn if he knew what it was about her, but every fiber, nerve, muscle, bone, and monster in him wanted her. Wanted to claim and own her. It was a dangerous path, one he knew he would never recover from if he let himself stray. But it was more than that. It was the fear of hurting her that had him tightening the chains.

"Killian?" Juliette lifted her head, her face shadowed by tendrils of tangled hair. "What's wrong?"

Rather than tell her the truth or tell her to run fast and run far, he grabbed the silver foil from his wallet and slammed the drawer shut. She didn't ask again as he made his way back around behind her. He tore the packet open with his teeth while yanking his trousers down the rest of the way with his free hand.

He plunged inside her with a single, powerful thrust. The momentum drove her up onto her toes. It rattled the monitor on his desk dangerously. There was no warning, no restraint but the bruising clamps of his fingers on her hips, holding her prisoner to his needs. Her sharp sob destroyed him. It rang through the room in a sweet symphony that sang to his very core. The tangle of pain and pleasure clawed down his spine, propelling him deeper. His heart screamed between his ears, a deafening sound of triumph. His cock throbbed as it settled in the velvet case of her body.

Panting, he held himself a moment, giving her time to adjust, needing her to brace before he lost himself again.

"Don't stop!"

The plea was followed by the frantic wiggle of her ass, by the push back of her hips, and the greedy ripple of her muscles around his cock. Any restraint he could have possibly hoped for snapped. Every ounce of his control vanished as he pumped inside her, thrusting deeper and harder each time until she was screaming and coming in a wild flail.

He fisted her hair. The damp tendrils formed a beautiful knot around his hand as he jerked her head back. His free hand snaked around her middle and found the pulsing bundle between slick lips.

"Again!" he hissed.

She did with a guttural sound that tore from her chest. Killian released her hair and her head fell forward as though her neck could no longer support its weight. A fine sheen of sweat had formed along the jagged line of her spine. It seemed to shimmer with every ragged heave of her back. Killian smirked to himself as bucked his hips three more times and came.

Thick, white cream gleamed along his cock when he withdrew from her. He was tempted to make her clean it off him and even started to reach for her when his phone buzzed across the smooth surface of his desk with a noisy clatter. Juliette stirred and forced herself up onto her feet. She glanced at the phone before turning to him, still braced against the desk as though her legs hadn't returned to their full function. Her lips parted in a smile, a smug, satisfied sort of smile that tightened a knot in the pit of his stomach.

The sight of her pinkened cheeks, her swollen mouth and her lack of clothes did odd things to his insides. It filled him with an arrogance he hadn't bothered with in the past. His lovers always left gratified, but it was different with Juliette. With her, there was a sort of pride swelling up in his chest at the knowledge that he had pleased her.

"I guess that's our cue that our time is up," she said. "You should probably get back to work, huh?"

He wanted to tell her he worked when he wanted to and whoever was calling could wait, but he knew that if he touched her again, he'd drag her into the bedroom and neither of them would leave for a very long time. The need for her hadn't been quenched. If anything, nearly destroying his desk had been more of a snack than an actual meal. Already he could feel himself hardening for another round.

"Marco will take you home," he said instead. "He'll stay with you for the day and bring you back here tonight."

She blinked. "Tonight?"

Common sense abandoning him, he closed the space separating him from her and trapped her between him and the desk. The heels of his hands dug into the edges of the table on either side of her hips as he leaned in close enough to skim her lips with his.

"I want to see your new clothes," he whispered against her mouth. "And we're not done."

To prove it, he ground his rock hard shaft into the soft flesh of her belly, smearing her juices across the skin of both their stomachs. Her weak gasp burned against his chin. Her pupils diluted. She lifted her hands and anchored her fingers into his shoulders.

"Can we—?"

"Tonight," he cut in before she could steal anymore of his control.

Her bottom lip puckered, but she grudgingly obeyed. "Can I borrow some clothes then? You ripped all of mine."

A grin worked up around his mouth no matter how hard he fought to hold it at bay. He drew back. His fingers drifted to the buttons on his dress shirt. The material came undone easily and he shrugged out of it.

"I don't think you'd fit in my trousers," he told her. "But this should be long enough to cover most of you."

Fighting back her own grin, Juliette accepted the top and eased into it, her eyes never leaving his. She did up the buttons and held out her arms.

"How do I look?"

Illegal.

It covered all the things that needed covering. The sleeves fell well over her hands and the hem stopped just at her knees, but nothing about it deterred the imagination. Maybe it was because he knew she wore nothing but a bra underneath, but he could picture every curve as though the material was transparent. Also, there was something mystifyingly enticing about her in his clothes that he couldn't quite put his finger on. All he knew was that she looked sexy as all fuck and the penis he had yet to tuck away took great pleasure in noticing.

"I take it that you like it," she teased, eyeing his shiny, new erection.

He glowered at her and stuffed himself back inside his pants. "Go."

Catching her bottom lip between her teeth to contain the laughter he could see shining in her eyes, Juliette skirted around him and quickly gathered her clothes. She pressed them to her chest as she turned back to him.

"I'll see you tonight."

"I'll be here," he promised.

With a wave, she hurried to the doors. They had been shut at some point. She might not have noticed as she yanked them open, but he did.

Frank, he thought.

True enough, the other man stepped into the room only moments after Juliette had left. If he had any thoughts on what he may have witnessed, it never showed on his face.

"Ryan Keating phoned," he declared evenly. "He apparently tried you first, but you were preoccupied."

Killian dragged his phone over and checked the missed call. Sure enough, there was one voicemail from his lawyer.

"He has the rest of those papers you asked for," Frank finished.

"Tell him to fax them over," Killian said, already moving towards the doors. "I'll look at them in a moment. Also, tell Marco to take Juliette and her sister wherever they need to go for the rest of the evening and bring her back here. Have John and Tyson go with them."

"John and Tyson, sir?"

Killian paused on the threshold and glanced back. "I don't want her left alone."

Frank inclined his head. "Yes sir."

He took a quick shower before dressing in fresh clothes and returning to the office. Frank was exactly where Killian had left him. But he must have left at some point, because there was a stack of papers on Killian's desk when he took his seat. He hoisted them up and flipped through them quickly. He would do a more thorough reading later, but at first glance, everything seemed in order.

"This is everything?"

Frank nodded. "The Twin Peaks Hotel is officially yours, sir."

Chapter 12

Remembering how to shop was like remembering how to ride a bike, Juliette realized as she hefted her bags more securely along her forearms. Their weight was beginning to cut strips into her skin, but she refused to let the two men tailing her take them for her.

They were nice enough, she supposed. Neither said very much, but it was their silence and watchful eyes that was most disturbing. They followed her from store to store without complaint and occasionally would deter other customers from the changing area when she wanted to try something on. Juliette was almost positive the entire mall thought she was some kind of celebrity. One boy even grabbed his cellphone to snap a photo before the one named John intervened and took the phone away. Juliette had tried to apologize and get the shadow to give the boy his phone back, but Tyson had gently taken her arm and maneuvered her from the store while John stayed to talk things over with the boy.

As embarrassing moments went, it was probably the worst.

Ultimately, she opted to ignore the pair and finish her shopping. Had she not been starting her new position the next morning, she would have just gone home. No. She would have gone to Killian and yelled at him for sending the two in the first place. She wasn't sure what their purpose was. Had he sent them to spy on her? To see where she was going and who she was seeing? The very idea was insulting and filled her with an anger that made her want to kick someone. But she saved it. Saved every ounce of her rage for the person responsible.

"I've got it!" she snapped when Tyson reached for her bags as they approached the gleaming SUV. "I'm perfectly capable of handling my own luggage."

If her manner or tone in any way affected the pair, neither showed it. They remained perfectly mute and impassive. Part of her couldn't help wondering if there was a robot hidden beneath their human skin.

Both were well over six feet tall with narrow, swimmer bodies and dark suits. Tyson had skin the warm color of chocolate and John looked like he'd never even heard of sunlight. Neither wore sunglasses, which made her eternally grateful. But they did have those plastic earbud things and every so often, she'd catch one muttering into the second half tucked inside the sleeve of their blazers. There were bulges under their jackets that she suspected were weapons, guns, no doubt and it only amplified her anger.

At the house, both men jumped out of the SUV before she could. Tyson held the door open for her while John grabbed her things. It was a well-oiled system that she would have found quite impressive any other time. But instead, she let John hang on to her bags. What was he going to do? Try on her bras? Besides, she had bigger fish to fry, namely Killian McClary.

The pair followed her up the stairs, keeping perfect time with her furious strides. Neither of them stopped her, which she found refreshing from the last time they'd chased her down with their guns drawn.

"You had me followed?"

She stomped into his office and found him, as she's suspected, seated behind his enormous desk, the same desk he'd had her bent over just that morning. The memory sent a tingle through her she had to shove aside.

"Hello darling," Killian said without glancing up from the papers in his hands. "How was your afternoon?"

Juliette glowered at him, not that it mattered; he still hadn't glanced up.

"It was fine until your ... goons, started shadowing me everywhere. What were you hoping they'd report back to you? That I bought underwear?"

That caught his attention and his head came up. Those magnetic eyes roamed over her in slow interest.

"Are you wearing them now?"

"Killian!"

With a sigh, he set the papers down and got to his feet.

"They weren't there to report anything back to me," he said evenly. "John and Tyson were there to protect you and I'm not sure they appreciate being called my goons."

Juliette opted to ignore the latter. "Protect me? From what? A boy and his phone?"

Killian's gaze shot past her to the two men as though silently asking what boy? What phone?

"There was a harmless incident," the one named Tyson reported in a very official tone. "The situation was handled."

"Handled!" Juliette barked. "They stole his phone and threatened him with bodily harm. He was barely fifteen! I'm surprised they didn't pummel him into the ground and pull him into a choke hold."

Killian looked on the verge of laughing, but he must have noticed the warning flashing in her eyes, because he wisely smothered it behind the hand he rubbed over his mouth. He fixed his attention on the two men over Juliette's shoulder.

"Thank you," he said. "Just put those in my room."

Inclining their heads, the two turned on their heels and stalked from the room. Tyson paused just long enough to shut the door behind them, locking her in with the man watching her.

"Why did you send them?" she demanded. "I don't appreciate being spied on, Killian, especially when I have never warranted your distrust."

There was no amusement on his face now, just a weary sort of contemplation bordering on a touch of defeat she really didn't like seeing.

"I meant it," he said. "I wasn't spying on you. I was trying to keep you safe."

"From what?" she stressed, feeling her anger draining away to confusion.

Killian turned away and started back to his desk. For a moment, she thought he'd return to his papers. Instead, he turned and propped his ass against the edge and stared across the room at her.

"Who do you think you're involved with, Juliette? Do you think I'm a banker or a teacher? Someone safe and harmless?"

A frown wrinkled the place between her brows. "Of course not."

He looked tired, she realized. Like he hadn't slept in days. There were dark shadows beneath his eyes and fine lines bracketing the corners of his mouth. Part of her wondered why she hadn't noticed them that morning. Maybe because he always held himself with such confidence. It was odd to see him show this sort of weakness. Or maybe she was just a bad person who never paid attention. Whatever it was, she didn't like it.

"I'm not a good person," he told her with a tension that insisted she understand what he was trying to tell her. "I have enemies. Lots and lots of enemies. Some who would not hesitate to destroy me and everyone I have ever met. Had you been any other woman, that first night would have been the beginning and end of us. I would have sent you home and never thought of you again, because that is how I like my relationships. Because that is how I keep them safe."

"Because you're cursed," she whispered, remembering his words over lunch the other day.

His chin lowered so he was peering down at his feet. "People I get close to die horribly and you..." He raised his head to fix her with an intensity that dried the spit in her mouth. "You are the only woman I can't seem to let go and that makes me the most selfish son of a bitch in the world, but it also means that I will do everything in my power to keep you safe, even if it means having you angry with me."

But she wasn't angry, not anymore. She was sad, frustrated, and a whole lot tired.

"They're not very friendly," she mumbled. "And they scare people."

The left corner of his mouth quirked. "That's their job."

She sighed. "What about Vi and Mrs. Tompkins? If I'm not safe then they're not safe."

He pushed to his feet. "I have men stationed by the house and another watching over your sister."

Men stationed by the house. Men following her, following Vi. Men with guns and watchful eyes. It was all too much. Her own life had never meant overly much to her, but she had sacrificed everything to keep her sister safe. Instead, she had put them both in a position that required those men and those guns.

"Juliette?"

One hand pressed flat to her pounding chest, she put the other up to ward him off when he took a step towards her.

"I … I need a minute."

She turned away, but there was nowhere to go except to walk into the doors. So she stood there and stared at the slabs of wood, at the three squares carved down each one and the gold handles. Her chest ached where her heart kept repeatedly slamming into muscle and bone. But no matter how hard she tried, her brain had become a wasteland of nothing. Its blankness fueled the impatience and fear she was fighting so hard to keep at bay and she hated herself. Hated the weakness. The inability to think of a way out of what was possibly eminent death.

"Make them disappear." She spun on her heels and peered at the man across the room. "Can you do that?"

Confusion tugged his brows together. "You want me to kill them?"

Juliette blinked. "What? No! I meant put them somewhere safe. Give them new identities or something. Hide them somewhere far away. I'll stay with you. I'll put up with your men following me, but Vi and Mrs. Tompkins ... I can't put their lives at risk because I can't let you go either."

A muscle tightened in the set slash of his jaw. "You won't ever see her again if I do. She can't ever come back."

The knot in her stomach tightened until she nearly blacked out from the pain. But she breathed through it slowly.

"You said you'd do anything for me if I let you." She started towards him. "This is what I want, Killian. If the time ever comes and something happens to me, promise me you'll keep my sister safe."

Anger flickered across opaque eyes, hot and formidable. It flared in his nostrils and turned his beautiful mouth into a thin, white line.

"I promise to keep her safe, but if the day comes when I have to pick between saving you or saving her—"

"You will pick her!"

"No, Juliette. I won't."

Dread settled on her heart, causing it to crash down to her ankles in a messy splatter.

"Killian, please. She's sixteen." Juliette crossed to stand before him. "She didn't ask for this. I'm the one who put her in danger."

He turned away. His shoes clipped softly as he made his way around the desk and lowered himself down into his chair. Springs creaked with his weight. He settled back and steepled his fingers. He watched her over the tips for several agonizingly long minutes.

"I'll handle it."

She didn't know what that meant, but it sounded like an agreement and that was how she would take it, because deep down, she knew Killian would follow through on his word. He may not have been a *nice person*, as he put it, but he was someone who honored a promise and that was what she needed.

Juliette sucked in a breath. "Thank you." She expelled the breath and willed herself to relax a fraction. "I'm sorry for calling your men goons. That wasn't very nice of me."

His facial muscles softened. "No, it wasn't. Tyson looked pretty hurt."

Chuckling, she glanced down at the papers still sitting on his desk. A thick wad of very official looking documents she couldn't hope to comprehend.

"I keep interrupting your work."

Killian followed the line of her gaze. "Aye, but you're far more interesting than a merger agreement."

"What are you merging?"

He leaned back in his chair and motioned her around to his side of the desk. Juliette went and was tugged by gentle hands into his lap. Up close, the papers looked no less official or complex, but there were two names on the cover letter that she did recognize.

"You own Off The Shelf Books?"

Off The Shelf Books was a three story bookstore large enough to be its own city. Juliette had never had the time to go inside and explore, but she'd heard the place actually came with a map and that alone had landed the place on her *must see before I die* list.

"No, I own the bistro next door."

"Pause."

Another place she'd never visited, but not because she didn't enjoy coffee or lacked the commitment to stand in line for two hours for a cup. It was the cost of said brew that kept her away; unless the cup came dipped in gold and the brew was some exotic blend of alien blood and unicorn shavings, she didn't see the need to pay ten bucks a pop.

"So you're merging the two?" she asked.

Killian nodded. "Off The Shelf wants to bring coffee to its customers. I happen to own one that shares a wall and makes good business."

Juliette made a humming sound of agreement. "Smart." She leaned back against the chest cradling her back and rested her head against his broad shoulder. Against her abdomen, his intertwined fingers tightened. "I've never been to either," she confessed. "But I hear good things about both so I think it's a great idea. Not that I'm telling you how to run your business." She yawned mid speech, but kept talking around it with one hand pressed to her mouth. "That would go against the contract."

"Tired?" Killian's lips brushed her temple, tickling the skin with his stubble.

"I'd forgotten how exhausting shopping can be," she admitted. "But I got a ton of really cute outfits so that makes me excited."

"Did you and Vi have fun?"

All thoughts of sleep vanished at the mention of her sister. Eyes she'd closed in relaxation popped open and she stared at the door across the room.

"She couldn't make it," she said, trying not to show just how much that fact hurt her. "She was busy."

It wasn't necessarily a lie. Juliette had rushed home, excited to share her great news with Mrs. Tompkins and Vi only to have her sister tell her she had more important things to do than shop with someone who had no taste. Apparently she'd made plans with her friends and wouldn't be home until late. Juliette hadn't stopped her. She'd gone upstairs to shower and change and head to the mall alone. It wasn't until she'd walked through the familiar glass doors that she realized just how pathetic she was. Only years earlier, she'd stalked through those shops with her friends as though she owned the entire damn building. Now, she couldn't even get her kid sister to join her. But at least she'd had John and Tyson, who, in a strange sort of way, had kind of made her feel not so alone.

"Well, I want to see them," he murmured in that low, guttural voice of his.

Juliette tipped her head back and peered up into his face. "I might have gone a bit overboard."

He shrugged the shoulder she wasn't using as a pillow. "I have time."

"What about the merger?"

"It's not going anywhere."

As crazy as it was, his offer was actually endearing. What man went out of his way to sit with a woman while she tried on clothes? But the fact that he wanted to returned the excitement Vi had killed with her careless disregard.

"Really?"

He lifted a hand to touch her chin lightly. "Really."

Elated, she pushed out of his lap and dragged him along with her as she started for the door. He pushed them open as she chatted on about all the different outfits she had to go through to find the ones she really liked. He listened patiently the whole way to the bedroom where her bags had been set on the bed.

"This is overboard?" he asked as she shut the door behind them. "There's only five bags here."

Juliette frowned at him without heat. "That is overboard for someone who hasn't bought a stitch of anything new in seven years! Now, sit somewhere. I'll show you what I have."

Hands up in surrender, Killian claimed a spot at the foot of the bed and watched as she scooped up the bags and hurried into the bathroom.

The clothing bonus hadn't offered very many options, but she had made do with two skirts, two blouses, a dress and one pair of sandals and a pair of knee high boots. The combination was interchangeable and enough until her first paycheck. She could buy a new outfit with every pay and build her closet from there. But for now…

She wiggled into the pearl gray pencil skirt and black blouse with the sandals. The four inch heels were pinchy around the toes, but they made her legs look fantastic and that kind of made up for the minor pain. She twisted her hair up, more to keep it out of the way then a fashion thing. Then she reached for the door and tugged it open.

Killian hadn't moved from his spot when she stepped out. He looked up when she walked towards him.

"What do you think?" she asked, twirling once so he could see the back.

"I'd hire you," he said, making her laugh.

"As what?" she wondered.

He shrugged and gave his head a shake. "Doesn't matter. Just to see you walk around in that."

Still laughing, she walked back into the bathroom.

The second skirt was shorter, coming mid-thigh with a sliver of a slit at the back. She topped it off with a fat, gold belt and a scarlet blouse and the boots.

"I'd leave your hair down with that one," Killian stated when she showed him the second outfit. "Curly."

Juliette arched an eyebrow. "You seem to know quite a bit about women's fashion. Something you'd like to share?"

He offered her a dry glower. "It's how I would like to see it."

Grinning, Juliette turned away. "One more."

"Only one?" He seemed genuinely confused. "That's only three outfits."

She paused in the doorway of the bathroom and glanced back. "They didn't give me a platinum credit card with unlimited funds. I had to make do with the amount I was given. No!" she warned when his frown deepened. She jabbed a finger at him. "Don't you pull any strings or do your hocus pocus whatever it is you do. This is fine."

With that, she ducked back into the bathroom to pull on the final outfit. Her favorite one. The moment she'd seen it, she knew she had to have it, even if it cost the entire bonus. Thankfully, it was part of some summer line and was knocked down by fifty percent, making it practically a steal. It only solidified her reasoning that it was meant to be hers, that and the fact that there was only one left and it was in her size. Absolute destiny.

The form fitting pencil dress came a sexy three inches off her knees and hugged every hill and curve of her body to perfection. The plaited front was cinched together by a gold clip that matched the one resting cool and shiny just below her collarbone, serving to keep the bodice together. A diamond peek-a-boo hole was cut into the material, plunging just low enough to show the hint of cleavage without becoming improper for work. Short sleeves hugged her arms and had little V-shaped slits to the shoulders. She added the sandals and the little something she'd picked up on a whim with Killian in mind. As an afterthought, she let down her hair and shook it out. She checked her face for smudged makeup before turning to the door.

Nervous for reasons unknown, she was less excited about her final reveal. Not that she didn't think Killian would like the dress. It was only a dress after all. But it was the other thing, the surprise that made her palms sweat.

"Okay!" she called out before reaching for the doorknob. "I'm coming out."

Knees wobbling, she stepped out into the bedroom and paused. Killian took her in, everything from her feet all the way up to the top of her head. His expression gave nothing away and that only intensified the anxiety clawing its way up into her throat.

"What do you think?" she asked, nervously.

"Sexy," he said. "The body hugging material suits you."

Her hands trembled as she ran them down the front of the dress. "Thanks. I really like this one." She licked her lips. "Can … can you help me with the zipper? I can always get it up, but never down."

Praying to God she didn't stumble, or worse, face plant, she made her way towards him slowly on shaky legs. She scooped her hair up and over one shoulder. Her heart hammered in her chest as he rose and met her halfway. She turned, offering him the zipper running down her back. Her entire body seemed to vibrate with pent up anticipation. Her skin tingled all over. She held her breath and waited.

The first brush of his fingers along the nape of her neck nearly sent her clean out of her skin. She gave a violent jolt she hoped he hadn't noticed. If he did, he never let on as he caught the tongue and rolled the zipper downward. The fabric gave inch by inch until the sleeves slipped down her arms. Juliette let the whole thing ripple to the ground in a puddle of black fabric. She stepped free and turned slowly to face the man behind her.

Her eyes locked with his.

"I also bought this," she whispered, brushing a hand over the lacy scrap of fabric hugging her hips.

It matched the gel filled cups plumping up her breasts to firm, sexy globes. Both had cost her more than the dress and the shoes, but the look on Killian's face … oh the look was worth every penny. It was raw lust in its truest form. It was feral and dangerous and she was in the center of all of it. It was enough to make a girl orgasm.

"Do you like it?" She reached for the first button on his dress shirt, her eyes never leaving his. "I thought of you when I picked it out."

The second button gave as easily as the first. Then the third and fourth.

He never stopped her, nor did he speak. He watched her the way a hawk watches a mouse, with a focus that was both unnerving and arousing. She could feel herself growing wet. The bit of string tucked between her ass cheeks rubbed uncomfortably against her moist folds and she honestly couldn't wait to be rid of it. But in the meantime…

She tore his top free from the waistband of his trousers, growing bolder the longer he didn't stop her; there was something profoundly naughty about taking control of a man like Killian. Watching the play of fire and restraint across his face and knowing she was the cause. It was the sort of power that propelled her to lean forward and graze a kiss to the masterpiece that was his chest. Then another and another, all the way to his neck and the erratic little pulse giving away just how much she was affecting him.

Driven by her new found powers, she drew back and planted a palm against the center of his chest. His heart beat in a chaotic rhythm beneath her palm. The hot, toned skin made her want to explore all of him inch by inch, but she wasn't sure how much she could push him before he regained control. For now, she had to use her time wisely. Next time, she'd look into getting scarves or handcuffs.

Delighted by the idea of tying him down and having her way with him slowly, she grinned and earned a raised eyebrow from him that she ignored as she nudged him backwards to the bed. He went without complaint and dropped on the mattress when his knees caught the edge. Juliette went down with him on her knees between his parted feet. Realization widened his eyes. But he didn't stop her when she reached for his fastens and unleashed his erection.

It jutted out from between the V of his trousers. Thick and proud, it stood at attention with its fat cap and hard shaft. Veins crisscrossed beneath soft, pink skin. They pulsed beneath the palm she wrapped around the base.

Above her, Killian hissed. His knuckles whitened around the edges of the mattress. Juliette raised her chin just enough to peer up at him through her lashes. The intense set of his jaw radiated in the heat of his eyes as he bore down at her.

Leaning forward, she grazed the top with an open mouth kiss. The appendage gave a jerk in her hand that she took delight in as she continued her progress down the length to the base. Then she worked her way back up with the flat of her tongue all the way up to circle the hood. Clear liquid had begun to trickle free and she lapped it up before taking just the top into her mouth and sucking lightly. She flicked with her tongue and earned a low grunt from the man.

"Juliette…"

Ignoring the plea, she made a slow descent, taking him deep into the hot cave of her mouth until there was about an inch between her lips and his base. She drew back, dragging her tongue along the shaft. She nipped at the hood once before working her way down again, faster.

After a moment, she worked a pretty good rhythm, using her hand and tongue and sometimes teeth until his labored panting was all that filled the room. It was a talent listening for the exact moment to really start the torture while concentrating, but Stan had been a five minute pumper and she knew when to recognize lift off.

When his gasps became choked groans, Juliette eased her hand inside his trousers and cupped the heavy weight of his balls. The violent jerk of his body almost made her grin if she hadn't been focusing so hard. Instead, she gripped them, tugging and massaging gently in time to her sucking and pumping. The vein along the base beat faster. His hips began to jerk like all he wanted to do was thrust up and end his own suffering. But she tightened her grip on his cock, warning him not to do anything that might accidentally get him bit off.

She was the boss now.

"Juliette…"

The low, tortured whimper was just what she'd been waiting for. The hand cradling his sac clamped firmly around the skin connecting them to his body and squeezed just as he started to come. His cock twitched wildly, but nothing happened. She had made him stop coming.

"Fuck!" he snarled. "Fuck! What … Jesus … fucking … fuck!"

Ignoring his incoherent swear fest, Juliette sucked on the sensitive cap. She licked and nibbled. Each one had him swearing louder and thrashing faster, but not to get away. He dropped back against the mattress, hands flying to his face as he threatened and begged her to stop. To not stop. To please … *please* end it.

Juliette smirked. "Patience."

His growl almost made her laugh in giddy delight. She focused on working the purple cock in her hand until she was certain he wouldn't come.

She released him and got to her feet. Hastily, she shoved her panties to the ground and stepped out of them and her sandals. She reached for the nightstand closest to her and yanked it open.

No condoms.

Muttering a curse, she scrambled up on the bed. One leg was throw across Killian's hips and she straddled his prone body while reaching across to the other nightstand. Her fingers closed around the box and she tugged it free of the drawer. Silver packets spilled across the sheets. She fumbled to tear one free of its row without leaving her place on Killian's abdomen.

Why hadn't she thought to do this before she started?

Exasperated, she got one and sat back on hard, corded thighs and tried to figure out how to put it on him. The circular bit of rubber came with no instructions. She vaguely remembered something from high school health class about the pointy end going up ... or was it down? What pointy end?

A chuckle from her companion had her glancing up to find Killian watching her. His amused expression was tight, but amused nonetheless. He took the thing from her and nimbly did the job himself.

"Not a word!" she warned as she adjusted herself to take him.

He was still grinning, but wisely said nothing.

Planting both palms on his chest, she arched her hips and wiggled, trying to get his cock to slide in. It was there. She could feel it bumping against the hard muscle of her clit and nudging against her wet opening, but it kept dodging her attempts when she tried to get on it.

Frustration welled up inside her, infuriating her enough to draw tears. This was not how she'd wanted to seduce him.

"Are you doing that on purpose?" she accused sharply when he missed again. "No!" she snapped when his hands lifted off the mattress. "I've got it."

He let his hands drop.

Determined now, she reached down between her legs and held him. *Let's see you try and escape now!* She thought with a wild sort of cackle in her head as she gripped him firmly and guided the head to her opening.

Once the cap broke through, the rest followed seamlessly. He stretched her in all the places that made her head rock back and her body shudder. Her nails dug into hot skin, anchoring her to the only solid thing in the room as everything else drifted away, except how fucking amazing he felt.

Hard, calloused hands settled on her hips and eyes she had no recollection of shutting flew open. Her head snapped down to find him watching her, his face burning with the same wild fire as the one raging through her.

"You feel so good," she whispered, unable to stop herself.

Her hips rocked, not sure if it was his doing or hers, but the sensation of pure bliss amplified. It surged up through her hot and unsteady like whiskey on an empty stomach. Every nerve ending in her body seemed to come alive.

"Faster."

Following his quiet command, Juliette bucked. She rose up over him and plunged down again and again, working up a pace that had her tightening and her core throbbing as it approached a too soon end.

"Killian...?"

His answer was to push up and band her middle with both arms. In that position, she was drawn into his lap, her legs circled his waist and her own arms went around his shoulders. But it was the depth of his cock and the angle ... Christ the fucking angle. Every thrust and pull dragged his shaft along the tight nub holding her together. It pushed her each time a little closer until she was nothing more than a mindless bundle of nerves straining for release. She couldn't think or speak except to pant his name and beg him not to stop.

She had a vague recollection of her bra being snapped open and her breasts freed to his hand. She hurriedly tossed the article of clothing aside as the nipples were stroked by clever fingers. Then pinched and rolled and just when she wasn't sure she could take anymore, he was sucking and nipping and with a harsh cry, Juliette came. Her head fell back as her whole body shuddered and rolled over his. Her nails tore skin off his back, but he didn't seem to notice, too preoccupied by the tongue he was tracing around each nipple.

She came down slowly from her high. His arms were still there, holding her close, holding her together. His mouth moved up to her neck and he nipped lightly at her pulse.

Lax and incredibly sated, Juliette clasped him to her and let him work out his own release. Every so often, she'd move her hips against his, enjoying the sensitivity of her own body. Killian didn't seem to mind. He didn't seem to be in any hurry either. He let his hands and mouth move over every inch of her that he could touch and she loved that too. His hands were magical. Every caress had her skin tingling and her insides fluttering. She honestly never wanted him to stop. But he came with a grunt that he stamped into the slope of her shoulder. Blunt fingers dug into her shoulder blades as he panted into her skin. His cock jerked uncontrollably a few times before falling still. Against her chest, his rose and fell rapidly. His hot breath fanned across the curve of her neck.

Juliette grinned into the warm flesh of his shoulder. "I think this is my favorite position."

His shoulders jerked in a silent chuckle. "Don't say that until we've tried them all."

A warm thrill raced through her at the thought of trying all manner of positions with him.

"Definitely top five then," she amended, drawing back to peer into his face. "Was it good for you?"

One dark eyebrow lifted in dry amusement. "Are you asking if it was top five for me?"

"Do you have a top five?"

"In general or with us?"

She had to think about that a moment. It was an interesting question and she had to really debate whether or not she wanted to know his favorite position with other women.

"In general," she decided, curious to know what he liked.

His answer was the feather light rake of his fingers down her back from shoulder to ass where they curled, lifted her hips and pulled her more firmly down over the hard length of him still buried inside her.

"I would rather show you."

Juliette's eyes widened. "Is that ... are you...?"

"Aye, it is." The corner of his mouth lifted. "Doesn't seem to want to go down when you're around."

A molten, hot shiver sliced through her. It poured over the embers left behind from only moments ago, igniting the flames to new heights. Her walls rippled around him, bathing him in a fresh wave of arousal. Her breathing quickened.

"I ... I guess we should do something about that," she decided.

Something dark flickered across his features that had her insides quivering.

"Oh, I insist."

It was well after two in the morning when Juliette slipped out from beneath Killian's slumbering embrace and crept across the room. Her limbs were still jittering from the earth shattering climax she'd experienced only minutes earlier, but she moved quickly gathering her things and getting dressed. Killian had passed out the moment he'd rolled off her. He'd hooked an arm around her middle just long enough to tuck her into the curve of his body, but it had taken no time at all before his slow, even breaths were burning into the back of her neck. She'd waited just long enough to be sure he wouldn't wake up before untangling herself and sneaking out of the room.

It was in the contract, she told the guilt ridden voice when it whined about just leaving without a note. It had stated very clearly she wasn't to spend the night. But it was more than that. She had to wake up early for her new position and she still needed to toss her new clothes into the washer. Plus ... God help her, but spending the night with him scared the shit out of her. It was an intimacy she wasn't sure she'd be able to walk away from in twelve months. It was just easier for all if she followed the rules.

At the bottom of the stairs, standing on either side of the front doors, Tyson and John straightened to attention. They squared their shoulders and watched her solemnly as she approached.

"Ma'am," Tyson said, inclining his head.

Painfully aware of how bedraggled and rumpled she looked, Juliette fidgeted anxiously. "Shouldn't you two be sleeping?"

"No ma'am," John said curtly.

"We have been assigned to stay with you," Tyson added, taking the bags from her.

Juliette's eyes widened. "Stay with me? Like ... everywhere?"

"Yes ma'am," they said on unison.

She started to protest, but stopped herself. It was what she'd agreed to, after all. It was in the contract, Killian doing all that was in his power to protect her.

"Fine," she muttered, trudging past them towards the door John quickly yanked open.

They took the same SUV as earlier. It hadn't been put away, she noticed. But sat gleaming under the night sky and the lights that never seemed to turn off around the property.

Next to it, the fountain of Killian's mom sat bubbling quietly, filling the stillness with a sort of calm. Juliette paused to stare up into the other woman's ivory face and thought of what Killian had told her about how his mother had died. It must have killed Killian and his father to see the statue every day, standing like a reminder of how they'd lost someone so important. But maybe it also helped ease the pain. There was a picture of her own mother, before the cancer had taken her health and youth and ultimately her life, on the mantel in the living room that Juliette used to stare at all the time after her mom had passed. Maybe it was the same thing.

"Ma'am?" John was holding the car door open for her.

With a last glance at the fountain, Juliette ducked into the backseat of the SUV and let herself be propelled home.

"Are you stupid?" Blue eyes blazing with contempt, Celina snatched the pen from Juliette's hand. "The year goes first. Then the month. Then the day."

It was a task not to snatch the pen back and jab it right in the other woman's eye. It would have certainly made Juliette feel better after being bullied, threatened, belittled, and yelled at for most of the morning and afternoon.

From the moment Juliette had walked into the hotel lobby, Celina had been on her case over just about everything from Juliette's selection of clothing to the fact that Juliette had even gotten the job, which was Celina's favorite topic to shout about when no one was around to hear it.

"Does it really matter which goes first?" Juliette demanded. "The form doesn't even specify."

"It does matter!" Celina shot back, looking practically unhinged at the very idea. "I have worked here for five years and that is how I've always done it and that is how it should be done." Sucking in a breath that heaved her ample bosoms dangerously close to the neckline of her low cut blouse, Celina tried again. "Year, month, day. In that order."

Resisting the urge to roll her eyes, Juliette turned back to the practice form Celina had her filling out.

It was simple enough. Most of it was done on the computer anyway and all she had to do was put in the guest's information and hand them over a key. But Celina made it sound like she was singlehandedly responsible for the saving the world.

"Tell me again how you got my job," Celina hounded, not for the first time. "I'm the one in charge of new hosts and I didn't hire you."

"Harold did," Juliette said yet again without glancing up from the form. "He called me in yesterday and told me it was mine."

"See, I don't believe you." Celina folded her arms. "The whole thing smells fishy. Harold would tell me if there would be a change like this and he would not put *me* on nights!"

Juliette shrugged. "You'll have to ask him."

"Oh, I will."

Juliette didn't doubt it. But what scared her was Celina twisting Harold's arm into firing Juliette. Sleeping with the manager came with perks like that. All Celina would have to do was bat those pretty blue eyes and suck Harold's cock and no doubt get him to do whatever she wanted. But what did that mean for Juliette? Would he fire her? Would he make her go back to being a maid? Unlikely. Celina would probably get her kicked out of the hotel for good. The very idea had her insides writhing and her skin going clammy. But she kept a cool composure, refusing to let the other woman get to her.

"Guests," Celina muttered.

Juliette raised her head and watched as an elderly couple made their way to the counter. Both were smiling kindly and immediately put Juliette at ease. She straightened and returned the smile while positioning herself in front of the computer.

"Hello, welcome to the Twin Peaks Hotel. Do you have a reservation?"

The man, tall and thin with a thick mustache and warm hazel eyes, reached into the inside pocket of his suede coat. His bushy eyebrows furrowed when he didn't find what he was looking for. His hands went to his pockets. His frown deepened.

The wife, short and round with a lovely face and bright red lips, chuckled. "Henry, what are you looking for?"

Still patting down his person, Henry huffed. "I can't find my wallet."

Shaking her head, the wife dug into her purse and drew the worn leather out. "This wallet? The one you gave me so you wouldn't forget it?"

Henry blushed and took the thing from her. "I knew that." He flipped it open. "I was just seeing if you remembered."

The woman rolled her eyes affectionately.

Endeared by the pair of them, Juliette chuckled.

A moment later, several pieces of ID and a reservation print out was set on the counter. Juliette followed the steps Celina had given her. She pulled up the online reservation form and found the man's name and room number. All the while, Celina breathed down her throat, watching her every move like a hawk. But she must not have done anything wrong, because she managed to get through the whole process without getting yelled at.

Mr. and Mrs. Therrien were sent off to find their rooms and Juliette was left alone with the queen of bitching once more.

"Are you sleeping with Harold?"

The question was so out of the blue and so surprising, Juliette wasn't fast enough to conceal her disgust.

"Oh, ew!" she blurted without thinking.

Realistically, there was nothing wrong with Harold. He was young and attractive in a car sales men sort of way. But Juliette had never found his dimpled smiles and twinkling green eyes overly enticing, not when she had someone like Killian to compare him to. Harold honestly never stood a chance.

"Who then?" Celina pressed on.

"That is hardly any of your business!" Juliette retorted sharply.

"It is my business when you stole my job!" Celina practically shrieked. "Who the hell are you anyway? What makes you qualified to run the front desk? Do you have any idea—?"

"Look," Juliette cut her off before the woman had an aneurysm. "I don't know how I got the job, okay? I've been applying for four years and I guess I finally got lucky."

Celina actually snorted like the very idea was ridiculous. "You did not get lucky. I pick who works at the front and who doesn't and I did not select you."

Juliette had nothing to say to that so she kept her mouth shut. Not that it mattered. Celina was on one of her rolls again.

"Furthermore, I would most certainly not let you take my place!" Her pretty alabaster complexion went blotchy beneath her flawless makeup and her eyes shone. "I don't work nights! I have a social life and I won't sit here in an empty hotel lobby, waiting…" She sniffled and turned away. Juliette felt a pang of guilt and sympathy and started reaching for the other woman in comfort. "I'm too young and hot to be locked up where no one can see me!"

Guilt and sympathy died instantaneously. Juliette dropped her hand and shook her head.

At five, Celina packed her things, cast Juliette a scathing glower and stalked out of the hotel. Juliette was left alone for an hour before Evan arrived for the night shift. She took the time to unwind from the nightmare that had been her first day. Her head was thrumming and her back ached, but it was her feet that made her want to cry. They hurt like a mother and she was pretty certain she had blisters where the straps on her sandals were cutting into her ankle. But Celina wouldn't let her sit down for longer than a minute before pointing out how lazy she was being.

Only nine more days to go, she told herself as a motivational pep talk. Celina's training would eventually end and Juliette would finally be free of the woman. She just needed to bide her time and not commit murder before then.

That was easier said than done when tomorrow would be another day.

John and Tyson were waiting for her when Juliette finally left. The two had taken turns all day sitting in the lobby. Seeing them filled her with a whole new surge of guilt.

"I'm sorry," she told the pair. "You guys must hate being stuck with me."

"No ma'am," Tyson said almost immediately.

"It's our job," John added.

She didn't believe either of them. Who wanted to spend their entire day watching the weather channel in a hotel lobby? The very idea bored her to tears.

"Look, if you guys want to take a break, get some coffee…"

"We're fine," John said. "Thank you."

Juliette sighed. "I'm just going home. You don't have to follow me there."

"We go where you go."

Awesome.

Not pressing the matter, she let herself be led to the SUV. Tyson drove while John sat in the back with her. The moment they started driving, Juliette undid the buckles on her shoes and kicked the torture devices off with great relish. She groaned as her feet straightened to their normal flatness. Her toes cracked. Sure enough, there was a blister on the big toe of her left foot and a cut from the strap on her right ankle. Both throbbed.

"Remind me to set those on fire," she told John, who inclined his head.

"Yes ma'am."

Juliette grimaced. "It's Juliette. Ma'am makes me feel all … matrony."

John bowed his head again. "Yes ma'am."

With an exasperated sigh, she dropped the subject.

"Roger." Tyson said unexpectedly from behind the wheel. He lowered the wrist he'd had up by his mouth. "Boss wants to see you," he said, peering at Juliette through the rearview mirror.

"Me?" Juliette asked. "Why?"

"Don't know, ma'am," was all the answer she got as he turned the car around and headed back towards the estate.

Frank met her at the entrance. His enormous frame took up the entire doorway in a hulking, black shape silhouette against the light coming from the foyer. He regarded her with a perfectly blank expression Juliette was beginning to wonder if they taught at some fancy bodyguard school.

"Hello," she said. "Frank, right?"

The giant inclined his head. "Yes ma'am."

Oh good, she thought with a tight lipped smile. *Another one.*

"I'm Juliette," she said. "It's nice to meet you."

Something shifted across the man's soft, brown eyes. A smile maybe.

"Likewise, ma'am." He stepped back and gestured her into the foyer. "Mr. McClary has asked me to take you to his room. He's finishing up some business and will be with you shortly."

She followed him up the stairs. John and Tyson didn't follow. They stayed downstairs and she wondered if they would finally relax now that she was in a heavily guarded fortress.

    Frank stopped just outside the bedroom. Juliette thanked him before ducking inside. The doors were shut behind her and she simply stood there with no idea what to do next. Did he want her to strip and wait for him on the bed? Was she supposed to get herself wet and ready? In the end, she padded over to the bed and dropped down on it, her exhaustion winning. She pulled the pillow under her head and watched the door for Killian's arrival.

Chapter 13

It was odd that a life of crime would take up so much after hour negotiation, but as Killian watched the little clock on the right side of his monitor, it seemed like it would never end. The hour kept getting later and the five faces on his screen continued to shout and argue through their webcams about all the necessary precautions they needed to take now that the authorities had upped their force.

None of it made a lick of difference to him. But it was required so he listened with only a quarter of his attention span and waited for the moment he could leave to find Juliette. Frank had already told him she'd arrived and, ever since, his skin had been prickling to go to her. It was the oddest sensation, but one he was quickly becoming accustomed to where she was concerned.

"Why should we offer our planes for your garbage, Lozano?" Theresa Maynard, CEO of Hanmark Corporation by day, gun smuggler by night, curled her pretty red lips in disgust.

As shrewd and evil went, she was probably one of the worst. Cut throat and cold to the core. But maybe one had to be when they put guns in the hands of children. Like Killian, it was a family business. One that had been passed down into her manicured hands. She was the youngest of three, and Killian had met her older brothers, but Theresa was molded in their father's image, ruthless and cunning. It was no surprise when the company had been put in her name.

Marcus Lozano wasn't the head of any business or corporation. He was second in command to William Lozano, his father. But William had no patience for the petty back and forth that took place once a month, every month like clockwork. Honestly, if Killian had a second in command, he would do the same thing. But the truth was that he liked knowing where his enemies stood. He liked knowing their game plan, even if they all lied.

Most nights, watching the five squabble and toss around idle threats was mildly entertaining, but Killian couldn't stand it any longer. The feeling coursing through him, the itchy sensation scuttling beneath his skin made him want to leap up and pace. Hell, it made him want to leave the room and let them sort it out on their own. It wasn't like they really needed him there. He wasn't even participating, just sitting there, waiting for someone to say something useful.

"Gentlemen, and ladies," he added quickly, inclining his head to the only two women in the chat. "I unfortunately have another meeting that requires my attention. Please send me an email when a decision has been made. Goodnight."

He shut off before anyone could think to protest or attempt to make him stay. The moment the screen went blank, he became profoundly aware of the humming inside his skull. But he ignored it as he got to his feet and made his way to the door. Frank was nowhere in sight, but Killian knew it only took a murmur of his name to summon the man from wherever he was lurking.

Strides quick, he made his way to his room in no time at all. But something made him turn the knob quietly, like a part of him had almost expected to find Juliette curled up on the bed, asleep.

She wore the black skirt with the red blouse. Her bare legs were curled almost to her chest. One hand was loosely curled next to her slightly parted mouth. But it was her hair he was most fascinated with. It was unbound, a chaotic mess of waves spilling across the pillow. In the dim light of the setting sun, the strands shone like spun gold.

Moving to her side, Killian perched on the corner of the mattress and studied the play of colors that only seemed to come out in different lighting. In the approaching hours of dusk, he could just make out hints of auburn and dark brown.

He lightly plucked up a coil that had been resting along the curve of her neck and wound the silky texture around his finger. All blonde with just a hint of brown.

Juliette sighed in her sleep. Her sooty lashes fluttered but remained splayed across the soft contours of her cheeks. She shifted half onto her back, tugging the strand of hair from his grasp when she turned her head away from him.

He let it go, his focus captured by the firm swell of one breast peeking out through the gap in her blouse. The voice in his head wondered if she was wearing that lacy bra she'd bought to torture him with. The one that had held her breasts to their full perfection and had converted his brain to soup upon sight. It was an image that had haunted him all day, scattering his thoughts mid conversation and making him lose hours at a time just reminiscing. But it was her mouth that had enslaved him. The things she had done with just her tongue. Christ.

"Full of surprises," he murmured quietly to himself as he peered down at the slip of a woman taking up far too much time and space in his head. "What am I going to do with you?"

Juliette didn't answer. He wasn't expecting one, but he continued to study her, taking note of just how vulnerable she looked in sleep. Such a change from the fierce, passionate woman who claimed his bed or stormed into his office like she'd like nothing better than to take a switch to his ass. The very idea was hilarious, he was twice her size, but in that moment, she seemed capable of just about anything.

Killian chuckled quietly to himself and realized with a start that he'd been doing that a lot lately. Laughing, chuckling ... smiling. While he knew he wasn't incapable, he truly couldn't recall the last time he'd done any of those things. Maybe not since his mother's death. There hadn't been much to be happy about after that.

"Killian?" Juliette opened bleary eyes and squinted up at him. A small smile turned up the corners of her mouth. "Hi."

Every muscle in his stomach clinched at that simple gesture. His chest cavity seemed to shrink, compressing his lungs and heart until both were struggling to keep him alive.

How did she do that?

"Hi," he breathed out around the constriction.

She yawned behind her hand and struggled upright. The left side of her face, the one that had been mashed into the pillow, was pink and streaked with lines. It took all his willpower not to reach out and stroke the skin, to feel the warmth of it.

"I must have dozed off," she murmured, casting a glance over to the window and the navy blue creeping across the heavens. "Is it very late?"

"No." He rose to his feet, needing a modicum of space to regain some of his composure. "Are you hungry?"

"I'm all right," she said a bit too fast. "I can wait until I get home."

Frustration lifted his shoulders in a deep exhale. "Are you hungry?" he repeated, more firmly.

She looked up at him. "I can wait—"

"Christ, woman! It's a simple enough question. Are you hungry?"

Her lips pursed in an annoyance that all too quickly dissolved into a smile that turned into a laugh.

"If you're so adamant to feed me, then yes, I'm hungry."

Glowering without heat, he offered her his hand and helped ease her off the bed. He kept his fingers locked around hers as he led them down towards the kitchen. It wasn't until they reached the hall of windows that he noticed how short she was walking next to him. Most people usually were compared to him, but she normally came to his shoulders. She was now barely at the center of his chest.

"Where are your shoes?" he asked, realizing she wasn't wearing any.

Juliette shrugged nonchalantly. "John is probably setting the devils on fire."

Killian blinked. "What?"

She peered up at him, her eyes shining with mischief. "They hurt my feet. They had to die."

Maybe it was her sly little grin or the way her nose crinkled just a bit when she said *die*, but something in him cracked and he was reaching for her before he could stop himself. His hands closed around her arms and he jerked her into his chest. Her gasp was swallowed by the mouth he slanted down hard over hers. His hand closed in her hair to cup the base of her skull. He crushed her to him as he devoured the sweet taste of her like a man starved.

Juliette moaned and melted into him. The sound vibrated against his lips as thin arms wound their way around his shoulders. Firm breasts mashed into his chest, the nipples hard points of arousal stabbing through both their tops. Toned thighs cradled up against his until she was perfectly aligned with every inch of him. Yet it wasn't even close to being enough.

"Christ!" he groaned, his hold tightening on her.

Slim fingers tangled through his hair, holding his mouth over hers as she nipped lightly on his bottom lip.

"Take me back to bed, Killian."

The very core of his being agreed with her husky murmur. His hands even started lifting her up into his arms. But that part of him, that little voice that reminded him her wellbeing needed to come before his needs, propelled him back to sanity.

"No." Breathing hard, he jerked back just enough to breathe in something other than her sweet, musky scent. "You need to eat first."

Brown eyes shimmered up at him with the sort of dark hunger that implied that she would be eating if he did what she asked. It was nearly impossible to ignore.

"Stop it!" Drawing back his hand, he swatted her smartly on the left ass cheek, making her yelp and blink with surprise. "Food first."

The corner of her mouth twisted downward, but she didn't protest when he led her the rest of the way to the kitchen.

Leaving her to find a spot at the island, Killian made his way to the fridge. Molly's neatly labeled containers sat in several neat rows in the freezer. Any one of them would take mere minutes to heat up, but something stopped him. Maybe it was because he was tired of stew and broth. Maybe it was because he just didn't want to stay home, but he turned to Juliette and found her gone. The kitchen was empty, save for him.

Bemused, he shut the freezer door and went in search of her and found the French doors open to the garden. Something tightened in his gut, a swell of dread that had no grounds. Aside from the gardener and himself, no one had ever been out there, not since his mom.

Moving carefully, he stepped out onto the stone patio and spotted Juliette almost immediately.

She stood at the railings overlooking a soft landscape of neatly trimmed grass surrounded by an array of flowers and shrubbery. A stone pathway cut along the side of the house and disappeared around back to where the garden really started, but she stayed on the patio.

"It goes on," he told her, breaking the silence.

Juliette turned her head and met his gaze. "Show me?"

He should have said no. His home had too many ghosts and he didn't care to share them with anyone. Instead, he found himself moving towards her. Found his hand slipping into hers. He guided her down the steps to the path.

The humid day had cooled to a soft, whispering breeze that wafted through the branches of a nearby oak tree. The leaves shivered, flashing almost silver in the fading light.

Alongside him, Juliette's bare feet made no sound at all as they turned the corner and came upon the main part of the garden.

"Oh my God!"

While most people had swimming pools and tennis courts in their backyard, his mother had built a paradise. Her own personal Eden, she'd called it. Growing up, Killian remembered being dragged across the globe in search of new ideas to bring home to their backyard. His mother had taken a bit of every place and somehow made it all possible right there in a breathtaking jungle of wonder. Flowers in all shapes, colors, and sizes ran rampant on either side of the path that wound deep into the heart of the maze. Trees and shrubbery loomed high and powerful in makeshift alcoves for sitting. A creek cut beneath a bridge that branched off into different sections. Each one held a new secret, secrets even Killian hadn't discovered. It was three hundred and thirty acres of magic just waiting to be explored.

"This is … incredible!" Juliette breathed. Her hand slipped from his and she started forward. "It must have taken years to create."

Thirteen, to be exact. His mom had started plans for the garden before the house was even built.

"A while," he said, following her. "My mom loved the smell of soil. She liked the feel of it wet between her fingers. She'd spend hours out here, weeding and planting and growing things, even though she had an army of gardeners."

Juliette shook her head. "No, something like this, you need to do it yourself to really feel pride in it. You can tell she loved what she was doing."

"You should see the conservatory," he said.

Juliette chuckled. "If I ever leave this place." She exhaled. "I would have loved to be here as a little girl. It's like a fairy garden."

"That's what my mom used to call it. She'd tell me that at night, when I was sleeping, all manner of creatures would crawl out of their hiding places and duel to see who was stronger. The elves, who were good and just, would battle the trolls, who wanted to destroy everything beautiful. During the summer, the elves would win and everything would bloom. Come fall, the trolls would dominate and everything would die. In the winter, both sides would hibernate, collecting their strength until spring when the elves would beat the trolls and unleash beauty on earth once more."

Juliette laughed. "Your mom was clever, and very creative. I like that story."

Killian gave a silent chuckle. "She was full of stories."

"My mom used to read from books," Juliette recalled. "Shakespeare mostly. She loved Shakespeare. She used to say that was why she married my dad, because the second she heard his last name, Romero, she knew he'd been meant for her. She'd climb into my bed and we had this fat book of Shakespearian plays and she'd say how Vi and I were both named after her favorite characters." Her tone had taken on a wistful tone that made him want to draw her into his arms. "What were your parents like?"

It was strange, but no one had ever asked him that before. Most of the people he knew had known his parents. The rest ... well, it wasn't their business. So it took him a moment to think of something to say.

"Mom was beautiful," he began. "Everyone loved her. It was hard not to. She had this aura around her that pulled people to her. She was kind and so giving. My dad used to tease that she would give her soul away if it meant saving another person. She loved to laugh. I remember her laughing and dancing a lot when I was growing up. But she had a temper." He heard himself laugh. "Her Irish was strong, my dad would say. God help the poor soul that got in her way when she got her head fixed on something. My dad ... he was a good man. He was fair and kind. He loved his family. I can't remember a single time when he didn't drop whatever he was doing to play with me. I never got told one minute or later. Nothing was more important than me and my mom."

He broke off, horrified not just by how hot the skin around his face had grown, but by how easily she had coaxed something out of him that he hadn't shared with anyone. The memories burned behind his eyes and lodged in his throat. He stared hard at the path beneath his feet and tried not to curse.

A small, cool hand slipped into his, silent, but screaming with so much emotion he almost jerked back. That simple gesture slammed into him with the weight of an iron fist; it had been so long since anyone had given him comfort, he had no fucking idea what he was supposed to say.

But she didn't seem to want any words. Her fingers threaded through his and they walked on in absolute quiet.

Nearly an hour later, they returned to the estate. Killian shut the terrace doors and turned to the woman next to him. She was peering down at her feet, at the dirt clinging to pale skin. Her nail polish had chipped in several places, he noted when she wiggled her toes. Her head came up and her eyes met his.

"I should clean up before I get dirt all over you floor."

It didn't bother him, but he showed her to the washroom and left her there while he decided on supper. Molly's care packages were out and it was too late to get a reservation anywhere decent. He decided on takeout, Chinese, preferably. He made the call quickly, ordering two of everything off the menu before walking down the hall to leave money with the guard stationed outside.

He was about to head back inside when he caught sight of John leaning against the side of the SUV parked out front. He had a cigarette in one hand and his phone in the other and was idly flipping through it. Killian wondered if he should ask the other man how Juliette's first day had gone, if anyone had given her any trouble, if she was able to fit in, and if she was happy. But he opted against it. Instead, he shut the door and ventured back to the kitchen just as Juliette left the washroom—her feet clean.

"I am ready to eat a horse," she declared.

"I am out of horse, but I do have beef and broccoli on the way if that works for you."

Her eyes lit up. "Chinese? I love Chinese!" Her eyes narrowed. "Molly is not going to appreciate you not eating her home cooked meals."

"I'll eat them," he muttered. "And whose side are you on anyway?"

The little witch didn't even pause to consider her answer.

"Hers."

Killian glowered. "And why is that?"

Juliette shrugged. "Because she scares me."

"And I don't?"

Her head bent to one side and she regarded him with a soft sort of smile. "You did that first night."

He wanted to tell her that was only a few weeks ago, that she couldn't possibly stop being scared of someone in that short of time. But then he hadn't expected to like her as much as he did in that time frame either so maybe it was the same thing. Plus the idea of her being afraid of him bothered him.

"Well, that's unacceptable," he stated.

She simply laughed and started for the kitchen. Killian followed, watching the sway of her hips and the bounce of her hair along her back. She walked with purpose. It wasn't exactly graceful or sexy, but it was captivating. It was the strides of someone who had no time for bullshit. He liked that.

At the island, she spun around on her heels and faced him.

"So, what do we do to pass the time?"

Anything but talk, he thought miserably. Already he'd divulged more in a single hour than he felt comfortable with. She had a way of drawing him into her web and it was dangerous. Not just for him, but for her. Somehow, he needed to remind her that what they shared out in the garden—clearly a huge mistake on his part—could never happen again. There could never be another heart to heart. Their arrangement needed to remain indifferent and physical only. Emotional attachments could get her killed; and, God help him, but he knew he'd lose his fucking mind if he let that happen.

Killian kissed her. He didn't mean to, but every ounce of his frustration seemed to pour into the single melding of mouths. His hands framed her face, holding her to him as he forced her back. She made a sound, like a squeak when her back came up against the island. Killian released her long enough to grab her hips. He lifted her up onto the smooth marble.

She didn't protest or try to stop him. Her eyes were dark and watchful, waiting to see what he'd do next.

"Undo your blouse," he told her.

His own hands moved up the soft, warm flesh of her outer thighs to the lush curve of her hips. His gaze stayed on her hands as they fluttered with ease to the first button. He vaguely recalled the first time he'd asked her to remove her top, back in the limo their first night. He remembered how her fingers had trembled and how tight her jaw had gotten. There was none of that now as she slipped button after button through the neat holes.

Crimson fabric parted to pale skin. Each new inch dipped lower to expose high, beautiful breasts. The bra, he noted with some disappointment, wasn't the one she'd bought the day before. It was a simple, cotton material in faded black, but in no way did it take away from the sight.

"Christ, you're beautiful." He'd meant the words to stay in his head, but they filled the kitchen in a guttural whisper.

Her chest swelled with her sharp exhale. The bit of fabric covering her strained, revealing the tight, hard outlines of her nipples. A warm flush crawled up her chest to soak into her cheeks and he followed the line with his lips from the valley between her breasts all the way up to her waiting mouth. His hands curled into the strips of material curving around her hips and he dragged her panties down her legs. She kicked them off and widened her knees.

"Lie back," he told her, resting his hands on her thighs.

She did a quick check behind her to make sure nothing was there before reclining. Her blouse parted on either side of her like red wings. Her stomach and chest seemed to heave with every ragged breath. But Killian's only focus was her thighs, her toned, slender thighs, the delicate color of milk. He loved her legs. Hell if he knew why. He'd never been a leg guy before. Breasts, yes. Lips, yes. But never legs. Yet hers fascinated him. He loved how they grabbed him when he was deep inside her and how they tensed and quivered when she was about to come. Her thighs said more than her entire body and it was why he always seemed to start with kissing them first.

Bending his neck, he pressed several open mouthed kisses to her inner thighs in a row up to the junction. The thick, musky scent of her arousal met him before he was even close and he felt himself harden against the front of his trousers; knowing she was already wet and ready for him always drove him crazy.

Lifting his head, he reached over and flipped the rest of her skirt up and over her stomach, baring her to the room and him. Her neatly kempt mound beckoned him. The engorged little bundle at the top peeked out from between plump, pink lips, tempting his fingers to stroke and tease. But he occupied his attention with littering kisses up and along the line of her pelvis. He nipped at her hipbones and drew just close enough to where she wanted him to make her twitch and whimper. His fingers made slow circles mere inches from her core. He let his thumb lightly brush her clit and she swore violently. Her legs jerked on either side of him.

He hadn't been lying when he'd told her he had a thing for eating pussy. The female body had always been a weakness. But the center of a woman's body, the apex of her pleasure had always made him curious enough to learn everything he possibly could about it. The number of past lovers was immeasurable, but they had all been a critical part of his discovery. They had all been different, but they all had one thing in common—the fact that they had a pussy. Yet none of them, not one, had tasted like Juliette. They hadn't felt like her ether, which was understandable, because they weren't her. With her, everything felt new, like he was learning it all from ground zero.

Carefully, he swept apart her lips to the wet, pink center. Her opening gleamed beneath the pool of her arousal. It trickled in a clear stream to the second little hole, the one he had yet to discover, but had every intention of doing so.

"Will you let me have your ass?" he wondered out loud.

"My ass?"

Gingerly, he brought a finger to the puckered rosebud already glistening and slick from her juices. He circled it once before giving just a hint of pressure.

Juliette cried out. Her hips jerked, but not to get away.

He pressed a little harder and watched her back tear off the counter. Her pussy clenched and more fluid expelled to coat his exploring fingers.

"I want to be in here," he told her, careful to keep his voice low.

He waited for no reaction or response when lowering his head and flicking a tongue over her clit before moving down to circle her opening with just the tip. The delicious taste of her filled his mouth with every ravenous sweep. His finger continued to tease her back entrance. Her cream mixed with his saliva, creating a slippery enough lubricant to push just past the first bend in his finger. The hot, tight ring gripped him as its owner wailed. It was becoming a task holding her flailing hips steady long enough to lift his mouth to her clit. His free hand left her twitching thigh to plunge two fingers deep inside her pussy.

As multitasking went, Killian was kind of proud of himself. He was somehow able to keep her from leaping off the counter while pumping two fingers in one hole, one finger in the second hole and still maintaining a steady suction on her clit. All the while, Juliette was a writhing, screaming, incoherent mess. Her body was hot enough to cook off of and she was clawing at his head, dragging him close enough to suffocate. But he let her, because there wasn't a fucking thing sexier than his woman lost in her own pleasure because of him.

"Do it!" she sobbed. "Do it! Do it!"

He didn't ask what she meant. He didn't need to.

He turned his fingers to the top of her vagina, to the wet, velvety walls and rubbed in slow, even drags against the bump.

Juliette came apart with a scream that could have shattered glass. She broke with a violence that nearly scalped him when her entire body seized. But he kept pumping and sucking right until she stopped convulsing and her sobs had calmed to pathetic whimpers. Only then did he pull free. The hands tangled in his hair dropped limply to her sides. She lay perfectly immobile except for the brutal rise and fall of her chest and the occasional jolt of her body.

Satisfied by his handiwork, Killian reached for his back pocket and pulled out his wallet and the fresh condom he'd tucked inside. But he was beginning to think he should just start carrying an entire box around with him. Grinning to himself, he tore open his pants and rolled on the rubber. Juliette was still barely coherent when he hoisted himself up on the island with her. Passion glazed eyes opened a slit to peer up at him. That was all he got until he thrust up inside her. The plunge widened her eyes. She gave a weak whine as her sensitive body gripped him with a ferocity that was almost painful. Her hands flew to his hips. Her legs lifted and wound around his ribs.

"Harder," she croaked, emphasizing her demand with the anchoring of her nails into the clenched muscles of his ass.

He was nothing if not compliant.

He fucked her. Hard.

He pounded into her until they were both drenched in sweat and crying out with release. Only then did he slump down over her, crushing her. Their bodies heaved against the others, a symphony of trembling limbs and cracking hearts. It was Juliette going rigid under him that propelled him up onto the balls of his hands to peer down at her.

She was so still, her enormous eyes the only color on her otherwise ashen complexion.

"Juliette?"

She stared up at him like the devil himself had materialized in the room. "Do you think anyone heard us?"

It was on the tip of his tongue to tell her the next city over probably heard them, but the horror in her eyes stopped him.

"I don't think we were that loud," he said instead.

She pressed a hand over her mouth. "I'd be mortified if your men…"

"They are paid very well to turn a deaf ear," he assured her.

"Oh my God…"

"Hey." He lowered the second hand she raised to cover her eyes. "Watching you come alive for me, fall apart for me…" He sucked in a deep breath through his nostrils. "I'm not stopping that for anyone."

Her cheeks continued to glow an alarming red, but she no longer looked horrified. She gave him a pained little smile though, which he took as success.

"It was really nice," she admitted.

He kissed her, long and slow. "Aye, it was."

Drawing back, he dropped down off the island and reached for her. She landed in front of him and quickly began straightening her clothes. He left her just long enough to dispose of the condom and fasten his own clothes before returning. He scooped her panties off the floor before she could and held them open for her to step into.

Juliette stopped. She stared at him with a raised eyebrow.

"Really?"

Killian shrugged. "Gallant, remember?"

Chuckling and shaking her head, she took hold of his shoulders for balance and stepped into the article. He dragged them up her legs and settled them neatly on her hips. He smoothed her skirt over top and stepped back.

"Thank you," she said.

He inclined his head. "Let's see if our food has arrived."

She made a quiet humming sound. "Might want to eat somewhere else though."

Killian burst out laughing. Actual laughing. The sound exploded from somewhere deep in his belly with such a force that it actually startled him. Juliette giggled watching him.

Soft footsteps had them glancing towards the doorway just as Frank stepped into the room. The bigger man paused on the threshold, eyebrows lifted high to a nonexistent hairline. He glanced from Juliette—who fidgeted and brushed nervously at her skirt—to Killian—who cleared his throat and tried to act composed.

"Your food is here, sir," Frank said.

"We'll take it in the dining room," he told the man. "Thank you, Frank."

Bowing his head once, Frank turned and left them.

"I should probably leave afterwards," Juliette said once they were alone. "I haven't been home all day and Vi has a tendency to take that as permission to give Mrs. Tompkins a hard time."

He didn't like that plan. He didn't want her to leave, not until he'd gone to sleep. It might have been a fluke or simple exhaustion, but he'd slept the night before. He'd slept the whole night until dawn. He hadn't jolted awake drowning in his own sweat. He hadn't scrambled to the edge of the mattress and thrown up with the severity of his nightmares. He needed that. He needed her to stay for a few more hours.

"Are you sure you can't stay a few more hours?" he coaxed, cupping her chin and tracing a thumb over her mouth.

TRANSCENDING DARKNESS

She chuckled. "Can you go another round?"
Killian grinned darkly. "You know I can."

Chapter 14

Fall slammed down over them with a vengeance that seemed unwarranted considering what a beautiful summer they'd been having. Vicious cold winds ripped leaves from their branches and turned manicured lawns to a brittle wasteland of frost. It was practically winter without the snow, not that that was too far off.

Juliette normally hated winter. Hated the cold and bulky clothes. She still did, but at least she no longer had to wait for the bus to arrive or leave early to make said bus and be at work on time. John and Tyson arrived promptly every morning in their shiny SUV and drove her wherever she needed to go. A second car, a BMW—also in black—arrived for Vi, which she absolutely loved. Juliette wasn't certain what she told people about why there was a hulking man following her around, but she never complained about it. It probably made her feel like some kind of celebrity. A third car, a van, sat parked outside the house, watching over Mrs. Tompkins. Juliette couldn't imagine what Killian was paying for all the security, but she was grateful for it.

October descended with a flurry of activity at the hotel. Every day was a new request to book the banquet hall for a party. Some were even booking for Christmas, which was lucky as most of the slots were already full. But with the new season and the approaching holidays, more and more people flocked the front counter or kept the phone lines buzzing with hopes of booking a room. Juliette no longer had the assistance of one prickly Celina Swanson so the task was left solely to her to accomplish. Being overwhelmed was an understatement. Her only saving grace was the evenings she spent with Killian, the nights he helped de-stress her in the most amazing and wicked ways. But like all good things, she would leave the warmth of his arms and head home in the predawn hours while he slept. She wouldn't necessarily say it was unfair, because those were their terms of agreement, but there were times she wondered what he would do if she stayed. If she just shut her eyes and let herself sleep the whole night with him. It was the fear of breaking their contract that kept her from finding out. It was the fear of losing him. Sleeping over was just not worth that.

Not that it mattered really.

The months were going by too quickly. It was a sinking comprehension every time she tore a new page off the calendar and realized just how little time she had left with him. It was a cold, sickening sort of slap that filled her with the need to burst into tears or hunt down a wizard to turn the time back. Each time, she was forced to remind herself there were more months left than they'd already used and she shouldn't worry about it. She knew she couldn't use that pep talk forever, but it worked for now.

Halloween was chaos. She never thought a hotel could get busy on a holiday not many people celebrated anymore, but it was absolute madness.

People in various costumes barged in, laughing and barely staying upright as they searched for the many parties being thrown in the rooms upstairs or in the banquet hall. Children scurried in with their plastic pumpkins demanding treats or else and the occasional normal guest looking for a place to crash for the night. It was such insanity that Harold had to get Celina to help Juliette man the front, Celina who had yet to forgive Juliette for taking her job. She and Harold were no longer sleeping together, which Harold seemed to regret more than Celina. Juliette kept feeling like she was in a teenage love story the way he kept watching Celina, like his entire world had been shattered while she went on to flirt with anything on two legs. Juliette didn't know who she wanted to hit more.

By the end of the night, she was ready to bang her head against the nearest wall and hope for a concussion. Her nerves were frayed. She was exhausted and hungry and all she wanted was to curl up in Killian's arms and let him make it all better. But the clocks had banded together to torment her. They ticked by with a slowness that was pure torture.

"Oh, I'll take him!" Celina blurted suddenly just as Juliette was contemplating a nap under the counter.

Her head came up just as a tall, beautiful man stopped directly in front of her.

"Killian!"

Her heart leaped. Her face blossomed into an unstoppable smile that lifted the exhaustion off her shoulders and chased away the gloom in her eyes. Had there not been customers in the lobby, she probably would have catapulted herself over the counter, straight into his arms.

"Hello love," he said in that panty-melting drawl of his. "Long night?"

Juliette exhaled, the sound thick with all her joy at seeing him. "The longest." She looked him over, taking in his dark trousers tucked beneath a long, wool coat. "Are you headed to a party?"

"Without you?" He raised an eyebrow. "Not likely." He reached into the front of his coat. "I'm here to get a room."

Juliette blinked. "A room? Here? Why?"

He withdrew his wallet and eyed her. "It's Halloween," he said like that answered everything, but it didn't. At least, not to her. "Is that all right?"

"Of course it's all right." Celina hip chucked her way next to Juliette. Had Juliette not been semi braced, she would have fallen over. "I'm sure we can find you something ... suitable."

Juliette opened her mouth to tell the woman to go deep throat a bottle somewhere, when the hotel doors opened and a crack of plastic filled the lobby. All heads turned as a boy of five came barreling in, plastic guns waving and snapping in the air. He was dressed head to toe as a cowboy, right down to the leather chaps and boots. Behind him, a tired woman staggered in just as the boy held out his guns at Juliette.

"Give me candy and no one gets hurt!" he declared from behind his red bandana.

Juliette had to bite down on her lip to keep from laughing as he bolted forward. His straw hat slipped down over his eyes as he ran and he had to nudge it into place with the barrels of his gun. He stopped on the other side of the counter, barely high enough for Juliette to see more than the top of his hat as he tipped his head far back to meet her gaze.

"Justin." His mother came up behind him. "You didn't say please."

"Don't use my name!" the boy exclaimed. "I'm an outlaw."

The mom, rubbing a hand over her face, exhaled. "Say please, Outlaw."

Justin turned back to the counter. "No one gets hurt … please!" He turned back to his mom. "Bag, Mom!"

She passed him over a homemade sack with a dollar sign stitched into the front. He gave her one of his guns and motioned her to pick him up. She did and perched him on her hip.

"In the bag, lady!" he demanded, holding out his bag.

"You best do it," Killian mused. "The man's clearly serious."

"I am serious!" Justin declared, even as his hat slipped down over his eyes again.

Practically in tears with her efforts not to burst out laughing, Juliette pulled out the bowl of candy and dumped a fistful into his sack.

He tipped his hat. "Much obleragated, ma'am."

"Obliged," his mom corrected, setting him down.

Not caring either way, Justin gave her the bag, took his gun and ran for the door, ignoring his mother when she called him back. Groaning, she quickly thanked Juliette and hurried after him. But Justin reached the doors, stopped, spun on his heels and ran back. He shoved his hat as far back over his forehead as possible so Juliette could see his big, blue eyes and a wisp of blonde hair.

"Thank you!" he said, then ran off again.

The two left and Juliette finally gave in.

"He was so cute!" she declared.

"He's a tiny criminal waiting to happen," Celina muttered. "Guns? Really? Is the world not violent enough?"

"Oh come on," Juliette said. "He was adorable and just a kid."

Scoffing, Celina went back to the computer. She opened a new reservation form and began putting in Killian's information. Juliette let her, too caught up in his burning scrutiny to think properly anyway.

"I've already reserved a room," he told Celina without taking his eyes off Juliette.

He gave over his license and waited while his name was searched. Juliette glanced over as Celina pulled up his reservation and her eyebrows rose at the six figures he'd paid for one night in the executive penthouse suite.

"Why do you need a room?" she demanded. "You live twenty minutes away."

"I told you," Killian said calmly as he took his room key and ID. "It's Halloween."

With a devilish grin, he gave her a wink before stalking with fluid grace to the elevators.

"We do not ask guests why they need a room!" Celina hissed once he was gone and Juliette was alone with her once more.

Juliette ignored her, too busy wondering what Killian was up to.

By midnight, there were no more children barging through the doors, but there were plenty of drunken adults. The majority stumbled their way to the counter, demanding keys to their rooms, but had no idea which room or where they put their wallets. It was an absolute nightmare trying to determine if they were really guests in the hotel or lost individuals that needed someone to call them a cab. She was in the process of assuring one man that yes, he had his pants on and no, she had no idea where his wallet had gone to when the phone rang. Juliette lunged on it before Celina could even think of moving.

"Front desk. Juliette speaking."

"Come here," the dark, husky voice murmured in such a gravely purr that her pussy automatically clenched in response.

"I can't just come up," she hissed into the receiver, careful to keep her voice low and her back to Celina. "I still have—"

"Now, Juliette. I want my pussy."

Christ.

Hot liquid need rushed free of her body to soak into her panties.

"Killian..."

"I won't ask again. Bring her to me or I'll come down there and fuck you where you stand."

The line went dead.

Juliette swallowed hard. Her fingers tightened around the plastic as her entire body vibrated with excitement. She knew he wasn't joking. She knew he would do exactly what he promised.

"Who was that?" Celina demanded.

Breathing uneven, Juliette turned to her. "A guest." She licked her lips. "He has a complaint about the room, asked to have someone come up and—"

"Bullshit." Celina narrowed her eyes. "It's that guy that was here, isn't it?"

Juliette darted a frantic glance at the clock behind the desk; he hadn't specified just how much time she had, but it couldn't be very much.

"I don't know what you're talking about," she told the other woman. "I'll be right back."

"I'm reporting this!" Celina shouted after her. "You can't just fuck your boyfriend while you're still on the clock."

Slivers of anger worked through the arousal thrumming through her. Part of it was aimed at Celina for being such a monumental bitch, but the majority of it was aimed at Killian for summoning her like some ... whore when he knew she was working. Didn't he know her job wasn't like his where she could just take an hour off for a quickie? He was going to get her fired damn it!

Fuming by the time she reached his floor, Juliette stormed down the plush corridor to the only suite with the door standing ajar. She slapped it open and marched inside.

Darkness met her. She stumbled into it and staggered to a stop as her eyes struggled to adjust.

"Killian?"

Silence as thick as the endless black crackled around her. Her heart began to hammer as fear crept through the array of emotions she seemed to be going through in a matter of a few minutes. Sweat slickened her palms as she moved them through the space around her, blindly fumbling for something solid.

"Killian, this isn't fun—"

A bang from behind her made her jump six feet into the air. Her scream was swallowed by the hand that clapped over her mouth. Terror coursed fast and hard through her, isolating everything else as she was forcibly dragged deeper into the darkness. She fought, punching and kicking and digging her heels into the carpet. But her captor was stronger.

With a powerful shove, she was sent sprawling face down on what felt like clouds. Her entire body sunk into the folds of what was a mattress. She would have marveled at its softness if her body wasn't humming with adrenaline.

She scrambled up on all fours and made a wild dash to the other side of the bed, not caring if she tumbled off the edge and broke an arm. But her captor, who seemed incredibly apt at seeing in the dark, grabbed her ankle and hauled her back. The momentum sent her down on her face once more. She tried to scream, but the hand was back. The bed dipped as her captor climbed on top of her, straddling the back of her legs. A hard chest pressed into her heaving back as he bent in close.

"Quiet," a painfully familiar voice whispered directly into her ear. The hand on her mouth lifted and stroked lovingly against her cheek, another familiar gesture that had her heart racing with a mind numbing sort of relief. "Or I'll have to punish you."

"Killi—"

A bit of twisted fabric was forced between her lips, silencing her. It was fastened at the back of her head. Her wrists were caught off the mattress and chained together at the small of her back with rope. It was all done so quickly. She had barely taken two breaths and she was restrained.

Behind her, something heavy struck the floor. There was a rustle of fabric and she knew he was undressing. She heard the tear of foil, the snap of rubber and shivered.

They had never played this game before, but she would play her part.

Twisting over, she kicked out, not hard, but hard enough to earn a pained grunt when her foot caught some part of him. Not waiting to see what would happen next, she rolled sideways towards the other side of the bed. But he was faster. His hands twisted in the material of her skirt and she was dragged back to him, kicking and screaming. She was forced onto her back and crushed by the weight he settled over her. He was naked and hot. And God she wanted him.

Heart palpitating in a tangled mess of excitement, arousal and fear, Juliette thrashed, ignoring the pain in her shoulders from having her arms trapped under her. She garbled insults at him that he no doubt couldn't understand. The fabric was soaked with her spit and was chaffing the corners of her mouth, but she didn't care.

"Naughty lamb," he growled into the side of her throat, his hips grounding a rock hard cock against the apex of her thighs. "I warned you."

The tear of fabric echoed through the room as he tore her clothes apart with his bare hands. Her cry of outrage was not fake this time. She bucked wildly, but he was on her thighs and her arms were useless.

"I am going to kill you!" she shrieked, but it came out unintelligible and was ignored.

Sharp teeth closed around her bare nipple. The sweet pain scattered across her skin and added to the fire roaring in her belly. There was nothing gentle about the way he was assaulting her. Every nip, suck, caress was designed to leave marks and she was whimpering for more.

She gasped when his hands were on her again, pulling and adjusting her across the bed, twisting her around so her face was mashed into the mattress and her ass was in the air. The cool air whispered against the wetness between her legs, sending a shiver through her.

Then he was inside her, fast and hard and without any warning. Her muffled cry burned into fabric. The familiar feel of his cock stretching her sang up her spine and her body immediately tightened around him, welcoming him, sucking him in deeper.

Her captor groaned. His grip cut bruises into her hips as he pistoned wildly inside her. Blunt fingers reached around and fondled her blood filled clit, coaxing her over the edge with him. She came with his name burning into the gag. Her channel rippled around his cock, triggering his release.

He withdrew and moved away just long enough to snap the lamp on. Juliette groaned as the sudden explosion of light punched her in the eyes. The bed dipped once more and Killian turned her over gently. He pried the gag free and wiped the sides of her mouth with his thumbs.

"All right?" he asked, searching her face intently.

She glowered at him. "No, I'm not all right!" she snapped. "You tore my clothes, you animal!"

The asshole actually smirked. "I warned you not to fight me." His hand closed around her ankle and she was dragged lower on the mattress. Her leg was tossed across his lap so she was splayed open wide with him between her calves. "I told you to be a good girl and let me…" He bent over her pussy and kissed her lips. Juliette groaned, her hips reflexively twitching. "Fuck you."

He worked her clit with his tongue until she was thrashing all over again. Her heel dug into the mattress as she writhed and pushed against him. It was harder to do with her hands bound and one foot resting in his lap, but she was sure she'd die if he stopped, which he did. Then he rose and stood over the bed to study her.

She must have looked an absolute mess what with her clothes in tattered pieces hanging off her and her legs lewdly thrown open wide. With her arms at her back, her chest was pushed out, the nipples sharp points begging for his attention. But the way he was watching her, she could have been a giant steak and he was starving.

He took his cock in hand, full reawakened and leaking. Juliette watched the steady pump of his fist, her core muscles flexing. Her hips wiggled across the sheets, wishing her hands were free so she could at least ease some of the pressure. Killian grinned, knowing perfectly well what he was doing to her. He reached for the dresser and pulled on a new condom. Her knees parted wide even before he climbed over her.

"Now!" she breathed, desperate. "Now, Killian. Please!"

Without missing a beat, he joined them. Slowly. So very slowly. It took ages for his full length to be sheathed inside her. Ages that had her head spinning and her whole body quivering wildly. Killian watched her as though she were some experiment he just couldn't understand. His features never lost their dark hunger, but it was underlined by fascination and something else. On either side of her head, his arms trembled with his restraint, but he seemed in no hurry to end either of their suffering.

He pulled all the way out before feeding himself back in. He did this so many times Juliette was practically in tears.

"No more!" she begged. "Please. Please, Killian."

His elbows creaked as he lowered himself on his forearms. His weight settled more comfortably over her. He bent his head and kissed her, gently at first. But the kiss increased as his thrusts did, until both were brutal and angry. Juliette welcomed it all as her body finally caught the release it had been begging for.

Against her neck, he muttered something she couldn't understand as he came. His body shuddered and went momentarily limp before he quickly shot up and reached to untie her hands.

Relief prickled the raw skin around her wrists and the soreness in her shoulders. The lines were faint, but she rubbed them anyway and peered up at the man watching her.

"That was different."

The corner of his mouth lifted. "Thought you'd like it."

She shrugged, her mouth twisting up at the corners. "I did once I got over being scared out of my mind. Thanks for that, by the way."

His hand lifted to the side of her face in a loving caress that made her insides flutter. "I would never let that happen. I would kill anyone who ever touched you like that."

Not sure what possessed her to do it, maybe it was just the tangle of fierce anger and determination glowing across his face, but she scooted over to him and climbed into his lap. Her arms went around his shoulders and she nuzzled into his neck where the skin smelled of spices and something wild she could never put her fingers on.

He held her back. He closed her up in his arms and cradled her to his chest.

It was a rare thing, this moment of absolute intimacy. He hadn't really held her since the afternoon he told her he'd saved her from Arlo. Being held during sex or a few minutes after wasn't the same thing. Normally, she never initiated it either for the same reason she couldn't look at a calendar without her stomach hurting. It was mind fucking and dangerous. But neither of them pulled away.

"I should go," she murmured at last. "I have an hour left, not that it matters." Carefully, she got to her feet. "I'm pretty sure I'm fired."

"You're not fired." He rose and moved to a chair pushed up next to the window in the corner of a beautiful bedroom. He picked up a pretty black and pink box and returned to her. "And you're not going back tonight. I have other plans."

Frowning, she took the box and set it on the bed. Killian moved aside to let her push back the pink tissue paper.

The fabric shimmered as she drew it from its resting place. It spilled through her fingers in a ripple of white satin woven through with fine, silver threads that matched the thick silver straps that ran lengthwise from under the left arm down the right hip. It circled around the back in three ropes that hooped over the right shoulder. At a first glance it almost reminded her of the light dresses Greek women used to wear, but the front was plated beneath the strips and there was a long cut up the right leg that went dangerously close to her hipbone.

Dress still in hand, she turned to Killian. "This is a bit ... fancy for a hotel clerk."

Beautifully naked, Killian moved with fluid confidence to the settee opposite the chair and hooked a finger through the hanger of a garment bag. He lifted it to study closely before turning to her.

"I told you, you're not going back tonight," he told her simply.

"Killian..." Her exasperated sigh was met with a carefully neutral expression from him. "By now, Celina is probably having a fit in Harold's office about me running up here to screw my boyfriend, which by the way, I did not appreciate!"

An eyebrow rose. "Getting screwed by your boyfriend?"

"You know what I mean!" she shot back. "You calling down there and threatening to fuck me in the middle of the foyer just because you were horny and couldn't wait two hours."

"Oh sweetheart." He moved towards her and stopped once he had her face properly tipped up to his. "That wasn't a threat. That was a very clear promise."

"Killian!" She set the dress down before she dropped the thing that probably cost more than her entire house. "This is my job! You can't just—"

"I can when your shift was over and you were free to get fucked."

Juliette frowned. "What are you talking about? I know my schedule. I had two hours."

"I promise you didn't."

Leaving him watching, she stalked to the phone on the nightstand and called down to the front. She braced herself for Celina's sultry purr to answer.

"It's me, Celina," Juliette said, doing her best not to grit her teeth. "Can you check my schedule for tonight?"

"I made an official report!" the woman retorted venomously. *"So it doesn't really matter—"*

"Can you please just check?" Juliette snapped.

She heard Celina's huff. Then the click of keys. Then there was a too long silence that made her nervous.

"This can't be right..." Celina muttered at long last. *"I checked yesterday and it said you were working until three."*

"So, I'm not working until three?" Juliette asked cautiously.

"It says you were off at one."

Juliette turned to look at Killian who was watching her with an almost catlike grin.

"This doesn't make sense!" Celina said. *"I saw it—"*

"Thank you, Celina." Juliette hung up and faced the man behind her fully. "What did you do?"

Killian blinked. "Why do you always assume I did something?"

"Because Celina and I both know I was supposed to work until three. Somehow, mysteriously, that time was changed so I could get off early, which is convenient since you arrived and summoned me upstairs."

"I didn't summon," he mumbled, looking genuinely offended. "I requested your presence."

"Killian, you can't do stuff like that!" She hated the frustrated whine in her tone, hated that she wanted to stomp her feet and scream at him. "You are going to get me fired and I am going to be so pissed that I might set all your clothes on fire."

He visibly recoiled. "That's a little excessive, isn't it?"

"No!" she barked. "It's not. It's self-preservation and since you like to meddle in my affairs ... you know what," she broke off, realizing something. "In the contract you stated perfectly well that I was not allowed to interfere with your business. So why do you get to come meddle in mine?"

The garment bag was tossed down on the bed next to her dress and he folded his arms, his posture as angry as hers.

"I have not meddled in your business," he said with a deadly calm that almost made her back down.

"Then explain the lost two hours," she shot back.

"Poor scheduling. A typo."

The anger washed out of her, not because there was a possibility that he could be right, which he could have been, mistakes happened. But because she was inexplicably exhausted. No part of her wanted to be upright anymore. Maybe it was adrenaline from being scared wearing off or the rush that always came with having mind blowing sex finally waning, but all she wanted to do was crawl into bed and sleep.

Instead, she walked over to where he'd tossed his white dress shirt neatly over his folded trousers and pulled it on. Then she gathered up her ruined clothes and tossed them into the trash. Half under the bed, a pair of heavy duty night vision goggles lay forgotten. That must have been the thud she heard and how he was able to see so clearly in the dark. She left them there.

"Juliette…"

She shook her head. "I'm fine," she lied.

"You're angry," he argued.

She stopped to meet his gaze. "I'm not. I'm not sure what I am."

He studied her with those calculating eyes, no doubt trying to assess just how to go about handling the situation.

"What part of this upset you the most?" he asked at last. "Tell me and I'll fix it."

Because that was what he did. He fixed things. He was forever fixing problems for her and while it was so good to finally not have to do them herself for once, she knew she needed to put a stop to it before she became so dependent on him that when their time was up, she didn't recognize herself.

"I just want the truth."

He considered that solemnly and gave a curt nod. "All right. I changed your schedule."

Some of the tightness loosened around her chest. "Why?"

"Because I wanted to take you somewhere and it was supposed to be a surprise."

Her gaze went to the dress. "Why not just tell me that? I could have booked the time off—"

He shook his head. "That defeats the purpose of a surprise."

She knew she could have given him a hundred different ways he could have gone about the situation, but another question came to mind.

"How? How did you get it changed?"

He opened his mouth. Closed it. A sort of grudging acceptance tightening his mouth.

"I asked Harold to do it."

"And he just did it?"

Killian nodded. "Basically, yes."

A more disturbing thought occurred to her. "Tell me you didn't get me the promotion," she whispered.

"I didn't get you the promotion," he mimicked without missing a beat.

"Promise!"

"I promise."

Inclined to believe him, having no reason not to, she relented. Her gaze went to the dress, her curiosity getting the better of her.

"What was the surprise?" she asked.

"A party," he said with a deep exhale. "But we might have missed that train."

She followed his gaze to the alarm clock next to the bed. It was already creeping to nearly three.

"It's over?" she asked.

"If it's not, it will be soon," he answered.

Guilt tugged at her chest. "I'm sorry."

Killian shrugged. "It won't be the first or the last."

It was said flippantly, like it didn't bother him either way, but she could see it in his eyes before he turned away. He had really wanted to take her, had gone through the trouble of getting her a dress and making sure she had the time off. He had even come to her, to her hotel so they could spend some time together before they left.

"Killian…" She went to him. Her hands lifted to his face and she arched on her toes to meet his mouth. She kissed him softly. "I love the dress."

Dark pools lingered over her face, moved over her mouth before settling on her eyes. "You'll have to try it on for me."

She started to, but stopped. She turned back to him with her lip caught between her teeth.

"How about I make it up to you instead?"

A dark eyebrow quirked in clear interest. "I'm listening."

Grinning, she picked up the dress, folded it neatly, and lay it down amongst the tissue once more. She replaced the lid and faced him once more.

"That'll be my surprise."

His eyes glinted. "I do like your surprises."

Chuckling, she went back to him and circled his shoulders with her arms. "Good. Now kiss me."

Firm hands settled on her sides and drew her more securely against his naked chest. "Such a demanding witch."

His mouth dropped to hers.

Juliette left Killian face down across the hotel mattress, naked and fast asleep as she pulled his dress shirt and boxers on. It was mortifying, and nothing fit, but having to roll the waistband of the boxers a few times was better than sneaking out of the hotel naked. She picked up his phone off the nightstand, found Frank's number and sent a quick text to bring Killian fresh clothes … when he had the chance. Please and thank you. She hit send, set the phone down and gathered her shoes and the box with the dress before sneaking out of the room.

After being a maid for the last four years, the extravagance of the suite no longer impressed her as she tiptoed across the sitting area towards the door. Everything was ivory and gold and gleamed to a stubborn sheen and felt as impersonal as it could possibly get.

Glancing back over her shoulder once, Juliette wrenched open the front door and skirted out quickly.

"Miss Romero?"

Juliette yelped in fright at the deep, rumbling voice that seemed impossibly loud in the deafening silence. The box and her shoes flew from her grasp as she whirled around. They hit the ground with a noisy clatter as both hands jumped to her chest.

Frank regarded her coolly.

"Jesus!" she hissed. "You scared the crap out of me, Frank."

He had the decency to tip his chin down a notch. "My apologies, ma'am. I received your message."

Still struggling to force her heart out of her throat and back into her chest, Juliette turned and gathered her things back up. She stood once more and faced the man.

"I had an accident with my clothes," she explained, not sure why, but being embarrassed enough not to be able to stop herself. "So I'm borrowing Killian's. He's sleeping right now, but I'm sure he'll want clothes for when he leaves."

He inclined his head. "I will see to it." He motioned her towards the elevators. "Please allow me to walk you to the car."

Juliette hesitated. "Is it safe to leave Killian alone? I mean, I'm sure it is. The hotel has cameras, but I'm okay to walk down alone. Thank you."

Frank studied her a long moment. "Mr. McClary would insist," he said at last.

Juliette glanced at the closed door and thought of Killian in bed, alone and vulnerable.

"Maybe you could walk me to the elevators and have John and Tyson meet me at the bottom?" she suggested. "I don't want him left alone," she whispered and immediately felt foolish.

The guy was in a hotel. What could possibly happen? But if Frank thought she was being overdramatic and ridiculous, he never said as much. He raised his left wrist to his mouth and spoke calmly and clearly into the device, all the while watching her.

"Rendezvous to the elevators," he said.

If someone responded, Juliette didn't hear it. But Frank nodded his head and motioned her to start walking.

At the elevators, he pushed the button and then waited with her while the cart rolled up. When it arrived and the door opened, John greeted her. He bowed his head once.

Juliette turned to Frank. "Thank you."

"Goodnight, ma'am."

Casting a glance down the hallway in the direction of Killian's room, she stepped into the cart and watched the door roll shut.

Tyson was waiting below for them. The pair flagged either side of her as they made a quick beeline for the front doors. Juliette paused long enough to slip her feet into her shoes before following the two to the SUV parked outside.

The van was still across the street from her house when they rolled into her driveway next to Phil's BMW. Juliette glanced at it as she hopped out. John closed the door behind her and started guiding her to the front door, but she dug her heels in.

"John?"

"Yes ma'am?"

Juliette peered at the van again and then the BMW where Phil was rolling down the driver's side window to talk to Tyson. It had never dawned on her, but standing there, seeing the cars and how they never seemed to move unless she or Vi were headed somewhere, she couldn't help wondering if the men ever left or did they stay there and wait? All that time, she'd been under the impression that they left really late and arrived really early. Now, she wasn't so sure.

"Where do you guys sleep?" she asked.

"Ma'am?" John looked genuinely perplexed.

She faced him. "Do you guys go home? Or do you go to Killian's?"

"No ma'am."

Juliette started. "Are you telling me that you guys live in my driveway? I mean, what about the bathroom and meals and … sleep? How do you sleep?"

John shifted uncomfortably. "We sleep in shifts, ma'am."

Juliette frowned. "In the car?"

"Yes ma'am."

"That … that is horrible!" she gasped. "I have a spare room inside and a sofa and I can get some air mattresses—"

John's face softened for the first time since she'd met him. "That's real kind of you, ma'am, but it's our job."

"That's ridiculous," she protested. "How can you do your jobs properly when you're exhausted and hungry? No. I insist. Don't argue with me!" she warned when he opened his mouth.

Not waiting for him to respond again, she marched to the van and knocked on the backdoor. It opened almost immediately and two faces peered back at her.

"Come inside," she told the men she couldn't remember the names of. "Both of you." She stalked back to the driveway, pausing only long enough to catch Phil's eye. "You too."

She stormed inside as quietly as one can storm without waking everyone up. She left the door open as she kicked out of her shoes and hurried to the hallway closet. She tore out blankets and pillows. In the foyer, she could hear the shuffle of feet as the group entered the house.

Arms full of everything they could use to sleep on, she charged into the living room and dumped it all on the sofa. Breathing hard, she swiped hair back from her face and eyed the crowd.

"I'll get air mattresses tomorrow, or cots. For tonight, I have a bed upstairs if you don't mind doubling up and there's the sofa and unfortunately the floor. The bathroom is just down the hall, same with the kitchen. Help yourselves to whatever."

With that, she turned and left them staring after her as she headed upstairs to shower and climb into bed.

"They're there to protect you, not shack up with you, Juliette!"

Juliette stared hard at the man glowering back at her from the expense of his shiny office. Her own arms were folded, her lips pursed thin. She wasn't sure how he found out, but she guessed one of his men had thought to inform him of her change in his orders.

"They're not *shacking up* with me," she retorted hotly. "But it's cruel to let them sleep outside in a car when they are there because of me. Plus, what difference does it make, Killian? Outside, inside, they can still do their job, but at least they'll be fed and rested. Besides, I have the room for it! Please don't make them go back out there."

With a vicious growl that made her think she'd maybe won, he scrubbed hard at his face with a palm. He pinched the bridge of his nose and squeezed his eyes shut tight.

"They are not puppies," he bit out finally.

"Exactly. They are men who are putting their lives on the line to protect someone they don't even know." She sighed and moved closer a step. "Please let them stay."

His hand dropped and he peered at her for what felt like hours. He looked no closer to thinking what she'd done was right, but the lines around his face weren't as harsh and she took that as a good sign.

"You're impossible, you know that, right?"

Knowing a win when she heard one, Juliette beamed. She crossed the rest of the space between them and kissed him.

"Thank you."

He continued to scowl. "I'll want something back for this," he informed her.

Grinning, she reached up and tugged lightly on his tie the way she'd wanted to do since she'd arrived. The burgundy strip running down the length of his white dress shirt made her think of fresh blood. Seeing it against his chest closed a fist of ice around her chest. So she felt no guilt tearing it off and tossing it somewhere over her shoulder. With it gone, her hands were free to glide up the toned valley of his beautiful chest to curl over his shoulders.

"I have a meeting—"

"A different tie," she whispered. "Any other color. Not red."

If he thought her request as odd, he never questioned it. Instead, his hands settled on the curve of her hips and she was drawn forward.

"What will you do today?" he asked.

"I promised the boys air mattresses," she said, skimming her fingers over the hot skin along the back of his neck between collar and hairline. "And we need food in the house."

"So you're going to spend your first day off shopping?"

Her mouth curved and she hummed softly. "I guess so."

His fingers skated up the length of her spine, traced each bump up the span to cup the back of her neck with five strips of heat that sent a wave of electricity through her. He kissed her lightly. The kind of kiss that had her toes curling and her heart dancing. It was the kind of kiss she loved and hated coming from him. It said too much when she knew it shouldn't.

"Come back when you're finished," he murmured against her mouth. "Wait for me in my room."

Her eyes opened and she found herself caught in the endless black of his. "I will."

His head began to lower once more when a scuffle from the doorway had them pulling apart.

Frank in his navy blue suit and a deep scowl stood blocking a group of men Juliette didn't recognize. Whoever they were, their presence had Killian stiffening and his arms quickly dropping from around her. The unexpected abandonment had Juliette staggering back a step in confusion.

"Leave," he said to her quietly, his eyes full of something that curdled all the happiness inside her. "Now!"

Not asking, Juliette ducked her head and walked out at a quick pace without looking at anyone. She knew enough about that part of Killian's life not to linger. Whoever these men were, they were not men she wanted memorizing her face or why she was with Killian.

"You're early, Mr. Smith," was the last thing she heard Killian say before she hit the hallway at a near run.

John and Tyson moved to her side the moment she tumbled to the bottom of the stairs. The front doors were open wide to a group of men, men who didn't belong to Killian and men who did. They seemed to be in a silent battle on the threshold that filled the air with a ripple of tension so thick, it was a near, physical heat wave washing over her skin. Sweat dampened her spine and her strides faltered.

John grabbed her elbow and hauled her the rest of the way by force to the SUV.

"Is he safe?" she demanded.

"My orders are to remove you off the premises," was her brisk answer.

"John!"

She was shoved into the back and the door was slammed shut behind her. John jumped in behind the wheel as Tyson took the seat next to her. The wheels screeched on marble as they tore through the open gates.

"John!" she shouted again. "Is Killian going to be okay? Who were those men?"

Nobody answered. Honestly, she wasn't expecting one.

It was ridiculous to be concerned for the safety of a person who had chosen that life, who had chosen to bring that kind of evil into his own home, but she was scared numb, scared of what was happening, but more scared of losing Killian. She tried to tell herself that *Mr. Smith*—if that really was his name—was in Killian's territory, which meant that Killian would have the higher hand. But it didn't matter. He was in there with what was clearly a threat and Juliette had no way of knowing if he was all right.

"Ma'am?" John was watching her through the rearview mirror, his hazel eyes apologetic, but calm. "Where would you like to go?"

Home.

That was her first thought and it even worked its way to her throat before she swallowed it down; going home wasn't going to make her worry any less. In fact, she was pretty certain she would spend all her time pacing and badgering everyone if there had been any news.

"The mall," she whispered in a sort of garble when her tongue refused to unglue from the roof of her mouth. "The mall, please," she repeated once she had regained control of her mouth.

John inclined his head.

"We will be informed when it will be safe to return you," Tyson said from beside her in a gruff, almost accented tone she couldn't quite place.

"You mean when those men are gone," she guessed.

Tyson said nothing, but she got a feeling he was trying to make her feel better. While she appreciated the gesture, it made no dent in her giant wall of worry.

The trip through the mall ended with her packing five heavy duty cots, foam mattresses, blankets and pillows into three carts. Tyson and John helped push the heavier one. The woman at the front asked if they were going camping and Juliette could only smile, because she could think of no answer. It wasn't until she was hit with the total that she realized she hadn't thought her plan out well enough. Mind lost in thoughts of Killian, she hadn't done her normal, diligent shopping. The one that involved price checking and comparing. There was no way she had enough.

She started to open her mouth when Tyson handed over a familiar, black card to the cashier, who happily took it before Juliette could get her wits about her.

"I know that card!" Juliette burst out, glowering accusingly at Tyson. "What are you doing with it?"

"We were asked to hold on to it in the event that you would need it," Tyson said as though reciting something he'd read.

"Unbelievable," Juliette muttered. "I told him I didn't want the thing."

The cashier looked uncertainly from Juliette to Tyson, the card trembling slightly between her fingers.

"So ... would you like to use a different—?"

"No," Juliette grumbled miserably, knowing full well her card would definitely not cover the cost. Plus, she had promised the men proper sleeping arrangements. "It's fine. But I still don't want it," she told Tyson, who said nothing.

When it was time to sign, Tyson scribbled something unintelligible across the slip and passed it back to the cashier. They loaded their things back into the carts and left the mall.

"We need to make a run to the store," she told the two. "If that's all right?"

"Yes ma'am," John said as he and Tyson packed their purchases into the back of the SUV.

It turned out that she would need Killian's ten grand credit card a second time that day. With five grown men in the house, plus Juliette, Vi and Mrs. Tompkins, her normal tiny grocery bill had blossomed to digits she would never have thought possible if she hadn't seen it with her own eyes. The SUV was stuffed in all manner of places, like a game of Tetris until there was just enough room for the three of them to sit, and even then, Juliette was forced to put her feet up on a case of Mac and Cheese.

"Have you heard anything from Killian or Frank?" she asked Tyson as they drove home.

Tyson shook his head. "No ma'am."

"Do his meetings normally take this long?"

"I wouldn't know, ma'am."

Not sure what else to do, she sat back and watched as the city morphed into the quiet of the suburbs. The children were just getting home from school when they finally turned up her street. Phil's BMW was parked in the driveway, a clear indication that Vi had come straight home rather than go anywhere with her friends ... again. It was becoming a habit that was beginning to concern Juliette. It was as odd as the other subtle little changes she wasn't sure what to do with.

Grabbing several items, she hopped out and hurried inside. The two men from the van, Javier and Laurence, had set up camp in the front room. They had pushed a plastic fold out table against the bay window overlooking the street and sat taking notes. No doubt they knew more about her neighbors than even she did. Neither glanced up when Juliette marched in and made a straight line to the kitchen in the back.

Vi was there, bent over the island, listening to Mrs. Tompkins as the woman went on about some boy she'd known as a girl. The thing that perplexed Juliette beyond reasoning was the fact that Vi was actually listening. No. She was smiling and listening. There wasn't a sneer or insult in sight.

Across the room, standing straight and immobile, was Phil with his salt and pepper hair, kind blue eyes and built frame. He wore the same navy suit as all of Killian's men, but he had a folded, white, napkin tucked into the breast pocket of his blazer. He stood watching the scene with a sort of amusement the others never showed. Granted, the others didn't show much of any emotion. Not even Frank. But Phil had laugh lines around his eyes and a perpetual sort of grin around his mouth. He looked more like someone's really handsome father than a bodyguard.

"Hey," Juliette said, taking her bags to the counter and setting them down. "You're home."

Vi shrugged. "I had homework."

It didn't matter how many times she heard it, the phenomenon never failed to make her want to check Vi's forehead for a temperature.

"So, did you do it? Your homework."

Vi gave a brisk bob of her head. "Yup."

"I watched her do it," Mrs. Tompkins vouched, kneading a large ball of dough.

Impressed, but severely disturbed, Juliette nodded. "Well, great! I bought groceries so I think I'll start on supper."

"You?" Vi blurted, darting up. "You're going to make supper? Like yourself?"

Juliette scowled. "I have made supper before."

Vi spun towards Phil. One finger shot out and jabbed straight at Juliette.

"She's trying to poison us. Tackle her, Phil."

The lines around Phil's mouth deepened in the ghost of a smile, but he didn't speak.

Juliette sputtered. "What?"

Vi speared her hips with her fists. "Do you even remember how to cook?"

"I can cook!" Juliette protested, as John and Tyson shuffled in carrying more bags. They dumped them down in front of the island and trudged out to get the rest. "I've cooked before."

"The last thing you made was pasta and it smelled like burnt feet."

"I could make a chicken casserole," Mrs. Tompkins offered.

"No!" Vi and Juliette shouted on unison.

"Thank you," Juliette added quickly. "But you've already done so much."

Mrs. Tompkins went back to her dough.

"We should order pizza," Vi decided. "We haven't had it in ages."

It was true. Juliette couldn't even remember the last time they ordered anything.

"But I just spent a fortune on groceries!" she protested.

Vi shrugged. "So? It's food. It's not like it's going to go to waste. We'll just put it all away and order pizza tonight."

It wasn't the wisdom behind the rationality that convinced her. It was the almost cuteness of her sister's hopeful face when Vi puckered her bottom lip and did that doe-eyed begging thing that was impossible to ignore.

"Fine!" Juliette muttered. "But only tonight and only because you did your homework without a fuss ... again."

With a squeal, Vi bolted from the room, yelling something about putting in the call. Phil started to follow her, but Juliette stopped him.

"What's going on with her?" she asked.

"Ma'am?"

He had a nice voice, she thought. Masculine and deep.

"Well, I know my sister and that is not her," Juliette said, motioning with the jerk of her chin in the direction her sister had taken. "Did you sell her to aliens?"

Phil gave a silent chuckle. "No ma'am."

"If you did, you can tell them to keep her. I like this one better."

With an inclination of his head, he followed Vi into the next room. Juliette went to finish helping John and Tyson bring in the groceries. Most of it had been brought in and left on the kitchen floor, but there was still the bedding to haul in. Then there was the process of instructing the men to shove the dining room table to one corner and set the cots up in its place in a makeshift bedroom. She let them sort out who got which bed and where they wanted to set up while she put the groceries away.

Forty five minutes later, the pizza arrived. The doorbell rang and it was like a bomb went off as everyone scrambled into position. Javier moved to the door as Laurence shifted to brace in the doorway between the foyer and the living room with his gun drawn. Tyson took his place next to Juliette as John stood on the threshold of the kitchen. Everyone had a gun.

"Is that necessary?" Juliette demanded of no one in particular.

"I'll get it!" Vi scrambled down the stairs at that exact moment with Phil right on her heels.

He grabbed her arm and tugged her to a stop three steps from the bottom. He said something and she made no move to continue. Juliette would have been severely impressed if Javier hadn't taken that moment to yank open the door.

The thing Juliette found hilarious about the whole situation wasn't the look of stunned horror on the pizza boy's face at having guns aimed at his face or that he would no doubt go back to work and tell them about the crazy house, but that Mrs. Tompkins continued to roll and thump on her clump of dough like nothing weird was happening. It was the same sort of indifference she'd given when Juliette had explained why there was a van parked outside or why Vi needed an escort everywhere she went. She had been honest with both of them and yet Mrs. Tompkins had taken it with a nod of her head and nothing else. Vi had been furious at the very idea of being followed anywhere. She had threatened to run away, to never speak to Juliette again. But one day with Phil and she had forgotten all about her rage. Juliette didn't want to question a good thing, but she was beginning to wonder if maybe Killian had found a way to implant people with chips designed to make them do whatever he wanted. In Vi and Mrs. Tompkins'ss case, to not fight the transition. To accept that they would be protected. She knew that was impossible and still she couldn't help wonder.

The pizza was brought into the kitchen and set on the counter. Plates were handed out and everyone grabbed a slice. Everyone, except Juliette. She kept glancing at the clock, watching the minutes sift away and still nothing from Killian. It had been hours. How could he not be finished?

"Have you heard anything from Killian?" she asked Tyson, who set his pizza down, chewed, and swallowed before answering.

"No ma'am."

The knot in her stomach tightened. She stared at the front door and tried not to let her imagination go wild.

"Can I have the keys to the SUV, please?" she asked him, holding out her palm.

Tyson peered at her. "I can't do that, ma'am. We were given orders to keep you here until further instructions."

She curled her fingers and drew her hand back. "Fine. I'll find my own way there."

Leaving the kitchen, she stalked down the hall. She made it as far as midway to the door when her path was blocked by John.

"We can't allow you to go there, ma'am," he told her in that infuriatingly calm manner.

"You can't stop me!" she shot back. "He could be hurt or worse and we may never know if we're sitting here doing nothing."

"There are protocols—"

"I don't give a shit about your protocols. I just care about making sure Killian's all right. It's been hours and no meeting takes this long. It means something has happened, something horrible or someone would have already gotten in touch. Now, you can take me or you can get out of my way."

John never so much as batted an eye. "I'm sorry, ma'am."

"Don't sorry me!" she practically screamed. "Just move."

"Can't do that, ma'am."

Maddeningly close to tears, Juliette glowered at him. Her balled fists trembled at her sides with the need to punch someone, but she knew it was pointless. He was bigger and perfectly capable of restraining her if need be.

"Juliette." Gentle hands took her arm and she was tugged away from the wall of muscle keeping her from the door. Vi peered at her with an ocean of sympathy Juliette had never once seen on her sister's face. "Come on," she said, motioning with the jerk of her head towards the stairs.

She let herself be led away. No one stopped them, not even Phil, who followed, but stayed in the hall when Vi pulled Juliette into her bedroom and shut the door behind them.

"You're not going to get through them," she told Juliette. "They're black ops, like top of the line almost assassins. Phil told me," she explained when Juliette stared at her. "They're highly trained killing machines, or something. Anyway, they won't let you leave if they don't want to."

The thought of being held captive in her own home terrified her. It made her wonder what the hell she'd gotten them into, and if something had happened to Killian, how was she going to get them out?

"They're not bad guys," Vi said quickly. "But they'll follow their orders or die."

"I need to see Killian," she said, and heard the desperation in her own voice. "He could be in trouble."

Vi raised an eyebrow. "The guy *is* trouble, Juliette. He's like grade A, crime lord trouble."

"No!" Juliette said too quickly. "He's not. I mean, he is, but he's not a bad person. He's really sweet and kind and one of the most—"

"You love him!" Vi's gasp startled her.

"What? No! No, it's not like that."

"Right, because I constantly worry about people I don't love, you know, just for the hell of it."

"I care about him," Juliette admitted. "He's been very good to us in ways you cannot possibly imagine. We both owe him our lives. I know I do and there isn't any way I can ever repay him."

"Oh, I don't know." Vi grinned at her. "I'm sure you'll find a way."

"Vi!"

"I meant a nice batch of homemade cookies, you pervert." But the mischievous glint in her eyes said otherwise and Juliette laughed.

Juliette sobered and eyed her sister. "This is nice," she said. "Why have we never done this before?"

"You mean sisterly bonding?" Vi teased. "Oh, probably because Mom got sick and I was left alone to take care of her while you and Dad continued to live your lives like nothing was happening. Then, she died and Dad threw himself into a bottle and then in front of a bullet and you just sort of forgot I existed."

All humor vanished. "What? That's not true! Everything I did was for us and what do you mean you had to take care of Mom?"

Vi turned away and moved to flopped down on her bed. "It's like I said, Mom got sick and you went off with your friends and Dad stopped coming home. At least the first few years. Then Dad started gambling and Mom got sicker and you started staying home more. When she was finally at peace, you couldn't get far enough away from me. It's all right though. I was really angry about it for a long time, being abandoned and all, but I worked it out."

It was a tossup what part of all that upset her more, the flat, emotionless tone or the weight behind what she was being told.

Vi had been five when their mother had gotten sick. The first couple of years, their mother had been well enough to carry on in whatever mothers did. It wasn't until the third year that the cancer got too strong for the chemo to fight. By that time, they had already been told they would lose her and there was nothing anyone could do. Juliette remembered needing to get away, away from having to watch the person she loved slowly die before her eyes. She had thrown herself into Stan and her friends and let them help her not think about the bleak future ahead. It was the phone calls on the machine, the ones from the bank and collection agencies and the school that made Juliette begin to see she couldn't keep running. That Vi and her mother needed her.

"Why did you never tell me?"

Vi shrugged. "I didn't think it would matter. You hated me."

"I never..." she trailed off, because as much as she loved her sister, she had also always hated her. From the moment Vi had been brought home, Juliette had never wanted her. "Vi..."

"It's okay. I'm not angry anymore."

Juliette frowned. "Why? I was a horrible sister."

"Phil." There was a softness to her tone when she said his name that prickled along Juliette's neck. "Helped me realize a few things."

Juliette blinked. "Phil?" She jerked a thumb over her shoulder towards the door. "Phil-Phil?"

"Yeah, Phil-Phil. He's been really good to me the last few months."

"Vi..."

Something in Juliette's voice must have given away just how concerned she was becoming, because Vi's head jerked up. Her eyes widened and then narrowed in disgust.

"Don't be gross! He's old enough to be my dad for God sakes. It's just nice to have one of those again, one that doesn't ignore or yell at you for waking him up when he's hungover."

Feeling guilty, Juliette shifted. "Sorry. I just ... I feel like I don't really know you and this new you is so different from the one I'm used to."

Vi snorted. "That's Phil's doing also. He made me see that being angry at the world doesn't bring my family back. The only person I'm hurting is myself."

"Wow," Juliette murmured, hating the bitter tang of jealousy that actually reared its head. "You and Phil talk a lot, huh?"

Vi shrugged. "A bit. I do spend about ninety percent of my time with the guy. I hated that at first. He was always there, you know? Lurking in the shadows, watching my every move. But he grew on me. Now, he's kind of the only friend I've got."

That hurt.

While it wasn't said maliciously, it carved into Juliette like a dagger. It had never dawned on her that Vi would feel alone and abandoned. She had always had an army of friends following her around like loyal puppies. She had a life. How could she possibly feel unwanted?

"But sisterly bonding isn't why I brought you up here." Vi hopped off the bed and rose. "I'm going to help you get out."

It took Juliette a moment to change gears on the conversation.

"What?"

Vi moved quickly to the window across the room and tugged on the lever. The window swung inward soundlessly. Someone—possibly Vi—had sprayed the hinges with WD-40, because everything else in the house squeaked like spirits being tortured. Reaching in, she grabbed the window and tugged. The latches gave seamlessly and the window popped out of the frame, leaving a neat, square hole in the wall. Vi set the window down and turned to Juliette.

"There is a ledge right on the other side," she said in a quick, hushed voice. "Brace your weight there and turn your waist just enough to grab the tree branch. From there, you have to creep across and down, but watch the bottom, there's a root that rises from the ground and my foot gets caught almost all the time. But once you're on the ground, turn left and go into the Ricor's backyard. Their back light doesn't work."

Juliette honestly had no idea what to say or how to react. A part of her was horrified that her sister was so apt at escaping her bedroom. Another part was impressed by the ingenuity and cleverness behind it. But a much larger part was thrilled.

"How long have you—?"

"Since like the fifth grade." Vi smirked. "You didn't honestly think I was up here doing homework, did you?"

Yeah, she kind of had. Now she just felt really stupid.

"I can't believe—"

"Are you going to go or what? They're going to come in here and check soon and you'll miss your chance."

Thinking fast, Juliette hurried to the window. She braced her hands on the ledge and peered over into the darkness below. The ground had become one giant black void that threatened to suck her in. But she didn't think about it. She threw one leg over and then the other and searched for the ledge Vi had mentioned. There was nothing but air for several seconds and then her heel caught it. She twisted her body, hands on the windowsill, and tucked her toes on the lip.

"You're doing great!" Vi encouraged in a low hiss.

Heart palpitating, hands slick with sweat, Juliette stretched her body just enough to turn and grab the thick branch resting on the roof. She wondered if that was something nature had done, or something Vi had done. She decided that now wasn't the time to think about that.

Gingerly, she lifted one foot and stretched it to the thick branch a full two feet away. Her stomach somersaulted and she wondered how the hell Vi did this every night in heels. Breath held, she gave one good shove and propelled herself onto the branch. The thing creaked and wobbled under her weight and it took all her willpower not to squeak.

Vi stuck her head out of the opening in the wall. "Watch for the root!" she reminded her.

Juliette braved a quick nod and started her slow climb downward. She didn't actually let out her breath until her foot hit bottom. Only then did she double over and wheeze. The cool night air swept around her, tearing at her clothes and licking at the sweat soaking her skin. She tried not to pay attention to it as she sprinted across the yard to the low, wooden fence the Ricor's had put up a few years back when they'd gotten their Pomeranian Muffy. She climbed over quickly and made her way up the side of the house to the driveway.

From there, she just ran.

Chapter 15

Getting shot had a unique sort of pain that most other injuries didn't. There was the initial burn as hot metal pierced through flesh. Then the temporary numbness where the brain hasn't fully caught up to what happened. Finally, there was the crippling sting of a fresh burn and the raging throb of being stabbed. It was probably why most criminals preferred guns to knives.

Killian had been shot before so the sensation was a familiar one, yet it never felt better. It still hurt like a mother. But at least the bullet had gone straight through. Digging fragments out was a whole other process he did not want to think about.

"Sir?" Frank entered Killian's bedroom, a phone in one hand and a blood soaked towel in the other, pressed down on the knife wound on his shoulder. "The cleanup crew will be here in an hour for the bodies."

Killian nodded. He heaved one leg down off the bed. Then the other. His body screamed in protest. His skin seemed to be on fire around the hole Frank had stitched up, which seemed to have pissed off the injury. It thrummed with a sort of malicious glee that crawled up the rest of him to antagonize the colorful rainbow splattered across his torso.

Christ, he wanted to throw up.

"Sir, maybe you should stay in bed," Frank advised.

Killian shook his head. "Need to check on the men." He shoved unsteadily to his feet and felt the room tilt. He squeezed his eyes shut as his bearings settled. "How many did we lose?"

He heard Frank exhale heavily. "Five."

Killian opened his eyes, his anger boiling to the very cusp of his control. "Smith?"

"Dead, sir. As are his men. Sir, perhaps you should stay—"

"I'm fine!"

His snarl was like a punch in the gut. It tugged at the stitches beneath the simple slap on bandage and Killian doubled over. Frank's meaty hands were there, grabbing him and hauling him back into bed.

"You are not well enough to go anywhere," Frank stated flatly. "I will see to the men—"

"No, they are my men." But he didn't try getting up again, all his energy having been vaporized. "I will see to them myself."

"Perhaps in the morning then," Frank suggested.

Killian started to shake his head. "No, I need to do it now—"

Frank stiffened. He jerked back with one hand going to the plastic bit in his ear. He said nothing as he listened.

"What?" Killian struggled to get up, but Frank held him down. "Frank!"

Frank lowered the hand. His dark eyes met Killian's.

"It's Miss Romero, sir."

Killian's entire world tilted this time. He felt the very air flicker between black and red. Blood roared Hot between his ears, deafening him to everything but the madness he could feel clawing through him.

"No..." He shoved the other man back with strengths he shouldn't possibly possess considering he could barely keep his eyes open. "Where is she? Where's Juliette?"

"Sir!"

But Killian was already on his feet, his pain numb in the blinding terror pounding through him as he staggered to the door.

Please, God, please don't let her be dead, he prayed over and over again through the thick haze clouding his thoughts. The corridor he'd walked a million times bobbed and swayed in a sick sort of game that twisted his insides. He tried to squeeze his eyes shut and will everything right, but that only amplified the splotches of gray weaving around the corners of his vision. His heart pounded in a wild and frantic tempo of war drums. Each beat resounded through his very bones. But it didn't matter. Not the pain. Not the hot waves crawling up his skin. Not the possibility of tearing his stitches. None of it, except finding Juliette. He needed to find her. He needed to make sure she was all right. The rest wasn't important if he'd lost her.

"Killian!"

Her voice echoed through the hollows of his subconscious, sounding small and far away. He tried to blink, but that only made everything blurrier.

"Juliette…"

Something gave. Maybe it was his legs or his whole body, but everything spun in a cartwheel then the ground vanished from beneath him. There was nothing but a strange floating sensation for several seconds or minutes or hours before he hit the ground with a muffled thud.

"Killian!"

A shadow leapt into the path of the ceiling lights, shielding him from their sharpness. Soft, cold hands cradled his hot cheeks, swept back his damp hair while a broken voice called his name over and over again. Raindrops hit his skin, each one stinging like acid upon contact. He tried to raise a hand or speak, but it hurt to even breathe. Instead, all he could do was close his eyes and give himself over to the numb nothingness on the other side. Eyes the sweet color of caramel were the last things he saw before everything faded to black.

Time was a funny thing when one was running a fever. Everything was a fuzzy, groggy mess between dream and reality. For most of the three days, Killian had no idea which was which. It was all a sickening blur of voices and colors. But the thing they all shared, the singular, solid presence was always Juliette. She seemed to be in every snippet of memory.

Her voice was the thing that kept drawing him back to consciousness. At least, what felt like consciousness; it was the one that came equipped with the blinding pain.

By the fourth day, some of that had dulled to an almost bearable hum. The hole still radiated with its own heat and felt like it was vibrating with its own unique brand of agony, but the rest of him was less tender. He knew because someone kept fussing over him, coaxing food and water into him.

It wasn't until almost a week later that he finally opened his eyes. The room was dark, except for the lamp next to the bed. Beneath it, the alarm clock read three AM. But it was the figure curled up in the chair that caught his attention.

Juliette.

She wasn't hurt. She was there, squished in an uncomfortable position, but alive. Unless she was a figment of his feverish imagination, something his sick mind had conjured to help ease him into acceptance. Not that there was such a thing. There was no peace or accepting that loss. The damn girl had burrowed herself so deep beneath his skin that he couldn't even process anything different.

He studied her in the fine whispers of light spilling through the messy knot of hair confined to the top of her head. It glided along the flushed curve of her cheek, the one not resting on her folded arms. She wore white tights under a loose, white top. Her feet were bare, exposing her dainty toes painted a light purple. Her knees were raised to hold her arms and she had her head tilted to one side. It was a wonder how she was able to sleep that way. He'd have already fallen face first to the ground. But it also made him wonder how long she'd been there. Had she really sat there the entire week, waiting for him to wake up? The thought made his chest hurt, a sort of hurt that had nothing to do with being pummeled by six guys or shot.

Damn it, Juliette. What are you doing?

Taking a deep breath, he called her name. Softly at first. Then louder when she didn't budge right away. She came awake with a start. One leg slipped out from under her and she staggered forward, barely catching herself on the corner of the end table. Her wide eyes jumped around the room before settling on him.

"Killian!" She threw herself out of the chair and perched on the edge of the mattress, next to his hip. Her hands went to his face. One rested on his cheek. The other went to his brow. "How are you? How are you feeling?"

He stared up at her, at the worry crinkling her brows and the fear darkening her eyes. Her face was chalky and drawn and held the resemblance of not enough sleep.

"What are you doing?" he heard himself ask.

The question seemed to confuse her before she realized something. She straightened, taking her hands with her. He felt their loss immediately.

"I couldn't leave you," she said quietly. "Not when you'd been beaten and … and shot. I know I'm not allowed to worry about you, but damn it, Killian, you were shot!" She broke off when her voice quivered.

"I meant what are you doing in that chair," he murmured.

Her head jerked up. The lamplight caught the dampness in her eyes and the sight of her tears hit him like a fist.

"You told me not to stay the night," she whispered. "It's not staying the night if I don't sleep in a bed."

Her logic was ridiculous, but it was a sharp spear in his gut and he wondered how many different ways she could possibly tear up his insides without lifting a finger.

"Jesus, Juliette." He tugged down the corner of the sheets. "Come to bed."

She seemed to shrink back a notch. "Maybe I should get Frank—"

"Bed!" he said louder. "Get in."

Hesitance still stiffened her shoulders, but she carefully slid over him and climbed into the empty space on his other side. He drew the sheets up over her.

"Come here."

"But you're hurt—"

"Damn it, woman!"

She wiggled into his side, the one away from his injuries and carefully snaked an arm across his ribs. Her head nestled against his shoulder.

Killian closed his eyes as her sweet scent washed over him, as her familiar weight and heat settled against his side. Seeing her when he woke up was one thing, but to feel her, to hold her and know she wasn't his imagination was a reality that shook him to the core.

"I thought something happened to you," he murmured into the top of her head. "I don't think I've ever been so scared."

"You scared?" she croaked. "I came in and you ... you were covered in blood and so white. Then..." Her voice caught. The hand on his chest balled into a trembling fist. "I was so sure…"

Hot, wet tears burned into his skin where her cheek lay. Against his palm, her back shuddered with her silent sobs and his heart broke.

"Juliette…"

"I know. I'm sorry. I'm trying to stop."

It was a bit of an effort getting both arms around her and not turning on his side. Already the movement was tugging at the stitching in his side, but he ignored it as he crushed her to him.

"Ah, darling lamb." He kissed the crown of her head. "What am I going to do with you?"

Juliette was gone when Killian woke up again. The room was soaked in bright, warm sunshine that hurt the eyes and the sheets had been drawn securely about his waist, but the place next to him was cool and empty. The sight of it annoyed him far more than it probably should have. She'd been quietly leaving his bed for months while he slept and, while he assured himself it was what she was supposed to do, it still prickled at him whenever he reached for her and his fingers closed in air.

Carefully, he tossed the sheets back and lowered his feet to the soft carpet. His muscles only twanged slightly with the motion, which he took as a good sign. He padded to the washroom and shut the door behind him.

He didn't look half as bad as he felt, he noted as he surveyed his injuries in the wall of mirror next to the shower. Aside from the weeks' worth of beard making his face itch, the kaleidoscope of colors in various shades of purple, black, green, yellow and blue had mostly faded. His ribs and back had taken the worst of it, possibly from the kicking. There were a few blotches along his thighs, his arms and stomach, but they would all heal eventually. Even the bullet wound, which was a raw, painful mess of stitches and flesh.

Killian exhaled slowly, his best attempt at tapering the boiling rage he could feel writhing like cobras deep in the very dark place inside him. Yet the anger had nothing to do with getting shot, it was the nerve of Smith and his pathetic group of morons who thought that they could waltz into his home and attack him. Had he honestly thought he would win?

Discarding the pajama bottoms someone—possibly Frank—had dressed him in, he stepped into the full sized shower and shut the glass door behind him. There were six different sprays stationed around the eight by five cubical, but he only ever used one, the one with the pressure massage. The hard jets struck him in all the right places, softening the pained muscles while he scrubbed furiously at the rest of him.

Half an hour later, he was showered, shaved and dressed once more. His side continued to pang, but he slapped on a fresh bandage and left.

Frank met him at the end of the hall. Juliette must have told him Killian was awake, because he seemed unsurprised to see his employer on his feet.

"There are a few matters that require—"

"Where's Juliette?"

Frank fell into an easy step alongside him as they headed towards the office.

"Miss Romero has gone to work. She left early this morning, but will return later this evening."

"How did she get here? Who brought her without my direct orders?"

He reached his office and stalked straight to his desk.

Frank hesitated by the door. "She arrived on her own, sir. Apparently she climbed through a bedroom window."

Killian staggered to a stop and spun around. "What?"

Frank straightened his shoulders and clasped his hands in front of him. "The team had secured the house. Miss Romero requested to speak to you, but our communication hadn't yet gone up and she took matters into her own hands ... sir."

Killian dropped his face into his hand and slowly shook his head. "That woman is going to be the end of me," he muttered to himself.

"What would you like me to do, sir?"

"Fire them." He lowered his hand. "If they can't watch over a single woman when there are two of them, I have no use for them."

Frank blinked. "Sir?"

"Bring them to me," he decided instead. "I want to hear what happened from them."

"Yes sir."

Killian leaned against the side of his desk as all strength in his limbs disintegrated, leaving him unnaturally exhausted and weak. But he stayed steady when he spoke again.

"The men we lost, have the families been contacted?"

Frank nodded. "Yes sir. The funerals have been arranged."

"Make sure the families are taken care of and bring me their numbers. I'd like to speak with them personally."

"Yes sir."

Forcing himself up, Killian moved to his chair and lowered himself into it. "This can't go unaddressed, Frank. Not just for my men, but because this is my home. They came into my home!" He shook his head. "No, this needs to be handled."

"Yes sir." Frank moved deeper into the room, phone in hand. "What would you like to do?"

"Bring me John and Tyson first," he instructed. "Get Jake and Melton to stay with Juliette. Then set up a meeting with Kinch."

Frank inclined his head, his fingers already moving over the keys on his phone. Finally, he straightened and lifted his head.

"Anything else, sir?"

He stared at the top of his desk. The underground cleanup crew had scrubbed the place clean of bodies and blood. It didn't even look like anyone had been shot, never mind killed in the middle of his office.

The knowledge that he was responsible for the death of another person never sat well with him. He wasn't a psychopath. But there wasn't any remorse either. Smith died by the hands of his own foolish stupidity and that was on him; although, the fault wasn't entirely with Smith, if Killian was honest with himself. He was just as much to blame.

His first mistake was holding the meeting with men he wasn't familiar with in his own home. But since Killian didn't have an office and hadn't wanted to leave the mountain of paperwork, he had figured it would kill two birds with one stone. His second mistake was turning his back.

Dan Smith, as he'd introduced himself was a semi known gambler with deep pockets. As owner of several of the cities more high end and well known gaming arenas, Killian had heard of the man in passing only. From their brief phone conversation the day before, Killian had been under the impression that Smith had a concern with one of Killian's fighting rings. He had agreed to meet the man to discuss it. At no time had he ever imagined that Smith would arrive with six heavily armed men and a head full of steam.

He'd stalked into Killian's office a full three hours ahead of their scheduled meet. It was a sign of control Killian recognized and appreciated about as much as getting kicked in the crotch. But he had tolerated it, had even offered the man a seat and a drink, both which were refused.

Smith had reminded Killian of an old, lumpy oil tycoon. He'd stood before Killian in his cowboy boots, plaid top, and ten gallon hat that matched his ten gallon gut. He'd even had a thick mustache the same steel wool gray as his slicked back hair. He'd stared across the ten feet to where Killian stood patiently waiting.

"Mr. McClary," he'd drawled lazily. "Let me just say what an honor this is. I am a big patron of your many establishments."

Killian had inclined his head politely. "Thank you. You said on the phone this matter was urgent."

"Yes, of course." He'd shifted his weight like his boots were hurting his feet. "I was frequenting your Man O Steel tournament the night before. It's one of my favorites." He'd offered Killian a grin like they shared a secret joke. "Nothing like two men boxing it out to get the blood pumping."

Killian had offered him a half smile.

Smith had continued, unfazed. "Now, as I said, I am a regular at most of your clubs. I was at the arena twice more this last week and I noticed that Nick Jameson, your newest fighter, hasn't lost once since he started, which I find extremely odd considering he's so green and his technique is deplorable. Yet, he's won three whole nights in a row. I just can't wrap my hat around it."

Killian had tried not to look at that enormous bucket on the man's head. "If you're insinuating that my fighter somehow cheated, Mr. Smith—"

"No! No, no, of course not. I would never, but I do think it's something worth looking into."

If that was all the man had come to say, Killian had been severely unimpressed. His gaze had drifted over the other five fanned out behind Smith and had wondered what their purpose was. No one went anywhere that heavily guarded unless they were the queen.

"Very well, Mr. Smith." He had returned his attention to the figure in front. "I will look into the matter. Thank you for bringing it to my attention."

Smith had bobbed his massive head. "Certainly, but there is another matter I wish to discuss."

Killian had waited, his patience waning.

"It's the matter of the amount I lost. I don't believe it's fair when the House clearly had the upper hand."

The House always has the upper hand, Killian had wanted to tell him, but he had been too busy scrutinizing the man watching him with those beady little eyes of his.

"I don't think I understand." Killian stared hard at the man. "Are you asking me to return the money you lost betting on the wrong fighter? Certainly that's not the case, is it, Mr. Smith? As someone who admits to frequenting my gaming rings regularly, I would hope you understand the rules of the games you are playing. There are no refunds."

Eyes the brittle cold of winter had peered into Killian, all good humor gone. The men behind him had shifted, but remained in place.

"It's only sportsmen-like, Mr. McClary," Smith had said in a manner that said very clearly that the matter was not some elaborate joke.

"I'm curious." Killian had moved several steps closer, his strides even and non-threatening. "Do you make it a habit of barging into people's homes, three hours before your appointment to cry about making bad choices? I certainly hope not, because if that is the case, I would feel inclined to ban you from my arenas. It's bad form to put money down on games knowing the odds could go either way and then complain when you lose. I am almost certain we would not be having this conversation if you had won. That said, I will talk to my gaming manager and he will investigate the matter. Should my fighter be in the wrong, as you claim, I will handle him accordingly. As for returning your loss, no. That is why it is called gambling."

Blood had welled beneath the doughy folds of skin on Smith's square face. It had reminded Killian of a walking tomato in cowboy getup.

"You are making a grave mistake, Mr. McClary." Smith's mouth had barely moved beneath the bushy patch of fur over his lip.

"The matter is closed, Mr. Smith," Killian had said, putting absolute finality in the words. "Perhaps you're better off trying your hand at the tables instead."

Killian's second mistake that day was turning his back to return to his desk. In normal business conversations that usually meant the meeting was over and the other party should leave.

The forearm had appeared out of nowhere and closed down with impossible strength across Killian's jugular. The pressure had pushed into his windpipe, blocking his airway and making his heart escalate to make up for the sudden loss of oxygen. A hard chest had pushed into his back, holding him prisoner as the door to his office was closed and locked with a quiet click.

In the background, he heard the *pop-pop* of gunfire, the shout of his men. Then the *boom* of weight slamming into his office doors; it wouldn't have taken Frank long to get in, but Killian didn't have the minutes.

"I think we should really renegotiate, Mr. McClary," Smith had drawled. "See, I'm not a man who is accustomed to the word no and I definitely don't like hearing it where my money is concerned. So, from one business man to the other, I would like for you to think very hard about your answer."

Killian's response had been the slam of his head into his captor's chin. The forearm had lifted just enough for him to bow forward, pull back his arm and drive his elbow into the other man's ribs. He'd grabbed the wrist connected to the arm holding him, twisted, ducked under, and wrenched it with enough momentum to hear the shoulder pop.

The other man had dropped with a howl. Killian had finished with a knee to his face that shattered his nose and sent him across the floor before rounding on the five gawking at him.

"My answer is still no," he had panted, pushing wisps of hair back off his brow. "Now, get the fuck outta my house."

A second man had flown forward, hands out like he'd wanted to wrap them around Killian's throat. Killian had dodged, ducked, and came up beneath the man's outstretched arms. He swung five clenched fingers into his side, ducked again, came up, grabbed an arm, and twisted it until there was a crack.

Something had slammed into Killian from behind, hard enough to send him down on his knees. A boot had planted into his ribs and he'd gone down. From there, there was no getting up again. It was four against one. The most he could do was curl up and cover his head as the blows rained down on him with a vengeance that made him see stars. Splotches of gray flickered across his vision and he'd known he didn't have long.

"I want my money, Mr. McClary," Smith had drawled as he made his way forward.

"Fuck you!" Killian had spat back before a foot caught him in the spine.

Smith had crouched down. His fat knees had popped as he'd bent to eyelevel with Killian. One stubby finger had knuckled his hat higher on his brow.

"Now, Mr. McClary, let's not be unreasonable. You give me what I want and we will have no more trouble." He'd paused a moment before adding, "Perhaps I need to find that pretty little cunt you had in here with you. Maybe she has my money."

Rage, blinding, flashing, blood red roared to life through every vein. It splattered across his vision like brain matter exploding across a wall. He felt the spray of it sear through him with a raw rage that knew no master.

He lunged with a roar that momentarily silenced everything else. The men jumped back in surprise and it was all he needed to close both hands around Smith's pale throat. The drive of Killian's weight threw Smith backwards, taking Killian with him. They landed in a heap with Killian gouging his knee into the man's chest.

All the pain had inexplicably vanished in the time it had taken to realize the bastard was threatening Juliette. Crimson waves had surged over the room, painting it a violent blur vibrating with his rage.

Beneath his palm, Smith's pulse had jumped, mirroring the terror in his wide eyes. His mouth had flapped, releasing a series of squeaks and squawks that meant nothing. The heel of his cowboy boots had cracked on marble with his flailing, but he wasn't going anywhere.

Killian had dug his thumbs into the soft tissues of the man's flabby neck, crushing the pipes and snaking under the sharp point of Smith's Adam's apple.

"You will never touch her!" Killian had snarled.

Out of their shock, the men had lunged into action. Hard, pointed shoes had drilled into his sides, his back, his legs, but his hold never loosened. Smith had writhed beneath him, a helpless worm on the end of a hook. His hands had grappled at Killian's wrists, his arms and shoulders, but Killian wasn't letting go for anything, not even when Smith had gone a frightening shade of purple.

His thrashing had slowed. Killian had known Smith had a few more minutes before there was no coming back and still ... if he let go and Smith lived, Juliette would be in danger. Smith would go after her and Killian could not allow that.

Over his shoulder, he had a vague recollection of a hammer being cocked back. The rattling sound of metal in the hands of someone unsteady had crackled in his ear. The stench of gunpowder had filled his senses, but it wasn't enough to make him pull back.

Two bangs had shaken the room simultaneously. Only one had metal piercing through him. Blood had sprayed in a crimson shower over the unmoving form of Dan Smith, staining his plaid shirt. Killian's hands had finally unraveled. His body had toppled off the other man as more bangs rattled the windows. He had lain there, staring at the ceiling as heat had pooled beneath him. Then Frank's calm face had appeared above his.

The rest was a blur of being mended, which was probably worse than being shot in the first place.

"Anyone we need to be concerned about looking for him?"

"I am looking into that now, sir. I will keep you notified. Anything else?"

"Yeah." Killian fixed his gaze on the other man. "How long was Juliette here for?"

"The whole time, sir. She took the week off to stay with you."

"You didn't think to offer her a bed?"

Frank visibly bristled. "I did, sir. She declined." He shifted his massive shoulders. "She's very stubborn, sir."

A grin turned the corner of Killian's mouth. "Aye, she is. It's one of the things that make her irresistible."

Frank straightened. "Sir, if I could speak freely?"

That was the oddest request Killian had ever heard coming from the man. Since when had he ever censored himself? Frank was Killian's conscience. The only person Killian trusted to give him the truth.

"Of course," he said, bemused.

"Perhaps it's time you considered a different source of employment."

A prickle of annoyance furrowed Killian's brows. "And what do you suggest? You know no one walks away from this life."

"Yes sir."

But there was more. Killian could see it on the man's face, in the muscle along his square jaw.

"What, Frank?"

Dark eyes swung just over Killian's head. "I'm not certain it's my place, sir."

Killian stared at the man for several heartbeats, his own mind churning.

"Frank? How long have you been in this family?"

The question seemed to surprise the other man. He blinked and then frowned as he tried to do the math.

"A while, sir," he said at last.

"Since I was in diapers," Killian said for him. "That's a damn long time."

Frank nodded slowly. "Yes sir."

"My dad trusted you and I trust you, probably more than anyone."

"Thank you, sir."

Killian ignored that. "So I think it's safe to say that you can pretty much say anything freely and I will listen."

A muscle flexed in Frank's rugged jaw, reminding Killian of someone chewing steel. The tension ran along his enormous shoulders and whitened at the knuckles clenched around his phone.

"It's about Miss Romero, sir."

Killian fought not to stiffen as he seemed to involuntarily do every time her name was spoken. "What about her?"

Frank sucked in a breath that expanded his massive chest before fixing his gaze squarely on Killian.

"I was there the day your parents met." A softness took over the harsh lines that usually hugged the sharp points of his features. "It was the first frost and her car fishtailed into the back of ours. She had been so embarrassed, but your father had laughed and said the only way he'd forgive her was if she had dinner with him. They were married six months later."

Killian had heard the story a million times before. It had been his favorite for a long time, but it had always changed depending on who was telling it. His father claimed she'd done it on purpose to get his attention, to which she would gasp in indignation and swat him. His mother used to say she'd been busy looking for a street and hadn't noticed the car stopping in front of her. It was interesting to hear it from a third party, even if it didn't explain what the other man was getting at.

"What are you saying, Frank?"

"That it's a rare thing to find someone who accepts the things we do, sir. For your father, it was your mother. She knew who he was and what he did and she still loved him. That love never faltered in fifteen years." He paused, seemingly bracing himself for what he was about to say next. "A man can't live alone forever and when a woman comes along who accepts him, his faults and demons, maybe it's time he reevaluates his future."

"Marriage and kids?" Killian guessed.

"Yes sir."

The idea of being with Juliette forever, of having little girls with their mother's eyes, hit him in all the places she had already made dents in his titanium wall. The impact had cracks splintering across the expense, but he held it together. He had to.

"You know why that can't happen. Even if I got out, you know you are never really out. For the rest of my life and theirs, I would have to look over our shoulders, always afraid that I might lose them if I'm not careful and when I'm gone, this is the life that would be left behind for them. It needs to die with me, Frank. My children will never know this life. They will never have to go through what I did."

Frank didn't look ready to let the matter drop, but he inclined his head. "Yes sir. I understand." The bigger man shifted, clearly uncomfortable. "Tyson and John are here."

Killian sat back gingerly. "Send them in."

———

He fired them both. It hadn't been a simple decision. For a moment, he had even considered letting it go this once, but life didn't work that way, especially when their vigilance was the reason he'd hired them in the first place. It didn't matter that Juliette was a grown woman. They were responsible for keeping an eye on her, keeping her safe, and they had failed. Because of them, she could have been hurt or worse and that was inexcusable no matter how loyal they were. He needed men who could do their job. Not that that would save Juliette once he got his hands on her. She had no idea what she'd be stumbling into and had foolishly put herself in incredible danger. It was pure luck that she'd arrived mere minutes after it was all over. Even an hour earlier and … Killian stiffened all over at the thought of Juliette in Smith's clutches.

Endy Kinch had been the head of Killian's gaming business for over eight years. He wasn't much to look at with his bulging brown eyes and squashed face, but he had a head for numbers and ran a fierce house. Killian had found him hustling tourists in the park with the tired ball under a cup trick. But he'd been good and made a solid grand a week. It was that sort of skill Killian had been looking for. He'd hired Kinch on the spot and had never once regretted it.

Nevertheless, Killian allowed the man to defend himself against the allegations Smith had made, even while Killian hadn't believed a word of it.

"He threw a fit and I kicked him out," Kinch explained simply. "There was no cheating. I check all the fighters before they go on and I checked Jameson like all the rest. I got video surveillance to prove it. He's just a good fighter, a bit sloppy, but decent."

"I want those tapes," Killian told him. "And I better not find anything I don't like on them, Kinch."

Kinch inclined his head. "I'll vouch for my fighters, sir. And the way I run my games. May not all be legal, but they're damn fair."

Killian believed him. It was hard not to when there was only one complaint in eight years.

There was nothing but a week's worth of paperwork waiting for him after Kinch left. A mountain that seemed impossibly high. Thankfully, Frank had taken care of most of the emails and phone calls in Killian's absence or it would have been much worse.

He was just beginning to get into the familiar rhythm when Juliette arrived. Her presence momentarily baffled him before he realized it was already after seven and the world outside had grown dark and gloomy in the early November night. He set his pen down as she headed towards his desk with a small smile. Her movement was it's usual hurried pace of someone on a mission, but he had enough time to enjoy the way her burgundy skirt clung to her hips and hugged her legs all the way to the calves before flaring out. Her coat was open to the soft, black blouse underneath and there were black heels strapped to her feet that cracked with every stride.

"You're up," she said in the way of greeting. "How are you feeling?"

"Better," he said, gathering his papers and tucking them into their folder. "How was work?"

She shrugged. "Busy, but nothing exciting happened." She watched him and he wondered if she was waiting for him to cry out in pain or pass out again. "I noticed John and Tyson are gone. Are they on holiday or...?"

He yanked open his drawer and stuffed the folders into them. He shut them in and rose to his feet.

"I fired them."

There was a flicker of confusion on her face, a fine wrinkle between her brows. "Why?"

"Because they didn't do their job," he told her simply. "They didn't watch you like they were supposed to so I have no need for them."

Her mouth parted in a silent O of stunned silence that radiated the horror shining in her wide eyes.

"What?" She shook her head like by doing so, it would make the situation less true. "Why would you ... that's ... it wasn't their fault! I'm the one who got away from them. You can't—"

"I can," he interrupted sharply. "I pay them to do a specific job and that job is to make sure you are safe."

"They were doing their job!" she cried, her eyes glistening with tears of anger. "It was my fault."

"Five men in a secured house and they couldn't keep an eye on you." His voice vibrated with a sort of rage that scared even him. "How can I trust that they can keep you safe when you're out? How can I trust that they will be efficient enough not to lose you in a crowded mall? Your safety was put into question and I won't have that, not when the thought of something happening to you is the only thing that can break me. You're my weakness, Juliette. You're my Achilles' heel, the key to bringing me down and I can't lose you."

She said nothing for so long, he wondered if she'd frozen in place. She studied him with those doe brown eyes filled with tears and something he wasn't entirely certain he wanted a name for. Finally, she pulled herself up. She dragged her coat together over her clothes and hugged her middle as though a chill had passed through the room.

"If that's your way of getting me to stop being angry, then it's very underhanded."

"No, love." He moved around the desk until he was directly in front of her. "That's me trying to keep you safe. Jake and Melton have their orders and you..." He took her warm face between his palms. "Are to follow them, do you hear me? If you ever pull anything as foolish and reckless as that again, I will put you over my knee and I promise you won't walk straight for a week."

Anger flashed across her eyes. "I was worried about you. No one was telling me if you were all right. What was I supposed to do?"

"Not climb fifteen feet down a tree!" he retorted, feeling his own anger climbing. "Never mind that you could have arrived here in the middle of what happened and gotten killed or captured, but what if you'd fallen and broken your fool neck? What then? I have half a mind to fire the whole group and—"

"No!" Her hands flew to the front of his shirt and fisted. "No! Please, please don't do that."

"Then I trust that we have an agreement? You will not dodge your security group again, right?"

"I won't," she said a bit too quickly. "I promise."

Killian narrowed his eyes. "While I love this complying side of you, I can't help feeling you have an ulterior motive for it."

She swallowed audibly. "Vi's grown very fond of Phil," she blurted quickly. "He seems to be very good for her. She's a completely different person, a good person since he's been with her."

"Juliette!" With a frustrated growl, he rubbed a palm over his face. "He's a bodyguard, not a ... a shrink!"

"I know, but please, you don't understand." She bore imploringly up at him. "We've been talking, Killian. Actually talking. That has never happened. She's always been so angry and I ... I never cared. Not once. Our entire lives I've considered her a burden, a pain in the ass that I had to deal with, that I never stopped to even try and understand her. But he did. He listened to her and did all the things I should have. I know it's selfish and pathetic, but if you take him away, I know she'll never forgive me."

"Jesus Christ!"

He moved away from her and went to stand at the window overlooking what had been his mother's garden. It was a wasteland of dirt and lonely structures.

"Killian, please," Juliette whispered. "I'll do whatever you want."

Tempting. Oh, so tempting. The number of things he wanted from her rolled around in his mind the way a toy catalogue would for a child just before Christmas.

"Come to the club with me tonight," he said instead, glancing back over his shoulder. "I have work and we can finish this discussion there."

Juliette seemed to consider this a moment before asking with a hint of wariness that almost amused him, "Does this mean Phil can stay?"

Killian turned back to the window. "For now."

Nodding reluctantly, she took a step back. "I'll run home and change then. I can meet you—"

"No need." He twisted around to face her fully. "I'll come with you."

Chapter 16

Before her parents had died and their house had been homey and furnished with nice things, Juliette had never had qualms about inviting people over; her mother had made the place like something out of a fancy catalogue. After having to sell the really nice stuff and replace some of it with ratty, used items, it looked more like a rundown crack house. At least in Juliette's opinion. Most of the rooms were bare and layered in dust while the rest held furniture no one ever wanted to sit on. It was a far cry from the extravagance of Killian's *manor*. Yet she could find no way to discourage him from crossing into her dark, dank world without coming off as insane, or worse, embarrassed, which she was. To herself, she could fully admit that she was devastatingly ashamed of her home, the place she'd grown up in, the place she'd fought like hell to keep.

Neither of them spoke as they hurtled through the city in the backseat of the black SUV with Melton and Frank sitting like mute statues in the front. Occasionally, she'd see Melton's arm turn as he twisted the wheel, but he was rigid otherwise. Jake had squished himself into the seat on Juliette's other side, forcing her between him and Killian. The latter she didn't mind so much, but her new companions were a different story. Neither had said a word to her since appearing on her doorstep to replace John and Tyson. They'd introduced themselves and told her they would be taking over, but that was all.

She missed John and Tyson. They hadn't been friendly or chatty, but she had grown fond of them in the three months they'd been together.

A sigh escaped her and she turned her head to stare out the window. The world was a muted blur behind the tint. Shops glinted and people roamed the sidewalks even as night packed around them. The sun had gone down several hours earlier, making the time appear much later than it was. Overhead, a thick overcast curdled across the heavens, threatening snow. Juliette inwardly cringed.

"There is an event I would like you to attend with me." Killian's voice drew her away from the depression weaving its way around her. "It's a Christmas party of sorts."

Juliette's eyebrows swung up. "Christmas party in November?" She considered it a moment. "I suppose that makes sense. Most of the days in December would be taken."

"No, the party isn't until the second week of December, but I know how you are with surprises and parties if you're not given proper notice."

She grimaced. "I still owe you for that, don't I?"

He made a quiet humming sound. "You can make it to me by wearing your new dress to this event."

"All right. You'll have to give me the date and time."

They pulled up in the driveway of her home. Unlike the others around it, hers sat dark and foreboding. A few of her neighbors had already hung their Christmas lights or at the very most, had their porch lit. The blinds were drawn over all her windows and no one had bothered with the porch light. Already the place made her cringe. Her stomach muscles tightened in dread as Jake held open her door. She managed a weak thank you as she slid out and made her way up the cracked walkway. Behind her, she was painfully aware of Killian's quiet presence.

They climbed up the steps together, but made it as far as the front door when it was jerked open by Laurence. He bowed his head to Killian before stepping aside to let them in.

The dining room with the sleeping cots sat in absolute darkness. On the other side of the foyer, the living room was lit solely by a single lamp that illuminated the lumpy sofa and faded wallpaper. Down the hall, the kitchen glowed the brightest. She went there.

"You've got to work it with your knuckles," Mrs. Tompkins was saying when Juliette stepped onto the threshold. "Really get in there."

The scene took Juliette a moment to figure out. For one, she couldn't fathom how the entire place could smell like warm, freshly baked bread *and* a donkey's ass, if said donkey's ass was made of burnt bread. For another, Vi was shoulder to shoulder with the older woman, sweater sleeves rolled up to her elbows as she pounded into a ball of slightly dry dough. Her forearms were caked in flour, as was her face, her hair and most of the kitchen. But she looked like she was having the time of her life.

"What's going on here?" Juliette wondered out loud as she braved a few more steps closer.

In the corner of the room, rigid and watchful, Phil caught her eye briefly and gave her the slightest of nods that she returned with a half-smile before focusing on the pair at the island again.

"I'm learning to make one of those knotted French breads," Vi declared, holding up her clump of dough. "I nearly made one earlier, but ... there was an accident."

Juliette glanced over at the chunk of crispy, black steaming on a rack on the counter by the sink.

"I see..." she mumbled. "I didn't realize you wanted to learn to bake."

"Oh, I don't." Vi laughed. "It's hard and messy." She smacked the dough down and smashed it with one fist. "But I get to beat on it so that kind of makes up for it."

Mrs. Tompkins chuckled. "Don't listen to her. She's a natural."

Juliette opened her mouth when a movement behind her reminded her that she had company.

Quickly, she stepped aside so Killian could step into the mess.

"Uh, Vi, Mrs. Tompkins, this is Killian McClary."

Vi's head shot up much faster than Mrs. Tompkins, who seemed unconcerned by yet another new person in their normally empty house.

She offered Killian a small, kind smile. "It's nice to meet you." was all she said to him, before turning her attention to Vi once more. "Add some water to your dough."

Vi wasn't listening. She was staring with wide eyed interest at Killian.

"You're Killian," she blurted, with the glimmer of a cat having finally spotted the elusive mouse. "Well, you're much better looking than I'd imagined."

"Vi!" Horrified, Juliette gawked at her sister's unabashed greeting.

"Thank you," Killian said with just a hint of amusement.

Vi nodded. "I always thought Columbian drug lords had greasy black hair and pockmarked skin and tattoos. But you are much better."

In the corner, Phil shifted and Vi's gaze darted to him before snapping back to Killian, who was biting his lip so hard Juliette was afraid he'd tear a hole in it.

"Crap, was that rude?" Vi hissed through her teeth. "I'm working on my filter. Sometimes I forget."

Killian burst out laughing. The sound was a rolling rumble that echoed through the house in waves. It coursed over Juliette in a warm caress that left her skin tingling.

"Killian isn't Columbian," Juliette murmured, biting back her own laughter as it bubbled up her chest. "He's Irish and he's not a drug lord ... are you?"

Killian shook his head, still grinning broadly. "No."

"Ah!" Vi said like that made much more sense. "That explains it then. Irish guys are stupid hot." She grabbed a box of yeast and shoved it towards Killian. "Read this."

It was a task not to face palm.

Killian took the box, but set it down carefully. His eyes shone with silent laughter as he regarded Vi.

"It's lovely to meet you, Viola."

Vi's jaw unhinged and a sort of hazy glaze crept across her eyes. "Wow ... have you got a brother? Preferably younger."

Juliette did face palm that time.

Killian chuckled. "Sorry. Just me."

Vi exhaled, the sound full of dejected sorrow. "Figures. Suppose I'll have to find my own gorgeous Irish guy. Wonder if I can order one online…"

"Water!" Mrs. Tompkins elbowed her and nudged the bowl of water closer with sticky, doughy fingers.

Vi shot her a glower before sprinkling a few drops over her flaking ball. She rubbed it in and kneaded the dough.

"Don't understand why we have to keep watering the damn thing," she muttered. "It's not a bloody flower…" She paused and considered that a moment. "The growing kind of … oh, never mind."

Juliette turned to Killian. "I'm sorry. I swear she's not normally like that. At least, not since recently."

Lips still quirked, Killian turned his head to her. "I like her."

Juliette arched a brow. "You would. She all but licked your ego."

"Mm," he purred just loud enough for her to hear. "I prefer you licking it anyway."

Her panties grew damp at the suggestive murmur that sent a ripple of heat working through her. Her cheeks warmed and she quickly averted her eyes before anyone else could notice.

"I should change," she mumbled.

"I'll come with you," Killian decided, body already turning towards the doorway. "I'm curious about your room."

"My ... room?"

Juliette hurried after him. No one stopped them as they climbed the steps to the second floor. Juliette led the way down the dark, narrow hallway to the very least for at the end.

"This is it," she murmured, reaching for the knob.

Killian plucked up one of the photos she'd pinned to the corkboard nailed to her door. They were old, as most of her photos were, but she kept them as a reminder that her life hadn't always been a nightmare. That there had been a time when she'd been happy. It was a collage of her with her friends. There were a few of her with her parents and even a couple with Stan that, despite everything, she couldn't bring herself to toss. Around it were words she'd cut out of magazines and friendship bracelets she no longer wore. But Killian went straight for the picture of her standing between a group of four other girls. He took it off the board to examine better.

It had been one of the last trips she'd taken with the girls. They stood just outside the iron gate guarding his hill. Looking back on it, she was stunned to realize that all that time, he'd been just on the other side.

"I used to dream of owning a house up there," she murmured. "My friends and I would drive up and pretend to house shop. We never went as far as the very top, but…"

Killian said nothing. He returned the photo and gave her a nod.

Gingerly, she pushed open the door and stepped inside with him at her heels.

"This is it," she proclaimed with a wave of her arm.

This, was a four poster bed she'd begged her parents for for nearly six months. It was the matching end tables, dresser, and vanity and their crown molding edges and white paint. The bed took up most of the room, but she had still managed to shove a desk into one corner, a bookshelf in the other and a wooden chest sat at the foot. On the other side of the dresser, was the door to her own personal bathroom. As bedrooms went, it was every teenagers dream. But Juliette hadn't been a teenage in years, nor had she had enough money to upgrade to something more … adult. Instead, she'd removed most of the girly pictures and posters and had tossed the stuffed animals she'd collected over the years. It no longer resembled a young girls room, but it wasn't glaring.

Killian wandered to her bed and sat, making her thankful she tidied up that morning, like a part of her had been expecting his visit. There wasn't a stray pair of pantries in sight.

"Tell me about your sister," he said, surprising her.

"Vi? Why?"

"Well, you said that's not normally how she is, so tell me what she's normally like."

The question was a reasonable one, maybe even expected, but Juliette had nothing. She stared at him while her mind raced with all the things she ought to know of her own sister, but didn't. Vi was a stranger.

"I don't know," she admitted, ashamed. "I don't know anything about her. I never wanted to." Dropping her gaze, she walked over and claimed the spot next to him. Her shoulder bumped his as she studied the knotted fingers in her lap. "I was seven when she was born. I was the only girl on both sides of the family and I was spoiled rotten and I loved it. I never wanted a sister. In my mind, she took away all that love and attention that had been mine from the beginning. I hated her. That hate never went away, not even after Mom died. It just turned into a sort of selfish need to protect the only person I had left. I never took time to see if she was okay. I hadn't cared that she'd lost her parents as well and was as alone as I was. I stuck her in school or with Mrs. Tompkins and considered my duties complete so long as she had food and a roof over her head."

"You didn't let Arlo have her," Killian pointed out softly. "It would have made your job easier if you had."

"No." She pushed a lock of hair behind her ear. "No matter what, she's still my sister. I would never have done that. I just abandoned and neglected her instead." She drew in a breath. "We might never be friends, but I have to fix some of the damage I've caused. Right now, that seems to be Phil. He's helped her way more than I've ever done. He didn't chalk her up as hopeless and ... she has changed so much in the last few months. I honestly don't even recognize her anymore." She fixed her eyes on the man sitting shoulder to shoulder with her. "I know he's a bodyguard and this isn't part of his job description, but she needs him."

Prodding black eyes searched hers with a quiet contemplation. "She needs you, love. She needs her sister."

"I don't know how to be that."

The bedsprings jingled with the shift of his weight as he reached over and lightly brushed the side of her face.

"You've got one of the kindest hearts I've seen in a long time, Juliette. You'll figure it out." He rose. "Get dressed. I'll wait downstairs."

He walked out and shut the door behind him. Juliette remained seated on her bed, thinking over what he'd said about Vi needing her and coming up empty; there was no way to right sixteen years of wrong. How could there be?

Heavy hearted, Juliette got to her feet and padded to her closet. She pulled out a pair of jeans and a sweater. Both were tossed down on the bed when the door opened. She expected it to be Killian, but Vi poked her head in.

"You needed to see me?"

Juliette frowned. "I did?"

Vi walked in. "Killian said you needed help picking out something to wear."

It wasn't exactly spelled out, but she understood what Killian was telling her: no time like the present to mend bridges.

She offered Vi her best smile. Even then, it felt horribly tight.

"Yeah." She motioned to the set she'd picked out. "What do you think?"

Vi frowned. "Where are you going?"

"Killian owns a club, Ice—"

"Shut up! Ice?" The look of pure elation on the girl's face insisted she'd heard of the place. "I've been ... I mean, I know a few people who have been dying to get in there!"

Juliette narrowed her eyes in amused disbelief. "Uh huh. So what do you think?"

"No! Definitely not. You need to look a lot sexier than that."

"I'm not going there to party!" She laughed.

"Still. Have you seen some of the girls in there? Not that I have," she added quickly. "But they are insanely hot. You need to make sure Killian only sees you."

She had a point.

"All right." Juliette stepped away from her closet. "What do you suggest?"

Vi laughed like that question was just adorable. "Absolutely nothing from your closet."

"Hey!"

Still grinning, Vi turned and headed for the door. "Come on," she said as she stepped into the hallway.

Juliette hesitated, not because she didn't want the help, but because following meant she was admitting that her clothes were not cool, which, granted, was true, but it still sucked, especially when she used to have such kickass taste once upon a time. The blow to her ego was astronomical.

Nevertheless, grudgingly, she shuffled after the other girl. Phil stood in the hallway, back against the wall, hands clasped in front of him. He glanced sideways at Juliette when she stepped into view. The look said very clearly not to try anything stupid ... a second time.

"At ease," Juliette muttered. "Just on my way to get the rest of my self-esteem destroyed."

Phil said nothing, but his mouth twitched a notch in a way that did nothing to ease her mood, but he went back to watching Vi's open door.

The girl in question stood buried to the waist in her closet. Random bits of clothing kept flying over her shoulder in arcs of color before creating pretty puddles across the floor. She seemed to be muttering to herself as she did it.

Several minutes passed before she finally emerged, arms laden by a pile of fabric. Unlike Juliette's closet that consisted of a handful of items, Vi's was overflowing, practically bursting at the seams. Most of it stuff Juliette had never seen, which always made her particularly uncomfortable.

Vi had been getting a weekly allowance of twenty dollars since she'd been twelve. That was hardly enough to buy a top, but it was all Juliette could afford to give her at the time. Yet she always managed to come home with new things.

"Where did you get all this stuff?" she asked as Vi dumped the items down on the bed.

"Places," was the vague response. "Here and there." She lifted a slinky tube dress in soft, navy blue that looked more like a headband. "Try this one on."

But Juliette wasn't ready to drop that matter.

"Vi…"

"Do you really want to know?" Vi rounded on her, hands going to her waists. "Really?"

That was the question. Part of her already felt like she knew, but did she really want validation?

"Don't do it anymore," she said instead. "I'll raise your allowance."

Vi narrowed her eyes. Her head bent to the side and she regarded Juliette quizzically.

"How much?"

Reaching out, Juliette took the dress. "Just promise me."

Vi shrugged. "All right."

Dress in hand, she turned and shut the door before undressing. She hopped and wiggled into the dress. The material was tight and clung to everything. It stopped just over the swell of her breasts, but barely. It felt more like it was clinging to her nipples to stay up. The hem rode up her thighs, giving barely any room for movement.

"Not sure about this one," Juliette voiced.

"Yeah, me neither." Vi thrust out a white dress. "Here. Try this one."

The white dress was no better. Neither was the green dress or the red dress or the purple dress. They all joined the small pile on the floor.

"All right, last one." Vi exhaled loudly. "If this doesn't work, we start on pants."

The cute black off the shoulder number worked. It molded over the hills and dips of her body like it had been painted on, but it was sexy as hell. Full sleeves ran down her arms and the hem stopped just below the curves of her ass. Vi added a pair of red heels much higher than any Juliette had worn in ages and a thin, red belt.

"That should do it." Vi stepped back to examine her handiwork. "Now for your hair and face."

"Vi." Juliette took her arm before she could hurry away. "Thank you."

Vi faltered. She looked from Juliette to the hand on her arm and Juliette quickly let go. Vi straightened. She scratched the back of her head as she turned away.

"Don't worry about it," she mumbled, making her way through the jungle of discarded clothes to the vanity tucked away under a mountain of makeup, hats, scarves and a pink feathered boa. "Let's finish you up, eh?"

Saying nothing else, Juliette let her hair get brushed, twisted, and pinned at the top of her head by a single strand Vi pulled away from her face. The rest was left around her shoulders. The makeup, Juliette did herself. She wasn't completely useless and still remembered how to apply the right amount of everything to make her face smooth and her eyes enormous. She added clear gloss to her lips and turned to her sister.

"Well?"

Vi nodded approvingly. "Nice. So, you're done."

She started to thank her again, but stopped herself. The first time had been awkward enough. But she smiled and headed for the door.

Phil was still standing there when she emerged. She offered him a half grin before making her way carefully down the stairs; it had been a damn long time since she'd worn heels that high. Halfway, she stopped and turned back, kicking herself for not having asked if she could help straighten some of the mess made on her behalf.

Phil was gone, she noted with some surprise. Vi's door was still open and she assumed he'd gone in to help her tidy up.

"She said she'd raise my allowance," Juliette heard Vi say softly. "I just have to stop five fingering my wardrobe."

There was a hint of self-deprecation in the remark.

"I warned you about that," Phil reminded her calmly. "Remember what happened last time?"

"Yeah, yeah," Vi grumbled.

"I know it's not what you wanted, but it's a small step in the right direction," Phil encouraged softly. "Don't give up."

"I don't know why I have to bother." Something thumped across the room. "This isn't going to work."

"It will. You need to be patient and—"

"Persistent. Yeah, I know. But it's so … weird. I'm not used to being … nice."

"Remember what not being nice got you?"

Vi exhaled. "What if it doesn't work?"

"Patience and—"

"If you say persistence, I will hit you."

Juliette turned away. She had no idea what they were talking about, but whatever it was, she would corner Phil about it later. Juliette was too tired for games and if there was something Vi needed, one of them needed to tell her. But later. Already an hour had passed and she had made Killian wait long enough.

Javier glanced up from his post at the table by the window when she hit the bottom landing. She offered him a nod before making her way towards the kitchen and the steady flow of chatter weaving through the corridor. Her heels clicked a bit too loudly in the rumbling emptiness of the place, sounding like firecrackers going off. But she made her way to the doorway and paused.

Her tiny kitchen was packed with people. Mrs. Tompkins and Killian stood at the island, chatting on like old friends while Killian's armed forces stood in various spots around them, guarding without looking like they were guarding. All heads lifted when she stepped over the threshold. The men looked away just as quickly.

Killian didn't.

He glanced back over his shoulder and faltered mid speech. The lines of his shoulders tightened even as he straightened. Eyes the infinite black of the night sky bore into her and carved deep grooves along every curve. She felt the weight of his desire wash over her like the slow rise of dawn creeping across the bed in the morning. It singed every inch of her.

"Apparently I have to make sure you don't look at other women while we're there," she told him with a teasing quirk of her mouth.

Amusement shimmered across the inky surface of his eyes. "Would it put your mind at ease if I assured you I haven't noticed another woman since you?"

It was funny, but the thought of Killian looking at other women had never bothered her. She hadn't even thought about it until Vi had pointed it out. Maybe it was because it had been stated in the contract that neither of them would see other people in their twelve months together or maybe because he had never given her a reason to worry, but … she hadn't. Oddly enough, she still wasn't worried. Nevertheless, his words sent a warm shiver through her.

"That so?"

"Aye, love." He crossed towards her in three long strides and stopped when he was close enough to lower his head and capture her mouth in a deep, toe curling kiss. She was breathless when he released her. "But you might want to bring a second dress."

The low growl against her ear rippled down her spine in rivulets of fire to burn in her belly. Her nipples hardened to sharp points that strained through the material of her dress. His gaze lingered on them before trailing back up to meet hers, darker, if possible. That simple gesture rocked through her as powerfully as though he'd reached out and stroked them.

"You ... you said you had work," she whispered.

Four deft fingers whispered feather light up the curve of her side. They moved to spread across the small of her back and bow her into him. Unbalanced by the motion and her heels, she hit his chest a bit harder than was necessary. Her hands flew to his shoulders. But he caught her easily.

"You ought to know how good I am at multitasking," he drawled lazily into her ear.

Her face heated up, but it was nothing compared to the spike in her temperature. Her entire body burst with an explosion of warmth triggered by the mere memories alone. She shifted as the hot rush of arousal trickled down the inside of her legs.

Killian eyed her questioningly when she mashed her lips together and grimaced with embarrassment.

"I'm ... I'm not wearing panties," she confessed in a whisper that was no more than the stiff movement of her lips. "The dress doesn't..." She broke off when his hands snaked down the curves of her hips, fingers dragging, possibly in search of elastic under the fabric. "It's too tight," she finished breathlessly once his palms had settled firmly over her backside.

"Christ, woman!" he snarled low under his breath.

Legs unstable, she tugged herself out of his bruising grip. "I have to make a quick bathroom run, but I'll meet you at the car, okay?"

He didn't say a word, but the look he gave her ... oh, the look raged with an inferno so wild she felt the flames lick strips off her skin. Lightheaded, she staggered back a step. Then another until she had extracted herself from his heat. She made a weaving path down the hall in the direction of the powder room. From the corner of her eye, she spotted Vi and Phil making their way downstairs. Laurence had joined Javier at the bay window. But no one paid her any attention as she slipped into the washroom and began to shut the door behind her only to have it fly out of her grasp. Another figure ducked in after her and closed them in with a resounding snick of the locks latching into place.

"Killian?"

His hands went to the fastens on his pants.

"We can't." She backed into the counter, not to escape, exactly, but to brace herself. "You're injured."

"I could be on my deathbed and I'd still fuck you," he panted, shoving his trousers down around his ankles.

The belt jingled loudly in the cramped space. It was followed by the snap of rubber as the condom went on down the hard length of his cock. His hands were on her then, grabbing her and lifting her. The cold marble came up against the bare skin of her backside as her skirt was bunched up around her waist. Bruising hands gripped her hips and she was yanked to the very edge. Juliette was given no time to react, not even to gasp when his mouth slammed down over hers, hot, hungry, and violent.

He pushed inside her with more gentleness than she knew he normally would have displayed. Their mutual sounds of satisfaction pulsed through the room as their bodies met in that beautifully perfect way. Juliette clutched him tight as he moved inside her in smooth, fluid strokes, hitting every nerve with brutal accuracy. Her fingers gouged into his shoulders, biting in deep as the world rocked beneath her. She came into the side of his neck with a cry of his name. He shuddered a split second after with a murmur of something in a language she didn't understand, but it sounded dark and possessive. He stayed buried inside her, even when he raised his head and peered down into her face. The beast continued to prowl just behind his eyes, still hungry, but temporarily sated.

Carefully, he pulled out, eliciting a whimper from her and a groan from him as the sensitive walls of her sex clutched at him, not wanting him to leave.

"I hate when you pull out," she whispered.

"Like me better deep inside you, do you?" he teased.

Juliette never wavered. "Yes."

The grin slipped into that predatory glint he got just before he ravaged the shit out of her. His fingers locked in her hair. He dragged her head back as far as it would go as he leaned in to nip hard on her bottom lip.

Juliette whined in delicious pain.

"Leave with me," he growled, running the tip of his tongue over the spot he'd assaulted.

Ready for him all over again, Juliette could only manage a weak, "Where?"

"I don't care." One hand slipped down to smooth over the fresh puddle filling over her opening. "Anywhere. Just name it."

Lost in the flick of his fingers, Juliette was barely listening. "Anywhere?"

"Anywhere."

She opened her eyes and peered up into his face mere inches from hers. "Can Vi and Mrs. Tompkins come?"

Two fingers worked deep inside her, replacing the loss of his cock, but barely. She still preferred him balls deep in her channel. Nevertheless, his fingers knew how to do that rubbing thing that made the top of her skull blow off.

"If you like."

"Rome," she decided, just for the hell of it. "I've always wanted to go. Or Venice."

"Both then," he offered, finding that magical spot that had her whining and begging. "All of Europe if you want."

She was no longer listening. With a tortured sob she could barely contain behind her teeth, she came, thrashing and rocking against his palm until the very last tremor. Satisfied, she slumped back against the mirror and shut her eyes, her body exhausted and so still buzzing. Between her thighs, Killian gingerly removed his fingers. Her eyes opened and she studied him through her lashes, a teasing grin curling her mouth.

"I had this weird mid orgasm dream where you said you wanted to go across Europe."

He chuckled as he moved to the toilet and discarded the condom. He leaned down and tugged his trousers back up. Once properly fastened, he reached for her. She allowed herself to be lowered to the ground. Her dress was smoothed back into place.

"I meant it."

Her eyes widened. "All of Europe? That could take months!"

He shrugged. "I have time."

A tour of Europe. It would be the greatest adventure she'd ever had. It would be the furthest she'd ever gone.

"Really?"

He nodded. "We can leave whenever you want."

A high pitch shriek escaped her as she flung herself into his arms. She pulled back a second later, happy mood momentarily overshadowed by doubt.

"What about work? Yours and mine? And Vi has school—"

He silenced her with a gentle finger against her lips. "Tell me when and I'll make it happen."

Woozy with excitement, Juliette beamed up at him. Her fingers tightened in the taut skin along the back of his neck as she pulled him close.

I love you!

The three little words came out of nowhere. They socked her square in the chest with the force of a steel studded fist. All the warmth drained out of her in a single swoop, taking along with it the blood from her face. Her eyes went enormous against the sudden pallor and he caught her when she swayed.

"Juliette?" Concern tightened his fingers on her as he pulled her into his chest. "What is it? What's wrong?"

I love you. Jesus Christ. I'm in love with you.

How the hell had that happened? When had that happened? How had she not noticed sooner? Better question, how was she going to keep him from finding out?

Chapter 17

Something was wrong. Killian could feel it every time their eyes met. There was a tremor in her gaze, a flicker of something that kept her from maintaining the contact for more than a second before focusing on something else. Plus she was unnaturally distracted. It worried him far more than he knew what to do with, especially when she refused to tell him so he could fix it.

"Have you changed your mind?" he asked one evening as they lay across the tangled expense of the bed, their damp bodies cooling.

As she so often did now, she had her back to him, which she did the moment he moved off her, as though she couldn't stand the sight of him.

"About what?" Her voice was barely audible.

"Europe."

She shook her head. "No, not unless you have."

He couldn't stand it anymore. "Juliette."

She flinched when he touched her. Actually flinched. It was such a slap that he could only sit there with his hand outstretched, his mind torn with disbelief and a swelling of hurt.

"I need the washroom," she whispered, already scrambling out of bed with the sheets and hurrying across the room.

What had he done? He couldn't think of a single thing. Had he hurt her? Wouldn't she tell him if he had? Was he asking for too much of her time? Did she need a rest? None of it made sense, because Juliette had never bottled up her feelings when she was angry with him or if he'd done something wrong. She had always been open and honest about everything. It made no sense why she was pulling away from him.

The bathroom door opened and she emerged. Dressed. He hadn't even seen her take her clothes with her.

"Juliette?" He sat up.

"I have some work to do at home," she whispered. "But I'll see you tomorrow."

"Juliette!" Her name snapped out of him in a warning growl before she could reach the door. "What is going on with you?"

"Nothing. I told you—"

"Bullshit." He threw himself off the bed and got to his feet. He made his way to where she stood, back rigid. "You've been running from me for days and I want to know why." He softened his voice. "Have I hurt you?"

He saw her fingers draw into tight fists at her sides. Her head lowered even as it rocked from side to side.

"No."

He barely heard her.

"Then what is it?" Carefully, terrified she'd flinch at his touch a second time, he took her arm and turned her slowly towards him. "Tell me."

"I've just been tired," she murmured, talking to her feet. "I'll do better."

"Stop it!" He gave her a gentle shake. "You know the only thing I care about is you."

Her chin lifted and he was sucker punched by the tears glistening in her eyes. There was raw agony shining beneath the gold that wrenched through him. His first instinct was to shake her again until she told him what the matter was. Instead, he found his fingers moving to frame her face.

"Do I need to kill someone?"

He'd meant it as a joke—partially. He'd hoped it would make her laugh. But her face crumpled. She jerked out of his hands and ran for the door. Then she was gone before he could even wrap his head around what he'd done wrong.

There was no sleep for him that night. Never mind that he didn't have her to lull him into unconsciousness, but couldn't stop seeing her face, the pain trembling along her bottom lip. Over and over he'd gone over every moment of the last few days, dissecting everything they'd done together and coming up with nothing. Their love making ... sex, damn it. Their sex had been as per usual. Since Halloween, he hadn't surprised her with anything overly new. He still made sure he took care to be reasonably gentle, to not let the beast get too carried away. But the question remained.

Sleep a mere illusion, he slipped out of bed and padded from the room. The corridor lights had been dimmed, but he knew the way down with his eyes closed. A deep sort of silence echoed through the place, the kind that demanded things he couldn't provide. His mother had designed the estate with children in mind. Lots and lots of children. She had always wanted a huge family, but could only have Killian. Her hopes had been that he would wind up giving her an army of grandchildren. Instead, he refused to give her even one. But she would understand. After what became of her and his father, she would know why it was important the McClary name died with him. Smith's attack was the perfect example. It might have been small in the scheme of things, but it was an attack inside Killian's home. Had he had a wife and children, had his men not been able to handle the situation ... the very thought of them coming to harm drenched him in cold sweat.

No. People like him didn't deserve a family. They didn't get a future. The most he could ask for was a kiss of happiness, a whisper of warmth to ease a cold existence. That happened to be Juliette. She was his one taste of peace. There would be none after her. How could there be when the thought of letting her go had become a fear worse than any nightmare he'd ever had? How could any woman ever possibly take that place? He loved her. Juliette had left him no choice. She had crashed into his world like a beautiful storm and disrupted everything. He could admit it to himself in the dark recess of his own mind. He had only ever loved one other woman, but he knew what it was even if it was completely different.

The conservatory doors opened with no effort. The hinges creaked on the weather worn frame. Stone slabs cut cold strips into the bottoms of his bare feet as he followed their path deeper into the darkness. Humidity clung to his skin, strangling the air in his lungs, but it was a familiar sort of pain, one he had visited often when sleep had become an elusive ghost.

Like his mother's garden, the conservatory held no rhythm or reason. There was no order other than the path that delved deeper into the madness. She had wanted a jungle, a beautiful chaos of colors and that was what she had created. Killian couldn't name even half of the blooms and foliage. They all looked the same to him. But he made certain nothing ever changed. Not a single plant. His father had done the same, except for the dais erected in the very heart of it all. The pedestal Killian visited on nights the world was caving in on him.

Pale fingers of light drifted down from the glass dome overhead to shower over the twin silver pots. It shone along the rims and spiked off the gold knobs on the lids. Killian lowered himself down on the only chair in the place and looked up at what was left of the parents who had given their lives for his.

"Hi Mom." He lowered his chin and peered down at his fingers hanging uselessly between his knees. "I know I promised to bring Juliette the next time I came, but that might not happen. I think she's had all she can of me. Not surprised, honestly. A woman like her wants forever and a man she can be assured a future with. I can only give her a year and that's too much." He scrubbed an agitated palm over his face and back through his hair. "It was a mistake keeping her. It was wrong of me to think ... I was selfish. Now she's going to walk away and I ... I'll have nothing."

Seconds closed as he tried to picture what he'd do when she ultimately walked out the door and never came back. Every day was one day less in their contract, one day closer to the end. It was only a matter of time when he would wake up to an empty bed and be alone forever.

"You'd've liked her," he told the concrete space between his feet. "Damn temper of hers would have made you proud." A soft chuckle escaped him. "And God she's a stubborn woman. Not a day goes by when I don't know whether I want to strangle her or kiss her." His smile slipped. "She's too good for the likes of me. She's too innocent and … I'd rather die alone than live without her."

He fell silent. The last of his words echoed in the muggy stillness. It faded. Then there was nothing, but creeping emptiness; his mother, if she had any advice, said nothing. The urn sat perfectly still on its wooden platform.

He stayed a few more minutes before saying goodbye and returning to the front of the house. Dawn was approaching, painting the sky a soft, pastel pink. The early morning air was chilly with the promise of snow. Killian paid no mind as made his way to the office, still bare foot and topless. He claimed the leather chair behind the desk and waited for Frank.

Chapter 18

There was no shortage to her stupidity, Juliette realized as she busied her hands sorting pens into different pen holders. It wasn't exactly a necessary job, nobody cared if the red, black and blue were mixed. But it was better than standing at an empty desk, waiting for the day to end so she could fix the monumental shit storm she'd caused.

What the hell was the matter with her? It was the same question she'd asked herself repeatedly since her dramatic fleeing earlier that morning from Killian. Yet no matter how many times the question was asked, she still had no response, except that she was an idiot.

So she loved the guy. Big deal. She wasn't some stupid hormonal teenager—at least, she wasn't supposed to act like one. She was a grown woman who knew how to control her damn emotions. So, just because she loved Killian, didn't mean it had to change anything. It wasn't like she needed to tell him. It could be her secret, and when the time came to say goodbye, she would, yet again, be a mature individual and ... accept that.

Her gut wrenched, but she told it to shut up. Her gaze flicked to the clock on the monitor and she breathed a sigh of relief to see she had five minutes left. Then she'd grab her things and head straight to Killian's estate where she would apologize and assure him she wasn't crazy.

Celina arrived promptly at six. She stalked straight past Juliette like she hadn't seen her and disappeared into the host room behind the desk. Juliette rolled her eyes, but made no mention of it as she turned and followed, not to make conversation, but to grab her things.

The host room was a much smaller version of the staff room. It was a closet sized bit of space with a square table, two chairs and a row of six lockers. Celina was at hers, hastily shoving her coat and purse inside. Juliette moved to the one at the very end, near the wall and removed her own coat and purse. The two finished their business without sharing a single word or glance. Celina had made it perfectly clear that she did not trust Juliette. That it was clear she was obviously sleeping with someone very important if she was able to keep her job after the *official* letter Celina had written to Harold, which had gone ignored. Juliette didn't give a shit.

She threw on her coat and marched from the room. She paused briefly to toss the master keys out of her pocket onto the table before making her way through the foyer.

Frank met her at the doors, a garment bag tossed carefully over one beefy arm. The sight of him had her automatically darting excited glances behind him, searching for the face she could never get out of her head. But he wasn't there. Neither was Jake or Melton.

"Mr. McClary has sent me to escort you, ma'am," Frank said coolly. "He wishes for you to join him for the evening."

Juliette faced the man. "Join him where?"

Frank held out the bag. "A place of his choosing, ma'am. He asks that you wear this."

Bemused, she took the hanger gingerly and glanced towards the bathroom. But rather than follow directions, she looked to Frank again.

"Who's watching him, Frank?"

"He is perfectly safe where he is," Frank assured her.

Juliette wasn't so sure, after all, his home was supposed to be safe and yet someone had managed to hurt him there.

The doubt must have shown on her face because his face softened. "I would not have left him otherwise."

Still unsure, but deciding not to waste time arguing about it, Juliette hurried to the bathroom. She locked herself up in one of the cubicles and began to undress.

There were shoes with the elegant, burgundy gown, strappy, silver things with five inches of heel. She pulled it all on before teetering her way out of the stall towards the mirror.

The Grecian gown was gorgeous with a single bunched bit of fabric over one shoulder and a sweetheart neckline. The chiffon material flowed from the cinched waist down in a flurry of shimmery movement. With the silver heels, it was absolutely stunning.

Needing to show off the cluster of diamonds pinned to the sash over her shoulder, she scooped up her hair and dug through her purse for the small Ziploc of hair things she kept inside. She pinned and fastened the blonde strands in a messy knot that left tendrils framing her face. She applied a fresh coat of makeup next before stuffing her old clothes into the garment bag and leaving to find Frank.

She didn't need to go far. He was waiting for her right outside the door.

He bowed his head once before taking the items from her.

"This way."

She followed him outside in the frigid November evening. Her gaze swung up as they crossed the parking lot to the SUV. The heavens were clear, but she knew it was only a matter of time before they were buried beneath a thick layer of snow.

"Where are we going, Frank?" she asked as he opened the back door for her.

"It's not far," was his smooth response.

Knowing better than to push, she slipped into the seat and watched him close the door behind her. He circled around and got behind the wheel.

He hadn't been lying about not going far. The drive couldn't have been more than fifteen minutes. When they stopped, he left the car idling as a short, beaming man hurried to open the door for her.

"Miss Romero?"

Juliette nodded.

The man's smile widened. "I'm Vince. Mr. McClary has asked me to take you inside."

Her gaze swept past the man to the building. It wasn't anything special, a squat, brick building in the middle of the warehouse district of town. But she let herself get helped out of the car.

"Frank, can I leave my purse with you?" she asked.

From behind the wheel, Frank inclined his head. "Yes ma'am."

Thanking him, she followed Vince through a set of metal doors. They opened in a cramped little stairway stained with graffiti and grime. It was not the sort of place she would have chosen to wear such a lovely dress, but Killian must have had a reason.

"This way."

Vince motioned her to follow him to the metal steps and up. There was three flights before the top. Juliette was breathless by the time they reached the green door at the top.

Vince beamed. Without a word, he jerked the door open and stepped aside for her to go in first.

Candles, dozens upon dozens of candles illuminated every square inch of loft space. Fairy lights twisted around wooden beams and ran rampant in loops from the rafters. In the center of it all, closed in from all sides by white, gauze drapes, sat an elegantly set table for two equipped by two long stemmed candles and delicate china.

Of all the things she'd expected, this was not it.

"You look gorgeous."

Startled, Juliette turned. Behind her, breathtaking in a black suit, Killian offered her a crooked smile that made her heart trip. His thick, wavy locks were swept off his brow and combed back to leave his freshly shaven face open. The ends curled over the crisp collar of his blazer. Beneath it, his shirt was a blinding white, a sharp contrast to the slash of silky black running down his chest to the gold buckle holding up his trousers. He reminded her of a model straight off the glossy pages of GQ.

"You look pretty nice yourself," she choked out, inexplicably breathless. She moistened her lips. "What is all this?"

He moved towards her in slow, even strides. His hands found their way into the depths of his trouser pockets. His dark eyes shimmered beneath the flickering candlelight.

"I thought we'd try something different tonight. If that's all right with you?"

While she liked going home to him and letting him work the stress out of every muscle in her body, a girl could hardly say no to a secret candlelight dinner.

"Oh, I'm sure I can manage," she said, offering him a teasing grin. Her smile softened and she reached for him. Her palm settled on the soft material of his blazer, just over his heart. "This is incredible. Thank you."

His hand closed over hers, swallowing her fingers as he drew her closer. "I merely oversaw the process."

She shook her head. "Doesn't matter. You could have just as easily taken us to a restaurant. There are a hundred fancy ones all over the city. Instead you did this." She looked over the room, still in absolute awe of its beauty. "I love it so much."

His eyes darkened. His fingers tightened around hers. "Good."

He led her to the table and drew out her chair. He waited until she was properly seated before rounding to his side.

Juliette waited until he was facing her before blurting the question that had been plaguing her.

"Is this because of this morning?" His eyes lowered, the only sign she needed to confirm her theory. "I promise that won't happen again. I am honestly so sorry for—"

"No," he cut in softly. "Don't be sorry. I haven't been very fair to you and that's my fault."

Juliette blinked. "What do you mean?"

He raised his gaze and fixed them on her face. "Doesn't matter. I don't want to talk about anything upsetting this evening. I just want to enjoy you."

A smile tugged on her heart. "I'm all for you enjoying me." She propped her elbows on the table, threaded her fingers together and perched her chin on her knuckles. "Tell me about your day."

Killian leaned back in his chair. "I did some work. Made some calls. Nothing out of the ordinary."

Juliette narrowed her eyes. "And somewhere between the working and call making, you put this together and bought me an amazing dress, which I absolutely love."

His lips quirked. "It's an all right dress. You make it beautiful."

Juliette laughed. "Are you trying to charm me into your bed, Mr. McClary? Because I have to warn you, I have a very long list of suitors vying for my affections."

One dark eyebrow lifted in amusement. "Have you now?"

"Worried?" she teased.

His grin was slow and brutally arrogant. "Ah darling, not at all. Your body will always belong to me. No other man will ever make it come apart the way I do."

Her body gave a shiver in agreement. All amusement becoming a hot, sticky rush of liquid soaking her panties. Her clit throbbed in longing.

He smirked with all the knowing grace of a man fully aware of his effect on his woman.

Juliette swallowed audibly. "You don't play fair."

He leaned forward and lowered his voice to that gravelly purr that drove her crazy. "You don't like it when I play fair. You like it when I'm dirty and rough. You like it when I rip off your panties, bend you over and fuck you until you can't walk for a week, or when I put my fingers deep inside your wet little pussy and make you scream. That's how you like me."

It was true. Fuck being fair. She lived for the nights when he tortured her mindless, when he had her so worked up she was certain she'd die if he didn't end the suffering. There was nothing fair or loving about those nights. It was all a brutal battle of hot, sweaty bodies colliding with one goal in mind—to fuck each other into exhaustion.

"Well, that can go both ways," she croaked out, willing her body to calm down before she upended the table to get to him. "I recall you begging a few times."

"I won't deny it, I am addicted to your pussy."

A second ticked.

Juliette laughed. "God, we sound like a pair of sex maniacs."

He drew in a deep breath and exhaled it slowly. "Only with you, love. Only ever with you."

Heart giving an undignified flip in her chest, Juliette started to open her mouth when a rumble filled the vast space around them. The sound tore her away from the deep yearning coiling deep inside her. Her head whipped around just in time to see the cargo elevator gate slide open and a stout little man hurry out pushing a silver cart. He bustled over, bowed low first to her, then to Killian. Without a word, he removed the dome off the tray, revealing two steaming plates, both holding the same sized slabs of filet mignon with a side order of asparagus. The dishes were set in front of them. The man bowed again and hurried away as quickly as he'd come.

"Thank you!" She called after him, but he was already lost behind the sliding door. She turned her attention forward and found Killian watching her quietly. She offered him a small smile. "This looks delicious," she murmured, needing to break the silence that had sweltered around them as hot and thick as a balmy July heatwave.

She picked up her knife and fork and cut into the tender meat. The silverware across from her clinked as they were lifted, but not utilized. She popped a bit of meat into her mouth and almost moaned as the seasoned flavor exploded across her tongue in a juicy rush. It took all her restraint not to wolf it all down, screw dignity.

"God, this might actually get you laid!" she blurted.

Killian laughed. "Well, as much as I would like to take credit, I can't say I had much hand in its preparation."

"Killian?" Juliette lifted her face. "Can I ask you something?"

He nodded. "Of course."

"Where's your sister?" she asked.

"Maraveet isn't exactly my sister," he corrected. "She's more of a self-appointed pain in my ass."

Juliette chuckled. "Got one of those too, eh?"

Killian snorted. "Our moms were best friends so I was always forced to play with her. Tea parties and dress up ... it was a bloody nightmare."

She had to bite back her laugh. "Not into tea parties and dress up?"

Dark eyes flicked to hers, narrowed with annoyance and a shimmer of amusement. "I think my hatred of tea and frilly dresses stemmed from those hot summer afternoons."

The laughter burst out of her in a roar she had to stifle behind her hand. The other went to her stomach as her body bowed forward.

"It's not funny," he grumbled, his own mouth twitching. "She'd parade me around the manor and chatter on about how many handsome gentlemen would ask us to dance at the ball later that evening."

Juliette sucked in enough air to ask, "There was a ball?"

"Every fucking night." He rubbed a hand over his eyes like the memory was forever burned behind his eyelids. "She'd bring out all her dolls and sit them around the room, then she'd make me spin her round and round…"

"I like her," Juliette decided. "She sounds like fun."

He lowered his hand. "Demanding, spoiled ... stubborn. Dear God she was fucking stubborn." He paused as a thought came to him. "I am forever surrounded by stubborn women."

"So, where is she?"

Killian shrugged. "Could be anywhere. I got a text from her a few months back from Paris. I might hear from her again in a week or month or year."

Her smile faded. "You guys aren't close anymore?"

"Oh, we're close, but with her line of work, she can't keep in close contact." His gaze lowered to the table cloth. "It's not safe for either of us to be close."

"That's so sad," she whispered, sitting back, food forgotten. "To not be able to ever have a family or anyone you can love. How do you stand it?"

"By not having a family or anyone to love," he murmured. "This life is a solitary one. There are a few, like our fathers, who think they can cheat their fate. They meet a woman, fall in love, and start a family, but ultimately, it never lasts. Their children become shadows of them and they ... they die."

A tightness filled her throat, making it impossible to breathe. "Where are Maraveet's parents?"

"They died in a car bombing when she was seven. Maraveet was staying with us, but she was supposed to be with them when it happened."

"Oh my God..."

"That is why I can't keep you for longer than a year, Juliette. This alone has put you in more danger than you can possibly imagine, but I needed this, need you, as selfish as that is."

Pushing back her chair, Juliette got to her feet and walked around to his side of the table. He was already expecting her. His hands closed around her hips and he drew her into his lap. Her arms went around his shoulders.

"Get out," she whispered into the warm stretch of skin along his neck. "Don't do this anymore." She hesitated a full heartbeat before adding in the quietest murmur, "Stay with me."

His arms around her tightened. His head turned to nuzzle his face into her chest.

"There is no out." His fingers tightened into her hip even as he burned the words into the soft material of her dress. "There will always be someone who will want what I have and eventually, one day, my luck will run out."

"Stop it!" The world tore out of her in a strangled growl. "Don't say that. There has to be a way." She drew back enough to peer into his eyes, her own filmy with tears. "You just … you need to find it." She touched the side of his cleanly shaven face. "I can't lose you, Killian."

He kissed her, but it was unlike all the other kisses he'd given her in the past. This one was too much like a goodbye that she jerked back. Her hand went to her lips, damp and trembling.

"Don't do that," she whispered, voice unusually choked. "Don't kiss me like you're saying goodbye."

For too long, he said nothing. The dark glint continued to play across his features in a knot of light and shadows. Everything about him was light and shadows, she realized. It was what had always called to her. His demons and angels.

"I've got something for you," he said unexpectedly, temporarily distracting her.

Juliette straightened a notch. "What?"

He gently nudged her off his lap and rose with her. He offered her his hand, which she took without hesitance.

"Well, you won't get it if you keep frowning at me," he told her as he walked with her backwards away from the table.

"I'm not frowning," she muttered. "I'm concerned. There's a difference."

He stopped and reached for her face. "Your concern has your eyebrows fighting." He rubbed lightly at the place between her eyebrows with the pad of his thumb, as though attempting to erase the crinkle there. "Come on. Smile for me."

It was hard to keep a straight face when someone says smile. It was an almost reflexive gesture. Immediately, her face softened and her mouth tilted.

"That's very nifty trick," she told him.

"Right?" Grinning, he pulled back. "All right, I'm going to show you how to waltz."

Juliette laughed. "Waltz? Are we in the seventeen hundreds?" Her eyes narrowed. "How do you know how to waltz?"

"I know many things," he remarked airily.

"Are you any good?" she wondered as he positioned her across from him.

"I am always good."

Juliette rolled her eyes. "Of course. All right. How do we start?"

"First, I need one hand here…" He took her left hand and set it on his shoulder. Once properly in place, he dropped his palm to her waist. "And the other here." He clasped her free hand in his. He positioned them a proper foot width away. "Now, you have to imagine a box on the floor around our feet. It's big enough for both of us to move easily around in it. When we start, I will move my left foot forward while you move your right foot back. Then we count three beats and move together right."

"My right or your right?"

"Mine."

Nodding that she understood, she braced herself.

"Ready? One … Two … three … and back…"

It wasn't so hard. It was basically line dancing, but in the same four spots, not that it stopped her from stomping on his toe or tripping over her own feet. Killian held her up and patiently guided her through the next step. The whole thing was made a hundred times better by the fact that he kept her laughing. Most of her missteps were due to her inability to keep upright when her body kept doubling over.

"I won't lie," Killian said at one point. "You are a horrible dancer."

"Shut up!" Panting, she wiggled her shoulders and tried to portray a look of confidence that was horribly skewered by the peal of giggles threatening to burst out. "Maybe you're just a horrible instructor."

He sniffed indignantly. "Unlikely. I'm a McClary and thus born with the natural graces of a swan."

There was no stopping the roar that exploded from her. Her head flung back as the sound exploded from deep in her thorax. Tears welled and spilled down her cheeks in a hot stream. Her legs abandoned her to be held up solely by his hands. Against her temple, Killian's chuckle warmed the skin. It ruffled her hair. His chest rumbled against hers as she sagged into him. At one point, she was no longer even making a sound, just an odd jittering that raked through her entire body.

"Okay..." She wheezed air into her lungs and struggled to straighten. "Okay, teach me that leg curvy thing."

"Leg curvy thing?"

Wiping her eyes, she nodded. "That thing with the leg going around her partner's leg."

He considered this a moment. "I think you're thinking of ballroom dancing. We're waltzing."

She wrinkled her nose at him. "Show me!"

His eyes narrowed warily. "I don't know if I want to. You might accidentally kick me in the crotch and I might strangle you."

She broke out in another fit of giggles at the thought. "I'll be careful."

He didn't look convinced, but he stepped back once he was certain she could stand on her own feet.

"I'll spin you out, then back in, and when I do, you hook your outer leg around mine."

Nodding that she understood, she waited for the tug as he spun her out fluidly under his arm. Then, with an equally perfect jerk, he spun her back into his chest. But rather than execute a flawless leg twist, she slammed into him, nearly sending them both to the ground.

"Again!" she demanded. "I almost had it."

It was his turn to laugh, but he obliged. He even did it slower so she had time, but it wasn't as easy as it always looked on TV. By the time her head stopped spinning, she'd missed her step, which was another tricky matter entirely. In the end, she never got it and wound up just hooking her leg around his hip for the hell of it without the turns.

"Do you think we're ready to compete professionally?"

Killian snorted a chuckle. "Maybe if you show a bit more leg."

"And boobs," she added.

"Definitely boobs," he agreed. "You certainly have nice ones."

Laughing, she pulled away. "Our food is cold."

"Do you want to eat or see what I have planned next?"

Juliette's eyes widened. "There's more?"

His answer was a grin as he took her hand and led her away from the magical room with the nearly melted candles. She paused at the door to glance back, wanting to imprint the moment forever to memory before following him down the stairs.

"I'm a little sad to leave," she admitted.

"We can come back again," he promised, squeezing her fingers.

The SUV with Frank in the front seat was exactly where she'd last seen it, parked out front with the engine running. Killian yanked open the back door before Frank could climb out and helped Juliette inside. He swung in after her and shut the door.

Without a word, Frank started driving.

"Where are we going?" she asked.

"You're not very good at this surprise thing, are you?" Killian mused.

She dug a teasing elbow into his side, but didn't ask again.

They drove for twenty minutes in the endless darkness that seemed to stretch forever along the highway. Next to her, Killian sat watching the window. His stoic profile hung in shadows and a tinge of green from the dashboard in front. Juliette studied him from the corner of her eye and wondered how he could be so calm doing what he did. She would have been a neurotic basket case. She couldn't imagine how anyone could get used to constantly being in danger. But he was right about one thing, she could never have a family with him, not like this. She could never bring a child into such an uncertain world. In the end, they really did only have less than a year. She didn't know what she'd do after that.

As though sensing her distress, her sadness, a hand settled lightly in her lap and curled around hers. Wordlessly, she turned her palm over and threaded their fingers together.

They came to a stop outside a single level building barely visible in the dark. Killian kept a hold on her fingers as he led her around the side to a set of double doors. Black drapes greeted them in a foyer no bigger than a closet. A single light gleamed down on them, sharp and hot. Killian swept the curtains aside and followed a narrow hall deeper into the semi darkness. More lights led their way to a door at the very end, painted in black.

"It's not one of those haunted houses at the fair, is it?" Juliette breathed, her fingers tightening around his. "I will not forgive you if it is."

"Why would I bring you to a haunted house?"

It was a good question, one she didn't have an answer to, but the queasy sensation didn't abate. He reached for the gold handle and she held her breath.

It opened to—surprise-surprise—more black walls and black curtains. But the room was larger and held a gilded mirror and two black chairs. There was a series of straps and hooks on the first one.

Killian led her in and shut the door behind them. Then he began to shrug out of his blazer. He undid the tie. Then the top two buttons on his dress shirt.

"What are you doing?" she asked when he undid his cuffs. "Oh my God, are we in a sex dungeon?"

Killian froze. His back was to her, but she could see the sudden tension snapping across the widths of his shoulders. His fingers ceased their unbuttoning and hovered over the gold knot. Slowly, he turned on the heel of one foot and faced her. His expression gave nothing away.

"A sex dungeon?" He said the words as though testing them across his tongue, like the very idea was foreign. "A sex dungeon," he repeated, still very slowly, but with a ribbon of amusement. "Would you like it to be?"

Juliette felt her cheeks prickle with heat. "Isn't it?"

He bent his head to one side and regarded her evenly. "That isn't answering my question."

"I ... I don't know," she stuttered awkwardly. "What would you do to me?"

The heat was unbearable shifting and flaring off him. It seemed to fill the room, stifling the air and making it impossible to breathe.

"Do you trust me?"

She nodded without hesitation. "Yes."

A sound escaped him, a low, rumbling growl that raked down the length of her spine.

"Come here."

She went. Her eyes never left his as she watched him reach for the straps on the chair. He pulled it to him and she realized the straps were sewn lengthwise across a thick vest. The thing was drawn down over her head. Her arms were passed through the holes and the straps slipped through the hooks tight.

Juliette knew nothing of bondage other than what Killian had done to her in the hotel room. She knew people did all sorts of crazy things with ropes and it was all supposed to be liberating and sensual, but she wasn't sure how she felt about the vest.

Nevertheless, Killian had never done anything she hadn't liked. Maybe this would be one of them.

He stepped back from her and her head shot up. He was still watching her with that sneaky grin of his. It made her insides knot.

"Should I take my dress off?" she asked.

"No."

Her shoulders drooped. "Are you going to rip it?" Her hands went over the fabric of her skirt. "I really like this dress."

Killian chuckled. "We'll try to keep it in one piece. If not, I will get you another one."

Exhaling in reluctant acceptance, she watched as he finished undoing the buttons on his cuff and rolling up his sleeve. Then he too tugged on a vest.

Her confusion must have shown on her face, because his smirk widened.

"Go on," he encouraged. "Tell me what you're thinking."

Juliette shook her head, her expression sour. "No, you're laughing at me."

He did laugh. "You're adorable," was all he said.

Straps secured, he motioned her to the wall on the other side of the mirror. His hand closed around a strip of white she'd mistaken for stripped paint and tugged. The hatch swung open seamlessly to reveal another room on the other side. Juliette's nerves whimpered as they were assaulted by the sharp scent of sweat. Her limbs trembled.

She'd heard of sex clubs where people played out their crazy fantasies of being tied up and ... who knew what. But she had never actually considered looking one up, not that she would know where to start looking. The thought of what she might see and what Killian might ask her to do rippled through her in electric currents of anxiety. She wasn't all together certain she even wanted to be there.

In the cramped little hallway with its purple carpet and black walls, Juliette stood trembling as she waited for Killian to give her further instructions. She fiddled nervously with the straps on her vest while casting furtive glances towards the bend at the end of the corridor.

"Killian, I don't know—" A helmet was set firmly on her head. "What…?"

His fingers brushed the underside of her chin as he fastened the strap.

"Hold still." The clip locked with a soft click. "There."

He turned away and tugged on his own black helmet. The lights overhead skated across the plastic flap fixed to the top. A face guard, she thought, watching as he did his own chin strap.

"What is this?" she demanded, no longer believing this was some weird sex dungeon.

A heavy bit of plastic and metal was dropped into her hands. A gun. She would have dropped it, except it looked nothing like a real gun. For one, it was too thick and the screws were fake. For another, there were lights inside and they were flashing different colors.

"Laser tag," he said, now that she no longer believed he was dragging her off to get gagged and flogged. "Not nearly as exciting as a sex dungeon, mind you, but I'm sure you'll enjoy it all the same."

Juliette gaped. "Laser tag?" She looked down at the gun before fixing him with her annoyance. "You had me believing…"

"That I was going to strip you naked and put you over my knee?" He smirked. "I still might, but you'll have to ask very nicely."

Her face exploded with colors. "Ass!"

"Don't be like that, my pervy little lamb." He took hold of her chin and lifted her face up for a hard kiss. "If it means that much to you, I'll build you your own playroom and we'll do whatever you like."

The thought was tempting.

"I'm not very good with surprises," she admitted a bit sheepishly.

One eyebrow lifted in mock disbelief. "You don't say. I could hardly tell."

She swatted at him. Laughing, he captured her hand and tugged her down the hall.

The bend opened to yet another door that led to an enormous arena made up entirely of foam walls, ramps, nets, pipes, mirrors and tiny crawl spaces. The overhead strobe lights swung in time to the heavy techno beat pounding through the chamber in a flurry of pink, blue and yellow. Everything was painted black with streaks of yellow. Even the floor had yellow arrows guiding people around the obstacles. But they were the only ones there.

"Have you done this before?" she asked, loud enough to be heard over the bass.

Killian shook his head, his face actually flushed with excitement. "I've always wanted to though."

It was hard to believe when faced with a man who ran an entire empire, a man who was always so confident and powerful, that he might actually still have a fun side. Unlike her, he'd never had a chance at childhood. Not a real one. Had he even had any friends other than Maraveet? She wondered with a touch of sadness. But she shook it away and forced herself to grin.

"Well, you're in trouble then, because I have." Skirt in one hand, gun in the other, she started for the opening. "Be prepared to lose, McClary."

In the end, she wound up ripping her own skirt while trying to roll out of a crouch and catching the hem under her foot. The score was two-three and she had no idea what she'd done to her heels. She vaguely recalled getting fed up and tossing them somewhere. But in the scheme of winning, they mattered little.

It was their last game. Juliette was up by one point. She'd lost sight of Killian somewhere by the foam pillars. Her plan had been to retreat before he recovered, circle around, and come up behind him, but so far, she'd lost sight of him and the clock was running out.

Against the stiff material of her light-up vest, her heart thundered with adrenaline and a tinge of fear that came with getting caught. Sweat slickened her grip on the gun. She tightened her fingers and edged closer to the end of the makeshift wall. The rubber material felt cold against her back as she pressed up against it and counted her breaths. Carefully, she slide forward and peered around the corner. A jungle of tangled ropes hung ahead, blocking her path to the tunnels on the other side. It was the perfect place to hide.

Holding the air in her lungs, she took a step forward.

"Not so fast." One toned forearm closed across her chest and yanked her back into a solid chest, eliciting a squeak from her. "Now you're mine, little lamb."

Heart going wild, Juliette laughed. "How did you get behind me?"

His lips grazed her ear. "You're not the only one who knows how to circle around."

"I was so close." She turned to face him. "One more game to break the tie?"

A streak of blue light shot across his face, illuminating his eyes. "Not tonight. It's late."

Juliette pouted. "But I was winning!"

He frowned and tugged lightly on a strand of hair that had escaped the helmet. "I think a tie means we were both winning."

"But I would have won," she clarified.

"Only because my injuries still hurt."

Juliette immediately stiffened. "Are you all right? You didn't rip the stitches, did you?"

"I'm only teasing, love." He took her hand. "Come." He led her towards the red sign marked EXIT. "Where are you shoes?"

She glanced down at her bare feet, then back at the obstacle course they were leaving behind.

"Not sure," she answered honestly. "In there somewhere."

Killian sighed. "Such an odd woman."

They reached the hallway and their helmets and guns were returned to the little shelves built into the wall. Their vests were hooked just underneath the cubicles and they pushed through the hidden door into the first room.

"I had fun," she said as Killian threw on his blazer and shoved his tie into his pocket.

He smiled. "Even if it wasn't the sex dungeon you had your heart set on?"

She elbowed him. "It was better."

In the foyer, he bent at the waist and easily swung her up into his arms.

"Can't having you walking on sharp rocks, now can we?" he said when she shot him a curious glance.

Frank stood by the SUV, holding the door open when they ducked out into the frigid night. Juliette hissed as the wintery air clawed at her sweat kissed skin. Killian pulled her closer to him, but it wasn't enough to save her from the cold. Hurriedly, he set her into the backseat and joined her in the warm cabin. Frank shut the door.

Juliette tugged her coat on, her teeth chattering. Her fingers trembled, but she managed to zip the material up to her chin. Killian wrapped an arm around her and dragged her into his side where she nuzzled her cold nose into the curve of his neck.

She must have dozed off, though she had no recollection of it, because when she opened her eyes again, they were rolling to a stop up the driveway of her house. The lights were all off, but she knew Javier or Laurence, or both would be at the window, watching.

She turned to the man still holding her, bemused.

He smiled gently. "Come on."

Groggy, she let herself get helped out of the car and up the stairs to her front porch. Frank followed with her purse and the garment bag with her original clothes. She took both and thanked him. He bowed his head before returning to the car, leaving her alone with Killian.

"Are we not going to your place tonight?" she asked, her voice hoarse with sleep.

Killian shook his head. "Not tonight. Tonight, I'm going to walk you to your door and kiss you goodnight."

Juliette frowned. "Why?"

He framed her chilled face between his warm palms. "Because tonight wasn't about getting you in bed." Then he kissed her, slow and gentle. It was barely a minute long, but they were both breathless. "Goodnight, Juliette."

Heart a wild bird beating against the cage of her ribs, Juliette swallowed weakly. "Night, Killian. Thank you for tonight."

She stepped back when he released her. Her fingers were unsteady when she reached for the doorknob. He was still standing there when she let herself inside. She gave him one final glance as he stood out there in the predawn, looking beautiful and rumpled before shutting the door."

Chapter 19

"All the arrangements have been made, sir."

Frank set the pages down on Killian's desk. Flight departures, hotel locations, and a clear map of all the places they would visit during their European getaway.

"Has Juliette seen these?"

Frank shook his head. "No sir. I only just received the final confirmation."

Killian held out the pages. "Have Juliette go over them when she gets here in a little while. Let her know to mark down anything she'd like added or removed. Then I want her to send you an exact number of bags she will be bringing along."

Frank took the papers. "Yes sir."

"How are we doing with Viola's school? Are they still refusing to give her the month off?"

The hard set of Frank's face said it before his mouth could answer. "Due to the state of her grades and the number of absences she's already accumulated, they think it would be unwise to give her the time off."

Killian sighed. "And Juliette refuses to leave without the girl. Tell them we will hire a tutor to come along with us and that we are willing to make a generous donation—"

Frank straightened, his attention no longer on Killian. One meaty hand had lifted to his ear, the other was lifted to his mouth. His thick brows had drawn together low over his eyes that were staring straight through Killian.

"Secure the gates!" he barked into the bit of plastic poking through the cuff of his sleeve. "Stay at your posts." He turned his dark gaze down towards Killian. "There has been an incident, sir. Please remain in your office."

With that, he turned on his heels and marched from the room, pausing only long enough to shut the doors behind him.

Killian watched him with one hand inching towards the drawer on his right, the one now heavy with his father's Desert Eagle, .357mag. It was loaded. He'd made sure of that the moment he'd retrieved it from the gun vault. He'd even started carrying it with him, something he'd always prayed he'd never have to do. But after Smith's attack, it had almost become a necessity. It had also become a task keeping it concealed from Juliette. The last thing he wanted was to further concern her. Lord knew she worried enough.

"Your men are absolutely hopeless, I hope you are aware."

Reflexes had the gun in his hand in the time it took to suck in a breath. The hammer cocked beneath his thumb even as his arm shot out, directing the barrel straight for the figure throwing open his office doors and stalking in like she owned the place.

His arm wavered once before dropping.

"Maraveet?"

Beautiful with hair the color of fire and eyes the enormous green of a jungle cat's, Maraveet Árnason smirked at him from over the rim of her aviator glasses. Her small mouth turned up in one corner.

"Hello little brother." She sauntered deeper into his office, her knee high boots cracking with every fluid stride. "Did you miss me?"

The gun hit the top of his desk with a loud clatter as he shot to his feet. He cleared the desk in three steps and hoisted her up into his arms. Her laugh tinkled in his ear and warmed the side of his face. Slender arms closed about his neck. She squeezed until he coughed.

"God, I've missed you," he breathed into her shoulder.

Her feet, dangling two feet off the ground, gave a little kick, her signal for him to put her down. He did gingerly, but kept his hands on her shoulders.

She was small, barely coming to his chest with a heart shaped face and peaches and cream complexion. Tiny freckles adorned the fine bridge of her upturned nose and scattered the smooth curves of her pinkened cheeks. A fine, white scar broke through the left eyebrow where he'd thrown a rock at her when they'd been children. His mother had been furious, but Maraveet had been the one to tell him to do it. It hadn't been his fault she couldn't catch.

"What are you doing here?" he asked, breaking away from her and moving back to his desk.

Maraveet followed him. "What did you expect me to do when I hear you'd been shot? I would have been here sooner, but I ran into a spot of trouble with the Peruvian government." She offered him a smirk. "Apparently they don't like it when foreigners visit their museums late at night."

"Can you blame them?"

She considered this a moment, shrugged. "I suppose not, but throwing a girl in jail for doing her job is a bit much, isn't it? I had the devil of a time getting out. You wouldn't know it by looking, but they are very well designed."

Her adventures no longer shocked him as it used to. There was a time when her texts would read, *guess where I just was ... Russian prison!* And he'd just about lose his damn mind with worry. But she'd been in and out of so many that he no longer felt inclined to make the fuss.

"At least it wasn't the Chinese prison," he pointed out and saw her shudder.

"Don't remind me."

Grinning to himself, he reached for his discarded weapon and gingerly set the safety back in place; it was a miracle he hadn't fired the thing when he'd dropped it.

"Is that the only reason you broke out of prison? Because I'd been shot?"

Maraveet perched jean clad hips against the edge of his desk as he returned the gun to the drawer. She watched him. He could feel her penetrating stare burning holes through his clothes in search of his injuries.

"Maybe not entirely." She folded her arms over the soft fabric of her stretchy sweater. "What's this rubbish I hear about you having a girlfriend?"

There it was. The real reason for the impromptu visit. He'd known, but it was nice to hear it from the horse's ... sister's mouth.

"Juliette isn't my girlfriend." He shut the drawer and faced her. "She's also none of your business."

"Is that how you want to play this?" She shot up to her feet. "Do I need to wave the history flag in your stupid face?"

Moving to his chair, Killian dropped into it. "History won't repeat itself, because it's not like that. We have an agreement."

Green eyes narrowed in various crinkles of suspicion and doubt. "You're lying. Your nose is doing that ridiculous wrinkling thing."

He had absolutely no idea what she was talking about, but it was the same thing she always said when she had apparently caught him lying. He would check, but his pride was on the line.

"It's not wrinkling. You're imagining things."

She huffed and glowered some more, like she was trying to glower the truth from him. He returned her fierce scowl with a perfectly blank one of his own.

"All right, fine." She straightened and averted her face. "Since I have no choice, but to believe you, I will—"

A scuffle from the doorway put a pause on whatever rant she'd been concocting the whole way there. They both glanced to the hallway as voices rose. Killian's initial thought was Frank. He was just preparing to intercept what could quite possibly be a bloodbath between his head of security and his security breaking sister when a voice cried out. The scuffle intensified. Something hit the wall with a heavy thud.

"Let go of me! Killian!"

Killian was out of his chair with speeds that sent it sailing backwards. It slammed into the wall behind his desk and twirled, forgotten as its owner stormed around the desk. Vaguely, he heard Maraveet call out to him, but his head was already thriving with all the noise of his purpose propelling him forward.

In the opening, Juliette swung into view, struggling against the hands curled into the sleeve of her coat. Blonde curls bounced wildly around her pale face. She kicked and swung viciously at the man trying to pull her away.

"Get your hands off her!"

His warning came too late. The seam at her shoulder came undone. The fabric tore with a loud rip that added to the violent buzzing between his ears. The man's hold slipped. Juliette hit the ground with a cry that spiked straight through the cavity of Killian's very existence. Her head ricocheted off the plaster with a crack and she whimpered.

Killian saw red. His heart roared as his blood sizzled in his veins. Knuckles popped as all ten fingers closed into two balls of violence. He closed the distance and swung. The blow burst against the man's mouth, breaking skin and snapping his head back. He flew off his feet and crashed into the wall where he slumped to the ground in a daze.

"You ever put your fucking hands on her again, I'll make sure you leave without them!"

Leaving him there, Killian hurried to where Juliette was struggling to sit up. Her big, brown eyes met his, brimming with a terror that seared through him. It brought him to his knees next to her and was immediately caught in the strangling circle of her arms.

"Killian..." her voice broke against his shoulder.

"It's all right," he promised into the side of her head. "I've got you now."

Against the palms of his hands, her back shuddered. Her head shook.

"I got here and there was smoke everywhere and strange men with guns and ..." she rasped. "They wouldn't let me see you."

"I'm fine." His free hand slide beneath the heavy curtain of hair at the back of her head and gingerly stroked the lump rising there. "You need an ice pack."

"No." She pulled away enough to touch the spot herself. "I'm all right." Her eyes searched his face. "Are you okay?"

Carefully, he eased to his feet, pulling her along with him. His gaze went to the tear in her coat before returning to her eyes.

"My sister came to visit," he explained, which probably made no sense to her, because she frowned.

"The one you haven't seen in years?"

He nodded.

With a hand placed gingerly on the small of her back, he led her into his office where Maraveet was watching them with an expression that suggested she was witnessing a horrible crash. There was no mistaking the disapproval etched into the tight lines bracketing her downturned lips, or the once over she gave Juliette.

"Juliette, my sister Maraveet," he introduced.

Juliette offered her a small smile. "It's nice to meet you. Killian's told me so much about you."

That only seemed to fill Maraveet with even more suspicion. Her green eyes snapped to Killian and narrowed into thin, murderous slits.

"Has he now?"

Juliette must have realized she'd said something wrong, because her smile faded. She glanced from Maraveet to Killian with a look of uncertainty.

"Only that you grew up together," she explained.

Maraveet was not appeased. She continued to burn holes into Killian.

"Odd thing to tell a person you have no real interest in."

Juliette blinked.

Killian kept his eyes on his sister. "Still none of your business."

"You're an idiot if you can't see it!" she bit back.

"There is nothing to see."

Fine nostrils flared as though Killian had cursed. Maraveet's chin went up.

"The fact that you can say that is cause enough for concern. As of right now, I cannot trust you to make any sort of decisions."

With that, she stalked towards the doors. She paused in the hallway to poke her bodyguard with the toe of her boots. When he only groaned, she stepped over him and disappeared from sight.

Juliette turned to Killian. "Did I miss something?"

Killian sighed. "Not even a little. Maraveet is … difficult to understand."

"I didn't offend her, did I?"

Killian laughed. "She's not easy to understand … or offend. She's just … Maraveet. Come on before she burns my kitchen to the ground."

With her hand firmly in his, he led her downstairs.

"Is she normally so exciting?" Juliette wondered as they reached the bottom and surveyed the small chaos taking place outside the open doors.

Plumes of gray smoke wound to the heavens, filling the air—and his house—with the stench of sulfur. His men were running around trying to clean up the mess, but there were scorch marks everywhere, staining the snow black. A short distance away, a cluster of men stood watching and grinning.

Killian growled low in his throat. "Unfortunately yes. But at least she didn't land on the roof via helicopter this time."

Juliette's eyebrows lifted. "That's different…"

"That's Maraveet. She never does anything easy." He stormed into the kitchen with Juliette hurrying to keep up with his long strides. "Did you set my house on fire?" he demanded of the woman rifling through his kitchen.

In the process of ransacking his cupboards, Maraveet snorted. "Of course not. I know how upset you get when I do that." She slammed one cupboard shut and yanked open another. "Just a few flash bombs and smoke grenades. Nothing harmful."

"Why can't you use the phone like a—"

Maraveet whirled around so fast, she was practically a blur. "Don't say it! You know how I hate the *N* word!"

Juliette looked at Killian. "The *N* word?"

Killian decided not to push his luck with his sister. She already looked like she wanted to start hurling knives at him ... again.

"I'll tell you later." he told Juliette.

"You should be thanking me!" Maraveet snapped. "Your men were utterly useless. The moment the bombs went off, they practically wet themselves. Had absolutely no idea what they were supposed to do next. I waltzed right past them. It was appalling. I could have killed you."

"My men aren't in the habit of getting bombed!" he shot back.

Maraveet smirked like he'd just proven her point for her. "Exactly. Shameful." She twirled back around to the cupboard hanging open. Jars and cans were shoved carelessly left and right. "Why in the bloody hell do you not own any tea?"

He was about to tell her the tea box was right in front of her face when she spotted it. The box was ripped down and she gawked at the thing was though it were personally responsible for the slaughter of helpless kittens.

Her head jerked up, her expression comical. "What is this?"

"Chai," he said as evenly as possible. "It's tea."

She shook it next to her ear like she expected to hear the whimper of lost souls begging to be let out.

"This is not tea," she decided, smacking the box down on the counter. "I don't know what this is, but I'm pretty sure it will give me hemorrhoids and influenza."

Killian sighed. "You are being irrationally overdramatic."

"It tastes best with milk." Juliette's quiet murmur reminded them she was still there, watching the scene unfold with one hand smothering her grin. "The chai," she explained when Killian and Maraveet both stared. "If you make it with milk…"

Maraveet shot the lowly little box a wary glance, but made no move to pick it up.

Frank took that moment to enter the room. His navy suit was streaked with black. His face was sweaty and his hands looked like he'd reached into a hearth full of ashes. Dark eyes, narrowed with more irritation than Killian had ever seen on his face rounded, on Maraveet, who conveniently pretended not to notice.

"Sir, it seems your sister has decided to drop in for a visit," Frank muttered.

"How are things outside?" Killian asked instead, smothering his own grin.

"Coming together slowly."

Maraveet nudged the tea box an inch to the right with the tip of her finger, still avoiding Frank's withering stare.

"I'll come out with you." Killian turned to Juliette. "I'm going to go make sure someone hasn't scorched holes into the side of the house. You can wait upstairs if you'd rather not have to deal with *that*."

"Oh, don't be like that." Maraveet pouted. "I promise not to eat your pretty bird."

Juliette laughed. "Go ahead. I'll be fine."

With a light touch of his fingers along her arm, Killian followed Frank out of the kitchen. He paused once they were far enough away not to be heard.

"Stay with them," he told the man. "Make sure Juliette doesn't kill my big mouthed sister."

Frank narrowed his eyes. "If you're sure, sir."

Killian chuckled. "She does make it tempting, doesn't she?"

Frank dutifully said nothing.

Chapter 20

"Come closer," Maraveet coaxed once they were alone. "I promise I've sheathed the claws." She rapped her blunt nails on the marble countertop as though to prove it.

Juliette smiled. "I'm not worried." She crossed to the island and took a seat on the stool. "Killian tells me you travel a lot."

"A bit." She continued to drum her fingers while eyeing the tea box.

"I can make that for you, if you like," Juliette offered.

"Lord, no." Snatching up the box, she shoved it back inside the cupboard and shut the doors with a crack. "I'd never forgive myself."

She was very pretty, Juliette observed, studying the other woman. Not exactly movie star gorgeous, but she had a sultry glow about her, like the sort of women who modeled *Victoria Secret* lingerie. She certainly had the figure for it. But it was her accent that intrigued Juliette most. It was every country and no country. It was as though every word that left her mouth held a different twang. Juliette had never met a person like that.

"What do you do?" she pressed on, fascinated by the only other person besides Molly that Killian had in his life.

Maraveet seemed to be lost in her own thoughts, because the question gave her a visible start. Her green eyes shot to Juliette with an almost accusatory frown.

"You're a bit nosy for someone who shouldn't be here."

The venom in the comment slapped her across the face. The burn of it stung her cheeks and her jaw dropped. She blinked at the woman.

"Excuse me?"

Maraveet's piercing stare intensified. Her mouth opened and Juliette instinctively braced herself. But whatever

Maraveet was about to say was silenced by the shuffle of feet. A moment later, the same man who had grabbed Juliette up by Killian's office ambled into the room. Blood was smeared across his chin. It streaked down the front of his dark coat. His eyes still seemed glazed, but he stood before them, sheepish.

"Ma'am, I—"

Maraveet put her hand up, stopping his apology. "No need for that, Robert. You're fired."

Juliette was stunned by the calm declaration. But Robert hung his head and staggered back out the way he'd come without a single word.

"That was a bit harsh, wasn't it?" Juliette remarked, horrified by how cold the other woman was.

"No," Maraveet said simply. "I hired him to protect me. Instead, he went down with one punch. I expect better of my men."

While understandable, Juliette still couldn't wrap her head around how easily she'd done it. It made her think of Killian firing John and Tyson for those exact same reasons.

Maraveet exhaled when several minutes passed and neither of them could think of a single thing to say. "How did you meet my brother anyway?"

"He saved my life."

"That's different. How?"

She found herself telling Maraveet the whole story. Everything from being indebted to Arlo to Killian offering her the contract. She wasn't sure what possessed her to do it. It wasn't as though it was any of the woman's business, but once she started, it all just poured out of her. At the end, she smiled softly and gave a little shrug.

"Like I said, saved my life."

Maraveet seemed unmoved, but Juliette could see thought churning behind those green eyes. She wondered if her story was getting analyzed and dissected, though she couldn't fathom for what.

"You probably reminded him of her." It was said so low, Juliette almost didn't hear it.

"Who?"

Maraveet straightened. Her head turned a fraction in Juliette's direction, pinning her to her stool.

"His mother."

Aside from the statue outside the front doors, Juliette hadn't seen any photos of Killian's parents. There were no photos at all, which hadn't seemed odd to her until that moment. But the statue's face didn't look a thing like Juliette's. She was fairly certain they didn't even share the same height. It made no sense to her how she could possibly remind Killian of a woman that looked nothing like her.

"I don't understand," she said at last. "What does his mom have to do with—?"

Maraveet's expression grew wary. She squinted at Juliette.

"He hasn't told you about what happened?"

Juliette involuntarily stiffened. "You mean about how she was attacked?"

"She wasn't attacked!" The outraged shout made Juliette jump. "She was brutalized. She was tortured and mutilated and raped for two solid weeks by a pack of gutless animals who only used her to make a point."

Juliette shuddered, not just from the image, but from the chill that seemed to be wafting off the other woman the way it rises off a chunk of ice. It swarmed around her, biting and fierce and Juliette shrank back in her seat.

"Saoirse McClary was murdered in the worst possible way any woman could ever die," Maraveet finished with a slight hitch in her voice.

"The people who…" She didn't want to say raped. She hated that word. Hated hearing it. The very sound of it felt violating. "Who hurt her, what happened to—?"

"Dead." Blunt and without mercy. "And the world is better off."

Juliette nodded in agreement. "Who were they?"

Maraveet averted her eyes, but Juliette saw the fire burning behind the green, turning them to polished emeralds.

"Yegor Yolvoski." The name spat from her lips the way one might spit out poison. "Inbred son of a bitch and his two good for nothing sons. There were others involved, but Yegor was the one who ordered the kidnapping. He took Saoirse right off the street."

The lunch she'd eaten hours before churned in the pit of her stomach. The contents felt soured and wrong. But she swallowed it back.

"Why?"

"Because of weapons and greed." Maraveet shook her head as though the thought disgusted her. "He and Callum, Killian's father, were in business together for years before Saoirse found out that Yegor was putting guns in the hands of children and her husband was helping transport it. Yegor was one of the most powerful arms dealers in the world. Nobody could touch him. But Saoirse would have none of it. She dragged me and Killian into Callum's office one afternoon and screamed at him about how would he like it if those were his children being armed, being killed. I had never seen her so angry. Callum just sat there staring at us. Killian and I were eight or nine so I didn't understand, but Callum broke his agreement with Yegor. He pulled his contract. I'm not sure how, but the coast guard got word of the weapons and Yegor got arrested. For years it was unclear whether Callum had given Yegor up or if his time had finally run out, but Yegor saw it as a betrayal."

"So he took Saoirse," Juliette murmured, mesmerized and horrified by the story.

Maraveet nodded. "He took videos of the things they were doing to her. Each day Killian would get a new one—"

"Killian?" Juliette felt her insides heave.

Maraveet didn't answer the question. "Callum took them. He wouldn't let us see, but Killian … Killian wouldn't let it go. He wouldn't stop. He knew there was something on those tapes regarding his mother and he wanted to see them."

"No…!"

A sad little grin twisted Maraveet's mouth. "We found them, hidden at the back of his father's closet." The smile slipped. A tinge of green spread up the curves of her face. "He wasn't the same after that. The nightmares … his screams…" A shaky hand was pressed to her mouth like the memory had followed her into the kitchen. "I still sometimes hear them late at night. They were the sound a wild animal would make while being tortured and I couldn't help him. The only person who could make him stop was Molly. She'd sit with him the entire night while he cried for his mother."

Something wet dropped on the back of her hand, startling Juliette. She looked down and was surprised to find she was crying. Tears were streaming down her face and raining off her chin. Her coat was stained with droplets. She wiped the rest away with her sleeves.

Maraveet didn't notice, too lost in the past.

"They dumped her outside those doors when they were done with her, right where that fountain now stands. She had fought them for a week before she'd given up, not that anyone can blame her. They had torn her apart in every way imaginable."

An image of herself on the side of a dark road, being grabbed and shook by Killian rose up in her mind. She remembered the urgency in his voice, the panic in his eyes as he'd made her swear never to give up. It had made no sense to her then, but now she understood.

"Oh, Killian…"

His name whispered from her lips, a sound of her heart hurting for him. The pain reverberated through every corner of her being. It was only the fear of having to explain why she was crying that kept her from finding him, from pulling him into her arms and promising never to let him go through that again.

"What happened to his father?"

Maraveet rubbed a hand over her tired face. "Yegor killed him, too." She exhaled heavily and let her hand drop. "The sniper was supposed to take out Killian, but Callum jumped in front of the bullet and died instantly in Killian's arms."

How was it possible for a person to have endured so much horror and heartache and not have gone completely insane? she wondered. How was Killian even functioning? To have seen that much at such a young age, it would have consumed her. She would have lost her mind.

"But at least he had you and Molly," she said to the woman across the island.

Maraveet shook her head. "He had Molly. I couldn't stay here anymore. This whole family felt cursed and I knew that if I stayed, either me or Killian would be next. So I took a job in Paris. I traveled. I stayed away, because getting close to anybody when you do the kind of work Killian and I do, will get you killed."

It should have made sense. Maraveet's logic was reasonable. She'd lost her parents in a gruesome manner as well, not as horribly as Killian, but traumatic nevertheless and she had every right to want to get away, yet it was wrong. It was so wrong. Juliette couldn't even wrap her head around the very concept of what she was being told.

"You left him?"

Maraveet looked up. "What?"

Slivers of fire had begun to heat the ice left behind by Maraveet's story. She could feel their gnawing as they worked to envelope her heart.

"You left him," she repeated, no longer a question. "He had his mother brutally torn away from him and his father just died in his arms and you ... his sister, left him. You just ... you..." She couldn't even speak through the hatred swelling up to close around her throat. "You abandoned him to this place full of all those demons and nightmares and never looked back.

Hooray for you that you got to travel the world and forget, but Killian stayed here. He walked these halls, halls that had once been full of everything that had meant anything to him. It's a wonder he didn't lose his mind. I can't believe how ... selfish you are, how ... horrible."

Maraveet jerked back so fast she almost stumbled. Her face had gone white, making her eyes appear even brighter. But Juliette wasn't finished.

"I'm sorry, but you are not a good person."

With that, Juliette slid off the stool and marched from the room before she did something truly unforgiveable, like beat all the rage and sadness she felt boiling up inside her into the other woman's face. Her spine tingled with the force of the tension working through the muscles. Her insides quivered between the urge to scream and break something or cry until the hurt stopped. Instead, she counted the *crack-crack-crack* of her heels snapping off the marble all the way to the front doors.

Someone had closed them to the swirling snow falling outside, but all she could think about was the fountain on the other side and the woman it immortalized. Her heart hurt all over again as she thought of Killian as a small boy, watching as the woman he loved was beaten and tortured. She thought of him waking up in the dead of night screaming for her. Then to have his father, the only person he had left, sacrifice himself to protect him and having to live with that ... how could so much unfairness happen to one person? It was no wonder he was afraid to love anyone. How could he when those he loved were either killed or they left him? But she wouldn't leave him. If he asked her to, she would stay with him forever.

"Miss."

A handkerchief—an honest to God square piece of fabric with an embroidered M—was pressed into her palm. She stared at it in wonder for a full second before she wiped at her eyes.

"There's nothing I can do, is there?" she whispered. "I can't help him. I can't fix what happened."

Kind, black eyes peered down at her with more pity than she liked. "You have already done far more than you realize."

It was hard to imagine how that was possible when she hadn't done anything, when Killian was still hurting, but arguing about it wouldn't do any good either.

"Perhaps you would like me to mend your coat," Frank offered when they both simply stood there in the echoing silence of the foyer.

Juliette had forgotten all about the tear in the shoulder where the wool gaped to reveal the satin fabric underneath.

She shook her head. "It's all right. I'll sew it when I get home." She sniffled and peered down at the mess she'd made of his handkerchief. Snot, tears, and smudged makeup had turned the once spotless bit of material into a disgusting sight. She grimaced sheepishly. "I'll get this cleaned for you."

The hint of a grin crinkled the corners of his eyes. "It's not a problem, ma'am."

She started to stuff the thing into her pocket when voices outside the door had her scrambling. She looked up at Frank with wide, panicked eyes.

"He can't see me like this," she blurted. "He'll ask and I…"

"I understand, miss."

Deftly, he caught her arm and guided her straight to a nearby washroom and stuffed her inside. He shut the door behind her.

On the other side, she heard Killian's voice giving instructions, the scuffle of several feet as they drew closer. It was ridiculous, but her heart gave a jitter of dread, like she was doing something she shouldn't be.

Shaking back the feeling, she moved to the sink and turned it on cold. Careful not to get her sleeves wet, she splashed her face. She reapplied a fresh coat of makeup, and double checked her reflection for any signs of her weeping before letting herself out.

"There you are." Killian was walking towards her from the corridor leading to the kitchen. "Everything all right?"

Forcing a smile she didn't feel, Juliette nodded. "Just needed the washroom."

Dark eyes searched her face before dropping to the torn sleeve. "You need a new coat."

Juliette wrinkled her nose. "Just needs a needle and thread. It'll be fine."

Attention was returned to her face. "Such an odd woman."

He gave her no chance to respond when his mouth slanted over hers. Warm, firm lips held hers for a full heartbeat before moving, coaxing hers apart. Strong hands glided up the curved length of her spine to tangle in her hair. He held her to him, melding their fronts and guiding her back into the doorframe. The strength of his body settled with a familiar, welcoming weight against hers in a way that showered her with an eruption of tingles. They worked along her skin to scatter in the pit of her stomach. Her mind spun, lost in his heady scent. A moan rippled between them and his arms tightened around her.

He pulled back, not far, just enough to torment her with how close he still was and not close enough. Her whine was met with a delicious curve of his lips in a taunting smirk.

"Food first. You'll need your energy for tonight."

Her chest hitched with her shaky gasp. Her eyes darted up to his.

"You're a horrible tease," she breathed, and earned a husky chuckle from him.

"Just getting you ready."

"Sir." Frank appeared over Killian's shoulder, his face set in a grim line. "Forgive the interruption, but there is a matter that requires your immediate attention."

Killian unwound his arms from around Juliette and turned to face the other man. "What matter?"

Frank had his phone in his hand, but he didn't glance at it as he spoke. "There was an incident at the Triend, sir."

"How bad?"

"The authorities were summoned, sir."

Killian exhaled. "Get Marco to bring the car around." He didn't wait to see Frank bow his head or leave. Killian had already turned back to Juliette. "I'm sorry."

Bottling back her disappointment, Juliette offered him a rueful little smile. "It's all right. It just means you owe me doubly later."

That brought a chuckle to his lips that shook his shoulders. "Oh, I would expect nothing less." His sobered, but his eyes continued to twinkle. "I might be a while."

She opted to leave, if for no other reason than because she didn't want to be there with Maraveet. The very thought of the woman had anger lancing up Juliette's spine.

"That's all right. I'm going to go make sure Vi's done her homework."

Warm, gentle fingers brushed the contour of her cheek, scratching the skin with the rough pads. "I'd rather you stay and keep the sheets warm until I return. It would be a great incentive to hurry."

It was Juliette's turn to laugh. "I'd wind up finishing on my own and turn you away."

Thick coils of warning snapped across the dark pools boring into her. The heat of them nipped at her skin. His hands found their way back in her hair, fisting, tugging until she was perfectly at his mercy.

His mouth parted, his jaw set.

"Sir." Frank's voice had returned and it said very clearly that it was time to go.

Killian didn't move. He devoured her with his eyes until there was nothing left of her but a hot, liquidy mess.

"Do not touch her," he warned with just enough tug of his fingers to nearly make her come on the spot. "I want to watch when you do."

Juliette's knees dissolved. She slumped into him, no longer in control of her own support. The apex of her thighs throbbed with a raw vengeance that left her shamelessly desperate for even a sliver of relief.

"God, please hurry," she whimpered.

He smirked the self-satisfied smirk of a cat who successfully had the bird in his grasp and no one was the wiser. He released her, but kept a secure arm about her waist as he guided her towards the front doors. Frank yanked them open and waited for them to pass.

Most of the scorch marks from the flash grenades had been shoveled away from the house. What couldn't be removed was being hosed and scrubbed off the frozen marble. The smoke had also cleared, she noted, glancing up at the cloudless sky. When she'd arrived, the place had resembled a warzone. Men had been shouting and running through thick plumes of black while bangs and flashes erupted all around them. Their cries were muffled by the stampede of panic as everyone tried to find their footing through the chaos.

Jake had just pulled through the gates as another riotous bang split the frigid cold. Their wheels had shrieked to a stop as a blinding light exploded mere feet from the hood.

"Back!" Melton had shouted, but Killian was in there.

Juliette had lunged from the backseat. Her foot had nearly slipped out from under her as she'd thrown herself blindly through the anarchy. Tears had burned her eyes, the smoke had clawed down her throat, yet somehow, she'd found her way to the doors. Another blast had rung out behind her, shaking the ground beneath her feet. Mounds of snow had erupted nearby in an explosion of jagged ice. The blinding flash had nearly sent her backwards off the steps. But she threw herself through the open doors and straight into a circle of men she'd never seen before.

Bulging was a lame term for men that towered seven feet into the air and could have doubled for WWF fighters. They had stood in a semi-circle around the front mat like it was perfectly normal to be there. Their eyes had bored into Juliette, surprised by her presence, but making no move to stop her.

"Excuse me," she'd said with all the courage she could muster.

The seven figures had exchanged glances, silently asking the others if this was part of the plan. Juliette hadn't waited for them to get their shit together. Dodging past them, she sprinted for the stairs.

"Hey! You can't go up there!" one of them had shouted.

Juliette didn't pause. She took the steps two at a time at a neck breaking run. The thunder of feet had followed close at her heels, but she had kept running.

In her head, Killian's warning about putting herself at risk played in a loop. She knew he was going to be furious, but it was too late to stop now.

Rounding the corner leading to his office, Juliette had slammed into a wall that hadn't been there before. The momentum had flung her backwards like a rubber ball. She had nearly gone down had an actual wall not cushioned her fall with a jarring crash.

Panting, Juliette had straightened, pushing coils of hair off her face. Behind her, the two who had been chasing her slowed to a stop. The human wall she'd collided with shifted.

"You can't go in there," he'd said, folding his massive arms to emphasize.

"Of course I'm going in there!" she gasped. "Killian's in there. I need to see him!"

Dark eyes had narrowed beneath thick, angry eyebrows. "You should leave."

Feeling cornered but determined, Juliette had planted her feet. "Where's Frank? I'm allowed to be here." She wasn't certain that was true, exactly, but no one had stopped her in the past. "Where's Killian?"

"Busy."

Her gaze had shot past his enormous frame to the open doorway just beyond and calculated her chances of reaching it before she was stopped.

She opted to go for it. Using her slenderness, she ducked past him at a run.

"Hey!"

A hard hand slammed down on her back. It fisted in her coat and she was tossed into the wall.

The bastard had ripped her favorite and only coat. She didn't feel sorry at all for him getting his lights knocked out by Killian. At the time, all she could feel was a crippling relief that Killian hadn't been shot or worse.

"Juliette?"

With a sharp intake of air, Juliette blinked out of the memory and focused on the man standing so close his heat was a toasty blanket against the sharp sting of cold nipping at her cheeks and the end of her nose.

"Sorry?"

"I said, I will let you know when I'm done," Killian repeated slowly.

They had reached the SUV with a sullen faced Jake standing next to the driver's door. He deliberately kept his face pointed straight, but she knew he was upset that she'd taken off on him. She made a mental note to apologize.

Meanwhile, she turned to Killian. She touched the center of his chest with an ungloved hand and raised her face to his, hoping for a kiss, but not sure he'd appreciate it in front of his men.

"Be safe and hurry back, okay?"

His features softened. "Always."

With a final glance, she let Jake help her into the back of the SUV. The door was shut between them and they set off almost immediate. The last thing she saw before the vehicle passed the gates was Killian's dark figure watching her drive away.

The house was quiet when she made it through the front door. Most of the lights were kept off, except the one in the kitchen, but the dining room was lit, which surprised her; Javier and Laurence weren't keen on too much activity that might suggest people actually lived in the house. It was a security issue, apparently. They kept the front of the house dark. But Javier, a short, bald man with a perpetual scowl, sat hunched over the plastic table tucked beneath the sitting room window. Several empty mugs sat in a cluster around a legal pad full of scribbles. Juliette wasn't sure what kind of notes the two kept taking, but they watched the front of the house as though certain they would be attacked at any moment.

He glanced up when Juliette stalked into the foyer, kicking off snow from her boots and undoing the zipper of her coat. Laurence poked his head out of the kitchen almost a split second later, a fresh mug in his hand.

Where Javier was short and round, Laurence was tall and thin and reminded Juliette of someone who spent a great deal of time reading. All he needed was a knitted sweater vest and cargo pants.

"Hello!" she called out as Jake and Melton stomped in after her.

"In here!" came a voice from the dining room.

Shrugging out of her coat, Juliette followed the voice and found Vi and Phil bent over a glass chess set. None of the pieces had been moved, but both were staring so intently at it, she half expected them to move on their own.

"What's going on here?" Juliette asked, dumping her purse and coat on a nearby chair.

"I'm learning the fine art of chess," Vi declared, never taking her eyes off the set. "I'm winning."

Juliette peered at the board, at the neat row of glass figures in their perfect formation. She was no expert at the game, but she was almost certain someone needed to move.

"You are not winning," Phil mumbled in that gruff, smoker voice.

"Sure I am, by refusing to partake in a senseless massacre."

Phil sighed as though this was an argument they'd had way too many times already.

"Don't you huff at me!" Vi warned, narrowing her eyes at the man. "My little pawns don't want to fight the queen's war. If the two feel so strongly about it, they should do what normal people do and get a reality TV show where they make bad choices and fight like real women."

Juliette mashed her lips together to keep from laughing.

"I think that makes me the bigger person here," Vi finished with a definite nod.

"Then why did you want to learn chess if you didn't want to play?" Phil muttered, his tone barely controlled.

"That was before you brought these little guys out." She picked up a pawn and held it up for Juliette to see. "Look how adorable they are! How can I ever send them into war? This is Mike. He's married to Gina and they're expecting their first baby. Do you really want the father of her unborn child to get killed?"

Juliette could have sworn a muscle ticked just beneath Phil's left eye.

"You ... named them?"

Vi blinked. "You didn't?"

Phil rose. "Okay, I think we're done."

Vi watched with just the right amount of blank innocence to make Juliette suspect her sister was playing the poor man. Phil gathered up the pieces and gingerly set them back in their velvet box. He shut the lid and walked away with them tucked under his arm.

Vi snickered. "He's so fun to mess with."

"You're horrible."

Vi's cackles only grew. "I know." She turned brown eyes to Juliette. "How was your trip to the Big House?"

Juliette shrugged. "It was ... crazy."

In less time than it took to actually experience the whole thing, she rehashed the whole day's event to the girl, leaving nothing out—except the part about Killian's promise to hurry back so they could finish what he'd started. She didn't think Vi would want to hear that part.

"Wow, the sister is a grade A twat canoe."

"Viola!"

Vi, unfazed, gave a delicate shrug. "You were thinking it."

She couldn't deny that. She had been thinking it, not so much in those words, but close.

Casting her sister a disapproving frown anyway, she started for the door. "Any ideas on supper?"

"God, anything but chicken casserole," Vi groaned. "I swear, I will run away from home."

While Juliette didn't say as much, she had to agree. It was kind of Mrs. Tompkins to take the time to prepare them supper every night for the last three years, but that was three years of chicken casseroles. She was fairly certain it wasn't healthy to eat that much chicken. Occasionally, it was tuna or pasta, but if Mrs. Tompkins could get her hands on chicken, it was made into chicken casserole. But, in all fairness, Mrs. Tompkins was the only one who knew how to cook. It was part of their agreement since Juliette didn't charge her for rent and she would only be cooking for Vi the majority of the time. But even she had gotten tired of the dish.

Mrs. Tompkins was in the kitchen when Juliette walked in. All her usual items were laid out across the counter and she was humming softly as she got ready to start.

"Hello Mrs. Tompkins." Juliette offered her a smile.

"Hello dear, how was your day?"

Juliette nodded. "It was fine. Thank you." She watched as the woman began reaching for the knife. "Mrs. Tompkins, why don't you let me handle supper tonight?"

That got her the expected response—confusion.

"You, dear?"

The bemuse pulling all the folds on the woman's face together was insulting.

"Well…" Juliette had no response.

She was saved when Vi skipped into the room, followed almost immediately by Phil; the man certainly took his job seriously, Juliette thought. Even Jake and Melton didn't follow her around that religiously.

"What's for supper?" Vi asked.

Juliette turned to her. "I was just telling Mrs. Tompkins to take the night off while I cooked something."

Vi's expression did the exact same wrinkle of confusion that was further insult to injury when she cocked her head to the side and regarded Juliette like she'd inexplicably begun singing in German.

"All right then, Miss Smarty-Pants, what do you suggest?"

"Grilled cheese," she decided. "I'll handle the actual cooking, but you can butter the bread."

Mrs. Tompkins, who'd been watching the scene unfold, stepped aside as Vi marched to the cupboard and freed three loaves of bread. Juliette grabbed the butter and cheese from the cupboard and everything was dumped on the already cluttered island. As one, as though reading the other's mind, they cleaned away Mrs. Tompkins'ss near attempt at chicken casserole.

"It's nice to see you girls working together," the woman said as the grilled cheese making process began.

"We just thought it would be a nice break for you," Juliette said evenly. "You're always making supper."

"Always making chicken casserole," Vi muttered under her breath and got kicked under the island by Juliette.

Mrs. Tompkins didn't seem to hear her, to which Juliette was thankful. "You girls are such dolls. I'm certainly going to miss you both when I'm gone."

Juliette chuckled uncertainly. "Gone? Gone where?"

She thought maybe the woman meant dead, but she still had loads of time left before thinking about that.

"My daughter wants me to move in with her," the woman surprised them by saying. "She's been asking for ages, but it wasn't time."

The buttering of bread was forgotten as both Juliette and Vi stared at her.

"But you said no, right?" Vi broke in. "I mean, you're not going to go live with them, are you?"

But Juliette could see the flash of guilt in the woman's eyes even before she lowered them to the counter.

"I don't have very long in this world," she said instead. "Each day is one day closer to when I won't be here anymore. You girls have been my family for three years and I wouldn't change that for anything, but I miss my children and grandchildren … and great grandchildren," she added with a chuckle. "I think it's time I spent some time with them now."

"That's rubbish!" Vi blurted. "We need you here."

"No," Juliette cut in softly. "I think it's a wonderful idea."

Vi rounded on her. "What?"

Juliette kept her attention on Mrs. Tompkins. "You're always welcome to come back anytime."

Relief loosened the knots along Mrs. Tompkins's thin shoulders. They lowered from their place at her ears and she offered them a tiny smile.

"I will miss you girls," she admitted, her gray eyes glistening. "I was worried about leaving you alone here, but the last few weeks have really changed my mind. You're both so happy and finally working together. It really warms my heart."

"Well, you're a crazy old lady," Vi muttered, grabbing two slices of buttered bread and turning away, but not before

Juliette caught her sweep quickly at her cheek. "Just abandoning us to run off with your real family."

The pan hissed as the slices were thrown down on the hot surface, drowning out whatever else Vi was grumbling.

"Don't listen to her," Juliette told Mrs. Tompkins. "She's just naturally miserable."

Mrs. Tompkins laughed. "I hope you'll consider coming down to see me once in a while. It's only one city over."

Juliette agreed. Vi stayed over the pan, grudgingly jabbing the bread with the tip of her spatula.

It was well after everyone had eaten and Vi had stalked off to her room and Mrs. Tompkins had retired for the night that Juliette realized Killian never called. Granted, she still didn't have her own phone—the cost was just not worth it—but he usually sent some kind of word with Jake or Melton and neither had said a word.

Wiping her wet hands on a dishrag, she padded from the kitchen in search of her guards. She found them in a small huddle with Javier, Laurence, and Phil in the sitting room. The five were talking in low whispers that made the back of her neck tingle.

"I'm sure of it," Javier was saying, his close set eyes a little too focused. "Same one about ten minutes after you arrive each time."

Jake and Melton exchanged glances.

"We haven't seen anything," Melton said at last.

"Maybe it's someone that lives in the area," Phil suggested.

Laurence shook his head. "I checked all the cars in a nine block radius. Doesn't match the description."

"Guest, maybe?"

Javier shook his head. "Drives by the house exactly ten minutes each time."

"Did you report it?" Jake asked.

Laurence nodded. "Called it into Frank an hour ago. No response yet."

"There was a fight at one of the casinos," Jake explained. "I heard it was messy. Guy got shot."

Juliette shivered and stepped away from the doorway. Her gaze jumped to the front door, closed and secured by three locks and a deadbolt and still she wondered if it was enough. What if someone still managed to get in, especially now that there was a possibility that someone was following them? Was Vi safe? Maybe they needed to go to ... where? The police? A hotel? There was nothing the police could do that Killian's men couldn't and a hotel was just out of the question.

"Ma'am?"

She jumped at the unexpected intrusion to her inner panic. Her head jerked up to find Jake standing a few feet away from her, arm extended. A phone was nestled on his palm.

"A call for you," he said, seeming unperturbed by the fact that she was clearly eavesdropping.

Swallowing audibly, she took the device and thanked him. He inclined his head and left her alone. She pressed the phone to her ear.

"Hello?"

His response was immediate, warm and soothing. It rushed over her with the power of a fluffy blanket, enveloping her and chasing away the chill and dread.

"Hey."

Her heart danced a tango of relief and the flutter of girlish delight. "How was the incident?"

She hurried up the stairs to her room. She shut the door behind her and went to the bed.

"Messy," he replied with a tired little sigh.

"What happened?" she pressed as she crawled onto the stiff mattress and propped her back against the headboard.

"Nothing you need to hear about before bed. What are you wearing?"

Her laugh filled her tiny room. "I think you should come over and find out."

His low groan sent shivers scattering across her skin, raising pimples and making her nipples harden. *"I'd be there in a heartbeat, except I was thinking of spending some time with Mar before she up and vanishes again. I'm not even wholly certain she'll be at the house when I get there."*

Rancorous bitterness swelled in her chest, filling her with a sort of loathing she hated herself for feeling.

"That's a nice idea," she forced herself to grind out. "We can always meet up tomorrow."

"Angry?"

She shook her head, even though he couldn't see it. "No, it's good you spend time with your sister. I know you haven't seen her in a while so…"

"Thank you, darling." There was a pause, followed by his sigh. *"I'm nearly at the house now. When do you work tomorrow?"*

Disappointment an iron weight hanging from her neck, Juliette stared across her room at her closet as she answered, "Later in the afternoon at the diner. It's my first day back in a week and I've only got four hours right after lunch, but before supper, which is the deadest time in the whole day. It's going to be awful."

"Why do you stay there?" he asked.

"Can't leave." She picked at a loose thread on her comforter. "I still owe them money from all the advances."

"I can—"

"No, you can't!" she broke in quickly. "It's fine. It's days I don't work at the hotel anyway so it saves me from having nothing to do all day."

"You know what I would really like?" He didn't want for an answer, but went on. *"A woman who actually lets me do things for her."*

Juliette raised an eyebrow he couldn't see. "Haven't you done enough for me? Besides, I only keep you around for one purpose and it's not to buy me things."

There was a pause, then an amused, *"That so? And what purpose is that?"*

She drew in a deep, exaggerated breath. "It's obvious, isn't it? Clearly so I can beat you at laser tag and make myself feel better."

His laughter filled her ear and made her chuckle. *"Nice try, but it was a tie so you didn't beat me."*

She hissed through her teeth. "That's just what I wanted you to think." In the background, she heard a car door slamming shut. Then the crunch of feet on snow and she realized he must have just arrived home. "Guess you have to go now, huh?" she murmured, unable to keep the pout from her voice.

"Aye, but I'll see you tomorrow. I promise."

With a sigh, she said goodbye and hung up. She set the phone on the end table and stared at it a long while before dragging herself off the bed and into the bathroom. After a quick shower, she dressed in a long t-shirt and climbed into bed.

The fire was slow burning, working its hot, greedy tongue up the length of her body in deft little flicks that had her writhing in anticipation for more. It consumed miles of flesh in a lazy trail that seemed to take forever to reach her apex. A choked sound forced its way up her chest and pooled at the back of her throat as her back arched to the languid dance of pressure gliding over and around her throbbing clit.

"Killian!"

His name tangled with the whimper that finally escaped its confinement. The tongue faltered as though startled by the sound, but it quickly renewed its insistence with a vigor.

Juliette gasped and reached for the hungry mouth lapping at her, guiding her effortlessly to the edge. Her fingers curled into thick, wavy strands of silk. Her knees lifted and fell apart in open invitation for more. Her companion groaned appreciatively. The sound vibrated against her core, giving it just the right push to send her over with a wail she stifled between her teeth.

The mouth vanished and she whined at the loss only to have her arms filled with broad shoulders and a familiar weight.

He drove inside her without a pause. The invasion popped her eyes open. It tore her back off the mattress with a strangled cry. Her gaze met dark ones on a face painted in shadows, but unmistakable. Her heart leapt and her mouth cracked into a smile in delight.

"Killian."

He kissed her. He tasted like chocolate and her. She welcomed it, welcomed him as she wound her legs around his hips, drawing him in deeper.

The kiss intensified with his every demanding thrust. She met every one. Every kiss. Every thrust. She let him swallow her moans as his body rode hers expertly to a second climax that was met a moment later by his.

His weight settled comfortably on her, but she knew it wasn't all of him. His face nuzzled the side of her neck as she littered tiny kisses along the seam of his shoulder. Her arms clasped him tightly to her.

"Please don't be a dream," she whispered against his skin.

His response was the turn of his head and the violent claim of his mouth over hers in a kiss that dissolved her bones and sent the room spinning all over again.

"I can't believe you're really here," she murmured some time later as they lay in a tangled mess across the rumpled expense of her bed.

She lay partially on top of him as he traced the bumps of her spine with lazy fingertips. Her head rested against his chest and she could feel the steady patter of his heart thumping beneath her cheek. One leg tucked comfortably through his as she drew lazy circles against his exposed skin with a finger.

"Wasn't going to," he said quietly into the top of her head. "But I couldn't think of anything, except to see you again."

She lifted her head and peered down at him. His beautiful face was barely visible beneath the curtain of darkness, but his eyes shone with their own inner light that never failed to mesmerize her.

"Stay the night?" she asked.

Fingers smoothed stray locks of hair behind her ear. "For a few hours."

Juliette's heart sank. Her shoulders drooped.

"None of that now," he said. "What kind of example would we be setting for your sister if I stayed?"

He was right and she was ashamed that she hadn't even thought of Vi.

"I'm sorry," she whispered. "You're right."

Even concealed, she could see his features softening. She felt it in the gentle glide of his fingers tracing the side of her face.

"I would if I could."

With a sigh, she lowered her head and rested her brow against his chin. "Thank you for coming." She raised her face and peered down at him. "I missed you." She flattened her hand against his cheek and pressed her thumb over his lips before he could speak. "I know you're going to tell me I shouldn't—"

He took hold of her wrist and gently drew her hand away. "God help me, but I missed you, too."

Elation sent her heart tap dancing in her chest. His words stole all her senses, even disappointment over him leaving in a few short hours. Juliette beamed as she dropped her mouth and kissed him.

He was gone when Juliette woke up only a short few hours later. The blankets had been drawn tightly around her, but the heat of his body was no longer enveloping her. If it wasn't for the sweet thrum between her thighs and the fact that she was naked, she might have mistaken the previous night for a dream.

Grabbing her clothes, she quickly dressed before the rest of the house could wake up. She righted her room. She was in the process of tossing her roped sheets into the hamper when she spotted the thin, black box on the nightstand, next to a card and Jake's phone. A fat, red ribbon circled the case, contrasting brightly against the dark velvet. Juliette stared at the thing. She knew full well that it hadn't been there when she'd gone to bed. Her heart skipped a beat as she reached for the card and turned it over.

Her name winked up at her from the back in perfect, scrawling penmanship and nothing else. She set the card down and reached for the box. It was real velvet, not the sort that anyone could just buy at the dollar store. It bristled lightly against her skin and she had to suppress the urge to stroke it to her cheek. Instead, she turned her focus to easing a finger beneath the bronze little latch. The top popped open with only a slight squeak from the hinges. More velvet filled inside with a layer of silk. Against the navy bed lay the most beautiful pendent Juliette had ever laid eyes on.

Early morning light danced off the elegant curve surrounding a flawless sphere and caught on each of the four stones embedded in a bed of gleaming silver. Vines twisted in jagged knots around the pale face of a beautiful girl in a

Victorian gown. Her long, unbound curls lay in perfect waves around bare shoulders and was held in place by a lily pinned to the side of her head. Juliette turned the cameo in her hand and early light skated along the swirling scripture etched into the silver slat on the back.

"Your happiness drives me."

The writing was faded, like it had been done years ago and she wondered if Killian had found it in a pawn shop or some antique dealer. It didn't even matter. The pendent was by far the most thoughtful gift anyone had given her in years. She'd almost forgotten what that felt like.

Moving quickly into the bathroom, she slipped the delicate chain about her throat. The cool metal settled lightly against her skin. The pendent nestled just inches below her collarbone. She fingered the carved gemstone and grinned at her own reflection.

Excitement thrumming, she grabbed Jake's phone and sprinted downstairs. Jake, Phil, and Melton were in the kitchen, surrounding the island with steaming mugs of coffee when she rushed in. All three jumped. Melton hissed when scalding liquid sloshed over the rim of his cup and burned his hand.

"Sorry!" she said, unable to stop grinning. "Do you think you're up for a drive?"

Jake set his cup down. "Ma'am, we go whenever you're ready."

Too geared up to tell them she didn't mind waiting until they were finished their coffee, she handed Jake his phone and nodded.

"I'm ready."

Leaving them, she hurried to where she'd left her coat and purse in the dining room. She moved quietly to avoid waking Javier, who most likely got the nightshift. Laurence glanced up from his position at the window when she stepped into the foyer, swinging her things on.

"Ma'am," he said in the way of greeting.

She smiled at him. "Morning."

Jake and Melton were on the front porch when she joined them. Together, they marched down the walkway to the SUV. Melton held the door open and she scrambled inside.

Maybe it was because she was practically crawling out of her skin with anticipation, but the drive seemed to take forever. It wasn't until Jake took an odd turn off the major road and through a deserted side street that she realized they were changing routes.

"Is there really someone following us?" she asked.

"It's only precaution, ma'am," Melton answered.

No one said anything else as they ambled their way up the side of Killian's hill. The gates opened at the top with a rusty shriek and they pulled to a stop next to the fountain. Juliette opened her own door. She hopped out and darted up the steps.

Despite having left her bed in the wee hours of the morning, Killian was showered and dressed and wide awake when she poked her head into his office. There was a black mug on the desk, no longer steaming, so she wondered how long it had been sitting there forgotten. The owner had his face buried in a stack of papers. He had his serious face on as he scanned the pages. It was the one that puckered the place between his eyebrows and pulled at the corners of his mouth. He didn't notice her walk in until she cleared her throat.

His face shot up and the lines on his brow immediately vanished. "Juliette?"

In a handful of determined strides, she closed the space separating them and took his face between her hands. There was a split second of surprise on his part, but the moment her mouth closed over his, it had dissolved into a look of pure satisfaction.

"I take it you got my gift," he teased once she'd drawn back.

Slightly breathless, Juliette grinned. Her hand went into the collar of her coat and she pulled the pendent free for him to see.

"It's so beautiful," she breathed, smoothing the pad of her thumb over the girl's delicate features. "I love it so much. Thank you."

Killian said nothing for several long minutes as he studied the cameo. He filled the silence by taking her hips and perching her gingerly on the edge of his desk. His chair hinges squeaked as he rose to tower over her. He lightly nipped the zipper of her coat and tugged it down the rest of the way. But his intentions apparently weren't to disrobe her. It was to get a better look at her wearing the gem.

"It was my great, great grandmothers," he murmured at long last. "My great, great grandfather had bought it during a trip to London and thought his then pregnant wife would like it. She brought it with her from Ireland and gave it to my great grandmother, who gave it to my grandmother, who never had a daughter and gave it to my dad." He paused to touch the jagged frame around the girl. "He got it engraved and gave it to my mom when she had me. It was her favorite piece."

Warmed by significance of such a treasured item, Juliette settled her hand over his and caught his eye. "Are you sure you want to part with something so precious?"

"Aye." Fingers still caught in hers, he turned his wrist a notch and lightly traced the line of her throat all the way to the hollow with just his thumb. "I wouldn't want it to be worn by anyone else."

Words failing her, Juliette reached for him when a light cough from the doorway broke through the moment, shattering it.

"Forgive my interruption, sir." Frank stayed on the threshold, hands clasped at his back, his expression professionally blank. "Your sister is in the kitchen and she seems to be having some ... difficulties."

Killian checked his watch. "It's only nine. She ought to be comatose for a few more hours."

A muscle twitched in Frank's jaw, the only outwards show of his barely suppressed irritation. "That doesn't appear likely, sir."

Helping Juliette off the desk, Killian led her after Frank to the kitchen where Maraveet stood in all her barely clad glory, rifling through his cupboards once more.

She wore a nightgown of purple silk and lace so fine, it was practically transparent. The thing clung to her generous breasts by dainty cups about two times too small. It cinched at the middle before flaring out in shimmering wave. Her long, slender arms were bare beneath the thin straps keeping the entire ensemble in place. She was muttering to herself and slamming the cupboards hard enough to rattle the others along the row. Her three inch slippers skidded and cracked against the floor with her uneven movement. Her unbound hair fluttered down her back in a curtain of glistening auburn.

She looked gorgeous … and pissed.

"Looking for something?" Killian hedged.

Shutting her most recently opened cupboard, Maraveet turned. She pinned groggy, green eyes on Killian and bared her teeth.

"It's nine in the bloody morning," she stated as though that were somehow Killian's fault. "An ungodly hour for any type of person and yet…" She threw open her arms to indicate all her near nakedness. "Here I am. Awake."

"Most people are at work," Killian countered.

Without makeup, Maraveet appeared considerably younger, which was why, when she batted her eyes rapidly, she reminded Juliette of a confused baby owl.

"I work nights!" she snarled. "Something I can't do here, which would be fine if the person who made me swear not to liberate the city museum of its precious items had the decency to stock a proper box of tea!"

"Not the bloody tea again!" Killian groaned. "For Christ sakes, Mara, send one of your men to get you your blasted tea."

"You're a robber?" Juliette blurted without thinking.

Both sets of eyes rounded on her as though the wall had started speaking. Their undivided attention was unnerving, but not nearly as terrifying as the look on Maraveet's face when she spotted the pendent still visible between the V of Juliette's coat.

"Is that..." She blinked and squinted like that would somehow make it less true. "Is that..." She couldn't seem to bring herself to say the words.

"Mom's pendent," Killian finished for her. "Aye."

"But I don't..." she trailed off, resembling someone who just got smacked in the face with a dead fish.

"I think we ought to deal with one problem at a time, which currently seems to be..."

It was Killian's turn to falter mid-sentence. But it wasn't just his unexpected silence that had Juliette turning her head; he'd gone rigid. His gaze had fastened to the fridge. His face had taken on that look of intense concentration, like there was something about the appliance that he was supposed to remember and he couldn't bring it to the forefront of his mind.

"Killian?"

Without saying a word, he turned on his heel and marched to the doorway, calling Frank's name.

Frank, who had been just outside, stepped into view.

"Sir?"

"When was the last time Molly was here?"

It was only when mentioned that Juliette realized she hadn't seen the woman in a while. The previous three times, Juliette had been at work and Killian had mentioned it in passing that Molly had swung by to drop off his care packages. The last little while, they hadn't stayed home to eat so she hadn't even thought of the neatly boxed meals or the lady who delivered them.

But Frank pulled out his phone, flipped through it carefully before responding.

"My records show two weeks, sir."

Killian's head drew back slowly. "Call her, Frank."

With an inclination of his neck, Frank left the room, phone already at his ear.

"You're still talking to Molly?" The hardness in Maraveet's voice surprised Juliette, but it mirrored the taut darkness that had settled over the woman's face. "What were you thinking?"

Killian said nothing, but Juliette could see the hard lines of his jaw bunch as though Maraveet had punched him in the gut.

"Why shouldn't he?" Juliette broke in. "Molly stayed with him and took care of him. He'd have to be a selfish asshole to toss her aside after that."

Maraveet's green eyes burned into hers. "Don't talk of things you don't understand," she ground out through straight, white teeth. "You've barely been here a week and no doubt spent most of it in his bed."

"Maraveet!" Killian rounded on his sister. "Enough."

That only turned her wrath on him. "If something has happened to Molly, it will be on your head, Killian. You know that."

With that, she stormed from the room with a vengeance that made every retreating stride crack through the house like gunfire. The vibration echoed all the way to the top of the stairs before carpet muffled her heels. Then there was silence.

"She's wrong, you know," Juliette murmured to the quiet man standing a few feet away. "It's not your fault. Molly's probably gone on vacation or she's been sick. There's a bad flu—"

"She's not wrong." Killian raised his head and she struck by the force of his anguish. It roiled in a dark tangle across his face. It creased the lines around his mouth and settled ruthlessly on his shoulders, stooping them. "She warned me years ago to cut ties and I didn't listen."

"That's insane, Killian!" She hurried to him. "You can't cut people from your life. You need people. You need family."

He didn't seem to be listening to her anymore. There was an unfocused glaze over his eyes as he stared unseeingly across the room. The hands tucked absently in his pockets bulged through the fabric in tight fists. Juliette ached seeing him that way and having no idea how to fix it. She wanted to touch him, her hands ached with it, but he didn't seem like he wanted that.

"Killian…"

Frank returned to the room, phone in hand. His grim expression closed an icy finger around Juliette's gut.

"There was no answer, sir."

It was as though someone had let all the hope out of Killian. His body sagged forward, taking his chin to his chest. One hand lifted to close over his eyes. His shoulders rose once before settling.

"Get the car, Frank."

There was nothing in his voice. The hollowness of it sent a cold chill through Juliette. His hand lowered and the emptiness in his eyes was even worse.

Frank left without a word and Juliette was left to find a way to pull Killian back from the chasm only she seemed to be able to see looming wide and open mere inches from his toes. He was teetering so close she was afraid to breathe in case it startled him. The helplessness closed around her chest with an intensity that made her ribs hurt.

"Killian…" Moving with the restrained hesitance of one trying not to spook a frightened animal, Juliette edged closer. Her hand lifted away from her side and gingerly reached for him. "It'll—"

"You should go home."

Her fingers lightly grazed his arm. When he didn't pull away, she closed them around his hand. The coldness of his clashed with hers, but she held on.

"I'm not going anywhere," she whispered.

Something in her words seemed to finally register. His eyes slid to hers finally and stayed. The face around them seemed permanently etched in blankness, but his eyes gleamed. They roared and clashed with every emotion she could feel thrashing around inside him. It took all her willpower not to reach out to him, to not soothe the torment twisting him up.

"Molly's dead," he stated with a bluntness that made her flinch. "You don't want to see that."

Her fingers tightened around his. "You can't know that. It's insane to think just because someone doesn't answer their phone—"

"She's dead," he repeated more slowly, like she needed to understand and accept. "I've known Molly since before I was born. Not once in twenty two years has she ever missed a Saturday and she hasn't been here in two weeks."

Maybe it was the enormous gap that separated their worlds, but in hers, people went without talking for months and it didn't mean they were dead. It just meant they were busy. But she wasn't entirely schooled in his world rules. Maybe he knew something she didn't.

"I'm still not leaving," she whispered.

He didn't try to talk her out of it. They walked silently to the foyer. Frank stood with Killian's coat tossed neatly over one arm. Juliette relinquished her grip on him just long enough to allow him to throw it on before reclaiming his hand. He let her, although she wasn't entirely certain he even noticed. He seemed so lost in the swirl of guilt and grief that swept around him.

They made a path to the SUV and climbed in. The door was shut behind them and they were off with Marco behind the wheel and Frank next to him. A secondary SUV rumbled along behind them with a small army of men. She wasn't sure what they expected to happen. No doubt they'd give Molly a heart attack when they stormed into her house for no reason.

It was the thought she clung to as they tore through the city. It was the image of Molly giving Killian an earful for being so neurotic and paranoid, not to mention for thinking she was dead without a shred of evidence.

Nevertheless, she held on to his hand, gripping it tight in case he even considered breaking away. But he didn't. He sat in rigid silence as the scenery changed from towering skyscrapers to neat little homes tucked against a gloomy backdrop of white and gray fields.

Molly's home was a two story colonial revival with a built in garage surrounded by a crisp blanket of snow. Juniper bushes hugged the sides, running beneath wide picture windows and complimenting the mint green shutters and door. It sat alone on a strip of road miles out of the city overlooking a rolling field. The closest neighbor was a tiny hint of a roof in the far distance. Juliette guessed about a fifteen minute walk. Not exactly far, but when it had been snowing nonstop for days, no one tended to notice that there was a mountain of ice and snow blocking visitors from the pathway leading to the front door, or that the two cars parked in the driveway were practically buried. It could have meant anything, but Killian's fingers nearly broke hers.

"Tactical formation," Frank barked to the men scrambling out of the second SUV. "Secure the perimeter. Red team, flank rear. Blue team, take the front."

It must have been something they did often, because they moved with the precision and grace of a very deadly ballet. The group of six branched off at the front curb. Three immediately started around the side while the rest climbed over mounds to reach the front door, guns Juliette had only ever seen in movies lifted to their shoulder. Frank stayed by the first SUV with Juliette and Killian. Marco remained in the car, probably waiting for Frank's orders to take Killian and leave immediately. Juliette stayed close to Killian's side, her fingers laced tight through his. Her insides writhed with a force that terrified her. It didn't seem to matter how many logical explanations her mind came up with as to why the snow around the house was undisturbed or why Molly wasn't answering the phone. All Juliette knew was that Molly had to be okay. She had to. For Killian's sake.

"Red team, report." Frank's gruff voice made her jump.

Her head snapped back to the house to watch as the team in front paused on the front steps. One pulled away from the rest and edged along the side, to the window. He paused at the corner and peered carefully inside.

"Repeat, red team," Frank said. Red team must have been the one at the back, Juliette realized, because the men at the front of the house weren't talking. "Blue team, prepare to intercept."

The guy at the window scrambled back to the door. The two covering him pivoted to flank either side of him as he hopped back onto the front step and reached for the doorknob.

Juliette held her breath. She prayed to God this was where they would barge in and hear a deafening scream from Molly. Then outraged cussing for barging into her house.

There was nothing.

Silence descended around them with a force that was definitely impossible. Everything from the wind snapping bare branches to the hum of traffic several streets over stopped. There was nothing but the murmur of her own prayers repeating inside her head.

"Sir?" Frank glanced at Killian. "The backdoor is open. It looks like forced entry. Would you like us to proceed?"

Killian didn't move. He didn't utter a word. Had his coat flaps not been trembling under the wind's vicious attack, she would have thought he'd frozen to the spot. But he must have given Frank some kind of signal, because Frank brought his wrist to his mouth and gave the command.

The front door was kicked in and the team charged.

Chapter 21

Sixteen years ago…

"I told you to get the hell outta my house!" Desperation cracked his voice, making him sound as young and ridiculous as he felt trying to be something he had no right being. "Your services are no longer required."

The steady chopping continued without pause. Whole bushels of parsley disappeared under the knife and came out perfectly minced. It was scooped up by capable hands and dumped into the pot.

"Did you hear me?"

Molly sighed. "Darling child, I'm old. Not deaf. Of course I heard ya. I just chose to ignore it."

Irritation prickled the back of his sweaty neck. The kitchen was a sauna, sweltering and nearly unbearable thanks to the four pots boiling steadily on the stove and the red hot oven baking bread. She'd been at it since dawn, cooking and baking as though preparing some lavish feast for a king. All the gleaming pots and platters lined neatly along every available stretch of space perfumed the air with their delicious aroma, and all Killian wanted to do was upend the lot of it across the floor. He wanted to stomp everything into the ground. But he refrained, not because he was better, but because, despite his rage and need to tear that entire day to pieces, Molly would be upset and he couldn't destroy all her hard work.

"I'm your employer," he shot back. "And I am ordering you—"

Molly scoffed. "Orderin' me? Don't forget, it was only yesterday I was cleanin' your nappies. I don't take orders from the likes of you."

A mortifying truth.

"I pay your salary—"

"You haven't paid me a shilling in your sixteen years, boy. Now quite wastin' my time. I've got guests arrivin' within the hour."

Heat swelled beneath his cheeks. *"My parents hired..."*

Molly looked up for the first time and only when his voice had cracked. Her stern features softened.

"Go get your clothes on like a good little lamb, eh? You'll want to look your best."

The hands he'd set on the counter between them balled. The whitened knuckles blurred behind the tears he'd been fighting for the better part of the day. All he kept thinking was how he wasn't ready. He was supposed to have years before becoming the master of the McClary Organization. He didn't know how to be an adult and that was what all those people were looking for.

"They only want to come and gawk," he muttered. *"They don't care. None of them. He hasn't been buried a day and the vultures have already started picking at whatever part of him they can get."*

"That's the way of things." Molly went to the pot and quickly stirred whatever was bubbling over the rim. *"Only people who will mourn ya are the ones who have stood in the fire by your side. Your da was a good man. Plenty will miss him for that alone."* She wiped her hands on her apron and faced him once more. *"Where's the girl?"*

He hadn't seen Maraveet since the afternoon he'd come home covered in his father's blood. She'd taken one look at him and ran from the room. He hadn't seen her since and that was nearly a week ago.

"Still refuses to leave her room."

Molly sighed. *"Well, let her be. You go on and get out of those clothes. I want you here in ten minutes looking like your da would want."*

His feet began to take him away. He made it all the way to the doorway before remembering why he'd been there in the first place.

"You're still fired," he told her.

She speared a loose fist against her hip. *"And you're still not dressed. Be gone with ya before I get the spoon."*

Damn woman refused to listen to reason, but he would make her. He would get her out of that house one way or another. He couldn't risk losing her too.

Present day...

He never could get her to leave. Even when he'd threatened her with Frank, she'd rolled her eyes and told him to stop wasting her time, or Frank's. Damn woman had wedged herself into his life like burrs in his hair, getting herself tangled and embedded so deep that he'd given up trying. He'd reluctantly accepted her presence, had accepted that if he limited her presence in his life to one day a week, nothing bad could possibly happen to her, that she would be safe. And she had been. For twenty two years, she had walked into his home with her cloth bag of precooked meals and he had let her. He had let her because she had been his anchor, the glimmer of light keeping the darkness at bay. She had kept the walls from closing in on him and the nightmares from consuming him and, God help him, he had been too weak to say no. Now, his reckless selfishness had taken away yet another person from his life.

"Sir?" Frank's deep rumbling tone snapped through the cold, jolting Killian back. "The backdoor is open. It looks like forced entry. Would you like us to proceed?"

Yes. It stayed lodged in the torn muscles of his esophagus, caught in the sticky paste collecting at the back of his throat, but it didn't need to be said. Frank knew. He always knew.

Against his side, Juliette's shoulder brushed his lightly. The quiet whisper of fabric sounded much too loud, but the subtle reminder that he wasn't standing in the cold alone had his body shifting closer. In his hand, hers felt so delicate. The fingers little sticks of ice clinging to his. An almost absent part of him had to resist the urge to pull her into his chest and shield her from the serrated edges of the cruel wind. But he wasn't sure he could trust himself. He wasn't sure he'd be able to let go again.

In the distance, the men pushed into the house, a well-oiled machine trained by Frank himself. The pounding of their feet echoed through the distance, somehow deafening. It was several seconds later that he realized the drumming was his own heart and it had taken residence between his ears. He muddled past it, needing to focus. His eyes burned, but he refused to blink. Vaguely, he was aware of Juliette setting her other hand over top of the one she was already holding. Her body turned into his side. Still, Killian couldn't move.

"Killian…"

Her quiet whisper was interrupted by the figure that bolted out of the house at a near run, stumbled down the steps and vomited all over Molly's junipers. The sheer force of his stress echoed all through the street.

Killian felt his vision waver. The edges frayed to a dull gray. He struggled not to blink, terrified that he might close his eyes and find himself on the ground.

"Sir."

There was a hand on his shoulder. A massive hand with long, thick fingers that could cover a man's entire face. It was gentle, but the weight of it held Killian in place and he realized he'd started towards the house.

"I must insist you leave this matter to me," Frank finished, his voice oddly distant. "I will bring you my report tomorrow."

Killian shook his head. "I'm not leaving."

Frank knew better than to push it. He quietly accepted Killian's decision and waited.

Juliette was another matter.

"There's nothing you can do here," she whispered. "Come home. We'll call the police and—"

"We're not calling the police." Killian muttered, watching as his men stumbled out of the house one by one. "Clean it up, Frank."

Juliette stiffened. "No, you can't touch it. The police—"

"There is nothing they can do." He finally forced his neck to the side to peer down at her. "This was a message for me and I need to handle it."

"Handle it? What are you talking about? This is a job for the authorities!"

Any other time, the bewilderment on her face would have been comical. It was clear that she had faith in the system. She honestly believed they would be able to handle this and he didn't have the heart to tell her they couldn't. He didn't have the energy to do anything.

"You should go home," he decided.

Juliette immediately recoiled like the very idea disgusted her. "No! I won't leave you like this."

But he didn't want her there. He didn't want her to see him like that. He couldn't think or let himself grieve properly when he worried about scaring her or letting her see a side of him he never wanted her to see. He couldn't be himself when she was there.

"You need to leave," he told her with as much patience and cogency as he could muster without actually snarling at her. "You need to leave now."

She shook her head. "No, please, don't." Tears crystalized along her lashes. "You don't have to do this. You don't have to … you're not alone this time. I'm here. Please let me … no!" She tore away from the hand Frank settled lightly on her arm. "I'm not leaving, damn it! Please just talk to me! Let me in. We can get through this. Please, Killian!"

Get through this.

He wondered for a moment what that meant. What was she thinking? Did she honestly believe he could walk away? That he could let this go unanswered? Did she really think he'd be able to sleep knowing he'd failed Molly twice? Maybe she expected him to grieve like a normal person, to take flowers to Molly's headstone once a week and pray she was in a better place. That was what people expected, he supposed. They put their faith in the authorities and trusted their problems would be solved.

It didn't work that way in his world. They couldn't do a damn when his mother had been kidnapped. They hadn't done anything when his father was shot. He really didn't believe they would do anything now and Molly deserved better.

Small hands curled into the soft material of his lapel. Wide, brown eyes peered up at him imploringly.

"You're better than this."

He froze at that. Not because of the words themselves, but because of the absolute conviction in her eyes. She genuinely believed he was worthy of redemption. No doubt she worried about tainting his soul further, but he still wasn't so sure he had a soul and if he did, it was beyond saving. Truthfully, he couldn't give a shit about it. Let the devil take it. What good was it to him anyway? The only one concerned about it was her and she needed to stop. She needed to stop trying to save him. She needed to stop being there. Her insistence to stay by his side infuriated him beyond reason. It made him want to punch a wall. How could she still want to stay after this? How could she not see that Molly had stayed? She had fought him too. She had refused his every demand she stay away. Now, there was no one left. He was alone. Again.

"Killian..."

"Leave." The single word ripped from his very gut. It rang low, but with an unmistakable clarity. "Now." Juliette started to open her mouth. He could see the protest and refusal and he snapped. "Leave!"

His snarl had the required affect. Her mouth closed. Her fingers loosened their crushing grip on his coat. She seemed to rock back onto her heels. The motion barely put a sliver of space between them, but it could have been the world for the way his insides dipped. Color that had nothing to do with the cold kissed her cheeks pink under the stray wisps of hair drifting lazily across her face.

Her hands dropped to her sides with her deliberate step back. It was just a foot, but, with the absence of her heat. The space seemed to crackle with ice.

"There is nothing down this road for you," she whispered at last, filling the void with a white plume of breath. "But I'm here and I care about you."

With that, she walked away from him and climbed into the back of the SUV. Frank said something to Marco. Then they were gone. She was gone. He should have been relieved.

"Sir—"

"Don't." The warning sizzled in the air between them. "Find who did this. Then find out where I can get my hands on them."

Maraveet was gone when Killian got home. He knew she would be. His sister wouldn't stay to face another death, especially not when she'd warned him it would happen. For years Maraveet had been chiding him for his attachment to things. She'd berated him for his weakness, his need for a semblance of normality.

"We're not normal," she was forever telling him. *"We can't afford to pretend."*

She'd been right. If he had listened, Molly wouldn't need a pine box.

Frank hadn't let him go in. Killian could have anyway. Ultimately, he was the boss. But he hadn't. He couldn't. Torn to pieces was not how he wanted to remember her. That was how she was brought out, in thick, black bags along with her husband. They had filled too many to be one whole piece.

Someone had taken their time. Had enjoyed themselves. They had made sure there was no doubt in Killian's mind that he'd pissed someone off. It was an unmistakable message and Killian knew all about leaving this type of message.

He'd been sixteen when his father's throne had become his. He hadn't even lost his virginity and yet he was responsible for an entire empire and expected to run it as well, if not better. But he had accepted. He had claimed his future out of sheer greed and vengeance. It was with the knowledge that with his family's extensive contact list and resources, he would find the people responsible for the slaughter of his parents and put an end to them. He was certain that had it not been for Frank and Molly, he would have gone crazy. That the darkness would have driven him even deeper into that place no child should ever have to face. But they had held him grounded. Frank had protected his body, but Molly had been his sanity. She had saved his life.

No one understood the pain of walking into the place he had always considered his haven and feeling the walls shift around him. No one understood why he couldn't even walk past his parent's bedroom or why the places their pictures had once hung lay barren. They weren't there the nights he'd wake up and swear blood was oozing from the cracks in the ceiling. Molly had begged him to leave the estate, to sell it, to get away from that life before it was too late, but that was just it. It was already too late. There was no help for him.

By nineteen he'd already had more blood on his hands than anyone his age ever should. He had basked in the deaths of his enemies. He had thrived on their pleas, on their suffering and, oh, had he made sure they suffered. He had left no one.

Word of what he'd done spread like gasoline on open flames. It ignited a frenzy of rumors that were beyond ridiculous, everything from him bathing in their blood to putting their mutilated bodies on spikes outside their homes.

None of which was true, but he never corrected them. Before long, he was The Scarlet Wolf and he never corrected that either.

Let them fear me, he thought. *Let them know what I am capable of, what I will do if anyone comes against me.*

What he also never did was admit to anything. He let everyone believe what they wanted, except Juliette. He had told her the afternoon she'd asked if he'd murdered anyone. He hadn't lied to her. He found he never could. Frank had been right about one thing, she had accepted him. Even knowing what he was, she never turned away. To most, that would make her special, someone who embraced all of him. It made her someone he should hold on to.

It didn't.

It made her vulnerable. It made her susceptible to all the evils of his world. It left her open. He couldn't have that. He couldn't stand outside another house and wait for his men to vomit in the bushes. Molly was bad enough, but if he lost Juliette … Christ, if he lost her there would be nothing left. He would demolish the fucking city, the world if he had to, to find the person responsible because he loved her. In the solitary darkness of his own mind, he could openly admit it to himself. He loved her. He loved everything about her. He loved how she made him feel, loved how she could make him laugh. He loved how she could make him forget the monster crouched inside him. But more than all that, he loved how she could walk into a room and make him forget everything he'd done. Maybe she was his second chance. Maybe he was an idiot for not grabbing hold with both hands. But if it was a contest between his sanity and her life, there was no question.

He didn't need his sanity anyway.

Chapter 22

It was three days before Juliette heard from Killian again. Three days of being left completely in the dark. Three days of worrying and badgering Jake and Melton for information and getting nothing in response. The pair were given orders to keep her away from the manor until further notice and no one knew how long that would be.

The wait was killing her, but she allowed it. She hoped Killian was taking the time to grieve and work through what the right course of action was from there. She hoped the distance was being used to put Molly to rest properly and not plotting revenge. Somehow she doubted it, but nevertheless, she was optimistic.

That night, Jake and Melton drove her home as they always did, neither saying a word … as they also always did. In the backseat, Juliette curled and uncurled her toes inside her pumps. The stiff joints creaked, reminding her she'd been standing in four inch heels for the better part of nine hours. She considered slipping them off, but then she'd have to get them back on and there was no point; they were pulling up in front of the house anyway.

All thoughts of discomfort vanished the moment she spotted the black Escalade parked in the driveway. The sight of it immediately had her heart racing and excitement diving through her. Killian's name burst out of her even as she threw open her door and scrambled heedlessly out of the SUV. Her pumps clacked noisily in her haste. Part of her was thankful one of the men had thought to shovel the walkway and porch at some point earlier that day. The cleared path made it easier to reach the front door.

"Killian?"

She scrambled into the foyer. Her purse struck the floor to the table by the door and slumped over forgotten. Her heels hit the hardwood all the way to the center of the foyer before she felt it.

The absence.

No one was there. Javier and Laurence were missing from their usual place at the window. Their table was still there with a small pile of things sitting on top. Phil and Vi were nowhere to be seen. Mrs. Tompkins had gone to her daughter's house two days earlier so Juliette wasn't expecting to see her, but everyone else…

"Hello?" she called.

Her own voice carried back through the darkness. Images of finding their massacred bodies somewhere at the back of the house had her scrambling backwards. She hit the front porch and twisted to see the driveway where Jake and Melton should have been.

The SUV Jake and Melton normally drove was gone. Its place was an empty square of wet concrete and shadows. Next to it, the SUV she'd seen on arrival sat parked exactly where it had been, the windows dark, but she knew no one was inside. Her gaze swung over the street, clinging to the hope that they'd parked at the curb.

But the black SUV was gone.

Heart a frantic knot in her chest, Juliette hurried back inside. Her heels struck the place next to her purse and she padded bare foot into the sitting room. Most of it was bathed in darkness, except for the plastic table by the window. The light from outside spilled across the white surface, making the rectangle glow. The three items sat in the very middle, in a small pile.

A phone, a set of keys she suspected belonged to the SUV parked outside and an envelope. She tore into the latter.

It was signed by Killian. His graceful penmanship looped across the bottom. His company logo burned at the top, making it all nice and official. But the series of words were wrong, no matter how many times she made herself reread the single page. It registered and she understood and still it made no sense.

In continuation of the original Agreement, this document is legal and binding between two consenting parties. Effective immediately, I, Killian McClary, hereby annul the contract called The Agreement previously decided upon with Juliette Romero. By doing so, both parties acknowledge that the termination is immediate, nonnegotiable, and without prejudice. As per accordance to The Agreement, section iii, paragraph twelve, failure to provide the appropriate thirty day notice, The Primary accepts the penalties and charges as stands:

- *One mobile device.*
- *One fully functioning vehicle.*
- *One lump sum of ten million dollars to be deposited in The Secondary's desired account.*

By accepting, The Secondary relinquish her rights to the original agreement. All parties are to refrain from further contact henceforth. Failure to do so will result in severe penalties.

Signed and dated by Killian McClary.

It was all so straightforward and to the point and yet she refused to believe he would do this, that he would break their contract without even talking to her. How could he even possibly think she would accept this without a fight?

Pitching the letter down, she turned and sprinted upstairs. She changed quickly out of her work clothes and drew on a thick sweater and jeans. She strapped her feet into a pair of comfy boots, threw on her coat, grabbed the phone, car keys, and letter, and stormed from the house.

It had been seven years since she'd driven a car. The Escalade was definitely bigger and more luxurious than her mother's old Neon, but it suited her immediate needs. The warm leather cradled her body as though designed for her. The inside smelled of new car and pine. It was nice, but not nice enough to stave off the chill that refused to be subdued no matter how high she turned the heater. It seemed to be radiating from deep inside her own bones. The phone and letter felt like a weights in her pocket and she had to refrain from pitching both out the window.

But she did pull out the phone and dialed Vi's number. The built in Bluetooth in the car immediately picked up the call and the ringer shrieked through the cabin. Juliette held her breath as she waited for someone to pick up.

"Hello?" Vi's voice filled her ears.

Juliette exhaled. "Thank goodness you're all right."

"*Juliette?*" There was a short pause, then, "*Why wouldn't I be?*"

Juliette shook her head. "Nothing. Where are you?"

There was loud chatter in the background, the low hum of too many people in a single place.

"*The mall with Phil. Why? Everything okay?*"

Juliette frowned. "Phil's with you?"

"*Yeah, we're at the food court. He got a call he had to take so he's wandering around somewhere. He'll be back in bit though. Why?*"

Confusion built in Juliette's chest, a sensation that insisted she was missing something. Why would Vi still have her security detail and not Juliette?

"*Juliette?*"

"Nothing," she said quickly. "I was just curious. You wouldn't happen to know what happened to Javier and Laurence, would you? They're not at the house."

"*Well, you can't expect them to stick around when Mrs. Tompkins is no longer there, can you? They must have been recalled or whatever happens to bodyguards that aren't needed.*"

She should have known that, Juliette realized with some embarrassment. Of course they were called back. They couldn't stay when they had no one to watch. But that didn't explain where Jake and Melton went off to. The pair hadn't left her side since they were appointed as her detail.

"I'm going to Killian's for a minute," she told her sister. "But I'll be back later tonight, all right?"

She could almost hear Vi shrug. *"All right. Have fun."*

The line went dead with a soft click. Juliette put her whole focus on driving rather than worrying herself sick. It was a blessing that the roads were clear. A light flurry had started and snow swirled around the streetlights, making the halos of light shimmer. They blew against Juliette's windshield, forcing her to start the wipers. Ice was beginning to form, turning the road into a rink. Her fingers tightened on the wheel.

The winding hill leading to Killian's estate hadn't been shoveled and snow spun out beneath the tires. Even with her high beams, the road was dark, forcing her to an almost snail's pace. At the top, the gates opened, which surprised her. She hadn't been sure what sort of greeting she would get. Pulling into park next to the fountain, she tore out the keys, grabbed the phone, and hopped out. The grounds were brightly illuminated, but she still didn't see any of the stationed guards. She knew they were there, watching. She could feel their eyes. She ignored the prickling sensation and sprinted to the front doors.

They opened as she had expected them to, but it was Frank looming on the threshold, his face that perfect blankness only he knew how to pull off.

"I need to see him, please," she blurted at once.

"I'm sorry, but Mr. McClary isn't taking visitors at the moment."

Juliette actually flinched at *visitors*, but she kept her voice even when she spoke. "Please, Frank. He can't go on the way he is. It's going to get him killed. Please just let me talk to him for five minutes—"

"I'm sorry, miss, but I have my orders."

"I love him, Frank," she said so fast she almost cut her tongue when it caught between her chattering teeth. "It would kill me if something happens to him and I didn't at least try."

If he felt anything at all by her declaration, his features gave nothing away. He stared at her with the same careful vacancy as ever.

"I'm sorry," he said again, sounding like he genuinely meant it. "There is nothing I can do. Please excuse me while I prepare for the shift change in five minutes."

With that, the door was shut in her face. She stood under the soft glow of light streaming from the bulb above her head. Flakes of snow danced around her, glittering as they caught on her clothes and hair. She stared at the piece of wood keeping her from the pigheaded man inside and wondered if it was possible for someone to be so smart and yet so stupid.

Vision blurring, she began to turn away. Her foot lifted when Frank's words hit her.

Five minutes. There would be no one guarding the door in five minutes!

Elated, she snapped back around and stayed where she was. The door had no peephole so she felt confident no one could see her and if they knew she was there, she hoped they wouldn't say anything. She waited, ignoring the sting in her cheeks where the wind kept nipping at the same spot. She stuffed her trembling hands into her pockets and did a little bounce, like that could somehow warm her up. It was the longest five minutes of her life, but it arrived. She wasted no time reaching for the doorknob. It felt oddly warm against the frozen state of her hand. The door gave easily and she scrambled inside.

The warmth made her whimper. It enveloped her in its familiar scent of floor cleaner, wood polish, and cinnamon. She breathed it in quickly before shutting the door and hurrying to the stairs. Her heart drummed anxiously between her ears, sounding impossibly loud in the deserted corridor. She knew the men did routine tours of all the floors, but during shift change, everyone met downstairs before splitting off. That gave her no time at all to get to Killian before she was seen.

Legs lengthening to widen her strides, she practically ran through the northern part of the house. Her every breath came out in choked pants that seemed to be in competition with her heart to see who could be louder. She glanced over her shoulder once before rounding the final corner and coming to a stop at the open doors leading into Killian's office.

He wasn't at his desk. The sight of the empty chair made her stomach muscles tense. She had been so sure he would be there. He always was. It made no sense ... then she spotted him by the window, nearly concealed in the ring of darkness the single light on his desk had created. He stood with his back to the door, his shoulders unnaturally straight. His aura alone broke her heart. It radiated heat the way an open wound would. Its viciousness rippled through the room, filling it with a heaviness that seemed almost animated. Part of her wondered if she could feel it like an invisible wall if she reached out. But she knew she had very little time before she was spotted.

Moving quickly, she darted into the room and shut the doors behind her. The lock snapped into place with a deft flick of her wrist. Her heart cracked wildly in her chest as she spun to face the man turning away from the window slowly.

Giving him no time to react, she marched to his desk and tore the cord out of the phone. She scooped it and his cell up and ran with them to the bathroom. Both were tossed a bit carelessly into the sink with a noisy clatter. The lock was flicked into place and she shut the door, locking his communication devices inside.

Then she faced the man watching her through the thick folds of black. The shadows painted over his features, turning him into one of their own. But she could just make out the glimmer of his eyes and the white flutter of his dress shirt.

"I don't accept," she panted.

He said nothing.

Swallowing down the paste collecting at her throat, she closed the distance between them, but stopped when a good length of space still remained. She dug into her pocket and unearthed the letter.

"You can't break our contract," she pressed on. "Not ... not like this. Not like what we had meant nothing." Her voice broke, but she plowed on. "I have done everything you asked me to. I followed every line of the contract you wrote. I never once gave you a reason to regret me." Her bottom lip trembled and she bit down hard on it. Still, the tears slipped, beyond her control. "You are not allowed to throw us away. I won't let you, and this ... this stupid letter..." The single sheet of paper tore too easily in her brutal grasp despite the heavy weight of its contents. "It goes against the contract." The annulment papers fluttered like fat snowflakes to the ground at her feet. She sniffled. "You said yourself that the only way to end our contract was with a very good reason in writing. You never stated your reason so I don't accept it."

Seconds were counted with every thump of her heart waiting for him to ease the pain. Her own labored breaths was the only sound in the room. The deafening silence loomed as thick and vast as the darkness keeping him in its clutches. Around her in a dim halo, the desk lamp shone, leaving her painfully exposed while he kept his features concealed. There was some kind of twisted poetry in the scene, she mused dully. Him in the folds of dark and she desperately beckoning him into the light with her, because a part of her knew that if she could just get him closer, he'd see that she was more important than his revenge. She needed that. She needed him to pick her, to pick life and happiness. To pick a future together. All he had to do was move into the circle.

"There is and never was an *us*." Said low and yet those words hissed the way a knife did against stone. She felt the cold slice all the way through her. "From the very beginning, I warned you there wouldn't be. This was never a relationship and you assured me that you understood. That alone defaults the contract. As to a reason, I don't require one. I opted to pay the penalties."

"By ... by giving me things I don't want?" she threw back. "When have I ever wanted your money or ... things? I don't want any of it. I just want you."

There was a subtle shift in his posture. It was quick so she wasn't sure if she imagined it or if it had been a play of shadows.

"That was never a possibility."

"Why?" She started forward, but came to an abrupt halt when he visibly jerked back. The gesture hurt worse than his rejection. "I don't understand why. What did I do?"

Light kissed the side of his face he turned towards the window. Thick lines painted most of it, but she saw enough there to make her hope maybe...

"You broke me." The light slipped away with just a shift of his head back in her direction. "You took away everything that I was, everything that made me strong. You made me forget what I was and why. Because of my carelessness, it took me two weeks to realize Molly was missing. That was my fault. I let myself be drawn into something I have always known I could never have, but it was because of you. You're not good for me, Juliette. You're the thing I need to keep away from if I am to keep fighting. You make me weak and weak men die."

She didn't know what to say. He hadn't shouted and yet they slammed into her one syllable at a time like a metal fist. Pain reverberated through her in waves.

He wasn't finished. "Now, I must ask you to leave and not return. I will not take kindly to you barging into my office again, Miss Romero. Our arrangement is over and I expect there to be nothing else."

Her face lifted. "That's it? You're just going to let me go?" She continued when he said nothing. "Did you ever think that maybe all the things you think you lost were things you never needed? I'm not an expert on relationships, but I know that if someone feels right—"

"There is a reason I don't pick women like you, virgins with no idea how to tell apart lust with love. We had sex. Lots of sex. It was great sex, I won't lie. But a real woman knows the difference, knows not to confuse the two. I apologize if you thought I would ever love you, but it's not something I am capable of."

So curt. So professional. It rang of just how delusional she'd been. It really had only been a business venture for him. Now that business was over and she was no longer needed. He was done with her.

White hot agony tore into her. It sank razor blades talons deep into her chest and ripped out her heart. She half expected it to be on the floor alongside the torn pieces of her dignity. Yet the saddest part wasn't that she couldn't seem to be able to feel her legs in order to move. It was the fact that she still loved him. That she would probably always love him even after this. She had foolishly given herself, all of herself, to a man who only saw her as a scratch to be itched. How could none of what they'd shared mean nothing to him? How had he not felt it?

Carefully, with fingers she could barely feel, she undid the chain from around her neck. The pendent slid free of her coat and swung once, catching in the light before she gathered it gently in her palm. She stared at the tiny girl with her gem face and felt her insides crack open. A tear exploded across the pendant's surface. Juliette wiped it away before setting the necklace on his desk.

"I don't want it back."

Maybe it was her imagination—the one that had betrayed and lied to her so far—but she could have sworn it was anguish she heard in his quiet murmur. She would have believed it if he hadn't just finished telling her she'd meant nothing to him.

She stepped away from the desk, away from the lamplight and into the darkness with him. It blanketed her, hiding her tears and the breath she seemed unable to catch. Barbwires had wound themselves around her chest, tearing into flesh and suffocating her oxygen. A hand flattened against her stomach. The other went to her mouth in some pitiful attempt to stifle the sob ledged in her throat.

"Don't ... Juliette..."

She was already running to the door, her ears ringing too loudly for her to be sure whether or not he'd actually spoken. But if he had, he didn't stop her. He didn't come after her, not even when she hit the bottom of the stairs. He wasn't coming, she realized with a fresh surge of pain. He was letting her go.

The sad, pathetic part of her actually waited, hoping that at any moment, he would appear, that he would charge down, scoop her up into his arms, and beg her not to go.

He didn't.

Devastated, Juliette reached into her pocket and removed the phone and car keys. She was about to set them on the console table tucked against the corner of the foyer when movement out of the corner of her eye. Her head jerked up and her heart plummeted. Frank eyed her, silent and watchful. She wondered if maybe he'd expected Killian to reject her. Maybe he'd hoped that by doing so, she wouldn't bother showing up at the manor anymore. Or maybe he had honestly hoped she would talk sense into Killian, which she hadn't. She hadn't even come close. But what did it matter? He hadn't wanted her so why would he give up his need for retribution for her?

Humiliated and shattered, Juliette went to him. She put the items into his massive palm without looking into those unfathomable eyes.

"Please take care of him, Frank," she whispered. "Don't let anything happen to him, okay?"

Not waiting for a response, she turned and hurried to the door.

"Miss Romero, please allow me to get a car to drive you—"

She shook her head. "You've already done so much. Thank you for everything."

Without a backwards glance, she threw open the door and threw herself into the night. The soft swirl of snow had turned into an almost blizzard. The wind howled and lashed against her with gleeful hatred. It ripped at her wet cheeks, turning her tears into shards of ice. Her lashes immediately hardened into spiky crystals. She ducked her head, but the frigid fingers swooped beneath her hem and raked at every inch of bare skin it could find. Little demons gnawed on the ends of her ears, making them burn. She tried to cover them with her hands, only to have her fingers instantly go numb. Forgoing that idea, she stuffed her balled fists into her pockets and ran.

There was a convenience store at the bottom of the hill. If she could get there, she'd call a cab, she told herself. If she didn't fall off the edge of the cliff first or get run over or die of hypothermia or exposure. Her cheerful thoughts kept her company all the way to the bottom. Every so often, she kept glancing back, hoping to see Killian's car hurrying after her as he had the first night. It didn't and that only further twisted the knife in her chest. By the time she hit the winding streets leading through the upper class suburban neighborhood, she had finally accepted that Killian wasn't coming for her. That he really had let her go. That it was over. In no way did her acknowledgement dull the pain, but it gave her new focus—to wait until she got home before crying.

Ahead, through the lashing swirl of snow, the lights of the 7-11 blinked and flickered. Just the sight of it nearly had her whimpering. She began to sprint, ignoring the numbness in her thighs where the cold had seeped through her jeans. Behind her, the roar of engine filled the otherwise slumbering night. She knew it was stupid, but she still stopped and glanced back.

The black SUV broke through the storm with the ease of a great shark. Lamplight sparked off the steel grill and glinted across the hood. Juliette's heart picked up immediately in a premature dance of joy; for all she knew, Frank had sent someone to take her home out of pity.

But the vehicle rolled to a stop and a familiar face hopped out of the driver's side. Head bent, he jogged around to join her on the curb.

"Mr. McClary has asked me to bring you back, miss," he said, practically shouting to be heard.

"Are you sure?"

He nodded. "Please."

It dawned on her to say no. To tell *Mr. McClary* to go take a flying leap off a high cliff. But that didn't happen. She let herself get propelled to the back door. It was yanked open and she started to climb inside when a hand shot out in front of her and closed over her mouth. Her muffled scream was swallowed with the wind as her head was forced back against his shoulder. Something sharp pierced the side of her neck and darkness jumped up to swallow her.

The resounding *bong* resonated through the shallow waters of sleep. The unwelcome intrusion vibrated along her body, making her acutely aware of every ache and pain. She was also aware of the paste in her mouth and the foul stench of urine, sweat, fish and bleach making her gag reflexes go haywire. Her cheekbone throbbed as she shifted against her uncomfortable position.

"Juliette?" the low hiss seemed as distant and unfamiliar as the persistent echo of metal vibrations under water. "Juliette, are you awake?"

Woozy and harboring the mother of all headaches, Juliette pried open one eye. She blinked at the white film blurring the odd shapes stretching out before her. Beneath her palm, the floor radiated with its own arctic coldness. The crippling chill worked through all the places she lay in contact.

One arm's length away from her face, vertical bars of iron shot up to the ceiling. On the other side, a dark figure kept shifting.

"Killian?"

"Get up!" the voice hissed, still barely above a whisper, but it was the necessity in the command that urged Juliette to pull herself together.

Gradually, inch by horrifying inch, the room swayed into view and it was a room she had never seen before. The entire structure was sheets of steel bolted together and stamped into concrete. Against one wall were three cages separated by thick bars and big enough to fit a fully grown gorilla. On the other side of the room was a series of wooden stairs that led up to nothing, but a wall. There was nothing else. No beds, not even a blanket. But there was a bucket in one corner of her cage.

"Hey!"

Terrified, Juliette faced her companion and her jaw dropped. "Maraveet?"

The woman looked nothing like Juliette remembered. Her auburn mane was a tangled, matted mess. Her face was drawn, streaked with makeup and pale. She wore jeans and a black coat, but her clothes were wrinkled. She sat on the floor of her cage, her green eyes enormous peering at Juliette through the bars.

"Are you hurt?"

The question took Juliette a moment to answer while she examined her own body. There was a crick in her neck from sleeping on cold cement and her cheek was throbbing, but...

"No, I think I'm okay." She touched a hand to her brow. "Where are we?"

Maraveet shook her head. "I don't know. This is where I woke up too."

Juliette did another survey of their surroundings, noting that there were no windows or doors.

"I don't understand." She licked her lips. "What's going on?"

"Someone's trying to get Killian's attention," the other woman stated. "I wasn't sure at first, I have my own share of people who want me ... out of the way, but I'm positive now that you're here."

"Me?" The room kept spinning. She wasn't sure if that was the after effect of the drugs or the situation, but Juliette squeezed her eyes shut tight and willed it to stop. "What do I have to do with—?"

"They killed Molly," Maraveet interrupted. "I don't know that for sure, but I'd bet my last dollar on it. Now I'm here and you're here, the last two people Killian cares about."

"They? Who's they?" Juliette demanded, eyes opening and focusing on the other woman.

Maraveet shook her head. Her green eyes shot to the stairs then back.

"I haven't been let out of this cage since I was brought in. I've seen four men. They take turns coming in twice a day with food and once to get the bucket. They don't speak and they're careful not to set a routine so I have no idea how long I've been here."

Mind reasonably clearer, Juliette paused to think. "How long have I been here?"

"A few hours at the most."

Juliette swallowed. "We went to see Molly three days ago."

"Three days," Maraveet muttered. "It felt longer."

"Well, it's okay, because Killian will know you're missing and he'll—"

Maraveet shook her head. "I left when you guys did. He has no idea where I am and he won't look."

Juliette blinked. "You ... you left him ... again?"

Green eyes narrowed. "This is why! We're dangerous together. I thought I would have time to leave the country before whoever killed Molly came for me."

"So you ran."

Rather than answer, Maraveet heaved herself into the corner between the bars they shared and the wall. Her legs rolled out in front of her and she leaned her head back.

"I don't expect you to understand. You've been protected and sheltered your entire life. How would you know the fears of dying?"

Juliette opened her mouth to remind the woman of Arlo, but the time for arguing about useless things would have to wait until later. They had a bigger problem.

"Where are we?" she asked instead.

"I think a boat. I can feel the room moving sometimes when it's windy."

Gingerly, Juliette shuffled to her feet and moved to the bar door and shook it once, just to see if maybe it would open. It didn't. She tipped her head back and peered at the ceiling with its inbuilt lights and smooth, metal surfacing.

"How did they get us in here? Where's the door?"

Maraveet pointed with one finger to the stairs. "It's a concealed hatch. No doubt used to smuggle people across international waters without getting caught."

Juliette snapped her neck around. "Smuggle people? They're human traffickers?"

Maraveet shrugged. "Possibly. Why else would you build a hidden room with cages under your boat?"

A cold wave of terror plowed into her, sending her crashing into the bars. She hit the floor on both knees as icy claws skated along every nerve ending in her body, turning them numb. Balls of air lodged in her chest, withholding every breath until she was sure she'd pass out.

"Hey." Maraveet scurried on all fours to the other side of her cage so she knelt just on Juliette's left side. "Slow breaths. We're going to get out of here."

The absolute confidence in the woman's voice momentarily made her forget the panic threatening to consume her.

"How do you—"

"Because Killian will know you're missing."

Juliette shook her head. "No, he won't. He told me never to come back. He told me I meant nothing to him." The memories doubled the anxiety already gnawing through her. Tears spilled in a steady flow to stain the front of her coat. "He won't look for us."

"He will," Maraveet insisted in that same confidence. "Trust me. I know my brother. He won't let you disappear, no matter what he might have said. Hey." She reached through the bars and grabbed Juliette's hand. "He's coming. I know he is."

Juliette broke down. She normally wasn't the sort to shatter under pressure, but between losing Killian and being kidnapped, her emotions refused to hold together anymore. They dissolved in a fit of sobs she hadn't ever allowed herself. Maraveet said nothing. She didn't tell her to be quiet or stop being a baby. She gripped Juliette's hand and waited.

"Done?" she asked, not unkindly once Juliette had run out of tears.

Juliette nodded, wiping her eyes on the sleeve of her coat. "I'm sorry."

Maraveet shook her head. "It's fine, but that is the only cry you're going to get, understand? After this moment, you're going to bottle it all up, all your feelings and never allow them to see you break. You're going to become the perfect little mute doll, got it?"

Sniffling, Juliette frowned. "I don't understand."

Intensity shone in the other woman's eyes, a green fire that washed through the chill in the room. "They will try to make us talk, to tell them whatever they want to know, but the minute we do, we will no longer be needed, do you understand? Give them nothing. No matter what they do to you or to me. The longer we hold on, the more time Killian has to find us."

Cold bile tightened around Juliette's throat. "You sound like you've done this before."

Maraveet grinned. "A few times." Her smile faded. "Just be strong and remember it won't be forever."

Juliette opened her mouth to ask how she knew that when a soft click filled the room. It was followed by the sound of decompressing air. The square patch of wall disconnected from the rest just above the stairs and a door swung into view. A man, rail thin and dressed in jeans and a leather coat, ambled down the stairs, making sure to hit every step with a vibrating thump. He reached the bottom and stopped at the sight of Juliette.

"You're awake! Good." He ambled closer. "The boss was wondering when you'd be up."

He reached for a set of keys hooked to his belt loop. He flipped through several before finding the right one. The rest jingled together loudly as he unlocked her door.

Juliette scrambled back, moving closer towards Maraveet. The other woman's fingers tightened around hers, but the man marched in without missing a beat and grabbed Juliette's free arm. He yanked her up and away.

The last thing Juliette saw before she was dragged up the stairs was Maraveet's intense green eyes watching her through the bars, willing her to be strong.

Juliette had always considered herself reasonably strong. She had faced things most people would never dream of and she had survived. But everything in that moment felt lost and hopeless and shrouded with an impossibility she wasn't equipped to handle. Not knowing what lay beyond the hidden door didn't help. Not knowing what or who ... no, she knew who. She remembered his face, his familiar, safe face. She had trusted him. Killian had trusted him. He'd betrayed them both. He'd brought her to that place and left her in a cage. Now, he was going to torture and possibly kill her.

The door opened to a spacious cabin straight out of the very concept of luxury. Maraveet hadn't been wrong, they were in a boat, but not a freighter or fishing boat as Juliette has expected. It was a yacht, a grand, beautiful length of space draped in rich satin. Crystal drops glittered from the ceiling, showering the mahogany furniture with their golden light. The dark wood complimented the peacock blue throws adorning leather sofas. An iron stairway twisted up from the center of the room and opened to the second floor above. Outside, through windows draped in gossamer drapes, the heavens were as navy as the carpets beneath their feet and dotted by a swirl of snow that obscured any landmarks that might have helped pinpoint their location.

Despite the early hour, the cabin was occupied by a small handful of men. None of which she recognized as she was led closer.

"Juliette." The voice could have been cut from silk. "You cannot possibly imagine how long I have been waiting for the moment when we would finally meet."

Chapter 23

Vile, unstoppable hated scuttled along Killian's skin, reminding him of a hundred spider legs creeping beneath his clothes. The sensation had his stomach churning, his skin crawling and his temper rearing its head. In the black slate of his window, his reflection glowered at him. Accusation and loathing oozed through the pane. It was a look of disgust and it was warranted. The things he'd said to Juliette would haunt him for the rest of his life. It would forever be the new reason he no longer slept. The excruciating look of heartbreak twisting her beautiful face had been all he could take. Had she stayed for even a second longer, it would have been the end of him. It would have sent him to her, the need to protect her be, damned.

In his trouser pocket, the jagged corners of the pendent cut into his palm. The metal and gem felt ridiculously hot in his freezing clutches. Every so often, he'd run the pad of his thumb over the face of the girl and think of Juliette's when he'd given it to her. The glow of elation in her eyes. The smile.

I had to do it, the pitiful voice insisted. *She would have been next.*

You don't know that! The second voice screamed. *I could have kept her safe.*

It was the same war, the same argument and neither side was any closer to winning. But Killian agreed with the first. He had no guarantee he could protect her. He couldn't trust that he wouldn't lose her the way he'd lost Molly, Molly who he barely saw. If they went after her because of him, what was stopping them from going after Juliette? What was stopping them from taking her, hurting her ... breaking her?

A new coldness gnawed at the pit of his stomach, the sort of sensation one got when drinking ice water on an empty stomach. It made the snakes there writhe in fury at being disturbed.

Losing her forever was a price he was willing to pay if it meant she would live. He would live with the agony so long as he knew she was somewhere out there, possibly happy.

A soft shuffle alerted him to the second figure hovering in the open doorway of his dark office. The harsh, yellow light from the hallway panted his enormous silhouette a murky black, but Killian would recognize Frank anywhere.

"You let her in," Killian said quietly. "Those gates don't open without your approval, nor does anyone, not even me, know the exact moment the staff change happens, except you. You disobeyed my orders."

Frank never moved. "I did, sir."

"Don't ever do it again."

Frank inclined his head. "Yes sir, but there is something you might want to know about Miss Romero when she left the manor—"

"I don't." He turned away from the window. "She is no longer my concern. You will never bring her up again, do you understand?"

"Sir, if I might—"

The man's insistence only fueled Killian's impatience. "I said no, Frank!"

The reluctance was unmistakable, even if his face was concealed in shadows. Killian could see it in the tightening of the man's frame. But he relented grudgingly.

"Yes sir."

Killian returned to the window, to the darkness and the company of his own miserable reflection.

"The Mishimoto Company is still waiting for your response to their offer to buy out the … sir?"

Killian blinked and raised his head. Frank was watching him from the other side of his desk, a large stack of papers gripped in both meaty hands.

"Yes, all right." Killian straightened in his seat. "Just set it down and I'll go over them when I'm done."

Frank wisely said nothing as the folder was set gingerly on top of a teetering stack of other files and paperwork Killian should have finished days ago. The entire surface of his desk had become one wrong sneeze away from a paper avalanche. The OCD claustrophobic in him shrieked at the sight of his once immaculate work space. But the rest of him had no energy to give a shit.

"Sir, perhaps you would like to head out for a couple of hours?" Frank suggested. "We could head into Ice and—"

Killian shook his head. "I have too much to do here."

But he sat and studied the same contract he'd been staring at for the better part of four hours. He still had no idea what it was about or what he was supposed to do. His pen lay across the first page, waiting to be utilized.

"Sir, if I may, it's been three days since…" He quickly bit back what he'd been about to say when Killian's gaze shot up to him warningly. "Since you've been out of this house and a few hours in fresh air…" He trailed off. His hand going to his earpiece.

Killian watched him, studying the hard lines pulling dark eyebrows together into a deep frown.

Frank exhaled. "Sir, there is a situation in the courtyard that requires your immediate attention."

Killian frowned. "This isn't a ploy to get me out of this office, is it?"

Frank shook his head. "No sir."

His ass muscles grumbled in protest as Killian rose from his chair. Stiff leg muscles creaked and tingled with every stride he took following the giant out the door. He couldn't remember the last time he'd actually left his chair, except to use the washroom and take the occasional shower. A time or two, he'd even napped in the damn thing. A few more days of that and he could probably make a mold of his ass off the leather. But it wasn't as though he had anywhere really to go and sleep was out of the question anyway. He might not be getting any work done either, but at least he was pretending. It was better than glancing at the phone and wondering if Juliette would pick up if he called. A time or two, he'd even dialed the number before coming to his senses. The whole matter was humiliating. He was pining like a teenage girl after losing her first crush. And she kind of was. He'd found women attractive in the past, but he'd never burned so completely for them. He hadn't lost his head and his heart. So, maybe that did make her his first crush. Who knew? The whole thing was ridiculous. He was too damn old and too damn tired to be lovesick.

Halfway to the stairs, he heard it, the deafening shriek of a female voice. There were other voices, louder, but the words were unintelligible.

"No!" Frank snapped unexpectedly. "Don't touch her. That is an order!"

Juliette!

It had to be. Who else would be on his front step making all that ruckus?

It was more than simply a ruckus, he realized when he reached the top of the stairs and heard the crash of glass shattering. It was followed quickly by a thump against the side of the house. The female voice screamed again and he tore down the steps. He hit the bottom just as a brick smashed through the bay windows of the formal sitting room. Glass exploded, glittering like diamonds in the afternoon sunlight before scattering across his mother's antique rug. The brick itself slammed into the glass coffee table and more glass exploded.

"What in God's name…"

Killian charged to the open front door. He reached the threshold and narrowly got a chunk of rock straight in the face. Pure reflexes had him ducking just in the nick of time. The rock sailed over his head and cracked across the foyer floor and rolled beneath the stairs.

"Where is he?" the voice shrieked. "I want to see him now or I swear to God I will break every bloody window in the place!"

For a moment, for just a split second, he almost thought it was Juliette. Long, wavy blonde hair rippled around a delicate face and small shoulders. Dominating brown eyes sparked with a fury unlike any other. But it wasn't her.

"Viola?"

The girl stood on the edge of his mother's fountain, a stick in one hand a broken brick in the other. His men were fanned out around her, edging closer, but making no effort to grab her. There was a small arsenal of rocks, bricks and bottles piled at her feet. There was more in the backpack lying open at the bottom of the fountain. She looked as fierce and dangerous as any of the warriors his mom used to tell him about. Her golden eyes found his and flashed.

"Where is she, you son of a bitch?" She slashed her stick in his direction. "Where's Juliette?"

The brick soared out of her grasp with deadly accuracy. It nailed him in the shoulder before any of his men could even think to block it. The pain exploded across his chest and splintered down his arm in ribbons of fire. Something hot and wet blossomed beneath his dress shirt and soaked through the fabric in a red bloom. Killian would have cursed if he could think past her words.

"What?" he demanded.

"Don't bullshit me, you Irish bastard!" She swooped down and snatched up a green bottle. "I know you've got her. She told me she was on her way to see you and then nothing for three fucking days. What have you done with her? Where is she? Where's my sister?" The last part was said in a scream that echoed through the courtyard.

Something jackknifed in his chest with such brutal force he nearly went down with it. The pain in his shoulder was immediately replaced by a slow burn of heat and cold that crashed through him in rapid succession. He spun on his heels to where Frank stood behind him.

"Find her." His voice nearly broke. "Find her now!"

He whirled to the girl who had lost all the color in her face. The bottle and stick hung limply at her sides, the fire gone from her. Her brown eyes were enormous and shining with all the fear curdling deep inside him.

"You ... you don't have her?"

Closing the distance between them in three wide strides, Killian grabbed Vi by the wrist and dragged her off the fountain. She went willingly and let herself be hauled into the manor. He took her to the sitting room she hadn't destroyed and shoved her into a chair.

"Tell me what happened," he snarled at her. "Where's Juliette?"

"I ... I don't know!" she choked out. The stick and bottle slipped out of her hands and struck the carpet beneath her feet. "She called me three days ago and said she was on her way to see you. She sounded weird, but I didn't think anything of it. But she never came home that night or the next. I went to her work, both of them and no one has seen her. So, I came here and your douchebag doorman said he had no idea who I was talking about. That he'd never even heard of Juliette. I thought..." She lowered her eyes, her cheeks a guilty pink.

"That I'd hurt her," he finished for her.

Vi nodded. "Juliette wouldn't just disappear. She'd never leave me. Something happened to her."

Killian began to promise he'd find her. No matter what he had to do or who he had to kill, he would bring Juliette home when Frank stalked into the room, his phone in hand.

"Sir, no one's seen her. I've called her work and she's missed three days."

The sour taste of rotten milk filled his throat, making him want to throw up where he stood. But he held firm. Juliette needed him to keep it together. He needed to find her.

"Track the GPS in the car or her phone," he ordered. "Call whoever you need to get the—"

Frank shifted. "That won't work, sir. Miss Romero didn't take the car or the phone when she left here the other night."

Killian stiffened. "What?"

"She didn't take—"

"I heard you!" he snapped. "How did she get home?"

A muscle tightened in Frank's jaw. "I suppose she walked, sir. I offered to have someone drive her, but she insisted."

"It was below zero degrees that night." Each word ripped through his tightly clenched teeth as fury and panic wound tight inside him. "She could be dead along the side of the road for all we know."

Frank said nothing, but Vi gasped. Her hands shot to her mouth to stifle the sound, but it was too late.

Killian ignored her. "Why didn't you tell me?"

Tension wove across the other man's shoulders. "I tried, sir. You asked me never to speak of her again."

He remembered Frank's insistence that night. It was the first time in years the man had ever vehemently insisted to be heard despite being told to stop. Killian wanted to kick himself.

"Find her," he continued in the same sharp tone. "Even if you have to knock on every door in the city, find her, Frank. Bring her back!"

With a deep inclination of his head, Frank turned and hurried from the room. Killian stood watching the spot the man had occupied with his heart in his throat and his stomach somewhere between his ankles. Haunting images of Juliette frozen to death somewhere alongside the road, hidden beneath a mound of snow hurled into his gut, making him nearly double over.

"What did he mean you told him not to speak of her again?" Vi demanded.

He'd almost forgotten about the girl. "I have work that requires—"

Vi was out of her seat in a flash and hurrying to block his path. "Work? Seriously? You're the last person to see my sister alive and you're concerned about your stupid work? She could be dead and … do you even care?"

"Of course I care!" The words ripped free of him in a growl that widened her eyes. "I've never cared more about anything than I do about your sister. I would easily give my life for hers, but if I continue to stand here and think of her out there hurt or worse, I will lose my fucking mind, do you understand me?"

The smooth column of her throat bobbed. She nodded. She didn't stop him when he edged around her and stalked from the room. The front doors were closed, but there were men inside and out cleaning the mess Vi had made. Killian couldn't even bring himself to be upset about that. He didn't care about a few pieces of broken glass when Juliette had been gone for three days and he hadn't known. Three fucking days.

A second set of feet behind him had him glancing back. He blinked in surprise to find Vi following him upstairs.

"What are you doing?"

It was her turn to look bemused. "Until Juliette's brought home, I'm not leaving your side," she stated simply. "I go where you go."

He opened his mouth, decided against speaking, closed it, and kept walking. Vi followed.

In his office, he went straight for his window. Vi took a seat in one of the chairs facing his desk and waited. Neither of them spoke and he'd never been so relieved.

The moment didn't last.

"What did you do?" the girl asked.

Killian forced his gaze away from the swaying treetops. "What?"

"To Juliette," Vi explained. "What did you do to her?"

It was on the edge of his nerves to tell her to mind her own business, to even be offended that she would assume he would ever do anything to hurt Juliette. But he had. He had hurt her. He'd deliberately and maliciously hit her where he knew it would wound her the most. Did it matter that he'd done it to protect her? Did it matter that he'd had her best intentions at heart? Did it matter that he would give his soul to have her back with him? She was gone. She'd been gone for days and he'd done nothing. If she was lost somewhere in the snow, he'd had two days to find her, to save her, and he hadn't. If she was...

"The hospitals!" he blurted, more to himself than Vi. "Did you—"

"Of course I did," Vi muttered. "I'm not an idiot. I called the hospitals, the police, the hotel. I even called Uncle Jim."

That knowledge made him pause. "You have an Uncle Jim?"

Vi nodded. "He's Dad's brother. He has a farm out in Alberta."

The way Juliette had gone on, he'd assumed it was just her and Vi in the world.

"Why didn't he...?"

Vi arched an eyebrow. "Take us in when we had no one?" she finished for him, her tone dripping with sarcasm. "None of them did. Dad owed them too much money. They weren't going to add to that debt by taking on his kids. Thank God Juliette was eighteen when Dad finally died, otherwise we'd both probably be lost in the system or something. Uncle Jim was the only one that sort of offered, but he's a total pervert. Likes little girls. Not that anyone in the family would ever say it out loud. Juliette refused." She shook her head. "Anyway, what did you do to Juliette? Why did she leave?"

Killian turned back to the window, unable to keep looking into those golden eyes. "Because I told her to. It was the only way I knew how to keep her safe."

"Safe from what?"

"Me."

"Sir."

Frank appeared in the doorway, his movement hurried. He was breathing hard like he'd ran all the way there. Every hard bulge of muscle was rigid, as tense as the muscles on his face. In his hand was a yellow envelope.

Killian's entire world jittered, going in and out of focus between black and white and color. The room shifted between present and past as he remembered being ten and standing where Vi was, watching as Frank brought that same yellow envelope to his father. Then the room was back and Vi was on her feet and Frank was watching Killian with the same grim expression he'd given all those years ago.

"No..."

Vi, as white as the snow outside the window, peered from one to the other with the frantic desperation of a spooked rabbit. Her hands were shaking as they lifted and clapped over her mouth.

"What?" Her voice wobbled. "What is it?"

Frank never looked away from Killian. "What would you like me to do, sir?"

Burn it! Break it! He wanted to scream. *Destroy it.* It couldn't be true if no one saw it. But he knew it didn't work that way. Things weren't less true just because he wished it.

"Sir?"

No. No. God, no he couldn't. Not again.

"Is it about Juliette?" Vi demanded of Frank. "Is it a ransom demand? I'm calling the police—"

In five long strides, Frank was next to the girl. Her phone was taken from her before the numbers could be dialed.

"Give that back!" Vi screamed at him. "We have to call the police!"

"They can't help her," Frank told her calmly, but with stern authority.

Tears rained along her cheeks, looking silver in the light. Her brown eyes went from Frank to Killian and hardened. She flew at him, hands fisted. With a shriek, she slammed both into his chest.

"Find her! Find her!" Every scream was followed by another crack of her fists raining down on Killian's chest, his shoulders, arms and even his face. He felt none of it. "You did this! This is your fault!"

Frank pulled her off, kicking and screaming loud enough to bring the house down. Killian stayed frozen in his own nightmare as the girl was hauled from the room. He had no idea what happened next, but the floor was suddenly beneath his hands and knees and everything he'd eaten that day, which thankfully wasn't much, came up with a violence that took bits of his stomach lining with it. Hot and cold waves rushed along the heaving curve of his spine, plastering his top to his back. Sweat dampened his temples and rolled into his already burning eyes and still the attacks continued.

Another scream echoed, one that only he could hear. The high pitched wail of his mother, begging her captors to stop. The shriek of her pain as they'd carved into her, as they'd taken turns doing things no one should ever have to endure. Those images had come in an envelope just like the one Frank was bringing to him now.

"It's not possible," he wheezed. "It's not possible."

Frank's large, capable hands tucked beneath his arms and Killian was lifted to his feet. He was taken to his chair and seated. Frank left his side and returned a moment later with a damp washcloth. Killian used it to wipe his face and mouth.

"It's not possible," he said again, slightly calmer. "I killed them. I killed all of them. There was no one left." He raised his eyes to the other man. "I left no one, Frank."

"Perhaps someone—"

Killian shook his head. "No, no, it's not possible. It's not…" A sound between a sob and a groan left him. "They have Juliette. God, they have her."

He felt sick all over again. More images he'd fought and buried for the last twenty two years rode over him, digging talons and barbs into his soul. Images of the bright afternoon his father's scream had woken him from a fitful slumber, of running downstairs only to be grabbed by Frank, but not soon enough to be saved the sight of his mother's bloody, broken, and naked body cradled in his father's lap. That would be Juliette. He would wake in the wee hours of the morning to find her...

"Sir!" Frank's sharp commanding voice spiked through the vortex Killian had been steadily sinking into. It shattered through the choppy film of his past and brought him slamming back into a cold reality he wanted nothing to do with. "May I suggest you watch the video? It's only the first."

Not many would understand that. Telling someone it was the first torture video in a long line of more to come wasn't a comfort. But Killian understood. His mother's video hadn't been more than her sitting in front of the camera as a male voice warned of her fate. She'd been so pale. Her dark hair had been in tangles, but it was her eyes that had held so much defiance. She had been the picture of calm.

The first video was a lie to lure him into believing he stood a chance at saving her, just like his father had. But it would still assure him she was safe, even if it was temporary.

Frank tore the envelope open. Killian didn't watch. He stared at the mountain of papers across his desk, but the sound made him flinch. His fingers creaked around the facecloth. Frank inserted the disk into the driver and the video automatically began playing.

Juliette, wearing the same clothes he'd seen her in last, sat on a metal chair. A concrete wall, one that could be found in just about any basement, stood at her back. Her blonde hair was matted and hung around her drawn face. There was a gash on her lower lip that he recognized as self-inflected. Harsh beams of light blazed down on her with a ferocity that made her squint against it.

"*Now!*" a voice hissed off camera.

Juliette blinked a few times and struggled to focus. "*My name is Juliette Romero,*" she began, her voice weak and hoarse. "*And I am ... what does that say?*"

The camera gave a shudder.

"*Uninjured!*" the same gruff voice hissed.

Juliette gave a small nod. "*And I am uninjured, for now. I have not been mistreated. I am given food and ... water?*"

"*Yes!*"

"*Water. But all of that can change if you don't find me.*"

The screen went dark.

Neither Killian nor Frank moved, not even when the video started from the beginning on a loop. He watched it run through twice more before turning it off. He pulled the CD out of the drive, set it gently back in its plastic case and held it out to Frank.

"Find someone who can tear that apart and tell me everything about it," he ordered. "I want to know what camera was used, when, where, and by whom."

Frank took the video.

Unlike his mother's abduction, Killian had technology on his side. He would track that mother fucker to the ends of the earth.

Chapter 24

"Mar?"

The iron bars bit into Juliette's shoulder and mashed into the side of her face and still she was no closer to reaching the other woman lying on her side. She managed to graze the very tip of her middle finger the calf of Maraveet's right leg, but they had deliberately placed her too far, too far for Juliette to do anything besides trying desperately to somehow squeeze through the bars.

She knew the woman was alive. Her back would shudder occasionally, slight convulsions that were followed by a dry, rattling sound of someone with pneumonia. They'd taken Juliette's watch, so she couldn't even say for sure if it had been minutes or hours since they'd hauled Maraveet through the door and down the stairs. They hadn't even been gentle about it. The two men had lugged her between them and then dumped her without care across the floor of her cell. They hadn't even looked at Juliette and had ignored her when she'd tried to ask them for water.

"Mar, please wake up," she begged, unashamed that her voice was a weak, shaky plea.

The days and nights in that place varied. It was impossible to tell without windows or even a watch, but Juliette knew it had been days, possibly weeks since their capture. It was the third day of Maraveet's beatings, or it was all in a single day, evenly spaced out. She had no idea. But it was the third time they'd pulled the woman from her cage, forcibly marched her upstairs in one piece and brought her back in several.

Psychological torture. Maraveet had warned her they would try that, but she hadn't said just how awful it would be to witness. The guilt was overwhelming. The need to do something was suffocating. Juliette couldn't even pretend to be brave when she knew that at any moment, some asshole would thunder down the stairs, snatch Maraveet up, and take off with her to do God knew what all to get Juliette to talk. She wasn't sure what they thought she knew, but she wasn't wholly certain she wouldn't tell them if they asked, which they hadn't. They hadn't called her back since the video session. They hadn't asked her anything, yet they continued to terrorize them. Well, her mostly. Maraveet seemed highly unconcerned about the entire thing, like somehow they were intruding on her personal time. The woman had guts to spare. Juliette envied that, but more than anything, she needed it to motivate herself to keep going.

"He's coming," Maraveet kept insisting whenever Juliette began to feel herself slipping. *"Just hang on."*

She never asked who *he* was, but she knew. It could be no one else, except, if Killian was coming, he was taking his damn time.

"Maraveet!" She raised her voice to a sharp whisper that seemed much louder in the metal box.

"Stop shouting," came a low, raspy grumble. Maraveet's left foot twitched. "I'm trying to sleep."

Relief surged through her and she let her arm lower. The cold metal kissed her brow as she lowered her head and murmured a prayer of thanks.

"Are you all right? How bad is it?"

"Bad," the other woman groaned. "They haven't got any tea at all. Savages."

"Don't joke," Juliette begged. "I thought they'd killed you this time."

"They're not going to kill me." Her back rose and shuddered all the way down. "They need me to make you squirm, so stop squirming. I've felt worse."

Juliette never knew what to say or think when Maraveet spoke like that. She wasn't sure if the woman was just trying to make her feel better or if she meant it. She had a feeling the latter. She had learned enough about Maraveet to put the pieces together.

"Like what?" she blurted, needing the other woman to keep talking, to stay awake. "What do you do?"

Maraveet's shoulders trembled. For a moment, Juliette thought she was coughing or having some kind of fit. But she was laughing.

"Haven't figured it out yet?"

Juliette shuffled back and settled herself in the corner where the bars met the wall. "I've guessed you're some kind of collector."

The laughter was more pronounced when Maraveet spoke. "A collector. I like that. I suppose it's close enough." She exhaled. "I'm an obtainer. I obtain things for people who can afford my services."

"You're a smuggler."

She made an almost purring sound. "No, I merely retrieve the item. The smuggling gets handled by someone else."

Juliette thought about that a moment. "How did you get into something like that?"

"Family business," Maraveet said without pause. "My parents were obtainers. Well, my father was. My mother was the one who did the smuggling. It was how they met."

Juliette raised an eyebrow. "How romantic."

"He loved her though," Maraveet went on, quieter now. "Said it never made sense how someone so small could be so dangerous. I was seven when they died. The last thing they ever said to me was, *Be a good girl for your aunt and uncle, Mara. Mommy and Daddy will be home before you know it.* Never saw them again. But I had Killian's parents and I loved them just as much so it wasn't too bad. Callum ran my father's company until the day I was old enough to take over."

"How did your parents know each other?" she asked.

Maraveet grunted as she tried to shift into a more comfortable position. "Callum's family has always been in the import-export business. They own several large ports over land, sea, and air. My mother used to use him to move things. Somehow, she met Saoirse McClary and the two became best friends."

Juliette peered down at her knees. She drew them up and wound her arms around them.

"What's your sister like?" Maraveet asked.

"I honestly don't know," Juliette said softly. "I spent the better part of sixteen years wishing she didn't exist."

"Why?"

Juliette picked at the fur around the tops of her boots. "Because I was an awful person before my mom died. Actually, I was an awful person even after she died, but before that, it was all about me. For seven years, I was the center of my parent's world and I loved it. When Vi was born, I hated her for taking the spotlight away. I was terrible to her. Never gave her the time of day. When Mom got sick, I couldn't deal with it. I couldn't be anywhere near her while she deteriorated and faded away. I started to spend all my time with my friends and my boyfriend. I stayed away from home as much as possible, never realizing that Dad was doing the same, leaving Vi alone to take care of Mom during some of the worst of it. By the time I realized we were losing Dad too, Mom was in the hospital. I left school, got a job, and continued to stay as far away from Vi and Dad and home as possible."

"Why?" The question was asked so low, Juliette almost didn't hear it.

"I don't know," she admitted. "I guess a part of me hated her for not having to deal with any of the stuff I did. She was just some kid. She didn't understand. But I was now responsible for her so I did what I thought she needed, a home, food, clothes ... school. I worked and tried to keep us surviving day by day. Then Dad was killed and Arlo showed up on our front porch, so I did what I thought was right and protected her from it. When she started acting out, I thought she was just being a spoiled little bitch, ungrateful and just..." she trailed off, shaking her head. "It never dawned on me that maybe she was just lonely and acting out was the only way she could get my attention." She paused to give a quiet chuckle. "I don't even know what kind of person that makes me."

"It doesn't matter," Maraveet murmured quietly. "It's what you do after this that makes the difference."

Juliette snorted to distract herself from the lump in her throat. "You mean if we ever get out of here?"

"We will," Maraveet said with that same unwavering confidence. "I know my brother and I know he won't ever stop looking for you."

Juliette shook her head. "I don't know. He made it very clear that I wasn't anything more than a passing amusement."

"He gave you his mother's pendent," Maraveet cut in. "Do you think he gives that kind of stuff away to just anyone?"

Instinctively, her hand went to the bare skin at her throat and her throat muscles tightened even further.

"He said such terrible things," she whispered.

Maraveet sighed. "Probably to keep you from falling into this sort of situation," she mumbled. "He knew you wouldn't leave otherwise."

He would have been right, Juliette thought miserably. She would have stayed with him forever if he'd asked her to.

Juliette opened her mouth to tell the other woman as much when the door opened with a distinct pop of air pressure being released. The sound never failed to close abusive hands around her throat. Her spine prickled with awareness and she edged even closer to the wall.

In the cage over, Maraveet never moved. She didn't speak either. Juliette wondered if her eyes were open, but couldn't bring herself to care as scuffed boots began their descent. Jean clad legs appeared, then the wiry build of the man who brought them food. There was no tray in his grasp, which usually meant he'd been sent to retrieve one of them. Juliette prayed it wouldn't be Maraveet. They'd only just brought her back.

The man was younger than the others. Clean cut and dressed in jeans and a black sweater, he could have passed for handsome or mildly attractive in that unmemorable sort of way. He wasn't someone she would offer a second glance, but compared to the other three men, he was practically a model with his shortly cropped cap of sandy brown hair and matching eyes. At his hip, the keyring jingled with every cruel stride forward.

"Boss wants to see you," he said, stopping at Juliette's door and idly flipping through the ring. He found the key he was looking for and jammed it into the lock. "Got big plans."

The bar door swung open and he stepped aside in clear indication. Juliette shuffled to her feet. She cast a nervous glance towards Maraveet, who hadn't moved a muscle before edging her way towards the man waiting. He said nothing, but he grabbed her arm once she was close enough, even though she wasn't struggling. Juliette practically had to run to keep up.

The change never failed to disorientate her. It was an entirely different world from the one she'd been held captive in. Topside, everything was bright and beautiful. The colors were vibrant, the textures intense and captivating, a huge difference from the dull steel she was quickly becoming accustomed to. But it was the smell that made Juliette want to cry. It was the crisp scent of winter, the decadent aroma of warm, melted butter and fried meat lathered in spices and clean. God, it smelled so clean. Yet despite all that, she would rather be in the cage with Maraveet—or home—than be upstairs with men who eyed her as though she were a prized cattle for the slaughter. Their attention crawled along her grimy skin, making her want to dive back downstairs and lock herself in. Her captor's grip on her elbow tightened. Maybe he sensed her desires.

She was propelled across the plush carpet to the sitting area made up just beneath the spiraling stairs. The two sofas and two arm chairs cluttered the space, but no one seemed to mind. Four figures were already there, waiting for her. Juliette had eyes for only one.

"Hello Juliette."

The voice was as soft and beautiful as its owner. Juliette didn't recognize him. He barely looked out of his early twenties with skin so white, he could almost be translucent and hair the downy white-gold of corn silk. It framed an elven face with a tapered chin and high cheekbones and lidded eyes the crystal blue of a clear, summer sky. He reminded her of an animation, too perfect to be real, too clean. Way too clean to be sitting surrounded by men who looked like they couldn't tell a bar of soap from a brick. Every line was flawlessly proportioned. He had the slender build of a pubescent child draped in an expensive suit the exact metallic gray as the sheets bolted around her cage. There was a baby pink dress shirt beneath the blazer and white loafers on his feet. She could just make out a hint of skin between the hem and the expensive bit of leather to notice he wasn't wearing socks. He sat regally with long legs crossed beneath a gold halo of the light spilling from above. In the surrounding darkness, he could have passed for an angel.

Eyes hooded lazily from a face lax with comfort lifted and fixed on her with that same arrogant, amused glint he'd given her the first time.

"How are you?"

People like him and Arlo liked asking that question when they knew perfectly well that they were the ones inflicting the pain and hearing it made them feel powerful and in control. She also knew that he didn't really care one way or another how she really was. She opted to say nothing at all.

True to her assumption, he carried on without a response from her.

"I truly feel terrible for putting you through all this. It wasn't like you asked for it." His head bent ever so slightly to the side, knocking a wisp of baby-fine hair across his brow. "Or perhaps you did in a roundabout way. How does that saying go? You're judged by your bedmates?" He waved a pale, dainty hand. Light caught the clear coating on his neatly manicured nails and glinted. "Something like that."

"I don't know anything," Juliette blurted, unable to hold her tongue any longer. "I would tell you if I did."

He smiled beautifully, all pearly white teeth and a tiny dimple against his left cheek. "I know you would," he soothed the way one would pacify a small child. "I know you would tell me whatever I wanted to know, because, unlike your friend, you're not strong, are you, Juliette? You're not a fighter."

While perfectly true, Juliette inwardly winced at the verbal slap. The fact that he knew that about her from the single conversation they'd had made her feel beaten and ashamed.

Juliette had always tried to be brave. She had fought to keep Arlo away from Vi, she had struggled to keep a roof over their heads and food on the table. She had done so unwaveringly for seven years. Before that, she'd had an entire high school to deal with, which most days felt like the greatest challenge of her life. Yet none of that had prepared her for being kidnapped by human traffickers. There was a unique sort of fear that came with being at the absolute mercy of someone without a conscious.

"Is that why you're hurting her?" she forced herself to ask. "So she doesn't fight?"

"More so she doesn't cause any problems," he corrected. "Just a little sedation technique. But that isn't why I asked you here. I need you to make me another video."

Automatically, Juliette's gaze jumped to the corner of the ship, the cramped square of space housing a clunky camera on a tripod. It faced a fabric curtain depicting a concrete wall and a metal chair. Behind the camera was a set of construction floodlights and a table harboring a laptop. Her skin prickled just from the mere memory of having their beams burning into her.

"Who are you sending the videos to?" she asked, hoping to prolong having to sit in that chair. "Is it to Killian?"

"Not any of your concern, is it? Just be a good girl and make my video. When you're finished, I've got a surprise for you."

Whatever it was, she didn't want it. She started to tell him as much when her elbow was captured in a bruising vice and she was forcibly twisted around. Her struggles proved futile when she was shoved into the seat with enough push to send the legs teetering backwards. Juliette flailed as she struggled not to get thrown. The floodlights were snapped on. The bulbs behind the glass hummed as the wires blazed to life. The burn scorched into her skin. She could feel her pupils shrinking to pinpricks. She winced, but could do nothing more than sit there as her guard prepared.

Like the last time, two of the men started the show. One clicked on the laptop while the other maneuvered the camera. He was also the one in charge of the cue cards.

"Just like last time," he told her as he stepped over the tripod legs and ducked behind the camera. "Read the cards."

Someone else must have written them, she realized with some relief. The old set had barely been legible. The words had been sloppy, misspelled, and some of the letters had been backwards. It was the workings of a six year old.

The little red light just beneath the fat lens blinked on. Her guard adjusted the lever, getting the camera angle just right before poking his head around and giving her the nod.

"Go!"

Juliette took a deep breath and started. "My name is Juliette Romero and I have not been injured. Not yet. But my time is running out. If you ever wish to see me alive again, I will be waiting for you under the golden arches."

The guard hit the switch and the red light flicked off. The flood lights were shut off next, leaving little bulbs popping across Juliette's vision. She stumbled as she got awkwardly to her feet. The cords and wires bunched around her feet caught her ankle and her guard caught her before she could take the camera down. She was returned before the assembly. The computer guy remained behind to put her video together and ready to send.

"Beautifully done," Man-Child praised. "You're a natural." His subtle mockery toyed at the corners of his thin mouth. "I think you've earned your treat."

"Why are you doing this?" Juliette demanded. "Who are you?"

"I am Cyril Konstantinov," he replied without a second of hesitation. "But we will save the reason you are here for another day."

With a curt bob of his head, he motioned to the man on Juliette's left. The man rose and ambled to the compartment door without a word. Juliette watched with growing panic as he flicked the switch cleverly disguised as a strip of paneling and disappeared down the stairs. Concern for Maraveet had Juliette starting after him. She got two steps only to have her arm grabbed by her guard. He smirked, clearly amused by her unease. His dark eyes burned into hers with the same sick pleasure as the others.

She pulled away. He let her.

"What is he doing?" Juliette turned to Cyril.

He didn't need to answer. The man returned with a semi-conscious Maraveet being dragged along at his side. Juliette rushed forward and the other woman was unceremoniously tossed into her arms. The weight nearly took them both down had Juliette not braced her feet. Maraveet cried out on impact. Her entire body seized with the pain and Juliette had to tighten her grip. She shifted Maraveet higher and elicited another groan.

"Can't a girl sleep in peace?" Maraveet rasped, lifting her head enough to glower at Cyril.

He seemed unperturbed by her lip. Maybe he was used to it. Juliette had no idea what the two talked about when Cyril brought Maraveet up.

"Alcorn and Calhoun will take you up for a shower," Cyril said, ignoring Maraveet's comment entirely. "Your smell is beginning to put me off my supper."

Alcorn was their guard. Calhoun was the beefy man who had brought Maraveet upstairs. He reminded Juliette of a young Santa Claus with too much gut straining the front of his knitted sweater and a permanent flush to his round cheeks. His brown hair was matted to his scalp and there was just a hint of an unfinished mustache along his upper lip that she could never seem to take seriously. The straggly patches were missing in places and thick in others. Not a shaving job gone wrong, but more like he was still waiting for the rest to grow in.

He moved forward. Alcorn flagged their other side and the two herded Juliette and Maraveet up the winding stairs. It was a long process when Juliette had to practically carry the other woman. They were both sweaty and breathless by the time they reached the top. Juliette adjusted her grip under Maraveet's arm and guided her the rest of the way to a small, three piece washroom.

It was clear immediately that this was something they did often. The white room was sparse. Just a sink, a toilet, and a bathtub. There wasn't even a mirror. The only color came from the pile of fabric dumped inside the porcelain bowl. The forest green outfits were clearly meant for them to wear, but there were no towels, she noted.

"You got ten minutes," Calhoun told them.

"Ten minutes?" Juliette panted. "That's barely enough—"

"Nine," he prompted.

Juliette didn't speak again. She took Maraveet to the toilet and gingerly set her down. Behind her, Calhoun snickered and shut the door.

At least they're giving us privacy, Juliette thought bitterly.

Sucking in a deep breath, she turned to Maraveet. "You go first," she said, already reaching for the woman's coat. "You've been here the longest."

Maraveet arched an eyebrow. "Are you saying I smell worse than you?"

Juliette started. "What? No, I was just—"

"Because you don't smell like a basket of roses yourself," the woman finished.

It took Juliette a second to realize she was being teased. She rolled her eyes with a grin and hoisted the woman up. Maraveet gripped the lip of the sink as Juliette quickly stripped her. The ruined clothes were tossed into the corner in a dirty, smelly pile and forgotten.

"Ready?"

Not waiting, she got Maraveet into the tub, helped her kneel and started the water. There wasn't any shampoo or razors, but there was a bar of soap and Juliette used it liberally.

The jets hit the array of colored skin and rained down into the bottom of the tub in a dark gray smear. The majority of her injuries were collected like badges across her torso. Sharp blossoms of blue, black, red, purple, yellow and green sprung up beneath the pale surface of her skin, a beautiful spray of flowers in the winter. The colors ran along the curve of her waist and splotched along her thighs, back and arms. But none of that was anything compared to the scars. Those ran in deep rivulets across her entire body. Whole areas rose in thick, crude ropes. Others were shallow nicks and faint, shiny slits. Then there were the burn marks, old, but unmistakable. It all jumbled together in a mess of ruined flesh. The sight was horrific. Seeing them made Juliette wonder if maybe Cyril had been right. Maybe Maraveet was stronger than Juliette. She knew for a fact that she would not be nearly as put together had it been her on the receiving end of all that.

"As flattered as I am, I'm not into women."

Juliette blinked and focused on Maraveet, who was watching her through half lidded eyes. There was the hint of a grin on her face and Juliette realized, with some embarrassment, she'd been staring at the woman's breasts.

Flushing, Juliette quickly looked away. "I'm sorry. I wasn't—"

Maraveet snorted. "Although, give me a few more days in that cage and even you might look tempting."

Despite everything, Juliette laughed. "Come on. Let's get you out."

It took no time at all to get Maraveet washed, rinsed, and dressed in the green two piece suit that reminded her of prison attire. Juliette helped her down on the toilet once more before stripping and climbing into the shower herself. It was the fastest cleaning she'd ever done in her life, but she felt semi human by the time the door swung open. Juliette gathered hers and Maraveet's coats, left the rest and followed Alcorn and Calhoun back below with Maraveet using her as a crutch.

"Better," Cyril said. "Now get some sleep. We have a long day tomorrow."

Juliette had no idea what that meant, but whatever it was, Man-Child looked far too happy for her piece of mind.

Chapter 25

It was three days after the first video when the second one arrived with the morning mail. The yellow envelope held the sloppy penmanship of someone in a hurry. Blue ink bled across the front, carving Killian's name and address in mocking slants. There was no return address. No other name. Not even a stamp.

"It was hand delivered," Killian noted, prolonging the inevitable. "They came right to the house."

"I questioned the carrier personally," Frank said. "His deliveries are sorted at the office and are left waiting for him when he gets to work. The package was there when he picked up his haul this morning."

Next to Frank, on the other side of Killian's desk, Vi shifted anxiously. The floorboards creaked beneath her fidgeting feet. Her brown eyes stayed fixed on the envelope the way a dying person waited desperately for news of a cure. Her thumb nail was tucked between her teeth, the skin around it torn and bleeding.

She hadn't left Killian's office since her arrival. Even at night while everyone else slept, she sat curled up in the chair, occasionally dozing off for a few minutes before jerking awake. Her face had lost its vibrancy. There were dark bags beneath her eyes and deep grooves cut around her mouth. Occasionally, she'd stumble into his washroom to bathe, then she'd be right back to sitting and waiting for something to happen.

Killian hated her for it. Hated that she was a reminder that he wasn't doing enough, a reminder that Juliette still wasn't home. But he couldn't ask her to leave either. Not because she would refuse, but because he'd promised Juliette that he would protect her sister. It was a sick, cruel joke, asking him to do any such thing when he'd been incapable of protecting Juliette, but he was trying. Plus, it was nice to have someone else suffering with him.

"Are we going to watch it?" she asked, her voice barely a raspy whisper.

Frank looked to Killian, asking the same question without asking.

It was the second video, Killian assured himself while staring at the envelope as though it contained the exact date he would die. They wouldn't hurt her in the second video. But that wasn't entirely reassuring. They hadn't followed the script so far. With his mother, the videos were daily. One every day for two weeks. In a week, they had only sent Killian two. He wasn't sure what to make of that, but it seemed infinitely important. Them not playing by the same rules, while simultaneously giving hints to it, left Killian in the dark, unable to foresee what would come next. It gave them an edge he didn't like.

"Sir?"

Killian pulled in a breath and exhaled. "Put it in."

Vi's breathing grew faster and thicker the longer it took Frank to insert the CD, to bring up the video and step aside. Her nostrils flared with every second that passed and nothing happened. Killian couldn't be sure, but he could have sworn he could hear her heart drumming in her chest, or was that his? Unsure and not caring, he turned his attention to the flicker of movement on his screen. The black opened to Juliette in that same chair, in front of that same, grimy wall. There was no color on her face, except her eyes. Whether it was the stress of what was happening or the harsh light drowning her, she reminded him of a ghost. She sat so small with her shoulders pulled up around her ears. Her hair was a tangled mess hanging limp along her back. She poked a tongue out and traced it unsteadily across dry, cracked lips.

"Go!" someone instructed.

The camera gave a slight jitter.

"My name is Juliette Romero and I have not been injured. Not yet. But my time is running out. If you ever wish to see me alive again, I will be waiting for you under the golden arches."

The hint was no help at all.

"She looked okay," Vi choked out, sounding shaken and relieved all at the same time. "Didn't she? I mean, she wasn't hurt or dead, so that's good, right?" She sucked on her bottom lip, pulling it in tight when her chin wobbled. "They still haven't asked for money. Aren't they supposed to…?"

"This isn't about money." Killian rose out of his chair and paced to the window and a world too big on the other side.

Bones popped as Vi cracked her knuckles and fretted. Frank stood stoic and silent next to her. But it was the look on the man's face that perked Killian's curiosity.

"What is it?" he asked.

Frank lowered his narrowed gaze to the table, but his brows remained knitted. "It could be nothing, sir."

"I don't care," he prompted. "Even the smallest thing might help us."

Frank inclined his head. "I was simply wondering if perhaps you were mistaken about … taking care of all that were involved."

Killian frowned. "I was very thorough. Whoever these people are, they are not the same ones from before."

"Are you sure, sir?"

He was about to tell the man that he was sure beyond a shadow of a doubt, when a thought came to him. It was distant and faded and so small in the sea of black he'd been crashing through since his father's death that it hadn't even properly registered.

"No…"

"Sir?"

It had been so long ago.

"There is someone," he murmured, mind lost in the cyclone of his own realization. "But I…"

"What?" Vi demanded. "Who?"

"Erik Yolvoski." His gaze fixed with Frank's. "He was just a boy the last time I saw him, but he died eight years ago. There was a flood and his car was washed over a bridge. I went to his funeral. It's not him."

"What do you think she meant by golden arches?" Vi looked to Killian. "Did you have a fight with Ronald McDonald?"

"Whatever the significance, it ties with something you have or haven't done, sir." Frank raised his eyebrows in question. "Is there any place in particular you recall that may or may not have arches?"

Killian shook his head. "None that want me dead."

Vi exhaled. "These guys clearly suck at hostage negotiation."

"That's because they're toying with me," Killian muttered, returning his attention to the window. "They have no intention of letting her go."

"So … so, what then?" Vi whispered. "What do they want?"

Killian shook his head. "I have no idea, but we're going to find out."

With that, he turned and marched back to his desk. Frank moved out of the way as Killian made a straight line to his chair. He dropped into it and wheeled himself beneath the desk. He reached for a pad and pen and tossed both to Vi.

"Sit down. You're going to help me."

She didn't ask how. Her butt hit the chair before he'd stopped speaking. The pen and pad were in her hand, one poised over the other as she waited for his next instructions.

"I'm going to give you a list of names," he told her as he pulled open his bottom drawer. "You're going to write them down and then cross them off after I've called them."

Again, she asked no questions, but nodded obediently.

Killian removed the thick, leather bound book nestled at the very bottom and set it down on the desk. Over his shoulder, he heard Frank suck in a breath, but he too said nothing.

The book was as old as his name was. It had belonged to the very first McClary back before his family had moved from Ireland, back before cars and reality TV shows, back when homes were built out of sticks and mud. It was generations old and had been passed down ever since. Each McClary had taken turns marking the pages with names and dates next to a neat description of what they were owed. The thing was the size of a large phonebook and weighed a little more than a bowling ball, but it would be the thing that saved Juliette. It had to be.

Mind set, Killian opened to the first page and began to read the names out loud. The scratch of Vi's pen filled the room. Frank stood silent as Killian worked. When it was finished, Killian closed the book and tucked it away once more. But rather than ask Vi to give him the first name, he turned to his computer. He called an emergency meeting amongst the other five organization members. None were happy about being summoned, but they listened as Killian explained the situation. It was in their right to say no and power off, but he knew they wouldn't, not when it meant the opportunity to have Killian McClary in their debt. All five agreed to get their men in on the search. They would fan across their territories for even the hint of Juliette's name.

"We will do this," Theresa said once the matter had been finalized. *"But I hope the north realizes what a risk we're taking sending our men away from their posts."*

Killian had to suppress the urge to remind the woman that they'd taken an oath to protect each other against outside threats. But that was how the game was played.

"You will all be compensated for your time and assistance," Killian replied, fighting to keep his voice even. "Please bring the people responsible to me, unharmed."

Heads bobbed once before the square boxes blinked out, leaving his screen dark once more.

That finished, he dragged his phone over to him.

"Give me the first name on the list," he instructed.

Vi did quickly and he dialed the number.

He hadn't given her all the names in the book. That would have been insane, plus a lot of them were already dead. But the ones he'd selected were the eyes and ears of the underground. They knew all the right people and had all the right information. He knew mostly likely that they would not refuse. Like the organization, they stood to gain substantially from doing business with him. But that wasn't what had made him hesitate to use the book.

"I don't believe this is a good idea, sir," Frank ventured. "You are well aware of the request they will make—"

"I don't care," Killian interrupted. "I will give them whatever they want if they can find Juliette."

"Yes sir, but—"

"The city means nothing to me without her," Killian said softly. "They can have it."

Frank shut his mouth, but Killian knew exactly what the other man was thinking. Any other time, he would agree. Being the line of defense between the innocents of the city and the underbelly was a job his family had taken on for centuries. Even his father hadn't used them to find his mother. But that was an example Killian wasn't going to follow.

"What?" Vi glanced from one to the other. "What's happening? Who are these people?"

Killian avoided her eye. "Give me the next number."

These people, were the men and women Killian's family had forcibly shoved away from the city and kept securely locked behind the shadows of the outer walls. He knew by eliciting their help, they would want their run of the city he'd fought to keep clean and protected and he was prepared to give the whole thing back to them if they brought Juliette back. To top it all off, he offered five million to the person who found her alive. That would ensure a lot of eyes to search and ears to listen.

When it was all said and done and he'd sold the last bit of his soul, Killian got to his feet just as a figure stalked into the room.

Aaron still wore his coat. There were clumps of snow clinging to his boots and his face was flushed from the cold, but he looked determined as he charged forward.

"Sir, you need to see this."

It was Frank who stepped forward to accept the CD the man held. It wasn't in a yellow envelope, but from the look on Aaron's face, Killian knew he wouldn't like whatever was on it.

"What is it?" Killian demanded as Frank popped the case open and reached to exchange one CD for another.

Aaron met his gaze, his expression tight. "It's the surveillance video from the convenience store down on Helm Street, sir. One of my men uncovered it during our search. It shows Miss Romero getting into a black SUV."

Killian's muscles tightened even as his eyes shot down to the screen Frank was adjusting. "Do we know who the car belongs to?"

Aaron nodded. "Yes sir." He paused for a full heartbeat. "It's one of ours."

Chapter 26

"I think we can take them." Juliette adjusted her legs, pulling one up to her chest while the other unfurled for circulation. "We'll just save all these bricks and throw them at their heads when they come to get us. We'll add it to the plan."

On the other side of the bars, Maraveet snorted. The Styrofoam plate balanced on the palm of her hand trembled slightly as she scooped slimy peas up with her plastic spoon. Unlike Juliette, who still wasn't used to the disgusting meals, Maraveet didn't seem to have any trouble shoveling soggy salad, runny peas, and burnt hamburger patties into her mouth. It didn't seem to matter that she was starving. Her gag reflexes refused to let her force anything that revolting down.

"You won't be able to throw anything if you don't eat," Maraveet advised.

Juliette nudged the patty with her finger. "I don't know how you're able to keep this stuff down."

"The trick is not to look at it." Maraveet took her patty up with her fingers and bit into it, filling the silence with a crunch. "Close your eyes if you have to."

Somehow, Juliette doubted that would help. The stench coming off the slab of meat was bad enough to make the hairs in her nostril shrivel up and cower.

She set her plate down. "How long do you think it's been?"

"Don't think about it." Maraveet chewed and swallowed. "You'll just drive yourself crazy."

Juliette glanced over at the other woman, her curiosity getting the better of her. "How many times have you been in this kind of situation?"

Maraveet raised her head. "A few."

"How did you get out?"

Plate all but licked clean, Maraveet set it aside and dropped her spoon down on top of it. "Not easily."

Her tone said very clearly that that was a topic they would never discuss. Honestly, Juliette couldn't blame her. Being there in that prison was bad enough. She couldn't imagine being in more than one.

"Occupational hazard, huh?" she said instead.

Maraveet nodded slowly. "Something like that." She dusted her hands and peered through the bars at the stairs. "This actually isn't so bad."

Juliette didn't want to know what could be worse than living in that cage and knowing their time was running out.

"Do you recognize the leader?" she asked.

Maraveet shook his head. "He's just a kid. Can't imagine what Killian could have done to piss him off this badly."

"He hasn't asked for anything," Juliette murmured. "In the videos, I mean. He just keeps making these stupid riddles and they're barely five seconds long and make no sense. If he's trying to get Killian to find him, he's doing a horrible job of it."

"Yeah." But the woman seemed distracted. She was staring at her spoon, turning it slowly between her fingers.

"What?"

"Give me your spoon," she said instead.

"What?" Juliette repeated.

Maraveet looked up. "Give me your spoon!"

Bemused, Juliette passed her spoon over and watched as the bowls were snapped off and pitched unceremoniously into the bucket in the corner. The handle pieces were pressed together. Then she reached behind her and pulled out two more broken handles and joined them.

"Give me your elastic," she demanded, hand already outstretched.

Not asking any questions, Juliette slid the band from her hair and dropped it into the open palm. She watched as it was wrapped around the plastic.

Secured firmly, she turned the jagged ends over and began grinding them slowly against the concrete. She kept doing this until a small pile of plastic shavings had collected beneath her hands and the plastic had been rubbed down to a sharp point on one end. Maraveet paused to blow the excess shavings away before examining her handiwork.

"It's not the best, but it'll do." She passed it through the bars to Juliette. "You can probably get one or two good uses out of that if you're really careful. Plan your attack and make sure you don't miss!"

Juliette's mouth went dry even as her palms began to sweat. She stared from the jagged weapon to the woman watching her through the bars.

"What … are you serious?"

"Do you want to get out of here?" Maraveet countered. At Juliette hesitant nod, she continued. "Time your attack," she said again. "If you strike too early, you'll get stopped early and you'll lose the element of surprise. But if you wait and time it, you can maybe even get three."

Get three.

What did that even mean? Kill them? Was she supposed to stab them with the crudely shaped weapon?

"You can do this." Something in her face must have given away her fears, because Maraveet reached through the bars and grabbed her arm. "You *have to* do this, Juliette. Do you understand?"

Juliette swallowed. "What about you? You seem to know what you're doing—"

"Because there is nothing they can do to me that I haven't already been through before." Something about the deadpan way she said it made Juliette's blood run cold. "But I won't let you go through the same. I'm going to make sure you get out of here."

The bit of plastic bit into Juliette's clammy palm. "Why?"

Maraveet never wavered. "Because my brother loves you and losing you would kill him."

While the idea of being loved that deeply by Killian made her heart patter just a little faster, Juliette couldn't shake the doubt his words had cut into her. But there was no point bringing that up now.

"You don't think he'd be hurt to lose you?"

"He better be." The woman drew back. "I'll haunt him if he isn't, but I'm not you and he needs you, so you need to make sure you get back to him."

Her gaze lowered to sharp point of hope resting in the palm of her hand. "How do I even use this thing?"

Maraveet shifted closer. "Grip it firm and when you do use it, go for soft tissue."

"Soft ... tissue?"

Maraveet nodded like she was explaining a complex recipe. "The eyes, throat, and genitals are the best places and ensure they won't get up any time soon."

The very idea of jamming that thing into another person's eye made Juliette's insides waver. Bile shot up into her throat before she swallowed it down.

"I don't know about this..."

"It's them or you," Maraveet said with a bite. "And trust me, the games are only just beginning.

Chapter 27

The betrayal was a crippling lance sweeping through him with a cruelty that made his insides feel torn. There were no words for the hurt and shock that came with the knowledge that someone he knew, someone he trusted would hate him so much that they longed to destroy him.

"I trusted you."

Brown eyes darkened by dilated irises, eyes Killian had looked into since he was a boy peered up at him from a face he had once trusted without question. He sat tense in the chair. His navy suit unusually rumpled, revealing his loosened tie and wrinkled dress shirt. He hadn't made a run for it, which had surprised Killian. Instead, he sat hunched and defeated in the chair, staring down at his knees.

"Why would you do this?" Killian asked, unable to bring himself to care that all his pain was radiating through his words, weakening them. Weakening him. "I don't understand."

Marco said nothing.

"Sir, perhaps I can have a few words with him?" Frank offered.

Killian shook his head. "No, please leave us."

Aside from Frank, Vi was there, as well as Aaron, Dominic, and Jacob. His men left promptly without question. Vi hesitated, but she relented and followed the others out. Frank shut the doors behind them.

Neither Killian nor Marco moved. The silent battle of wills only hurt all the more. A part of him wanted to lunge across the desk, wrap his hands around the man's throat, and squeeze until he told Killian where Juliette was. Another part of him couldn't seem to wrap his head around the fact that someone he trusted would do something so horrible.

Climbing out of his chair, Killian started around the desk separating them. He stopped once he was directly in front of the other man. The table edge settled along his ass cheeks.

"Where's Juliette?" he asked quietly. "Where did you take her?"

Marco remained stubbornly silent. His pale face was tight with fear and guilt. Killian leaned back. His feet flattened on the floor as he rose. His hands curled into the ledge. It was all the restraint he would allow himself.

"I could have you tortured until you talk," he mused softly. "I could do many terrible things to you and I want to. I want you to suffer for what you did, for what you're doing to her right now. It's only the fact that you've been part of my family since I was a boy that is saving you. It's the only reason I am willing to give you a chance to tell me where you took her and who has her. If you tell me, you won't die a slow and horrible death. If you don't..." he let his words trail off. "You know what I am capable of. You know the things I will not hesitate to do to people who hurt those I care about. Juliette is mine and I will take down anyone who stands in my way of getting her back. So, what will it be?"

Marco shifted. His eyes lowered to his knees. He seemed no closer to speaking, but Killian would fix that.

"Do you want to know something amusing?" Killian paced away from the desk and circled around the man in slow, even strides. Each clip, he noted, nudged a subtle flinch from his driver. "Had Juliette been here, she would have probably asked me to spare your life. She would insist on it. Not for your sake, but because she has this insane notion that she can save my soul." He made a full round and stopped in the same spot. "She keeps insisting I have one, which I can't honestly say I believe. But she does. Do you believe you have a soul, Marco?"

The sharp point of Marco's Adam's apple bobbed.

"I don't think people like you and I are allowed to own a soul," he continued. "We're not good people. We live by laws that are not permitted through the gates of heaven so I can see why one might not care how they live the rest of their lives when their eternal fate is already sealed. There is blood on both our hands, but unlike yours, mine was never the blood of the innocent. I have not made the world a lesser place by taking a life worth living. But you … Juliette is innocent. She is good and pure and untainted by the things we have done to survive. Taking her, hurting her, will not bring you peace. It will, however, bring you me and, while I will not kill you, I will let you will live every day in hell where I will bring you to the doors of death in the most excruciating methods imaginable, but I will never let you pass through. So, I will ask you again, one final time, where is Juliette?"

There was a tremor in Marco's hands as he slid them along the leather armrests. He had yet to raise his eyes, but his breathing had quickened. His entire body seemed to vibrate beneath the layers of his clothing. Sweat glistened along his brow, plastering dark strands to hollowed temples. Knuckles bulged white beneath the pulled skin of his knuckles. But no explanation passed his pale lips.

Killian straightened. "If that is your answer…"

He began towards the doors.

"I don't know!" Marco's frantic voice stopped Killian after only three measured steps. "I wasn't told where they were taking her."

Killian turned and went back to the desk. "By who? Who took her?"

Marco hesitated. "I don't know."

Anger welled beneath the calm he struggled to maintain. The edges of his limits must have shown in the clenched set of his jaw and the dark fury writhing behind his eyes, because Marco visibly recoiled. All the blood vanished from his face. It bleached his lips white and his eyes were enormous.

"I never met the person in charge." His chin lowered. "He sent me a text with a location and instructions."

Killian perched on the edge of the desk once more and studied the other man carefully. "Some person you've never met texted you with instructions to kidnap Juliette and you just hopped to it?"

If possible, Marco seemed to shrink even more in his seat. "It was the same message I got the first time."

Killian's fist left his side before he could pull it back. It flew into Marco's jaw with a satisfying crack and nearly sent him flying backwards, chair and all. His knuckles blazed with pain that rocketed up the length of his entire arm, but it was worth it.

"I am getting very tired of your half assed answers, Marco," Killian bit out. "I'm not going to play fifty questions with you. Tell me everything or so help me God, I will skin you alive across this desk."

Looking dazed, Marco scrambled higher in his chair, one hand clutching the side of his face. His wide, stunned eyes shot up to Killian.

"I … I'm sorry…" He moistened his lips quickly. "I never wanted any of this to happen. I never wanted to hurt anyone." His deep inhale shuddered through the room. "The first time they sent the message, it was pinned beneath the windshield wipers of your father's town car. I thought it was one of the security details playing a joke so I ignored it—"

"What did the message say?" Killian cut in.

Marco frowned. "Something about being chosen. It made no sense so I threw it away. A few weeks later, another one appeared. This one more detailed. It went on to explain I was hand selected to fulfill a great task and that by accepting, I would get everything I ever wanted. But if I didn't, I would be sorry. I had a day to decide by signing the bottom of the page and putting it beneath my wipers. Once again, I chalked it up as bullshit and tossed it." He broke off to stare at his hands. "A few days later, I came home to find Lisa missing. All her things were still in their places, her car in the driveway, but she was gone. I looked everywhere, called everyone we knew and nothing. No one had seen her."

Killian vaguely remembered hearing something about Marco's wife leaving him years before. He hadn't paid much attention to the gossip. At the time, his mother had gone missing and his mind had been preoccupied. Later on, it was just concluded that she'd left him and no one ever asked again.

"What are you saying?"

Brown eyes shone beneath the tears clinging to damp lashes. "They took her. The same people who have Juliette." A tear squeezed free when he shut his eyes. "They left another note telling me that I had a week to do what they said or I would never see Lisa again. So, I agreed. I had no choice. They had my wife … and our son." He rubbed a shaky hand over his face. "Lisa was pregnant when they took her. I had to get them back. I had to."

Killian's frown deepened. "That was years ago. What does it have to do with Juliette?"

Veins throbbed along Marco's jaw. They pulsed at his temples. He licked his lips, but it made no difference.

Sniffling, he cleared his throat. "Because it was the same people who asked me to take your mother."

The weak confession brought the world screeching to a halt. An electric silence descended, turning the air thick and sweltering. Currents crackled along his skin, burning and making the hairs rise.

"What?"

"Yegor Yolvoski had my family," Marco explained hurriedly. "He said my wife for Callum's, but he never gave her back and I was too afraid to tell your father so I said nothing. I had hoped that when your mother was found, my Lisa would be too." He lowered his head. Dark strands tumbled over his downcast eyes. "Saoirse was given back. I never saw Lisa again."

"You gave them my mother? You took her?"

It was the one thing Killian had never considered. When his mother had been taken, it had simply been assumed that one of Yolvoski's men had ambushed her detail and taken her. No one ever considered the possibility that it was someone on the inside. But now that Marco was telling the story, Killian saw it. He remembered how his mother's guards hadn't even drawn their guns. There had been no struggle, because they had known their attacker, had trusted him. Killian's mother had trusted him.

"You took her?" The vicious growl tore through Killian's esophagus.

Marco blanched. "They had Lisa..." he croaked. "What would you have done?"

Even while a part of him already knew the answer to that, knew he would give whatever they wanted to get Juliette back, the rage remained. It continued to blanket him even as his mind fought with the two scenarios. He wondered if he would have been more forgiving if it had been a stranger and not his mother. Would it have made a difference to him? Would it have made the situation any less horrible? Marco had been in the exact position Killian was in now, only he'd lost two people simultaneously. Did that justify the pain and suffering he'd caused Killian's entire family? Killian didn't think he was in the proper state of mind to consider those questions, not when there were more important ones to ask.

"Yolvoski is dead," Killian bit out, willing his rage to taper long enough to find out where Juliette was. After that... "He can't possibly have Juliette."

Marco nodded. "I don't know who this person is, but they knew about Lisa and what I'd done. They threatened to kill you if I didn't bring them the girl."

That momentarily surprised him. He had expected a great number of reasons for the treasury, but not that.

"And why would you care about what happens to me after what you've done?" Killian demanded.

Marco's head slipped even lower on his neck so the sharp bones along the back jutted out beneath the pale skin. He was practically doubled over in his chair with his face in his hands and his elbows digging into his knees.

"I lost my son that day." His muffled confession was barely above a whisper. Marco sniffled and raised his head a notch. "After they were gone, I thought of you as a—"

"Don't you dare!" the snarl lashed out of him before he could stop it. "You kidnapped my mother. You let her get tortured and murdered and you knew all along who had her and you did nothing! Now you've taken Juliette. You took the woman I love and gave her to men who are doing God knows what to her right now. Don't you dare sit there and tell me you thought of me as your son."

Marco's head lowered all over again, but he said nothing.

"Where did you take her? Who contacted you? What else did they tell you?"

While he waited for a response, he charged past the broken man and stalked to the doors. He yanked them open and motioned only Frank inside. But Vi sprinted in after him. Killian started to tell her to wait outside, but opted against it. He just left the door open behind her as he returned with Frank to his desk.

"Where did you take her?" he asked Marco again.

Marco straightened a notch. "They gave me a street address. A van was waiting there and two men jumped out and took her."

"And you let them?" Vi blurted. "You just … let them?"

Marco said nothing.

"How could you do that?" Vi went on.

"Viola." Killian put his hand up to stop the girl. "Now isn't the time. I promise he will get exactly what he deserves once we get Juliette back."

Vi said nothing else, but stood glowering at Marco like she wanted nothing more than to jam a pen in his eye.

"Where did you meet the van?" Killian turned his attention back to Marco.

"On the corner of Easten and Broad. Right next to an old bakery. There are no cameras there. They were careful."

Killian ignored that. "Assemble a crew," he told Frank. "We're going to the location. I want every inch of it searched."

Frank started to incline his head when a movement in the doorway had them all turning. Jake, Melton, Laurence, Javier, Phil, John, and Tyson stood in a loose cluster on the threshold. They were already in their Kevlar and camo. Their guns were tucked into holsters strapped to their legs, across their chests and anchored at their ribs. They were dressed ready for war.

"What's this?" Killian demanded, although he had a feeling he already knew.

John stepped forward. "With all due respect, sir, but we'd like to be that crew."

Something in the determined lines of their faces, the hard strength of their shoulders, and the fire burning in their eyes filled Killian with a burst of pride and a hint of amusement that he concealed behind a frown.

"I'm fairly certain I fired two of you," he said evenly. "Why would you want to help?"

"You did, but Miss Romero was good to us, sir," John answered. "We owe it to her to find her and bring her home."

The other six nodded in agreement. But Killian turned to Frank, waiting for his analysis. He was the head of security. He knew the men better than Killian did and Killian wanted the best out there to get Juliette back.

"I vouch for them, sir," Frank assured him. "They're the ones I would pick."

Killian nodded. "All right. Get my coat. We leave now."

The men nodded.

Frank stepped forward. "With all due respect, sir, it would be best if you remained here."

Killian blinked. "Here?"

"This could be a trap to get you out in the open," Frank explained. "We should tread wisely until we have something more concrete."

The notion was sound, but Killian had been in that house since before Juliette was taken. He'd suffered inside every inch of those four walls. Remaining behind when Juliette needed him was a notion he did not want to even consider.

"You would be a risk to the mission, sir," Frank added.

Killian conceded. "Fine, do whatever you deem necessary. Bring her home safely."

"With your permission, sir, I would like to run point from here."

"What?" Killian frowned. "No. I want you out there looking."

"I understand, sir, but my first and only priority is to protect you."

Killian nodded. "But I'm ordering you to find and protect Juliette. She is your charge now."

Frank's thick eyebrows furrowed in clear disapproval, but he bobbed his head once more before turning on his heel and marching to the doors. The crew followed him.

"What can I do?" Vi demanded. "I want to do something. I need to do something. I'm going crazy."

Killian started to open his mouth when Frank returned, his expression tight. "Sir, there's someone here to see you."

That someone, much to Killian's surprise, turned out to be Arlo and Juan. The two were followed closely by no less than eight fully armed men in black attire and cold features. Their impromptu visit had Killian's suspicions rising. It had him moving to put himself between Vi and the newcomers. The girl's big, brown eyes shot to his, filled with question, but she wisely kept her mouth shut.

"If I tell you to leave, leave," he told her quietly under his breath. "Understand?"

Vi nodded.

Killian turned just as the group came to a halt in a small cluster inside the door. Juan, in his loose trousers and gray coat, tore off his leather gloves and stuffed them into his pockets. Next to him, Arlo had the sour expression of someone who'd been force fed cockroach clusters. His bright, red coat was zipped all the way to his chin and he had both hands shoved into his pockets. He reminded Killian of a sullen teenager, which was almost entertaining.

"Juan." Killian stepped forward to shake the other man's hand. "To what do I owe to this pleasure?"

"Killian." He took Killian's palm in a firm shake. "I have come to offer my services in your time of need." He motioned with his free hand to the men waiting for his instructions. "They are my best and will do what they can to help find your woman."

At *your woman* Arlo shifted and averted his gaze. No one paid any attention, but Killian noticed. He also noticed the glance Arlo cast Vi. It was barely a sideways flick of his brown eyes, but there was no mistaking the spark of interest. It made Killian wonder if he'd ever seen Vi before or even knew who she was. He might have. Maybe he was just surprised to see her in Killian's home. Whatever the case was, Killian had to suppress the urge to tell Arlo not to even think about it. Even without his promise to Juliette, he still wouldn't allow assholes like Arlo near her. Not that it mattered. Vi caught the glance and shot Arlo the curled lip of disgust, followed by the aversion of her gaze.

"Thank you." Killian turned his attention back to the man standing before him. "That is quite generous of you."

Juan nodded and stepped back. "When one is attacked, we are all attacked. We must unite in times such as this and prove that we do not go down quietly."

He inclined his head. "Thank you."

"Arlo will also stay to make sure my orders are followed," Juan added.

The last thing Killian wanted was Arlo, but to decline would be to insult the other man and Killian had enough problems. Not that he believed this unexpected act of kindness came from somewhere deep in the man's heart. No one ever did anything without a price. Juan would eventually ask for something and Killian had a feeling he knew exactly what that would be. For now, however, Killian let it slide.

"Thank you."

With a brisk nod, Juan faced his son. He said something in Spanish that sounded like an order. Arlo frowned, but he nodded and muttered something back. Killian had never been any good at picking up other languages, not like his father, but he suspected Juan was telling his son not to fuck up. He relayed the same message to the men before turning and marching out the way he'd come in with three of the eight men following. Arlo met Killian's eye and the two exchanged a mutual displeasure over the situation before Arlo's attention was drawn over Killian's shoulder to Vi again. Vi caught his glance a second time and her frown was even more vicious than the first time.

"Got a problem, pal?" she muttered.

A smirk tweaked the corner of Arlo's mouth, darkening his eyes. "I got something." The remark was followed by the lazy glide of his gaze down the length of her. Killian felt his annoyance prickle and was about to tell the shithead to keep his eyes to himself when Vi beat him to it.

"I don't *something* outside my species. Might want to find someone with low self-esteem issues and bad eyesight."

With that, she folded her arms and stomped over to her usual haunting grounds, only to find her seat occupied. Killian hadn't forgotten about Marco. He just wasn't sure what the hell to do with him now. Normally, a slow and agonizing death came to mind, but this was Marco. He used to help Killian into the car when he was too small to get in by himself. He used to help with his seatbelt and made sure it was done up tight. He'd been in the family since before Frank. Since before Killian's parents had even met. He was family. Had been. He had been family.

"Dominic!" Killian called without taking his eyes off the man waiting for his execution.

Dominic stepped on the threshold, hands clasped neatly in front of him. "Sir?"

Killian jerked a nod towards Marco. "Take him to the basement. Keep him there until I say otherwise."

Bowing his head once, Dominic hurried forward. Marco was already on his feet, waiting. Neither man said a word as Marco was led out.

Killian glanced up and met Frank's hard expression. There were extra folds on his face that hadn't been there before and a flicker of grief in his dark eyes that Killian understood; he wasn't the only person Marco had betrayed.

"You should go, Frank," he said quietly.

Frank squared his large shoulders, lifted his chin, and gave a quick nod. "Yes sir."

"Take Arlo and his men with you as backup." Anything to get them out of his house.

"Yes sir."

He stomped forward and the group fell into step in an efficient cluster out the door, leaving Killian alone with Vi.

"He took Juliette?" the girl asked.

Killian moved to his desk. "That's what he says."

Vi narrowed her eyes. "You don't believe him?"

"I do." He took a seat and stared at his monitor. "He doesn't know who he gave her to."

Vi edged closer and perched tentatively in her favorite chair. "Yeah, I heard that part. Phil said he'd been with you for ages. Did you piss him off?"

Killian looked up. "Why would you think I would piss him off?"

The girl shrugged. "Isn't that how it usually works? Jaded employee kidnaps boss's girlfriend to get even."

It was almost laughable, but he knew she was being serious.

"Marco was my dad's driver," he explained. "He'd been working for us for years. He was family."

"Well, I hope you kill him," Vi decided without missing a beat. "No offense, but he's the reason Juliette is missing and possibly hurt. I don't feel sorry for him at all."

How different the sisters were, Killian thought, studying the girl. Juliette would have begged him to spare Marco's life, to forgive and forget. Or maybe not so different. He remembered telling her about killing Yolvoski and she had accepted that without batting an eye. The woman was forever surprising him.

"Do you think we'll find her?" Vi's voice was small and housed all the insecurities and doubts Killian had been struggling with.

"Aye," he answered without hesitation. "I won't lose her."

The third video arrived two days later. Killian stood at his desk, surrounded by Arlo's men, his men, and Vi. A map of the city lay open across the cleared surface and lines had been drawn in thick, red marker.

The last place Marco had seen Juliette was an abandoned district on the outskirts of the city near the river. Its only inhabitants were the homeless, drug pushers, and the occasional strung out prostitutes. Marco hadn't lied about there being no surveillance. Frank and the crew had returned with absolutely nothing to show for it.

"I have some men in that area," Arlo stated. "I'll make some calls and see if anyone saw a van around in the last couple of weeks."

Killian nodded. "Tell them the van would have been heading east. West is blocked off after the bridge collapsed."

"Well, that doesn't really mean anything," Vi piped in. "Boats can still pass through in the spring when the lake isn't frozen."

Killian looked at her. "Boats?"

The girl shrugged. "Why not? You can easily get a van down that incline to the waterline and then get on a boat."

She had the attention of everyone in the room. A slight tinge of pink worked up into her cheeks, but she remained firm.

"*À la française,*" she said like it was supposed to mean something to any of them. "Really?" she snapped when no one seemed to know what she was talking about. "I am the youngest person here and I rarely even bother going to school." When it became apparent that she would need to explain, she huffed loudly. "*À la française* is basically French Style or In French Style, which I personally don't understand, but I guess it's supposed to be romantic. It was that whole district." She tapped the map where Killian had drawn a ring around the spot Marco had dropped Juliette off at. "Back in the day, when the bridge wasn't a heap of scrap metal dumped into disgusting brown waters, *à la française* was like the New Orleans of the city. Parties every night, lots of sex, drugs, and midnight cruises across Harrison Lake. People would pay big bucks to get pampered and dine on one of the glamorous yachts. Around like the turn of the century or something, the bridge structure collapsed and the thing crumpled into the lake and the whole district was reduced to garbage and bums."

"I remember something about that," one of Arlo's men pipped in. "Not so much the pampering, but a lot of the sections used to use the bridge to push their product. They would smuggle it to the water's edge and..." He followed the blue gash of the Harrison up stream and stopped just where the lake branched off. "Unload around here. Caused a lot of turf wars."

Arlo nodded. "That stopped when the bridge went down, cutting the lake in half and making it impossible to cross."

"But you can still get around that," Vi chimed up quickly. She snatched a pen out of the cup holder and bent over the map. "There's an opening where the bridge ends meet the shore. Here." She circled the spot and straightened. "You can easily walk through it to the other side. From there, it's a ten minute walk to this really cute beach. It's not really a beach, obviously, but it's very romantic late at night when…" she trailed off when she glanced up and found everyone watching her. Her cheeks darkened. "Not that I've ever been there or anything."

Killian stared at her, eyes narrowed. "I'm guessing Juliette doesn't know about your … discovery?"

Vi faltered. "No…" She grimaced. "But aren't you glad I never listen?"

Killian had to bite back his grin as he took his pen back and turned to the map. "If Viola is right, then there's a good chance the van will still be there. We might be able to follow the path down the lake—"

"Oh my God!" Vi's unexpected scream caused everyone to jump, including Killian, whose hand tightened around the pen as though anticipating an attack, which he got when Vi punched him in the arm. It was hard enough to make him wince. "Golden arches! Golden arches!" She grabbed his arm, the one she'd assaulted and shook him. "Arches!"

"Calm down, woman!" He dislodged himself. "What are you on about?"

"The bridge!" She smacked the map. "The bridge, originally, before it turned an ugly red and went into the river, had been painted yellow!"

"But that's only one arch," one of Arlo's men piped in.

In no way did this deter Vi. "It's still a golden fucking arch! And it's winter!" she added hurriedly. "Which means the lake will be frozen so they can't go anywhere."

The first sliver of hope bloomed in Killian's chest. It shot splinters across his entire being, thawing the shards of ice that had crystalized in his blood. He felt it working through his muscles and finally soaking into his heart. He would have laughed and hugged the girl if there hadn't been an entire room of armed men watching the moment.

Instead, he put on his boss face and turned to the crew. "That's where we're going then," Killian stated. "We'll drive out immediately and—"

Frank jerked. His hand flew to his earpiece, as did Dominic and Aaron. Their faces went from confused to stunned in five full seconds. Eyes went to Frank, waiting for instructions.

"What?" Killian demanded as Frank lowered his hand, his face a subtle shade of white under the dark skin.

His throat muscles bobbed, but he straightened. "Excuse me, sir. There is a matter in the basement that requires your attention."

It took Killian a second to realize what in the basement could possibly require his attention and have his men look like someone had died. His heart plummeted. He could feel it hitting the floor around his ankles, crushing every ounce of the hope he'd been basking in only mere seconds before.

"Are you sure?"

Frank nodded. "Yes sir."

"Is there a problem?" Arlo cut in.

"No." Killian turned to the group. "Have someone handle the situation in the basement until I return. In the meantime, we—"

A soft knock sounded on the doors of his office, turning all heads away from Killian to Jacob, whose face said it even before he lifted a hand and showed them the yellow envelope. And just like that, it didn't feel like he would ever get a break. What spark of hope he'd been clinging on to after the news of Marco's self-inflected death in the basement crashed into a pit of jagged rocks. Killian could feel himself dying a little inside, could feel his stomach rising up his chest. The weight crushed his lungs, making it impossible to breathe. Beside him, Vi's fingers tightened around his arm. The color washed from her face. Her eyes met his for the smallest of seconds and the terror in them matched the one clawing through him.

Frank went to get it. He brought it back to the table. Killian didn't touch it and Frank didn't offer it to him.

"If you gentlemen will please excuse us," Frank told the group, taking charge when Killian couldn't even remember his own name. "Please get yourselves ready for the trip out in about twenty."

The men dispersed immediately. They marched quickly to the door and out. Vi stayed. Killian hadn't expected her to leave. But Arlo stayed as well. His gaze kept darting between the envelope and Vi like he couldn't figure out which one needed his attention more.

"Mr. Cruz." Frank motioned him to the door.

Arlo actually hesitated. His eyes were on Vi. But he caught himself, tore his gaze away and marched quickly from the room.

Frank shut the door behind him before returning to the desk. He circled to Killian's side and reached for the CD drive in the tower. It slid open, the gears making a world of noise. Vi shifted closer to Killian, whether for comfort or to get a better view of the monitor as it flickered to life was beyond him. Frank stepped back and the whole room seemed to hold its breath.

Juliette sat in the same metal chair. The concrete wall was behind her. The harsh lights turned her face a fierce white. Her hair was around her shoulders, brushing the stiff material of her green pajama style uniform. She seemed to be waiting for something. Her expression was uncertain and fearful. Her brown eyes darted back and forth at something behind the camera.

"*Am ... am I supposed to say something?*" she asked quietly.

The picture shuddered, but no one answered beyond the rustle of material. There was a thump. The camera was nudged again and then two figures stepped into view to block her. Every line of Killian's body stiffened. His heart thumped in his chest, loud and panicked as his instinct warned him what was about to happen. Next to him, Vi's small hand curled sharp little nails into his upper arm. The pain was a welcome change to the numbness creeping up his limbs, paralyzing him from doing a damn thing, except stand there and watch helplessly as Juliette was cornered.

"*What are you doing? No! Stop it!*"

Scuffling made the image blur. Snippets of light broke through the cracks every time the hulking figures shifted. Occasionally, they could see flashes of Juliette's arm or head as she fought the hands grabbing her. Then the bodies moved and Juliette was forced between them, each arm restrained out on either side of her. The chair was kicked aside and sent clattering somewhere to the left. Without it, the space was wide enough to jerk Juliette backwards. She was slammed into the concrete wall with enough force to make her cry out. They never released her arms, but held them just over her head.

"*Let go!*" she snarled, yanking and struggling against the confines. She kicked at one, but missed. "*What are you...?*"

A third figure stepped into view. Juliette's eyes widened even as she tensed. Her struggling slowed to panicked jerks. A choked sound rose over the scuffle of feet.

"*Been waiting a long time for this,*" a male voice drawled with a sickening sort of pleasure.

It was impossible to see in the video with his back to the camera, but there was no mistaking the sound of unfastening jeans, the jingle of a belt buckle being undone and the rustle of fabric. Juliette was no longer struggling, but she had flattened herself as far back into the wall as humanly possible without breaking through to the other side.

"Don't come near me!" Even to Killian's ears, the warning was weak and laced with terror. It mirrored the green tinge working up the column of her throat to seep into her cheeks. *"Please ... don't..."*

Her desperate whimper tore through Killian. It drenched his insides with a molten red rumble of fury that exploded from somewhere deep inside him. It cascaded in an avalanche of rage so intense, he almost screamed.

"Be a good girl and we'll make this real good for you."

Juliette was visibly crying now and thrashing. The sound wreaked madness through him. It toyed with his sanity until he was sure he'd never recover.

One of the men cackled, amused by her suffering, by the helpless struggle of her body. The one in the middle reached for the triangle of space where her top had lifted, exposing a sliver of skin. His fingers hooked into the elastic waistband and Killian's stomach dropped. His vision twisted in a blurry mess of gray. He was vaguely aware of Vi's quiet sobs at his side. They escalated into blood curdling screams when Juliette's trousers were forced down and the camera closed to black.

"No!" Vi lunged at the monitor, as though she could somehow reach in and pull her sister out. The screen teetered and tumbled backwards off the desk. It crashed to the floor and shattered into pieces of plastic and glass.

Killian didn't notice. He couldn't move or breathe. The whole world had stuffed itself in his chest, a jagged ball of steel and glass. The suffocation nearly sent the floor swaying beneath his feet. He barely managed to grab the desk corner when his vision blurred.

"Killian!" Someone was shaking him. "Do something!" Vi was hysterical. Her pretty face was a blotchy crimson smeared in tears. "Stop them!"

Like some sick joke, his eyes went to the destroyed monitor, his mind replaying Juliette's screams.

How old was the video? Two, three days? That morning? What state was Juliette in now?

"Get the men." The voice was his, but he had no idea who was speaking. "We're going to find her even if we have to burn the fucking city to the ground."

Chapter 28

All the world's cold had found its way deep into the marrow of her bones, paralyzing her muscles and making Juliette all but useless sitting huddled in the corner of her cell. It had been hours since they'd dragged her down and dumped her where they'd found her, but her limbs refused to stop shaking. Her heart refused to stop threatening to burst free of her chest. There were tears burning the back of her eyes, but even they refused to fall. All she could do was sit and shiver and try not to think of Alcorn's hands on her.

"Juliette." On the other side of the bars, Maraveet sat with her shoulder pressed into Juliette's. It was all the contact the other woman would give, to which Juliette was eternally grateful. "Tell me what they did."

Juliette, face buried in the folds of her arms, shook her head rapidly. "They didn't do anything," she choked out for the tenth time.

Maraveet exhaled. "It wasn't your fault."

Juliette raised her head. "They didn't do anything," she repeated. "They started to, I think … I think for the camera…" Her voice warbled. "But they stopped and threw me back down here."

A soft sound escaped the other woman. It was so quiet Juliette almost didn't hear it. But it was brimming with relief and dread. Neither had to say it, but they both knew that next time, she wouldn't be so lucky.

"We're going to get out of here," Maraveet promised. "We just need to figure out how."

The door opened and the soft hiss of air punched into Juliette's chest. Her arms tightened around her drawn knees and she prayed to God they were only bringing food.

There was no food, just Alcorn with his scuffed boots and smirking mouth. His hands hung at his sides and Juliette flinched at the sight of them. The bits of skin he'd touched throbbed like an agitated burn and she had to resist the urge to rub at the spot.

"Boss wants to see you," he drawled, peering through the bars at Juliette.

The keys jingled as he found the one and inserted it into the lock. The sound mirrored the wild drumming of Juliette's heart. Her head snapped towards Maraveet, but the other woman was glowering at Alcorn.

"It amazes me how someone who looks as smart as you would work for a boy," she said. "But I guess getting paid in lollipops and special favors work best for pedophiles."

Alcorn was unfazed by the jab. He laughed as he threw open Juliette's door and stepped inside.

"Do you think I haven't heard worse?" Shaking his head, he stalked to where Juliette sat and hoisted her up by the arm. "You girls never think of anything new to say."

With that, he dragged Juliette from the cell. She had just enough time to glance back before they hit the stairs. The last thing she saw was Maraveet pointing at her pocket and mouthing something that looked like *use it*.

Juliette's numb brain took longer than necessary to register that. Her fingers slipped into the pocket of her coat and curled around the makeshift weapon she'd tucked away. It wasn't exactly as though she'd forgotten the thing, but they hadn't let her take her coat when she'd gone up earlier. Possibly to make their assault appear more authentic without a bulky jacket getting in the way. But they didn't tell her to leave it behind now and she clung to the weapon with all her might. Carefully, she tucked the flat end up her sleeve for better access.

Cyril sat in the same place he had been from the very first day, small and almost doll-like in his perfection. He wore a peach colored suit with a white shirt and white shoes. His pale hair was combed back, leaving those unfathomable blue eyes dominating his face like clear pools on white, sandy beaches. He watched her approach with the faint outline of a grin turning up the corner of his mouth.

"How are you feeling?" he asked.

Juliette said nothing as she was shoved forward to stand in the center of the room. The other men sat in chairs on either side of her, making her feel surrounded and cornered.

Plan your attack and make sure you don't miss. Plan your attack and make sure you don't miss.

Maraveet's words echoed in her ear, drowning out the words Cyril was speaking. His mouth continued to move and Juliette had to force herself to listen.

"Well?"

Juliette swallowed. "Sorry?"

A mild flicker of irritation shone across his porcelain face. "I asked, what you thought of the videos."

The very mention of them made her insides roil, but she answered, "You haven't asked for anything and you haven't given any clues as to where we are even though you keep asking Killian to find you. So they are pointless if you're trying to get what you want."

Someone shifted in their seat. The wood groaned under their weight, but no one spoke.

"Clever," Cyril murmured. "But I'm already getting what I want and I honestly couldn't care less if he finds us or not."

Juliette frowned. "I don't understand. Then why are you doing this?"

"Because he took something very valuable from me years ago and I tend to hold a grudge."

Her frown deepened. "Years ago? You can't possibly be old enough—"

"I'm twenty three, but I'm told I look much younger. It comes in handy when dealing with certain people. They always mistake the appearance of youth for stupidity."

"Okay, but why haven't you asked for whatever Killian took back? Just tell me what it is and I'll—"

"Unfortunately, that isn't how it works." He rose fluidly with the faintest whisper of silk. His feet barely made a sound as he started around her and headed for the bar. No one else moved, except Juliette, who turned to watch him. "My asking won't give me quite the same satisfaction and I have waited too long for this moment to squander what little enjoyment I can garner from his misery."

"It must be horrible holding such bitterness towards a single person," Juliette muttered, no doubt a very bad idea, but he laughed.

"It has been." He drummed nimble fingers on the table while he contemplated the rest of his words carefully. "For ten years I've waited and plotted and bided my time for this moment, the moment when I would finally have the Scarlet Wolf at my mercy." He snorted and shook his head slowly. "I honestly never believed it would happen. Years I've watched while women paraded through his bed, one after another and nothing. I was just beginning to wonder if I needed to put him out of his misery and be done with it when the most remarkable thing happened." Blue eyes glimmered like sunlight off clear waters as they lifted and fixed on her. "You." He left his place at the bar and wandered back to her. "You, my beautiful Juliette, walked into his life and all that was missing was the heavens opening up and the angels singing the hallelujah chorus. Granted in the beginning I thought that you would be like all the others, just another whore to be cast aside, but then I saw it. I saw the way he looked at you. The way he touched you. I saw it all right there and it was like Christmas. You brought the beast to his knees and tamed him. You made him love you. You weakened him and left him completely open and vulnerable."

You make me weak and weak men die. Killian's final words to her echoed between her ears. They rebounded off every bone until it was ringing throughout her entire body in ripples of truth and guilt.

"Thanks to you, he will now know what it feels like to lose something so incredibly precious that the very thought of living another day without it is unbearable. He will know genuine pain as his entire world is ripped apart. I have dreamt of this moment for ten years and you helped make it happen."

He was practically panting, practically glowing. Happiness radiated soft pink blossoms in his cheeks and danced behind the enormous smile stretching his face. His delight in Killian's misery made her stomach hurt. It made her anger prickle and she had to resist the urge to punch her weapon straight into those wide eyes.

"You're crazy if you think I'll ever help you hurt Killian," she whispered instead.

Straight, white teeth flashed in an almost Cheshire cat smile. "Oh, but you already have. Those videos you've been kind enough to help us make, what did you think they were for? My personal amusement? I'm fairly certain he's beside himself watching that last one, wondering just what we're doing to you right now. It will eat him up alive. It will destroy him. By the time I am through, Killian McClary will be on his knees, begging me to end his suffering."

The hatred turning his features demonic was terrifying. It twisted his perfect features into something evil and frightening. It was as though his hatred could manifest itself in human form and it was a terrible sight to behold.

"Why are you doing this?" she asked again. "What has he done that was so horrible it justifies kidnapping and murder?"

He turned away from her slowly and made his way back to the bar. He drew down a crystal tumbler and set it on the table with a resounding crack. A bottle of whiskey was brought out and placed next to it. The amber liquid sloshed in its confines, reminding her of liquid honey.

"I've got my reasons and believe me, they are quite justified."

Ice cubes struck the bottom of the glass with a rattling clink and was drowned by whiskey. The bottle was set aside. The cap twisted back into place. He raised the drink. Light lanced off the rim as he brought it to his lips.

"If you let me talk to him, I am sure I can get back whatever was taken," she urged. "I know he will. Please, you don't have to hurt anyone."

"Have you ever heard the story of Tantalus?"

The question threw her. It was said so unexpectedly that for a moment, she could only stare at him in confusion.

"I'm sorry?"

Drink in hand, Cyril made his way back to the sofa. He sat with flawless grace, folding one leg over the other and observing her over the rim of his drink.

"Tantalus," he repeated like saying it a second time might help jog her memory.

Juliette shook her head. "No, who—?"

"Tantalus betrayed the Gods by divulging their secrets and stealing from them. But the worst betrayal was the day he killed his son Pelops and cooked him in a meal, which he served to the Gods. They of course knew and didn't eat it, except Demeter who accidentally ate a part of Pelops' shoulder. But as punishment, they cast Tantalus into the deepest part of Tartarus where he was to remain in the middle of a large lake with an apple branch dangling just over his head. He would stay there forever, unable to eat, despite the apples and unable to drink, despite an entire lake at his feet. All because of one little betrayal. It's a powerful and horrible tool that can destroy everything."

Juliette had never heard of the story, but it sounded completely disgusting.

"I don't understand."

She prayed to God that wasn't how he was planning to end his game, by cooking her and feeding her to Killian.

"The moral of the story is how Tantalus treated the Gods, who were so good to him. They cared for him and no matter what he did, they forgave him and continued to give him their favor. But it wasn't enough. He was greedy and selfish. In the end, it consumed him."

No matter how much he said, he seemed to make less sense the longer Juliette listened. His riddles were only making her head hurt and she needed to focus in case she missed something important.

"That was how it all began, with Callum McClary betraying my father, ruining him and his reputation after my father made Callum what he was, for treating him like family. But it wasn't enough. Callum got greedy. He sold my father out, got him arrested like some common criminal and thrown in jail. It didn't matter what my father did after that. No one wanted to work with him. No one trusted that he could deliver. So of course my father was angry. He had every right to be."

"Yegor Yolvoski," Juliette whispered, not sure how she knew, but knowing without a shadow of a doubt.

Cyril's head lifted, surprise stilled his drink halfway to his lips. "So you've heard the story."

Juliette swallowed. "It was an accident. Callum didn't call the authorities. They just—"

"They were tipped off," Cyril cut in, taking up his drink once more and downing a large mouthful. "Someone told them where the ship would be. It was also highly suspicious that the minute Callum McClary broke their contract my father would get caught immediately after."

"But that was so long ago," she stressed. "Everyone involved is dead. Can't you let it—?"

"They are dead because your boyfriend killed them." He set his drink down with a deafening crack on the end table next to his elbow. "He slaughtered my entire family in a single night. Everyone, but me."

His bitter hostilities towards that fact caught Juliette by surprise. It was as though the worst thing Killian ever did was let him live.

"Your father tortured and brutalized his mother and killed his father," she pointed out. "Maybe it's time to end this."

"No!" Temper turned his cheeks a harsh, sunburned red. With his soft, pink suit, he reminded her of a fancy lobster. "His father betrayed mine. Mine got even. That is where it should have ended. It was over. Callum broke the code. My father let him live. That should have been enough. But Killian sought vengeance instead and I am amazed by how unperturbed you are by his viciousness while when I seek the same justice, you get upset. Is it because I want your life?" The genuine confusion in the question had his head cocking to the side. "Would you be less distressed if I were to take someone else in your place?"

Juliette gave her head a shake. "I don't want it to be anyone. I just want to go home."

"To him?"

She didn't pretend to misunderstand. "Yes."

Even if Killian didn't want her.

Cyril's arm lowered slowly. The ice in his glass rattled softly as his hand settled neatly in his lap and he regarded her with open puzzlement.

"Is he home? That murderer? That … monster?"

"Yes," Juliette whispered again. "He's not the way you say. I know he's not. Killian isn't a monster."

He stared at her. A faint dent appeared between his furrowed eyebrows and was shadowed by the wisps of hair that had escaped across his brow. There was a question in his eyes she didn't understand.

"It was him," he insisted at last, refusing to believe her. "I saw him with my own eyes, standing over my mother, drenched in my father and brothers' blood. It was a sight I will never forget." Pale lashes lowered. He peered at the glass in his hand like all his memories lay within next to the abandoned chunks of ice. "My father had been doubling security for weeks since the systematic murder of his men the last two months.

He'd known it was only a matter of time before the threat came to our doors. That night, when the alarms sounded, my mother put me in a closet. She made me promise not to come out no matter what I heard. Then she kissed me, said she loved me, and left. That was the last time she would ever say those words to me." The hatred in his eyes when they lifted to bore into her curdled the contents of her stomach. "I broke my promise and left the cupboard. I'd already heard my brothers being killed, heard the weight of their bodies hitting the ground, their screams ... I'd heard my father begging for my mother's life and I knew she was next. So, I ran to her, not caring if I was killed too. She was on the floor, surrounded by the bodies of my family. My eldest brother was pulled into her lap and she was sobbing like I had never heard before. The sound was horrible. I wasn't even sure it was human. But Killian stood over her like an angel of death descending on my family. But I couldn't let him have her, not my mother. I threw myself between them. I swore I would kill him if he touched her and he just stood there, staring at me with those black eyes, his face splattered with blood. I was so sure he would kill me too. But he didn't. Even then, he was mocking me. It was a game to him, poetic justice. My father spared him, so he would spare me so I would live on knowing his pain."

"No!" Juliette blurted. "You were a child. You had nothing to do with what happened to his mother. He would never have hurt you."

"That was his mistake, wasn't it?" Cyril set his glass aside. "He gave me ten years to study him, to learn his weaknesses, waiting for the day I would finally put an end to him." His nostrils flared. "I lost everything that night and I will make him lose everything. Starting with you. Once I am satisfied I have tortured him enough, I will start all over again with his sister. I would have kept that fat cow of his for the same purpose, but she disgusted me too much."

Juliette gasped. "You killed Molly?"

Cyril grunted, lips curling back. "Cutting into her was like slaughtering a pig. She practically exploded. Had a harder time with her husband. All bones," he explained like that too was appalling. "Nevertheless, while it wasn't exactly satisfying, I enjoyed watching Killian's misery."

You need help! Juliette wanted to scream.

"Killian will kill you," she said instead. "If you hurt me or Maraveet, there won't be anywhere you can hide."

Cyril seemed unfazed by her declaration. He sighed quietly and turned his head away in clear boredom.

"What time is it, Delgado?" he asked the man on his right.

The man checked his watch. "Nearly one, sir."

Cyril pursed his lips. "We've wasted enough time. Let's get started."

Juliette stiffened. "Start what? What's going on?"

Cyril fixed his attention back on her even as Alcorn and Calhoun rose to their feet. "Our man inside has gone silent. While I don't think we'll be found here, I don't relish being proven wrong."

"Man inside?" Juliette mimicked, needing to keep him talking. "You mean Marco? How did you get him to work for you?"

"I didn't. He used to work for my father. I found his name in my father's old records. I knew one day, he might come in handy. Clearly, I was right."

The heel of her boot nearly caught the carpet when she shuffled back a step, a pathetic attempt at putting distance between herself and the men closing in on her. Her heart drummed between her ears, a sound of panic and desperation that was clouding her thoughts.

"What ... what about your mother?" she blurted. "Surely she doesn't want this kind of life for you."

All traces of emotion erased from Cyril's face. Even the arrogance washed away. He stared at her with dead, doll eyes that seemed to drill straight into her.

"He killed her," he stated evenly. "By destroying her family, he took away her desire to live. She ended the suffering three months later."

"I'm so sorry," she whispered, actually meaning it. "You were so young."

His lashes drooped, severing the connection. "Doesn't matter now. I have finally accomplished what I promised her I would and she will finally rest in peace. But that is enough of that. The time for talking has ended, Juliette. We're going to make one final video to leave behind just in case he does find us."

Another video. A follow up to the one they'd made just earlier that day. She wasn't stupid enough not to realize what was coming.

She staggered back, her heart trapped in her throat as paralyzing numbness washed through her veins. Cyril remained seated, watching the show with mild interest while idly tapping one finger on the armrest.

"It'll be less painful if you don't fight," he remarked casually.

Bells shrieked in her ear, drowning everything but the roar of her own blood humming between the walls of her skull. Cold sweat dampened her top beneath her coat and yet the bile that rose up her chest felt scalding hot.

"Please don't."

Her plea for even a hint of humanity went ignored. The four advanced, a pack of wolves at the scent of blood. Their eyes seemed to reflect, the eyes of predators stalking out of the shadows in the night. Their dark, inner light prickled along her skin in phantom chills. They pressed forward in a half circle, driving her back into the bar. The sharp corner stabbed into her back, holding her at point without room to escape. Her rapid panting was the only sound amongst them.

"Finally," Alcorn murmured with a lick of his lips. "Been waiting for this."

His hands were already undoing his jeans. The belt jingled loudly in the deafening silence. The zipper hissed and the V parted to a thick cock jutting out from a circle of straggly, sandy brown hair. The others began removing their sweaters and unfastening their own pants.

"Get her to the camera first for Christ sakes!" Cyril commanded, irritation making his voice high.

"With pleasure."

Alcorn made a grab for her arm and something inside her snapped. It roared over her in a thick film of desperation, an animal instinct that drove her to fight. The entire room seemed to fade. Everything, except the four hulking figures threatening her sanity. Time itself seemed to creep to a standstill as her heart pumped adrenaline through her veins like crack from a needle.

Juliette thrust. She didn't pause to consider where. She just let sheer panic propel her as she drew back her arm and drove her makeshift weapon out of her sleeve and straight into the soft bit of skin just above Alcorn's cock. The jagged point pierced through skin with disturbing ease. Blood welled and then gushed with the jerk of her hand. It poured down the front of his jeans, turning the powder blue to dark red. Alcorn screamed, the sound chilling as it recoiled off the walls. It raked over her nerves the way the sound of nails on chalkboard would. He grabbed at his crotch, his face absolutely void of color and dropped to his knees. His howls continued as blood continued to rush freely from between his fingers.

The others shot back in surprise, maybe even fear. Juliette didn't wait for them to regain their senses. She ducked around Calhoun and tore towards the other side of the ship, away from the secret hatch. The patio doors glinted as though beaconing her to them, but she knew she would never make it. There were too many obstacles in between, too many unnecessary seats and sofas and tables. Getting around them would take too much time and she couldn't trust her legs to leap over them.

At the last second, she veered right, going straight for the makeshift film studio and the number of items she could use as a weapon.

"Get her!"

Cyril's bellow was muffled by the clack of the tripod legs as she snapped them shut. She hefted the hefty weight over her shoulder swung blindly. She hadn't expected to make contact, but the bulky camera collided with the side of Calhoun's face with a glorious crunch of bones and plastic. His grunt was a spray of blood as his head snapped to the side. The momentum flung him backwards and he crashed into Delgado. The pair went down in a tangled heap of limbs.

"Harmon! Get her!"

Cyril sounded downright enraged. He was on his feet, his face the exact shade of red as the blood pooling rapidly around Alcorn's writhing body. His pale hair was not so neat as it was abused beneath his agitated hands. Seeing him coming undone only urged her further to escape, to get help, to get Killian.

"Stay away from me!" she warned as Harmon, the only one standing, advanced on her. "I mean it!"

They'd taken her by surprise the first time. They had lured her into the chair, into the corner and she'd had no chance to fight back. But no fucking way was she going to let them touch her again, not without a damn good fight.

She swung again, hoping to at least deter Harmon's persistent approach. But the swing was too wide, he ducked beneath it and launched himself at her middle. They staggered backwards with the impact. The wall slammed into her back and the camera, tripod and all, were torn from her fingers. The edges cut into her palms but the pain was mute compared to the crash of camera striking the wall and smashing to the floor in a ruined heap of shattered glass and broken plastic.

Cyril roared. "You idiot!"

The sound of his boss's rage had Harmon faltering in his capture. His hold weakened and Juliette shoved him with all her strength, using the wall as leverage to drive him backwards. The jungle of cords caught the heel of his boots and gravity caught him. He went down, taking the spotlights with him in a deafening crash of exploding bulbs. Sparks flew, distracting Cyril and Harmon away from Juliette just long enough for her to grab the metal chair, close it and slam it down on Harmon's head four times before he stopped moving.

Panting and wheezing, Juliette dropped the chair and staggered back. A choked sob left her, but she bottled the rest back up as she tried to hold it together. She whirled around, but wasn't fast enough. Tight arms banded around her from behind, caging her to Delgado's hard chest. The collision nearly sent them both to the ground, but her captor held on, cracking ribs and breathing hot, sour breath on her neck.

"No!"

Her screams went ignored as Calhoun shuffled to his feet, no longer in a heap with Delgado. His face was a ghastly mask of smeared blood and rage that blazed behind his eyes. Blood stained his teeth and darkened the front of his coat. He wiped under his nose with his forearm, making the mess worse, but not caring as he descended on her.

"You stupid fucking whore!"

His hand flew back, palm open. Juliette reflexively flinched. Her entire body seized, bracing for the blow, for the sharp explosion of lights and the daze that would follow. She remembered all too well how Arlo's beating had felt, had remembered how paralyzed and useless she'd become. But this was worse. If they got even a pinch of an upper hand, she was done. They would win and they would not go easy.

A sound rang out, a bang that shook the room and rattled the windows. For a moment, no one moved, time itself seemed to pull to a stop as the sound reverberated the way thunder did after the crack of lightning. Juliette's eyes met Calhoun's wide ones for just a split second and something like shock passed between them before they both simultaneously glanced down at the red blossom spreading across the front of his coat. It had nothing to do with the broken nose she'd given him and they both knew it. His head jerked up and their gazes locked a second time, this time with horror as he went down at her feet.

"One down, four to go." A gun was cocked. "Who wants to piss me off next?"

It was a tossup who was more stunned by the figure standing just inside the patio doors, smoking gun raised. Juliette was the first to break out of her shock.

"Arlo?" By far the very last person in the world she ever expected to see coming to her rescue. "What…?"

Brown eyes never wavering from her, he raised the hand not holding the gun and brought it to his mouth.

"Got her. Sixth boat. Don't even," he warned when Delgado began pulling Juliette backwards. "Let her go."

Delgado's arms only tightened further, crushing her. Their feet tangled as he continued guiding her further away towards the secret compartment at the back. Juliette dug her heels in. She put all her weight down, refusing to be taken anywhere.

Another bang exploded and a perfect, black hole smoldered inches from Delgado's foot.

"Not going to say it again," Arlo said, twisting the hammer back. "Let her go."

Against her shoulder blade, Delgado's heart hammered. His hot breath washed along the back of her neck, making her skin prickle. She tried to jerk away. She tried stomping on his foot and clawing at his arms, but he was adamant about keeping her as his own personal human shield.

"Counting to three," Arlo went on. "One … two—"

"Juliette?"

Like a beautiful sunrise over a majestic landscape, Killian charged through the patio doors behind Arlo and immediately took possession of all the air in the room. His very presence shrank all her fears. It smothered every ounce of the nightmare she'd been living the last couple of weeks.

Suddenly, there was no room for anything but an unimaginable happiness at the sight of him.

"Killian!"

Dark eyes found hers. They roamed over her once before noticing the man holding her. They went impossibly black with rage. His chin rose a notch as every hard line of his body stiffened. Before her eyes, he seemed to grow in size as power and dominance radiated off him in dangerous waves.

"You're surrounded," he stated evenly. "There are roughly twenty men aboard this ship at this very moment. The odds of you making it off alive are very slim either way, but if you don't get your hands off her, I can promise you'll wish I'd killed you."

Delgado released her instantly. For good measure, he staggered back and nearly fell over the unconscious—or possibly dead—body of Alcorn.

Juliette didn't let him get very far. Bolting forward, she snatched the laptop off the table and swung it across his head. The machine made a distinct crack as the screen shattered and snapped off. Delgado flew backwards, tripped over Alcorn and hit the ground with a sickening crunch as his head ricocheted off the bar.

Panting, Juliette dropped the bit of computer she still held and stomped on it, breaking off keys and cracking plastic. Not sure if that was enough to destroy the files, she grabbed the whiskey bottle off the counter and dumped the whole thing on top.

"Juliette..."

Shivering and rapidly falling apart, Juliette spun and flung herself into Killian's waiting arms. One hooked around her middle while the hand on the other closed in her hair, mashing her face into his shoulder. Her own arms locked around his ribs. Her hands fisted in the fabric of his coat as she inhaled his soothing scent. She clasped him close to stifle the broken sounds struggling up her throat, the ones that rocked through her very core in violent waves. Tears burned, amplifying the urge to break and just sob for all she was worth. But not yet. She couldn't. She needed to hold on a little longer.

"Are you hurt?" The question was an uneven growl.

Juliette shook her head. "You came." Her breath caught around the words. Her voice broke. "You really came."

"Nothing was going to stop me." His arms tightened. "God, Juliette."

A bang made them both jump. Something shattered.

"Don't you even," Arlo warned, gun aimed at Cyril. Broken pieces of glass lay at his feet from the lamp Arlo had shot. "I've got a clear shot at your head and no one'll miss you."

"Oh!"

Pulling out of Killian's embrace, Juliette hurried to Alcorn. She dropped down and unhooked the ring of keys from his damp belt loop. She ignored the smear of blood as she tore them free.

"Juliette, what…?"

Ignoring the question, she ran to the compartment door. It took some fiddling and prodding before she found the secret panel that unlatched the door. It hissed open.

"It's okay." She promised when Killian started after her. Not waiting, she sprinted down the stairs. "Maraveet? Maraveet, get up!"

The woman's head shot up out of her folded arms and she blinked her green eyes. They widened at the sight of Juliette. Then shot past her to the open door.

"What…?"

"Come on!" Juliette urged, flipping through the keys until she found the right one. She undid the door and rushed inside to help Maraveet to her feet. "It's okay," she said. "Killian's here."

"Killian?" A grin spread across the woman's face. "I knew he'd come."

Panting, Juliette tightened her grip as they shuffled to the stairs. "Don't forget the plan."

Maraveet growled under her breath. "It's a stupid plan! Let Killian kill them all."

"No! You promised!"

Maraveet shook her head. "There's something wrong with you. Fine," she muttered when Juliette stopped walking. "I'll follow the plan."

Relieved that Killian would be one less thing she would need to worry about, Juliette started onward, dragging Maraveet up each step carefully. Her mind was a painfully organized compartment of everything she needed to do before the sun came up, everything she'd dutifully worked over and practiced in her head for the last two weeks. It didn't even dawn on her that it wasn't normal to be *that* calm about such a situation. In a reality, she should have been a mess. And she would be. Just not in that moment.

The revolting crack of flesh on bone greeted them at the top. The shrill cry of pain with every clap. The grunts that followed. Certain Cyril's men had somehow gotten the upperhand, Juliette hurled herself and Maraveet through the door and into the second level.

Arlo stood exactly where she'd left him, by the patio doors, holding his gun out at men who weren't even moving. Frank was at his shoulder, calmly watching the scene unfolding in the sitting area where Killian had Cyril pinned to the carpet. One knee was gouged into the younger man's thin chest, spearing him to the ground as Killian beat all ten, balled fingers into his beautiful face, or what used to be beautiful. It was a broken, bloody mess.

"Killian!"

Juliette's cry jarred him from the spell he seemed to be under, the one that had his face as dark as his eyes and his teeth bared like a wolf's. His head snapped up, his nostrils flared as though anticipating the thought of beating the hell out of someone else. When he spotted no other threat, he let his hands drop. The torn and bleeding fingers unfurled at his sides.

"Mar?" Killian's face went slack with shock. He pushed up, making sure to put his weight on the knee crushing Cyril's chest. The boy gasped and curled onto his side. His entire body jerked with every cough. Blood speckled the ground by his face. Killian didn't notice as he bound over the body and hurried to his sister. "What the hell are ... what did they do to you?"

Maraveet groaned. "Had a tea party. They served the wrong tea. Things got real."

"I'm going to fucking kill him!" he snarled, already turning back.

"No!" Juliette cried. "Maraveet needs a doctor. She's hurt badly."

That made him pause. His murderous gaze shot from Maraveet to Cyril, his mind visibly torn between helping his sister and killing the bastard who put her in the position. The right choice won when he reached for Maraveet with a frustrated growl.

"Come on."

"God bless you." Maraveet went into her brother's arms. He scooped her up against his chest, and while the gesture was gentle, Maraveet cried out. "Gentle!" she snapped. "I'm fragile."

Her teasing was met with a frown from Killian as he carted her to the patio doors. Another figure moved in as though anticipating and took Maraveet from him. He set her gently into the arms of one of his men and instructed him to take her straight to the car. Then he turned and motioned Juliette over.

"Go with them," he ordered.

Juliette shook her head. "No, Marco—"

"I know." His gaze flicked away from her, but not before she caught the pain in them. It radiated along the set slant of his jaw and ticked in the muscle in his cheek. "He's not around anymore."

Juliette tensed. "Did ... did you...?"

Killian looked away, his jaw set. "No, he did it himself. Guilt and shame, I guess."

She didn't want to know what that meant, but she had a feeling that hurt Killian more than Marco's betrayal had.

"Come with me," she urged. "We'll phone the police and—"

Frank stepped into the space behind Arlo, his massive frame filling the threshold.

"The ship has been cleared, sir. There were only the..." he trailed off as he studied the unmoving bodies strewn throughout the place with more than a little surprise. "Five men," he finished lamely.

Killian nodded. "Get everyone restrained. Take Juliette to a car and drive her to the hospital straightaway. I will meet you there once I am finished here."

"No!" Juliette turned to him. "I'm not going anywhere."

It was ridiculous, only moments earlier, she couldn't wait to get off that ship without a body bag. But she knew if she left, Killian would kill Cyril and all his men and, while they might deserve it, they didn't deserve that piece of him. There had already been too much killing. It needed to stop. Someone needed to make it stop.

"You need to be seen," Killian said firmly.

"I'm fine," she insisted. "But please don't do this. There has already been so much bloodshed and pointless deaths and it will never stop if you don't stop it."

"I say kill him," Arlo piped in, his gun barrel never wavering from Cyril, who had struggled to his feet, his face bloody and his pretty suit ruined. His right eye had already swollen shut. "Toss him overboard and let someone find him in the spring."

Killian never took his eyes off Juliette, his features thoughtful, his gaze searching. "If I let him live, he will come back. He will never stop. This is the only way."

"No!" Her fingers tightened on his sleeves. "No, just call the police, let them take him in. I will testify. I will make sure he goes in—"

"He won't stay there forever, Juliette," Killian broke in. "And he deserves to die for what he did to you."

And Molly and Maraveet, the voice in her head chimed.

"He and his family don't deserve another piece of you," she whispered. "Don't give him what he wants."

Killian frowned. "Family?"

"Fascinating, isn't it?" Cyril's voice broke through the silence that followed Juliette's plea. "You can almost believe for a moment that she really could save you."

Killian raised his eyes over Juliette's head and pinned them on the man standing five feet away. He seemed to really be looking at him for the first time. Juliette couldn't help wondering if he'd even said two words to Cyril before beating the shit out of him.

"Who…?" It seemed to dawn on him slowly. She could see the confusion melting into shock and confusion. The lines deepened as his eyes widened and his eyebrows lifted into his hairline. "Erik Yolvoski. How is this possible? You're dead."

Cyril smirked around a swollen mouth. "Perhaps I am a ghost." He spread his arms out to his sides. "How else can I possibly be here, hmm?"

Killian's shock wore down to annoyance that tightened the corners of his mouth. "I was at your funeral. I watched them put you into the ground."

Cyril blinked. His head bent to one side as he regarded Killian with a new sort of suspicion.

"You went?" His lips curled back. "Why? To gloat?"

"You were fifteen. What pleasure was I to derive from your death?" Killian countered. "I went to pay my respects to a child who died too soon."

"Or was it guilt?" Cyril spat back. Blood dribbled from his lip in a long, pinkish ooze of spit to stain his ruined top.

"After all, you were the reason I needed to die, needed to erase myself from the world and start fresh."

Killian's shoulders lifted in a deep inhale that flared his nostrils. "I can't help being disappointed," he said at last, sadness weaving through the tight confession. "In my mind, I always saw you as that thirteen year old boy who threw himself in front of danger to protect his mother. The boy with so much potential. I honestly believed you would better yourself, change the course laid out before you. I thought perhaps seeing what happened would show you just how senseless this life really is. But here you are, doing exactly what your father would have."

"My father was a great man!" Cyril snarled through clenched teeth. "He was a loving father and a good husband and he—"

"Died begging for his life!" Killian interjected with a snarl. "He was a coward. He was a murderer, a rapist, and a coward. You might have turned him into a martyr to justify the things you have done, but you could have been better. I had hoped you would be better." Dark eyes snapped over and found Juliette's. They exchanged silent glances for a full minute before he faced Cyril once more. "I would like nothing better than to kill you. The world is a horrible enough place without you in it. Fortunately for you, Juliette has appointed herself the savior of my soul and she has asked me to let you live. So, I will. For now. But you will not leave this ship in one piece—" He ignored Juliette squeak of protest. "—not even Juliette will save you there. It will be the sort of pain you cannot even imagine. I can promise that. I will make sure you regret ever touching her and when I am done, I will dedicate my life to watching your every move very closely. If I get so much as a whisper of something I don't like, I will personally put a bullet through your head. Do you understand?"

The frothing fury swirling around Cyril crackled like livewires, but it was splintered with fear. Sparks flashed across his eyes and the look on his face was sheer rage in its purest form.

"Tamed," he hissed around a disgusted curl of his lips. "The great Killian McClary, the Scarlet Wolf, the monster everyone speaks of in hushed whispers, tamed by his bitch. Oh, how the mighty have fallen. You are weak and so long as you are, your kingdom will crumble down around you while you lay dying amongst the rubble. I might not be the one to end you, but I will relish the day you die."

Juliette didn't know what possessed her. Maybe it was being tortured for the last several weeks. Maybe it was being called a bitch, or maybe it was just to shut him up, but she was marching forward before she knew it. Her arm snapped back and she drove five balled fingers of hatred straight into the delicate line of his slender jaw. The impact sang up her arm in a flurry of pain, but the snap of his teeth, the crack of his neck as his head flew back was a sound she would bask in for a very long time. He crashed to the floor with a weak cry. Fresh blood welled over his puffy lip and dribbled down his chin and she hoped she'd broken a few of his teeth.

"That's for Molly," she decided. "And this..." She pulled back her leg and let it swing forward with all her strength behind it right between his legs. The sound he made was one of air being let out of a balloon. His entire face went a frightening shade of purple and red as he curled onto his side, clutching his gut. In that state, he was neither beautiful nor regal. He was pathetic. "That's for Maraveet."

Satisfied, she turned and hurried back to the patio doors, so ready to get the hell off that stupid boat. Arlo, Frank, and Killian watched her as she joined them. Arlo's gun wielding arm dropped down to his side now that there was no one to point it at. His expression was something between amused and impressed. Frank had no expression at all, but his eyes did twinkle, which made her feel good. Killian simply met her gaze, the dark fire in his eyes shot through with a liquid heat she recognized as arousal. She said nothing to any of them as she hurried out onto the deck.

The cold predawn air clawed at her, licking at the sweat dampening her skin and making her shiver. It had begun to snow, adding a fresh layer across the city. She breathed it in, letting the cruel fingers of winter burn into all her exposed skin and become a reminder that she'd made it. That Cyril had been wrong. That she wasn't weak. The world of shadows and darkness hadn't claimed her. She had fought and won. It was the greatest victory a person could ever accomplish and she had done it. Granted, not alone, but she had survived. More importantly, she hadn't given up.

There was an almost skip to her steps as she hurried down the frozen plank onto the docks. Her boots thumped as she ran down the path in the direction of the lights ahead. It was far, but she didn't stop. She pumped her legs and let the cold cut into her lungs like serrated shards of glass. The wood ended on icy dirt running alongside the frozen river. She ducked beneath a series of broken beams that had once been a bridge and kept running until she was at the incline leading up to a parking lot filled with cars and lights and voices.

"Miss Romero!" John jogged over to her, his coat flapping in the night like wings.

Juliette laughed and hurried to meet him halfway. She hugged him. She didn't care that he tensed all over as though she'd suddenly grown a second head and tried to eat him. He was a sight for sore eyes.

He patted her awkwardly on the back before carefully detaching and taking a step away.

"It's good to see you," he said.

Juliette smiled. "Thank you for finding us."

He looked away. "Didn't do overly much, ma'am. But we're glad you're safe."

"We?"

He stepped aside to reveal the other five figures silhouette against the headlights of a parked SUV. The sight of her little group brought tears to her eyes. It tightened the muscles of her throat until she couldn't breathe. John took her elbow gently and guided her forward.

"You guys came." The words came out in a strangled croak.

"Just doing our duty, ma'am," Tyson murmured.

She embraced each of them in turn before stepping back and smiling sheepishly at their uncomfortable shifting.

"Thank you."

There were nods, but no one spoke.

Jake finally stepped forward. "We have been given orders to take you to the hospital."

Juliette didn't protest. Going to the hospital was all part of the plan. It was where she needed to be if she was to save Killian and put Cyril behind bars. She let herself be guided to the SUV and helped inside the cozy interior. Jake climbed in behind the wheel while Melton claimed the passenger's seat. John and Tyson squeezed in on either side of Juliette, flagging her. She wasn't sure where Javier and Laurence went off to, but she suspected to get a second SUV to follow them.

Juliette relaxed against the warm leather. "Where's Maraveet?"

"Miss Árnason insisted she be taken to the hospital," Tyson answered.

Good! Juliette thought. Step one was complete.

"Where's my sister? Has anyone checked on her? Is she all right?"

"Miss Romero will meet us at the hospital," Jake assured her. "She's been informed of your safe recovery and is on her way with Phil."

Juliette exhaled. She lay her head back and closed her eyes.

It was over. It was finally over.

Chapter 29

Killian didn't care what anyone said, hospitals were portals into limbo. It was the place tormented souls went to wait and wither to nothing. It was the place run by Satan and his white clad minions with their needles and sour faces. The whole lot of them made him want to strangle somebody, quite possibly the pissy little nurse who kept telling him to please wait. If he heard those two words one more time, he might forget his promise to Juliette not to commit anymore murders.

Square slabs of moonlight punched into the speckled linoleum between his feet. The brightness made his eyes water, but he continued to sit hunched over, elbows braced on his knees to study the glow. Around him, people went about their business, rushing in the way only people in the hospital did, with hurried strides and set faces. No one gave him a second glance. Overhead, some woman kept buzzing doctors to this room or that in a dry monotone drawl that grated on his nerves. Then there was the god awful stench of floor cleaner, antiseptic and misery. The latter was oddly the worst. It seemed to be pouring from the ceiling and oozing down the walls. Yet, he remained. He sat waiting for the elusive and possibly invisible doctor to finish twiddling his thumbs long enough to tell Killian Maraveet's status. It had been hours and not a single person had gone in or out of those doors. Were they all taking a coffee break together?

He was just about to go harass the frazzled woman at the front counter again when the magical doors finally swung open and a nurse hurried out. Her head was bent over a clipboard, but she looked up, looked around and spotted him. Her small face lit up.

"Mr. Hutchinson?"

Killian glanced over his shoulder at the row of empty chairs. Then back at the woman, certain she had the wrong person.

"Sorry?"

Smile melting into uncertainty, the nurse peeked at her notes again. "Callum Hutchinson?"

It took him a second to connect Maraveet's very clever dots, but he caught on quick enough and got to his feet.

"Aye?" He moved closer. "Is my...?" he trailed off, not sure what Maraveet had stated him as.

"Sister?" the nurse hedged carefully, like she wasn't entirely sure either and wasn't sure why he wasn't sure.

"My sister, yes. How is she?" Killian said quickly.

Blue eyes dropped down to the forms in her hands. "The doctors just left her after running multiple tests to make sure there was no internal damage. They did several x-rays and blood work that hasn't come in yet, but—"

"Is my sister all right?" he cut in.

She smiled. "She'll be fine. She's banged up a little, but nothing to be worried about. The police are in there with her now, but if you—"

Killian stiffened. "The police?"

Her smile faded. "Yes, she insisted we call—"

He moved past her and charged through the doors, ignoring her when she called after him. It took several aggravating minutes of searching before he found her, nearly at the end of a very long hallway.

Sure enough, there were two police officers standing at her bedside, both in full uniform. Maraveet sat propped against a mountain of pillows while she listened to whatever the shorter of the two was saying. He expected her to be in cuffs, but they were talking to her as though she were the victim. In a sense, she was, but if they knew who she was, the situation would change very quickly.

"And you didn't recognize the men?"

Maraveet shook her head. "No."

"Is there anything else you can tell us?" the taller one asked.

"No, I'm sorry."

"And the other woman?"

"Juliette? They brought her in a couple of weeks ago."

"And you didn't know her before then?"

"No."

The shorter one jotted her response down while his partner continued to ask his questions. Maraveet was light on her answers, sticking to yes and no and only giving short explanations when absolutely necessary. Her posture was relaxed, but he could just make out the slight twitch in her fingers. He had no idea what she was playing at, but it was a dangerous game calling the police in. He was stunned that she would. Maraveet hated the police and they hated her with good reason; criminals and cops would never see eye to eye.

"Thank you." He tucked his notepad away and the two took a step away from the bed. "We'll keep in touch if we hear anything else."

Killian ducked out of the doorway and made his way to a bulletin board against the far wall. He kept his back turned until the clip of footsteps faded somewhere in the opposite direction. Once certain they weren't coming back, he stepped into Maraveet's room and shut the door behind him.

"What was that?" Killian asked, moving to take their place next to Maraveet's bed.

"That was your girlfriend's idea," she hissed through her teeth. The calm façade she'd been holding onto for the police was gone. In its place was a sheen of sweat across her brow and trembling hands. "She's a bloody menace, you know that right? An absolute nut."

"What idea?" he demanded.

Maraveet ignored him as she picked at the tape holding her IV needle in place along the back of her hand. "Should never have listened. It was pity is what it was," she grumbled to herself. "I felt bad so I agreed. Never doing that again. Bloody cops."

"Maraveet!" Killian snapped. "What did you two do?"

"Apparently we told the truth to save you!" she cried with great exaggeration.

"What truth?"

She tore the needle out and pitched it aside. Her hand closed around the blankets next as she struggled to heave herself off the bed.

"Ask her!" She rolled to her feet and swayed. "It was her stupid idea." Moving with a slight limp, she hurried to the folded chair containing her coat and shoes and tossed both on. The coat took a bit longer without jostling her ribs. "They'll return the second they find my prints on that boat and I don't intend to stick around." She paused and glanced at him. "I'll wait for you at home."

Killian nodded. "Be careful."

She rushed to the door and peered out. The coast must have been clear, because she was gone before he could blink.

At least she's all right, he told himself with a weary sigh.

He left the room and made his way to the other end of the hospital, the end where they were holding Juliette. Every stride was quick and determined, carrying him through the enormous structure at a near run. He told himself it was because he wanted to know what kind of scheme she and Maraveet had cooked up, but the truth of the matter was that he needed to see her, needed to know she was all right. His quick glimpse of her on the boat hadn't assured him of anything. He still had no idea just how extensive her injuries were, not just beneath her clothes, but in her mind. Something like that left dark prints on the soul. It was like rot beneath the glossy peel of an apple, hidden from sight, but slowly devouring the fruit until it was festering. He couldn't allow that to become Juliette. It would be just one more evil he'd brought into her life and he couldn't stand it.

He caught sight of Frank first. He stood at the end of the hall, away from Juliette's room, but close enough to keep an eye on her door. Sitting or leaning along that same wall was Phil, John, Melton, Tyson, and Jake who were void of their weapons, but still wore their cargo pants and black coats. And since Phil was there, Killian suspected Vi was somewhere inside with Juliette.

"What's the news?" He stopped next to Frank.

"Cops," was all the other man said, his face set as he watched the doorway leading into Juliette's room. "They had questions for Miss Romero."

Killian nodded. "They just finished talking to Maraveet. She's gone." He added when Frank looked over at him. Killian exhaled. "Any idea what the questions are?"

Frank shook his head. "I don't understand how they knew. The letter we left with young Yolvoski said nothing of Miss Romero or Miss Árnason. Do you think he told them?"

Killian shook his head. "Erik wouldn't know we would take Juliette or Maraveet to the hospital and he's not stupid enough to confess to his crimes."

"Then how...?"

"Juliette," Killian muttered. "Maraveet said this was all part of her plan."

Frank frowned. "Her plan?"

Killian only shrugged, not understanding that woman either. "How is she?"

"I overheard the doctor say she was fine. Dehydrated mostly. A few bruises. But she'll be okay."

"She seemed okay," Killian mused.

Frank nodded very slowly, dark eyes pinned to the open doorway. "Young Cruz may have mentioned that Miss Romero had already incapacitated the men before you arrived."

Memories of how beautiful and fierce Juliette had been on that boat swelled over him like a warm flood of sunlight. It laced with pride and a smug sort of satisfaction he really had no right to feel, but couldn't stop. She hadn't let them take her down without a fight. She had stood her ground and kicked the shit out of them. If he wasn't already madly in love with her, that would have solidified his resolve.

"Aye, she did. She was amazing."

"She's very special," Frank went on casually. "Not the kind of woman you're likely to find again."

Killian shot him a sidelong glance. "Are you trying to say something, Frank?"

"No sir. Just making an observation."

The officers left Juliette's room. Killian tilted his head away until they were out of sight.

He contemplated walking away, just leaving and not looking back. It would have certainly made things easier, not just for him, but for Juliette who wouldn't have been in the hospital had it not been for him. It was his fault her life had become so fucked up. But his body had all but shut his brain off, refusing to listen as it started forward. The sweet sound of Juliette's laughter greeted him before he reached the threshold. It tangled with Vi's voice as she explained all the things Juliette had missed in her absence.

"That is horrible!" Juliette was saying in between fits of giggles. "He must have been so angry."

"No!" Vi said. "I mean, I totally expected him to strangle me, but he didn't."

"There might still be time for that later." Juliette laughed. "I hope you apologized at least."

"I might have momentarily considered it."

The two burst out in giggles again that made Killian shake his head slightly in amusement. But at least she sounded happy, he thought. She would never forget what happened, but at least she hadn't let it darken her ability to move past it. That was what he wanted, for her not to live in those couple of weeks. If he had his way, he'd make her forget it entirely.

Then maybe you should let her go, said the sensible voice in his head, the one pinning him to the floor right outside the room. *Seeing you would only bring back everything that happened to her. It will remind her of what you did and how you weren't able to keep her safe.*

His body drew away from the door, no longer only aching to see her, but wanting to save her from further pain.

"Killian?" From the wide eyed look of surprise on Vi's face, she hadn't been expecting to find anyone blocking the doorway. She exhaled a bit nervously and offered him a sheepish little smile. "You're here."

He didn't know what to say, so he gave a slight nod.

Vi licked her lips and shot a glance towards the side of the room where he suspected the bed was. Her brows drew together for a second before she was looking at him again with an innocence he didn't buy.

"I'm just on my way to get some poison in a cup so I'll let you guys talk."

He heard a hiss from the room that could have been words, but she ignored it as she skipped through the door. Killian moved to let her pass, but she stopped in front of him and threw both arms around his shoulders.

"Thank you for bringing her back," she whispered in his ear before letting him go and stepping back. She offered him a crooked smile. "You should have brought chocolates."

Killian blinked. His gaze dropped to his empty hands like he had no idea where they'd come from. Vi laughed as she sprinted past him and hurried down the hall with Phil falling into step alongside her. Killian remained, staring at his palms and wondering if he should get something from the gift shop. That was what normal people did when visiting someone in the hospital, wasn't it? But it was too late for that now. He was already there and she knew he was there.

Drawing in a breath, he stepped into the room.

It was the exact replica of Maraveet's room. Dull white walls, crude, blinding lights, a window overlooking the parking lot, and a bed bracketed by two end tables. Juliette sat in the center of it, hooked to an IV and wearing a green gown that matched the blankets tossed over her lap. Her face was streaked with dirt and her hair was matted, but she was still the most beautiful woman he'd ever seen.

"Hey," she whispered.

He dared a single step closer. "Hi."

She fidgeted slightly with the blankets, tucked a lank curl behind her ear and swallowed before speaking again. "How are you?"

Killian almost laughed. "Shouldn't I be asking you that?"

God, why was this so hard? Every moment thrummed with tension and unease and he didn't understand it. He couldn't recall a single moment between them that had ever felt so intense or awkward. Not even their first time and that had been an odd experience for him.

She broke the silence.

"How's Maraveet?"

"Good." He moved to the foot of her bed and braced his palms on the plastic footboard. "She already left."

Juliette nodded. "Good. I'm glad she did."

"She mentioned a plan."

Her cheeks flushed and she chuckled.

"What was it?" he pressed when she didn't elaborate.

She peered up at him with a sheepish half smile. "That we tell the police everything. That we were taken and held captive on that ship by Cyril and his men. That they were going to sell us, but we managed to take them by surprise and we ran. I made sure Maraveet told them we'd never met before and she was supposed to use a different name, just in case. But at least they got her statement and that will help put Cyril away. I also made sure none of this was traced back to you. I doubt Cyril will tell them you killed his parents, not without revealing that his killed yours first, or that he'd spent the last ten years plotting revenge. I also didn't mention Marco. I said I didn't see who grabbed me so … as far as the police are concerned, Cyril was a human trafficker and we were victims that got away. I'm also kind of hoping his men won't talk, but if they do, it's their word against mine and they're criminals so I'm hoping it doesn't come to that."

Something tightened in his chest. It coursed through him, propelling his body to do something completely crazy like go to her and gather her up into his arms. The weight of the last couple of weeks hadn't diminished, not even in that moment. It sat heavy on his chest, a suffocating force crushing his lungs. It killed him to see her there and not be able to go to her, or touch her, or love her. It hurt to stand there and not know what to do.

"That's very elaborate," he mumbled. "You really thought it through."

Juliette gave a little shrug. "I had a few weeks to really perfect it, on the off chance we actually escaped." She peered at him. "You didn't kill him, did you?"

Kill him? No. Cyril was still very much alive, if not seriously rethinking his life choices. Killian may have promised Juliette he wouldn't kill the little fuck. But even she wouldn't have been able to stop Killian from beating the last two weeks into him.

Killian shook his head. "Tied him and his men up and left a note for the police. Frank stayed to make sure the police got them all when they arrived."

She exhaled her relief. "Okay good." She nibbled on her lip, a frown knitting her eyebrows. "What was Arlo doing there?"

He almost laughed at the disgruntled question. "Would you believe me if I told you he was there to help find you?"

Her eyes narrowed. "At what price?"

That was the question. Arlo hadn't said anything when he and Killian parted ways by the ship, but he knew the Dragons would expect some kind of thank you gift, especially since Arlo was the one who actually found Juliette.

To Juliette, Killian shook his head. "Doesn't matter. You're safe. That's all I care about."

Her gaze lowered to her lap. "Thank you for taking care of Vi. I'm really sorry about your windows. I'll pay for the damages."

Killian shook his head. "It's not important."

"Still, I should—"

"I don't care about the windows." The sharpness in his voice had her eyes lifting back to him and the sadness in them punched him in the chest. "The only thing I wanted was to get you back," he murmured. "I know I said some things I shouldn't have, but I'll always be here for you." His head dropped forward so he was staring at the twin peaks of her feet under the blankets. "You can come to me for anything. I won't ever turn you away."

"Thank you," she whispered.

Thank you. That was it. But what had he expected? That she'd tell him she loved him and wanted to be with him forever? That she'd forgiven him for the horrible things he'd said to her? Even if she did, that didn't mean he could bring her back into his world. Not ever again.

He drew in a breath. "Goodbye, Juliette."

Her brown eyes held his and no matter how hard she fought to keep her face smooth, the gathering tears tore at him. It reflected in the tremor of her chin and in her white knuckled grip around the blanket. A pink tongue snuck out and wet her lips before disappearing once more.

"Goodbye, Killian."

It was incredible how something so tiny could feel like she'd taken a bazooka to his chest. Two little words that it felt as hollow as her voice. The plastic beneath his hands creaked under the force of his grip. He relinquished it quickly and pushed back. He began to turn away, needing to leave before he did something infinitely stupid like beg her take it back, but he stopped. He reached into his pocket and withdrew his mother's pendent. He set it gently on the foot of the bed, not trusting himself any closer to her.

"Take care of it for me," he murmured, unable to look at her, knowing that if he did and she was crying, he'd never leave. "It'll just collect dust if I keep it. You could give it to your children one day." Children she wouldn't have with him.

Children she'd create with some other man, someone who could give her children, someone who could give her the normal life Killian couldn't. Someone who would get into bed with her at night and touch her and hold her and make her come apart. The man didn't even exist yet and Killian could already feel his blood boiling. The very idea of this faceless person touching Juliette made his vision go red. But he didn't take it back. Instead, he turned on his heel and stalked to the door.

"Don't go."

He couldn't be sure if it was a voice in his head or if the words had actually been spoken, but when he glanced back, Juliette was staring out the window, her eyes unblinking and bright. Her arms were clasped tight around her and she was cutting a gash in her bottom lip.

She looked up when he stopped. Her eyes met his and a tear cut down the curve of her cheek to cling to the corner of her lips. Something hard kicked him in the stomach, hard enough to nearly send him to his knees. His chest tightened and he was sure he was about to die of asphyxiation. Her lips parted and Killian left. He ran before she could let the words he could see in her eyes spill through the room and further destroy him.

Chapter 30

Juliette waited until his footsteps had faded before letting the walls crash down around her in a flood of agony. The pain of watching him walk away devoured her all over again with a fresh urgency that made her insides feel hollowed out. It cut into all the tender places that were already torn open from their original break up and ripped the crude stitching wide open. She reached for the pendant and broke into a fit of sobs that mostly had nothing to do with Killian. It was as though the dam she'd built during her captivity burst and she was swamped with everything she'd kept locked behind it. It flooded over her, pulling her under until she was sure she would die. Even to her own ears, the sounds escaping her weren't quite normal. They were the wails of someone under immense torture, which was exactly how it felt.

"Hey." Thin arms wound their way around her, pulling her forward into a body that smelled of orchards and citrus. "It's all right," Vi whispered. "It's going to be all right."

Juliette couldn't even push away the wild drumming beating down on her long enough to give an answer. She didn't even know what she could say that would justify her complete meltdown. How could she explain that she was only just starting to feel the full impact of the terror she should have felt during her stint in the cage? How could she possibly make anyone understand what she'd gone through? They may not have beaten her like Maraveet or raped and tortured her like Killian's mom, but the never knowing what they would do was a sort of torture beyond words. It was waking up and wondering if that would be the day they would finally break her. It was the prayers that went unanswered and the guilt of being powerless. Tangled amongst all of that was the loss she felt at losing Killian and knowing it was the right thing. She couldn't stay with him when he refused to leave that life that had put her in the hospital in the first place. She couldn't stay with him knowing it was a possibility that she could be taken again. She couldn't stay when her presence in his world made him weak. He'd said as much himself and Cyril had confirmed it. She would be his death and she would never allow that.

"When can I go home?" She lifted her wet, blotchy, and swollen face off Vi's damp shoulder. "I need my bed."

Vi gave her a sad little smile. "Not until tomorrow, but I'm going to stay right here with you, okay? So, just lie down and rest for now."

She did, not because she'd been told to, but because the thought of sleeping the hours away made the idea seem logical. Only a few more hours and she'd be in her own bed, dressed in her own clothes and walking through her own home. It had been so long that she almost ached with the need to be surrounded by all the familiar things she'd always took for granted.

"What's that?"

Juliette followed the line of Vi's pointing finger at the pendant she still held clutched in one hand. She unfurled her fingers so the girl could see.

"Killian gave it to me," she whispered. "It belonged to his mother."

"It's beautiful!" Vi gasped. "Where is Killian? I thought for sure he'd still be here."

Her fingers closed around the cameo. "He left."

Vi blinked. "Oh, when is he coming back?"

"He's not." Hot tears trickled from the corners of her eyes and soaked into the pillow. "He's gone."

"What?" There was a bemused chuckle in the question. "Why?"

"Because he could never love someone like me." That was what he'd said, someone like her, someone inexperienced and stupid in the ways of love and sex.

"No, that's not right. The guy is crazy about you. Trust me, I know. I was there when you were taken."

Juliette had nothing to say to that, no explanation. Even if she had, she was in no mood to do so. She shut her eyes instead and willed herself to sleep.

True to her promise, Vi was still there when Juliette opened her eyes again. The sun was already high in the sky and it filled the room with a pale, white light that chased away the cold gloom of the night before. Vi sat slumped forward in a plastic chair. Her arms were folded on the bed next to Juliette's hip and she was sound asleep. In the doorway, she could just make out Phil's somber profile and wondered if he'd been there the whole night. But it was the pendant still clutched in her hand that really pulled her attention. She peered down at the ivory face of the girl with the flower and thought of Killian. She wondered where he was and what he was doing and if she would ever see him again. She doubted it. The night before when he'd walked out of the hospital had been their final goodbye. The thought was devastating, but she knew there was nothing she could do, but let him go.

Next to her, Vi shifted and sat up yawning. The right side of her face was a maze of welts from her coat sleeve. Her makeup had smudged, leaving thick, black mascara rings across her cheeks. She squinted at the window across the room, then turned to peer at Juliette.

"It's morning."

Juliette smiled at the hoarse croak. "Yup, looks that way."

Groaning, Vi pushed back the chair and rose, straining her entire body towards the ceiling. She yawned loudly and bowed backwards with her arms above her head, her fingers interlocked. She straightened and let her arms drop down at her sides.

"I need coffee and an Advil." Grunting, she glowered down at the chair. "You'd think they'd make those things more comfortable." She rubbed her ass. "My butt is killing me." She exhaled and glanced at the door. "Hey, Phil's still here."

Juliette nodded. "I think he's been here the whole night."

Vi huh'd. "I guess he really feels bad."

"About what?"

The girl turned to Juliette. "For abandoning me at the mall."

"He what?" Juliette's voice carried across the room, drawing Phil's attention. He peered inside briefly before going back to standing guard. "He what?" Juliette repeated quieter.

"Remember that night you called and I said I was at the mall?" At Juliette's nod, Vi continued. "Well, remember how I said Phil got a phone call and would be right back? Well, he didn't. He got called back by Killian or whoever's in charge and he just left without a damn word."

"He what?" Juliette's snarl was followed by the struggle to untangle herself from the blankets.

Vi stopped her. "Calm down. It's fine. I was pretty pissed myself, but whatever. I always knew he wouldn't be around forever. Not like he's really my dad or anything. He's just some guy paid to stick around. It was my fault that I..." she trailed off to study the diamond pattern sewn into the blankets. "I'm over it."

Juliette ceased her struggling and peered at the girl standing before her with her tangled locks and drawn features. Maybe it was because she had never really seen her sister, but looking at her now, it was impossible not to see just how lonely she was. Everything about her screamed for affection and companionship and Juliette had never once stopped to give her either.

"Hey." Reaching out with the hand not hooked to an empty bag of fluid, Juliette took Vi's fingers. She gave them a light squeeze. "We're going to be okay. I promise. You and me."

Brown eyes lifted and peered at her with apprehension and a timid glimmer of hope. "Yeah?"

"Promise," Juliette said again. "Things are going to change. We'll make sure they do. We have each other no matter what."

A hint of a half-smile tugged the corner of Vi's mouth. "I like the sound of that."

Juliette beamed. "Good. Now go get us some coffees while I hunt down the doctors and hopefully get the hell outta here."

Laughing, Vi hurried from the room.

Juliette watched her go before reaching for the call button hanging off the side of her bed and hitting it ... repeatedly.

"Yes?" came a grumpy voice from the speaker mounted on the wall.

"Hi, I was just wondering when I'll be discharged?"

A moment passed, then, *"The doctor will make his rounds shortly. Please just be patient."*

She hated bothering anyone, especially people who held her life in their hands, but there was nothing wrong with her and she wanted to go home.

"You wouldn't happen to know how long that will be, would you?"

"No," came the abrupt response, then a click as the connection was severed.

"Thanks a lot," Juliette grumbled.

With nothing to do, Juliette sat there and stared at the opposite wall, trying not to think of anything, except going back to her normal routine as quickly as possible, which meant calling the hotel and the diner and begging them not to fire her. Charis would take some convincing, but the hotel might still take her back once she explained the situation. She didn't even want to think about what might happen if neither took her back on top of everything else. The very thought was soul crushing.

Nevertheless, she grabbed the hospital phone and began dialing.

As she suspected, the moment Charis answered and Juliette said hi, the woman fired her. It wasn't even done nicely or apologetically.

"We've already hired someone competent and reliable," the woman sneered into the line. *"Drop your uniform off and don't even bother asking for your last pay as you still owe us."*

The line went dead promptly after the short rant.

Juliette sighed. Oddly enough, she felt no remorse over not having to go back. If anything, she was sort of relieved.

She called Harold next.

He picked up on the third ring.

"I completely understand," he told her after she'd finished explaining the situation. *"We're just so relieved you're all right. Can't believe such a thing even happens outside of movies. But yes, of course you still have a position here whenever you're ready to come back to it."*

The relief was astronomical. She wasn't sure what she'd done to deserve that sort of break, but she wasn't going to question it.

Mrs. Tompkins was her final call. She was still at her daughter's house—thank God—so Juliette decided not to tell her about anything that had happened. They chatted a few minutes, mostly about Mrs. Tompkins's move before hanging up. She was setting the phone back on the end table when Vi returned with a paper bag in one hand and a drink tray with two plastic cups in the other. She bounded into the room and set the items down next to the phone.

"I found bagels," she declared. "No peanut butter, but they had cream cheese and jam."

"Tell me what happened with your friends," Juliette said after a stretch of silence that was filled with cream cheese spreading and coffee sipping.

Vi looked down at her bagel with cream cheese and jam, her mouth twisted in grimace.

"They're assholes," she mumbled. "I always knew it, but…"

Juliette stopped eating. "What happened?"

Vi set her half-eaten bagel down on the wrapper and dusted the crumbs off her fingers. She continued to stare at her breakfast rather than Juliette.

"They dared me to take something from a store in the mall. It wasn't anything special, a lipstick that wasn't even my color, but it was something we used to do all the time so it wasn't a big deal—" Juliette opted to let that comment go for the time being. "—so I did it. I took the lipstick and started to walk out when Brittany went running to the clerk and ratted me out. I mean, dead on told the girl I took the lipstick. I was stopped and searched and obviously I had the thing so I got busted."

"Vi!"

Vi rolled her eyes. "I know. Stupid. Anyway, Phil got me out. He talked to the woman, said he was my dad and I wasn't stealing. I was waiting for him and must have forgotten to pay for it. The woman let us go and we left. I felt about two inches tall. I'd never been caught before. I was also pissed. They were supposed to be my friends. That's when Phil kind of set me straight, told me I was being a shit and I needed to clean up my act. He made me swear not to take anything anymore or he'd arrest me himself. Kind of started liking him after that."

No longer hungry, Juliette set her bagel down and wiped her hands on a napkin. She reached for her coffee and cradled the warmth between her palms.

"You should have told me," she said.

"I hardly saw you," Vi countered. "I mean even before Killian, you were never home and when you were, you were yelling at me or sleeping. Besides, I knew you were only going to lecture me on stealing and I'd already learned my lesson."

Juliette exhaled. "I've been so unfair to you, haven't I? Probably the worst sister on the planet and I am so sorry. I have no excuse."

Vi nodded slowly. "Yeah, you were, but it's either you or Uncle Jim and you won't make me wear frilly panties."

Gagging, Juliette recoiled. "That is disgusting!"

Vi grinned. "And yet so true."

Laughing, Juliette shook her head. "Okay, enough of that. Let's talk about what we're going to do."

"Do with what?"

"Everything." She shrugged. "We have nothing to worry about anymore. The hotel doesn't exactly pay in gold bricks, but we're going to be okay if we're careful—"

Voices in the hallway had them both glancing back just in time to see Arlo stride into the room, followed closely by Phil. The two stopped at the foot of the bed, Phil with a scowl.

"Hey there, Juliette," Arlo said in that tone she had never wanted to hear again. "They told me you were awake."

Juliette nodded. "Yeah."

"Excellent." His brown eyes flicked over to Vi, lingered in a way that made Juliette's skin prickle before returning to her. "Glad to hear it."

"What are you doing here?" she demanded with more bite than was necessary.

"Just coming to check on my favorite person. You had the entire underground community looking for you. McClary is probably happy to have you back." His gaze slid to Vi again, who stared back at him without a trace of emotion. "Also came to see when they were letting you out."

Juliette frowned. "Why?"

He shrugged. "Curiosity."

"It's none of your business," she retorted.

He fixed her with an arched eyebrow. "Seriously? That's the attitude I get for saving your life?"

A muscle tightened in the pit of Juliette's stomach as a sickening realization crept home; was he going to strong arm her into owing him all over again? Was that why he was there?

"I won't come back to you," she hissed. "Not ever."

Arlo rolled his eyes. "Calm down. I don't want you back. My father was already compensated for his help in your rescue, which means you get to go on and live your boring little life."

"Compensated how? By whom?"

"McClary," he said simply. "Gave my dad the deed to the ports."

Juliette remembered all too well how badly Arlo had wanted the port papers signed, enough so that he'd knocked the shit out of her for it.

"Lucky you," she muttered.

"Yup." He stuffed his hands into his pockets and rocked back on his heels. "I personally think we got the better end of the deal, but whatever." He slanted his gaze towards Vi again. "Hey, walk me out."

"No!" Coffee sloshed over the rim of her cup when she shot up and grabbed Vi's arm. "She's not going anywhere with you."

"It's okay." Vi detached herself from the hold and rose. "I'll be right back."

Arlo smirked at Juliette. "I'll see you around, Juliette."

With an arrogant salute, he spun on his heels and led the way out of the room with Vi right behind him. Juliette met Phil's angry gaze.

"Follow them. Don't let him touch her."

Phil didn't even hesitate.

Juliette set her cup down and hurriedly kicked the blankets off. She scooted to the edge of the bed and tossed her legs over. The cold tiles bit into her bare feet as she hopped down. She reached for the IV pole and was about to follow when Vi returned.

"What are you doing out of bed?" the girl demanded.

"What are you doing following that asshole?" Juliette shot back. "Do you have any idea what level of bad news—"

"Chill!" Vi laughed. "Trust me, nothing will ever happen between me and that guy. Like ever. I know exactly what he is and what he wants and I'm not an idiot."

Juliette jerked back in surprise. "Really?"

Vi nodded as she made her way back to the bed. "I can overlook a lot of things about a guy, but selling, beating, and degrading women is where I draw the line. So, yeah." She flopped down on the stiff mattress and reached for her bagel. "No sexy fun time for him."

Juliette blanched. "Ew!" Gingerly, she regained her seat. "So, what did he want?"

Vi bit into her breakfast, chewed, and swallowed before speaking. "A kiss."

Thank God she was already sitting or she would have fallen over.

"What?"

Vi snorted. "He made me this promise before they set off to find you the other night, that if he found you first, I owed him a kiss."

"And you said…?"

"What do you think I said? Obviously no. I know what he did to you, what he made you do. He told me everything."

Juliette blinked. "He *told* you?"

"Yeah, we were stuck together in Killian's house for like days and there was nothing to do. So, we talked. He was honest about everything."

None of it made sense. The last thing Juliette ever expected was honesty from Arlo, never mind his inexplicable interest in her sister, which irritated the shit out of her.

"Well, stay away from him," she mumbled. "He's not like Killian. He's definitely not the good guy."

"I know." Vi stuffed the rest of her bagel into her mouth. "I'm pretty sure that's the last time we'll ever see him."

Juliette could only hope.

Chapter 31

Five months later...

"I honestly couldn't care how you get it done. Get that wall down and put a door in."

Killian scribbled his name on the contract before him while cradling the phone between his ear and shoulder. The cord kept getting caught on his arm, but he hoped the conversation would end soon so he could get back to actual work.

"I understand, sir, but there are shelves on this side—"

"Get the shelves down," he said with great exasperation. "Honestly, what am I paying you for?" He hung up, took the contract he'd finished writing and set it with the others and rose. "Frank! Where is the finance report for Ice?"

The figure that stepped into the room wasn't Frank nor did Killian need to glance up to recognize the steady click of heels crossing the floor.

"How much longer are you going to hide in here?" Maraveet propped a hip against the edge of his desk and regarded him with annoyance furrowing her brows. "I would like to spend some time with you, especially considering you're the one who asked me to stay."

"Not now," he muttered, rifling through the papers across his desk. "I don't have time. Frank!"

"You never have time!" Maraveet interjected with a slight whine in her voice. "You sit in this bloody office all day, making phone calls and whatever all this is." She waved a hand over the mess. "I haven't seen hide nor hair of you in months! Honestly, what are you doing in here?"

"Work." Leaving her there, he marched to the door and stuck his head out into the corridor. "Frank! Where the hell is he?"

Maraveet huffed. "He's outside doing a parameter check, if you must know so stop shouting."

Exasperated, Killian marched back to his desk and tore through his papers a second time. He knew the damn thing was there somewhere. He'd seen it only that morning. Unless Frank moved it.

With a deep inhale, Maraveet rose. "Fine. I'm going out. I don't know when I'll be back, not that you'll worry or care."

He let her walk out, in no mood for her whining. Lord knew he loved the woman, but he had no time to sit and do nothing. He didn't have the courage. The moment he had even a second of free time, he was engulfed by thoughts of Juliette and as soon as that happened, days could pass in a swirling mess of depression and he wouldn't notice. His every waking and sleeping hour would be consumed by images of her face, the lilt of her voice, and the consistent wondering if she was all right. He knew she was still working at the hotel, but that was all he would allow himself.

Frank appeared in the doorway. "You were looking for me?"

Relieved, Killian straightened. "Where is the finance report for Ice?"

"I filed it away, as per your request."

Killian had no memory of this, but he let it go. "Bring them to me please, along with the end of year tax forms for—"

The phone rang, interrupting his thoughts. Part of him contemplated letting it ring, just in case it was that idiot contractor. The other part knew he needed to answer, especially if it was the idiot contractor.

"McClary," he barked into the receiver.

"Mr. McClary, this is Susan Compton, we spoke last week about the charity benefit you're throwing this weekend."

Killian nodded, even though she couldn't see it. "Yes, hello Ms. Compton. What can I do for you?"

"I'm just calling to inform you that everything has been organized. We've sold a little over nine hundred tables and the botanical garden is set for the big day. I do have a few questions regarding catering and if you would like anything special served, but otherwise, we're well ahead of the game."

Killian never once doubted the woman's abilities to throw a successful charity event together at the drop of a hat. She was the best in her field and her lengthy cliental list spoke for itself. But he really wished she would phone Frank. He had more patience.

"Call whoever you think would do the best job and I have no specific requests." He rapped his pen on the desk. "If you have any further questions, you can contact—"

"I won't," Susan assured him. "As I said, we're all finished with everything else. I will see you at the event, Mr. McClary. Have a wonderful week."

With that, she hung up.

Resisting the urge to gouge his fingertips into his temples, Killian set the phone down and faced Frank.

"Can you locate my dinner tux and make sure it's ready for this weekend? Also, bring me those files I requested. I'd like to go over them again before I have that meeting with the head of—"

His phone rang again and he cursed.

It wasn't anything new. It had been a steady rotation of calls and meetings, when he wasn't writing, signing or reading over a contract, form, or whatever else that needed his life signed away. The whole thing was a mess, but it kept him going. It kept him occupied. There were times he stayed up for days at a time, bringing himself to the brink of exhaustion before falling face down on the bed. Any other way would have him lying there, staring at the empty space next to him and wishing things he had no right wishing for. Nearly killing himself seemed to be the only way to get any rest, even if it was restless and plagued by all the wrongs in his world.

It was dinner time when Maraveet returned home. Killian didn't ask her where she'd been, but she found her way into his office as he was finishing up the last of the tax forms for the previous year. She wore a black dress over black leggings and brown boots. Her hair bounced around her shoulders like flames. She stalked to his desk and stopped to glower down at him.

"Are you done now?" she demanded.

Killian sighed. "Why is it so important I finish?"

Maraveet's green eyes narrowed. "Because I've had this crazy notion of actually seeing you before I leave."

"Leave?" Killian rose. "Leave where?"

"Oh, do you care now?"

"Don't be a shit, Mar. I haven't got the patience."

Maraveet huffed. "You know what? I don't think I'll tell you. You clearly know everything already. But I won't stick around to be ignored by you either. So, goodbye and good luck."

"Mar, wait." He rounded the desk before she could storm off. "I'm sorry, all right? I've got a lot on my mind lately."

Her face softened. "Juliette."

He didn't bother denying it. "Yes, but not entirely."

Maraveet sighed heavily. "Then why don't you go talk to her? Get her back. I know she misses you."

Something in that sent a spike through his chest.

"Have you spoken to her?" He knew he shouldn't ask and yet he needed to know. "Is she all right?"

"No, she's not."

His heart dropped into his stomach like a stone and was picked at by the bubbling acid. "Why? What's wrong?"

"How could you not know? You're not really so blind, are you, little brother?"

"Damn it, Maraveet! Just tell me."

Her look was pitying and slightly disgusted. "She's in love with an absolute moron. It's any wonder she's so heartbroken. She keeps hoping you'll come to your senses and pick her over this life that you don't even belong in and you never do." She folded her arms. "She's dating you know. She's seeing this handsome fellow named Randy."

He turned away and headed back to his desk. "Why do I need to hear this?"

"Because, you idiot, you're going to lose her if you don't get your fat head out of your ass! This Randy person is nice and all that, but he's not you and that's who she wants."

Killian stopped and glowered at her from over his shoulder. "You've got problems, you know that? For years you've been telling me to keep away from people, to never fall in love, to never let myself be happy. When I finally listen, you're telling me I should drag Juliette back to this nightmare and put her in danger all over again. I can't honestly decide whether you hate me or her."

"I don't hate either of you!" she cried. "I love you both is why I'm here. You haven't been the same since she left. Honestly, I hate this person you've become. You're arrogant and selfish, and worse, you're bitter. My brother, no matter what, had always been kind and wonderful and always thinking of others. Now, you're just an asshole behind a fancy desk."

He whirled around, his temper clashing with the pain prickling at his temples. "What do you want from me, eh? You can't seem to make up your bloody mind!"

"I want you to be happy!" she screamed back at him, her cheeks red with exertion. "I want you not to be here anymore. I want you to give up this life that isn't yours. You don't belong here, Killian. You never belonged. Your mother knew that. Do you think she would want you to lock yourself in here day after day, night after night, killing yourself for nothing? She wanted you to be happy. She wanted grandchildren. She wanted you to find your fairytale and you have. You found Juliette. She's the one meant for you and you're pushing her away."

"I almost lost her," he reminded her, fighting to keep his voice in check. "I came so fucking close, Mar."

"I know, but—"

"No, you don't. You have no idea how much I hate this. You have no idea how badly I want her back, or the things I would happily do to make it happen. I miss her, Mar. I miss her so much it fucking hurts. But every time I pick up the phone to call her, or even think about having her back, I remember the envelopes. I remember how completely useless and helpless I felt not knowing what they were doing to her. I did that to her. I put her right in their hands and I can't do that again. I can't … God, I can't!" He sagged against his desk and clapped a hand over his burning eyes. "Just let me rot in here. I'd rather die alone and miserable than to live forever knowing she's not out there."

"Fine!" Her chin warbled. "But know that I hate you so much right now."

Spinning on the points of her heels, Maraveet stormed from the room, leaving Killian alone in his misery.

Chapter 32

"Hey, want to hit a movie with me tonight?"

Randy Sawyer smiled at Juliette from across the counter. Anticipation and hope glittered in his blue eyes, giving his beautifully chiseled features an almost boyish glint.

"A movie sounds nice," Juliette lied, forcing herself to smile. "I'd like that."

That wasn't entirely a lie. She liked movies and she liked Randy and sometimes, it was nice to do things she liked that didn't involve sleeping or walking around her house in her pajamas. The only problem was that she couldn't bring herself to like-like Randy the way he seemed to like-like her and that made the whole dating thing awkward.

It had been two weeks since their first date and she still wasn't sure why she kept saying yes when all she wanted was to die a lonely death wallowing in her own desolation. Maybe it was because Vi refused to let her or the fact that every time he asked, her mouth automatically said yes, like if she said it often enough, eventually her heart would notice that, hey, there's a really sweet, good looking guy over here who deserves a chance. It made her the worst person in the world, but her brain had already decided that she needed to move on and let go. Her heart was a whole other matter. It was still adamant that it wanted Killian and only Killian and no one else would ever do. The two refused to see eye to eye on anything and Randy was taking the hits. But she figured if she forced herself to take more notice and open up to the possibility, then maybe, eventually, the pain would fade. That hadn't happened yet.

Dimples winked from a smile made for toothpaste commercials. "Great! I'll pick you up at six."

"Why don't I meet you at my place?" she suggested. "That way I can change."

Randy nodded. "Okay, but I can drop you off so you don't have to grab the bus."

His kindness made her hate herself a little more.

"It's okay. I like the bus. Besides, you'll still be working when I get off."

Randy was a masseur in the hotel spa. She'd never seen him before the day he walked up to her counter and asked for her number. The sheer size of him, those dimples, and the unexpected approach had bulked her into complying.

He relented. "Okay, well, then I'll pick you up at seven."

Juliette agreed and watched as he ambled away.

I can do this! She willed herself to believe. Honestly, how hard was it to find someone else? People did it all the time. They broke up, ate chocolate, and moved on to someone new. It wasn't even as though she and Killian had been dating. It had only been sex, for God sakes. Letting go should not be that hard, and yet, five months later, she was still unable to do so, even with a guy who was as amazing and sweet and safe as Randy. There was something wrong with her, clearly. She had problems.

"You have problems!" Vi smacked the dishcloth down on the island and stormed to the fridge. "You're insane and I am no longer feeding your crazy."

"Vi, please!" Juliette begged. "If I have to listen to one more awkward silence, I will kill myself."

"But go on your date?" the girl cried, whirling around. "Do you have any idea how weird that is? God, Jewels, he's going to think we're some kinky sister love package."

"Oh ew!" Juliette flinched. "That's disgusting."

"Then don't invite me to your date!"

Groaning, Juliette dropped into a stool at the island and dropped her face into her folded arms. "I don't know what to say to him when we're together," she mumbled. She lifted her face and peered imploringly at her sister. "He keeps asking me things."

The look Vi shot her was one of profound disgust. "Yeah, because you're dating!" She threw up her hands. "Why are you if you can't even stand to have a conversation with him?"

"It's not that I can't stand to talk to him," Juliette argued. "It's because I don't…"

"What?" Vi demanded when she trailed off.

Juliette sighed. "Because I don't want to talk to him. I mean I do. He's such a great guy and—"

"And he really likes you," Vi chimed in, being no help at all.

"But I don't feel anything," Juliette whispered. "When he takes my hand or when he kisses me—"

Vi raised a brow. "You mean that very awkward peck on the cheek that nearly sent you out of your skin? Okay, fine, sorry. Not helping. Go on," she mumbled when Juliette shot her a frown.

"I keep hoping something will just spark and I'm getting nothing."

"Then clearly you need to say goodbye and find someone else," Vi said sagely.

"What if no one else wants me?" Juliette cringed at the pathetic note in her voice. "What if Killian…" Just saying his name hurt. "What if he was the only one and—"

"You're right." Vi sighed. "Well, there's only one thing to do now. We need to get you a cat."

She pitched the dishrag at Vi's face.

The girl caught it, grinning. "We'll call him Ginger."

"Will you shut up?" Juliette rose.

"And we'll get him a little bell on his little collar," Vi went on relentlessly. "Then, we'll get him a girlfriend and call her Whiskers. Then Ginger and Whiskers can have little baby kittens and—"

"I hate you." She stumbled out of the room with Vi's story of Juliette's future following her to the stairs. "You're still coming with me tonight!" she called over her shoulder.

"Can Daisy and Mr. Pickles come too?" Vi chased her down the hall. "You know how they hate being away from you. Plus they'll want to meet their new daddy. Oh!" Clapping her hands, Vi skipped up the first step after Juliette. "We'll get you one of those cat purses and you can take all your babies with you everywhere! Or a kitty stroller."

"I will push you down the stairs, I swear to God."

Vi's cackling followed them all the way to the top.

Randy arrived promptly at seven in his Dodge Ram and clean, pressed jeans and black coat. His hair was still damp at the ends as though he'd left straight after his shower. The smell of soap and shaving cream wafted off him when he moved in to brush a kiss to Juliette's cheek.

"Hi."

Forcing her mouth to obey, Juliette smiled up at him. "Hey, you don't mind if Vi tags along, do you? She had nothing to do and I felt bad leaving her alone."

"No! Not at all. It'll be great to get to really meet her." He looked past her to Vi, who was taking an unnecessary long time to lock the front door. "Hey Vi, how are you?"

Pocketing her keys, Vi joined them at the bottom of the steps. "Good. I'm good. Excited, actually."

Randy's eyebrows went up with interest. "Yeah? What's up?"

Vi's arm snaked through Juliette's. "Juliette has agreed to get a kitten."

Juliette shoved her.

"She's always wanted a kitten," Vi went on, unfazed.

"I will cut you," Juliette warned under her breath.

Vi simply grinned.

Randy peered from one to the other, genuinely baffled. "Oh, well, that's great. I love cats."

Vi elbowed Juliette. "Daddy!"

"Okay, can we go please?" Juliette marched towards the truck with the other two following behind her.

They drove to the movie theater in silence. In the backseat, Vi's simmering disapproval coiled through the cabin, making the air bitterly uncomfortable. Juliette wondered if Randy could feel it too, but at a glance, he seemed only focused on the road. There was a calmness to his profile she envied. The sunlight toyed with the ends of his damp hair, making the rich strands shine. It highlighted the fine curves of his lashes to delicate gold. Juliette never understood the term Adonis like, but if she could picture anyone as the deity, it was Randy. He fit the persona, the Hercules body and Adonis's face. Any girl would be lucky to have him.

The thought curdled something in her chest, turning what little happiness she still harbored into guilt and self-loathing. She was a bad person. There was no other explanation for it.

"Oh, I nearly forgot." Randy pulled to a stop at a red light and turned his head to Juliette. "I won tickets today at work for that new botanical gardens that's opening up this weekend."

Juliette's eyebrows lifted. "Wow! Really?"

He nodded. "I didn't even know we had a contest going or anything, but my boss just walked up to me and said *here, you won.*"

"That's so great!" Juliette said, meaning it. "I've been wanting to go since I heard about it."

That seemed to perk Randy up. He grinned as the light turned green and he put the truck into drive.

"Yeah? Well, good, because I was hoping you'd go with me."

Juliette stiffened. "Oh…"

"Vi can come," Randy said quickly. "I only have two tickets, but I'm sure we can pick another one up—"

"No, that is totally cool!" Vi piped in from the backseat. "I don't even like flowers. You guys should go."

Say yes! The voice urged when Juliette could only sit and stare at her hands curled in her lap. This was what she wanted. It was what she needed. She had to make this work.

"I would love to go," she heard herself say, and the hollowness in her voice was painfully evident even to her own ears.

Bad person. Such a horrible, miserable, rotten person. She didn't deserve Randy. He certainly didn't deserve the screwed up mess that she was. He'd been nothing but good to her and all she could think about was how wrong it felt being in that truck with him. She should tell him. He needed to know that there was a very good possibility that she might never love him. That they might never be more than two awkward strangers.

"Juliette?" She must have made a sound, because Randy was darting concerned glances her way. "You okay?"

Tell him!

But the words remained stubbornly lodged in her throat. Instead, she was smiling and nodding as though she wasn't an absolute coward.

They arrived at the theater and did what they always did; they got their tickets, their popcorns, and made their way to the proper door. Juliette had no idea what movie they'd decided on. She didn't even watch it. She spent the entire hour trying not to stare at Randy's arm taking up the entire armrest. She knew he wasn't doing it to be an ass. He was no doubt hoping she'd do the normal thing and put hers next to it and she should, because that was what people dating did. They held hands at the movies. They kissed. They cuddled. What they didn't do was flinch every time their shoulders brushed.

The movie ended and everyone rose. She followed Randy's back down the aisle with Vi right on her heels.

"Are you guys hungry?" Randy asked as they left the theater and made their way to the truck.

"I have school tomorrow and homework to finish," Vi said. "But if you guys—"

"I actually have to start work really early tomorrow," Juliette blurted. "I should make sure I have clean clothes."

Randy nodded. "Fair enough." They arrived at the truck and he yanked open her door. "But we're still on for this weekend? The event starts at like eight so I can get you at seven, if that works for you?"

Juliette nodded. "I'd really like that."

Chapter 33

The low chatter of voices, the soothing hum of flutes and violins rolled along the smooth sheets of glass sweeping high into the evening sky in a gleaming dome over a breathtaking sea of colors. The conservatory brimmed with people Killian had never met and had no desire to meet now, but he remained and greeted each one politely. Somewhere in the mess was Maraveet. She hadn't spoken to him since their argument, but he could feel her frothing anger and disappointment like an icy breeze. He made a mental note to track her down before the night was over and hopefully calm some of her feathers.

In the meantime, he circled the room, playing the ever gracious host. He laughed and talked like his bowtie wasn't choking him, like his suit wasn't uncomfortably too tight. It was all in his head, but it still made him want to tear it all off and go home.

"Killian McClary!" Nelson Miles cut through the crowd of silk and gems, large palm extended. "Good to see you again."

Killian plastered on his required smile and turned to greet the man. "Mr. Mayor, I'm glad you could make it."

"Of course. Of course!" He released Killian's hand. "Wouldn't miss it. Nora couldn't stop talking about it for weeks."

Small and fairy-like in her green sequined gown, Nora smiled at Killian. "A garden is just what this city needed. It's absolutely gorgeous."

Killian offered her a smile and the inclination of his head. "Not nearly as beautiful as you look tonight, Mrs. Miles."

Her pale cheeks flushed. "You're too kind."

Mayor Miles tucked a gentle arm around his wife's tiny waist and drew her comfortably into his side. It wasn't a possessive gesture, but one that spoke of a long, happy relationship.

"She does look stunning this evening, doesn't she?"

The color on his wife's face amplified, but the shimmer of pleasure in her green eyes contradicted the playful swat she gave her husband.

"Stop that."

Chuckling, Mayor Miles turned back to Killian. "Tell me what made you think of building such a splendor."

"My mother," Killian answered honestly. "She had a love of flowers and gardens. I wanted to share that love with the city."

"Oh how sweet," Mrs. Miles whispered. "Well, you did a wonderful job. I'm sure she would have loved it."

Killian started to open his mouth to respond when a movement by the entrance caught his attention. The words he'd been formulating dissolved in a fog that settled thick across his brain. His mouth went dry even as his heart gave a violent jolt in his chest.

Juliette.

She wore the dress he'd given her on Halloween. The Grecian gown rippled along her lithe frame in a wave of white satin and glittering gems. The silver threads glistened with her unhurried movement. She'd done her hair up in a twisted updo that left her shoulders bared and her face framed by subtle curls. She wore no jewelry, except his mother's pendant and the sight of it nestled against the soft skin of her chest was nearly his undoing. Then he spotted the hulking figure standing next to her, one hand settled lightly on the small of her back and the burst of joy he'd felt at seeing her thawed into a dark plume of rage.

"Killian?" Mrs. Miles had a dainty hand on his arm and he realized, with a shock, that his fingers had balled into fists. "Is everything all right?"

Forcing himself not to do something absolutely insane like grab the bastard who had his hands on Juliette and pitch him straight into the pond.

"Yes, forgive me, but I must find someone."

Excusing himself, he headed in the opposite direction of Juliette. He fought to keep his strides slow and even when all he wanted to do was plow through the whole crowd in search of his meddling sister.

Maraveet stood by a fountain, a flute of champagne in one hand, her clutch in the other. The lights built under the water reflected off her gold gown, making the sequins glitter, which in turn reflected off her skin in shivering sparkles. She glanced up when Killian approached.

"Why?" he demanded without missing a beat.

"Sorry?"

He moved in closer, hoping the short distance would remind him to keep his voice low. "Why did you invite her?"

Maraveet blinked. "Who?"

"You know who!" he hissed through his teeth. "Juliette."

Maraveet's face went from surprised to absolutely blank in the second it took for him to blink. "I don't know what you're talking about. If she is here, then maybe she bought a ticket like everyone else. It is a public event, after all."

He hadn't considered that. He hadn't considered ever seeing her again, especially not at a charity event, not with another man.

"She needs to leave," he decided, more to himself than Maraveet.

"All right." She raised her glass to her red lips and took a sip. "You tell her."

Just like that, Maraveet turned on her heels and slinked through the crowd, leaving him alone to figure it out. He glanced over the room, wondering if it was large enough to avoid her. There were certainly enough people and if he just paid attention to where she was the entire night, he could easily keep out of her way.

That was easier said than done when paying attention meant watching as the ape at her side kept touching her, kept bending low to murmur into her ear. The guy was all over her, giving her food, passing her drinks ... asking her to dance.

He couldn't do it. Not without committing murder before all those people. No, he needed to leave. Susan could take over, make sure the rest of the night went smoothly. He was a busy man after all and no one expected him to stay and party. He could sneak out the back and no one...

Juliette tugged away from her companion, said something, and then made a quick escape off the dance floor in the opposite direction. Her strides were hurried, practically a near run as she ducked through the open terrace doors and disappeared into the gardens.

Don't! His brain warned sharply, but his feet refused to listen.

He hurried after her.

Chapter 34

This was a bad idea. It was such a bad idea. She should never have come. What had she been thinking? Of course Randy would want to dance and enjoy the evening. Of course he would want to touch and act like all the other couples around them. And why wouldn't he? No, it was done. She couldn't do this anymore. It wasn't fair, not to Randy. She had to end it. There was nothing else for it.

"Juliette!"

As though conjured from the very depths of her turmoil, Randy jogged after her. His blond hair caught the light from the row of lamps flagging the cobblestone path and shone like a beacon in the cool evening. His cheeks were pink from the chase and his blue eyes were bright with worry that only made her feel worse.

"What's wrong?"

Juliette exhaled, wishing the floor would just open up and swallow her. "I'm so sorry, Randy. I'm an awful person."

He slowed two feet from her and stopped. "What are you talking about? You're not awful."

She nodded. "I am and I can't ... I can't do this to you anymore. I tried so hard to be the kind of person you deserve and I can't. I will never be that person because I can't make myself want you the way I know I should and I tried, I really, really tried so hard to do this, but I can't..."

"Whoa, slow down." He offered her a small, weak chuckle. "What are you talking about?"

"I love someone else." She squeezed her eyes shut tight. "It makes me the biggest fool on the planet, because he doesn't love me back, but I can't keep seeing you when..."

"When you love someone else," he finished for her softly.

Her eyes opened and she peered at him through a layer of tears. "I'm so sorry."

Randy shook his head. "No, I get it. I figured it was something like that, but I thought that if I tried…"

Her heart tore all over again. "I'm sorry," she croaked for the hundredth time. "I'm so, so sorry."

"No, it's not your fault." He offered her a half grin. "We can't help who we love. It wasn't like I expected you to fall hopelessly in love with me in two weeks. Doesn't work that way."

It had taken less time for her to fall for Killian, but Randy didn't need to know that.

"Randy—"

"Please don't say you're sorry again," he teased with a chuckle. "It's okay. It was fun, right?"

She nodded, because she didn't know what else to do.

"Okay then." He stuffed his hands into his pockets. "Can I at least drive you back home?"

She shook her head. The last thing she wanted was a painfully awkward drive back.

"I'll find my own way. Thank you."

With a slow nod, he took a step back. "So, I'll see you around, right?"

"Yeah."

He turned on his heels and started back the way he'd come. Halfway, he stopped and glanced back.

"For the record, you're not the fool. He is."

Then he was gone and she was completely alone in the second most beautiful garden she'd ever been in and all she wanted to do was cry. Instead, she tugged her phone out of her clutch and dialed home. Vi answered on the third ring.

"You can't already be bored."

"I told him," she blurted. "I told him and he left."

"Whoa, what?"

"Randy." Breathing hard, Juliette paced further along the path. "I told him about Killian."

"You told him about Killian?" Vi's exclamation nearly pierced her eardrums. *"Are you crazy? Why would you do that?"*

"Because he asked me to dance and I said yes and we were on the floor and he was holding me and all I could think about was the time I danced with Killian and how I'm wearing the dress he'd given me and—"

"Juliette, breathe!"

But it was beyond that, she was passing mildly hysterical straight into the place of no return.

"And I realized that was how it was always going to be. He'll ask me something and I'll say yes because I really don't want to be alone and I'll wind up married to him and have a million babies and I'll keep living every day comparing him to Killian and he'll fail. He will always fail because I love Killian and I will never love Randy and—"

The phone disappeared out of her hand before she could finish her meltdown. The absence of it had her spinning on her heels and coming face to face with the very last man she ever expected to see again. Her heart skyrocketed even as her stomach dropped.

"Killian?"

Dark eyes locked with hers, sharp and penetrating as he lifted her phone to his ear. She could vaguely hear Vi calling her name on the other end.

"She'll call you back."

There was a split second pause from her sister, then, *"Killian?"*

Without responding, he hung up and stuffed Juliette's phone into his pocket. She followed the hand with her eyes, struck dumb, except to point and mutter, "You hung up on her," stupidly.

"She'll understand."

Unspoken thoughts scattered over in all directions, a spilled basket of thread unwinding and unraveling and tangling across the floor. She knew she needed to say something, but she wasn't entirely certain she was awake or if he was just another figment of her imagination.

Bathed in the soft glow from lights around them, he seemed so surreal, like so many of her dreams. Shadows molded around him as comfortably as his dark suit. His face hung somewhere in between the light and darkness, but the contemplation blazed bright in the unwavering contours of his eyes.

"What are you doing here?" she blurted at last, when it became apparent that he wasn't a dream.

"It's my charity event," he answered evenly.

He didn't seem at all surprised to see her there, which made her wonder…

"Did you send Randy the tickets?"

He shook his head. "No, I wouldn't."

Of course not. Why would he? He didn't want to see her again so why would he invite her and her boyfriend? The realization sank into her chest like claws burrowing through flesh and bone to close around her heart.

"I was about to leave," she said, already skirting around him. "Have a nice evening."

"You look beautiful."

His quiet compliment stilled her retreat. Her gaze lifted to his and found his closed of all emotion.

"Thank you." Her hand tumbled unsteadily down the front of her dress. "I didn't want it to go to waste and the invitation said formal."

"I didn't mean the dress."

Her lungs hitched, driving the fluttering in her stomach crazy. "I should go. Can I have my phone back please?"

Rather than comply, he closed what little space there was between them. The two steps she would have taken were devoured by only one of his and he was suddenly there, in front of her, tall and impossibly beautiful stealing her oxygen.

"If you answer something for me first."

His proximities wreaking havoc on her, she could only swallow audibly and nod.

"Did you mean what you said?"

Her heart jumped in panic. It hadn't even dawned on her that he might have overheard everything she'd said to Randy or Vi. She hadn't considered he would even be there. Why would she? What were the odds? But that wasn't her problem anymore. How much had he heard?

"What?" she forced out at last.

"The things you said." His lashes lowered, shadowing his eyes as he surveyed her parted lips. "Did you mean them?"

"Did you?" she heard herself ask back. "The things you said in your office, did you mean them?"

His gaze lifted to hers and latched.

"I wanted to."

His quiet confession splintered through her, denting her resolve.

"But did you?"

It took longer for him to answer. His jaw was clenched so tight, she almost feared his teeth would shatter. His eyes blazed with his inner turmoil. Tension vibrated off him to fill the cool air around them.

"Damn it, Juliette!" he growled at last, his calm mask cracking. "Don't do this." Black eyes burned into hers, flashing and crackling with fear, anger, and so much longing it nearly destroyed her. "Don't ask me that."

Heartbroken, she started to draw away from him. "Then it doesn't matter if I meant what I said, does it?" She broke the connection and turned away. "Goodb—"

His hand closed over her mouth from behind. "Don't!" he breathed into her ear. "Don't say that again. I can't stand it." His fingers relaxed and his hand slipped away. But even without him holding her, she could feel the brush of his chest against her back, the whisper of his breath along her skin. He was so close his heat was a warm blanket around her bare shoulders. "Every voice in my head is telling me I should let you go." It was only the vibration of those words across her back that assured her she hadn't misheard. It was the kick of his heart against her shoulder blade. "That yes, I meant every word and I should tell you to leave."

Juliette struggled to regulate every breath, too afraid the smallest movement might jar him back to his senses.

"Is that what you want?" She licked her lips. "Do you want me to leave?"

"Yes." He didn't even hesitate.

The single word shot through her like rusted daggers. Pain and embarrassment heated beneath her cheeks and she began to pull away.

"Ask me what I need, Juliette."

Her heart cracked against her ribs, a helpless boat in an angry storm.

"What do you need?" It was said in barely above a choked whisper.

"I need to breathe again." Each word vibrated as though torn from his very soul. They wrapped around her with their thorny edges and cut in deep. "I need to feel what it's like not to be dying inside." The tip of his nose grazed the side of her face lightly, barely even a whisper. "I need you."

Juliette didn't stop to let him finish. She spun on her heels and threw herself into his arms, arms that wasted no time gathering her up against his chest. Her ribs cracked, but she didn't care.

"I didn't," he whispered into her ear. "I didn't mean a damn word I said that night."

"I meant what I said," she whispered into the side of his neck. "I love you."

The arms tightened, crushing and painful. "Jesus, Juliette." His ragged breath burned into the bare skin of her shoulder. "Jesus, I love you." He drew back to take her face between his hands. Urgency and desperation blazed bright behind his eyes, brightening them with a deep inner light. "I don't know how, but I'm going to make this work. I'll do whatever I have to do to keep you. I swear it."

She started to tell him she believed him when they were interrupted by the hurried click of heels on stone. They both glanced up just as Maraveet rounded a row of bushes and clipped into view, a phone clasped to her ear. Her golden gown shimmered beneath the lights. The sequins glittered with every fluid motion. She spotted them and jogged forward.

"I found them," she said into the phone. "No, no one's hurt or naked. Right?" She snickered before turning green eyes on them. "Your sister says a little warning would be nice next time you hang up on her. Also, she's ... hold on." She paused to listen to whatever Vi was saying on the other end. "Right. Okay, hold on." Pulling the phone away, she hit speaker and Vi's voice filled the silence. "All right, go on."

"About time! Do you have any idea how hard it was to get the two of you in the same place at the same time? You owe us big. I would like my thank you in hundred dollar bills or a nice Porsche, just an FYI."

Juliette exchanged bemused glances with Killian before facing the other woman. "What is this? What did you two do?"

"What we did?" Maraveet huffed. "We saved our own sanities is what we did."

"You two are the biggest babies on the planet," Vi chimed in. *"Someone had to do something."*

"I don't understand! How do you two even know each other?" Juliette demanded.

"We met for coffee," Maraveet answered as though it were the most normal thing in the world. "We had a few words and decided we had a few things in common."

"Yeah, like two totally unreasonable, emo siblings," vi piped in.

Juliette sighed. "So the tickets. That was you?" She looked hard at Maraveet.

"It was me actually." Vi snickered. *"Mar gave them to me, but I was the one who gave them to Randy's boss and told*

him Randy had won best employee of the month or some such nonsense. Idiot actually believed me."

Juliette shook her head. "But why?"

"Because Killian has been an absolute nightmare and he wouldn't do it himself," Maraveet muttered. "I thought that if he saw you with another man, he might get his act together and do the right thing. Clearly, I was right."

"What if it hadn't worked?" Juliette demanded. "What if it had ended badly?"

There was a pause, and then simultaneously, both Vi and Maraveet asked, *"How?"*

Clearly the notion of things not going their way had never occurred to them, which kind of scared Juliette.

"Perhaps we should finish this talk at home," Killian advised, glowering at his sister. "Tell Viola I'll have someone pick her up and bring her to the manor. I believe it's time for a family meeting."

Without waiting for Vi or Maraveet to say a word, Killian took Juliette's hand and led her back towards the conservatory. Along the way, he released her and slipped that same hand around her back. His fingers curved at her waist, burning her through the thin material of her dress. That single touch worked along every inch of skin, raising goose bumps and reminding her just how badly she'd missed his hands on her.

"Killian?"

He glanced down at her, his face illuminated by the glowing lights pouring over them from the approaching terrace. She waited until they'd climbed the ivory steps to the top before turning to face him.

"What happens now?" She glanced down at the arm hooked gently, but with a near possessiveness about her waist. "What does this mean? Is this going to be only sex again?"

"No." The fingers on the hand not holding her lifted to ghost lightly along the side of her face. "I meant what I said. I will find a way to keep you. It's selfish and dangerous and it scares the hell out of me, but I can't let you go again, not unless it's what you want."

"Are you going to keep being the Scarlet Wolf?" she asked.

Killian paused to consider her question. "I don't understand."

Emotion tightened around her windpipe, making words and breathing impossible, but she forced them out with a strangled gasp.

"I can't live in your world," she choked out. "I can't run and hide every time the doorbell rings and sneak around to see you in some nondisclosed location for a quickie. I want babies, Killian, and I want to be able to raise them without being afraid something might happen. I want to be with someone I won't worry about every time he leaves the house. I want normal."

He didn't pull away, but she could feel the air shifting, filling the cracks between them with cool fingers.

"Babies," he mused quietly.

Juliette nodded. "Not tomorrow, but one day, yeah."

"I can't give you babies." His hands dropped away and she gasped at the loss. "Not because I don't want to, but I … I can't."

"Because you won't give up being the wolf," she finished quietly for him.

"Not won't," he corrected sharply. "I can't. You can't leave this life. My father left Yegor Yolvoski and you know how that ended. Getting in is easy, but you never leave. Not unless you're dead."

She drew in a breath even as her heart cracked all over again. "I guess that answers my question, huh?"

"Juliette…"

Shaking her head, Juliette turned and hurried through the doors of the conservatory. Her heels clicked loudly despite the chatter and music. No one paid her any attention as she hurried towards the entrance.

It was only when she found herself standing on the sidewalk overlooking a packed parking lot that she realized she had no car and her great escape was ruined by having to wait for a cab, which she couldn't call, because Killian still had her phone.

"Fuck!" she snapped to no one in particular.

The glass doors behind her flew open and Killian jogged out.

"Juliette, wait."

She rounded on him. "Give me my phone back!"

"I will, but let me explain first."

Her eyes narrowed. "Explain what? What is there to explain? We can't be together. We can never be together. No matter how much we want to or how much it hurts to be apart, a fish can't live with a bird."

"You can if you have a sister like me." Maraveet followed Killian out, a wide, sneaky grin on her face. "Just say the words and I'll be your *Redbull*."

Chapter 35

"That is the worst idea ever!" Juliette paced away from the group. She'd taken her shoes off—Killian had no idea what became of them—but she padded around the empty shipping container with her skirt trailing after her in the thin layer of dust. "I'm pretty sure that's not even legal! And why are we in this box?"

"It's the only way I can guarantee you can live the rest of your lives as normal and boring as humanly possible," Maraveet argued. "And because we can't trust that someone won't overhear us anywhere else. My family owns this cargo dock so I know we're safe to talk."

"Okay, but this idea of yours..."

"The decision is entirely up to you, obviously, but I promise it'll work."

The idea was disturbingly ingenious. Killian could find no flaws no matter how he turned it over in his head. It was perfect, too perfect, the kind of perfect that came with years of planning.

"And this idea just came to you overnight?" he asked, eyeing his sister.

Maraveet looked away. "It's something I've had in the works for a while, okay? It's a one time showstopper so either we do it all the way through or not at all."

Juliette shook her head. "I don't even know how you'd ever pull this off."

"It's all about timing and commitment," Maraveet answered.

Next to Killian, Vi stood silent and pensive. She hadn't said a word throughout the entire exchange and her silence worried him.

"What do you think?" he asked her. "I know Juliette won't do this without you and neither would I, but it doesn't have to happen if you don't want."

Juliette ceased her pacing and turned to the girl. "He's right. I won't do it without you."

Vi shrugged. "I've got nothing here. No reason to stay."

"Are you sure?" Juliette demanded. "You have to be sure, because if we do this, we can never come back here. You'd leave your school, your friends … Mrs. Tompkins."

Vi pushed off the wall she'd been helping Killian hold up and stood. "There are other schools. I haven't got any friends and Mrs. Tompkins is with her family. Like I said, nothing here worth staying for."

Killian studied Juliette. Even in the dull light, her eyes were enormous with fear. Her face was pale and drawn. She'd begun to cut a gash along her bottom lip with her teeth and it was the sight of blood that had him going to her.

"Juliette." He took her cold cheeks between his palms. Her brown eyes lifted to his face, dilated with fear. "It's all right, love."

"I'm scared," she blurted. "It all sounds so risky and final and…"

"Are you afraid you'll change your mind about me later?" he wondered out loud.

Her head rocked wildly. "That you'll regret it. That you'll look back one day and realize it wasn't worth giving up for me."

"I'm not giving it up for you." He smoothed back a lock of hair caught at the corner of her lip. "I would never have taken on the business if it wasn't for Yolvoski. I never wanted it. But I need you. I need the rest of my future with you." He kissed her lightly. "And I need those babies you mentioned. I want them with you. Lots of them. As many as you'll give me."

Tears and apprehension shone in her eyes as she searched his. Her hands settled over top of his, holding his palms to her cheeks.

"But what about your house? Your mother's garden? The fountain and all your businesses and money?"

A grin turned up the corner of his mouth. "I promise I'll keep you well cushioned in all the nothings you allow me to shower you with. I already told you what will happen to the business and the property. Charites mostly. As for the rest, stuff. Lots and lots of stuff tainted with memories I don't want anymore. I lived in that nightmare long enough. I want new ones with you. But if you want to stay here, then I'm okay with that too. I'll figure out another way."

A tear slipped and he caught it with his finger. He smoothed it away gently, but kept peering into her eyes, willing her to see just how much he needed her to take this step with him. How much he needed her to help him forget.

"Okay," she whispered at last. "Let's do it."

He kissed her lightly. "I won't let you regret this," he whispered against her mouth.

She peered up into his face with a small smile. "I won't. I want this." She touched the side of his face with cool fingertips. "I want you."

"All right now." Maraveet moved forward. "That's enough of that. There's only so much I can stomach. Besides, we've got work to do if everyone's in agreement."

Vi nodded before anyone else. "I'm in."

"Me too," Juliette murmured.

Killian only nodded when his sister caught his eye.

"Lovely." Maraveet clapped her hands once and rubbed them. "Well, that's our meeting for tonight. Everyone off to bed. We've got a full day tomorrow."

Pulling out of his arms, Juliette hurried to Vi and tugged her out of the metal container. Killian watched them a moment before turning to his own sister.

"How long have you had this in the works?" he asked.

Maraveet shrugged. "A while. Every great escape artist needs a final act."

"Does this mean you'll be joining us?"

Her nose wrinkled. "Not yet. I've got plenty of plundering left in me before I take the final plunge."

Killian went to her, stopping when she had to tilt her head back. "You know what that'll mean if you don't."

Her eyes lowered, but he saw the pain in them. "I know, but it won't be forever. I'll still find ways to see you."

"Come with us, Mar. Hang up your hat. This could be a second chance for both of us."

Her gaze went to where Juliette and Vi stood. "Not sure I'm ready for that."

He knew pushing would make no difference, so he relented. "Don't take too long."

There were tears in her eyes when they rose up to his. She gave him a lopsided grin. "Think you'd be getting rid of me that easily, little brother?"

He pulled her into his arms. "Better not."

They stood that way for several minutes before she drew back, sniffling and rubbing at her cheeks.

"Do something for me?" At his nod, she pressed on. "Don't do anything stupid, okay? I can only make you disappear once and if you screw it up…"

"I won't," he promised. "I'm done with all of this. I just want her."

She expelled a sharp breath. "Good."

She hurried past him to stand with Juliette and Vi in the filmy shimmer of twilight. Killian watched the trio with a sense of tightness blossoming in his chest. Fear and uncertainty coiled beneath a plume of excitement and joy. He could feel himself shedding tens of thousands of pounds as the weight of the world shifted off his shoulders. He felt no loss at the prospect of never having the things he now possessed. He felt no sadness for walking away from the chains binding him to the past. If anything, the anticipation made him want to break down and sob like a baby.

It was over. The nightmares were gone. He was finally free.

"Hey you." Juliette crossed over to him, a teasing smile making her eyes twinkle. "What are you looking so happy about over here?"

Without missing a beat, he took her hand and spun her in a flawless twirl straight into his arms. Her squeal echoed off the metal containers around them, followed by the sweet chime of her laughter as she collided with his chest. Her arms went around his neck and she peered up at him with so much love shining in her eyes he felt momentarily dizzy.

"Are you sure you want this?" she asked him softly. "I'm so afraid you'll come to hate me later for—"

"I could never hate you," he broke in. "And I have never wanted anything more than I want this."

She exhaled. "Okay, good, because I want to be with you for the rest of my life and the thought of you not feeling the same—"

"You are never getting rid of me."

Her head rested on his shoulder. "I'm holding you to that."

He made love to her that night in his bed. He held her close through every thrust, every delicate bow of her body, and every gasp of his name. He held her long after she'd fallen asleep curled up in his arms. It would be the last time they'd be in that bed together. The last time their joined satisfaction would fill those walls. He waited for some shred of regret, a whisper of uncertainty, but nothing came. If anything, he felt like a prisoner finally getting out of a twenty two year long sentence. He couldn't wait for dawn.

Stroking a kiss to Juliette's mouth, he slipped out of bed. He pulled on his trousers and quietly left the room. Silence followed him through the familiar corridors, but it rang differently. It felt foreign and complex. He ignored it all the way to the conservatory. The cold stones nipped at his bare feet as he padded to the heart of his mother's pride and joy.

Three urns greeted him. One for each of the people he'd lost. Unlike his mother and father's, Molly's glinted like a shiny coin.

"I'm leaving," he told them quietly. "I'm going to marry Juliette and have as many babies as she'll give me and I am never coming back."

He couldn't see it, but he felt the shift in the air. While he didn't believe in ghosts or spirits, he liked to think his parents were happy with his decision. That they supported it.

Carefully, he gathered the three pots up and took them with him from their stand. He tucked them away inside the hallway closet; he'd promised Maraveet he wouldn't bring anything with him, but he wouldn't leave those behind.

That done, he returned to his room, to Juliette who hadn't moved in his absence. He shut the door and padded back to the bed. The rustle of his pants sliding down his legs had her stirring. She turned her head and squinted through the predawn glow at him.

"Why are you out of bed? Something wrong?"

Kicking off his trousers, he went to her. His fingers hooked in the sheets covering her and he tugged them free. Immediately, her eyes darkened. Her breathing quickened. She was reaching for him even before the condom had snapped properly in place.

"Nothing." He climbed between her legs and cradled her to him as he pushed inside her. Her low groan pulsed through him as her willing body gripped him tight. "Not a damn thing."

He took her with slow, even thrusts, working her the way to the very brink before letting her tumble over with a quiet whimper of his name whispered in his ear. Her heat engulfed him, sucking him deeper into her folds. He took his time building her up a second time. Building her up only to demolish her all over again. Only he went with her this time. He let himself get lost in the silky confines of her beautiful body as dragged the very last shudder out of both of them and collapsed in her arms.

"I'm going to miss this bed," she whispered, her fingers lovingly stroking his hair as he nuzzled into her chest. "It holds so many good orgasm memories."

Killian burst out laughing. The sound echoed through the room and tangled with hers. He raised his head and peered down into her partially shadowed features.

"We'll make new orgasm memories in a new bed," he promised. "And in the showers, floors, and all the walls and tables."

"Wow! You've really thought this through."

Lowering his head, he kissed her lightly. "I am always thinking of ways to get inside you."

She giggled and caressed the side of his face with gentle fingers. Her eyes searched his as her body stayed firmly closed around him. Killian did not mind. Being enclosed in her arms, her legs, her sex and lips was the only place he ever wanted to be again.

"How does it feel knowing you've tamed the wolf, little lamb?"

He expected her to laugh or tell him great. That she was done with the beast. But she kissed him softly and whispered, "I don't want to tame him. I fell in love with him first."

Chapter 36

As nerves went, hers were shot. Every second thrummed with a rigid anticipation that made her want to be sick. The late spring morning was bright with so much possibility it hurt to even look at. The breeze was cool as it whispered around them, encouraging or deterring, she wasn't sure, but it danced through her unbound hair, sending the curtain across her face. She shoved the strands behind her ear and went back to cradling herself.

"It'll be all right, love," Killian whispered into the back of her head. His arms tightened around her from behind, compressing her already queasy stomach with his clasped hands. "Just a few more minutes."

He'd been saying that for nearly an hour. She was beginning to think he didn't know she could tell time. But she didn't push. She let him hold her as they stood far below his home, hidden from view in a tucked away road surrounded by trees, watching as the sun rose over the top of his hill. It crashed into the walls of his home and pooled into the fountain of his mother. The whole thing made Juliette want to cry and it wasn't even her house.

In the car, a non-descript two door Coupe in an unassuming white, Vi was peering up at the estate through the back window. Her face was set, but Juliette could just make out the tense lines around her mouth and the slight twitch as she nibbled on the inside of her lips. She hadn't said a word since they loaded the car in the pre hours of butt crack dawn, other than to assure Juliette that she was fine. Juliette really wanted to believe her, because if she wasn't, then it would be Juliette's fault. She wasn't entirely sure Vi even fully understood what was happening. What if she regretted it later and resented Juliette for tearing her away from the only home she'd ever known? The thought made her sick. They'd finally begun to make progress. They were finally as close as sisters were supposed to be. She honestly didn't think she'd be able to handle it if the girl hated her.

"Vi—"

"If you ask me one more time if I'm okay, I will cut you," Vi muttered, without taking her eyes off the hilltop.

"That isn't what I was going to ask!" she protested, but the false cheer in her voice made her a liar. "Not only," she amended.

"Uh huh." Vi sighed. "How much longer now?"

"Five minutes," Killian said, preoccupying himself by nipping lazily at the column of Juliette's neck.

They couldn't leave. At least, that was what Maraveet told them. They had to wait for the exact right moment, which seemed like it would never arrive. But that wasn't even remotely the least odd command they'd been given as Maraveet shooed them away from the property and told them not to come back.

"Are you sure no one's home?" she asked anxiously. "Did all the men leave last night when you told them to?"

"I watched them all leave," Killian promised. "By the time they return, we'll be gone."

"What about Frank?"

"Frank left too. He wasn't happy about it, but I told him I wanted the house to myself and he was to return the next morning."

Juliette lifted her eyes up to his face. "He's going to be devastated when he arrives and—"

"Frank's smart. He'll know and he'll be okay. It's time for him to retire anyway. Move to the Bahamas or something and find a girlfriend."

"Does it have to be your house?" She sighed. "Mine is—"

The explosion ripped through the silence with a deafening boom that rocked the entire hill. Chunks of debris burst from the head of the great, crimson cloud and rained below. Black and red tangled together against the flawless blue in a war of fire and smoke clashing for dominance. Killian's beautiful manor crumbled like a house of cards to the ground, leaving nothing but hungry flames to devour what was left.

Juliette cried out. Her hands flew to her mouth to stifle the rest. Killian's arms tightened around her. His heart remained steady against her back even while hers raced. He nuzzled the side of her head with his face.

"Come," he murmured into her ear. "Let's go."

"Maraveet … she was up there…"

"She's long gone. Trust me."

He pulled open her door and gently tucked her inside. He never even paused to glance back as he circled the hood and got behind the wheel. They set off without speaking a word as everything he had ever known burned in the rear view mirror.

It was hours and miles later as they abandoned the steel and glass of the city for the flat nothing of the country that Juliette finally turned to him.

"Are you okay?"

An aura of calm had settled over him. Halos of black still clung to the edges, faint, barely there at all, but there was actual peace in the lines of his body, serenity in the curves of his face. He looked so happy that her question felt stupid.

"Never been better."

Something in his calm relaxed the weight settled on her chest. She relaxed in her seat and allowed herself to finally feel the excitement and relief of starting over, of leaving all her demons behind.

"So, any idea where we're going?"

Eyes never leaving the road, one hand abandoned the wheel to reach across and clasp hers. It was drawn over and a kiss was brushed against the heel.

"I promised you Europe."

Epilogue

Six years later...

"Dinner!"

Salty sea breeze wafted off the Mediterranean to wash her summons back in her face, dragging strands of hair with it to blind her as she squinted against the smudge of orange and red conjuring the heavens beyond the walls. Across the yard, the two figures sat unaware as the day melted into evening and their little corner of the world slowly settled. They sat in the heart of the garden they'd planted together, surrounded by an array of blossoms as the setting sun painted them in a soft, golden light. Seeing them never failed to make her heart miss a beat.

"Want me to get them, miss?" Aniela poked her head out through the open terrace doors, her gnarled hands twisted in a dishtowel. "The food is almost finished."

Juliette shook her head. "It's okay. I'll get them. Thank you."

Abandoning the patio, she picked her way down the steps and along the cobblestone path. Her slippers made no sound as she broke off and padded across the grass. Killian's low murmurs greeted her before she even reached them.

"That's how spring is made," he was saying when she got close enough.

"Trolls?" Four year old Callum peered up at his father with big and dark eyes. Locks of unruly black tumbled across his small brow, shadowing the furrow of concern knitting his eyebrows together. "Can they get under my bed?"

"No," Killian assured him. "That's what the elves are there for. They make sure the trolls stay far away from the house."

"I don't like trolls," Callum confessed.

Chuckling, Killian lowered his face and brushed a kiss to the top of their son's head. "Don't worry. I won't let anything hurt you."

"Or Mommy?"

"Or Mommy."

Satisfied, Callum slumped back against his father's chest and stared at the bush. She knew he would have a million questions about his day later when it was time for bed. There was never any shortage of the whys and hows of the world and she cherished those moments with him.

"Hey you two." She stopped when her shadow had draped over the pair, capturing their attention. "It's dinner time."

One eye closed against the sun, Callum tipped his head far back to peer at her. "Daddy was telling me about the trolls and the elves that live in the garden."

"Mm, that is a good one," she agreed. "But you still need to wash up. Go on."

Callum, with his father's assistance, got to his feet and hurried back to the house. Juliette watched him until he was safely inside before turning back to her husband.

"How many is that today?"

Dusting off his trousers—his new ones, she noted—Killian rose. "Only six today."

Juliette laughed. "Maybe you should write all your stories into a book that he can read himself."

Killian scoffed. "What fun is that?" He moved closer and locked his arms around her middle. She was pulled into his chest where she nuzzled happily. "How's my girls?"

"Exhausted," she confessed. "I can tell she's already going to be a spoiled princess just by how tired she makes me when I so much as lift a finger."

Chuckling, he kissed her lightly. His palms splayed along the side of her protruding belly, burning skin through the material of her light dress.

"I can't wait."

Her insides warmed as it always did at the joy that filled his eyes at the mention of their growing family. "You sure? You'll probably have to tell twelve stories a day with the two of them."

Killian shook his head. "Don't care. I've got two knees for a reason."

Six years and still Juliette never once regretted her decision to leave Juliette Romero behind in a brilliant inferno. Six years of being with the man she couldn't live without, living in a home they had created together, and raising a family neither of them ever expected they'd have. Just watching him with Callum tightened her resolve that she'd made the right choice leaving that day. She would do it again in a heartbeat given the chance. He'd given her so much more than just a new name in a new postal code. He'd given her a future with him and with their children. He'd given her safety and security and the kind of happiness written about only in books. It didn't seem to matter how many years passed, she only seemed to fall more in love with him with every passing day.

"What are you thinking about?" A finger hooked a strand of her hair and tucked it behind her ear.

"I can't tell you. It'll go to your head."

A dark eyebrow lifted. "And you say I'm the tease."

Laughing, Juliette took his hand and tugged him towards the house. Along the way, he released her fingers to slide his hand around her waist. He fit her into his side as they climbed the steps together. Their hips and shoulders bumped in that familiar way she was so used to from years of being tucked into that place of comfort.

"I got a postcard from Vi this morning," she remembered. "She's loving the museums in Paris and the art classes she's taking are coming along great."

Killian pressed a kiss to the side of her head before moving ahead of her to help a struggling Callum shut the faucet off. He grabbed a towel and lightly patted the boy's hands dry before scooping him off the stool and moving back to her.

"That's good. How's her French coming along? Any better?"

Juliette grinned as she pulled Callum's chair out. "Well, it's apparently good enough to land her a date with some smoking hot French guy. Her words, not mine."

Shaking his head in amusement, Killian set Callum into his booster and scooted his chair under the table. "Does this mean she's not with that British guy with the spiky hair?"

"I guess not."

Grinning, Killian turned to her. He opened his mouth when a cry ripped through the house. Aniela, her face was as white as her apron, tore into the room calling for Killian in frantic squeaks.

"Sir, there's a man at the door and he's trying to get in—"

"Get Callum." Killian didn't even wait for the maid to finish. He snatched a knife off the table. "Now, Juliette."

Heart hammering, she dragged the boy's chair back and scooped him into her arms.

"Mommy?"

"It's okay, baby." She clutched him tight. Her panicked gaze went to Killian's.

"Go," he told her, already circling the table towards the front door.

Not waiting to be told a second time, she took Callum and ran from the room. The place was designed for that exact situation. It was how they'd built it, with ways to get in and out that only they knew about. Juliette cut through the dining room and into the library. Her fingers trembled as she dragged the third bookcase open on its hinges and set Callum inside.

"Remember what we talked about?" she whispered, her voice rushed and urgent.

Callum nodded, his little face white beneath his freckles.

"I love you." She kissed him. "So much."

"Mommy...?" Dark eyes brimmed, breaking her heart.

"It's okay. I promise. It's okay. Just be very quiet until Mommy comes back, okay?"

His bottom lip quivered. A tear slid down his cheek, followed by a sob that she quickly shushed.

"Shhh, baby. It's okay."

With a last kiss, she shut the door. Then ran to the bronze lamp perched on an antique table. She tore the shade off, spun it around and hefted it against her shoulder. Her heart thundered in her throat, sounding ridiculously loud between her ears. It muffled the world around her, irritating her as she pushed her back against the bookcase and waited.

The wait wasn't long. She spotted the shadow before the footsteps. Her limbs trembled as she waited, breath held, counting every second.

"Juliette—"

With a scream, she swung. The figure lurched back just in time to keep from getting their brain splattered by the jagged base of the lamp. The metal rebounded off the wall, chipping paint and creating a hole.

"Juliette!" Killian grabbed her arms.

The lamp dropped from her grasp with a deafening thud. Her heart nearly stopped in her chest as she stared into her husband's face.

"Killian...?"

"Jesus, you're supposed to be in there with him!" But he hauled her into his arms, crushing her close as she trembled against him. His hands smoothed over her hair and down her back. "It's all right," he promised softly.

She pulled out of his arms and rushed to the bookcase. Callum peered up at them. His face tearstained and blotchy. His little arms flung up and she pulled him to her.

"I was quiet, Mommy," he croaked into her shoulder.

"You were," she whispered, her own voice wavering. "You were such a good boy." Her filmy eyes went to her husband. "Who ... who was it?" she stammered, fighting like crazy to keep from throwing up.

Rather than answer, Killian went to them and pulled them both into his arms. He kissed the side of Callum's head, then Juliette's lips before drawing back.

"Are you okay?" His palm settled on her stomach.

She nodded. "Just tell me who was at the door."

Pausing long enough to search her eyes, Killian took Callum from her, perched him on his hip and took her hand.

"You won't believe me if I tell you."

He was right. She wouldn't have believed him, not unless she'd seen it with her own two eyes and even then…

"Maraveet?"

The woman hadn't changed a freckle since they saw her all those years ago. Her hair was shorter, but her eyes were still that cat green Juliette envied. She wore tight jeans tucked into soft, leather boots and a flowy top that complimented her full chest. In her hands was a purse she dropped unceremoniously when she spotted Juliette.

"Surprise!"

That was an understatement. They hadn't seen the woman in six years. Occasionally, Killian would get a text on the untraceable phone Maraveet had given him the night they blow up his manor and set off into the sunrise. It never made any sense to Juliette, but he would tell her Maraveet was in China or Prague or Canada. It was always somewhere new. She knew Killian had told Maraveet where they were in that weird cryptic message of theirs, but Maraveet had never, not once dropped by.

"What are you doing here?" Juliette asked, still not fully steady from the scare Maraveet had given them. "And what the hell are you doing trying to break in? You scared the hell out of us."

Maraveet had the decency to grimace. "Just testing your reflexes."

Heart refusing to slow, Juliette could only glower at the woman.

"It wasn't funny," Killian said for her. He shifted Callum higher on his hip. His hand rested carefully against the boy's back. "You know that."

Maraveet was no longer listening. Her eyes had fixed on Callum with wide fascination. "Who is this?"

"This is Callum." Killian turned his body so she could catch a glimps of the face Callum had squished into Killian's neck. "Callum, this is your Aunt Maraveet."

Callum refused to move. His thin arms tightened around his father and he remained stubbornly hidden.

"He's shaken," Killian stated, looking hard at his sister. "Someone decided to break into his house."

"Well, how was I supposed to know he was here?" Maraveet demanded, still watching Callum like he were a unicorn. "I didn't know he existed." Her gaze went to Juliette's stomach. "Either of them." One corner of her mouth twisted. "Jesus, I'm an aunt! I'm an aunt twice!" With a giddy laugh, she turned to the man standing at her shoulder, tall and quiet "I'm an aunt!"

The man chuckled. It was a nice sound, a kind sound that matched his handsome face. He had the flawless tan of a European with thick, glossy black hair and golden brown eyes set in a movie star chiseled face. Juliette didn't recognize him, but the way he stuck to Maraveet's side, the way he had his hand settled on the small of her spine, she had a feeling they would be seeing a lot of him in the future.

"Here I thought I would be surprising you guys."

"I'm surprised," Killian said, chuckling. "So, who's your friend?"

That caught Maraveet's attention. Her cheeks flushed pink as she turned so they could see the seven foot man towering drastically over her.

"This is Pedro. We met in Spain."

Killian raised an eyebrow. "Is there a reason you brought Pedro from Spain or have you upped your business from things to people?"

The color on Maraveet's face darkened. "He and I might have gotten married."

"Married?" Killian's mouth opened and closed a few times before the rest of his exclamation poured out. "How? When?"

"Well, it's a bit of a story." Maraveet grimaced. "But basically, he was trying to arrest me and I seduced him."

"I wasn't trying," the man muttered with a dry little frown that was contradicted by the laughter in his eyes. "I did arrest you."

His rich, Hispanic purr was almost as delicious as Killian's Irish one. It rumbled flawlessly over the kitchen, tangling with the spicy scent of cooked meat.

"You're a cop?" Juliette blurted. "You married a cop?"

"I don't think what we did with those handcuffs can be construed as arresting," Maraveet said to her husband before turning her attention to Juliette. "Not anymore. I've converted him to the dark side..." she broke off when Pedro raised an eyebrow. "We might have converted each other. No more arresting for him, no more ... borrowing for me."

Killian glanced from one to the other, his expression bright with hope. "Does this mean...?"

Maraveet shrugged with a teasing grin. "I might have hung up my hat. Kind of had to..." With a bite of her lip, she touched her flat belly and Juliette squealed.

"Really?"

Giggling, Maraveet nodded. "Only just found out last month. Pedro and I decided it was time to get a house and a fence and maybe a dog, but a big one with lots of teeth."

"I think I need a drink." Killian blew out a breath.

"You're not leaving, are you?" Juliette asked. "Supper's already on the table and I want to hear more about how you guys got together." She turned her attention away from the pair to the baffled maid huddled just inside the doorway between the kitchen and the hallway. "Aniela, can you please set room for two more?"

Bobbing her head, Aniela peeled herself away from the doorframe and hurried to do as she was asked.

Maraveet glanced at Pedro. "We can stay a little bit, yes?"

Tawny eyes settled on her face with the absolute devotions of a man head over heels in love. "If you like."

Beaming, Maraveet took his hand, but looked to Juliette. "We'll stay."

Dinner was filled with talks of Maraveet's adventures, of Pedro's chase to capture the thief stealing art pieces all over Spain and him finally capturing her, only to fall captive himself. It was filled with laughter and all the things that Juliette had always wanted filling her home, love, friendship, and happiness. But also the promise of a tomorrow. She only wished Vi had been there. The table just wasn't complete without her.

Maraveet and Pedro stayed the night. Killian showed them to the guestroom as Juliette put Callum to bed. The boy had said very little since the incident. While he was normally a reasonably quiet child, she knew he would have had a million questions. They had told him of his Aunt Maraveet, had told him she was far away and it had taken them a week to answer all his questions. For him to be so sullen meant something was wrong and Juliette knew exactly what it was and it broke her heart that he had to go through it at all.

"Hey, want a story?" she asked as she drew the sheets around his tiny chest.

He shook his head.

Juliette sighed and perched on the mattress next to him. "Want to talk about what's making you sad?"

Dark eyes lifted and it always amazed her how much they reminded her of Killian's; they both had such open, expressive eyes.

"I didn't like the bookshelf," he whispered. "I don't want to go in there again."

With her pregnancy hormones, it was a task not to burst into tears at the solemn declaration. She stalled having to answer by brushing strands of hair off his brow.

"Mommy and Daddy will always protect you," was all she could promise. "We will never let anything hurt you or your sister."

"Will she have to go in the bookshelf?"

"Not if we can help it." Killian stepped into the room, his hands tucked casually into his pockets.

"I don't want her going in there." His small mouth pursed in determination. "She won't like it and I won't let her."

Juliette rose off the bed, her emotions overwhelming her as tears started a steady trickle down her cheeks. She quickly kissed Callum on the forehead, whispered she loved him before hurrying from the room.

She was standing by the terrace in the room she shared with Killian when he joined her. He shut the door and crossed over to stand behind her. His arms slipped around her middle and he drew her back against his chest.

"I hated that," she croaked.

"I know. Me too."

Her back shuddered with a quiet sob. "I never … ever wanted to do that."

His arms tightened. "It won't happen again. Maraveet didn't think. I'll talk to her. We're safe, Juliette. I promise you. You and our babies, I won't let anything happen to any of you."

Swallowing, she wiped her eyes and turned to face him. "I'll be okay. I'm just shaken. Plus the hormones, I'm a mess."

He took her face between his palms. "You're a beautiful mess." He smiled when she chuckled.

"How is he?"

Gentle hands brushed hairs off her damp cheeks. "He'll be okay. I promised him a hike along the beach tomorrow. We're going to look for mermaids."

"That sounds nice." She sighed. "I'm glad he's okay."

Nodding, he tugged her closer to him. "It's our anniversary this weekend. Any regrets so far?"

"Only one." She tangled her arms around his neck and peered up at him with a teasing grin. "Those five months—"

"Jesus, woman! Are you never going to let me live that down?"

Juliette shook her head. "Never. It's five months I didn't have you and it was your fault."

With a frustrated growl, he kissed her hard. His hands tangled in her hair as he gripped her viciously close and plundered her mouth until she was a burning ball of fire on the verge of imploding. Then, just as effortlessly, the kiss softened. It slowed to a gentle sweetness that melted her into weightless vapors.

"Then I will spend the rest of my life making it up to you, lamb," he vowed quietly against her swollen mouth. "Just give me forever with you."

Dizzy, Juliette raised her eyes to his. "If you insist."

His mouth broke into a dazzling smile. "I do."

THE END

About Airicka Phoenix

Self-proclaimed romance addict, Airicka Phoenix lives in a world where unicorns, fairies and mermaids run amok through her home on a daily basis. When she's not chasing after pixies and rounding up imps, also known as her four children, she can be found conjuring imaginary friends to play with. Airicka is the prolific author of over eighteen novels for those who crave strong, female leads, sexy alpha heroes and out of control desires. She's a multi genre author who writes young adult, new adult and adult contemporary and paranormal romance.

For more about Airicka and the realm she rules with an iron fist--and tons of chocolate--visit her at:

www.AirickaPhoenix.com
|| Facebook || Twitter || Goodreads || Google+ ||
AirickaPhoenix@gmail.com

Newsletter

Made in the USA
San Bernardino, CA
28 February 2018